# SAVAGE

I was rooted to the spot. The dreadful keening from the slaves in the hold seemed to permeate the ship.

"Garth, Garth," I cried, "make them stop. Please, make them stop!"

He strode over to me and pulled my hands from my ears. He dug his fingers into my flesh. The harder I struggled to get away the tighter he held me. The fire in his eyes made me tremble.

"Stop it," he said sharply. "Stop fighting me, Elise."

"No," I panted, "never. Not until I die!"

"You'd be no good to me dead," he said, and slid his arms around my waist. He began to kiss me, over and over again until I was breathless.

# SURRENDER

I could feel the old weakness creeping over me and I sagged against the table. I could feel his hands, unfastening, unlacing. I tried to suppress the rising tide of longing sweeping over me, but I might as well have commanded the sea to stop its strong, incessant movement.

With a despairing groan I lay back in his arms and let him scald me with his lips. I knew that the fire would have to rage until I was consumed. . . .

**From the gentility of a French chateau to the black nightmare of a slave ship; from lusty romance as a pirate's wench to brutal ravishment by a desperate fur trader, Elise Lesconflair meets her destiny as a woman of daring . . . a woman of bold desires . . . a woman of love in this tempestuous saga of thunderous adventure and lightning passions!**

# SAVAGE
# SURRENDER

## Natasha Peters

ace books
A Division of Charter Communications Inc.
A GROSSET & DUNLAP COMPANY
1120 Avenue of the Americas
New York, New York 10036

SAVAGE SURRENDER

Copyright © 1977 by Ace Books

An ACE Original

First Ace Printing: September 1977

Published simultaneously in Canada

Printed in U.S.A.

# SAVAGE SURRENDER

# I. The Betrothal

"Where have you been!" Françoise's voice was like thunder. "The Count is in a fever. He's been asking for you for hours, and we couldn't find you anywhere. Come on, child. Hurry!"

I skipped across the marble floor of the grand entrance hall of the Chateau Lesconflair and threw my arms around her neck. "Oh, Françoise, you look wonderful standing there with your hands on your hips, just like a fishwife who has wandered into the Louvre by mistake!" Her scowl deepened. "It's such a beautiful day, Françoise. I love summer! I love spring and the Chateau and Uncle Theo. I even love you!"

"Settle down, child, for the love of Heaven." She detached my arms. There was less severity in her tone than in her words. "You're a fright. Your hair—you look like a witch! Where are your ribbons? Where are your pins?"

A footman scuttled past. "He's been calling for you, Mademoiselle Elise. I told him I thought you had come in."

"Yes, yes." Françoise waved him away impatiently, as if she were the mistress of the Chateau instead of my nurse. "Tell him she'll be right along." She frowned at me again and jerked my puffed sleeves up on my shoulders. "Who told you to pull your gown down like that?"

"Don't be such a peasant, Françoise," I chided her fondly. "All the ladies in Paris——"

"Paris!" She snorted. "I know what goes on in Paris!" Producing a hairbrush from her apron pocket, she attacked my touseled black curls. "No one would ever know to

1

look at you that you were the daughter of a famous general, the niece of a count, and the goddaughter of Napoleon himself. You look just like a street wench.''

''What do street wenches look like, Françoise?'' I asked teasingly.

''Never mind,'' she muttered crossly. ''No time even to make you presentable. Been poking his head out of that library every five minutes, asking everyone he sees where you are.''

''But Uncle Theo saw me at lunch, Françoise, not two hours ago. Of course he didn't even look up from his *paté*; I could have been naked, and he wouldn't have noticed.''

''Hush! You might show proper respect for the man who has cared for you since you were a child. You and your scapegrace brothers! But I always said you were worse than either of them. I have you to thank for my gray hairs, Elise. No one else.''

She smoothed down my skirts and shook her head over the grass stains on the hem. Then she stood back and looked at me critically through narrowed eyes.

''Well, Françoise, do you like what you see?''

''I suppose you'll do,'' she said grudgingly. ''You're more like your mother every day, and she was a hundred times more beautiful than those pale scarecrows you see in Paris who are supposed to be beauties. Paris!''

I was still laughing at her prejudices when I tapped lightly on the library door and entered the room.

The library was my favorite place in the Chateau. It was not at all gloomy and dark like the libraries of English homes I had been in. The walls had been painted a pale shade of blue-gray, and large rectangular mirrors were set between ceiling-high book shelves to catch the light from the row of French windows behind Uncle Theo's desk. A large globe, with which I had spent many fascinated hours as a child, stood in one corner in front of the windows, and a fine bust by Houdon of my mother, "La Belle de Corsique," which everyone said looked just like me, stood in the other. The rug underfoot, an oriental patterned with flowers of blue and tangerine, felt thick and soft.

Best of all, the room was crowded with many things besides dull, dusty books; curios and figurines and novelties from around the world, splendid Chinese vases, intricate ivory carvings, weird shapes sculpted in wood and stone, miniature paintings of Lesconflairs and Bourbons and Marianis and Tugereaux, a David portrait of me, even a few archaic weapons, like a crossbow which had been wielded by a Lesconflair in some long ago siege, and ancient fossils and relics that had been found on the estate. Every available space—on the walls, between sets of books, on the mantelpiece, on top of Uncle Theo's desk, on sideboards and pedestals—was crammed with these momentoes and souvenirs of generations of Lesconflairs. While most of the other rooms in the Chateau were huge and hollow, decorated with faded tapestries and a few pieces of thin-legged furniture, the library seemed to be the living center of the house, not only the place where Uncle Theo ran the estates and charted the family history, but a kind of storehouse filled with the little things that the Lesconflairs had loved.

Uncle Theo rose from his desk and beamed at me. He still wore an old-fashioned powdered wig and satin knee breeches; a pearl-colored brocade waistcoat was stretched tightly over his round stomach. His blue eyes were shining, and his apple cheeks seemed even pinker than usual.

"Good afternoon, Uncle Theo. You wanted to see me?"

"Yes, child, yes. Sit down, please, here near my desk if you like." He smiled and chafed his plump hands together. "Elise, I shall come to the point at once. I have news, good news, excellent news. It concerns you." He picked up a square of paper from his desk and waved it excitedly, like a child waving a flag at a parade. He drew a breath and proceeded rather solemnly. "This morning, Elise, I received a letter from a noble gentleman asking for the honor of your hand in marriage. What a wonderful thing this is, Elise. I am delighted for you! He is very impressed with you. Just listen to how he praises your beauty: 'I have never beheld such a lovely form and face, nor found such exquisite beauty enhanced by so lively a mind. The finest qualities of your niece's French and Corsican ancestors have surely been bestowed upon this single radiant creature. Heaven must surely sing with joy that Mankind has at last achieved, in the person of dear Elise, a true pinnacle of perfection and a noble monument to Womankind and to Love!' " Uncle Theo sighed rapturously. "Isn't that exquisite, Elise? How proud you must be."

I couldn't contain my laughter. "Oh, I really do think I'm a bit young to be both a pinnacle and a monument, Uncle Theo," I gasped. "Why, Françoise says I am the worst behaved girl she has ever known, and even you have said—"

"Yes, yes. But the time has come to put girlish behavior behind you, Elise," said Uncle Theo irritably. "You are fast becoming a woman, my dear, and soon you will be assuming the responsibilities of marriage and motherhood. Heavens, Elise, you are seventeen already! Soon you will be quite unmarriageable, I fear. I tell you I was quite relieved to have this proposal."

"But Uncle," I protested, "it's not my first proposal, and I am sure it won't be my last."

"This is not the same thing as a passionate declaration made on the dance floor, Elise," Uncle Theo said sternly. "This," he held up the letter, "is the first man who is truly worthy of our consideration."

Ah, this one has money, I thought. "Oh, Uncle Theo, I don't want to get married yet," I said. "I'm having too much fun! But who is the letter from, pray? Not that pimply Marc Laurent!"

My uncle smiled and looked smug. "No, it is not young Laurent. It is none other than—" he paused, giving the announcement its full share of suspense and importance, "the Baron Friederich Rolland von Meier." He pulled down his waistcoat and looked at me expectantly.

I gasped with horror. "What? That porky, pompous, dreadful little man? I—I can't bear him, Uncle Theo! The Baron Freddy!" I jumped up and stood in front of Uncle Theo's desk. "Oh, Uncle Theo, he's awful, he really is. Why, I can hardly keep awake when he talks to me. He's so terribly dull, the way he goes on and on about shooting in Bavaria and the fat grouse on his estates and how keen his old hound is. And he's so ugly, Uncle Theo! Grotesquely ugly! That fat belly and those thin blond wisps of baby hair—yes, he looks just like a gigantic baby! And his breath stinks, too, haven't you noticed? I have seen you pulling away from him when he gets too close, Uncle. I can just barely keep myself from being rude to him—"

Uncle Theo stood up. "That's enough, Elise," he said sharply. "The Baron has done you a great honor by asking for your hand, and he is at least deserving of your respect. For shame! Will you continue in your irresponsible ways until you are an old woman? All this riding and racing after your brothers and acting like a wild thing! And your language, Elise! Sometimes I think you must have been raised in an army barracks."

I reached over the desk and squeezed his hand. "But I very nearly was, Uncle Theo. Father was a soldier—"

Uncle Theo drew himself up proudly. "Your father was an officer, Elise. A general. He died on the field of honor, and he gave his life for France." He fished in his pocket for a handkerchief and mopped his forehead. Not a puff of air came through the open windows, and the room felt uncomfortably close and warm. "Listen to me, Elise. I have done the best I could with you and your brothers. I have done what I thought your father and mother would have wanted me to do, and I assure you, it hasn't been easy for me. I am a lifelong bachelor, and I admit that my knowledge of children was rather limited. Still, I would like to think that you haven't grown up feeling unloved and unhappy."

I ran around the desk and flung my arms around his neck. "Oh, no, Uncle Theo! You have been a dear and wonderful uncle and I love you very much, you know I do. Please don't be upset with me. I'll be good and I'll marry whoever you say, but please don't make me marry the Baron Freddy." I dropped my voice. "Please, Uncle Theo. I'm not so uncivilized as you think I am, either. I love pretty gowns and nice things, and my year at court was just wonderful! And you know I get invited to all the balls and lots of handsome men pay court to me. Surely we don't even have to consider the Baron—"

"I have already answered the Baron, Elise," Uncle Theo said softly. "I have told him that you were delighted and honored, and that you accept his proposal. I expect him here in a few weeks. The wedding will take place around the first of November. Preparations are already under way."

I felt the blood drain out of my cheeks. I stood stock still and stared at him speechlessly for a full minute.

"No," I said hoarsely. "You can't be serious, Uncle Theo! Please! I'll—I'll kill myself!" I threw myself into an armchair and sobbed wildly.

"Your histrionics are futile," my uncle said stiffly.

"You are my ward and you will do as I say, Elise. I am only thinking of what is best for you, my dear."

"That's a lie!" I shouted. I knew he was having money problems. Repairs on the Chateau had to be postponed because my brother Philippe's commission and my season at court had cost him dearly. What if the Baron had not only waived a dowry—one does not necessarily expect to win a pinnacle and a monument and money as well —but had given Uncle Theo a loan at a low rate of interest with the understanding that the money would not have to be repaid if his suit were successful? But surely Uncle Theo was not in such desperate straits that he would have to accept a bribe for my hand! "I won't marry him! I can't. I realize that my opinion and what I want is of no importance under the law, but to be presented with a *fait accompli*—oh, Uncle Theo, how could you? It is so unlike you. I—I thought you loved me, but you don't! You want that man's money, and you don't care about my happiness at all! I hate you!" I pounded the top of the desk.

Uncle Theo said nothing. He was seated at his desk, and he suddenly looked old to me. For the first time I noticed how blue and prominent the veins on his hands were; how the lines around his mouth seemed deeper. My heart went out to him.

I rushed to his side and knelt beside him. "Oh, I'm so sorry, Uncle Theo! I could bite my tongue out. I didn't mean to hurt you, but it was such a shock, to think you even had to consider such an absurd proposal. Of course it was tempting, because he's so rich. And I'm such a wicked girl, I must deserve to be threatened with the Baron. I'm willful and undisciplined, I know, and I'd give anything to be sweet and docile like the Tourrand sisters, but I can't help myself. I have a terrible temper and the

nuns at school said I have a tongue like a rapier. I haven't
been trying very hard to improve myself, but I shall.
You'll see, I shall attract rich suitors from all over the
world. Perhaps I can marry one of the Emperor's cousins
or brothers and become Queen of Corsica. You know,
there are Bonapartes all over the place, and Napoleon
himself might even consider me, now that I'm grown up.
He always liked me, and when I was fourteen, he told me
my breasts were nearly as nice as Josephine's.''

"Elise!" Uncle Theo was shocked.

"Well, it's true," I insisted. "He did say it. If he can
marry two times, surely he can marry three. I'm far more
beautiful than the new Empress, everyone says so. I'm
one of the most beautiful women in France. Think of it,
Uncle Theo. Elise Lesconflair, Empress of France!''

Uncle Theo sighed, and then, in a tired voice, said,
''The Emperor himself has approved this match as advan-
tageous for France. He has even promised to attend the
wedding, and as your godfather he will escort you to the
altar. Napoleon admired and respected your father very
much, Elise. It's quite an honor.''

"An honor!" I whispered the word. "An honor? To
marry a man I loathe? And for what? To consolidate some
silly country where the people can't even speak French?
Why, the Emperor could move his soldiers in and annex it
any day he chose!''

"This is better for France," Uncle Theo said staunchly.

"Better for France!" I raged. "Better for Napoleon!
Better for Theo Lesconflair! Better for everyone except
me!''

I strode angrily to the open windows. The vista was
breathtakingly beautiful: broad, terraced lawns fell away
into wooded areas that seemed to stretch to the horizon.
Marble fountains shot sprays of water high into the air,
where the sun caught the droplets and transformed them

into a million tiny prisms. Tears came to my eyes as I gazed at the only home I had ever known. Yes, it was beautiful, and I was about to be sacrificed to the land like some poor victim in pagan times. Most terrifying of all, there was nothing I could do; my uncle's word was the law that governed me.

"I am truly sorry, Elise, that my plans do not meet with your approval." Uncle Theo cleared his throat noisily. "Ah, very often," he coughed, "the, ah, individual good must be subordinated to the general good in order for society to remain strong."

"Rubbish," I said. "For the Lesconflair coffers to remain full, you mean."

"Please let me finish. Your father, my younger brother, would have welcomed this marriage, Elise. He loved France and was happy to die in her service. He loved this house, of course, but more than that he loved the Lesconflair name, and the fine, stalwart men and women who have borne it through the centuries. They held their name above everything else, Elise, because they knew the name would endure long after they were gone. That spirit of pride was their greatest legacy to us.

"Scandal has never touched that name, Elise. I will confess that to some extent my decision has been influenced by monetary concerns. I am in severe financial straits because I had to act quickly to keep our name from being blackened. I sincerely hope that this unexpected drain on our fortune will not be repeated, but it has nonetheless left this family in a dangerous and precarious position."

I looked uncomprehendingly at him for a moment, and then the true meaning of what he was saying came to me. "Honoré," I whispered. Honoré was my other brother, two years older than Philippe, five years older than me, heir to the Lesconflair title and estates. I sat down.

"But—but I thought it was only a few francs. To his tailor and his bootmaker."

"The matter did not concern you, Elise," Uncle Theo said grimly. "However, I suppose it won't hurt for you to know, since you are now involved. Honoré's gambling debts amounted to fifty thousand francs. Plus another ten thousand to a young lady of decent family whose father I shall never be able to look in the face again."

"Oh, no." The room seemed to tilt. I closed my eyes until it righted itself. "I had no idea—"

"There was nothing you could do then, Elise, and I didn't want to worry you. I was unable to raise that last ten thousand. The Baron came to our aid. We have a great deal to thank him for."

We were silent for a few minutes, then I burst out, "But it's not fair! Why should I have to pay for Honoré's sins? How can you bear to leave him the house and lands after the way he has behaved? I thought you loved me, Uncle Theo, but I have been deceived. You love Honoré and the stupid Lesconflair name and this pile of rocks and timber better than me. You have no heart, Uncle Theo! You're not even human! Doesn't it matter to you that I'll be unhappy for the rest of my life? Did you think of me at all when you arranged this monstrous match? Oh, I'll never forgive you for this! Never, never!"

I hid my face in my hands and cried bitterly and loudly, as I had not cried since I was a child. Uncle Theo came over to me and rested his hand on my shoulder. I jerked away from him.

"I did think of you, Elise," he said softly. "If there is to be ruin and disgrace in our family I want you to be far away from it. The Baron is a kind man and I think you will come to love him in time. You have a good heart, and surely you can see that I have done what was best. Thank

God you are not devoid of sense, Elise. Please try to understand.''

''I understand only that this gross frog thinks he has fallen in love with me, for no other reason than that I am beautiful. Oh, I wish I were ugly, ugly and so stupid that I could actually believe the lies you have told me. Those silly, feather-brained girls at school could hardly wait to be married. They had their children named and their homes furnished before they had even met a man who would marry them! They would count themselves lucky over this, and they would even pretend to be in love. But I won't pretend. It is clear to me that there is no such thing as love, and that marriages are made on earth because it profits someone to make them, not in Heaven at all, as the nuns said. I'm so unhappy! I—I shall kill myself on my wedding night. I would die rather than let that—that gross pig touch me!''

Uncle Theo sighed deeply. ''It would indeed be ironic, Elise, if you, not Honoré, were to bring disgrace upon the family.''

''I don't care!'' I cried passionately. ''If that horrid man tries to touch me I shall kill him, too!''

My uncle shook his head slowly. ''When your father married your mother I had my doubts about the wisdom of his bringing Corsican blood into the family. I was right. You are a little savage.''

''I'm not!''

''Then act like the daughter of a noble family, and not like some Italian peasant bent on murder!'' he said crisply. We glared at each other. Uncle Theo sighed again. ''Dear Elise,'' he said wearily, ''you are too passionate. You are almost a woman and you're still acting like a spoiled, selfish child. I won't tolerate any more, Elise, and please remember that I don't have to!''

I ran for the door and paused with my hand on the knob. "I would rather be too passionate, Uncle Theo," I said in a husky voice, "than be dead and buried in the tomb of the Lesconflairs." I went out.

Honoré was standing in the hall. He looked at my tear-streaked face and flushed slightly.

"Oh, hello, Elise," he said with uncharacteristic kindness.

"Ah, and here we find the real culprit," I exclaimed wrathfully, "sulking in the halls, gloating over his victory. Traitor! Fiend!"

"Elise, I beg you," he said pleadingly. He held out his hands toward me. I slapped at them.

"I should have known that Uncle Theo was too kind to think up such a scheme on his own. You are at the root of this whole conspiracy, aren't you, Honoré? You put it into his head to accept the Baron's proposal, didn't you? And I'll wager you encouraged that—that moronic pig to offer for me in the first place! Didn't you? Didn't you?"

Honoré stiffened. "Certainly not. Give yourself a little credit, Sister. The Baron was besotted with you from the first moment he laid eyes on you, you know that. Every saucy turn of your raven head and every flash from those black eyes made his head spin. And I have not been in collusion with Uncle Theo. When he first mentioned the idea to me I was against it. Now I rather like it. Imagine the poor Baron's surprise when he finds out what he has really married. The sweet young daughter of a noble house? The convent-educated goddaughter of the Emperor? Hardly! You've a devil, Elise, we both know that. You're spoiled and headstrong and wild. It's a pity the Baron's not the man to tame you."

I flew at him. I hated him and I wanted to kill him. Honoré caught my wrists and held me tightly. I cursed him under my breath and struggled to escape.

"For God's sake, Elise, calm yourself! This isn't the end of the world. A wedding is, after all, the high point of a woman's life. You ought to thank—ouch! You blood-thirsty little bitch!"

I had bitten into his hand as hard as I could and he released me. We stood apart, eyeing each other suspiciously, while Honoré nursed his wound.

"And you ought to thank me, Honoré," I said through my teeth. "How would you be enjoying yourself right now if Uncle Theo hadn't come up with that last ten thousand francs?"

His color rose. "I don't know what you mean."

"You know very well what I mean! The oldest son and heir gets himself into a scrape and badly needs money to buy himself out of it, and where does the money come from? From me! From the only piece of salable goods left on the estate! Uncle Theo sold me to the Baron to save you, Honoré, and to rescue the family honor. Honor! I'm so sick of the word I could scream. What kind of honor is it that demands that a woman be sold like a slave to the highest bidder? Your luck held this time, Honoré. You can breathe easily, thanks to me. But don't expect me to thank you for what you've done. And don't you dare preach to me about weddings and happiness. I—I can't bear it!"

Tears rushed to my eyes. I ran blindly out of the hall and down the steps to the drive, across the terraced lawns where the marble fountains played, into the stand of pines that bordered the lawns on the west side. I threw myself onto the ground and cried furiously until I could scarcely breathe. I hated them, hated them all, the men who controlled and manipulated my life. Brothers, uncles, suitors, priests, emperors. Finally my tears ceased. I sat up and brushed the damp hair out of my face. I had no wish to go back to the Chateau yet. I felt hurt and humiliated, and I couldn't face them until I had myself under control.

I stood up and looked around resentfully. The sun was still shining brightly. The sky was still the same dazzling August blue. Birds sang cheerfully. A rabbit scampered into view, paused to look me over, then scurried into the underbrush. The world was oblivious to my suffering. Life had collapsed in ruins around me, and nobody cared.

Anger welled up inside of me and almost choked me. I began to walk hurriedly through the park, towards the wilder part of the forest out of sight of the Chateau, where the gardeners and their boys never penetrated. Why had I behaved so childishly? I should have remained calm. I might have been able to persuade Uncle Theo that there were better ways to repair his losses. But no. He had already accepted the Baron's proposal in my name, and the family honor demanded that I conform to his wishes. I recalled the humiliating encounter with my brother. I should have played on his sympathies, tried to win him over. But Honoré would surely side with Uncle Theo. They were both eager to have that rich pig in the family and they didn't care if they had to sacrifice me to get him.

I tramped for hours, not caring where I was going, not wanting to go home again, ever. My conversation with Uncle Theo kept coming back to me. He had said I was too passionate. Too passionate! Yes, and too alive, too vital, too demanding. I wanted too much from life, more than I had a right to expect, obviously.

Late in the afternoon I came to a place where fallen trees and floating debris had formed a natural dam across the stream that cut across the Lesconflair lands. The water spilled over the falls into a deep, crystal clear pool. It was a beautiful, enchanting spot, wild and unspoiled. Deer watered there, birds nested in the tall grass on the banks, and an ancient willow tree drooped elegantly over the water. We had swum there, Philippe and Honoré and I, when we first came to live with Uncle Theo, after our mother died. I missed Philippe terribly and wished he would come home. He would take my part against the other two. He loved me.

Dropping down on a rick by the pool's edge I kicked off my shoes and stockings and splashed my feet in the water. It felt delightful. In an instant I had shed my dress and chemise, and plunged naked into the pool. The water was icy cold, for the stream was fed by underground springs. The shock of immersing myself in it drove everything else from my mind. I floated lazily for a long time, reveling in the coolness of the water and the joy of being unencumbered by clothing. I ran my hands slowly over my swelling breasts and down my sides.

I was beautiful, and the Baron desired me. I shivered with disgust. A lot of men desired me. I had seen their eyes when they looked at me, scanning my rounded hips, my tiny waist, and the beautiful white breasts that swelled over the tops of my gowns. Why, I could run away to Paris and become a courtesan, a demimondaine. I could have hundreds of lovers, all young and handsome and rich. The Baron Freddy would be shocked, and Uncle Theo would be furious. Françoise would scold. The plan amused me, and I splashed delightedly in my private pool. Finally I drew myself ouf of the water and lay panting on the grassy bank. The low roar of the falls obscured all other sounds and lulled me to sleep.

"Well, I see old Neptune has tossed me up a tasty-looking fish."

I sat up with a start and rubbed my eyes. A man was standing near the pool, holding a horse that was drinking thirstily. He was staring boldly at me through pale ice-blue eyes.

I gaped at them. The horse, a giant chestnut covered with lather from hard riding, snorted and blew noisily as he drank. The man was tall and bare-headed. The sun glinted on his hair, making it shine richly like burnished gold. His face and neck and hands were quite tan. He wore no neckcloth and his loose-fitting shirt hung open, revealing a brown, muscular chest. His face was lean and hard with hollows under the cheekbones, and he had a fine, straight nose and high forehead. His lips were thin and firm, and at the moment they were curved into a cynical suggestion of a smile.

His clothing had been chosen for serious travel over rough roads. His coat was loose-fitting like his shirt, and dark brown in color. His fawn colored breeches clung tightly to his thighs and calves. His high boots were covered with dust.

"Your pardon, Mademoiselle Nymph." His voice was pleasant, warm and deep. "This is the way to the Angiers road, is it not?"

His eyes caressed my naked body. Only then did I come to my senses. Hoping that it might not be too late to salvage my modesty, I scrambled for my chemise and slid it over my head. Under his unwavering gaze my fingers fumbled ineptly with the ribbons on the bodice, and finally I drew the edges together over my breasts and knelt in the grass with my knees drawn up under me.

"Who are—what do—how dare you!" I sputtered.

He rested his arm casually on his horse's back. His smile grew broader. "How dare I water my horse at this lovely stream on the hottest day of the year?"

I felt tremors starting up and down my spine. "You are trespassing on private property," I snapped. "Go away from here at once or I shall have you arrested."

He laughed softly. "So I'm a trespasser, am I? And since I have drunk your water and breathed your air, I suppose I am a thief as well? I plead guilty, then. But before you hang me, you must permit me to dine on the luscious feast you and the gods have set before me."

I gasped, paralyzed for a moment as his meaning became clear. He turned away to tend to the horse, who, having drunk its fill, lifted its dripping muzzle as if to ask for praise. The man patted the horse, then dropped to one knee at the pool's edge and drank from cupped hands. Then he splashed his face and neck with water and ran his damp fingers through his hair.

I jumped up from my grassy bed and raced for the shelter of the woods. I thought I heard a low laugh, but I plunged on recklessly, impeded by rough tangles of briars and vines and sharp twigs and thorns that dug into the soles of my bare feet. I thrashed about in blind panic, telling myself that he wouldn't dare give chase. Then to my horror I heard the unmistakable thunder of hooves and the crashing of bushes as his horse plowed easily through the undergrowth that had made the way almost impassable for me.

In another moment they were upon me. I looked up and saw the powerful horse with its villainous rider bearing down on me, and in an instant the man leaned over and slipped his arm around my waist, lifting me onto the horse's back with one easy movement. I pushed feebly at his chest as I tried to catch my breath, and as I regained my strength I cursed him and struggled violently.

"I had no idea there were naked savages in these woods," he said with a little laugh. "So young and beautiful, too."

I tried to jam my elbow into his side, but his muscles were like iron. He pinned me against his chest with the arm that held the horse's reins, and with the other hand he opened the bodice of my chemise.

"Delightful!" he exclaimed. The touch of his fingers on my breasts inflamed me further.

"Let me go! Vulture! Dog! Let me go!"

He chuckled. "Ah, they heave like waves on the ocean

when you are angry. Only in France do the girls have such lovely, slender legs and such superb bosoms.''

I wriggled in his grasp. "Let me go," I panted. "Put me down at once!"

"I wouldn't let you go now if Napoleon's whole army were chasing me," he said. "Are you in a hurry to go home? I suppose your master is waiting for you, and for that I cannot blame him." His hand moved down to my stomach and he pulled me fiercely against him pinching my buttocks with his thighs.

A servant! He thought I was a servant! I was outraged. "I—I'll kill you for this!" I said in a choked voice.

"Never fear," he said mildly. "I shall make this afternoon worth your while."

I was so furious that I could hardly speak. A servant—and a whore!

When we reached the clearing near the stream he dismounted first, then reached up to lift me down. I saw a riding crop sticking out from one of his saddlebags, and I grabbed for it and brought it down on his upturned face with all the force I could muster. A bright red streak appeared on his cheek. He seemed astonished, but he made no move to touch his wound. I slid off the horse's back and darted past him.

His arm shot out and he grabbed me around the waist and pulled me to him. "I swear you are no nymph, girl, but a wildcat in need of taming."

"You are no better than—than a swine!" I hissed breathlessly. He laughed harshly and bent his head to kiss me. I bit him savagely on the lip. Suddenly he raised his hand and slapped me across the face. Tears smarted in my eyes.

"You have a taste for blood, don't you, my girl?" he demanded angrily. "We must indulge this taste at once."

Pinning my arms to my side, he covered my mouth

with his. I felt weak and breathless from running, and my cheek still smarted from the blow he had given me. His kiss drained me of my remaining strength. I tried vainly to keep my lips pressed tightly together, but he forced them apart with his tongue and ravished my mouth. When he released me I gasped for air. My head was throbbing.

He said, "I can see that you have never been kissed before. I find that almost impossible to believe. Are the men in this part of the country blind, perhaps, or are they idiots?"

I spat on the ground and wiped my mouth with the back of my hand. "They are gentlemen, not animals," I snapped.

He grinned. His gaze went to my bosom and moved slowly down my body. My bodice was hanging open to the waist. I pulled the thin fabric over myself, my face burning with shame and anger. I was keenly aware of my vulnerability.

"I would call them saints," he mused, "these poor, crude provincials. Or perhaps they are really cowards, afraid to tangle with a vicious spitfire who first entices them and then tries to blind them."

"I never enticed you!" I said hotly.

"Oh, but you did." His voice was low, hypnotic. He stepped closer to me, moving slowly like a hunter stalking a wild creature. I stared at him dumbly. My eyes felt as large and as round as dinner plates, but I could not pull them away from him. My brain was empty of all thought, and I was conscious of a hollow feeling in my body, then of shivers passing up the backs of my legs and into my middle. The heaviness in my legs weighed me down. I knew I could not run away from him.

"Don't—please don't hurt me, Monsieur," I whispered. My mouth felt as dry as dust.

He was very close to me. He loomed over me. I could

feel the heat of his body, and I could smell the traces of horse, sweat and leather that clung to him. He put his hands on my shoulders and looked searchingly into my eyes. The cruel little smile never left his lips. I shuddered and looked down, and I saw the greatness of his manhood straining at his breeches. I gave a little cry of horror and tried to jerk away.

"A man's anatomy betrays him every time," he said lightly. The hands on my shoulders tightened their grip. He was breathing hard. "But I don't know that that's such a bad thing."

His face came closer to mine, filling the field of my vision, obscuring everything but the terror I felt. I could see the blood caked on his cheek and the red blister on his lips where I had bitten him. His eyes were cold. They looked right through me, seeing only a wench he would use to break the monotony of his journey.

My hypnotic state faded for a moment, and I began to fight him. "Leave me alone! Let me go!"

The smile faded from his lips and he wrestled me easily to the ground. I fell heavily and he came down on top of me. He pinned my wildly thrashing arms and legs and he kissed me again and again. Each time his tongue seemed to go deeper until I was almost gagging with rage and fear.

"You don't like the way a man kisses?" he asked in a breathless whisper.

"I hate you!" I sobbed. "Let me go, damn you! Let me go!"

I could feel his heart pounding against my breast. The hard weight on my thighs made me tremble. I went limp for a moment and closed my eyes. I felt him relax his hold on my arms and I seized the chance to free my hands. I raked my fingernails down his cheeks, and nearly cried aloud with joy as he yelped with pain and pulled back. But my satisfaction was short-lived. He slapped me hard across the mouth and for a moment the world went black. I could hear a sighing sound in my ears, and I wondered if he had killed me.

When I opened my eyes I saw that his mouth was set in a grim line. His eyes were burning dangerously and I felt afraid, really afraid. I began to scream mindlessly, hysterically. He clapped his hand over my mouth and threw his whole weight down on top of me. He parted my legs with his knee, and then he drove into me. I felt my body splitting apart as the steel knife of his aroused manhood slashed me so fiercely that I swore I could feel my flesh ripping and tearing.

"Oh, God," I whispered. "God help me."

He framed my face with his strong hands and looked into my eyes. "Well, I am honored. How kind of you to have saved your virginity for me, little hellion. You have doubtless murdered a whole slew of stable boys in order to bring me this fine gift."

I was convulsed with pain and crying hysterically. He held me fast until I lay quiet in his arms. My fear and pain began to subside and I was consumed by a burning hatred. Then he began to move against me, slowly at first, almost gently. I bit my lips to keep from screaming. His movements became more violent, and finally, after what seemed like an eternity, it was over. He shuddered slightly and lay still.

He eased himself off me and stood up. I was shaking with shock and hatred, and I rolled over on my side and drew my legs up.

"You'll pay for this," I said thickly through my tears. "I swear by all that is holy you will pay for this with your life. I—I could kill you!"

"I'm sure you could," he said briskly. "I could cheerfully have murdered you, little Hellcat. I am astonished someone hasn't taught you to behave. How does your master tolerate your impudence? Farewell. The afternoon hasn't been entirely enjoyable, but at least I feel rested and refreshed." He gave a low laugh. I saw a glint of gold and I heard something fall in the dust near my face. A golden louis. I had sold my virginity for a single golden louis.

I leaped to my feet and hurled it after him, but he had already mounted his horse and was trotting towards the edge of the clearing.

"Fiend! Filthy scum!" I shouted after him. "I hate you! I hate you!"

The sound of his laughter drifted towards me but he did not turn his head. Then the forest enveloped him and I saw him no more. A wave of nausea swept over me. I fell on my knees, sobbing and retching. When I was calm I walked to the stream and bathed away the blood and dirt from my face and legs, then I retrieved my dress and shoes and stockings and put them on. I moved mechanically, without thinking. I felt no sorrow, no pain, no anger, nothing at all. I was lifeless and hollow, and I knew that the Elise who walked away from this place would not be the same one who had come here earlier. I left the clearing without even a backward glance at the crushed grass on the spot where he had violated me, and I went through the deepening shadows towards home.

## II.  The Wedding

I reached the Chateau after dark. I wanted to get to my room without being seen; I felt sick and I knew how dirty and dishevelled I looked. I managed to sneak up a back staircase and I was halfway down the hall when Honoré came bursting out of his room.

He stopped abruptly when he saw me. "My God, Elise, where have you been? We've been frantic. I was just about to go—"

His worried eyes took in my loose tangle of hair and soiled gown and tear-streaked cheeks. He grabbed my arm and looked into my face. "Are you all right, Elise?" I felt too numb to answer him. He gave me a little shake and demanded in a cracked voice, "Are you all right? For God's sake, say something!"

Tears came to my eyes. Honoré did love me after all. He had been genuinely concerned about me. "I—I'm fine, Honoré, really I am," I whispered. Then I started to cry softly.

"You're lying," he said grimly. "You say you're fine when you look like you've been dragged a mile through the dirt and muck. Why are you crying, Elise? Tell me what has happened."

"A man," I said shakily. "In the forest near the stream where we used to swim. You know the place."

Honoré dropped my arm. "Oh, my God," he said harshly. "This is all my fault. Did—did he hurt you?"

I knew what he meant. I looked at the floor. "Yes," I mumbled.

23

"Who was he?" he demanded, grabbing me by the shoulders. "I swear I'll kill him! Who was he?"

"I don't know, Honoré. I never saw him before."

"Oh, this is an outrage!" Honoré clutched at his hair. "I'll find him and kill him, Elise. I swear it!"

"Yes!" I gripped Honoré's hands tightly. "Yes, Honoré, find him and kill him for me! He was—it was so—." I collapsed in my brother's arms, and he picked me up and carried me to my room.

He placed me gently on my bed and said, "I'll send Françoise at once, and then I'll tell Uncle Theo."

"Oh, no, Honoré!" I looked at him beseechingly. I didn't want anyone to know my shame. Bad enough that I had encountered Honoré, but once he told Uncle Theo —why, the world would know what had happened to me!

"I must, Elise. You can't possibly marry the Baron now, surely you can see that. I shall tell Uncle Theo, and we will make every effort to find the dog who did this to you and execute him. I'll cut his heart out myself, I swear it."

The hatred that welled up inside me nearly choked me. "Yes, yes, Honoré," I said eagerly. "Find him, and cut his heart out!"

Uncle Theo was worried and upset by the incident, but to our astonishment he was adamant about not searching for my assailant. Under no circumstances would he permit a whisper of scandal to ruin the match with the Baron. Honoré pleaded for my honor, but Uncle Theo stood firm. The best way to salvage my honor was to marry me off as soon as possible to Baron Friederich and say a word of this to no one.

"And how," asked Honoré sarcastically, "are we going to keep the Baron in the dark after the wedding night? I know the man's not very bright, but even he—"

"The Baron," said Uncle Theo, "will have plenty of wine to drink at his wedding. I'll see to that. And the next day he will have no one but himself to blame for his poor memory."

"Perhaps I can procure a vial of chicken blood," Honoré suggested, "to help the illusion."

"That will do," Uncle Theo said sharply. "People like the Baron, who are good-hearted and without guile, see what they want to see and believe what they want to believe. We will need no help from you, Honoré, and I forbid you to make any attempt at all to find Elise's—ah, the man." He looked over at me. I felt my cheeks go crimson and I bit my lips to keep from crying. Uncle Theo said in a softer tone, "We are all to blame for this. You, me, and even Elise. I have warned her time and again not to go wandering off by herself."

"But—"

"I do not care to discuss the matter further." Uncle Theo pressed my hand and kissed my forehead. "Good night, child. I'm sorry this had to happen, but we cannot let it interfere with our plans, you can see that."

When we were alone again Honoré said bitterly, "Well, our placid and amiable Uncle Theo is turning out to have a will of iron." He continued to chafe at our uncle's decision, however, and a couple of weeks later when Philippe came home for the wedding, looking splendid in his military uniform, Honoré tried vainly to enlist his aid.

"Our sister's honor is at stake!" he argued passionately. "And our own!"

Philippe shook his golden head. "You should have thought about our honor long ago, Honoré, then none of this would have happened."

Honoré fumed. "You forget that we are half-Corsican, Brother, and honor means more to a Corsican than it does to a Frenchman. We cannot let this outrage go un-avenged.''

I looked at my brothers. Like me, Honoré favored the Corsican side of the family. We were small and dark, with fiery tempers and passionate natures. Philippe, on the other hand, took after the Lesconflairs. He was tall and fair, and he managed to retain a cool head in a crisis.

"But no Corsican," said Philippe calmly, "would be willing to sacrifice his sister's reputation for the sake of his own satisfaction. We don't have the slightest idea of who the fellow is, after all. If the two of us start making inquiries, armed only with Elise's description of him and the date and place he was seen, then everyone will know what's afoot. I assure you, Honoré, that if I ever meet the fellow I will run him through without a second thought and throw his carcass to the dogs. I am no coward, and I would give my life for Elise. But she would be better served by our love and discretion now than by our thirst for re-venge."

And there the matter rested. Uncle Theo wrote to the Baron and told him that the date of the wedding had been advanced because "Elise is so anxious and eager to be-come your bride." Wedding preparations were acceler-ated: a half dozen seamstresses worked feverishly on my trousseau and my wedding gown, repairmen and garden-ers crawled all over the Chateau, invitations went out and soon gifts began to pour in.

Uncle Theo was enormously relieved by Françoise's assurance that I would not have the seducer's child, but plans continued to speed ahead. The sooner I was wed, the less chance there was of something else going wrong and ruining our chances for a baronial connection. Six weeks after I lost my virginity to a stranger I would become the Baroness von Meier.

I spent my days reading or walking or riding occasionally with Honoré or Philippe. Most of the time I sat alone in the gardens or in my room, staring at nothing in particular. Uncle Theo had forbidden me to go out of sight of the Chateau unaccompanied, but he need not have worried. I felt too sick at heart to go anywhere or do anything. I hardly gave a thought to the Baron, and I took no interest at all in my approaching nuptials. More often than not I found myself thinking about that afternoon by the stream.

I couldn't put him out of my mind. I told myself that I hated him and that if I ever saw him again I would kill him, and I was furious with myself for remembering vividly everything about him: his broad shoulders and fine carriage, the smile that rested on his face until he was provoked to anger or to laughter, his strong hands, his deep voice and startlingly pale eyes. When I closed my eyes I could feel his hands on my body and his fiery lips on my breasts, and I shook with loathing. Or at least I told myself it was loathing. Several times I lay awake at night, feeling the new stirrings in my body and wondering at the currents of desire that ran through me now and again, especially when I thought of—him. In a few minutes I had been transformed from a girl into a woman, and I was still feeling the shock of what had happened.

I tried to picture the Baron as bridegroom. I was repulsed by his gross flesh, his oozing sweat and flabby face, his unattractive corpulence which I suspected was restrained during the day by bone corsets. The girls at school used to say, collapsing into giggles, that you could accurately guess the size of a man's Thing, as they called it, by looking at the length and shape of his fingers. I pictured the Baron's plump, formless digits and I shuddered.

During those weeks that preceded the wedding my

behaviour was spoiled and sullen. Françoise guessed that the true reason was not so much my distaste for the Baron as my inability to forget the stranger.

"You are no better than any other silly girl who falls in love with the very man who treats her badly and then runs off," she observed tartly. "I've never yet known a woman who would choose a good man over a bad one—if she could get him."

"Love him!" I raged. "I hate him! I hate him so much that—that I'm almost sick with hatred. I promise you, Françoise, that if I ever lay eyes on him again I shall kill him!"

"Well, I hope you never do find him. Men like that are nothing but trouble. My advice to you is to stop thinking about him. Forget him. When you get to be my age you'll care more about the roof over your head and food in your belly than you will about what a man puts between your legs, you'll see."

"Stop talking like that, Françoise!" I said angrily. "I do not think about him. I don't care about him! I hate him! I hate him!" I balled my hands into fists. "Oh, why am I so unhappy?"

I threw myself on my bed and wept bitterly. Françoise sat next to me and stroked my hair, and murmured words of consolation and assurance that went unheard and unheeded.

A grand ball was to be held at the Chateau on the Friday evening before the wedding day, Sunday, to celebrate the signing of the marriage contract. Guests from all over France had been invited for the weekend. Whole wings of the house which had been closed were thrown open and cleaned vigorously. A bridal suite was sumptuously outfitted and decorated in gold and white. Uncle Theo ordered tons of food and whole casks of wine for the occasion. Everyone expected the wedding and ball to be the most exciting events held outside Paris since the days of the *ancien régime*, thanks to the Baron's generosity.

On the afternoon of the ball I bathed and, at Françoise's insistence, powdered and perfumed myself generously. Then Françoise and her assistants labored for two hours, torturing my hair into thousands of tiny ringlets which they piled high, Grecian fashion, and fixed with diamond-studded gold combs, a gift from Uncle Theo. At eight o'clock I donned my ball gown. First I put on a sleeveless undergarment of the finest white silk which fitted tightly above the waist and then flared away to a hem that was just wide enough to dance in. Over the silk went a dress of the sheerest transparent gold gauze with flowing elbow-length sleeves. This was fastened under my bosom and hung open at the front to reveal the shimmering silk underneath.

Françoise and her helpers stood gaping for a full minute before they let loose with a chorus of rapturous sighs.

"Oh, Mademoiselle!"

"Ah, *chérie!*"

"She is so beautiful that I could cry!"

I twitched impatiently. "Well, let me see. Bring a mirror, somebody. It isn't every day that you get to see a lamb so gloriously arrayed for the slaughter."

Françoise tut-tutted disapprovingly, and the two maids brought in a chunky, full-length oval mirror, a relic from the days of the Sun King.

I lifted my chin, threw my shoulders back, and turned to inspect myself. I saw an Elise who was at once familiar and at the same time a stranger to me.

Black curls framed my face and stood around my head in high, sooty clouds. Diamonds winked among the curls like stars in a midnight sky. My eyes were gleaming like polished coals under the strong arch of my brows, and although my skin was pale, nearly as white as the silk chemise and the long gloves one of the maids handed me, patches of pink stood out on my cheeks like roses on snow, as Françoise said. My full lips were red and slightly parted. The face that I had known as attractive and interesting was now arresting and truly beautiful, with a new maturity and seriousness in its expression. And with the yards of shining gold gauze draped over my slender hips and shapely bosom I looked powerful and somehow unreachable, like a fairy queen, like a proud and wrathful Titania.

Tears welled up in my eyes, blurring the vision of the golden goddess I suddenly detested. I whirled and snatched up a weighty handmirror and hurled it at this new Elise with all my strength. Both mirrors shattered noisily. One of the maids screamed loudly and Françoise sucked in her breath.

"I hate her, I hate her!" I cried. I buried my face in my gloved hands and sobbed.

"Now you've done it," snapped Françoise, who was superstitious. "Not one mirror—oh, no, most people when they break a mirror would break only one—but not you! Two! Heaven only knows what will happen to you now."

"Oh, be quiet, you silly old woman!" I shouted at her. "Can't you see that I hate it, all of it? I don't want to marry that fat German peasant, that gross ape! I don't want to marry anyone. All this folderol, all this foolishness! He'll gloat and slobber over me—oh, I can't bear it!"

A knock sounded at the door. Françoise came up to me and shook me.

"You can bear it, child because you must. You're making yourself miserable for no good reason. You'll never be happy, Elise, because you can't see happiness when it's right under your nose. You never could. You keep waiting and wishing for something better, instead of being satisfied with what you have. Dry your eyes." The knock came again. "It's time to grow up, Elise. It's time to be a woman."

She strode to the door and threw it open. My faithful bridegroom stood on the threshold with an anxious smile on his face.

"It is permitted to pay my respects to Mademoiselle?" he asked in his formal way. "I have something to give, something it would give me great pleasure to—"

"Come in, then," said Françoise brusquely. She stood aside to let him enter. "You girls, out." She tossed her head at the two maids, who, still wide-eyed and open-mouthed from my tantrum, scurried into the hallway.

The Baron bowed his way past the departing maids—Honoré and I giggled furiously over his pathetic eagerness to please and the way he bowed democratically to everyone from the lowest bootblack and the clergy to Uncle Theo's most noble friends—and padded across the room to me. I glared at him without smiling.

"Ah, Mademoiselle, dearest Elise, may I say that you are truly radiant this evening?" he gushed, dropping to one fat knee and pressing my hand to his lips. "I can but kneel at your lovely feet, in humblest adoration—"

"Did you wish to see me about something, Friederich?"

"Ah! Yes! Indeed, yes." He struggled to his feet and proudly extended a large velvet coffer. He flipped open the lid. "A little something for you to wear tonight, my dearest." He was so pleased with himself that I wanted to kick him. Inside the coffer lay a necklace of huge diamonds in a grotesque Baroque setting of cupids and twirling ribbons, with matching earrings.

I gulped. "Friederich, really, you shouldn't." I had never seen such hideous jewelry.

He beamed. "My sainted mother's," he explained

fondly, setting the casket down and extracting the necklace. His pudgy hands trembled as he held it up to my chest and he sighed ecstatically. "Gold for my golden girl, and diamonds for one who shines brighter than any star!"

I looked past him to Françoise, who lifted a warning eyebrow at me and pulled her mouth into a tight, critical line. I swallowed hard and thanked the Baron as graciously as I could. "Oh, they are beautiful, Friederich. Please, put the necklace on for me."

Quivering with the joy of being so near his lady, the Baron fastened the horrid thing around my neck. I nearly sagged under its weight, but I smiled gamely and pretended to be thrilled with his gift. When he had kissed my hand another half-dozen times and taken himself away, I sighed with relief and looked sourly at my bosom.

"My God, Françoise, have you ever seen anything uglier?"

"No," Françoise admitted, "I haven't. At least you didn't throw it in his face."

"Not likely," I said glumly. "I can hardly lift it!"

Françoise laughed heartily. The sound was merry and infectious, and I joined in in spite of myself. When Philippe came in and asked for the pleasure of escorting me to the ball, I was smiling for the first time in weeks.

"Is it possible," he whispered as we descended the staircase to the main hall, "that you're actually becoming reconciled to marrying the Baron? Or did he purchase your affection with that digusting bijou?"

"He did not," I said crisply. "And neither am I reconciled to my fate. I think I am merely bored with sulking, Philippe. I have decided to put on a new face for the evening. Do you like it?"

"I have always liked it," he said fondly.

I kissed him and swept off to receive my guests.

The nuptial ball was a huge success. The drive to the

Chateau was filled with coaches and liveried grooms and footmen, and Uncle Theo had stationed small boys with lanterns every twenty feet or so to light the way for our guests. The Baron and I led the first dance at nine o'clock, and after that I danced and flirted with every man in the room. I downed countless glasses of champagne and grew flushed and witty with wine and warmth and dancing. Philippe claimed me for a mazurka at eleven o'clock.

"You're looking far too radiant, Sister," he said as we whirled around the floor. "The Baron is wearing a worried expression on his face, I see. He is proud of your success, yet I rather suspect that he wishes you would give him a little more attention."

"He'll have to get used to it," I said gaily. "After we are married I intend to have whole squads of admirers and sy—sycophants."

"Elise," said Philippe with mock disapproval, "I think you are a wee bit drunk."

"More than a wee bit." I tapped his shoulder with my fan. "A lot. But don't scold, Philippe. I am having a wonderful time. This is my last night of freedom, you know. I think I shall dance until dawn. Until noon tomorrow. I shall dance until tomorrow night, and then I shall fall into a faint and sleep—forever. Until I die, perhaps."

"Oh, come now, it's not that bad," Philippe laughed. "At least the poor devil's rich. And you can't fool me, Elise. You know you can wind him around your little finger. He'll probably let you stay in Paris year-round, if you like."

"I suppose so. Oh, Philippe, if only he weren't so awful to look at. He reminds me of a toad, all squat and warty. Ugh!" I lifted a glass of champagne off the tray of a passing footman and downed it in a single gulp.

Our mazurka came to an end. In the lull between dances

I heard old Derain, the butler, announce the arrival of a latecomer.

"My Lord Armand Charles Alexandre Valadon, Marquis de Pellissier."

I glanced up. I had never seen the Marquis, although I had heard his name. He spent most of his time abroad on diplomatic missions. My champagne glass crashed to the floor. Heads turned in my direction. A footman darted over to sweep up the mess.

"Elise, what's the matter? Are you ill? You're as white as a sheet."

"Philippe, take me out of here," I whispered hoarsely. "Now, at once!"

"But why—"

"Please! I beg you!" Philippe led me into the hall and sat me down on a bench in an alcove.

"Do you want an ice? A glass of water? Oh, why did you drink so much?"

"Philippe." I was trembling all over. He took my hands and cradled them in his. "That's him, Philippe. The—man in the forest."

"Who, Elise? Which man?"

"The Marquis de Pellissier, Philippe. He just arrived."

Philippe grew pale. "Oh, my God."

I looked at him beseechingly. "What shall we do, Philippe? If he sees me, he'll escape. Kill him! We—I—. Oh, Philippe, I hate him so! We've got to do something!"

Philippe frowned and stared at me for a long time without saying a word. "You're sure about this, Elise?" he said after a while. "There's no mistake?"

"No, Philippe, I swear it. It's the same man. I—I could even see the scar on his cheek where—where I struck him with the riding crop. Oh, God, Philippe, I think I'm going to faint."

Philippe passed his arm around my waist and helped me to stand up. "Try and be calm, Elise, and listen to me. Are you all right? Can you stand?" I nodded. "Then go to the library and wait for me there. I've got to find Honoré and tell him. Everything will be all right, I promise you. Now go quickly and we'll join you as soon as we can. This is a very serious matter. He is a nobleman, one of Napoleon's favorites. We must not act hastily."

I nodded again and when he left me I ran to the library. When I got inside I threw my weight against the door and closed my eyes. My heart was thumping wildly and I thought I was going to be sick. I stumbled to the French windows and threw them open. I sucked in great lungfuls of air and tried to calm myself. Soon I felt quite sober, and angry.

How dare he! How dare he enter this house on the eve of my wedding! He would pay for this with his life, I was sure. Philippe and Honoré would not let him escape. I knew I could depend on them to avenge my honor. Yes, they had had to comply with Uncle Theo's wishes that no search be made for the man, but when he fell into their hands this way, why, they would cut him down like the cruel animal that he was.

They wouldn't denounce him publicly. No, that would only embarrass me. Instead they would speak to him privately. Welcome to the Chateau Lesconflair, my Lord. We are delighted that you could be with us on the occasion of our sister's wedding. We understand that you and she have met. You think not? Think again, my Lord. Think back to a time about six weeks ago—

And then they would withdraw to a balcony, or somewhere far from the crush of servants and guests, and they would discuss the terms of the duel. Philippe, who was a fine swordsman, would issue the challenge. Honoré as his second would find weapons. Swords in hand, Philippe

Lesconflair and Armand Valadon, Marquis de Pellissier would face each other. I could almost hear the clanging of their blades, their heavy breathing, their determined footfalls. Philippe had taught me to fence a little, and I had no difficulty picturing each thrust and feint. Kill him for me, Philippe, I said to myself. Run the devil through, and bring me his heart on the point of your blade!

The door opened and I whirled around. The Marquis de Pellissier stood on the threshold with Philippe and Honoré in closed ranks behind him. He was undoubtedly alive, and worse, he still wore the cynical smile on his lips that had haunted me for weeks. His eyes seemed to find me where I stood in the shadows and they burned into my brain. He gave a jerky movement and stepped into the room. Philippe and Honoré followed and closed the door.

"Not too hard, I beg you, Monsieur," said de Pellissier. "This is my newest coat. I would hate to have the velvet spoiled."

"Rest easy, my Lord," said Philippe smoothly. "When you are waiting for burial no one will notice a tiny tear on the back of your coat. Instead they will be admiring how well you look in repose."

I saw then that Honoré was pressing the point of a knife into the Marquis' back.

"Philippe! Honoré!" I exclaimed. "What is the meaning of this?"

"Our sister, Elise, my Lord," said Honoré sharply, by way of introduction. "But you have met before."

"Have we? I do not recall the pleasure."

I stepped forward into the center of the room where the light was better. A slow smile of recognition spread over his face.

"But of course! I remember now. You were costumed differently then, Mademoiselle. If I could see—"

He broke off as Honoré prodded him. "You seem to

have left your manners, my Lord, in the same forest where my sister lost her honor,'' Honoré growled. ''But perhaps both of you might gain something this evening if my Lord can persuade himself to act like a gentleman. Can you recall our conversation of a few minutes ago, my Lord?'' he prompted the Marquis.

''Certainly. The point of your dagger brings swift remembrance, my friend,'' the Marquis replied. ''But surely there is no need for these crude tactics. We are not in Sicily now.''

''Corsica, my Lord,'' said Honoré grimly. ''The hot blood of Corsica runs in our veins, as it flows in the Emperor's. Like him, we do not forget a slight or an insult, but like him, we are willing to be reasonable.''

''We are negotiating with your life, my Lord,'' Philippe put in.

''Negotiating!'' I said. ''What is there to negotiate? Philippe, I must insist—''

''One moment, Elise,'' said Honoré. ''Well, my Lord? Have you reached your decision?''

''The word 'decision' implies choice,'' the Marquis remarked coolly. ''I have no choice, as I see it.''

He approached me. Hatred and revulsion flowed over me but I did not shrink away from him. I met his gaze with eyes as cold and steady as his own, although I was trembling inwardly. His presence filled the room. He seemed inevitable and inescapable, like Fate or Doom.

He bowed deeply. ''Mademoiselle Lesconflair, will you do me the honor of accepting my hand in marriage?''

''Marry—you?'' I gasped. I turned to my brothers. ''Is this how you avenge me, then?'' I demanded angrily. ''Cowards! Weaklings! Diplomats, bah! How can you suggest such a thing? I would rather die myself than marry this sneering villain. Give me your knife, Honoré.'' I extended my hand. ''I shall kill him myself, as I have vowed to kill him. Brothers, indeed! I would rather have two children in my service than you. What's the matter with you? Have you gone mad?''

"Elise.'' Honoré's face was flushed. "Control yourself. It was Philippe's idea. I was all for—''

"It was the best solution,'' said Philippe with icy calm. "To everything.''

"You're afraid!'' I said accusingly. "You're afraid of repercussions, of being punished by the Emperor! For shame. The country would be well rid of this worm. Marry him? The idea is absurd and insulting!''

"I am in complete agreement, Mademoiselle,'' said the Marquis with a little smile. "Perhaps we can reach an understanding, then—''

"I want no understanding,'' I said. "I want your blood!''

The Marquis yawned and settled himself into an arm chair. "I'll let you three fight this matter out. Let me know when you have reached your decision.''

"You will marry,'' said Philippe firmly. "Elise, you will wait here with his Lordship while Honoré and I make arrangements. You will have about an hour to become better acquainted before you marry.''

"Acquainted? Marry?'' I shouted. "Philippe, I won't! You must be joking.''

"Believe me, Elise,'' Philippe's face looked strained and tired, "this is the only way, the best way.'' He turned to my newest bridegroom. "Please don't try to leave this room, my Lord. I have stationed armed men at the doors and windows. They have orders to kill you if you emerge without the company of my brother and myself.''

The Marquis nodded and yawned again, then he closed his eyes. Honoré and Philippe went out, leaving me alone with him. I paced the floor nervously. At that moment I hated my brothers more than I hated this man. They had

betrayed me. I had no one to fight for me now. I glared at
the Marquis, who seemed completely at peace. His hands
were folded over his chest and he was snoring gently.

I stamped my foot. "How dare you sleep! Wake up at
once and get out of here!"

He opened one sleepy eye. "Forgive me, Mademoiselle. I have had an exhausting day, and the evening
promises to be even more exhausting."

"Get out!" I pointed at the door. "Do you hear me? Go
away! Now!"

He raised his eyebrows. "And be slain by your
brothers' henchmen? You'd like that, wouldn't you? No
thank you, Mademoiselle. I shall stay where I am."

"You—you are filth!" I said. "You are the lowest
worm, the dirtiest cad I have ever met. You disgust me,
you nauseate me!"

"I beg your pardon," he said mockingly. "I am sorry
that the sight of me stirs such appalling feelings in you.
Most women have quite a different reaction when they are
in my company."

"Most women," I sneered. "Poor ignorant bitches. I
have seen you in a different light, Monsieur, and I know
you for what you are: cruel, arrogant, and unfeeling. You
are a beast. You are an animal. You—you have no
manners!"

"No manners, you say?" he drawled. "Dear, dear.
Forgive me, Mademoiselle. I have never before been
accused of having no manners. I suit my manners to the
occasion, of course, and I confess the requirements of this
particular occasion defeat me. How does one address a
lady with whom one's acquaintance has been rather brief,
and who seems destined to become one's wife at any
moment? Particularly when one has met this lady under
quite different circumstances. I know you, Mademoiselle,
for what you are, just as you say you know me. You are

wanton, willful, and wild." He licked his lips at his
poetry. "Yes, you are a little savage, lady, and I must
admit that the prospect of marriage to you rather frightens
me."

"How dare you talk to me that way?" I stood in front of
him, my fists clenched. "You—you brutally attacked
me. I was only trying to defend myself! You arrogant
swine! Brutal fiend! Callous bastard!"

"Your vocabulary is impressive," he remarked. "I
seem to be a walking catalog of infamous traits."

"You are heinous, ugly, horrible!" He was laughing at
me!

He smiled. "I can hardly believe that in these enlight-
ened times, among educated persons, matrimony should
be the natural and immediate consequence of a minor
poolside dalliance. Still, this is a provincial backwater,
and I seem to have fallen into the clutches of some rather
ill-bred ruffians—"

I shook my fist at him. "It is you, Monsieur, who are
ill-bred!"

"—who insist on placing the blame for an insignificant
incident—"

"Insignificant!"

"—squarely on the shoulders of the victim." He
stood up and strolled around the room. I was speechless at
his audacity. "Very nice," he remarked as he looked up at
the David portrait of me as Diana the Huntress, done at
Napoleon's request on the occasion of my sixteenth birthday. "But not really accurate. But then it would take a
greater artist than David to capture the sparkle in your
eyes, the right tint of the flush on your cheeks, the glorious
swelling of your breasts when you are angry. This picture
of you is too serene, too innocent. You are not innocent,
Elise. You never were."

I dove for Uncle Theo's desk and picked up a heavy

silver inkwell and hurled it at his head. He saw it just in time and dodged out of the way, and the inkwell smashed one of Uncle Theo's favorite Dresden figurines. In a flash the Marquis was at my side, gripping my hands in his. I kicked out at him, but I was wearing thin kid slippers and I only succeeded in hurting myself.

"You are a spoiled, undisciplined child, Mademoiselle," he said. "I swear if you were mine I would beat you until you could not stand. I am not fond of the company of spoiled children—"

"Except when you want to rape them!" I said.

His smile broadened and he leered at me. "Exactly so." His fingers dug into my wrists. "You know, you lost your virginity because you nearly blinded me. You needed to be taught a lesson, little one."

"Liar!" I spat at him. "You would have—you would have done it anyway."

"Would I? You may be right, but then we'll never know, will we? You were a luscious, ripe fruit, ready for the plucking. Decent girls do not swim nude in secluded pools, nor do they lie on their backs in the sun, dreaming of love. You must forgive me for misconstruing the situation. But I am only, after all, a mere man and not a saint."

He let me go. I stood away from him, shaking with anger. I was so choked with rage that I could not speak. I massaged my wrists and glared at him wrathfully. He settled himself in a chair and crossed one leg over the other.

"We must be civilized about this, Mademoiselle Lesconflair, even though those around us are acting like barbarians. A marriage between us would be a grave mistake. What happened between us was nothing, the merest whiling away of a hot, dull afternoon." I gave a strangled cry. He went on. "You are to wed the Baron von Meier, I hear. Do it. Marry him and bear him ten fine sons and let us forget this foolishness. You must persuade your brothers to accept another form of restitution.''

''If I persuade them of anything,'' I said through my teeth, ''it will be to run you through. You think I welcome the thought of marrying you? I would welcome death more eagerly!''

The door opened. Philippe and Honoré came in, followed by an ancient prelate dressed in red robes who walked with two canes.

''We're in luck, Elise,'' cried Honoré. ''Cardinale Francesco Paolo de Guerrera from Rome is among the guests tonight. We have explained the situation to him and he has said that he would be delighted to lend his assistance.''

''No!'' I said sharply, then in a rising crescendo, ''no, no, no, no, no!'' My brothers stopped in their tracks. ''Don't you understand? I will not marry this monster tonight or ever! I would rather be married to the Devil himself than—''

''Oh, for Heaven's sake, don't throw one of your tantrums now, Elise,'' said Philippe impatiently. ''You've been moaning and groaning for weeks now because you had to marry the Baron, and now when you have a better offer you're still raging like a hornet.''

''And what about Honoré's debts?'' I demanded. ''You don't think for one moment that this wretch will stand behind you, do you?''

''That's none of your concern, Elise,'' said Honoré crisply. ''It's not important.''

Not important! Honoré's indiscretions had thrust me into one appalling alliance simply to avert scandal, and now that we were about to do something even more scandalous—it was none of my concern!

I put my hands up to my flaming cheeks. ''This is horrid! Insane!'' I said breathlessly.

The Marquis' voice cut through the air. "I couldn't agree with you more, Mademoiselle."

The aged Cardinale shuffled forward and said in a quavering voice, "We may begin now? Is there to be no music? Bless you, my children."

*"Si, Cardinale, si,"* Honoré said, bustling around arranging furniture and positioning the Marquis and me in front of the Cardinale.

"How beautiful is the morning," the old man sighed rapturously. *"Si?"*

"Good God, the man is senile," said the Marquis. "This is lunacy!"

We were married in Uncle Theo's library by a feeble Italian prelate with Honoré and Philippe as the two witnesses required by canon law. At the end the Cardinale produced a document from the depths of his robes. We all signed.

"Blessings of God on you both, *Barone e Baronessa,"* said the Cardinale grandly, offering his ring to be kissed. He squinted his rheumy eyes at us and beamed happily.

Armand Valadon laughed aloud. "He thinks I'm the Baron! This can't possibly be legal!"

"It's legal, all right," said Philippe coldly. "You may be sure of that."

At that moment Uncle Theo burst in with the real Baron in tow.

"Elise, where have you been?" Uncle Theo demanded. "Everyone's been asking—." He looked at the Cardinale and at the Marquis, and then he caught sight of the document that lay on his desk. He picked it up and scanned it quickly. "Great God in Heaven!" He mopped his brow and sat down heavily. The Baron began to sputter in German.

"The Marquis de Pellissier is the man for whom we have been searching," said Honoré. "He preferred marriage with Elise to instant death. The ceremony took place just a few minutes ago.''

''Are you mad?'' Uncle Theo pounded the arm of his chair. ''Do you have any idea of what you've done?''

''Don't worry, Uncle,'' said Honoré, ''the Baron will be repaid, I promise you.''

''A marriage! It's out of the question, do you hear? I shall procure an annullment! An annullment! I forbid this! I refuse to permit it.''

The Baron spoke up. ''Marriage? Death? Ceremony? I do not understand. What has my golden girl done?''

The fight was on. Uncle Theo ranted, the Baron wept disconsolately, Philippe and Honoré pleaded, and the Cardinale grinned benignly at us all. Armand Valadon stood at the open window, apart from the fray, and gazed placidly at the lights playing on the fountains. A glorious display of fireworks had been planned for midnight, to signal that the marriage contract had been signed and that the houses of von Meier and Lesconflair were joined. They went off as planned, unseen by everyone in the room except the Marquis.

When Uncle Theo discovered his shattered figurine he insisted that the Marquis take me away at once. It took Philippe nearly half an hour to persuade him to permit us to stay until the morning, when he and Honoré would escort us to the Marquis' estates south of Paris.

I went over to him and tried to embrace him, but he put me off, saying, ''No, no, it's all right, Elise. I should have known you would have your own way in the end. I was a fool to expect anything from you or your brothers. You are savages, you Corsicans, all savages. I have never known a Corsican who wasn't a savage, and that includes that upstart Bonaparte!''

We could tell when Uncle Theo was really upset when he began to vilify Napoleon. This time not even Philippe could soothe him. Finally my brothers escorted the Marquis and me out of the library. Philippe sighed deeply.

"I'll show you and Elise to the bridal chamber, my Lord," he said to the Marquis. My heart thumped painfully. Oh, God, I thought, not that.

"And shall you keep watch through the night to make sure that the marriage is consummated?" the Marquis asked calmly.

Philippe stiffened. "My Lord, this has been a trying night for all of us. I beg you, please remember that we are gentlemen—"

"Lest you prod me into remembrance with your swords and make your sister a widow before she is even a wife? I don't think you will do that." The Marquis turned to me. "Come, my dear, I think we should do something to celebrate this occasion. This ball is being given in honor of your wedding, is it not?" He placed a firm hand under my elbow and propelled me in the direction of the grand ballroom, where our guests, ignorant of what had just taken place in the library, were enjoying themselves to the full. "By all means let us attend—together."

"No!" I tried to jerk away and his grip tightened. I looked pleadingly at my brothers, who looked away. I was this man's wife now, his property. He could do what he liked with me, and no one dared interfere. "I beg you," I hissed at Valadon, "spare me the embarrassment of being seen with you in front of my guests."

He looked at me coldly and said, "Have you spared me this evening? We shall have to face society sometime, why not now? Are you embarrassed," he stressed the word unpleasantly, "to be my wife? Perhaps you are embarrassed at the suddenness with which this has all taken place. I cannot blame you for that. I am rather bemused, shall we say, myself. I have always found that the best way to deal with embarrassment is to ignore it, since it comes only when one is concerned with what others may think. But we don't care about that, do we, Elise, or we would not have behaved so shamefully in the woods. Are you still embarrassed about that? I, for one, would have guessed that you had no shame at all."

He dragged me down the long corridor towards the main entrance of the ballroom. I was aware of the surprised expressions on the faces of the people we passed. I wanted to die. I wanted to sink through the floor, to vanish, to disappear in a puff of smoke. I felt degraded, ridiculous, and wretched, but I held my head high as I swept along beside him.

We reached the top of the short flight of stairs that led down to the enormous dance floor. I held back. "No, I can't," I said under my breath. "I refuse to go in there."

"Madame." His voice carried over the din of the crowd and the orchestra. I cringed. "Kindly remember that you are my wife! In my brief acquaintance with you I have discerned in your character several alarming traits: you are willful, you are stubborn, you are headstrong, and you are accustomed to having your own way. Well I, Madame, am also accustomed to having my way. You will submit to me or you will suffer for it here and now, in front of these good people." His gaze swept over the room, which had fallen absolutely silent as he spoke. Even the musicians had stopped playing. "But forgive us, Mesdames and Messieurs," he said. "You have come here to celebrate a wedding and so you shall. Gentlemen Musicians, a *valse,* if you please."

The crowd fell back as we descended the stairs. The dance floor cleared, and an excited hum arose from the edges of the room. My husband pulled me around to face him. I lifted my right hand to slap him, but he caught it in mid-air and pressed my fingers to his lips. Then he passed his arm around my waist and we began to dance sedately in unnerving silence until the orchestra, recovering from its astonishment, began raggedly to play a waltz.

"I shall never forgive you for this," I said tightly.

"Never is a long time, Madame. Ah, you're doing splendidly. One, two, three. One, two, three. Very good."

"I hate you!" I said through clenched teeth. "I would sooner be married to an ape!"

"And I to a cobra," he said mildly. "But that is beside the point. Why don't you smile for all these wonderful people? I wonder what they are thinking."

"I don't give a damn what they think!"

He shook his head slightly. "I must cure you of your abominable language, Madame. It's quite shocking."

I opened my mouth to retort, but his arm tightened suddenly and he drew me closer. Our bodies touched, from chest to knee. The crowd gasped. Around and around we whirled, faster and faster. I ceased to be aware of the faces in the crowd. I ceased to care what they thought. We might have been spinning in some kind of vortex or in a gigantic whirlpool. I saw only him. I was aware only of the hard power of his body, his warmth, his grace, the warm breath on my cheek, the thrilling pressure of his arm. I closed my eyes. My head fell back and I felt his lips on my throat—.

The music ended abruptly. We came to a halt. My head was spinning and I would have fallen but for the support of his arm. He addressed the assembly:

"My wife and I appreciate your warm good wishes, but it is late and we are tired."

Then, to my horror, he swept me up in his arms and carried me out of the ballroom and up the stairs to the second floor landing. When we reached the top he turned and bellowed, "By God, will someone show us to the bridal chamber, or must I bed the lady in the hall?"

A wide-eyed footman darted up the stairs. "This way, my Lord."

Finally we were alone in the gorgeously decorated apartment. He set me down.

"Not bad." He glanced around. "A trifle overdone, but I suppose your Baron would not find it so. Ah, I see some kind person has supplied us with champagne. The brother with the sense of humor, no doubt. Philippe, was it? A shame we cannot be friends. Will you have some?" I glared at him. He shrugged. "Too bad. It's really excellent."

Sipping casually at his champagne, he strolled over and tested the softness of the bed with his hand. "The purpose of the champagne in the bridal chamber is, I imagine, to alleviate embarrassment," he leered at me, "calm the nerves, and dull the pain, should there be pain. But of course, you are no virgin—"

I found my voice. "Thanks to you, my Lord."

"Thanks to me. Indeed, we are old friends, you and I." He refilled his glass and stretched out on a chaise longue. "Yes, this impromptu wedding has caused me some inconvenience, Elise."

"I'm glad to hear it," I said.

He grinned. "It seems that whenever we meet I must delay a journey. If you were different, I might respect the somewhat unorthodox circumstances that have brought us together this night. You would like me to leave you untouched and the marriage unconsummated so that you could procure an annulment, wouldn't you? You could even marry again when the fuss died down, perhaps to that grotesque German."

"I want no favors from you," I told him.

"Nor are you likely to get any," he said. "I find you singularly undeserving of consideration. After all, a night spent in a splendid Chateau with a noble lady is much better than one spent in a small cramped room of some provincial inn, in the company of a street whore, don't you agree? Take off your gown, Mademoiselle—or rather, Madame, and let us get down to business.''

Fear knotted my stomach and sent shivers down the backs of my legs. I moistened my lips with my tongue and said, ''I shan't.''

''You must,'' he said bluntly. ''I have given an order and you will obey. You know very well that if you go running off to your brothers now they will send you back to me.'' He set down his empty glass and crossed his arms over his chest. ''Take off your clothes. I want another look at what I had to buy to save my neck.''

''No, Monsieur.'' I prayed that my voice would not betray the terror I felt. ''If you are such a depraved animal that you would bed me by force in these circumstances, I cannot stop you. But I will not help you. I will fight you with every ounce of strength I possess.''

A hundred candles filled the room with a brilliant yellow light. Armand Valadon stared at me for a while, then he got to his feet and walked to each candelabra and wall sconce in turn, blowing the candles out. When the room was dark except for a pale glimmer of moonlight he took off his own clothes and tossed them over a chair. He came towards me through the shimmering moonlight and stood in front of me.

I leaned back against a low dresser and braced myself with my hands. I held my breath and closed my eyes. When I felt the gentle weight of his hands on my shoulders I shuddered inwardly, but I vowed that I would not show my fear. I would not plead and beg this time. I would not scream and I would not weep. I would choose my time carefully, and then I would attack.

He grasped the edges of my bodice and slowly tore the silk and golden gauze away from my body. I stiffened, and when I judged him to be near enough I swiftly brought my knee up to his groin. He blocked it with one hand, and with the other he grabbed my hair and pulled my head back so roughly that I thought my neck would snap. He was holding me so close to him that I had no room to maneuver.

"None of that, Madame," he chuckled. "You don't want a worthless bridegroom, do you?"

"I hope you burn in hell!" I told him.

He removed the Baron's diamonds from my neck and earlobes. "Not part of your dowry, I trust," he said. He dropped the jewels carelessly to the floor. Then he took the combs and pins out of my hair and let it fall softly to my shoulders. He kissed my neck and my ears and my eyes, and his tongue found my mouth. A warm flush spread over me. When he lowered his head and kissed my breasts, I felt as though someone was driving a burning spike into my loins. My strength of purpose melted away. I was dizzy, weak, and as limp as a doll in his arms. He slid his hands down to my buttocks and kneaded them gently. I gasped audibly and tossed my head. Every nerve in my body was tingling and alive.

My hands twitched convulsively. I stroked him lightly and tentatively. His flesh felt firm and smooth, and cool. I ran my hands over his back and shoulders. His kisses grew deeper and more demanding. I wreathed my arms around his neck and laced my fingers through his thick hair. I could feel his fiery nakedness against the entire length of my body. He nudged me gently with his knee. I moaned deliriously and pressed closer to him.

He scooped me up and carried me to the bed. I closed my eyes and rested my cheek on his shoulder. He paused for a moment, then dumped me unceremoniously onto the coverlet. I looked up at him uncomprehendingly.

"Good night, Madame," he said. Even though I

couldn't see his face clearly I could tell he was grinning. He gathered up his clothes and slung them over his arm. He held his shoes in his hand.

"Where—where are you going?"

"To sleep in the dressing room, of course," he said. "Rest easy, my lady. I am not really a brute. I shall not rape you—tonight." He went out through the connecting door to the dressing room.

I threw myself face down on the bed and pummeled the pillow. His meaning was clear: he would not rape me because I was willing, all too willing, to give myself to him. I was utterly shameless and wanton. He was probably laughing himself silly now. Oh, I was such a fool! No doubt he thought that my behaviour absolved him from any guilt for what happened at the pool. In the right circumstances I really was no better than a street whore.

I tossed restlessly, starting at each bump and footfall as the wedding guests took themselves to bed. I could not ignore the deep hunger that gnawed at my vitals, and I could not put my husband out of my mind.

## III. The Honeymoon

We left the Chateau in the cold gray of early morning, before Uncle Theo and his guests arose. Armand Valadon, Marquis de Pellissier, was to travel with me in a small coach while Honoré and Philippe rode alongside to make sure the Marquis did not escape before I was safely installed as the new mistress of Pellissier. Honoré had armed himself with pistols, a rapier, and a poignard, and he flushed red to the roots of his black hair when the Marquis expressed an earnest wish that he would not hurt himself.

Françoise filled two trunks with the items from my trousseau that she thought I would need most. These were strapped on behind, and inside the coach I had a smaller valise with the garments and toiletries I would need during the journey.

I wore the costume that had been made for my trip to Bavaria, a soft jade green velvet traveling suit trimmed with black. A shower of fine lace at the throat softened the fashionably masculine cut of the jacket and provided a perfect setting, or so the seamstress had assured me, for my oval face. Françoise had dressed my hair so that clusters of curls bounced under the brim of my black bonnet. I carried a small reticule and an ebony walking stick.

Françoise begged Philippe and Honoré to allow her to accompany me. "It's unheard of, a young lady traveling all that way without another woman along!" she fumed. "If your Uncle were in his right mind he would never allow it."

"I'm sorry, Françoise," said Philippe kindly, "but Elise will send for you after she arrives. It will only take a week or so."

"We are more interested in speed than propriety, Françoise," said Honoré loftily, "and we want to keep the coach as light as possible." He eyed her considerable bulk. "Speed is of the essence."

"Your hide is of the essence, boy," she retorted grimly. "You'd better get it out of my sight before I forget you're supposed to be a man and give you a thrashing."

I hugged her tightly. "Oh, Françoise," I whispered despairingly, "why must I go away with such a brute?"

She patted my shoulder reassuringly. "There, child, things happen for the best, mark my words. You won't be sorry."

"I'm sorry already! I have never met such a loathsome creature, one that I detested so—so—." I glanced over to where my bridegroom was standing idly in the dirveway. He caught my eye and grinned lewdly at me. "Oh! I hate him!" I exclaimed audibly. I dropped my voice. "And he hates me."

Françoise chuckled. "Does he? He's angry because a man wants to choose his own time for marrying and his own woman. But you be sweet to him and he'll come around. Remember, you're the prettiest girl in all France, and in spite of your willful ways and your tantrums you're the sweetest. Give him a month and he won't trade you for all the coal in China."

"Tea, Françoise," I corrected her gently. "All the tea in China."

"Let's go, Elise." Honoré jerked impatiently at his horse's reins.

The Marquis opened the carriage door and offered his arm to help me in. I ignored it pointedly. I sat back on the cushions and watched the familiar scene roll past. The schools in London and Paris had been fine enough, and I had delighted in my season at court, but the Chateau Lesconflair was the only home I had ever known, and I knew I would miss it terribly. I straightened my back and lifted my chin. I was not afraid, I told myself. And I swore I would not let him see me cry.

When I removed my bonnet and laid it on the seat I noticed that my companion, who sat opposite me, had slumped down and appeared to be sleeping. All well and good, I thought. We had exchanged not a word, not even a polite greeting, and it was my intention to maintain silence until we reached our destination. Far be it from me to disturb his slumbers, I thought angrily.

I glared at him, and almost as though he could feel the power of my gaze, the corners of his mouth twitched into the merest suggestion of a smile. He was doubtless dreaming, I assured myself, of one of the legions of barmaids and harlots he had known. Well, he could soon go back to them. I wanted none of him.

The memory of the previous night burned in my brain and brought an angry flush to my cheeks. I thought unpleasantly that his enormous body as it swept down on mine was not unlike a vulture coming out of the sky to pick carrion. Then I remembered how I had responded to his skillful caresses, how I had practically begged him to take me! The memory was so degrading, so humiliating that I thrust it from my brain at once. Yet every once in a while brief flashes of how I had felt, how dreamlike and delicious certain moments had been, came to my mind. Any man who could make a woman feel such wanton abandon must surely be the Devil himself, I reasoned.

Still, he looked harmless enough in repose. His thick hair was clipped short and brushed forward into the Grecian style that was just beginning to become popular. The lines in his face were as hard as granite, even as he slept,

but they didn't look really—evil. It was a handsome,
powerful face. I found myself admiring the fine line of his
nose and the strength of his chin, and the way his ears lay
back against his head. He really was the handsomest, most
compelling man I had ever met. His long frame seemed to
fill the coach.

He probably loathed neckcloths and cravats, I thought,
for he wore an open-necked blouse, very full, and he had
allowed the collar points to lie outside the black velvet
jacket. His cuffs bore no lace, and he wore no hat, no
jewelry, and no rings on his gloveless fingers. He carried
no snuff box or quizzing-glass, as far as I could determine.
I looked at him disdainfully. Had the cut of his clothes not
been so obviously fine and the fabrics so expensive one
might almost take him for a peasant.

"If you have finished raping me with your eyes,
Mademoiselle—your pardon, Madame," he drawled
with his eyes still closed, "perhaps you will turn your
attention elsewhere and let me sleep."

"What rubbish," I snapped. "If you are unable to sleep
it is no fault of mine."

"Oh, but it is. The heat from those smouldering black
eyes is making me quite warm." He opened one sleepy
eye. "And when a man is warmed by the heat of a
woman's glance, his thoughts turn to love. Obviously."

I jumped and drew my skirts around my legs. "How
dare you suggest such a thing! Don't touch me! Don't
come near me!"

He grunted. "Ever the affronted virgin, aren't you,
Elise?"

Slowly and haughtily I turned away from him and gazed
out the window. After a few moments a gentle snore
issued from his corner of the carriage, and a furtive glance
at his tightly closed eyes and loose jaw assured me that he
really was asleep.

We stopped once in the course of the morning to change horses, and again in the afternoon for lunch. As we drove up to an inn not far from Tours I noted a large number of mounted soldiers milling around in the courtyard. Our coachman stayed clear of them, and after their leader approached us and spoke a word to Honoré and Philippe and peered into the interior of our coach, they rode off, scattering in different directions.

Philippe dismounted and opened the door on my side of the coach. "Quite a hive of activity in this part of the country," he remarked. "I hope they catch the fellow."

"Who, Philippe?" I asked as he helped me down.

"Some spy, apparently. He's made off with some battle plans, right under General de Boileau's nose. That was in Angiers, a few weeks ago. And two nights ago someone sabotaged an arms factory not far from here. They think it was the same fellow. An Englishman."

"How frightful!" I said with spirit. "They really are uncivilized, those English. Do you remember London, Philippe? Utterly squalid. And their food was inedible!"

"An abomination," Philippe agreed. "Do you concur, my Lord?" He looked over at the Marquis, who was yawning and stretching broadly in the sunshine.

"I suppose so," the Marquis said distractedly. "But you know, I find their servants much better behaved than ours. I think as a nation they are born to serve rather than to rule."

Philippe laughed heartily. "I hope we may have the pleasure of ruling them someday, then. You speak the language?"

"English?" My husband looked pained. "A wretched cacophony. I have never learned it, for my ears could not bear to listen to my tongue." At that moment Honoré joined us and we all walked towards the dining room.

After lunch Honoré came to sit inside the coach with

me, and Valadon rode with Philippe. Later Philippe and
Honoré changed places. From the occasional shouts of
laughter outside the coach I could tell that my brothers
were impressed with my husband. Their conviviality irritated me. I felt lonely and left out of this masculine
camaraderie. I suddenly felt that it was the Marquis'
intention to strip me of everything I had ever held dear,
even the affection of my family.

When we finally stopped for the night at a roadhouse
near Orleans, I was hot and tired and my body ached from
being jostled inside the coach. Philippe went to make
arrangements with the proprietor for two rooms. I was
sorely tempted to ask Philippe if I couldn't have a room to
myself, but I couldn't think of any really plausible reason
to give him. When he returned, he informed me that all the
rooms were taken for the night but one.

"For you and Armand," Philippe explained. Armand it
was now! "Honoré and I can sleep on benches in the
tavern or in the stable."

"The stable!"

He smiled. "We can have your room on the way back."

"Back? But Philippe, I thought you were going to
stay—"

"No, Elise. I have to get back to my regiment, and
Honoré must do the best he can to mollify Uncle Theo.
We'll stay long enough at Pellissier to see you comforta-
bly situated in your new home, and then—"

I put a reassuring hand on his arm. "Of course,
Philippe, I shouldn't have expected you to stay. It's
just—well—everything has happened so quickly. I
suppose I am not accustomed to being a wife, that's all."

Philippe gave a fond chuckle. "You're a lucky girl,
Elise. He's twice—three times the man the Baron is,
and you know it. I've heard that half the mothers in Paris
and Rome and Brussels have their eyes on him."

"And the fathers, too," I muttered.

"It's a match beyond our wildest expectations, Elise," Philippe said more seriously.

I smiled bitterly. "Especially since he never would have looked at a poor Lesconflair when he was ready for marriage. But Fate seems to have played him into our hands. In a way I can hardly blame him for hating me."

Philippe scoffed. "He doesn't hate you. How could he? And Uncle Theo will be truly delighted when he gets used to the idea. You'll see."

I followed a maid up the stairs to my room, where a tub of hot water was waiting. A couple of well-dressed ladies came out of a room near the top of the stairs. The hallway was narrow and I stood aside to let them pass.

The elder of the two was saying fretfully, "If only Armand Valadon would come back from Russia! You know, I've heard the Emperor himself has sent him on a secret mission to St. Petersburg. Very important. But it's so dull without him."

They rounded the corner and disappeared down the stairs. I stood gaping after them and only collected my wits when the maid stopped in front of a door at the far end of the hall and said, "This way, Madame." I hurried to catch up with her.

The room was small and quite cozy. The maid helped me to undress and carried my suit and shoes away to be cleaned. I sank gratefully into the tub of steaming water and closed my eyes. Just at that moment the door opened and the Marquis walked in.

I slid deeper into the water and covered my bosom with my hands. "What are you doing here?" I demanded angrily. "Can't you even knock?"

He said, "I've come up to scrub your back. It's so crude of your brothers to make you travel without a maid."

"We are a poor family," I said icily. "We have no

maids to spare. But I am sure your country home is filled with maids: up and down and in-between maids, maids for work and maids for play and maids that exist purely for decoration.''

He stood over me, looking down at me with his arms crossed over his chest. He grinned. ''It's a shame your tub is only large enough for one,'' he remarked.

I could feel perspiration beading up on my forehead and upper lip. ''Why don't you get out of here? How can you have the audacity to even speak to me after—after—'' I felt myself blushing.

''After last night?'' He laughed softly. ''Surely you're not angry about that? I was only respecting your —virtue.'' He laughed again.

''Oh!'' I scooped up a double handful of water and threw it at him. He jumped nimbly away. ''I don't know what you're doing in this part of the country anyway,'' I said hotly. ''You're supposed to be in Russia.''

The smile faded from his lips. ''Oh, really? Who told you that?''

''Two women I saw in the hall. They spoke as if they knew you, and they are simply pining for your return from St. Petersburg. Poor fools! I should have told them that you had come back unexpectedly—unfortunately.''

''That's very interesting,'' he said slowly.

''It is indeed. I must tell them when I go down for dinner that their wish has been granted. They'll be delighted.''

He said, ''I have already ordered a tray. We will dine here, alone.''

''But I want to go downstairs,'' I protested. ''I am heartily sick of the sight of you, and I want—''

''No.'' He looked at me but I had the feeling that he hardly saw me. ''We will dine here and you will retire early. You have had a long day and you are tired.''

"I'm not!" In my anger I forgot myself and half rose from the protection of the bathtub.

Hoofs clattered on the cobblestones in the courtyard under the window. He turned his back on me and threw the window open.

"Well, well, another contingent of the Emperor's soldiers," he remarked under his breath. "This is becoming amusing." Then he strode purposefully to the door and left without even giving me another glance.

"Vile beast!" I shouted after him. "Wretched son of a—oh!" I hurled a sopping sponge at the door and hopped out of the tub. He could insult me and he could torment me, I muttered, but he could not order me around as though I were a serving girl. How dare he tell me what I could and could not do!

I dressed hastily, and when a servant appeared with our tray I told him to take it away. When I was ready to go down I threw open the door. The Marquis was standing in the hall, holding the supper tray in his hands.

"Going somewhere?" he asked.

"You know damned well where I'm going," I said briskly. "Please get out of my way."

"You shouldn't have been so eager to send this back. It will be quite cold by now."

"I don't care. Excuse me, but I am going to join my brothers in the dining room."

He pushed his way past me and set the tray down on a small table in the center of the room. He drew up two chairs. "Your brothers have already finished their meal, Madame. They are now enjoying their brandy in the taproom. Surely you don't want to join them there."

"Wretched pigs," I grumbled. "They couldn't even wait for me. I don't care. I'm going down anyway. I'll eat alone. In fact, I would prefer it." I started out the door.

He came after me and pulled me back into the room.

"And I would prefer it if you would stay here," he said smoothly. Before I knew what was happening, he had picked me up and set me down on a chair. He lifted the layer of toweling off the tray. A grayish congealed omelet and some unappetizing rolls greeted our eyes. A faint vinegary smell drifted up from the carafe of wine that accompanied the food.

"Ugh, hogswill," I snorted, starting to rise. "Surely you can't expect me to eat that!"

He clapped a heavy hand on my shoulder and pushed me down. "I advise you to try. You won't get anything else tonight."

With one quick motion of my arm I swept the tray off the table. Crockery and eggs went flying and wine spattered the walls and floor.

"Take your dinner to Hell, Monsieur le Marquis," I cried. "I want none of it!"

He lifted me out of the chair, sat down, and turned me over his knee. Shoving my gown and chemise up to my waist, he spanked my buttocks until they felt warm and numb. I shrieked and thrashed, but his blows continued to rain down mercilessly. When he set me on my feet again I rushed at him, claws bared, screeching wildly. He slapped me across the face rather sharply. My head snapped back and I fell silent.

I put my hand up to my cheek and stared at him. No one had ever treated me like this before in my life. It was unspeakable, reprehensible. I would run at once to Philippe and Honoré and tell them—. Tell them what? That my husband had beaten me? I would die rather than admit that.

I indulged in a torrent of piteous weeping. I threw myself face down on the hard bed and cried until I felt ill. After a minute I heard the door open and close and I knew that he had left me alone. I sat up quickly, fired with determination, and dried my eyes. I wouldn't stay here another moment. I would run away to Paris. I would join the circus, the theater. I would be a dancer, a singer, an acrobat; yes, I would even be a street whore before I would stay married to that maniacal bully a moment longer.

The maid came in, carrying my cleaned traveling suit and shoes. I changed my costume hurriedly, tied on my bonnet and picked up my dainty walking stick—it was the only weapon I had. I shoved the rest of my possessions into my small valise, wishing fervently that I had some money. Then I slipped out of the room and went quickly down the hall and down the stairs. I could hear laughter and voices in the taproom, which was situated on the other side of the downstairs hall from the dining room.

"Good God, Armand, you must be a madman!" I recognized Honoré's voice. They must be sitting right inside the door. "And you knew that her husband would return at any moment!"

"A man must be willing to take chances to win what he most desires," the Marquis observed. "I have always found that danger lends a truly distinctive flavor to an affair. Besides, one can learn more about battlefield strategy in the bedroom than in war."

My brothers laughed appreciatively. I could almost see them hoisting their tankards to him. The swine! I hated them, all of them.

I tiptoed towards the rear of the inn then raced through the kitchen—where the cook gave me no more notice than if I had been a cat—and darted out the back door into the night. What to do next? I had to escape quickly, before they found me gone and raised the alarm. A horse. I would have to steal a horse. I crept around to the other side of the building, for the stables were on the side of the courtyard opposite from the inn. I could still hear the roisterers inside. I bid them all a silent farewell, and walked straight into the Marquis' arms.

"Ah, my little bride. Taking the air?"

"What are you doing here? I—I had a headache, and I thought I would take a stroll."

He looked me over. "And you have brought your baggage and your stick, so that you would be ready for any emergency. How clever."

"Not clever," I retorted. "In these parts one never knows what ruffians one might encounter. Please let me pass." I brandished my stick at him.

He pulled the thing out of my hands and broke it over his knee. "Silly piece of trash," he remarked, tossing the broken bits aside. "I can't imagine what makes women dress the way they do."

I was speechless with fury. I began to punch and pummel him with all my might. My blows seemed to make no impression on him whatever. He brushed me off as easily as if I had been a bothersome mosquito and led me firmly to the courtyard.

"Since this inn doesn't appeal to you, I have decided that we should proceed immediately to my estates," he said. "Ah, and here is a conveyance. How convenient."

I saw a light curricle standing in front of the inn door. A silent groom held the horses' heads.

"What's all this?" I looked around. "Where are my trunks? Where are Honoré and Philippe? I don't understand."

"You don't have to understand, just get in," he said. Looking at him sharply, I saw that he was dressed for travel. "Your brothers will follow in the morning, after they have had a fine and restful sleep, and your trunks will be sent on." He slipped his hand under my elbow and half lifted me into the curricle.

"You're not going to drive us yourself!" I sat down on the narrow seat and tucked my valise under my feet. His little bag was there, too, and a fragrant sack which I guessed held food.

"Why not? Is not Armand Valadon the finest whip in the land?" He climbed up beside me. I sat as far away from him as I could. The groom handed him the reins and accepted a small stack of coins. "Thank you, my friend," said the Marquis. "I'll see that the horses are returned to you in good condition."

Ths man dipped his head. "Best of luck to you, sir, and to the lady."

We drove off. A full moon in a cloudless sky illuminated the road, and the horses moved along at a fairly brisk pace. The Marquis did not speak a word, so intent was he on his driving. After several impatient inquiries which brought no replies I, too, fell silent. The light vehicle bounced terribly on the road, but I felt suddenly overwhelmed by exhaustion. Soon my thoughts became incoherent, my worries dissolved, and my chin bumped on my chest.

It was not yet dawn when I awoke. I found that I had slumped down in my seat and that my head was resting comfortably on the Marquis' shoulder. I sat up quickly and straightened my bonnet. He smiled at me.

"Good morning," he said companionably. "Did you sleep well?"

"No. I am stiff and sore and hungry."

"There's some bread and cheese in that sack. Help yourself."

"I will not," I said with spirit. "I want coffee and brioche and ham and—"

"We won't be stopping for food," he said. "This is all you're goint to get today. Frankly, I don't care whether you eat or not."

I stared at him. "I think you must be mad," I said slowly. "If I were Napoleon, I wouldn't trust you with the laundry, much less with state secrets and diplomatic missions. You are the rudest, most arrogant man I have ever met. I—I don't want to be married to you, do you hear? Let go of me at once. Let go of me!"

"I'm in no mood for your fussing today, Elise," he said brusquely. "If you can't settle down and behave yourself I'll tie you up, is that clear?"

"You wouldn't—"

"Oh, no?" He shifted in his seat and faced me squarely. "Perhaps you would care to test my patience, Madame."

The hardness in his voice and the dangerous glint in his eyes silenced me momentarily. I could hear distant birdsong. As the darkness melted away, the shapes of farm houses and trees and rocks became more apparent.

"How rocky it is here," I remarked. "It looks more like Normandy than Orleans."

The wheel hit a rock and the curricle bounced and tilted. I clutched at the side to keep from falling out. Now that daylight was almost upon us, Valadon had whipped up the horses and we were flying over the ground so quickly that the roadside was only a blur.

He is certainly in a hurry, I thought to myself. Is he really that eager to introduce his new bride to his mother and sisters? Does he have a mother and sisters? I didn't know. I didn't know the first thing about him. I was tempted to question him, but the thunder of the horses' hooves on the roadbed and the rattle of the wheels made such a deafening din that I decided to save my voice. Then I noticed that the sun was at our backs. We were heading west, not east, towards Paris.

"Where are we going? Tell me!" I grabbed his sleeve and shouted into his ear. "Why couldn't we wait for

Honoré and Philippe? Why are we rushing so? We're not going to your home at all. We're going west—''

He shook me off. ''Sit still!'' he roared. ''Do you want to upset us?''

''Tell me!'' I insisted. ''What's going on? I have a right to know.''

''We're taking a little detour, that's all. Now for God's sake sit back and hold your tongue, Elise. I'll explain later.''

Suddenly I was terrified of this man. He was a stranger to me. We were fleeing together like common criminals. Why? Suppose—suppose he wasn't the Marquis de Pellissier at all? What if he was the English spy the soldiers were looking for?

I wet my lips. ''Where are you taking me, sir?'' I asked in my halting schoolgirl English. ''Do not try and deceive me further. I know who you are now.''

He glanced at me briefly, his mouth curled in the faintest of smiles, then he turned his attention to the road. We careened madly through the countryside, traveling faster than I had ever traveled before in my life, it seemed. If one of the horses should stumble, if one of the wheels suddenly came loose—I closed my eyes and prayed for deliverance. This maniac was riding to his death, and he was taking me with him.

The sun stood high in the sky when we finally stopped to change our lathered horses. Before we climbed down to stretch our cramped legs, the Marquis put a heavy hand on my arm and looked intently into my face. When he spoke his voice was low and humorless.

''Listen to me, Elise. You are not to say a word to anyone while we are stopped, is that clear?''

''I—'' I began to protest.

''If you disobey me you will die, instantly,'' he said. ''I promise you that. If anyone asks you how you feel you may smile and simper and blush prettily, but you may not speak. If you do—." He paused to let the full dangerous meaning of his words sink in. "Your life depends on this, Elise. Do you understand?"

I was desperate, terrified, and angry. He was actually threatening me! His hand tightened on my arm. It felt like an iron claw. His mouth was hard and tight, and it seemed to me that his eyes were red and hot, shining like livid coals in his face. He was serious. He would not hesitate to kill me, I knew. I gulped and whispered, "Yes, my Lord."

He released me. "All right, you may get down."

"Pretty well done in, these animals are." The hosteler eyed our horses critically. "You folks must be in a hurry to get someplace."

I felt the Marquis' arm slide around my waist. I looked up at him. He was smiling down at me, but his eyes were cold. "We are in a hurry, Monsieur," he said tenderly. Oh, the liar! The villain! I opened my mouth to denounce him but he placed a warning finger on my lips. "Oh, my sweet precious, don't worry. You see, Monsieur, we are eloping. This lady's family does not approve of me, and I fear her father and brothers are after us."

The man clicked his tongue sympathetically. "It's a bad business, this marrying in haste. You know what they say." He looked at me sharply. The arm on my waist tightened viciously until I thought I would be cut in two. I managed a weak smile. "Still," the man went on, "it's a shame her family's not agreeable. I never saw a handsomer couple, if you forgive me saying so. You so tall and fair, Monsieur, and the lady small and dark. Ah, it's a strange world, isn't it, Monsieur, when two people can't be allowed a little happiness."

He unhitched our poor horses and led them away.

"You're doing beautifully, my dear," said the Marquis encouragingly. "Just keep it up."

"You swinish villain," I said under my breath. "You'll pay for this, I promise you. Let me go this instant."

I wriggled in his grasp but he held me firmly. "Later. Be patient."

The hosteler promised not to tell anyone he had seen us. As we drove out of the courtyard I dropped my reticule over the side of the curricle. I hoped my brothers would see it when they came after us. I was sure I would be rescued, and as we drove I kept turning my head to see if Honoré and Philippe were in pursuit.

"Don't bother to look for your brothers," the Marquis said with a grim chuckle. "At this moment they're probably chasing us along the Paris road."

I bounced painfully at his side, and gradually the hope began to drain out of me. They would never find me. When this monster had finished with me he would surely slaughter me and roll my body into a ditch. The birds and scavenger animals would pick my bones clean. My brothers would abandon their search and forget me. The picture that came to my mind was so horrible and pathetic that I stifled a sob.

The night promised to be moonless and hazy, and the Marquis conceded that it would be impossible to travel after dark.

"Thank heavens," I sighed. "I am longing for a bath and a decent bed. And some real food."

"That won't be possible," he said. "We shall spend the night in the fields, far away from towns and inns."

The idea was so ludicrous that I laughed in his face. "You can't be serious!" I said after a moment. "You are mad! You must be an escaped lunatic, a raving idiot. I tell you right now, Monsieur le Marquis or whoever you are, I will not sleep on the ground like some—gypsy! In fact, I shall not go any further. Kill me now. I would rather die than spend one more minute in your presence."

"Don't tempt me, Elise," he said half-seriously. "I might forget that I need you."

"Need me? What do you mean, need me?"

Darkness began closing in and he was forced to slacken his speed. We drove into a grove of acacia trees near a stream.

"With you beside me and my highly plausible tale of romance and elopement," he said, "I can be fairly inconspicuous."

"You'll never get away with this," I told him. "They'll find you and hang you, and when they do I shall be right there, under the scaffold, cheering them on. Your face will grow purple and your eyes will pop out of your head, and I shall laugh!"

He raised his eyebrows. "Bloodthirsty little bitch, aren't you?" he remarked. He hopped down from the curricle and unharnessed the horses. When he had led them towards the stream and his back was towards me, I climbed down and raced for the shelter of the trees.

I ran until I thought my heart would burst, and when I heard him pounding along behind me I sank to my knees in despair and covered my face with my gloved hands. Without saying a word, he picked me up and carried me back to our campsite, and I was too weak and sad to resist him. He set me on my feet and wrapped his long cloak around me.

"We shall sleep side by side tonight, like husband and wife," he said. "Be certain, Elise, that if you try and escape in the night I shall know it."

I backed away from him. "You wouldn't dare touch me," I said in a low, furious voice. "Haven't you done enough to me already? You have brought me low, ruined me, wrecked my life. Isn't that enough for you? I will not sleep with you tonight, you—you cur. Kill me first.''

He sighed. ''You only make yourself more desirable when you are angry, Elise. Lie down and go to sleep, or I won't be held responsible for my actions.''

I sat down on the grass and folded my arms around my knees. ''I will not sleep at all, then. I will not lie with you.''

''Suit yourself,'' he shrugged. He squatted down and opened the food sack. He hadn't eaten a thing all day, and now he ate the stale bread and cheese greedily, as if it were caviar and hummingbirds' tongues. I watched him stuffing the food into his mouth, and at that moment I hated him more than ever. I was cold, hungry, and tired; and there he sat, gleefully filling his jaws, oblivious to my suffering. I couldn't take my eyes off him and his damned bread and cheese. ''Have some?'' he offered when he saw the sick longing in my eyes. I shook my head vigorously, turned my back on him, and lay down on the ground. My hollow stomach rumbled mournfully.

After a while he came and lay down beside me. I gasped and started to get up. He pulled me back down.

''In the interests of precaution,'' he said, throwing his arm over me. ''I need sleep and I won't get it if I have to play zookeeper all night. Just lie still and go to sleep, Elise.''

''Filthy, lying vermin,'' I said passionately. I twisted around and tried to spit in his face. ''Scum of the earth! Wretched mangy fly-covered dog! I hate you, Armand Valadon, I hate you so much that—that—.'' Words failed me. Quivering with fury, I clenched my fists and strained against him, trying to free myself.

He rolled over on top of me. My screams split the

night. "You were warned, lady," he said huskily. "Now let us have no more of your childish whining and complaining."

"Let me go!" I shrieked. "Let me go! I'll—I'll be quiet, I swear it, only don't—don't do this to me. I won't try to run away."

His warm breath fanned my face. I could feel the steady persistent thunder of his heart—or was it mine?

"Please," I said softly. Tears of weariness and self-pity ran down my cheeks. "Please don't hurt me, Monsieur. I'll behave, I promise."

He gave an exasperated grunt. "You know how to try a man's patience almost beyond endurance, Madame," he said. He slid off me. I hastily wrapped myself in the cloak and turned on my side, sniffing pathetically. "Goddamn it," he growled, "stop that noise."

I noted carefully that at least he was no different from other men I had known in one respect: he couldn't bear the sound of a woman's weeping.

Crickets and cicadas began their tuneless night songs. Heavy darkness absorbed us. I lay for a long time waiting for his breathing to become slow and deep, which would mean that he was asleep. As far as I could tell, there was no change in its rhythm or tempo, and finally, cursing him, I fell asleep myself. Towards morning the September air grew chill, and when I awakened I found that I had pressed close to him in the night. My head was resting on his shoulders and my knees were drawn up under his. His arms encircled me and the soft wind of his breath ruffled my hair.

I untangled myself and stood up. "How dare you!"

He stirred sleepily and grumbled, "On the contrary, Madame, how dare you?"

Shivering, I stumbled towards the stream. Every bone, every muscle throbbed painfully. The icy water on my face and neck made me shudder. When I searched my valise for my comb and brush I discovered I had left them at the inn. I sighed unhappily. It was going to be another dreadful day.

I was ravenously hungry and swallowed a portion of bread and cheese without complaint. We were on our way before sunrise. Only one incident made the second day of fast travel different from the first. On a little used country lane not far from a town called Veaux we encountered a pair of soldiers on horseback. I felt my companion stiffen, and he slowed our pace to a trot as we approached them. I saw his arm go to his side, and when his coat opened slightly I saw the butt end of one of Honoré's pistols sticking out of his belt. So this fine husband of mine had encouraged my ever-vigilant brother to drink himself into a stupor and then had relieved him of his pistols. He was dangerous and desperate, and all the more dangerous because he was clever. If I could give the soldiers some sign, some indication—

The Marquis saw me looking at him. "This is no time for heroics, Elise," he said icily. "If you behave yourself those soldiers will live. If you betray me to them, they will die and so, I am afraid, will you." He halted the curricle.

A sergeant trotted up and lifted his hat to me. I pulled myself together and snuggled close to the Marquis. "Bonjour, Messieurs!" I called gaily. "And where are you going on such a fine morning?"

He laughed. "Somewhere, anywhere, my Lady. Today Belgium, tomorrow Russia. Who knows?"

"Oh," I marvelled, "is this the road to Russia?"

"No," he said with a loud guffaw, "it is only the road to Veaux. And where are you bound?"

"To visit my in-laws," I said brightly. I looked up adoringly at my husband. "We are newly married, Messieurs. Isn't it wonderful?"

"Be quiet, chatterbox," said the Marquis fondly. "These good men are not interested in my troubles."

The soldiers roared, and I blushed and smiled. They rode away, wishing us good day and Godspeed.

The Marquis urged the horses on. "Well done, Elise. You have missed your calling."

"If you mean I would make a good spy," I said coldly, "I am not interested."

As we drove on, I thought I could smell the sea. "We're going to Nantes, aren't we?" I asked him. He made no reply except a noncommittal grunt. "I suppose this is where our journey will end," I said. "You think you are safe, and you can plunge a knife into my breast and toss me into a ditch."

"If we're going to Nantes I can just throw you into the harbor," he said innocently. "It's much more convenient."

Nantes reeked of rotting fish and the sea and humanity. The dark narrow streets were clotted with sailors—French, Portuguese, American, Spanish—and swarthy, dirty women and dirty children, burly stevedores and fat, prosperous-looking merchants, ragged beggars and uniformed soldiers. A row of inns and brothels and public houses rose up along the waterfront. We stopped in front of what appeared to be the worst of these and went in.

I wrinkled up my nose at the foul air and drew my skirts up. The landlord accepted the Marquis' money, rather surlily, I thought, and bade us follow him up a flight of dark, narrow stairs.

"I'm not going up there," I whispered at the Marquis' back.

"Then stay down here," he said over his shoulder.

I glanced through a doorway at the tavern, with its rough types, foul women, its dirt and stench. I hurried after him.

When we were alone in the tiny room he said, "I asked for a room that could be locked. Here is the key. I suggest you lock the door after me and don't let anyone in. A servant will come with some water and food, but if you want to be safe don't admit anyone else." He paused with his hand on the doorlatch. "Oh, I have my own key, so don't think you're safe from me, not yet." And he was gone.

I quickly turned the key in the lock and examined our quarters. The landlord had left us with two short candles, and in the dim light the room looked dingy and not too clean. It smelled of liquor and sweat and stale pipe smoke, and I hated to think what else. I wondered if I had been deliberately abandoned here. But no, the villain had left his traveling bag, which signalled his intention to return.

I knelt down and opened the bag. Perhaps I could find some clue to his identity, or to the purpose of his mission. But there was nothing out of the ordinary, only a few shirts, some handkerchiefs, one neckcloth, and a set of brushes with plain silver backs. I sat back on my heels with a sigh. Well, at least I could make good use of his brushes.

I knew that this was my chance to escape him. But I didn't relish being on my own in Nantes at night. I had no money to pay for a room, and I was not so naive that I believed men would respect me simply because I was a noblewoman and Napoleon's darling. And if I ran away now I would never find out who this person was and what he was doing masquerading as the Marquis de Pellissier. I could best serve France, I told myself, by biding my time and trying to find out all I could about him. I was suddenly filled with patriotic fervor, and in the back of my mind lurked the knowledge that society would not be too hard on me for being forced into marriage with a scoundrel if I could somehow bring about his capture.

By the time he returned I had washed my face and hands in a basin of tepid water, dined on an omelet and fish stew, brushed some of the dirt out of my hair, and put on a soft muslin nightgown with bands of lace at neck, cuffs and hem.

I stood watching silently as he sat on the edge of the bed and pulled off his boots, then lay back with a sigh and threw his arm over his eyes.

"Well, you came back," I said lamely. I couldn't hide the resentment I felt towards him, and I told myself I would have to do better if I wanted to get any information out of him. I needed to play along with him, get him to trust me, lull him into a false sense of security. I would even have to pretend to—to like him. I would need all my wits and all my courage. I gave a nervous little laugh, which sounded false and hollow even to my ears. "I thought you were going to desert me."

"You're still here, too, I see," he said. "We're both out of luck tonight."

I sighed plaintively. "What will become of me?" I wondered aloud. I crossed the room and sat on the corner of the bed farthest from him. "You have no feeling for me at all, do you?" I asked softly.

He thought a moment. "Feeling? What do you want me to feel? I suppose you're an attractive, desirable girl, when you're not being a screaming bitch, which is most of the time. You'll probably outgrow your willful ways. Too bad I won't be around to see it. You'll meet some stalwart fellow who will cheerfully plow you ten times a day. When you're saddled with a half dozen brats you won't have too much time to think about yourself."

I swallowed my anger with an effort. I wasn't getting anywhere, and time was growing short. I was sure he would make his move tonight. I forced myself to say evenly, "But you still think I'm—I'm desirable." I stretched out my hand and rested it on his leg.

He sat up slowly and laid his hand over mine. I steeled myself to his touch. "You're feeling very friendly tonight, Elise. Have you had a change of heart about me? Not ten hours ago you were treating me like a leper." He picked up my hand and placed it on the soft swelling between his legs. I gave a startled little cry, and tried to pull my hand away, but he held firm. I could feel my face growing red. "Little girls shouldn't start things they can't finish."

"I don't know what you mean."

"I mean if you're trying to seduce me you will succeed, but if you're trying to bleed me for information you're destined for failure. I've been tested by experts, lady. What makes you think a babe like you can win at this game?"

The sleeping manhood under my sweating palm was coming alive. I could feel it stretching and growing. My breath began to come in short little pants, and my whole body felt flushed and warm. I again tried to jerk my hand away but he held it steady with a firm hand. With his other hand he stroked my loose hair and caressed my face and neck.

"I'm not a babe," I said defensively. "Not any more. And I'm not playing a game. I realize that I have been nothing but an irritation and a trouble to you, and I'm sorry." He made a scornful noise. "No," I protested, "I really am." I bowed my head and said in a small voice, "If I were a different kind of person none of this would have happened. It's all my fault. I wish I could die."

I had the feeling he was suppressing his laughter, but I didn't dare raise my eyes to find out. He fingered the lace on my nightgown.

"Is that what this is supposed to be?" he teased. "A shroud?"

I smiled up at him through my lashes. "Don't you like it?" I asked coyly. "Françoise told me it was what ladies of breeding wore on their honeymoons."

"I think it's hideous."

"Well, please don't tear it off because it's the only one I have."

He laughed and gathered me into his arms. I wriggled out of the offending garment and he tossed it to the floor. His clothing followed immediately, and soon we were entwined in each other's arms, our bodies naked and shining in the dim yellow light. He kissed me deeply and a shudder like a sigh passed through me. I reminded myself sternly that I had a mission and that my determination must not flag, but his caresses took my breath away and drove everything out of my mind. He lightly stroked the insides of my thighs and all thought flew out of my brain. I felt hot and cold all at once. I wanted him to stop, and I wanted him to go on. I moaned softly and opened my legs.

"You are too greedy, lady," he said laughing. He kneaded my body with his great, skillful hands while his tongue darted serpent-like in and out of my mouth, teasing and inflaming me. I threw my head back and strained upwards against him, longing for the weight of his body on mine. But he waited until he had brought me nearly to the brink of madness with his lips and his tongue and his fingers. When he came into me the combined force of our passions created a fierce, explosive, all-encompassing world. It was a revelation to me.

He was like a golden stallion in the candlelight, I thought. A golden leaping pawing plunging stallion. When at last he fell away from me we lay gasping. Gradually my scattered wits began to return.

"I suppose you'll be leaving for England tonight," I asked in a throaty voice when I was at last able to speak again.

He laughed sleepily. "And if I am, how does that concern you?" he murmured. "You got what you wanted, Elise. Be quiet and go to sleep."

"But—" He sighed deeply and turned his back to me. In a moment he was asleep.

I raged inwardly. I had behaved like a wanton, a whore, a trollop, and what had I gotten for my pains? Nothing! Nothing but a warning to be quiet. He turned his back to me as though I were nothing. I hated him, and I was furious with myself. If I had hoped to get anything out of him, any clue, I had failed. He had known from the beginning what I was after, and he had let me make a fool of myself. I was sick with disappointment. I felt suddenly old, and at the same time very young. I closed my eyes. I had learned so much in the past few days, and yet I still knew so little.

Later, much later, when he thought I was asleep, he climbed out of bed and dressed himself. He stood for a second looking down at me where I lay sprawled half-naked on the pillows. Watching him through the fringe of my lashes as I pretended to sleep, I saw him toss something on the mattress. Then I heard the door open and close again. He was gone.

I sat up and reached for the object he had dropped on the bed. It was a fat purse. I dumped the contents into my hands. Louis d'or, about twenty gold pieces. Enough to hire a carriage to take me home, if I wasn't raped and killed in this awful place first.

I threw back the coverlet and dressed hurriedly. I swept my possessions into my valise and clapped my bonnet on my head. I wasn't going to stay in that filthy room another minute, and I wasn't about to let him get away without first finding out where he was going. I had to have something to tell the soldiers, and I only hoped I wasn't too late.

I tiptoed into the hallway and darted down the stairs. I paused in the shadows at the bottom when I heard his voice. He was speaking to the landlord.

"—and there will be hell to pay. She's the Emperor's goddaughter, the apple of his eye, my friend. He'll come down on you so fast—"

The landlord mumbled, "Oh, aye, aye, Monsieur, I'll look to the lady right enough. Pleasant journey to you."

The Marquis slipped out the door and the landlord returned to his patrons in the tavern. When the coast was clear I crossed the space between the bottom of the stairs and the door, and I ran out into the night. I looked up and down the street. Valadon was walking briskly towards the wharf. I followed him, keeping to the shadows, ready to press into doorways and alleys when I saw someone coming towards me. Thankfully the hour was late and few people were abroad.

By the time we reached the wharf I was gasping for breath. Hiding behind a huge bale of goods near the dock I saw my quarry disappear down a narrow flight of steps that led to the water's edge. I heard low voices, and then a bumping and creaking told me that he was stepping into a rowboat. As I thought, when he and his companion were about a hundred feet away from the dock I could see him sitting in the prow of the boat opposite the rower. They were heading for a ship that lay at anchor well out in the harbor. I could see her masts gleaming eerily in the moonlight like naked trees against a winter sky. A few lanterns winked from her decks.

A sailor approached me, walking unsteadily along the dock. I jumped out from behind the bale and accosted him.

"See here," I said sternly, "what ship is that? Tell me at once."

The man collected his wits and leered at me. "American ship, Ma'am. The *Charleston Belle*."

"American? Where is she going? Tell me."

He shrugged. "I don't rightly know. Spain, someone said it was."

Spain! Ah, that was a start. I wondered if the swine was planning to sabotage Napoleon's operations there. "I want to go out there," I told the sailor. "Right now, tonight. You must take me. It's all right, I can pay you."

He protested. "I don't want to go out there. It's not my ship. Let's you and me go someplace else, eh?"

"I'm not going anywhere with you unless it's out to that ship," I said firmly.

As we argued I became aware of a clatter of feminine voices behind us. The sailor grabbed my arm and shoved me towards the approaching women. "Those dames are going out there," he said. "You can go with them."

I looked at the jabbering females. I wondered for a moment if they were wives, going out to the *Charleston Belle* for one last farewell. But no, they didn't really resemble respectable married women. They were too loud, too lewdly dressed, too gay. I went up to a fat lady who seemed to be the leader.

"I beg your pardon, Madame," I said humbly. The women fell silent and stared at me. "I understand that you are going—out there." I indicated the ship.

"And what if we are?" one of them demanded. "Do you object, your ladyship?" Her friends tittered.

"Oh, no, not at all," I assured them. "In fact, I would like very much to accompany you, if you don't mind."

"And what would the likes of you want with common sailors?" They surrounded me, laughing broadly, fingering the cloth of my suit and the ribbons on my bonnet. I held my valise tightly against my chest.

I sniffed and said with what I hoped was convincing pathos, "It's my husband. He made me leave my home when he married me, and now he's leaving. I don't know anyone in this part of the country and I'm so frightened, and I thought if I could see him or talk to him I could at least get some money to take care of me and the—the baby," I added as a masterstroke.

They murmured sympathetically. The fat one patted my shoulder. "There, now, dearie, that's all right. Come along. There's no harm in asking him, I guess, but if I know sailors he's spent all he had."

We walked along the dock until we came to a place where a larger rowboat was tied. Two sailors were waiting impatiently. We clambered down a wooden ladder with some difficulty and stepped into the rocking boat.

"Hey, Jack," one of the sailors shouted to his companion in English. "This one's clean!" He pinched my buttock as I passed him. "They're sendin' us a higher class whore now."

I stopped and gaped at him, but the boat lurched and I stumbled down next to a scrawny woman who was wearing a decrepit shawl and a skirt and very little else. The sailor had been right; she smelled foul.

When we reached the *Charleston Belle* we climbed up rope ladders—with eager hands lending assistance from above and below—to the deck. Everyone seemed to reek of rum and sweat and what I now recognized as sex. In the riotous confusion on deck I managed to evade the drunken hands that grabbed at my bosom and thighs. I crept into the shadows to reconnoiter. I peered at the scene every so often, hoping to catch sight of Armand Valadon. I wanted to confront him with what I had learned, and I thought I could expose him to the Captain and crew of this vessel and persuade them to hand the scoundrel over to the proper authorities.

An arm shot out of the darkness and fumbled at the front of my bodice. "Ah," breathed a whiskey-soaked voice. "Look at this, look at this!"

I shrieked and twisted free of him. As I ran along the deck I could hear him gasping behind me. Then I heard a crashing sound, like a fall, and a stream of rich curses. I glanced back: my pursuer had tripped over a coil of rope and become hopelessly entangled. I found shelter in a dark corner between two enormous casks. I sat down on my valise and rested my head in my hands.

My plans weren't working out as I had hoped. Instead of denouncing a criminal I was running for my life. I rather suspected that at this time of night, with all the distractions at hand, none of these men would be willing to listen to my tale. God, I was tired. The sounds of revelry grew fainter and gradually I ceased to hear them altogether. Soon I would try and find that rascal Valadon, after I had rested a bit. What madness was this: stinking quayside inns and boats full of whores and squads of drunken sailors, all chasing me up and down a ship.

"Will you look at this! Wake up, gal. The Captain's chewing nails this morning, and he won't be happy to see you."

I got unsteadily to my feet and looked around. With horror I saw that it was day. The harbor was gone, there was no sign of other ships, Nantes had disappeared. We were rocking along on a gray ocean under a leaden sky. The bottom of my stomach dropped out.

"Where—where are we, Monsieur?" I asked slowly in English. "I didn't want—I didn't mean to stay here."

The sailor shook his head. "We sailed on the morning

tide, before sun-up. Come along now. The Captain likes to eat stowaways before breakfast. You'd better pray we meet a French ship before too long."

I opened my mouth. "But you don't understand. I have come here to find a man who is masquerading as the Marquis de Pellissier. I know he's here—"

"Sure, sure, lady. Come and tell your fancy tale to the Captain."

I went pale at the sight of Josiah Fowler, Captain of the *Charleston Belle*. He was rotund, bulky, hirsute, and he stank of rum, vomit, and salt water. I explained the situation as best I could in my stumbling English, and I wondered if he heard me at all. He kept his eyes fastened to my bosom during the whole course of my recital.

"—and I must tell you, Captain, the man is an imposter. His name isn't Armand Valadon at all. I don't know what his name is, but I am sure he is an English spy. Surely you have seen him." I described the Marquis. "I came out here last night. I followed him, and I know—"

The Captain scowled deeply. "Got no passengers aboard this ship. You're spinning me a yarn, and I'm in no mood to listen to it. Parker!" He called to the sailor who had found me. "Do something with this bitch. I'll have no whores on my ship, do you hear?"

"Captain," said Parker hesitantly, "there is one passenger. The American who came on board last night, Mr. McClelland. You remember, sir, it was arranged—"

"Oh," the Captain grunted. "Him. Get him in here, then. Now!"

Suppose Valadon had left the ship before it sailed? Suppose the passenger was someone else. American? He was no American, I could swear to that. I stood trembling with my eyes glued to the floor until the door to the Captain's cabin opened and Valadon stepped in with

Parker behind him. He glanced at me. The expression in his eyes was hard and angry, but I breathed a sigh of relief. At last I would be vindicated.

"That's him, Captain," I cried. "That's the man! He is a dirty spy, a traitor, an evil, cunning man. I demand that we return to Nantes at once and—"

"You know this female, McClelland," the Captain demanded. "Says she came on board last night with the whores. My man found her this morning, hiding behind the water barrels."

"I wasn't hiding," I protested. "It was an accident! I fell asleep."

The tall fair man looked at me and then at the Captain, who continued to stare intently at my breasts. My heart stopped. I was at the mercy of the very man I sought to capture. If he disclaimed any knowledge of me—. I glanced at the Captain. Saliva gathered on his lips and he wiped it away with the back of his hand. I shuddered visibly and looked beseechingly at the Marquis.

He blew out his breath. "Yes, I know her," he said wearily. His English, I noted, was flawless. "She is—my wife."

I allowed myself to breathe again. The Captain's frown grew still deeper.

"This ship is no place for a woman, man! If you want to keep her you can pay her passage. If you want her thrown overboard no one will be the wiser except me and Parker here, and we know how to keep quiet."

The cold blue eyes flickered over me. "It's a tempting offer, Captain, but I suppose I must keep her. I have no money, though——"

I fumbled in my bag. "I have money, Captain." I handed him the purse with the golden louis. "It's all I have." I avoided looking at the Marquis. "I hope it will be suff—suffi—" the word defeated me. "Enough."

The Captain hefted the purse. "Get her out of here, McClelland," he growled. "And keep her out of my sight. Why you'd want to go and marry a whore I'll never know. Women are trouble on a ship, nothing but trouble."

The man he called McClelland took my arm none too gently and led me silently out of the Captain's presence. I followed him down a narrow passage. He opened a door into a smaller cabin that was dark and low, hardly high enough for him to stand erect. It had a leaded glass window through which I could see the bleak ocean, a small table with two kegs that could be used as chairs, a washstand with a pewter bowl and pitcher, and a narrow berth with storage closets built underneath. A lantern swung crazily from a beam over the table. As I watched it I felt a tide of nausea rising in my throat. I choked it back down.

The man and I watched each other in hostile silence. He sat down on a keg.

"Have you ever heard of a bad penny, Elise?" he asked in English. I shook my head. "It doesn't matter. Welcome to your new home. It's not the Louvre or the Chateau Lesconflair, but it's small and easy to keep clean."

"Who are you?" I demanded in French.

He shook his head. "France is behind us," he said. "You'd better start brushing up on your English. By the way, my name is Garth McClelland. I'm an American."

"Bah! You are a dirty spy!"

He smiled. "Such patriotic fervor."

"Scum! Villain!" I cried. "Filthy saboteur! The Marquis of *nothing* is what you are!"

He lifted his eyebrows. "Why, Elise, you are a snob. Shame on you."

"Shame on me! Pig, dog, son of a jackass!" I shouted, scraping my English vocabulary for fitting adjectives.

"This cabin is hardly big enough for one of your spectacular scenes, Elise. Fortunately, there is very little for you to throw." He seemed very calm. "Believe me, I rue the day I ever set foot in the forests of the Lesconflairs. And I doubly regret the Fates that led me to an important rendezvous at your little fête, but we're going to be cabin mates for a long time, and—"

"Long time, pfui," I sneered. "You dirty rascal, just wait until we get to Spain—"

"Spain? Where did you get that idea? We're not going to Spain."

"But the sailor in Nantes said—"

"Drunken sailors are not responsible for what they tell whores, even well-dressed ones that look like ladies. Captain Fowler is a slaver. This is a slave ship. The next time you set foot on land it will be on the Slave Coast. And when you next experience what you think of as civilization—in about six months—you will be in Jamaica. So calm yourself and enjoy the voyage. We are going to Africa."

## IV. Slave Ship

The waves lapped innocently against the mossy hull and gentle swells lifted the anchored ship up and down. A sea gull screeched overhead and swooped low to retrieve an invisible morsel from the water before disappearing in the seaward horizon. Light gusts of wind from the land shook the ropes and rattled the furled sails in the masts. My skirts whipped around my legs. I wished that the wind would carry me away beyond the horizon with the sea gull.

I stood in the prow of the *Charleston Belle* watching the shore. A hot sun was burning through the haze that had shrouded the coast since dawn, blurring the details of the jungle into a solid green mass. The jungle smell, heavy with the stink of rotten vegetation and the perfume of blooming hibiscus, seemed to permeate the ship.

The second boatload of slaves came alongside with a little bump and a sailor on deck dropped a rope ladder into outstretched hands below. Five strong sailors armed with guns and sticks prodded twenty terrified Negroes up the ropes.

"We have to bring 'em in in small bunches, Ma'am," a sailor had told me. "Else they might panic and overturn the boat, and we'd lose 'em. Their fear is catching, like a disease."

I knew, for I had caught it. The previous day I had watched as a tall black man reached the top of the rope ladder, then suddenly turned and dove into the bay. A sailor fired at him and wounded him. As they rowed towards the struggling swimmer I saw a sudden turbulence and a pink stain spreading through the water. The men stopped rowing and watched while the sharks ripped the screaming man to shreds. I vomited my lunch over the side of the ship.

When the slaves came on board they were herded towards the hold. Soon their cries and groans joined those of the other captives below. Frightened women with bellies distended in pregnancy clasped small children to their legs, and others suckled babies at their breasts. Tall warriors with bizarre tattoos and others with jewels set into their noses and earlobes stood quivering with fear like wild beasts, while young boys and girls who had no idea of their fate saw it as an adventure and laughed as they swarmed up to the deck. Most were stark naked, some wore tiny breech cloths of beaten and woven bark; all —except for the very young—had the same look of hopeless bewilderment on their faces.

"How long will we be anchored here?" I asked one of the sailors.

"Maybe three more weeks," he said. "Maybe longer. The Sultan told the Captain that he had some more coming in from someplace, maybe another hundred."

I nodded without speaking.

"I bet you're the first woman ever to witness something like this," he said, nodding proudly at the natives that shuffled past us under the watchful eyes of armed white men.

"I sincerely hope," I said softly, "that I am the last." The sailor was watching the procession and seemed not to have heard. I moved to the other side of the ship and gazed at the horizon.

We had sailed into the Bight of Benin in the Gulf of Guinea in early October, having enjoyed remarkably good winds and fair weather after we left Nantes. My ex-Marquis husband, Garth McClelland, had told me that the international slave trade had been outlawed two years before in 1808, but slavery was a necessity to planters in America and the Indies who relied on slave smugglers like Captain Fowler for cheap labor. The first thing we saw when we neared the port of Ouidah was an enormous hut built on stilts, standing in the waters of the bay not far offshore. This factory, as they called it, was accessible only by boat, and was used to house captives who were awaiting the arrival of a slave ship. The Sultan of Dahomy sold these captives to merchants, mostly American or English, for guns, powder, and ammunition.

When the Captain had concluded his business with the Sultan he gave his permission for the crew to go ashore in small parties. Garth McClelland and I attached ourselves to a group of five sailors.

The African jungle seemed to grow right up to the shoreline. The sailors beached our rowboat on a strip of white sand and we looked up at towering trees, thickly covered with vines and flowers and fruits. Birds in garish, bright colors darted through the treetops, calling loudly to each other. I thought I heard a lion roaring deep in the forest. A few huts nestled among the greenery, and one stood out as larger than the rest. The Sultan, an obese man with a wide smile who was set apart from his people by his corpulence and his air of command, emerged from the large hut and came forward to greet us. He had completed his business with the Captain to his satisfaction, and he looked forward to celebrating with us in grand style. His people crept silently out of their huts and refuges and came shyly forward to inspect us. They seemed particularly taken with Garth's golden hair and my own pearl-white skin, which had had almost no exposure to the sun since I had been on ship. The natives surrounded us, touching us timidly and giggling at our odd appearance.

I began to think of the land as a sort of Paradise, and I forgot that the Sultan felt no compunction about selling his prisoners of war and those who had fallen out of favor with him to these slavers.

He invited us to examine the village, which was no more than a random collection of huts around a communal fire pit. As we were walking around the crude structures, one of the Sultan's henchmen brought out a new captive for us to admire. It was a woman, small and black as midnight, with a fine, delicately featured face and smooth, well-shaped limbs. One of the sailors grunted approvingly and quickly extended his pistol and his dagger to the Sultan. The Sultan looked at the goods doubtfully and shook his head. It was not enough for such a fine woman. Then the other four sailors, apparently struck with the idea of owning their own slave, pooled their weapons and their coins and made a collective offering to the Sultan. This he accepted, and he turned the girl over to the sailors, who made much of her, petting and stroking and admiring her, although the poor thing was stiff with fright.

As the sailors and their purchase moved away into the shadows of the trees along the water's edge, I saw the Sultan jabbering and gesticulating to Garth, occasionally glancing excitedly or pointing in my direction. Just as it came to me that the Sultan was trying to bargain with Garth for the beautiful white-skinned slave, we heard a desperate scream rising above the loud and raucous laughter of the American sailors.

I ran towards the sound, and came upon them scarcely out of sight of the village, the girl on her back in the sand, screeching with fear, and one of the sailors on top of her.

I made a movement towards them, but Garth, coming up behind me, caught my arm. "Don't be a fool. Leave them alone."

"Stop them, you must stop them," I begged. "It's brutal, terrible. Please."

"Do you want to be next?" he demanded. "I could do nothing to stop them if they decided they wanted you, too."

The men roared and tumbled on top of the girl, one after the other. Garth held me back or I would have rushed at them, screaming, ordering them to stop. I was sobbing but unaware of the tears coursing down my cheeks. Powerless to look away, I watched them plunging their red and swollen weapons into the girl's bleeding loins. The Sultan and his men watched with amusement as the white savages performed for them. One of the blacks shook his head and made a disparaging gesture with his hands to show that the girl was too small in the hips to make good babies.

In an incredibly short time the sex-starved sailors had satisfied their lust. Their laughter ceased and they stepped away from their victim. She lay spread-eagled on the ground, not moving. Her eyes were open and they stared sightlessly at the sky. The earth between her legs was stained with blood. I pulled away from Garth and ran to her. Falling on my knees at her side I picked up her limp wrist and felt desperately for a pulse.

"She's dead." I spoke softly but my voice carried far in the awful stillness that suddenly filled the clearing. I turned on the sailors accusingly. "You've killed her, you—you beasts. I hope you hang for this."

They looked shamefaced and resentful. They had been so intent on their pleasure that they had forgotten there was a woman in the audience. I saw a glimmer of hatred in their eyes. They would not soon forget, or forgive me for being present. I turned my back on them and ran to the edge of the sea. I was too numb to cry, too shocked by the horror of what I had just seen to feel anything.

Garth came up behind me. "That was a touching display," he said disgustedly. "Are you trying to get us killed?"

"Why didn't you stop them?" I faced him angrily. "You could have stopped them and you didn't. You're no better than they are, you filthy animal."

His eyes were cool. "That should come as no surprise to you. Come, get into the boat and I'll row you back to the ship. Someone else can come back for these men later."

"What will happen to them?" I asked as we pushed off from shore. I wanted to see them flogged until they were almost lifeless and hung from the highest yardarm on the ship.

"Nothing." Garth bent into the oars. "She was their property, after all."

Paradise had become Hell. I did not go ashore again, but stayed in my cabin, afraid of meeting the five sailors who had taken us ashore, afraid of meeting anyone for that matter. Every man on that ship looked at me with ill-disguised lust, and I could feel their savage hatred burning into me whenever I ventured up on deck. Just because I was a woman. The only woman. And they couldn't have me.

Occasionally I watched another pitiful parade of slaves come on board, and I wondered at human behavior. I had been so sheltered, so ignorant. My brain had been filled with Montaigne and Rousseau and the Noble Savage, and I was revolted by the way these flesh merchants could callously barter human lives. I felt that Hell existed on the *Charleston Belle* and that no one on that ship was free of the taint of evil, not even myself. Already I felt myself becoming hardened to their pain, inured to their suffering, and deaf to their cries.

The sea gull swooped low over the ship and then whirled away again. I pressed my hands over my eyes and told myself that I would not cry, I would not pity myself, I would not dwell on the past.

"Quite a change from the glitter of Paris and the pomp of the Imperial Court, isn't it?"

Garth McClelland joined me at the rail. It was dusk and few of the men were on deck, so I had sneaked out for a breath of air. I dropped my hands to my waist. I did not look at him, but kept my eyes fixed on the smudged line that divided sea and sky.

He went on. "Still, Captain Fowler is like a petty Bonaparte. You ought to feel quite at home."

"You think this is all very funny, don't you?" I said bitterly. "Brilliantly funny and ironic and oh, so wonderfully amusing. You would have laughed at the Inquisition."

He shrugged. The cynical detached smile never left his face. "I'm not responsible for your presence on board this ship."

"You would like to think so, Mr. McClelland," I said intensely. "Neither are you responsible for what is happening here, or for what happened to that girl back there. If I hadn't been there you would have joined them, wouldn't you?"

"Don't flatter yourself that you could ever keep me from doing what I wanted to do, Madame," he said. "But I've never gone in much for group activities."

"Don't worry. I don't flatter myself that you are concerned about me at all. If you hate me so much, why didn't you let the Captain throw me into the sea?"

"Perhaps I thought you might make the voyage more enjoyable. I couldn't have been more wrong."

I flushed. "I don't owe you anything, Monsieur. I certainly don't owe you wifely loyalty."

"Don't you? You married me in good faith—" I glared at him fiercely and he broke off. "Well, don't stay out too late if you don't want to feed the mosquitoes."

He strolled on down the deck, pausing for a moment to

puff on his pipe and to look up at the sky. The light wind ruffled his hair and the thick beard he had grown since we were at sea. He had said that of a choice between sweating under a beard as we neared the equator or trying to shave on a rolling ship, he would choose the first course, like most of the men on the *Charleston Belle*. He was so rough and uncivilized, so at home in this uncouth company, that I couldn't believe he was really the same man who had masqueraded brilliantly as a cultured, sophisticated French nobleman.

Gone was every vestige of Armand Valadon, Marquis de Pellissier. In his place stood this American giant who called himself Garth McClelland, who refused to speak a word of French to me and always answered me in English when I addressed him in French. He spent his days on deck with the common sailors, or conferring with the Captain on a problem of navigation. He gladly climbed to the very tops of the huge masts to mend sail ropes that had come apart. He drank whiskey, spoke roughly, and smoked foul-smelling tobacco in my presence. He spent most nights in the Captain's cabin, drinking and gambling. He would come in very late, long after I had retired, undress and lie down on the berth. After our first night out he didn't touch me.

My cheeks still burned when I recalled that night. I had spent that first day being very seasick. I had railed against my fate and berated Garth whenever I saw him for his part in what had happened to me. I refused all food and drink, and by the time darkness fell I was weak and almost feverish with agitation and fear.

When he went out of the cabin I undressed and put on my muslin nightdress. I settled down in the berth and the rolling of the ship soon rocked me to sleep. I awoke to find him standing naked at my side, about to join me under the covers.

"Don't you touch me," I yelped. I pulled the rough

blanket up to my chin and drew my knees up to my chest. "Don't you dare touch me. Keep away from me, you filth! Keep away from me or I'll scream."

He reached over and tore the blanket out of my hands. "It is my intention, Elise," he said, looming over me, "to avail myself fully of the opportunity you have given me. To do otherwise would be foolhardy." I could smell the whiskey on his breath. He's drunk, I thought helplessly. I had never seen him drunk before. He stretched out alongside of me and put his hand up to my face. "Kiss me, Elise," he murmured. "Come to me and kiss me."

I was trembling so violently that I could hardly speak. He slid his hand down between my breasts. I felt his nakedness as he rolled against me and flung one of his legs over me. Then my brain exploded. I fought him as I had never fought before. I wanted no part of him and his lovemaking. I scratched, kicked, bit and snarled like a trapped beast, and he could not subdue me. Finally he got to his feet and looked down at me. His manhood pointed at me angrily.

I sobbed incoherently and tried to tell him what I thought of him, while I tossed my head and flailed my limbs. I heard rapid footsteps outside our door, and then an anxious pounding. Garth slipped on his trousers and went to see who it was. I sat back, shivering from my frenzy, drenched with tears and sweat and saliva.

I heard mumbling in the corridor. Then Garth said clearly, "No, there is nothing the matter. Have you ever known a woman to become hysterical when there was anything the matter?" Laughter. Mumble, mumble. "No, thank you, Bo'sun, a cat o' nine tails won't be necessary this time. Unless you think she would benefit by being flogged publicly. Personally, I doubt it." Mumble. Laughter. Mumble. "I quite agree with you. Good night."

He closed the door and came over to the berth. I was

breathing hard and still crying softly. My hair was standing on end and my face was red and blotched and tear-streaked. I looked awful, and I felt worse. He said, "You've been working up to that all day, and now it's done. Maybe you'll calm down now. I'm going out for a little while. But I will not sleep on deck, Elise, and I will not make a rude bed on the floor. We will share this berth—"

"If you come near me again I'll kill you, I swear I'll kill you," I informed him.

He grunted. "May I remind you that I am the original occupant of this cabin. You, Madame, are the interloper."

"Interloper!" I squawked. "You—you abandoned me in that filthy pig sty in Nantes! You didn't care what happened to me, did you? Well, here I am and here I am doomed to stay, it appears. Since you have caused me nothing but heartache and misery, you owe me this berth."

"I owe you a beating, Madame," he said hotly, "and nothing more. Someday you will collect it, you may be sure."

He flung his shirt over his shoulder and stalked out of the cabin. As soon as he had gone I leaped out of the berth and looked for some way to barricade the door. There was no lock, only a latch that could be worked from the outside as well as the inside. The kegs were no good to me. They were too low and light to deter anyone, especially an enormous ape like Garth McClelland. Oh, why didn't this wretched ship have chairs?

The table. If I upended the table I could hook its edge under the latch and effectively prevent his entry. I worked feverishly for a few minutes. When at last I felt secure I returned to bed and pulled the coverlet up.

I hadn't even closed my eyes when I heard his step in the

passage. He pushed against the door and jiggled the latch.
My barricade held.

"Open the door, Elise," he said wearily. "Now."

I said nothing, but smiled grimly at his vain efforts to
gain admittance. I hoped he would freeze up on deck.

He threw his weight at the door. The bottom of the table
slipped an inch. With a couple more blows he would have
the door open. I jumped out of bed and ran to shore up my
shaky buttress.

"Elise," his voice was calm but dangerous, "if you
don't remove the obstruction at once I shall break the door
down."

I moistened my parched lips. "Go ahead and try," I
said bravely.

He threw himself at the door once, twice. I was leaning
with all my weight against the table and I could feel myself
sliding with each blow. On the third try the table went
flying and so did I. I sprawled on the floor with my legs in
the air.

"Better cover up," he said. "You might catch cold."

I yanked my nightgown down and glared at him. He
paid no attention, but stripped his clothes off and climbed
into the berth.

"Get out of there!" I shouted. "That's my berth!"

"You may share it if you wish," he offered. "There's
plenty of room."

"Go to hell," I said through my teeth.

I made a bed for myself on the floor in the farthest
corner of the room from him. The straw mattress on the
berth had been lumpy and uncomfortable, but the floor
boards felt as hard and cold as marble. I gritted my teeth
and silently catalogued the offenses he had committed
against me. Someday, I vowed, he would pay for each one
of them.

When morning came Garth rose and dressed. After he

had left I dragged myself to the vacant berth and lay down.
I slept soundly until evening. After that I would frequently
occupy the berth during the day and then lie awake all
night, listening to the gentle thunder of his breathing. If he
stayed very late with the Captain, I enjoyed the comforts
of that horrid bed until his return, when I sullenly would
take myself elsewhere.

During the first week I would scream at him whenever I
saw him. "This ship is disgusting, unbearable. I have
never seen such ugly men. And the food! Ugh, the food is
poisonous!"

"Perhaps I'll be lucky and you'll die before we reach
our destination," he said.

"Oh, you think I don't pray for death? Every waking
hour! You are nothing but a heartless monster, a counterfeit noble!"

"And you are a counterfeit lady, Elise," he said lazily.
"What of it?"

"Boor! Pig! I will not permit you to insult me this way.
You have no breeding, no manners. You are no better than
any of the rest of these—these swine. I won't put up
with this another day. You must order the Captain to turn
back to France at once. I must get off this ship!"

He looked at me pityingly, which only inflamed my
anger, and strolled out of the cabin. He knew that I would
hesitate to follow him up on deck, for even in the beginning I had felt uncomfortable in the heavy silence that fell
over the men when they saw me. They watched and
waited, and even when I was in the cabin I could feel them
lurking just outside, waiting, longing, biding their time.

Several times I tried without success to find out why
Garth, an American, had been a spy and saboteur in
France.

"I do not understand," I argued. "America is a neutral

country. She has no quarrel with France, not like England.''

"Your knowledge of current events is quite dazzling, Elise,'' he observed. "Really, one would think you had been a student of diplomatic affairs all your young life.''

I bristled. "I know as much about it as anyone. Perhaps you were in the pay of the British. That would explain everything. Were you?''

"Perhaps.''

"Oh, you are the most irritating man! I suppose you were just rampaging around France in disguise for the sheer fun of it, and that you really admire and love Napoleon and think he is the greatest leader the world has ever seen.''

"In my humble opinion,'' he drawled, "Napoleon is just one more petty tyrant trying to get his name in the history books. I do think, however, that he should keep his eyes off the New World until he has done conquering the old.''

"Ah, ha!'' I cried triumphantly. "Then you admit you were a spy!''

"Not at all. I was merely expressing my opinion. I recall that your uncle had no great love for his Emperor.''

I waved my hand. "Oh, that's only because Uncle Theo has known Bonaparte ever since he and my father were cadets together. They served together, and when Napoleon became First Consul he made my father a general. Uncle Theo considers him an upstart because he's young. Napoleon says all the great leaders have been upstarts: Alexander the Great and Caesar. But then Uncle Theo never got over the Revolution. That was why we are so poor.''

He stifled a smile. "Because Napoleon is an upstart?''

"Because of the Revolution,'' I explained impatiently.

"Most of the Lesconflair lands were confiscated, but Uncle Theo's father buried all the family treasures until after it was all over. He says Napoleon climbed to power on the bones of France's finest and oldest families, and that he deliberately fomented chaos so that when he restored calm he would look like a great savior."

"Your uncle is very astute," he admitted.

"Yes, he is. But you keep distracting me from the subject. We both know what you are. Surely the need for secrecy is done. How could I possibly endanger your mission now, here in the middle of the ocean, surrounded by your countrymen? Why won't you tell me what you were doing?"

He shrugged. "Because it's none of your business or anybody else's."

I stormed and pouted, to no avail. I was no farther along on my quest for information than I had been. Yes, he was most infuriating.

We lay at anchor off the coast of Africa for nearly two months before the Captain was satisfied with the number of slaves in the hold and we were able to sail. The Sultan's additional hundred slaves arrived from the interior a few days before we weighed anchor, and they were added to the already overcrowded hold.

Garth warned me constantly to stay out of the Captain's way, and he forbade me to go near the hold. One day, however, the groaning and moaning from below seeped into my brain, tormenting me so that I could hardly bear it. I slipped up on deck, determined to see for myself the conditions that this living cargo had to endure. I walked boldly towards the hold. Although there was usually a guard stationed at the hatch, no one was around now. I lifted the heavy hatch with some difficulty, and descended the short ladder into the bowels of the ship.

The stench that greeted my nostrils was so overpowering that I fell backwards a step and pressed the hem of my skirt over my nose and mouth. Keening and moaning filled my ears, and with it the clank and rattle of chains. I forced myself to stay until my eyes became accustomed to the gloom and I could see better the Hades in which I had found myself. I moved slowly down a narrow aisle between layers of bodies that rose up on either side of me. Huge shelves had been built, one on top of the other, to accommodate up to five slaves apiece. The poor creatures lay there, like items in some grotesque shop, unable to sit up or even move around. Once a day they were taken up on deck in small groups for air and force feeding, like so many geese being readied for *fois gras*. If they refused to eat they were beaten. That short trip was their only exercise, and the rest of the time, twenty-three and a half hours out of every day, they lay here, tossing and wailing and dying.

I proceeded slowly along this ghastly corridor of death, feeling the bile rise in my throat. I became dimly aware that I was walking through a running stream of stinking muck that could only have been human excrement. I grew cold with the horror of it all. My leg knocked against something that felt like a spar. I reached down and felt a human foot and leg, stiff and cold. A baby cried weakly and I heard small children sniffling and fretting. The women seemed to be separated from the men, and I wondered if, being smaller, they had been packed in even tighter than the men on the rough plank shelves.

The Captain had said that he had taken four hundred on board. Four hundred, in a space no bigger than Uncle Theo's library. He had also said, ''Even two hundred will bring a fat profit.'' The monster fully expected to lose half of these people to starvation, disease, suffocation. Every day the sailors tossed a new corpse into the sea.

A groaning louder than any other filled my ears. I

realized that it was me, and that if I didn't get out of that wretched hole I would go mad. I stumbled back, through the slime and the muck, towards the hatch. My teeth were chattering and I was babbling prayers in French, prayers I hadn't said since I was a child. Then suddenly I heard the slam of the hatch door and I was plunged into total darkness, stumbling along towards the ladder I knew lay ahead of me. The rolling of the ship pitched me from side to side, and I knocked against the flanks of bodies. Recoiling from the writhing, stinking, crawling flesh, I lost my balance and fell headlong into the filth. Hands came at me out of the foul blackness, hands plucked at my hair and my face and my gown, hands begging for release, for salvation, for death. Hands groped for light, for air, for freedom. I was screaming when I reached the foot of the ladder, screaming as I pounded my fists against the underside of the hatch.

Finally it was flung open. Dazzling sunlight flooded my face and nearly blinded me. Brutal arms pulled me to the deck, and I looked into the grinning face of Captain Josiah Fowler.

"How did you like our hold, Madame?" he sneered. He shook me roughly. "I've got half a notion to chain you down there with the rest of 'em, if you're so fond of 'em. Damned interferin' bitch."

I began retching and he threw me away from him. I fell in a gagging stinking heap on the deck.

A strong arm lifted me to my feet. "Come on, Elise, let's go back to the cabin."

I looked up into Garth's face. "Horrible, horrible," I murmured. "Worse than animals, Garth. They live like pigs in a sty, only it's worse, much worse. It's a nightmare."

"By God, McClelland, if I ever see that wench around here again I'll flog the both of you. You keep her out of my sight, you hear me? Next time I'll throw her down there and keep her there until we reach Jamaica.''

"Let's go, Elise." Garth dragged me away, still crying and babbling incoherently and praying feverishly. When we were in our cabin he stripped all the clothes off my body and washed me from head to toe with water and strong soap. I stood shivering in the middle of the room while he worked over me, scrubbing the smell out of my hair and off every inch of my body. He wasn't particularly gentle with me.

"Why didn't you stand up to him?" I demanded through my tears. "Why do you always take his part, not mine? You should go down there, Garth, and see for yourself what that man is doing. It's a disgrace, it's shameful. I never dreamed a man could behave that way, treating people, human beings like swine!"

"Hold your tongue, Elise," he said sharply. "For the love of God, just be quiet."

I stared at him for half a second, then burst into a torrent of noisy weeping. He pulled my nightdress over my head and managed to work my hands and arms through the sleeves.

"If you don't calm down I'm going to hit you," he said.

"You—you wouldn't!"

"Don't push me any farther, Elise," he said warningly. "Your stupidity almost cost us our lives."

"Pooh! Liar!" I spat. "We're paying passengers, aren't we? He—he wouldn't dare lay a hand on either of us."

Garth shook his head. "You're so—young," he said in an exasperated tone. "Haven't you learned anything by what happened today? Don't you know that a man who is capable of running this kind of operation, of smuggling and trading human lives, is capable of anything? Do you think that just because we've given him a few coins to take us along that he would hesitate to get rid of us if we became a nuisance? Use your head, Elise. Try thinking like a woman instead of a feather-brained ingenue. He's involved in a dangerous and desperate profession, and he's a dangerous and desperate man.''

I looked at him. ''So were you, when I met you. And I managed to survive that.''

''So you did,'' he sighed. ''Why don't you try looking on this as another test of your wits and strength. Try and see if you can survive this voyage and Captain Fowler. Stay away from the hold and stay away from him. He is a stupid and ignorant man. He really believes that women on a ship are bad luck, and in a sense he's right. Do you realize what the presence of one woman on board a vessel carrying a hundred men can do to them? Don't you know by now what they're thinking about when they look at you, what they would do to you if they had half a chance? Remember that girl in Dahomy, Elise. She died because those sailors had been penned up on a ship for nearly six weeks with a beautiful woman and they couldn't touch her.''

''You can't blame that girl's death on me!'' I cried. ''That's preposterous.''

''Is it? I'm just telling you, Elise, to be on your guard. I'm not joking and I'm not teasing this time: stay away from Fowler and don't interfere with the slaves.''

''You're afraid of him, aren't you?'' I sneered. ''You're a coward after all, but then I always suspected it.''

His mouth hardened. ''I'm not a coward, but neither am I a fool. You are, Elise. My advice to you is to grow up. Put away your dreams and your illusions about human decency and accept the reality of the situation.''

I said stiffly, ''When I want your advice I'll ask for it.''

''As you please. But don't come crying to me when

you're hurt and disappointed. You didn't have to see what was in that hold. Your brain should have told you. You won't get any sympathy from me and you aren't going to enlist my aid in cleaning up conditions below decks. I'm not a saint or a crusader and neither are you. Forget it. Forget the slaves and what you've seen.''

"Never!" I said passionately. "I'll never forget them and I'll never forgive you for being so cold-hearted and unfeeling about them. I'm not a saint and I'm not a crusader, but I am a human being and my heart cries out when I see other human beings in pain. I can't believe that you feel nothing, no anger, no rage, no sorrow. What kind of man are you, Garth McClelland? I'm glad I'm a fool, if being a fool means that I'm not like you. Where are you going with those?''

He had scooped my soiled clothing into a pewter basin and was walking towards the door.

"I'm going to dump them over the side.''

"No!" I protested. "I have so few things—and my shoes!—please, I beg you, don't do that. I'll clean them myself, Garth. Don't throw them away.''

He set basin and contents down and bowed mockingly. "As my lady wishes,'' he said. "If you busy yourself with domestic chores perhaps you can curb your troublesome humanitarian impulses.'' Then he opened the door and went out.

I sank onto the berth and buried my face in my arms. I didn't know how much more of this I could endure, and I had the feeling that there was worse to come. I was right.

The next few days passed uneventfully enough. But the grisly obbligato of moans and sobs from the hold never stopped, day or night. It accompanied my every thought, my every action, until it seemed like the ship itself was mourning as it rocked along over the waves under flat gray skies.

I suspected that even Garth was not unaffected by the atmosphere. His face lost its habitual smile of cool disdain and took on a worried frown. He spent longer hours away from the cabin, not, I surmised, in the company of Captain Fowler, and frequently he did not come to sleep at all. When I tried to make conversation or ask questions he answered with curt one-word replies, and it was obvious that he didn't want to be bothered with me. He was more remote and cold than ever, and I actually longed for the days when he raged and insulted me and told me what to do. I hated being ignored, and even insults are better than no attention at all.

The crew was edgy and nervous. It was clear to me that they hated Captain Fowler and detested their duties. When the slaves grew noticeably weaker, the ship's doctor became alarmed and urged the Captain to permit longer periods on deck. The Captain agreed, and further decreed that the hold be cleaned out daily and washed out with sea water. The men hated that job most of all.

Then a sickness broke out in the hold and scores of captives—mostly the older ones and the very young children—died. After a week the plague had run its course below decks, leaving over seventy-five slaves dead, and it spread to the crew. Most of the afflicted sailors recovered, but the cabin boy and several others died, and half a dozen more were unfit for work for a week or more.

The Captain prowled the decks relentlessly, whip in hand, looking distraught and wild-eyed. Every slave meant money lost. Dead and incapacitated crew members meant that the already overworked sailors who remained well had to shoulder extra responsibility. Fowler kept a watchful eye on his men and discouraged malingerers by flogging them in public. If anything, the iron-clad discipline aboard the *Charleston Belle* became more rigid.

Slaves and sailors alike paid heavily for mistakes and misconduct.

In mid-December, when we were about two weeks out of Ouidah, we were buffeted by strong winds and heavy squalls which swamped the decks and carried off one of our precious barrels of fresh water. During one violent thunderstorm the foremast was struck by lightning and the top half snapped off. This slowed our progress considerably, and the Captain raged against the injustice of Nature. When the bilge pumps ceased to function the hold was flooded and we began to founder. More slaves died before the water was baled out and the pumps put to rights, drowned as they lay chained to their crude bunks at the bottom of the hold.

This run of bad luck left everyone unnerved. The Captain's behavior became more violent and more savage. There were floggings every day. One evening when I was up on deck I saw him heave a tiny black child overboard because it had gotten under his feet. Although my heart cried out in anguish, I forced myself to hold my tongue and return to my cabin. Garth was right: this man would stop at nothing now, and I dared not risk a complaint or protest.

One afternoon, unable to bear my captivity any longer, I went up on deck while Captain Fowler was administering a particularly vicious flogging to a huge black man who stood chained to the mainmast with his hands tied high over his head. I crept up unseen behind a silent group of onlookers.

"Be-Jesus," one sailor muttered to his neighbor, "the poor bastard's had twenty strokes already and he's still on his feet."

"He's hardly bleedin'," the other whispered. "Hides like leather, these slaves got. And not a peep out of him yet."

I stood on tiptoe and craned my neck to watch. Every lash seemed to bite into my own flesh. The men around me moved their lips silently as they counted: twenty-six, twenty-seven, twenty-eight——

When the Captain's arm grew sore he turned his whip over to the bo'sun. "Lay into the son-of-a-bitch. He's enjoyin' it too much," he ordered, standing back to watch the show. "Harder!"

The black man never whimpered. Thirty. Thirty-one. Thirty-two. The crew grew excited at the man's stamina and started betting on which lash he would fall. Forty. Forty-one. At last the man slumped and his head dropped forward.

"Bring him to," the Captain snarled. Someone sloshed a bucket of water in the slave's face. He groaned and sputtered. "Keep goin, Bo'sun," the Captain said. "I want to hear the bastard scream."

The flogging continued. I was sweating, even though the wind over the decks was brisk and cold. My fingernails dug into the palms of my hands. Keep a hold on yourself, I kept saying. Garth is right. Don't be stupid. It took every ounce of courage and self-control I had just to stand there and do nothing. This was real, this was life, and it was ugly.

Twice more the slave fainted, twice more he was revived. At sixty lashes the Captain called a halt. The man's back was a red pulp. Blood ran over his naked buttocks and down the backs of his legs. The Captain seized him by the hair and jerked his head back.

"Goddamn," he said gleefully, "he's still conscious. Come on, boys, let's wash a little of this mess away. Get some salt water."

I gasped and closed my eyes, and jammed my fist into my mouth so that I would not cry out. I heard the bumping of the bucket as it was lowered for seawater and drawn up again, then the slosh and the sharp intake of the black man's breath, like a sob, as they poured the brine over his raw flesh.

"Cut him down," the Captain ordered brusquely. "He won't be tryin' to jump over the side again. If he goes it will be because I've thrown him over. Are those others watchin' this?" he barked. For the first time I noticed that a frightened group of slaves was observing this horror from a far corner of the deck. "Is he still conscious?"

"No, Cap'n, he's passed out."

"Jesus, some of them are hard to kill," the Captain snorted. "Tell Doc Hawthorne to get up here and see to him. I don't know if he's worth savin' or not. It'll keep these others from gettin' ideas."

I wasn't sure about that. It seemed to me that death by drowning was infinitely preferable to this fate. The Captain and his crew dispersed, leaving their sport behind. I ran to the wounded man and knelt at his side. He lay huddled on the deck in pools of his own blood. He looked obscene, like the invention of a sick, artistic mind. But he was real, too real. I wanted to help him, but I hardly knew where to start.

Doctor Hawthorne came up and knelt beside me. "Is he dead?" he asked wearily. Doctor Hawthorne was kindly and old and dizzy from drink most of the time, but he was the only man on the ship that I wasn't afraid of.

"I—I can't tell. I don't know what to do."

The Doctor flipped back a black eyelid and pressed his finger under the man's ear.

"Poor devil," he muttered. "We might as well throw him over the side. He's bled gallons. Look out, you'll get your dress in it."

"No, no, that's all right. It doesn't matter. Is he dead?"

"Not yet. It's just a matter of hours."

"Why can't we save him? Please, Doctor, can't we at least try?"

The Doctor squinted at me. "Save him for what, Ma'am? For more of the same? You think their lives on those plantations are any better than they are here, on this death ship?"

I shook my head. "I don't know. But he'd be *alive*, wouldn't he?"

The old man sighed. "I'm sorry, Ma'am. I've no place to put him. If we leave him out he'll die of exposure. If we put him back in the hold he'll be dead before morning."

I put a hand on his arm. "We'll put him in my cabin and I can take care of him."

"But your husband—"

I flushed and said quickly, "It's all right, he won't mind."

"Well, I suppose we could do it. The Captain will raise holy hell, you know."

"We don't have to tell him right away," I said. "If this man dies, we've lost nothing. If he lives, well, perhaps I can buy him myself. And then the Captain will get the best of the deal."

We cleansed the terrible wounds as best we could and applied some ointment and a light dressing, just enough to keep the wounds clean. I went to find Garth. It took all my powers to persuade him to help us. Finally the three of us managed to drag the unconscious form into the cabin.

The Doctor refused to put him on the berth. "The floor is good enough," he said to my protests. "They're not used to better, even in their own homes. We'll fix a pallet, and he'll be all right there, out of the sun and the rain. He'll probably be feverish tonight."

Garth watched silently as the Doctor and I made our patient comfortable. When Hawthorne left us alone he said, "You don't really expect to get away with this."

''But they were going to throw him overboard, Garth,''
I said. ''I couldn't let them do that, I just couldn't. And it
was the first time I felt that I could help one of them. I want
so badly to do something. I know you can't understand,
but it's very important to me.''

''The Captain—''

I cut him short. ''The Captain can be persuaded, really,
he can. I have it all worked out. When we get to the Indies
you can lend me a little money and I can buy Joseph—''

''Who?''

''Joseph. I have named him Joseph, after Joseph
Bonaparte, you know. He was always very nice to me, and
I think this Joseph resembles him a little, don't you
agree?''

Garth looked at the black man critically. ''Only around
the mouth. The rest of him looks like Jerome.''

''You think so? Oh—oh, you are teasing me! I
should have known you would treat this whole thing as a
joke. I should have known!''

He shrugged. ''I'm not interested in how you occupy
yourself on this voyage, Elise, as long as you don't disobey my instructions and cause trouble for me.'' He
turned to go.

''I cannot believe you are as hard-hearted as you pretend to be. I cannot believe it!''

His eyes burned into me. ''Believe it. For your own
sake, Elise,'' he said softly, ''believe that I am everything
you think I am.''

At the end of the third day Joseph's fever subsided and
he was able to take some water. The wounds on his back
healed a little and they did not seem to be infected. When
he opened his eyes he shrank away from me. I tried to
comfort him.

''It's all right, Joseph,'' I said soothingly, ''you're safe
here. You are going to live.''

As if he understood what I was saying, he smiled

weakly and closed his eyes. At that moment the cabin door flew open.

"You goddamn thievin' little wench!" The Captain stood on the threshold. "What in hell do you think you're doing!"

"How dare you enter this cabin without knocking," I said angrily. "Don't you know how to behave like a human being instead of an animal?"

His eyes gleamed and he wet his lips with his tongue. Although I was fully clad I had an urge to cover my body, to hide myself from those small, red-rimmed eyes and those wet pink lips.

"You have somethin' that belongs to me, wench. I've come to take it back."

I stared at him stupidly for a second or two before I realized that he was referring to Joseph. "Why, this man was near death, Captain. The Doctor was about to give up on him, and I asked if he could bring him here. That's all. I meant no harm, I just didn't want to see him die. You may have him back when he is strong and fit, and I shall buy him from you when we get to Jamaica."

Fowler prodded the sick man with his boot and said sneeringly, "You've taken quite a liking to him, haven't you, wench? Well, I'll be goddamned if I'm going to let you keep him here just because that husband of yours is too stupid to know how to keep a female like you in line. I know how to treat a bitch like you, and you need a lesson."

I jumped up. "How dare you talk to me that way. Get out of here this instant before I scream this ship down. Get out!"

I flew at his face, shrieking like a *tricoteuse* at a guillotining. He backed away a step and shouted over his shoulder for two sailors who were waiting in the passage. They came in, and without saying a word picked the black man up and carried him out of the cabin. Joseph groaned audibly and the Captain chuckled.

"Finally got some noise out of that fellow," he grunted. "Thanks to you, Ma'am." His eyes lingered on my bosom a moment longer, then he snorted disgustedly and followed his men out of the cabin.

Throwing caution aside, I ran after him and caught his sleeve. My heart was racing, and I was filled with anger that I could hardly speak. "Don't you have any pity in your heart at all?" I demanded. "Doesn't a human life mean anything to you?"

"No," he said in a low, lascivious whisper, "only when there's a hot-fleshed little woman connected to it." He locked his heavy arms around my waist and kissed me clumsily. He reeked of whiskey and tobacco. I squirmed and kicked until he released me. "What's the matter," he asked, wiping his mouth on the back of his hand, "don't you like the way a real man kisses, whore? I notice that half-man of yours is spending his nights up on deck, lookin' at the stars." He grabbed at me again and squeezed my breasts painfully with his hands. "I'm thinkin' that I ought to take his place in that bed of yours. He won't care—"

"You—you filth!" I spat in his face. My voice and expression must have revealed the deep revulsion I felt, for suddenly hatred as well as lust shone in his eyes. I felt afraid of him, truly afraid.

"Good afternoon, Captain. There's no trouble here, I hope?"

Garth appeared in the narrow passage. I nearly sobbed with relief when I saw him.

"Trouble?" the Captain snarled, releasing me. "Yes, there's trouble, McClelland. This bitch of yours is nothing but trouble. You know, it surprises me, McClelland, that a big fellow like you would leave his wife alone with one of those filthy slaves. He's been with her two nights, while you've been topside star-gazin'.''

Garth laughed and said smoothly, "Really, Captain, the man was hardly in any condition—"

I didn't want to hear any more. I ran into the cabin and slammed the door. Pressing my hands over my eyes I breathed deeply and tried to force down the feelings of rage and nausea that rose up within me.

Garth came in. "What happened?"

"He—he burst in here and took Joseph, and when I tried to reason with him—"

"I can just imagine how you tried to reason with him," Garth said dryly. "Next time it will be worse. I tried to warn you and you wouldn't listen to me. You had to go your own stupid, headstrong way." Even though he spoke calmly I could hear the rage in his voice. "I was the fool this time, though. I never should have allowed you to bring that man in here."

I whirled on him in a fury. " 'Never should have allowed!' " I raged. "You make me sick, Garth McClelland. If I hadn't brought him here he would have died, and you know it. Not that he won't die now. That Fowler is an unspeakable villain, an inhuman monster. Oh, I would cheerfully kill him if I could. And you are no better. You make me sick, the two of you."

I tried to push my way past him. He stepped in front of me. "Where do you think you're going?"

"I need some air. The stink of your cowardice is making me sick."

"Listen to me, Elise—"

"No." I stepped back a pace and faced him squarely. "No, you listen. I will not be penned up in this cabin for another ninute. I can defend myself against that disgusting man, better than you can defend me, I'm sure. He doesn't frighten me for a moment, and neither do you. I hate you and I hate this death ship. There isn't a day since I've been here that I haven't wished that I was blind and deaf and dead. This is hateful to me, do you understand? Hateful! The moaning and crying, day afer day, it tears my heart out, and we, civilized people, we sit and do nothing. Well, I'm not sorry that I tried to help one of them, and if the opportunity arises I will do it again and again and again. I'm sick of being pushed around by you and the Captain. Let me pass."

To my surprise he walked away from the door and stood staring out the window. "Do you honestly believe that I enjoy this? Can you honestly believe that a day passes when I don't want to shove my fists into his stupid face and make him bleed? Go on, then. Get the hell out of here. I don't care what happens to you." He turned and shouted, "Go on, get out!"

I was rooted to the spot. I stood staring into his fathomless eyes, wishing that I could see into his soul. The ship rolled heavily and I had to clutch at the table for support. The dreadful keening from the hold seemed to permeate the ship. I put my hands over my ears and still I heard it, that wrenching, sorrowful sound.

"Oh, dear God," I said, "make them stop. For the love of God, make them stop."

Garth strode over to me and pulled my hands away from my ears. The moaning grew louder again. He dug his fingers into my flesh. The harder I struggled to get away from him the tighter he held me. The fire in his eyes made me tremble.

"Stop it," he said sharply. "Stop fighting me, Elise."

"No," I panted, "Never. Not until I die!"

"You'd be no good to me dead," he said roughly. He slid his arms around my waist and kissed me over and over again until I was breathless and exhausted. I could feel the old weakness creeping over me and I sagged against the table. I could feel his hands on my bodice, unfastening it, unlacing the ribbons that closed the top of my chemise, fondling my breasts. "You're so beautiful," he murmured. "So soft, so lovely."

Not five minutes earlier that animal Fowler had behaved almost identically and I had loathed it, but now—. It was different with Garth, much, much different. I tried to suppress the rising tide of longing that was sweeping over me, but I might as well have commanded the sea to stop its strong, incessant movement. With a despairing groan I lay back in his arms and let him move his scalding lips over my face and neck and breasts. I couldn't fight him any more. I didn't want to. My resolve was being destroyed by the slow fire he had ignited in my depths. I knew that the fire would have to rage until I was consumed.

I closed my eyes while he undressed me and ran his hands over every inch of me. I was sharply conscious of our two bodies, of the powerful sensations that engulfed us. He stripped his clothes off and guided my hands over his body. I marveled again at the muscular hardness of his arms, his back, his buttocks. I raked my fingers through his hair and returned his kisses eagerly.

He picked me up and bore me to the berth, and I gave myself to him freely, hungrily, without hesitation and without struggle. His fiery blade pierced me to the quick, but the anguish I felt was beautiful and thrilling. I ceased to be aware of anything else: the cries of the slaves, the Captain's horrible lust, the woman-starved men working on the ship only a few feet away from us. I let Garth take me into the dark sensual caverns of love where pleasure ruled and pain and distress were soon forgotten.

When we lay spent and breathless in each other's arms he nuzzled my hair and said, "No more nights on the floor, Hellcat. We've wasted too much time as it is."

Passion's blinding, deafening spell faded away. The dismal sounds of the ship reached my ears once again. I raised myself up on my elbow and looked into his face. I saw him once again not as the bearer of pleasure and forgetfulness, but as the man who had beaten and violated and humiliated me. I was furious with myself for yielding to him, but I knew that I was powerless to refuse him now. He repulsed and attracted me. I drew away from him.

"I hate you," I said, gritting my teeth. "More than ever. Nothing has changed between us, nothing!"

He rubbed my cheek with the back of his hand. "No, you're wrong about that, Elise. Everything has changed."

And with that he rolled over and went to sleep.

# V.   Josiah Fowler

The *Charleston Belle* had weathered the severest
storms the older sailors had ever seen, storms that had set
the ancient tub nearly on her side and swamped her decks
with waves that swelled to fifty feet and higher. Her
human cargo shrieked and cried with terror as the ship
bucketed and tossed, and the water rose in the hold as fast
as the sailors could bale it out. Even though we were near
the equator, the storms brought icy winds that felt like
blasts from the heart of Hell. Even seasoned mariners
couldn't stay on deck for long periods of time, and the
slaves, who had never known any but tropical tempera-
tures, suffered as much from the cold as they did from the
unceasing violent pitching of the ship.

I rattled around in the cabin like a pea in a pail, looking
desperately for a stable surface that I could cling to in the
madly tilting chamber, wondering at the utter madness
that possessed men who sailed the seas. During occasional
lulls I would collapse on my berth, bruised and battered
and seasick.

"What's the matter with you, Elise?" Garth asked as I
lay clutching my stomach and groaning during one terrible
siege of illness. "You used to be a pretty fair sailor, but
now you're no better than those poor wretches in the
hold."

"Thank you for your kind solicitude, Monsieur," I
moaned sarcastically. "Sometimes I find your goodness
overwhelming. Oh, God, why can't I just die? Kill me,
Garth, and put an end to my suffering."

He laughed callously. I shot him a withering glance.

"You'll get over it," he said. "The sea will probably be calmer tomorrow. I'll take you up on deck and let the sun put the roses back in your cheeks."

"I wish you would just go away. You can't even allow me the dignity of being ill in private. Oh, God," I gasped as the ship rolled heavily. The table skittered from one side of the cabin to the other, the kegs we used for chairs rolled around the floor like marbles, but Garth McClelland stood next to the berth grinning down at me, as solid and secure as a mountain. "I wish you would take your ugly face away from here," I said. "Just looking at you makes me feel a thousand times worse."

He laughed and went out whistling. I clung to the sides of the berth to keep from falling out, calling him every kind of name I could think of.

The storm abated during the night and I crept up on deck the next morning for a breath of fresh air. The seas were still heavy, and when I glanced up at the masts and saw them careening against the gray sky my stomach heaved and I ran for the rail. I heard a shout over my head and saw Garth climbing down from the mizzenmast.

"Feeling better?" he asked with no real evidence of concern. "You behaved very badly last night. I could hardly sleep a wink."

"That's too bad," I said, straightening up and wiping my mouth with my handkerchief. "Why didn't you go someplace else?"

"Why, Elise," he sounded disappointed, "you know there's no better place to be in the world than by your side. And I couldn't desert you in your hour of need, could I?"

"I hope you fall out of the rigging and break your stupid neck," I said with feeling. "Nothing would give me more pleasure than to see your wretched body sprawled all over the deck, broken and bloody. I want to see your brains

scattered to the four winds, your arms and legs fed to the
sharks, your—''

He stood against my back and kissed my neck. A thrill
of pleasure traveled up and down my spine. ''Death is
very final and very dull, my dear Elise,'' he murmured.
''Remember that.''

I flushed angrily and slipped away from him. ''I pray
hourly for death, Garth. Yours or mine. It wouldn't make
any difference. Either way I would be free of you.''

I made my way below once again. The cabin reeked of
sweat and vomit and stale lovemaking. I threw the small
window open and pulled the covers off the berth to air,
then I got down on my hands and knees with a pail of salt
water and a rag and started to scrub the floor.

''Meet Mademoiselle Elise Lesconflair,'' I grumbled
as I worked. ''Charwoman, whore, adventuress. Born of
noble blood, educated at the finest schools in England and
France, darling of the court and of the Emperor himself
—and now, reduced to this! Oh, I hate him. God knows
how much I hate him.''

A wave of nausea passed over me and I had to stop
momentarily and close my eyes. What was the matter with
me? I had been a good sailor, but lately—. Perhaps I
was dying, I thought ruefully. Not that it mattered. Death
was infinitely preferable to the kind of degrading life I was
being forced to lead.

When the cabin was relatively clean and smelling better
I stripped off all my clothes and washed them as best I
could, then I sponged myself off with ice cold seawater,
shivering constantly, and dressed in a clean chemise and
frock. My clothes were in a shocking state: I had worn my
traveling suit until it was threadbare and soiled, and my
lingerie was all stained and torn. I had begged Garth one
day to find me a needle. He had done so, then laughingly

claimed his reward. Now I threaded the needle and jabbed it into a rent in my green skirt, and I meditated on how far I had fallen. To be forced to give my body in exchange for a needle. I pricked my finger and sucked at the puncture. Damn! Damn that man to eternal fire!

He came in while I was sewing. I looked up sullenly, then returned to my work.

"I'm glad to see you've tidied up," he said. "This place was beginning to reek."

I bit my lips and vowed that I wouldn't scream at him. He sat at the other side of the table and watched me silently for a few moments. "You'll make some man a fine wife, Elise," he said. "I don't suppose you can cook, too?"

I lifted my chin. "Certainly not."

"Oh, excuse me," he said elaborately. "I didn't realize that was an insult. I wonder what I should do with you when we get to the Indies. You can probably find a position as governess in one of the planters' homes. Perhaps you might even marry one of them. But the English are very selective about whom they marry. You might do better in the States, where men are more democratic. You know, half the citizens in Louisiana are descended from French convict girls, although you would never get them to admit it. I'm sure you can find some dull fellow who would be willing to overlook your bad temper and your viper's tongue."

"I do not have a bad temper!" I protested loudly. I took a breath and stabbed my needle in and out of the cloth at random. I would have to take it apart and do it all over again, but I had to show him he couldn't succeed in baiting me. "You would try the patience of Job himself," I said more calmly.

"I would take you home with me," he went on, "but I can't really afford servants. All I have is a little shack back in the bayous—that's what they call Louisiana swamps—and the alligators come right up to the door when the water is high. The insects are rather annoying, too. The mosquitoes are as big as mice, and the snakes are so numerous that I've used a string of them to curtain off a doorway.'' I knew he was teasing me, but in spite of myself I shivered. ''No, you wouldn't like life in the swamps, Elise,'' he said decisively. ''You're too civilized to be able to appreciate unspoiled beauty. Of course, you can always set yourself up in New Orleans. A girl of your obvious charms shouldn't have—''

I threw down my sewing and stood up. ''Why can't you leave me alone!'' I shouted at him. I was near tears. ''Isn't it enough for you that you've taken me away from my home and my family and the only life I have ever known—''

''The fact that you had to leave your home was no fault of mine,'' he said.

''And you think that that exonerates you from any blame for what happens to me, isn't that right?'' I stormed at him. ''What a low, vicious worm you are, Garth. You have stripped me of everything, and still that's not enough for you. You have to torment and plague me every minute of the day, because hurting people gives you pleasure.''

He grabbed my hand and pulled me onto his lap. ''Oh, for God's sake, Elise, I was just having a little fun—''

I squirmed and kicked at him and tried to claw his eyes with my fingernails. He caught my hands and held them behind my back. ''Let me go,'' I panted. ''I'll kill you, I swear I'll kill you!''

''Will you, now,'' he chuckled. ''Well, no man could die a happier death, I'm sure.'' He buried his face in my neck and slid his hand under my skirts.

I pretended to yield to him. He freed my hands after a while and I wound one arm around his neck and kissed him eagerly, while with the other I felt for my sewing on the table top and found my needle. I ripped it loose, and then plunged it deep into his arm. He gave a cry of surprise and anger, and I broke free and ran for the door. I tore into the dank passage and raced up the short ladder towards the deck. I fully intended to throw myself into the sea, for I felt that I could no longer bear to live with him.

Captain Fowler stood at the top of the gangway. I almost collided with him, and when he reached out for me with a swinish grin on his face I fell back and rolled to the bottom of the ladder.

"You must be in some kind of hurry, Frenchie," he said. He started to come down after me. I gasped with horror and quickly scrambled to my feet. I heard Garth approaching me from the other end of the passage. I looked from one to the other of them in a daze, then I covered my face and sobbed.

"Jesus," the Captain muttered disgustedly. "Get that female out of my sight, McClelland. She's worse than a yowlin' banshee."

"She is, indeed, Captain," Garth agreed. "Come along, Elise." He put a proprietary hand on my shoulder. I shrugged him off and raced back in the direction of the cabin.

I could hear the two of them laughing scornfully as I ran, and when my legs became entangled in my skirts and I stumbled and nearly fell, the Captain roared delightedly and made a sneering remark about how after all this time I hadn't even found my sea legs. When I was safe in the cabin I threw myself on the berth and sobbed inconsolably until I felt sick. Even after my tears had stopped I lay shivering and choking, wallowing in self-pity and despair.

Garth came in and crouched near the berth. I expected another mocking tirade, but he rested his hand gently on my damp forehead and said, "Forgive me, Elise. I shouldn't have teased you. I deserved your barb. I'm just thankful you didn't have a knife hidden in your skirts somewhere."

His unexpected kindness only provoked more tears. I cried and cried. He sat on the edge of the berth and helped me into a sitting position. Then he lifted a flask of brandy to my lips.

"Drink this," he said. "You'll feel better."

I shook my head and tried to move away from him, but he held me firmly and urged me to drink. Finally I obeyed. "That's not armagnac," I said, making a face.

"You're damned right it's not." He put the flask away and gathered me into his arms. I resisted only slightly, then closed my eyes and rested my head on his chest, drawing comfort from his warmth and nearness. I snuggled close to him, forgetting for the moment that he was my sworn enemy, my merciless tormenter. He brushed the hair away from my face and murmured soothing words, the first I had ever heard from him. He caressed me tenderly, and once again I felt myself responding to his touch.

My brain whirled and I could feel tongues of fire licking at my loins. I melted into his embrace and we made quiet, tender love. Only when we finished did I see the satisfied gleam in his ice blue eyes, and I realized that once again I had allowed him to use me, to exploit and manipulate and maneuver me. I hated him, and I hated and cursed myself, but I knew that I could no more live without him now than I could survive without food and water.

His kindness had been a sham, a fake, a pose. I should have known better than to believe in him, but I suppose that I wanted to believe that he really had some feeling for me, that he wasn't just toying with me to pass the time and forget the horrors of the *Charleston Belle*. I had to admit to myself that I was using him for the same reason: to forget for a little while. I loathed and despised him, but still I gave myself to him eagerly. Than made me no better than a slut, and I didn't care. If desire could bring even a short interlude of forgetfulness and oblivion, then I was all too grateful to him for wanting me.

"Feeling better?" he asked solicitously. His falseness was all too evident now.

"You're a fine actor, Garth," I said bitterly. "The Garrick of your time. And you know just how to get around a woman's tantrums, don't you? A kind word, a loving touch, and pouf! I open to you like a flower to a bee. It's disgusting."

He smiled. "It's nature, Elise. You can't fight nature. Don't be ashamed because you like the way a man feels inside you."

I reddened. "I'm not ashamed. But there should be love as well as desire. Desire without love is—is—"

"Is delightful and amusing," he finished for me. "You're fortunate, Elise. You have all of Love's joys with none of Love's pain and anguish. No jealousy, no fear of being abandoned, no worries about losing your looks. Count yourself lucky, my dear, and enjoy it. I do."

I studied him thoughtfully. "You have enjoyed a great many women, haven't you, Garth? And I'll bet you haven't loved one of them, not one. You don't even know what love is. And you don't want to know, do you? I'm almost sorry for you."

His mouth curled into a condescending smile. "Save your pity for those who want it, Elise. I do what I do because I like it. And if my heart remains untouched, so much the better."

He stretched lazily. The candlelight gleamed on his firm flesh and tawny hair and beard. He was so handsome. I could feel the twist in my heart even as I looked at him. I realized then how easy it would be to fall in love with a man like him. If his tenderness had been real, if he had given me the slightest encouragement, I would have pledged my heart to him forever.

As it was, he was cold, brutal, and disdainful. I told myself how lucky I was that I felt nothing for him but an all-consuming dislike and deep loathing.

I sat up with a start. What was I doing, even thinking about falling in love with a man like him? Was I mad? A woman would have to be an utter fool to lose her heart to such a monster. I climbed out of the berth and went to the open window. The sharp wind cut into my lungs and cleared my head. I breathed deeply and swept the hair back from my face. I would continue to use him, I decided, just as he was using me. My heart would not become involved. I would never allow myself to forget how low I had fallen, thanks to him.

Toward the end of February, Captain Fowler went on a rampage, flogging slaves and sailors alike at double his normal rate, ranting at Garth and blaming everything that went wrong on my presence on board. He stood outside my cabin and screamed at every sailor who passed, exhorting them in the foulest, most suggestive language to stop thinking about me, until they could think of nothing else.

"You've got to stop him, Garth," I pleaded. "He's driving me mad, carrying on that way. Do something, please."

Garth frowned deeply. "What would you like me to do?" he asked caustically. "Ask him politely to cease and desist? He'll get tired of the game after a while and go to his cabin and sleep it off, don't worry."

"But he's mad, Garth, he must be. Oh, God." I sat down heavily at the table and rested my head in my hands.

"I can't take much more of this. I'm going mad, too, and you do nothing to help me. You are just as bestial as he is."

"You've got to stop thinking of every man who wants to get under your skirts as a beast, Elise," he said. "It's really a compliment, you know."

I glared at him. He was so arrogant, so sure of himself. And so sure of me. My anger sprang to life. I picked up a heavy tankard and hurled it at his head. "I hate you, you miserable fiend," I shrieked. "I hate you!" I started throwing everything I could get my hands on—shoes, plates, knives. He dodged the barrage successfully and pinned my arms to my sides.

"Stop it, Elise," he ordered. "Stop it at once!" I continued to scream and thrash as he held me. He struck me sharply across the face and my words died in my throat. I looked at him with a shocked, hurt expression on my face, then I fell on his chest and wept.

"Why did you have to do that? Why? No one ever hit me in my life before I met you. Why?"

His arms tightened around me. I could feel his soft breath on my hair. Outside the window we could hear Fowler's raucous voice, chanting its crude litany against me.

"I'll murder that man some day, so help me God," Garth said in a tired voice. "If we ever get off this barge alive, I'll strangle him with my bare hands."

The next day Garth came into the cabin and said, "You can come up on deck now, if you like."

"But Fowler—"

"He drank himself into a stupor last night. The Bo'sun had to put him to bed. It's all right, the coast is clear."

We crept past Fowler's cabin and into the sunlight on deck. A fine, stiff wind was blowing us towards the Indies and the sun was almost blinding in its brightness. Garth took me to a sheltered place on the foredeck.

"You can sit here for a while. No one will bother you."

I looked up at him. "Thank you," I said grudgingly.

He pinched my cheek. "You're losing your looks, Elise. I won't be able to marry you off if you're ugly. Well, enjoy yourself. I'll come for you if there's any sign of him."

I swallowed a retort. I had been nagging him for days to let me come on deck, and now that my chance had come I didn't want to spoil it. I might have known he would have an ulterior motive, though. He was probably planning to sell me when we got to Jamaica. I sighed deeply and wondered what would become of me when we landed. I tried to think ahead to the time when Garth McClelland would no longer play a part in my life, but it wasn't easy. I felt that there had never been a time in my life when I hadn't known—and hated him.

I was aware of some commotion around me. Men were running and shouting for the Captain, and I heard a voice calling, "A sail, a sail!" I went to the rail and squinted into the sun. I could barely make out a small speck on the horizon. Hope fluttered in my breast. What if it were a French ship! They would take me away from the *Charleston Belle*, back to France. I began to pray feverishly for salvation.

Garth stood at my side and peered at the ship through his glass. "British," he said. The flame of hope died in me. "I can't make out her name, but it looks like a warship."

The Captain stumbled towards us. Ignoring me, he grabbed the glass from Garth and looked at the approaching vessel.

"She's doing about thirteen knots, I wager," Garth said. "And all her guns are out."

"And us with a couple of goddamn twenty-pounders we haven't fired since we left Charleston," Fowler growled. "Damned redcoats."

As the ship drew nearer we could make out her sleek lines and the rows of guns bristling from her sides. The Union Jack waved gallantly from her topsail, and eventually I could make out the name painted on her prow: the *Eureka*.

"The enemy," I breathed.

"To you, Elise," Garth corrected me, "but not to us. If they board us, for God's sake keep your mouth shut. I wouldn't want them to think we're carrying French spies."

"My English is perfectly good," I said tartly.

"It is indeed, but that's no reason to show it off to His Majesty's Navy."

"What do they want?" I asked.

"Nothing, I hope. Maybe they just want to see who's sailing in this part of the world. But they have been known to impress American sailors into service when they're short-handed."

"Impress? What's that?"

"It means to kidnap, the way you and your brothers impressed me into marrying you."

He moved away, cutting off my reply. The other ship signalled that they wanted to come aboard. I saw them lower two small boats over the side. Blue-clad figures climbed down ropes and picked up their oars. Our own sailors were milling around on deck, crowding the rails to watch the boarding party. I found Garth and stayed at his side when the Bo'sun blew his whistle for all hands. Captain and crew gathered amidships to greet the visitors.

I saw that the group of slaves that had come up for their daily meal and exercise included Joseph. I smiled at him and his eyes flickered recognition.

Captain Fowler greeted the Britishers coldly. The

leader of the party, a man I guessed to be an officer, addressed him in a voice that we could all hear.

"Captain, we regret having to interrupt your voyage, but we have reason to believe that certain seamen of His Majesty's Navy are hiding on board your ship, posing as Americans."

"That's their usual excuse," Garth told me softly. "Conditions in His Majesty's Navy are so bad that men desert by the hundreds whenever they reach port."

The officer handed the Captain a paper. "These are the men we think may be among the company of the *Charleston Belle*."

The Captain scanned the sheet and returned it. "No. None of these men is aboard my ship."

"Then we must assume that they are known to you by other names. Conroy." He summoned one of his men. "Pass among those assembled and see if you recognize the blighters."

"I don't understand," I said to Garth. "Are those men here?"

"No, but he'll find them anyway. Wait and see."

My stomach knotted and my legs turned to water. I felt afraid. I looked at Garth. His face was tense and drawn.

Conroy stopped in front of a young sailor.

"I know you, sailor," he said. "Your name's Wainwright. You jumped ship in Gibraltar, didn't you, sailor, and you're hiding out with this filthy gang of slave haulers. Come on, sailor, the game is up."

The terrified man tried to bolt and run, but two of His Majesty's men pounced on him in a flash. They manacled his hands and dragged him to the rail to wait for their departure.

"Dirty, filthy swine," the young man shouted. "Rotten kidnappers! My name's Jeremy Booth and always has been."

He received a blow across the mouth.

"Ye'll have more respect for the members of the King's
Navy," a burly British seaman told him. "Now hold yer
bleedin' tongue or I'll knock yer teeth clear down yer
throat."

Conroy approached us. When he saw me his eyes widened and he grinned broadly. "Well, well, what have we
here? Why, you're the Charleston Belle in person, aren't
you, little lady? You wouldn't by any chance be a seaman
named Jones, would you?" He laughed heartily. His
mates joined him.

I shook my head and shrank away from him. Conroy
looked at Garth. "But you're Jones, aren't you, mate? I
thought I recognized you."

"No, I am not," Garth replied coolly. "My name is
McClelland. This lady is my wife, and we have the misfortune to be passengers on board this ship."

"Your wife? Passengers! Oh, ho! These Yankee slavers are getting a mite fancy, aren't they, mates? And you,
lady, how do you like being a 'passenger' on a tub that's
hauling a lot of dirty wogs, eh?"

He rubbed my cheek with his hand, then yanked me
away from Garth and kissed me hard on the mouth. Garth
leaped at him and pulled him away from me, then hit him a
mighty blow on the jaw. Conroy fell to the deck, stunned.

"Garth, no!" I screamed.

Five British sailors jumped to the aid of their fallen
companion. Garth knocked down two more of them before they overpowered him and threw him to the deck.
They manacled his hands behind his back, and one of them
struck him across the face with the butt of his pistol,
opening a wide cut that bled freely. I ran to him, crying
and calling his name, but strong arms tore me away from
him and sent me sprawling.

They took two more sailors after that and two strong
blacks. One of them was Joseph.

They admired the scars on his back. "This one's been flogged by the Devil himself, mates, and lived to tell about it. Haven't you, mate? Gawd, look at that. Isn't often you get a man that's been tested like that."

Someone, I think it was Doctor Hawthorne, kept a strong hold on my arm as the British sailors marshalled their captives and took them away. They freed Garth's hands long enough for him to go down the ropes to the boats that were waiting to take them all back to the *Eureka*, then they manacled him again.

I broke free and rushed to the rail to watch. I could see his golden head shining among the rest as the little boats bobbed over the waves. As they drew farther away I could feel the numbness of disbelief settling over me. Surely this wasn't happening. It was all a hideous nightmare. They wouldn't be taking him away, they couldn't.

"Would you like my glass, Ma'am?" The Captain held out his spyglass to me.

Without thinking, I took it and raised it to my eye. I could see Garth more clearly then, being prodded up the side of the *Eureka*, stumbling when he reached the deck, lashing out with his fists and feet at an officer, who raised a club and beat him around the head and shoulders. He fell to the deck in a heap, and still they beat him and kicked him viciously. As they dragged him away, he was limp and unconscious.

The Captain took the glass out of my hands, but I was hardly aware of him. I still gazed after the *Eureka*, which had hoisted her sails and drawn up her anchor, and headed boldly into the wind.

"That poor bastard will never live through the day," the Captain remarked with satisfaction. "They'll beat the fight out of him and then they'll beat the life out of him."

I looked at him, horrified. His eyes were gleaming evilly as he stared at me. The snake of fear that uncoiled in my belly felt the true horror of my situation before my brain grasped it. Only Garth had stood between me and this man. And now Garth was gone.

I turned abruptly and ran to my cabin. There was only that small latch on the door, which served to keep it from banging and swinging in rough seas. When I heard his step in the corridor I threw myself against the door, sobbing and panting in sheer panic. Never in my life had I been so terrified. My heart was bursting in my breast and I could taste the fear in my mouth.

He threw the door open, sending me flying across the room.

"I've come to pay my respects," he said, smiling lewdly. "It's a damn shame about your fellow, isn't it? I came to console the little widow."

"Please go away, Captain," I said hoarsely. "I'm all right, I promise you." He was advancing on me. "Just go. Please. I appreciate your sympathy, but—. Get out! Get out of here this instant!"

He came closer. I backed away from him. "You don't look all right, Frenchie." He roared with laughter. "You're scared, ain't you? You're afraid of what I'm going to do to you!" He was shouting, his face a distorted mask of animal passion. Saliva ran down his chin.

He unbuckled his belt and ripped open the front of his breeches. I stared at him unbelievingly. "And you're right," he said. "I'm going to teach you some things that star-gazer never heard of."

"Please go, Captain, I beg you," I said, sobbing and incoherent. "I would like to be alone now, if you don't mind. Perhaps we could discuss this later—"

"We ain't discussin' nothin', bitch," he growled. He reached out and touched my hair. I ducked away and tried to run past him, but he grabbed a fistful of hair and hauled me back. I fell on my knees and struggled to rise.

He chuckled gleefully, and placing a meaty hand on my shoulder, he pushed me down to the floor. His ugly, purple-veined bludgeon was raised to strike me out of the stinking, black-matted filthiness of his groin. I drew in my breath and closed my eyes and prayed to faint, but as he came down on me with all of his considerable weight, nearly three times my own, I was horribly conscious. I fought and scratched, but my fingernails made no impression on his tough hands, and when I tried to scratch his eyes he slammed my head against the floor and hit me in the face again and again with the back of his hand. Tears poured down my cheeks and I nearly choked on my own blood.

"Damned bitch. Two-bit French whore," he snarled. "You could be high and mighty and treat me like dirt when you had your pretty boy to stick up for you. Now you don't even have the fancy slave you saved, do you?" He laughed. "Don't think I didn't know what was going on down here, bitch. Now you're going to learn how to take care of a real man. You're going to do everything I tell you to do, and when you finish you're going to beg for more. You're mine now, bitch. Mine."

He had shoved my skirts up to my waist and wrenched my legs apart. His face was close to mine and I could smell the putrid breath and hear his grunts of pleasure as his rotten stump assaulted my flesh.

In desperation I closed my eyes and tried to pretend it was Garth, that Garth and I were together again, making the fine violent-tender love that left us weak and warm and one.

But this raving beast was not Garth. I felt no desire, only revulsion and pain, humiliation and disgust. He heaved and snorted and grappled me, and I sobbed and winced and prayed to God to stop him.

As if in answer to my prayer, he finished quickly

enough. Thank God, his kind have no ability to prolong
their pleasure. He sat back on his heels and crowed over
me. I could feel his rough hands on my thighs, kneading
and stroking me. I groaned and rolled painfully onto my
side, and pulled my legs up while I covered my face with
my arms.

"Eh, we're going to have a lot of fun from now on,
Frenchie, you and me." He pawed my buttocks. I whimpered and tried to cover myself. "We've got a long way to
go yet, another month, maybe more. Time for lots of fun."

And so it began, an interminable desecration at the
hands of this loathsome creature. He violated not only
my body, but my soul and my mind as well. I became ugly
and timid; I stopped believing in a God that would permit
this to happen to me; my dreams were dominated by blood
and death.

I was more of a slave than any of those in the hold.
Captain Fowler locked me in my cabin and watched me
constantly. He refused to allow me to go up on deck for air
because once I had tried to throw myself over the side into
the peace and silence of the ocean. In a way, the curtail-
ment of my freedom was a blessing: I couldn't bear the
looks on the faces of the sailors. Envious, evil, lusting, or
even sympathetic, I couldn't tell them apart any more. I
was an object to them, and I could hardly tolerate the
shame and degradation I felt. The slime and dirt that
Josiah Fowler left on me made me unfit for any other
companionship: I felt dirty and befouled to my very bones.

Fowler took his meals with me. He was as obscene and
revolting when he ate as he was when he satisfied his other
physical drives. He even slept with me in the berth that
Garth and I had shared. He took me—abused me
—constantly, in an astonishing variety of ways. I did
things that I hadn't dreamed existed a few months before,

and I did them even though they disgusted and nauseated
me. After that single attempt to do away with myself, I no
longer contemplated suicide. Somewhere in my innermost
depths I decided that I wanted to live, that I could survive
and would survive. I would do anything. And I had to do
everything.

When I protested I got the back of his hand across my
face. Sometimes he kicked me with his heavy boots,
kicked me as I lay grovelling at his feet like a whipped
dog. Garth had been kicked like that, I thought in my
agony. Perhaps Garth survived, and perhaps I would survive, too.

I'm sure no one tried to dissuade Fowler from the course
he had taken with me. They were all terrified of him. I
wondered if this crazed lust of his was a new face, one he
had never exhibited to them before. They saw it and
trembled as I trembled, for we all knew that he dealt out
death with no more thought than he gave to opening the
front of his breeches. Killing was just another perverted
pleasure for him. The sailors may even have been grateful
for his attentions to me: every moment he spent torturing
me was one less he would spend haranguing them. Floggings above deck decreased in inverse proportion to the
rise of violence in my cabin.

He broke my pride. I tried everything I could think of to
change his attitude, to quell his raging brutishness. I cried,
I wept prayerfully, I pleaded with him. To my greatest
shame, I even tried to flaunt myself in front of him so that
he might see me in a different way, perhaps as a beautiful
woman who deserved to be treated more gently. I tried to
call him Josiah, and I forced myself to smile sweetly at
him and inquire, as dutifully and sincerely as any wife, if
he had had a nice day.

"Trying to sweeten me up, are you, bitch?" He

laughed unpleasantly. "I'll be damned if you're not tryin'
to impress me with your fancy ways so that I'll treat you
like a goddamn lady."

"Not at all." I smiled weakly. "I am interested in your
work, that's all. You're an experienced seaman, a real
veteran, so of course—"

He gripped my face in his hand and twisted my flesh so
that the insides of my cheeks were bruised from grinding
against my teeth. "A real veteran, am I? I'll show you
what I'm a veteran of. Just shut your mouth." He hit me
hard, knocking me back against the berth. "Get those
stinkin' rags off and lie down on your ugly face." Trembling, I removed my clothes and lay down. "Damn it, I
said face down." And then he proceeded to abuse me until
I thought my lungs would burst from my screaming.

Just when I thought he had run the gamut of horrible
things to do to me, he thought up something new. He came
into my cabin one day, pushing a terrified young Negro
girl in front of him.

"You had such a good time watching the boys and that
bitch back in Dahomy," he said gloatingly. "See how you
like this."

She screamed weakly as he leaped at her and threw her
down, then forced her legs apart. She had no strength to
fight him, but went limp in a moment, and she didn't even
cry when he eased himself off her and kicked her viciously
in the groin.

"Did you like that?" he demanded, panting. "Next
time she can watch while I do it to you," he added for me.

Next time, next time. He kept his promise. That woman
witnessed my shame, and so did several others at one time
or another—after I had witnessed theirs. He even brought
in a small boy, who screamed and vomited all over the
floor and bled so badly that I was sure he would die on the
spot.

I dreamed of killing him. Not by sword or gun, but by torturing him slowly as he had tortured me, so that life would drain out of him, drop by drop. If I could spill his blood, I thought, I would wallow in it and rejoice.

I fought with all my strength to stay alive. How much that fight was costing me I did not know until one day when I tried futilely to cajole my persecutor into treating me kindly.

"So it's another Josiah Dear day, is it?" He wagged his head and creased his face into a grimace. "You stupid French whore. Josiah has had about enough of you. You stink and I'm sick of the sight of you. Do you want to see why?" He shouted with maniacal laughter and ran out of the cabin, returning in a moment with a small shaving mirror. "That's why!" He held it up in front of my face, smirking with triumph.

I did not recognize myself. I squinted at the reflection for half a minute, trying to make out a vestige of my former self. My black eyes looked enormous in my skull-like head. They were sunken and dull, ringed with purple from exhaustion and the repeated beatings around my face and head. My once smooth cheeks were hollow, and the tone of my skin was dull and lifeless. Lips that had been full and merry were now cracked and scabby. And my hair, my beautiful, glorious hair that Garth had said reminded him of a night sky after a storm, now stood around my head in crazy tufts, rough and tangled and knotted between patches of bare scalp where it had fallen or been pulled out.

I was more terrifying than any witch.

I raised a hand, a claw, on which the veins stood out like strands of blue cord on a field of red-blotched white, and I touched my face. Then I started to laugh, loudly, madly. I laughed and laughed at the ironies of life. I had thought that my life was over because Uncle Theo wanted me to marry a rich baron! Oh, that was delicious! And how angry I had been, how enraged, when I had looked at myself in the mirror on the night of my wedding ball, because I was too beautiful! Oh, it was funny! Madly, wickedly, wonderfully funny!

"Oh, Josiah, look, look at what you have created!" I shrieked. I waved my stick-like arms at him. "A witch! A real black sea-witch, Josiah!" I saw him pale and step away from me, and I persisted in my madness. I dropped my voice to a gravelly whisper. "I have new powers now, Josiah." I rolled my eyes. "Powers to heal and powers to curse. And I curse *you*, Josiah Fowler! I curse you, I curse you, I curse you!"

I scrambled after him, howling like a fiend. and he scuttled out the door. I lay back on the berth and laughed. He was really frightened of me, the fool! Oh, why hadn't I thought of it before? Sailors are superstitious, and even captains are not immune. I had put the fear of demons into him. I laughed again, and the sound that came to my ears was wild and lonely. Lonely. I turned over and wept deeply, from the soul, as I had never wept before.

Fowler's visits were less frequent after that. As we neared Jamaica he spent more time supervising the feeding and exercising of the slaves so they would present a fine appearance as they stepped off the boat and fetch a high price. He took to sleeping in his own cabin, for which I was thankful. Although he still used me to satisfy his uncontrollable cravings, he eyed me warily now, half believing that I had turned into a witch. I mumbled to myself in French a lot because he hated it. It was worth a cuff or a blow to see him go red with anger and then white with fear.

"Stop that damned jargon, do you hear?" he would shout. "Or by God—"

*"Ah, que vous êtes l'animal le plus gros et despicable*

*de tout le monde,''* I would croon. I had a weapon now, and I did not hesitate to use it. I discovered that incantations in Latin, muttered low while gazing at him out of the corner of my eye, were even more effective. I racked my brain for snatches of schoolgirl Latin and drove him to distraction, even when he was on top of me, with *amo, amas, amat* and *veni, vidi, vici.*

I knew that my danger was becoming more acute as we neared the end of our journey. I did not think for a moment that he would let me live to see civilization so that I could expose his brutality to the world. And his sailors, who had a stake in this voyage, too, would certainly stand behind him.

One day I taunted him too gleefully, and I was surprised and appalled when he hauled me to my feet and began pulling me towards the passage, saying, ''I'm going to throw you to the real sharks today. You're gonna scream like you ain't never screamed before.''

I unleashed the full range of my curses at him, but he dragged me along, unheeding, unafraid. Down the narrow corridor amidships, up the gangway to the deck. Into the sunlight. I gasped and covered my eyes with my hands, stumbling blindly in the glare. I had lived like a mole for—I had no idea how many days. The air felt warmer, warmer than it had been on that wintry day when they had taken Garth away and given me Josiah Fowler in his place.

The Captain gave me a shove and I fell heavily on my knees. ''All hands, all hands,'' he shouted.

I heard murmurs of surprise and wonder, and the clatter of footfalls on the boards. The sails billowed and rustled above me: I could hear them bellying noisily as they caught the wind and lost it and caught it again, ballooning and deflating. I rubbed my eyes and looked around me. A forest of legs and feet, some shod, some not. Some hairy, some smooth. Breeches, most in rags. Heavy belts and open shirts revealing grimy manly chests, some muscular, some scrawny. And faces, filled with curiosity and dismay and fear. The crew had gathered.

"Mrs. McClelland." Murmurs of wonder and amazement. "Mrs. McClelland has been ill, gentlemen." A few chuckles. He couldn't pull the wool over their eyes as easily as that. "Ill, I said. She can't remember she's a woman, isn't that strange? I think she needs a reminder from some of you fellows. A gentle reminder." Genuine laughter now. They could see how gently I had been treated.

They shuffled their feet, shifting their weight from one leg to the other in nervous schoolboy fashion. They had caught the lust from him now. They had the scent of woman in their nostrils, white flesh as opposed to the black flesh they had been grabbing in the hold.

"You see this coin, mates?" I looked up and caught the glint of gold in the Captain's hand. One of my gold louis. "This coin goes to the first man who has the goodness and pity in him to cure this lady of her sad affliction."

They were frozen for a moment as the bribe sank in. They circled me slowly like a pack of hungry wolves. Their eyes were bright and cold. I knew what held them back: they thought I was a witch and they were afraid. Nonetheless, I was amazed that the twin bribes of gold and a woman failed to move them.

"Are ye frightened of a damned whore?" the Captain bellowed angrily. "By God, you cowards! A coin to *each* man who cures the lady, then!"

I went down under them like a lame caribou falling to the wolf pack that has been stalking her for days. Hands ripped away every shred of my dress and grabbed eagerly at my flesh and my hair and my face. They wanted their reward badly enough now.

I must have started to bleed almost immediately. Soon

they fell back, muttering. Then the real pains began. From the silent depths of my agony I brought forth a spine-curdling, tortured scream. My body writhed and twisted from this new pain, and my tormentors looked down on me as I jerked and gasped. Then a broadsword cut into my loins and slashed me again and again. I shouted and screeched my pain for all of them to hear.

"Jesus, what's happening?"

"She's a goner now for sure, Captain."

"Goddamn it! Find that bastard Hawthorne!" I could feel him standing over me, straddling me, hating me. "You're all to blame now, you swine," he cried. "You've killed her this time for certain."

"What is all this?" A kneeling figure at my side. Comforting whiskey breath. "What have—oh, my God!"

The broadsword twisted in my bowels. I heaved and screamed.

"Take her below at once, now! Don't just stand there like a pack of fools. You're all responsible for this, God help you. Come on, hurry!"

And then merciful oblivion.

The ship rocked gently, a cradle in the deep. I slept. Then the rocking became a violent pitching. More heaving and spewing out my insides. Tears and sweat, but not, in spite of the pain, not Death. Had I cheated Death? Or had Death cheated me?

"Doctor Hawthorne?" I groped for his hand.

"Yes, child, I'm here."

"What's happening?"

"A storm, that's all. Some heavy winds and high water. The usual thing. It looks like a good blow this time. Just lie back now and rest. You'll be all right, Elise, just try and rest."

Elise? I hardly recognized my Christian name. I hadn't heard it since—since Garth. It made me cry. "Dirty, I feel so dirty," I moaned. The Doctor moistened my lips with water. "Please—please tell me what happened. I know about the men—the pain was so terrible."

His hand on my forehead was cool. "You lost your baby, Elise." I smothered a cry. "Didn't you know you were carrying a baby?"

"No. No," I gasped, shaking my head slightly. "I thought it was seasickness. Seasick so much, and I'd never been—thought I was just upset." I choked back a sob. To lose a child before you even knew you had it. It was so awful, so sad. "I'm glad, Doctor Hawthorne. Glad. I wouldn't have wanted—his baby."

The doctor was silent for a moment. "It was a large fetus, Elise. Almost four months along, I'd say. I think you may never be able to have another. I'm—I'm sorry."

A new abyss of sorrow opened up. It had been Garth's. I had lost Garth's child. Tears rolled down my cheeks. I wept not for Garth or for our child, but for myself.

The seas became calm again. The Doctor told me that we had been blown far off our course by the storm, but had sighted land. We were now anchored in a natural harbor, waiting for a party to return with casks of fresh water. The Captain, he said, was furious about the unforeseeable delay, for we had been within a few days' sail of Jamaica and these waters were alive with pirates.

I smiled feebly. "Surely not pirates, Doctor. In this day and age?"

"Oh, yes, indeed. In fact—"

I heard the cabin door open and Captain Fowler came into the room. I shrank back. "Get out, Hawthorne," he ordered.

The little man took a breath. "Captain, I should warn you that any further excitement—"

"Out, goddamn it!"

"—could have a serious effect on the patient, and if she dies, I promise you that you and you alone shall hang!"

"Go to Hell, Hawthorne. You haven't the guts of a clam. Nobody's going to hang if you keep your goddamn mouth shut."

I heard a shout and some scuffling and whining, then I knew I was alone with Josiah Fowler.

"I should never have taken you aboard this ship," he said tightly. I turned my face away from him. He grabbed my chin and jerked it towards him. "You'll look at me when I'm talking to you, bitch!" he snarled. "You're not going to tell anybody anything, and neither is that idiot Hawthorne, because neither of you is going to live through the night."

"*Non amo te, Sabidi—*" I chanted thickly.

"Stop that, stop that, do you hear me!" He lifted his arm and struck me full across the face.

"*—nec possum dicere quare—*"

He would have killed me right then, I know, but one of the sailors suddenly burst in crying, "Pirates, Captain! Pirates!"

Fowler ran out of the cabin. I laughed to myself. Cheating Death, cheating Death. Cheating Josiah Fowler. Then a pain shot through me, not as severe as before but bad enough, and I doubled up. Sweat was pouring off me, and I knew I was feverish. Perhaps I hadn't cheated Death at all. He was merely biding his time, waiting to take me in his own way. I lay in that stinking cabin, sick and alone, only dimly aware of the pounding of feet and the thunder of guns over my head.

The next thing I heard was a voice close to me, speaking in French, and then another replying from far away.

"Dear God, who is she? Is she dead, Pierre? She must be some octoroon, her skin is so light."

I moaned and struggled to speak. It was like one of those nightmares when you know you're in danger and yet you can't move your feet or utter a sound. You struggle and strain to make yourself understood until you finally wake up and realize it was only a dream after all.

Then I decided I must be back home. I heard my own voice saying in French, "But I want to marry him, Uncle Theo, and he can live with us at the Chateau and we shall have champagne every night."

"Mother of God, Dominique, she's alive!"

Then the voices began to fade away. I felt strong arms come down and carry me clear up to Heaven, and when I got there I passed out and knew no more.

## VI. The Pirate Lafitte

"Lily, your hands have more healing magic than all the doctors in New Orleans. You've finally banished Mademoiselle's fever."

I floated in darkness, free of pain. I had no idea whether I was dead or alive, and I cared less. The half-mad face of Josiah Fowler danced around in my head, but my hate and my fear, so many feelings swirled numbly together, and I couldn't tell them apart. I must be dead, I thought. I had had nothing to live for. Men had destroyed my life, and if I had lived they would just have abused me and destroyed it again and again. I felt quite comfortable now. I basked in my death and the peace and warmth of my darkness.

Voices reached me again and irritated me a little. How dare they speak in the presence of the dead. Why didn't they show more respect? Why didn't they go away?

Someone laughed. A woman's warm laugh. "Oh, Mister Jean, she's comin' along jest fine. Ain't she a sorry lookin' little mite, though? It jest about tears my heart out lookin' at her! Jest like a little sick puppy!"

Go away, I thought. I don't want you to look at me.

"Yes, she's had a bad time of it, Lily. I hope she recovers. How old do you suppose she is?"

"Old enough," said Lily grimly.

"So it would appear." I could feel them flying around me in the darkness, web-winged bats with human voices. I could feel their wings beating against my face, and I wanted to brush them away. "She's getting restless, Lily. Do you think she's coming out of it?"

SAVAGE SURRENDER

"Wouldn't surprise me none. She's jest been lyin' there for the past week and a half. Her body's been restin' and healin' itself up, and now it's gettin' ready to wake up."

I won't wake up. I won't. A week? How long is a week? Is it longer than a day or shorter? A year, a month, a minute, an hour, what are they? Not important. I want to sleep. The darkness rocked a little. Someone sat on the edge of the bed.

"*Bonjour,* Mademoiselle." The man spoke. "Can you hear me? Do you want to awaken?"

"Go away," I muttered.

"Glory be, will you listen to her, Mister Jean. She's talkin'!" cried Lily.

My eyes opened and the darkness melted away. A large white field and some posts and veils. What kind of nonsense was this? My brain worked fast. Of course, I was in bed and the white was the ceiling and the veils were some kind of netting. "Where am I?" I heard a voice from far away and then realized I had spoken.

"You are quite safe, Mademoiselle." The voice was close, much closer than my own. I turned my head towards it and saw a man seated on the side of the bed. If I had been able to lift my hand I might have reached out and touched him. Then a shadow moved up behind him. A woman, a big chocolate-colored woman with a red scarf wrapped around her head. The man reached over and placed a cool hand on my forehead.

"Who are you?" I said. I couldn't make out the details of his face. My eyelids felt heavy and things were fuzzy, so fuzzy.

"My name is Jean Lafitte. This is my house."

"I see. I—I am sorry to be a trouble to you, Monsieur Lafitte. So sorry." I closed my eyes.

I felt the weight of his hand on mine. "Please do not

concern yourself, Mademoiselle. I assure you you are no trouble. You must concentrate on getting better.''

''No, no, too late. Too late—can't—rather sleep forever,'' I muttered drowsily.

He laughed softly. ''You have slept long enough, I think. When you—'' The voices faded away and then another wave tossed the boat lightly. ''—think she's asleep again. Let me know if there is anything I can do.'' I opened my eyes again and saw the man across the room now, at the door.

''Yes, Mister Jean, I will.'' The woman's gentle hands smoothed the coverlets and stroked my face and hair.

''I want—I want—'' I began to breathe harder, and I struggled to sit up. The woman helped me and supported me. I clung to her and looked past her at the man, who had turned back and was looking at me, surprised. ''I want—'' I gasped brokenly. ''Kill Josiah Fowler, and—and bring me his head on a platter, if you can!'' I laughed weakly, crazily. ''Kill him! For me!''

''Hush, now, child, don't you go gettin' yourself all wrought up like that,'' said the woman. I fell back on my pillows, exhausted, and sleep overtook me almost immediately.

But I heard the man say to the woman, ''It's a good sign, that hate. It will keep her alive.''

I began to have longer periods of consciousness every day. Lily encouraged me and praised my progress, even going so far as to declare that I was getting pretty.

''Oh, Missy, the swelling's about gone and your cuts are all healed up, and the bruises show just a teensy bit. You're going to be pretty as a picture again, jest you wait and see. You was pretty once, wasn't you? And you'll be pretty again, even prettier.''

I didn't believe her, but her words cheered me. I hadn't

been able to eat for two weeks, even the smell of food had made me nauseous, but finally my appetite began to return and I swallowed small portions of Lily's tempting soups and stews, to her great delight.

"Oh, you'll look jest fine when you get a little weight on you, Missy. I couldn't do much with your hair but cut the knots out and wash it, and it still looks kind of funny because of all the places where it was pulled out. My, what you must have been through!"

"Perhaps we could cut it all off," I suggested. I didn't want to talk about how it got that way. "And then it would all grow back at the same rate and not look so strange."

We debated the problem for a day or so, and finally Lily obliged and got to work with her scissors. She was thrilled with the result. "It looks jest fine, jest fine, and it's starting to curl up already in this heat. Why, maybe you'll start a new style, Missy, and be the talk of New Orleans. Do you want to see? I'll get the glass."

"No, no," I said quickly. "Please don't bother, Lily. I—I don't want to look, ever again." I could still see the face in the mirror held by Captain Josiah Fowler.

She shook her head sadly. "Aw, don't feel like that, Missy. You're alive, aren't you? And that's a lot more than you can say for some of those poor souls that come over on those ships, and you know that better than most."

Just then Monsieur Lafitte came into the room. I smiled up at him, for I always looked forward to his visits. He was very polite, even a little distant, and I had to admit he was devastatingly handsome. Lafitte was not tall, well under six feet, but his slenderness and erect carriage, his proud bearing and the cut of his clothes made him seem taller. His reddish brown hair was thick and straight, and he wore a moustache the same color. His brown eyes were always filled with warmth and concern when he looked at me, and only later did I learn that they could flash with anger and glare so fiercely that men twice his age and size would tremble. His face was lean and hard, but smooth except for a slight scar along the jawline. His dress was always immaculate. His shirts were dazzling in their whiteness, and generously ruffled at the cuffs and neck. Some would have called him a dandy, but his taste was far too good and he wore his beautiful clothes with a complete lack of self-consciousness; he was elegant, the most elegant man I had ever met—and at the French court I had met a good many men who affected elegance.

We spoke French, but he was fluent in English as well. I learned that he used both languages when dealing with his men and with merchants and business men in cosmopolitan New Orleans, and he also spoke the Cajun or Arcadian patois of the men who had grown up in the bayous of Louisiana with a language and customs that were uniquely their own.

Jean Lafitte's manners were impeccable. They were so much a part of him that he never slipped, never forgot himself; I was sure he would remain a gentleman in any situation.

When he approached my bed he took my hand and raised it to his lips. Then he stood back to study the effect of the thick short black curls that framed my white face.

"Most becoming, Mademoiselle. You are far too pretty to keep hidden away like this."

"You will turn my head with all your praise, Monsieur Lafitte," I said a little sadly. "I will grow vain as a peacock, like the king who didn't know he had ass's ears until it came to him in a whisper. I shall strut, and everyone will laugh at me."

"They will not laugh, Mademoiselle," he said firmly. "Come, it is time for you to see a bit of the world. I have had chairs set on the veranda outside your room."

"Oh, no! Please! I would much rather stay here. What if someone sees me? What if—"

Laughing at my protestations, he picked me up and

carried me out in his arms. I cringed as we neared the French windows that opened onto the second floor veranda, for I had not been out of the room since my arrival. I buried my face in the ruffles at his neck, and clung to him for dear life.

He deposited me in a vast wicker chair, and wrapped me with blankets even though the breeze from the water was warm. "You must stay warmly wrapped. If you have a relapse Lily will be furious with me. She is very proud of your progress. I believe it is she who is strutting!"

"She has been so kind. You have both been so kind." I looked around me. The house stood back on a flat beach, overlooking a wide expanse of blue water. "Is this New Orleans?" I asked.

"No, Mademoiselle, we are on an island known as Grand Terre, in an area which the early French settlers named Barataria in honor of Sancho Panza's island kingdom in *Don Quixote*. He could not reach his island, and the French could not penetrate here because of the thick trees and the swampy terrain underfoot. In front of you you see the Gulf of Mexico; behind us lies Barataria Bay. We are to the south of New Orleans, the finest city in the territory of Louisiana. You have never been there? No? Then you shall see for yourself someday."

"But why do you live here, Monsieur? Surely such swampland is not good for farming?"

Lafitte smiled politely. "I am not a farmer, Mademoiselle. I am an outlaw. So far I have not been hunted like a criminal, but there is always that chance, and it pays to be safe, no? A good many people would like to destroy me and my business. Grand Terre is easy to defend, and therefore I find it an ideal headquarters for me."

"Oh. And what is your business? Are you a pirate?" I asked wittily.

"A pirate?" Looking out over the gulf, he leaned on the rail of the veranda and folded his arms. "Pirate is a fine romantic name. Scoundrel is one I have often heard. Buccaneer is, I think, the most popular. But smuggler is the most accurate. I am a smuggler, then, which to some minds is equivalent to being a thief. Indeed, the chair on which you sit, the coverlet in which I have wrapped you, the bed you sleep in and the carpets on the floors and the foods you eat—all are stolen goods or goods bought with the profits of smuggling. In short, Mademoiselle, you have fallen in with a band of ruthless thieves. I hope you are appropriately frightened." He turned and looked at me without smiling.

"No, I'm not afraid of you," I confessed shyly. "I think that very little would frighten me now." But I felt old terrors and hatreds tearing at my soul as I stared out across the water. Josiah Fowler's image loomed before me and I remembered my raving to Monsieur Lafitte on my first day of consciousness. Was my tormentor dead? I could not force myself to ask. Surely Hell could be nothing compared to what I had been through.

"Perhaps, Mademoiselle," he said gently. "I think, however, that you are a little afraid of seeing other people?"

I nodded. "Yes, I am. I still feel rather—raw, and —unclean."

"Won't you tell me who you are and how you came to be on that ship?"

For a moment I said nothing. I realized then that this elegant polite stranger had been telling the truth about his business. He must really be a pirate, incongruous as it seemed. His ship had stopped the *Charleston Belle*, had stayed Captain Josiah Fowler's hand from killing me. It all came rushing back to me, and I saw the stinking cabin and the filthy, rotten whore I had become. I heard again the voices of the pirates speaking in French before I fainted, and I knew how I came to be in his man's house. He had rescued me from my Hell, he had seen me in that Hell.

"No. No, I couldn't. Please don't ask me. When I am well enough I shall go away and you must forget you ever saw me." I covered my face with my hands.

After a while he said, "There is no need to fear the past, Mademoiselle. It is over and done with, and it cannot hurt you. You are safe here. No one will harm you. I promise you, Mademoiselle, if any man touches you without your leave, he will die by my hand."

I looked up at him. "You—"

Monsieur Lafitte understood my unspoken thoughts. "Captain Fowler met with an unfortunate accident. He had gone quite mad, I believe, and when I was in New Orleans, after we had relieved the Captain of his ship and his cargo, he came to my house one day, brandishing pistols, and began firing wildly at me. I was forced to repulse him with my sword."

"So he is dead," I said slowly.

"I had no intention of killing him—the wound was not serious—but I thought I had better bring him back here and keep him out of sight until I decided what to do with him. Unfortunately, you had not yet spoken or I promise you I would have tortured him slowly, until the life drained out of him drop by drop—perhaps I would have brought you his head—" he smiled fleetingly, "—but I locked him in the hold of his own ship out in the harbor, as he was too revolting to keep on the island. To my sorrow, I was not responsible for his death: I believe that his madness had progressed so far that he was bent on self-destruction.

"That night, as I was sitting on the veranda, I saw a faint glow in the southern sky. I gathered Dominique and some of the men and we took out a couple of small boats, but by the time we cast off, the *Charleston Belle* was a blazing torch on the dark sea, and before we could reach her she sank into the gulf with her Captain aboard.

"The moon was fair, and we kept an eye out for floating timbers that could have supported a clinging survivor, but there was nothing. The evil that was Captain Fowler perished by fire and water at his own hand.

"The next morning your fever was gone, and you spoke your first words, Mademoiselle. You asked me to kill a dead man. I am sorry; I should have felt honored to kill him for you."

I sat without moving, stunned by his words.

"But life goes on, Mademoiselle, and that chapter of your life is finished forever, or it will be when you feel you trust me enough to tell me about it. Do you not think it is too big a burden to carry alone?" Without waiting for an answer, he said, "Come, let us go inside now. You are tired."

"Yes, I am." He bent over to pick me up. I rested my hand on his arm. "Monsieur Lafitte."

"Yes, Mademoiselle?"

"My name is Elise. Elise Antoinette Leonore Mariani Lesconflair. I—I would be honored if you would address me by my first name."

"Thank you, Elise. And you may call me Jean, if you like."

Lafitte left for New Orleans the next day on business. He expected to be gone a week, perhaps more. Lily was determined that when he returned I would greet him at the door standing on my own two feet and looking, as she put it, as pretty as a black-eyed Susan. She was a stern taskmaster, watching what I ate and making me take longer and longer walks every day.

"It feels good to walk on a surface that isn't tipping under my feet," I told her. "It's much easier, in fact."

I learned that the two pirates who had discovered me on the *Charleston Belle* were Jean Lafitte's older brothers. They came to visit me one day. Pierre, who was only two years older than Jean, was the same height as his brother but thicker in build and darker. He was careless in his dress—his shirt was torn and soiled, and he wore a knotted red handkerchief around his neck—but he had a kind of rough attractiveness that I found very appealing. Dominique You, ten years older than Pierre, was short, hardly taller than I was, with a dark swarthy face badly scarred on the left side by powder burns. His shoulders were broad and meaty, about twice the size of his brothers', and I could see why I had felt like a cloud, if his arms had carried me off the *Charleston Belle*. Dominique You looked like the cruelest, most dangerous villain imaginable, but when his face broke into a mirthful grin and his eyes twinkled at me, I could see that he wore his villainy like working clothes—to disguise his good heart. I thanked him for saving me from the *Charleston Belle*.

"Ah, Mademoiselle, it is always a pleasure to rescue a young lady from evil like that. And may I say you are looking quite dazzling today. Why, this island's never seen the likes of you before, has it, Pierre? Say, how did you come to be on that tub, anyway? That Captain got his desserts, I suppose Jean told you. Our Jean is a great one with a blade, and with words, too, as you have no doubt discovered."

Pierre spoke up. "Shut your trap, Dominique, for God's sake. Mademoiselle is too tired to listen to your yarns. My apologies for my brother, Mademoiselle. He did not have the benefit of the fine education Jean and I received, and he has spent so many years in the crude company of privateers and low waterfront types—"

"Few so crude as you, Pierre!"

"—that he has forgotten how to act with ladies of quality."

I barely managed to keep from giggling. "Thank you, Monsieur, but I find nothing at all objectionable about your brother's manners. You forget, I have spent a good deal of time myself in the company of low waterfront types, and I fear my quality has been somewhat tarnished."

"Never!"

"Unthinkable!" They chorused in protest. "Gold," Dominique asserted gallantly, "will always shine brightly when it is rubbed, even if it has the grime of centuries on it."

I couldn't help myself. I laughed merrily and said, "Thank you, Monsieur Dominique, for that delightful compliment. I have never had a nicer."

"You numbskull," Pierre growled. "Swords have two edges; compliments should never have more than one, much less three! But then who could expect a full-sized brain in a little sawed-off runt like—"

Dominique's eyes flashed. "Why you bandy-legged, two-bit bean smuggler. I'll give you both edges of my blade in your scrawny neck. I was chasing the British when you were still wearing baby dresses."

"Maybe so," Pierre retorted, "but did you catch any, grandpop?"

"Catch them! You bet your skinny ass I caught 'em, and I squeezed the life out of 'em and threw 'em overboard, just like I'm going to throw you over Mademoiselle's balcony." Quick as a flash Dominique had wrapped his huge arms around Pierre who, though brawny himself and a full head taller, struggled and shouted futilely while Dominique dragged him out on my balcony. I ran after them and tugged on Dominique's shirtsleeve.

"Where?" I asked breathlessly, hoping to prevent bloodshed. "Where did you chase the British, Dominique?"

"Ho, where haven't I, eh, Pierre?" Pierre affirmed with a sullen grunt, and Dominique released him. Then they began to tell me the story of the Lafitte brothers.

The Lafittes had been born on the island of Haiti, in the days when it was still a French possession, and before the bloody and bitter slave uprisings that had brought it to independence as a black nation in 1799. Alexandre, the oldest, became a privateer, and after the fashion of the other privateers of the times, he changed his name—to Dominique You.

As a privateer, Dominique carried letters of marque from French colonial governments which authorized him to stop and seize enemy vessels, mostly English and Spanish, in the name of the Emperor. Naturally, the spoils of war were the privateer's to keep, and Pierre and Jean were eager to follow Alexandre or Dominique You, into this most dangerous and lucrative profession.

Dominique sailed to France, where he won fame as a cannoneer in Napoleon's navy. The two younger brothers joined their cousin, Réné Beluche, who already had twelve years experience as a privateer. When the situation in Haiti during the slave rebellions became critical, Pierre and Jean evacuated many French refugees to New Orleans, and then set out to procure their own letters of marque and a ship of their own.

The American purchase of Louisiana put a different light on things. America was a neutral nation, not at war, like France, with England, Holland, and Spain. Under no circumstances could she condone privateering. But Jean decided, like many of the other privateers, to continue the lucrative but illegal operations. So, using Louisiana as their home base, Jean and Pierre became pirates, and when Dominique returned from France, he joined them.

The pirates took their prizes outright, without pursuing their claims through maritime court as they had done previously, and they smuggled their goods to New Orleans, where eager buyers awaited them. American restrictions on imports and the embargo on shipping in 1807 forced prices up in American markets. When the pirate-smugglers began to offer identical goods at lower prices, they found that the markets would take whatever they could supply. Hundreds of independent smugglers tried to cash in on the demand, and it soon became obvious that some sort of organization was necessary to channel their various nefarious talents properly and to keep prices competitive.

"For example," said Dominique, "you take some green, smart-assed young fellow in tight breeches who decides that he wants to be a pirate. He gets himself a boat, goes out after a big merchant ship, and the Devil drinks bilge water if he isn't so stupid that he sinks her! The merchant loses, the pirates lose, and the public loses. Hopeless!"

"And," Pierre added, "even if he does manage to capture the ship, where does he go to sell his goods? He doesn't have any connections, you see, and he tries to sell his bolts of silk cloth to some storekeeper who has a thousand bolts already and who offers him a dollar apiece for the bolts, saying, 'Well, I don't need your cloth, but I'll take it off your hands as a favor.' "

"Why, if you had enough goods you could create your own demand," I said, "by controlling the supply."

"You catch on pretty damn fast," said Dominique proudly. "Make a good pirate, this one, eh, Pierre?"

"So what did you do?" I asked. "What happened next?"

"We had ourselves a Pirates' Convention about six years ago, right here on Grand Terre. They all came, remember, Pierre? Vincent Gambie, and Réné, and that

Cut Nose Chighizola. Cut Nose and Vincent Gambie each thought they were gonna take over the whole empire, no matter how many throats they had to cut along the way, the bloodthirsty bastards. And every organization has to have a leader, you can see that.''

''Of course,'' I said, fascinated.

''Well, you can imagine the scene,'' said Dominique slowly, savoring his position as the center of my rapt attention. ''There we are, everybody with a sword in his mouth and a dagger in each hand, gathered together on this sand bar in the middle of nowhere like we were waiting for the second coming. And in a way we were. The way it works out there are four possible choices: Réné, Cut Nose, Gambie, and Jean. Pierre and I aren't in the running, because we know that Jean is smarter than any of them and he's smarter than us by a long shot, and neither do we relish working for Cut Nose or Gambie, the—. Well, never mind. Réné Beluche is all right, because he's a cousin, but Réné has always liked the sailing and whoring part best and he doesn't really want to run the show. Gambie wants it bad because he's just plain greedy, and Cut Nose wants to set himself up as the King of Barataria. We all know that both of 'em would cheat us blind, but they're hard men who would kill to stay on top. Thank the Holy Gates they hate each other's guts, because if they teamed up we'd all be working for nothing.'' Dominique shook his head.

''And then there was Jean, sitting there as cool as you please in the middle of all that scum. I can still see him, flicking out the ruffles on his cuffs and smiling as though he was stepping out to a ball. Some of them don't know him too well, and they look at him and decide he's soft. But Jean just watches them fight it out. Some of the boys line up behind Chighizola, and some of them behind Gambie, but Jean doesn't care.

"Two days of wraggling go by, and we're all tired and edgy, and then all of a sudden when they least expect it, Jean stands up and says in that soft voice of his that penetrates over the roar of a cannon, "Gentlemen,'—he always calls 'em gentlemen—'Gentlemen, you are wasting your time, if you will forgive me for saying so.' This brings on a bit of a stir and a rumble 'cause they don't like this young fellow gettin' up there insultin' 'em. 'You have come here to elect a leader,' he says, 'and instead it looks like you will follow either a thief, who will rob you'—that's Gambie—'or a knave who will use your talents and then throw you to the wolves'—that's Cut Nose.

"And then he tells 'em that if they want this thing run for profit it should be run like a business, and that takes a man with brains. He tells 'em exactly what has to be done: storing the goods, moving them, distributing and getting a fair return on 'em. And most of all, doing it so every man of us doesn't land in jail. They like it, we can tell, and it's quiet while they're listening, for the first time in two days it's quiet. You can feel the tide turning in Jean's favor, but there are two men there who don't like it, don't like it at all.

"So Jean is telling the boys how he'll do all this for them, and they're cheering and drinking to him and eating right out of his hand when he tells them that he'll make them twice as rich as they ever dreamed. And then Gambie comes up and throws his arm around Jean's shoulders and tells him how he thinks it's great and how he'll do all he can to help Jean, and so on. Nice gesture, isn't it? But there's steel in Gambie's other hand that nobody sees—Vincent always likes to carry a knife up his sleeve, just in case—and then quick as a flash Jean throws him down and gets his knife and sits on his chest, with the point of the knife just pricking Vincent's gullet."

I was spellbound with excitement, and Dominique smiled appreciatively.

" 'Monsieur Gambie,' he says all polite, 'I have always admired your courage and your abilities as a pirate, and I regret having to exclude you from this venture, but you leave me no choice.' He digs in with his knife a little harder and Vincent squalls like a baby and says he didn't mean it, he was only testing.

" 'And did I pass your test, Monsieur?' Jean asks him. His voice is as hard as flint, and all you can hear is the waves on the sand, everybody is that quiet. Vincent Gambie says yes, you pass. Then Jean stands up and hands him back his knife and turns his back on the man, to show he trusts him. That's what really wins the boys. And then Jean takes a sword and weighs it in his hand and says, 'Perhaps there is another among you who would like to test my mettle?' Not a sound. 'Very well,' says he, 'I agree to run this business for you. I am one of you, gentlemen. The man who cheats me cheats you; the man who crosses me betrays you; the man who kills me dissolves the organization and puts you all back where you started, squabbling and arguing like a bunch of hungry sea gulls. Is that clear?' It's clear. 'Then by God what are we waiting for? Let's drink to it!' he says. And they give him a cheer that can be heard in New Orleans.

"And that," said Dominique, settling back and beaming at me, "is the story of the Lafittes."

"It's a wonderful story," I breathed.

Pierre nodded. "And there isn't a soul in New Orleans who isn't involved in this thing one way or another. There's never been anything like it."

"Yes, and look at us now," Dominique said. "Six years later, and on Grand Terre alone we have forty warehouses, forty! Not to mention the ones in New Orleans and up and down the river as far as Donaldsonville.

And we got homes here for the boys that wants 'em, and a brothel and a tavern, and a hospital—''

"But no church?" I put in. They roared with laughter.

"No, no church! Hey, Pierre, we'll have to tell Jean that. He'll like it. And slave pens—"

"Slave pens?" I frowned. "You mean—"

"Of course. Why do you think we took that slave ship you were on, if not for the cargo? I know it's not nice for patriots like us to prey on an American ship, but that Captain was outside the law and he took the risk. You know what they do, these American slavers, they run up a Spanish flag when they come into American waters and nobody is supposed to touch 'em. Well, we touch 'em. Slavery is a big part of our business here. Did you know that a good slave buck brings five hundred dollars on the open market now? And a female three hundred?"

Lily came in and saw that I was looking tired.

"Now you boys know better than to talk this poor girl to death. Shame on you, Mister Dominique, and you too, Mister Pierre. You jest get on out of here now, 'fore I throws you out."

"Aw, Lily, we was just telling the young lady—"

"I knows what kind of trash you been tellin' her, now git!"

Somewhat abashed, they stood up, bowed stiffly, and shuffled out.

I was still exhilarated by the romantic history of the Lafittes, but discovering their involvement in slavery soured my enjoyment and made me feel bitter and depressed. But what, after all, had I expected?

"What you lookin' so low about, Missy?" Lily asked.

"It seems the bold buccaneer is just another slaver after all," I said sadly. "He's no different from Captain Fowler."

Lily frowned and turned her head on the side. "Slaver?

Mister Lafitte? Well, now, I suppose he is. But he didn't invent slavery, and he can't change it, and so he lives with it. We all do, Missy. You can love it or you can hate it, but you can't change it. Didn't they have no slaves where you come from?''

"Oh, no, Lily. We—they have servants, of course, who are paid a wage or given a place to live and their keep.''

"Well, that's what the slaves gets here, too, at least the lucky ones do. 'Course some of 'em are just about worked to death, from what you hear.''

"Are you a slave, Lily?''

The big woman put her hands on her hips and said haughtily, "Me? One of them ragtag good-for-nothin's? I should say not. Why, I'm married and I got four childern. My man's done been sailing for Mister Lafitte for the past five years. Now you rest. Those fools ain't got no business comin' up here and makin' you all tired and sad like this.''

What a strange country this was, I thought when I was alone. In addition to being a pirate, this Lafitte was a shrewd businessman who bought and sold human flesh. Now a shrewd man would not be guilty of making a poor investment. I wondered what he had in mind for me when he took me into his house and restored me to health. Would he sell me, too? Why, oh, why did the course of a woman's life seem to depend on the choices a man made concerning her?

The next day Lily brought me a beautiful sprigged muslin gown. "From Mister Lafitte," she said. "He put some women to sewin' for you before he left. And there's lots more, Missy. Dresses and night things and beautiful negligees, and oh, so many pretty things.''

I fingered the fine fabric. The soft white muslin was embroidered at the neck and hem with crimson rosebuds and trailing green vines. The neckline was cut modestly low, and the sleeves were softly puffed. Red ribbons attached to the sides crossed under my breasts and tied in a bow at the back. "It's lovely," I said.

"Here, put it on." Lily helped me out of my convalescent robes and into the lovely soft gown. "Oh, Missy, that's beautiful!" The full skirts moved gracefully as I walked around the floor. I lifted the hem and marvelled at the tiny stitches. I had never seen such beautifully delicate handwork, not even in Paris. "I'll say one thing, Missy, you sure can wear the clothes. Yes, Mister Lafitte will be real happy. He likes his women to wear pretty things."

His women! I wondered again what kind of plans Monsieur Lafitte had in store for me.

"Would you like to look at yourself?"

"No, no, Lily, that's very kind of you, but I'd rather not. Mister Lafitte is very generous."

"He's a fine man," Lily declared staunchly. "Now you're too pretty to be sittin' 'round in a sickroom. Why don't you go and look around the house for a bit, and later I'll walk you down to the water."

I obeyed and ventured forth on my weak legs. The more I saw of Lafitte's mansion the more impressed I became with his taste as well as his wealth. The bedrooms on the second floor were arranged on all sides of the house around a central circular staircase with a leaded glass skylight above it. My room was done in shades of peach, and there were rooms decorated in gold, wine red, and pale blue. One of the corner rooms held an enormous bathtub—big enough for two, it seemed—and shelves loaded with flasks of perfumes and scented salts. I shook my head in amazement. It must take five men a whole day to bring up enough water to fill that tub, I thought. Then I opened a closet door and saw that a dumbwaiter had been installed for just that purpose. Most ingenious!

The room next to mine was the simplest of all, I noticed. Aside from a massive bed and an equally massive chiffonier and washstand, the only ornament in the room was a huge Titian canvas depicting a nude Venus with Mars. An old master for the master bedroom. How appropriate.

The rooms downstairs were equally tasteful and opulent. Fully one half of the ground floor was taken up by a ballroom of grand size, complete with musicians' balcony, crystal chandeliers, and beautifully designed inlaid wood flooring. The walls were lined with floor to ceiling mirrors. I caught the barest glimpse of myself and fled. I was being silly, I knew. I would have to face the truth about myself sometime, but perhaps later, when I felt stronger.

On the other side of the center front hall were drawing and dining rooms, and a comfortable looking library. I guessed that Jean Lafitte spent much of his time here. The shelves held a number of well-thumbed books, mostly French, but some English and Spanish authors as well. In the center of the room stood a large desk, loaded with a vast clutter of letters, receipts, log books and diaries, and account books. The mess reminded me of Uncle Theo's desk, without the knick-knacks.

Over the mantelpiece hung a painting that looked remarkably like a Rembrandt. I stepped closer to examine it.

"I hope it bears up to your inspection, Mademoiselle Elise," said a soft voice from the doorway. I whirled around and he smiled. "I would be most offended were I to discover that any of my treasures were not originals. The Rembrandt was on a ship that was destined for Kingston, and it was intended to grace the home of some fat colonial. I decided he couldn't possibly appreciate it as much as I and so I borrowed it. You're looking very well, Elise. And quite astonishingly pretty."

"Thank you, Monsieur Lafitte," I said politely. "And thank you for the dress. It's lovely."

He waved a hand. "Don't give it another thought, Elise. You needed something to wear, after all. Lily showed me the rags you had on when they found you."

"Not rags," I said. "My trousseau."

"Oh, you are Madame Lesconflair?"

"No, I—I have no husband."

"A great pity." He sat down in his desk chair and glumly surveyed the disorder on his desk. "What chaos. If only one could occupy two places at once. Have you ever felt that way, Elise? That there are too few hours in the day?"

"Not lately, Monsieur. If you will excuse me—"

"Not until you tell me why you have suddenly reverted to addressing me as 'Monsieur,' Elise. What have they been telling you about me? I suppose Dominique has been bragging to you about my sixteen mistresses, or some such nonsense."

"I have no great interest in your mistresses, Monsieur Lafitte. But I would like to know what you intend to do with me."

He frowned. "Do with you? What do you mean, 'do with you'?"

I faced him squarely. "Am I not part of your loot? Are you going to put me in one of your warehouses now that my condition is improved, or perhaps in one of your wretched slave pens with my companions from the *Charleston Belle*? How will you transport me to market? Gently, I trust, lest I be damaged in transit. How much will I bring? Three hundred dollars? Two hundred?" I pinched the flesh on my forearm. "I'm not strong yet, and I cannot bear children, you know, and worst of all I am ugly. What kind of woman is that? You'll be lucky to get

twenty dollars. Of course you can keep me here a little
longer to fatten me up—''

"I think you have said enough," he said in a low but
penetrating voice. His dark eyes flashed angrily.

Shame flooded over me. I sat down and hid my face
from him.

"I fear your experiences with men like Captain Fowler
have made you bitter and suspicious," he said quietly. "I
can quite understand that, Elise. But know this: at no time
have I thought of you as anything but an honored guest in
my home. You are free to go at any time. If you stay I
promise you that you will be as safe in this house and on
this island as if you were at home in France, and probably
safer. You have no family in this country? No one?'' I
shook my head. "Do you wish to return to France?'' I
could make no reply. "Or perhaps I can find a husband for
you. I am sure that would not be a difficult task.''

"I don't want a husband!'' I cried. "Oh, who would
want a woman like me? Dear God, after the things that
animal did to me, and what he made me do to him—.
I'm not even fit to look at anymore. I used to be really
beautiful, did you know that? And now I'm ugly, ugly,
ugly! Oh, why didn't I die, why? What do I have to live
for now?''

He stood over me, a puzzled expression on his face.
"Why, Elise, I believe you are trying to insult me. Surely
you have not discovered me looking at you with any
measure of distaste? Can you suppose I would permit you
in my house if you offended my artistic sensibilities?
Perhaps you think I have none? Come with me.''

Lafitte firmly drew me out of my chair and led me
across the hall to the ballroom with its hundreds of mirrors.

"No, no," I pleaded. "I beg of you! Please
don't—please don't do this to me!''

We halted in front of a mirror, but I pressed my hands tightly over my eyes. Gently but firmly he grasped my wrists and pulled my hands away from my face.

"Open your eyes, Elise. Perhaps it won't be as bad as you think."

I can't, I thought. —But you must. —All right, I can take it. I took a deep breath, clenched my teeth, and slowly opened my eyes.

I stared at the reflection, and slowly my irrational fear drained away. The face I saw was mine, really mine. The hideous, swollen, disfigured caricature that I had seen on the ship had returned almost to normal. I put my hand up and touched my skin: I traced the outline of my temples, my forehead, my chin and lips. Faint discoloration still showed around the eyes, and the cheeks were sunken and gaunt—all of me was too thin, in fact—but flushed patches on my cheekbones lent some color to the pale flesh. And in my eyes, the old jaunty gleam was dancing, perhaps somewhat sedately. The frame of black curls around my face looked very attractive indeed.

"I'm all right," I whispered softly with amazement. "It's me, Jean, really me!"

"Who else would it be, Elise?" said Lafitte. "Of course it's you. How do women conjure up such strange ideas, anyway? You are a beautiful, charming woman." Our eyes met in the mirror, and a little current of excitement ran through me. "It doesn't matter what happens to us, do you understand that, Elise? We are what we are in spite of what people do to us. If you can keep your mind and your soul, you can keep yourself." He stepped back, leaving me alone in the reflection. "You are what you are, Elise."

I contemplated the little figure that stared back at me and let out a long sigh. I had surmounted another barrier, and this one in my own imagination. The obstacles to happiness were unlimited, it seemed, but at least one more was down.

"Thank you, Jean," I said softly.

"You are more than welcome, Elise."

We returned to the library. I told him everything then, omitting only Garth's true name.

"But I might be able to trace him," Jean said, "if you would tell me who he was. There are many ways. No one ever disappears without a trace, even in the British navy."

"No, no. I don't want to know, Jean. I hate him and I never want to see him again. If we met I might—" I clenched my fists and whispered, "I would kill him. No. I want to put it all behind me. And start over."

Jean looked at me searchingly. "Whatever you wish, Elise. Only remember that I am always at your service. If ever you want him traced, or if there is anything else I can do for you, please do not hesitate to ask."

I thought for a moment. He would help me return to France if I wanted to go. France. France might have been a million miles away rather than several thousand. How far away, how long ago it all was. No, I was not yet ready to return to France, not ready to face my family after all that had happened, not ready for their tears and their pity. I had had enough tears and pity for the time being.

"If—if I could just stay here a little longer," I ventured.

"Of course, Elise. My house is yours for as long as you want. I would feel honored if you could learn to be happy once again in my part of the new world."

"I would like to learn to be useful again," I said shyly. "I wonder if I could help you in your—ah, business—if there was anything that I could do." My eyes went to the welter of papers on the desk.

He followed my gaze. "You astound me, Elise. Surely, with your beauty, you have not also an eye for business! I didn't know women knew anything about money and numbers. But I've been thinking of training a secretary, and no doubt you will do as well as any of these brawny lads who have bashed their brains around fighting and brawling.'' He shook his head in dismay at the jumble of books and documents. "I fear I may be all too willing to accept your offer, Elise. You know, I used to be able to keep up, but things have gotten rather out of hand lately. Many of the warehouses are overloaded, and the inventory lists are phenomenal. Perhaps we can begin later this week, if you feel rested.''

"I am so tired of resting, Jean. I would love to begin —today?''

He looked at me curiously. "I've never seen anyone so eager to work! Very well, we will begin immediately.''

Lafitte swatted the papers around a bit and complained about how boring the business end of smuggling was, but finally, searching methodically through the pile, he began to explain which log was which and what receipts went where. He even found a piece of heavily perfumed parchment which he scanned quickly and then tore into small bits before discarding.

"November, 1809! I can't imagine why this was never thrown away.''

I stifled a grin. Eventually we sorted things out and were ready to enter the figures in their appropriate books.

"This is quite enough for today,'' he said. "I am fatigued and all this dust has given me an uncontrollable thirst for fine wine. And look at the grime on my shirt! A good thing it is that you forced me to go to work before I had time to change it. And you, Mademoiselle Secretary, would not be so relieved if you were to gaze at your reflection now. The smudge of dirt on the end of your nose is nearly as black as your eyes. Allow me to wipe it off for you.''

Jean rubbed gently at the smut with a gorgeously embroidered handkerchief. "That's better. Elise, you are a good influence on me. I should have begun this months ago, but I always managed to persuade myself that the more exciting tasks were also more important. I trust, however, that you won't begin nagging me to keep at it. Nagging women are the scourge of the earth. I am tempted to beat them, and it would try my conscience sorely to beat a poor frail invalid like you. Do you nag?"

I smiled. "I should not be likely to admit to it after that threat!"

"But you do have a temper. I caught a nice glimpse of it a short while ago, when you professed not to be interested in my sixteen mistresses."

"I am far more interested in your warehouses, Monsieur Jean. But I do have a temper, I confess. I was the worst tempered girl in France."

"And now you wish to set Louisiana on fire as well, do you?"

"Certainly not," I said firmly. "I'm too old to be throwing tantrums and causing scenes."

"Well, we shall see. But now we must prepare to dine and to drink some of that fine wine. Will you join me for dinner tonight, Mademoiselle Elise? I imagine your uncle taught you to appreciate fine food and drink?"

"He did indeed. Dining was his greatest passion, aside from reciting the glories of the Lesconflairs."

"Wonderful. I am delighted at last to have found a woman who can not only read and write and count, and who can appreciate the finer things in life, but who is charming and strikingly beautiful to look at as well, when she doesn't have a smudge on her nose. Perhaps you would like to rest a little before dinner. You have done more than enough for one day."

I dropped a curtsy and left the room. I felt a bit amused

by Jean Lafitte's formal politeness, and a little tired. His
manners seemed to fit as tightly as his skin, unlike the men
of my previous experience. My recent distasteful adventures had not been peopled with gentlemen aspiring to the
social graces, and even the rigid impeccable formality at
the French court was a façade which the cavaliers of the
court would drop in a flash to banter obscenities with their
friends or to force their attentions on a young debutante.

However, Jean Lafitte seemed always sincere and serious, if distant. I wondered if spending time with his
brothers wouldn't be more relaxing and more fun. They
certainly didn't guard their tongues so carefully. But
perhaps Lafitte's formal manner was just as well. If I were
to work with him, having him leer at me would make
things difficult. I wasn't ready to think of men in that way
yet. I didn't know if I could bear to have a man's arms
around me again, or to feel the crushing weight—no, the
memories of Captain Josiah Fowler were too fresh in my
mind. Even thinking about him made me feel cold and
sick. Was he really dead?

No, Jean Lafitte would shower me with politeness to his
heart's content and treat me as if I were the male secretary
he had expected to have. I would do the best I could to
deserve his kindness and respect, but anything more than
that was unthinkable.

In the weeks that followed I learned the business end of
the Lafitte smuggling operations inside and out. A tour of
the warehouses on Grand Terre brought to life what I had
previously only heard about or seen on paper, and it left
me gaping in astonishment at the mind-boggling wealth
stored there and at other points along the Mississippi.

Grand Terre was as busy as a seaport. Its little harbor
was crowded with ships of varying sizes, many of them
captive vessels that the pirates had seized and brought
back for their own use. The *Charleston Belle*, as Jean

Lafitte had told me, had sunk to the bottom of the gulf. Had Josiah Fowler's corpse really been on board? God, I hoped so. I couldn't bear ever to set eyes on that ship or her master again. Even the smallest recollection of anything or anyone connected with those days set me trembling with a fear that I could not conquer.

Lafitte's mansion was the island's most imposing structure. The tropical sunshine, reflected doubly by the sky and the sea, glistened from white pillars and tall windows which opened from the lush bedrooms and the elegant rooms onto identical wide verandas that swept around the building on all four sides, one above the other.

Most of the pirates lived in single story dwellings built on Barataria Bay, on the north side of the island. Several of the men had brought their wives to Grand Terre; others brought their mistresses. All of the men loved to go to New Orleans for drinking and brawling and whoring. The trip took three days through the bayous and swamps and over a short stretch of land.

Jean Lafitte did not work me very hard, and the weeks of walking, and swimming in the gentle breakers of the gulf, and playing with the children on the island made me stronger and healthier than I ever had been. Dominique You adopted me after a fashion and took me on guided tours around the bayous in a little pirogue, a kind of flat-bottomed skiff that was ideal for navigating shallow swamp waters. Dominique loved Louisiana and he showed off her wild beauties proudly, as if he had had a hand in making them. I became reasonably accustomed to the infernal heat and humidity, and I even got to the point where I could tolerate the infinite varieties of insects. The bayous were thick with alligators. I had never seen such odd-looking creatures before, but Dominique warned me to stay away from them. One of the pirates had lost his leg to a 'gator, and some of them looked big enough to swallow a whole man.

I loved the mysterious gray veils of Spanish moss that draped everything in the swamps like witches' tresses; I loved the gnarled cypress trees that grew in the shallow bayous with all their little knees protruding out of the water like upside-down icicles. Most of all I loved the peace and freedom that came with living where few men dared to penetrate. The pirates had carved out their empire in a wilderness that was easy to defend because it was so inaccessible.

Dominique's proudest possession, and the one he loved best to show off, was his flagship *Tigre*. She was a trim little craft, laden with guns but fast and sleek.

"She can outrun any warship ever made," her captain boasted as we toured her. "Maybe I'll take you out on her someday."

"I'd love to go, Dominique. She's a beauty."

"You're not afraid of ships, then?" Everyone on the island knew or guessed my story by that time, and I found I didn't care too much. What they knew they didn't have to ask, and when they didn't ask I didn't have to answer.

"No, I'm not afraid of ships. Only of the men who sail them." I looked at Dominique sternly.

He chuckled. "You're a bold wench, Mademoiselle. You'd make a damn fine crewman, with some training."

I said nothing for a moment. Then I looked up at him. "Dominique," I said slowly, "will you teach me to shoot? Not guns like these, not cannons. Pistols. I want to learn to shoot."

He looked doubtful. "I don't know that that's such a good idea. You might blow your pretty head off."

"Oh, pooh, I wouldn't hurt myself, not if you trained me properly. And you're the best shot in Louisiana, everyone says so."

He nodded. "I know guns even better than I know ships. Big or small, the principle's the same. But Jean, he'd raise all kinds of Holy Hell."

I knew he would teach me. He realized it, too. "You know as well as I do that Jean lets me have the run of the island, Dominique. I can do anything I want. Please teach me, Dominique, please."

"Aw, fer God's sake, stop your grovellin'! You know in your hands I've got no more spine than a piece of seaweed. You knew before you even asked me that I couldn't say no."

"Oh, that's grand! Can we start today? And I want to learn to fence, too. My brother Philippe taught me a little when I was younger, but I want to be good, really good. Will you teach me that, too, Dominique? Please?"

Dominique shook his head. "No, not me, I won't. I'm no great hand with the blade, and you'd learn bad habits from me. Jean is the one to ask for that—he's the best swordsman in the country, or I'll chop up the *Tigre* and eat it piece by piece—but I can tell you right now what Jean will say. He won't do it."

"Of course he'll do it, if I ask nicely," I said confidently. "How could he refuse me?"

"Now, who in the Devil are you gettin' ready to wage war on, you little spitfire?" asked Dominique warily. "Something's brewin' up there in that bit of cotton you call a brain. I want to know what it is."

I looked hurt. "Why, Dominique, can't a woman learn to defend herself without raising all kinds of suspicions?"

He grunted. "A woman can't do nothin' without givin' a man the shakes. You know that. Now I have a sneakin' suspicion of what you're thinkin' about, and I won't have it. And I can tell you another thing, even if you got around me, Jean would sink every last one of our ships afore he'd let you do that. Why, if anything happened to you he'd slice us all to ribbons, every last one of us."

"What could happen?" I demanded.

"You're a stubborn wench, you are, but a damn pretty

one.'' He sighed. ''A regular full-blooded pirate's beauty.''

That afternoon he initiated me into the care and handling of firearms. I learned to clean, load, and fire a pistol, but my aim was terrible.

''You've got to open your barmy eyes when you shoot or you'll never hit a damn thing,'' said Dominique, exasperated.

''But it's so noisy, Dominique,'' I complained. ''I think I'm going deaf.''

''Screwin' up your eyes ain't gonna save your hearin'. Try it again now. Spill in a little powder first, that's right; now the ball. Poke it in good. Now raise it up—for God's sake relax your arm a little or you'll bust your shoulder —and squeeze the trigger. Well, that wasn't too bad. Just remember, Mademoiselle Hotshot, the gun doesn't know if the hand that's holding it is male or female, so bein' timid and ladylike isn't gonna help you. Try it again.''

By the end of the day I had at least learned the rudiments of shooting. But I felt very tired at dinner, and I must have dozed off at dessert.

''—a fine bouquet, but disappointing to the taste, and that is the true test, after all—. Why, Elise, you're not even listening.''

I pulled myself up. ''Oh, forgive me, Jean. I'm rather weary tonight, I'm afraid.''

''I hope you're not having a relapse. Perhaps I've been working you too hard.'' We got up from the table. ''I think I shall have my brandy on the veranda tonight. If you wish to retire—''

''No, Jean, really, I'm fully awake now. How boorish of me to nod off at the table! What must you think of me?''

''I think you are a wonderful, good-hearted, beautiful woman, you know that. You are tired, that is all. But even if you were so tired you fell in the soup tureen, I would still think you were wonderful. Please, don't feel you must keep me company this evening, Elise."

"No, I want to come out." We strolled out to the veranda. I sat on the railing while he settled himself in a broad wicker settee and swirled his brandy.

"Now," he said, lifting the snifter and inhaling the aromatic fumes, "you want to ask me for something. What is it?"

I stared. "How did you know?"

He smiled gently at me. "How does an old woman know when it's going to rain? From the pains in her knees. I, too, have my pains. A little bone here in my chest," he pointed to an area very close to his heart, "throbs alarmingly whenever a woman is about to ask me something. The harder it throbs the more she wants. Right now," he closed his eyes and concentrated, "it is only a medium throb. But I suspect it will become worse if we ignore it. So tell me, Elise, what can I do for you?"

"I want you to teach me how to fence."

He sat motionless, his brandy snifter poised in mid-air. "You astonish me, Elise. Really, you do. Fence! Why on earth do you want to learn to fence?"

"So I can defend myself," I said, lifting my chin.

"I pray to heaven that God's angels will defend us all. Do you women not have enough weapons in your arsenal? Do you need to borrow a man's as well? I assure you, Elise, you have no need to master the martial arts in order to defend yourself. I, Jean Lafitte, promise that I shall defend you to my dying breath. And all of my men will gladly give their lives for you. I know we Americans must seem like barbarians to you, but believe me, Elise, there is no need for you to take up arms against us. I have never heard of such a thing!"

I took a breath and said as levelly as I could, "If I had had the courage and the knowledge I would have killed

Josiah Fowler. I would have, Jean. And if ever again I find myself in a similar situation, I want to feel confident that I am well prepared. Oh, not with a woman's weapons—I tried those, Jean, and they don't always work. I need to know how to use weapons a man will understand, like the sword.''

"I should have taken you to New Orleans the minute you were well enough," Lafitte said sorrowfully. "I'm afraid living here among these ruffians has affected your mind. A sword is not a child's toy, Elise. It is an instrument of death, and when you deal out death to men you can expect them to deal it back to you. But," he sighed deeply, "the throbbing in my chest tells me that you are about to remind me that I said I would do anything in my power for you.''

"How acute your perception is," I remarked dryly.

"Elise, it's utterly impossible. I have never heard of a lady doing such a thing, and I refuse to be a party to such an outrageous undertaking.''

I threw back my head and laughed delightedly. "Oh, Jean, I'm not a lady anymore, and I don't know if I ever was! I'm a pirate's beauty, a regular full-blooded pirate's beauty! Dominique said so!'' I threw myself onto the settee next to him. "And beauties are notoriously headstrong and stubborn and maddeningly persistent. I should think pirate's beauties are even more so!''

Lafitte stared into his brandy. "This must be the part where you throw your arms around my neck and kiss me and call me 'Uncle Jean,' '' he said, lifting the snifter and draining the remainder of the pale amber liquid.

I obliged him. I hugged him tightly, kissed him tenderly on the cheek, and said sweetly, "Thank you, Uncle Jean.''

"At least I have the sense to know when I am beaten," he said wearily.

"I think you are wonderful!" I kissed him again.

"Women always do when they get their way." He sighed heavily and got to his feet. "It remains to be seen, however, how apt a pupil you will be."

"I shall work from dawn until dusk," I promised eagerly. "When my other tasks in the library are finished, of course."

He moved to the rail and looked out over the water. After a while he said, "You know, Elise, a weapon is a strange thing. It has no brains, no feelings, no judgment. It doesn't know if the hand that holds it—"

"—is male or female," I finished for him. "I know, Jean. I'll be careful, I promise you. But this is something I feel I must do, can you understand that?"

"No, but that doesn't matter, does it?" He sounded tired and sad. "And now you should go to bed. We shall start tomorrow morning at eight o'clock, in the ballroom."

"Thank you." I resisted the impulse to hug him again, but rested my hand on his arm and said softly, "Good night, Jean."

The next morning when I appeared in a skirt and blouse, Lafitte smirked and said, "Your costume may be a distinct disadvantage, Elise, if you wish to fight like a man."

"What do you mean?" I looked at myself. What else was I to wear?

"You force me to demonstrate." He grasped a sword and whipped it expertly through the air a few times. I gasped admiringly. "Pretend for a moment that we are facing one another as enemies. Perhaps you would like to hold a sword. To help the illusion."

He chose a weapon for me and handed it to me with a bow. The sword was heavy, and it threatened to drag my arm down, but I struggled stalwartly to hold it up.

"Now," he went on, "eye your opponent, me in this

case.'' He spread his arms and posed gracefully, one leg in front of the other. His body in its flowing white shirt and skin-tight breeches was as slim and supple as a boy's.

"You are beautiful, Jean," I exclaimed. "I think you make a beautiful target."

He frowned with annoyance. "I make a fair size target, Elise, but if I am quick enough to avoid your thrusts you will never touch me. Now look at yourself. You are an even smaller target than I am, but your skirts make you enormous. *Voilà!*"

Before I knew what was happening, he had wrapped the point of his sword in my skirts and forced me back. I lost my balance and fell to the floor.

"I seem to have lost my balance," I said wryly.

"Forgive me, Elise, but you forced me to demonstrate the point I am trying to make." He stood over me and looked down at me very seriously. "I hope you realize now that this is no sport for a woman."

"You did not even prick my skin," I said. I felt angry with him. I knew that he never had any intention of teaching me how to use a sword. He was trying to embarrass me into quitting in disgust.

"I have no desire to hurt you, Elise," he said. "But I wish you to understand the folly of your ways." He offered me a hand to help me up. I ignored it and jumped to my feet.

"If you will excuse me for a brief moment, Monsieur," I said, patting my dishevelled hair. "I seem to require some pins to keep my coiffure in order."

"Of course, Elise." He bowed and fell into a chair with a thoughtful expression on his face.

"You won't go away?" I asked anxiously.

He breathed deeply and looked up at me. "No, Elise, I won't go away. But I hardly see the point of continuing."

I would show him. I raced through the house to the kitchen, where Lily was kneading some dough.

"Lily, quick," I gasped. "You've got to find me a pair of breeches. Now!"

She looked up from her bread board and stared at me. "Breeches! On a girl? I never heard of no such thing."

"Please, Lily," I begged. "Monsieur Lafitte has promised to teach me to fence, but we're not getting anywhere because of my skirts and he's being just horrible to me. Oh, I want to learn so badly, I really do. I want to know how to defend myself, you see. Against men."

She chuckled. "Well, now, I ain't never had no trouble defending myself, 'cause I'm about twice your size and my George listens when I say boo. But you, Missy, you ain't much bigger than a Louisiana mosquito. Let me think. Miz Rollins' Albert is about your size. You wait right here."

She went out the back door towards the pirates' dwellings. I paced the floor nervously, and after what seemed like hours she returned, waving a small pair of gray breeches.

"Here we are, Missy. I got 'em off the line. So at least they's clean."

I tore off my skirt and petticoat and slid into the breeches. Albert must be quite small indeed, for his trousers fit me like a glove. Lily fussed around me, tucking in my blouse, and she found a length of red satin to wind around my waist for a sash.

"Oh, thank you, Lily!" I hugged her fiercely and ran back to the ballroom. I snatched up a sword and fell into the classic stance that Philippe had taught me years ago. "*Me voici*, Monsieur," I cried jubilantly. "*En garde!*"

Lafitte was leaning back in his chair with his hands locked behind his head and his eyes closed. At my words he sat straight up and gaped at me. His eyebrows nearly disappeared into his hairline. "You make me tremble, Mademoiselle. Let me look at you." He stood up and walked around me very slowly, eyeing every part of me in my revealing costume, almost as if I were a horse he considered buying. "Not very fashionable," he remarked, "and not particularly well cut—really you must let me recommend my tailor, Elise—but not altogether unattractive." I sighed impatiently and bore his inspection in silence. "And yet it is very strange," he mused. "For some reason you still look like a woman. I don't know if I shall be able to forget that."

"It is immaterial to me, Monsieur Lafitte, what you are able to forget and what you are able to remember," I said coldly. "I have come to fight, not to parade around in my starched shirt front and ruffled cuffs like a peacock."

He laughed out loud and clapped me on the back. *"Touché,* Mademoiselle Lesconflair, *touché. En garde!"*

That day we established a pattern which we followed in the weeks to come. We worked in the cool hours of the morning, and again, if nothing interfered, in the evening after the heat of the day had passed. He didn't spare me in our lessons; if anything he worked me harder than he would a boy, just to prove to me that I was too weak to stand up to the intensity of the training. I worked just as hard to prove that he was wrong. When I was alone I practiced for hours in front of the mirrors in the ballroom.

I never told Jean that I had persuaded Dominique to teach me to shoot, and Dominique did not realize that I was learning to use a sword. Hoisting the heavy pistols helped strengthen my wrists and arms, and the concentration I was learning from fencing helped improve my aim when I fired my pistols.

"Well, wench," said Dominique one day with a satisfied nod, "at least you're no worse now than any of my men, and you might even be a little bit better."

"Oh, Dominique, that's wonderful!"

"Not," he added, winking his eye meaningfully, "that you'll be any good as a pirate until you've learned to wield a blade, but someday—"

"Someday—" I whispered, hefting my pistol in my hand and firing at a rock down the beach, "Damn! Someday soon, Dominique. Very soon."

The day came when Jean admitted that my form showed considerable improvement and that I needed to focus my energies on keeping my wrists supple and improving my concentration. I felt that I had already won a victory. Our lesson on concentration was a memorable one.

"You cannot kill a man when you are thinking about something else," Jean said airily, waving his blade. "You must thrust as though you hated me, as though you meant it, Elise. Duelling is not a woman's game, you know. Even the greenest boy could disarm you the way you fight now, swish swish like a lady."

I fought to control my irritation. "But I don't want to hurt you, Jean."

"Well, if you don't want to hurt me, you'd better try to kill me. Or had you forgotten that killing is what this is all about? Don't worry about hurting me, Elise. Concentrate on killing. I can protect myself. *En garde*."

I lashed into him furiously, sparing nothing. He laughed delightedly and parried my blows, making some remark about finally getting some fun out of these lessons. I knew he was playing with me and I pressed my attack, ignoring the amused look on his face. I hated his slick confidence and his masculine arrogance. So he wanted me to kill him, did he? By God, I would do my best.

Just as I saw an opening his eyes flickered. I seized my chance and thrust my blade home. I only touched his shoulder with the point, but a red stain quickly spread over his snowy shirt front.

He looked down at the flow of blood. "God in Heaven," he breathed. "That's what I get for watching your derrière in the mirror."

I flung my sword aside and rushed to him. "Oh, Jean, oh, dear God, what have I done?" I sobbed. "I didn't mean to kill you, I really didn't. Oh, Jean, I shall never forgive myself, never. You have been so good to me, and I was angry because you have been acting so—so superior, and I don't know how it happened. I shall never fight you again, never!"

I tore his shirt away from the wound and staunched the blood with a wadded handkerchief. I made him sit down while I ran for a glass of brandy, and as he drank, I crooned over him, vowing to lay down my sword forever. Through it all he looked sheepish.

"Lay down your sword? And have the whole world think that when Lafitte was bested by a girl he refused to fight her again? No, my petite Amazon, I must fight you now whether I want to or not, simply in order to preserve my self-respect, which has been badly bruised by this little scratch. You have proved my point, though. About a woman having tricks in her arsenal that a man could never have. And about concentration. If only I hadn't been admiring your—" He reached out and gave a tender pat to the object that had caused his downfall.

I jumped back indignantly. "Why, Jean Lafitte, you're no different from any other man!"

He smiled shamelessly. "No, Elise, I may be better than many men, but at bottom I am no different."

## VII.   Queen of Barataria

Life on Grand Terre was good to me, and as I regained my health I achieved a new level of self-confidence and pride in my latest achievements. But I soon became dissatisfied with sitting around the island listening to the pirates tell tales of adventure that were forbidden to me. The Lafitte enterprises were interesting enough on paper, but I had seen their marauding ships return to the island with as many as six captured vessels stringing along behind, and I longed to see a battle first-hand.

I felt no great desire for the gold and the jewels—at this stage in my life wealth had ceased to have any importance for me—nonetheless the idea of stealing struck none of my moral nerves. More thrilling by far than the illicit wealth was the adventure which the ships carrying that wealth represented to me: battles at sea, flaming sails, the clash of blades and the thunder of guns, the taking of the prize, the cheers and the lusty merriment. Adventure.

I could see myself, as taut and strong as a tigress, climbing around the rigging, battling at Jean's side like a Fury, overwhelming my antagonists with my flashing blade and deadly aim, and shocking them speechless because I was a woman. It just didn't bother me that what Lafitte and his men were doing was against the law. The law had not helped me on the *Charleston Belle*, and I had lost my regard for it. I knew I could never again be accepted by society, a society that supposedly lived by the law, and I had gone too far to fit in with anyone's ideas of conventional womanhood now. I didn't want to go back to the old life. What did I care for their rules of behavior, their silly customs and strictures and limitations and meaningless social gestures? What did I care for their stares and recriminations? I was no longer one of them. I was my own woman, and I chose to be a pirate.

Jean's men doted on me and spoiled me shamelessly. I learned to like their rough bawdy talk, and when they told their tales of life on the sea and exotic ports and thrilling battles I clung desperately to every word. My thirst for excitement was becoming almost unbearable. I almost felt that I was one of the men, and when they said that they couldn't imagine Grand Terre without me, I felt that I had earned the right to fight with them.

Jean, too, seemed to enjoy my company. He went to New Orleans less frequently, and often he sent Pierre to do business in his place. Occasionally he entertained businessmen and other guests from town. I presided over his table as hostess, charming one and all with my manners and wit, before withdrawing discreetly after the meal and leaving them to their business discussions. Most evenings, however, Jean and I dined alone. He didn't mix freely with his men, although he knew them all by name and knew the names of their women and children as well. His position, he felt, required him to live apart. He had built his fabulous mansion not only as a luxurious and elegant refuge for the objects of art and refinement that he enjoyed, but also as a symbol of power and leadership to his men. They needed to stand in awe of him if they were to obey him, and the magnificent temple built of ill-gotten wealth reinforced his image. Even in his absence it stood to remind them of his absolute leadership.

In spite of Jean's unfailingly reserved manner, he did not lack a sense of humor, and during the many hours we spent together we cemented a wonderful platonic friendship. I sensed that I filled a void in his life. He had his women, I was sure, to satisfy his physical needs, and a wealth of other friends. But my natural taste and intelligence coupled with my education and a cultural exposure that rose far above even the most cultivated New Orleanians, satisfied a need in Jean Lafitte that seemed stronger than his physical ones. We talked about everything: art, beauty, philosophy, religion, medicine, even women in history and the life of a courtesan.

But we never discussed my being a pirate. I never even broached the subject, for I knew he would laugh at me. Fencing in a ballroom with a friend was one thing, but pitting one's strength to the death against seasoned fighting men was entirely different. He would never permit it, never. And because I knew he would never give in, I avoided the subject and told myself that I would find my own way in my own time, without his knowledge or permission.

One night Jean called a meeting of what he called his War Council, which included Pierre and Dominique, Réné Beluche, Cut Nose Chighizola and Vincent Gambie. They did not dine with us, but Jean excused himself immediately after dinner and went to the library, where they were waiting. I waited until everyone was closeted inside, then I tiptoed out to the veranda and crouched near the open French window. I could hear Jean telling them about a British merchant ship, the *Mary Rose*, which was expected to dock at Kingston, Jamaica, in a few days' time en route to New Orleans. I knew my hour had come.

"Relations with England are getting tense," Jean was saying. "If those idiots in Washington declare war that will put an end to merchant shipping for a long time."

"There will always be Spanish ships," Gambie put in.

"War with Britain means seas bristling with warships and frigates, and blockades at all the major ports. One of America's quarrels with England is free sea lanes and the right to control her own shipping. England will be more than happy to assert her strength in that respect and starve us all out."

"So we must go after the *Mary Rose,*" said Pierre, "as a kind of farewell gesture."

Jean said, "We are going to capture the *Mary Rose,* make no mistake about that, but it won't be easy. I have received word that she is heavily armed with up to twenty thirty-pounders, and perhaps more."

"A goddamn shooting gallery," grumbled Chighizola.

"And as if that wasn't enough," Jean went on, "she'll be escorted from Kingston to New Orleans by two of His Majesty's fine frigates, also heavily armed. It would seem that someone is afraid of someone else, would it not? Anyway, they've given us a pleasant little problem. Armed like that the *Mary Rose* is almost untouchable."

"Why don't we tackle her before she reaches Kingston?" Dominique suggested.

"And miss out on all that sugar and molasses and indigo?"

"They'll slaughter us," said Gambie grimly.

"Well, perhaps not—if we descend on them after they've started up the Mississippi to New Orleans," said Jean. I could hear the crackle of parchment as he unrolled his map of the Delta region.

"Get them on the river? That's damned crazy, Jean! The Governor will come down on you so hard—why, for a tenth of the provocation, he'd blow this island clear to Haiti!" As usual, Pierre believed in Jean's schemes only after they were carried out.

Jean spoke somewhat like a wounded innocent. "Come down on *me?* But I shall have nothing to do with this operation. In fact, I shall be in New Orleans, attending William Claiborne's very own Inaugural Ball. Everyone will see me there, and I shall be nauseatingly conspicuous the entire week. Yes, I shall bring Governor Claiborne the greetings and congratulations of the Baratarians in person.''

"Oh, God, let's hear this crazy plan."

"Look here," said Jean. I heard a bumping of chairs as they crowded around the map. ''The *Mary Rose* and her two bodyguards will have clear sailing after they enter the mouth of the Mississippi until they get to this point here. Now we arrange a little diversion—shots from the trees to occupy the *Mary Rose*, and one or two swift boats to act as gadflies and draw off the two frigates. Now we approach our target in skiffs.''

"Skiffs!" cried Cut Nose. "Who ever heard of boarding a ship from skiffs?"

''Nobody, I trust, Cut Nose. The attack surprises them, of course, and even supposing they man their guns while we're swarming up the sides, they'll still—''

"They'll fire right over our heads!" shouted Dominique excitedly.

''Exactly. Now, once the escort is distracted and we board the *Mary Rose*, we take her upriver about a mile and a half to where the Mississippi joins Bayou Laforce.''

"Bayou Laforce! But it's all silted up, Jean."

"It's too shallow."

''There's no channel, and besides, it's too narrow. And it's blocked up with trees.''

''We'll clear the trees—temporarily. And there is a channel, isn't there, Dominique? We took one of the ships up there last week. It's narrow, just barely wide enough for our purposes, but there's a current and the channel is sufficiently deep. We can send a squad to clear the pass ahead of time, and camouflage it with some rafts covered with weeds and moss. So we can take the *Mary Rose* upriver, squeeze through the pass, and then double back towards the gulf and *voilà*, up to Grand Terre.''

''But what's to stop those frigates from giving chase

down Bayou Laforce?'' Gambie demanded. ''The *Mary Rose* is an old tub, and with all those guns and cargo, too—why, we'll never get away from them.''

''The pass is narrow,'' said Jean patiently, ''and as I said, we are only going to clear her temporarily. The banks on either side are full of old logs, stumps, and debris, all very precariously placed. A strong powder charge would dislodge everything and close the pass again, certainly long enough for us to get safely back to Grand Terre.''

''We can load our camouflage rafts with the powder charges,'' Dominique said excitedly, ''and then fire at them once we get through—''

''It will never work,'' said Cut Nose.

''Oh, I think it will work,'' said Jean softly. ''Of course, if you don't want a share of this, Chighizola, just say so. We'll need all the men we can get, but we can do without you if you're not interested.''

''Don't get excited, Jean,'' said Cut Nose hastily. ''But there won't be anybody left to get shares if we're all blown up.''

''You leave that to me,'' said Dominique. ''Powder's my department.''

''Cut Nose,'' said Jean quietly, ''and you, too, Vincent, listen well. This is going to be a reasonably bloodless operation. When Dominique takes command of the *Mary Rose* he will set her captain and crew adrift on the Mississippi on the same skiffs we use to board her. The authorities are going to come down on us hard after this one, and we don't need charges of unnecessary murder added to our other sins.''

When the meeting broke up and the men were leaving, I waylaid Dominique. ''Listen,'' I hissed, ''you've got to take me with you.''

''Are you crazy, wench? Jean will have my skin. He'll

peel it off and fly it from the topmast of the *Tigre*, and—''

"Oh, be quiet and listen, Dominique," I said. "You know as well as I do that this is the chance I've been waiting for. Don't you understand, I want to be one of you, really one of you. I've got to do it. And part of it's for him, for Jean. I want to do something no other woman has done so that he'll be proud of me. Please, Dominique.''

"He'll flay you alive," growled Dominique. "A battle's no place for a women, you crazy wench. You've got to stay here, where it's safe.''

"I'm sick of being safe," I said. "And Jean won't have to know until it's all over. If I get killed I have only myself to blame, right? I'm ready, Dominique. You know I am. After all these months of learning to fight, I've got to do it for real. Just thinking about danger makes me feel more alive.''

He shook his head. "It's not right. It's not right for a girl to feel that way about killing.''

"I'm not a girl anymore, Dominique. I'm a woman and I know what I want. It's right, I know it is. You'll see.''

I wished him good night and went into the library. Jean was rolling up his maps.

"Did you have a nice meeting, Jean?''

He looked at me quizzically. "Yes, the meeting was satisfactory; our plans are progressing as smoothly as could be hoped. It's a shame that a mind like mine had to turn to crime, don't you think, Elise? I could have been—President!''

I laughed. "It's not too late. If you keep getting richer you can buy the Presidency.''

"I can think of better ways to spend my money," he said. "Tell me, how would you like to accompany me to the Governor's ball?''

I looked at my shoes and said slowly, "Oh, Jean, it's so

sweet of you to ask me. But I don't think I'm ready to meet people yet. I'd rather not, if you don't mind.''

He frowned. ''No, I don't mind, Elise, but I do think it's time you came out of your shell. Barataria is no place for a girl like you. You need lights and music and intimate girlfriends and cultured suitors, people who will pet and admire you. You need things to bring out the best of your womanhood. If you continue running like a tomboy with this pack of ruffians, you may forget you're a woman at all.''

I said meekly, ''I'm sorry, Jean.''

''You're not sorry at all,'' he grumbled. ''I shouldn't be surprised if you do it just to torment me.''

''Oh, how can you say that? You have no idea how I feel about anything. All you care about is yourself and how elegant and perfect you are.'' Lafitte turned a shade paler, and I was overcome with remorse at this outburst. ''I'm sorry, Jean. I promise, I'll go to New Orleans with you anytime you want, but not this time, all right?''

He had already recovered his composure. ''Elise, I think the heat of the Louisiana sun has curdled your brains. You would have a wonderful time in New Orleans society. It's sure to be great fun. But you can do as you please of course.''

''Well, there will be more fun another time. Good night, Jean.''

''Good night, Elise,'' he said thoughtfully.

A week later Jean went to New Orleans, after dispatching parties of men to clear the pass and conceal it again. I dogged Dominique with a grim determination, hounding him until he finally agreed to let me go along with Pierre on either the *Tigre* or the *Polidor,* the two ships that were to draw the frigates away from the *Mary Rose*. I wanted to go with the boarding party on the skiffs, but he refused to hear of it. We argued about it for days, and finally I pretended to give in. I promised to stay with the *Tigre*, which was dangerous enough.

Jean's spies brought word that the *Mary Rose* and her escort were only a few days away from the mouth of the river. Preparations intensified, and I felt my excitement mounting. I practiced constantly with my sword and my pistols. I felt ready—ready for anything.

At last the time was right. When the *Mary Rose* entered the mouth of the Mississippi, we had men staked out to watch her, and they reported on every mile of her progress towards New Orleans. Grand Terre hummed with activity. The grand scale of Jean Lafitte's scheme required the services of every available man. But no women. Dominique was in charge of the raiding parties, and Pierre and Vincent Gambie were to lead the diversionary maneuvers of the *Tigre* and the *Polidor* respectively. Dominique and I finally persuaded Pierre to take me along on the *Tigre*. But at the very last moment I told Pierre with a frightened look on my face that I wasn't feeling too well and had changed my mind and could not accompany him after all. He was greatly relieved.

Instead I surreptitiously joined Dominique's band of raiders. He didn't notice me among the groups of men who pushed off in a half dozen skiffs. I wore boy's dress and hid my short billowing curls under a bandana. The men in my skiff thought it was a great joke, and they didn't breathe a word of my presence to Dominique.

We traveled for two days to reach the river. I sat in the bottom of my skiff like some privileged Cleopatra while my mates took turns poling us through the dense swamps. I breathed in the heavy, pungent smell of the bayous and gazed at the canopy of browns and grays over my head as we glided over the still brackish waters under ancient cypress trees festooned with Spanish moss.

On the evening of the first day we camped on a small

island in the heart of the bayou. Dominique passed among the men while we were eating fresh fish and roasted fowl, washed down with wine from flasks the men had brought. When he saw me crouched in front of a campfire calmly dissecting a broiled fish the jokes died on his lips and he gaped. His face reddened and his eyes nearly popped out of his head.

"You! You! Hell's fire, you crazy, schemin' wench, I—I oughta flay you alive!" He sputtered and choked and fumed. "As if I hadn't already put my head in the noose by making Pierre take you on. He chewed me up one side and down the other for letting you get away with that much!"

"Oh, I fixed it with Pierre," I said, spitting out a fish bone. "I told him I changed my mind. I think he was actually glad about it, Dominique. My feelings were hurt."

"I'll bet they were," Dominique growled.

"Don't worry, Dominique," I said reassuringly. "I'll behave myself. I'll just board the *Mary Rose* with the rest of you and stay out of trouble until the ship is ours."

"Out of trouble! What do you think this is, girl, some kind of scuffle in an alley behind a tavern? You can't stay out of trouble on a ship, you're *in* it, there's no other place to be. I've got a notion to gag you and tie you to a tree right here until we come back. Might teach you some sense. Damn women! Damn all meddlesome females!"

The other men were watching this exchange with great amusement. "Oh, come on, Dominique," one of them said. "Elise will bring us luck!"

"It's not luck we need," he retorted, "but cool heads and keen eyes."

"I do have a cool head and keen eyes," I insisted. "And I dare you to prove otherwise."

We glared at each other until I broke the tension with a little laugh. "Poor Dominique, you trained me, after all. Don't you have any faith in yourself as a teacher?"

"By the good God, you're a hellion, wench," he said, shaking his head. "What are you bastards laughing at? Get yourselves to sleep. We have a long way to go tomorrow."

I watched him stalk off to his own campfire and I sighed heavily. I had won another skirmish, and now I was set for the big battle that lay ahead. All I had to do was keep my head and concentrate, I told myself. The rest would take care of itself. But already I could feel the fear in my stomach, and I wondered if I shouldn't have gone to New Orleans with Jean.

We traveled all the next day and camped on the west bank of the Mississippi that night. On the morning of the attack we awoke to find the river shrouded in heavy fog. Dominique was jubilant, for if the *Mary Rose* arrived before the fog lifted we could almost certainly approach it unseen. Our forces split up and regrouped on both sides of the river, south of the Bayou Laforce pass, to await the arrival of our prey. Dominique grumbled constantly about having to wet-nurse an infant pirate, but he kept me close to his side. He cursed when the darkness lifted and the sun threatened to burn off the fog.

I was shivering, with dampness or with fear I was not sure. "I don't know what's the matter with me," I told Dominique. "I feel like I'm on fire some of the time, or else I can barely keep my teeth from chattering. I'm about ready to explode, I'm so tense."

"It's the danger," he said. "It's like a drug, makes you hot and cold at the same time. You can start slow, but you get so you need more and more, and then you have to live like that all the time. Too many men like that, not happy unless they're about to get killed. It's terrible. No way to live."

"Jean's not like that, is he?"

"Oh, he is. We all are. And now you're gettin' it, too. It's a craziness, that love of danger. You go through it and wonder how you ever got out of it alive, and you swear to yourself never again. But after a while the old itch comes back, like a scratchin' in the bowels. And off you go again.'' He grunted. "Jean is going to murder you for disobeying him."

"Disobeying! He never told me I couldn't be a pirate. He never even mentioned it."

"And neither did you, eh, wench?"

I stifled a laugh.

Then we heard it through the fog, the unmistakable creak and groan of a ship under sail, the thud of billowing sails, the scattered voices from her decks that came to us in snatches over the water. We heard the crackle of gunfire, and an answering burst of cannon fire. As the *Mary Rose* drew abreast of us Dominique gave a signal and we pushed our skiffs off from shore and glided noiselessly towards her with our weapons ready. Not a man of us didn't give hearty thanks for the mist that shrouded us. Apparently the volley of shots aroused some excitement on the big ship, for sounds of frenzied running and shouting reached our ears.

As we drew alongside of her the men tossed up ropes with heavy weighted hooks to catch the bulwarks, and we swarmed up the blackened expanse of her hull to the decks. I was the last from our skiff to board the ship, except for a giant Haitian named François, who I imagined Dominique had ordered to help me up the ropes and keep me out of trouble when we reached the deck. François picked me up as easily as if I had been a sack of grain and carried me aloft.

The scene on deck was noisy and confusing. Men were fighting hand to hand and the air was thick with powder smoke. François clapped a huge hand on my shoulder and pushed me down behind an unmanned cannon before leaping into the fray. I crouched in my sheltered corner for a few moments, gazing numbly at the fight that was taking place under my very eyes. The stench of sweat and blood reached my nostrils, and I felt sick with fear as I watched men shouting and bleeding, and killing each other. Whatever I had imagined, I was wrong, terribly wrong. I had made a horrible mistake in thinking that I ever wanted to be part of something like this.

A man fell at my feet. He was bleeding profusely from a stomach wound, but he still had his pistol clutched in his hand, and when he saw me a wild look came into his pain-filled eyes and he lifted the weapon and pointed it at my face. Terrified, I brought the edge of my blade down on his outstretched arm, and I scampered away from my hiding place, dropping my sword as I ran.

I hardly knew which way to turn. My heart was pounding so rapidly that I felt it was about to fly out of my chest, and I thought the din in my ears would drive me mad. How in God's name did one fight? Did one slash and shoot wantonly until the enemy was decimated? Did one choose a likely-looking enemy and kill him while his back was turned, or did one wait and face him—like a gentleman? But these English sailors were not navy men; they wore no uniform, no hard, flat hats. I looked at a pair of combatants and for the life of me I couldn't tell which man was a pirate and which was a British sailor. Did one join a duel already in progress, and try to win the fight for one's own side? Was there a protocol to be observed?

Or did one just stand like a moron, pistols in hand, and wait for an opportunity to kill a man?

I heard a noise behind me and I whirled around. A huge sailor was bearing down on me with his dagger drawn. Instinctively I dropped to my knees and fired upward at him. I watched horrified as he clutched his chest and dropped heavily at my feet. I heard a roaring in my ears and wondered if I would be sick. I fought back the impulse to kneel beside the man and see if I had killed him or if there were still something I could do to save him. What a fool I was. As usual I had refused to listen to those who knew best. I followed my impulses without thinking —would I never learn?—and now I would have given anything to be off this ship and far, far away. What was a pirate after all, if not a robber who kills when he is cornered, when his own safety is at stake?

More than anything I wanted to escape the sights and sounds of the battle on the *Mary Rose*. I used my knowledge of the *Charleston Belle* to find my way below deck. I followed a dank passage until I came to a door which I thought might lead to the main cabin. I stopped just long enough to reload my pistols, then I pushed at the latch and kicked open the door.

The captain of the *Mary Rose* looked up from his desk and hastily closed the lid on a small chest. We faced each other for a moment, and then I cleared my throat and found my voice.

"Excuse me, Captain, but we missed you upstairs," I said smoothly, as I imagined Lafitte night have spoken to the man. My voice sounded painfully high-pitched and girlish.

A pistol materialized in his hand. As he fired I fell sideways, bringing up my own pistol as quickly as I could. I closed my eyes and fired. The door behind me was splintered by his ball, and when I opened my eyes I saw with astonishment that my shot had knocked his weapon from his hand. He stood holding his wounded hand to his chest, staggering toward me slowly.

"By God, boy," he said thickly, "you'll bloody well hang for this, I'll see to that."

I raised my other pistol and pointed it at his head. "And I promise you, Captain, that my next shot will take your head off," I said in a trembling voice. And I meant it. I was desperate, terrified of being killed. The knowledge that I would have killed him, swiftly and mindlessly, shook me more than anything that had happened thus far. I motioned him to stand against the wall while I searched the top of his desk. I found another loaded pistol hidden under some charts. I shoved it into my belt along with my spent pistol, and then I backed away from the desk and pressed my back against the wall to the right of the door. From that position I could watch not only him but the door as well.

"You're a fool, boy," the Captain said. "You'll never get out of this alive. I'll see you hang!"

I tried to shrug casually, and I swallowed deeply. "It's as good a way to die as any," I said with an easy conviction that I did not believe. "But hold your tongue. If your hand is paining you, it grieves me. Shall I send for the ship's doctor? You can suck on it if you like. Surely a little scratch like that doesn't hurt a big man like you."

He cursed me freely. By crouching down I could hold one of my empty pistols between my knees as I reloaded it while I kept the other pistol aimed at him. In a moment I had two of my own loaded pistols in my fists, and the one I had stolen from him in my belt. I prayed for something to happen soon. Surely I could not intimidate him for long. With every word I must be giving myself away as a green, scared kid. When he recovered from the shock of his wound he would make a move and I would have to shoot. I didn't want to kill him. Something in his tired, red face reminded me of Uncle Theo.

One of his men burst into the cabin. He took in the situation at a glance. Pointing one of my pistols at the intruder, I kept the other on the Captain and barked, "Order this man to drop his weapons to the floor. If he does not he will die. You will both die."

The Captain jerked his head at the man, who reluctantly did as I told him. What the Devil would I do if a third man came in, I wondered. I had three guns, but one of them was unfamiliar, and it would be easy for them to over-power me once my shots were spent. I might be quick on my feet and possess a truly deadly aim, but I had no illusions about my strength.

Then I had a thought. I ordered the sailor to kick his weapons over towards me, and I gathered them behind me. Finally I ordered the captain and his man to lie face down on the floor. Cursing sullenly, they complied. But the next sound I heard was Dominique's familiar roar in the passageway. I nearly fainted with relief. He and a pack of his men rushed into the cabin and halted abruptly when they saw me with my two captives.

"Now you've done it!" cried Dominique gleefully. "Taken the ship single-handed. Captain, you and your men are about to take a little trip in Louisiana skiffs. I hope you enjoy it."

The Captain glowered at me as they led him out. "You'll pay for this, boy. You'll pay, you filthy little ruffian."

"Don't go insulting our prize pupil," said Dominique, winking at me.

"Your prize pupil will hang for a thief before he reaches manhood," the Captain snapped.

The pirates grinned and took the two men away. Dominique walked over to the desk and lifted the lid of the chest. His eyebrows shot up.

"He was doing something with that when I came in," I told him, moving closer. "What's in it?" I peered over his shoulder.

"Gold," said Dominique reverently. I saw the warm yellow glint of the coins he cradled in his hand. "Gold sovereigns. Enough to buy Louisiana back from the United States, if we wanted to. I'll be damned." He dropped the coins back into the box and closed the lid. Then he put his arm around my shoulder and said, "Well,

Mademoiselle Pirate, how did you like your baptism by fire, eh?''

Suddenly, the awesomeness of what I had done struck me, and I began to tremble violently. I dropped my head onto Dominique's massive shoulder and burst into tears. ''Oh, it was horrible, dreadful! I have never been so frightened in all my life! Why, I think I killed a man, Dominique. Me! I—I can't believe it, even now.''

''What did you expect,'' he said roughly, ''champagne and rose petals? Come on, dry your eyes. Pirates don't cry. This adventure isn't even half over. We still have to get this tub to Grand Terre, and for all I know those frigates could be right on top of us.''

When we were under way I looked back at the Captain and his crew floating disconsolately in the little skiffs that had carried us out to her just a few minutes ago. Those minutes had seemed like hours to me. I would never forget them as long as I lived.

As we neared the pass we heard a burst of cannon fire. ''Come on, men!'' Dominique shouted. ''Get movin' up there and let's get this ship turned about. Move! There's time enough for yarns and drink when we get her through this blasted pass.'' The men ran to obey, and Dominique peered through the thinning mist with his glass. ''Jesus, those two bloody frigates, comin' after us like they had wings on. By the sails of Satan, there's another one! A warship!''

The pass was narrow, as Jean had said. As I looked over the side I could see land not ten feet away from the hull of the ship. I could have jumped to earth if I had wanted to. I saw the huge floating rafts of debris the men had constructed. The blunt prow of the *Mary Rose* nosed through them, pushing them gently aside. The men prayed that no spark would explode the powder charges hidden among the tangle of growth until we were well on our way down

Bayou Laforce. Two sailors jumped into the water and helped push the rafts aside, watching closely for alligators. Then they swam after us and clambered up the ropes again.

Just as we were almost through the narrowest part of the pass, I felt a crunch and the *Mary Rose* lurched and came to a halt. I was terrified. We could see the frigates now out on the river heading our way, just out of cannon fire range. Quickly all the men swarmed into the water. We had only touched lightly, and soon they had dug her loose and pried her free, and we were on the way again.

The frigates were already beginning to fire at us by the time Dominique judged we were far enough away from the treacherous rafts. He himself stood behind the gun at the stern of the ship and fired. His first shot fell short of the rafts, and he swore vehemently while the men reloaded the cannon and he took aim again. Just as he was ready to fire, a ball from one of His Majesty's frigates landed right on one of the rafts. After an agonizing moment, it exploded, sending a shower of mud and branches into the air. Sparks from the explosion caught the dry grasses and twigs on the other rafts, and three more resounding explosions filled our ears.

The men cheered wildly. We were now heading into deeper waters, and a brisk wind caught our sails and sent us speeding towards Barataria.

"Well," said Dominique with a satisfied grin, "if we haven't changed the course of the river, at least we've bought ourselves a few hours of time."

I smiled thankfully, found a corner sheltered from the harsh sun that had burned off most of the morning's mist, and went to sleep.

With the heavy tail winds, we reached Grand Terre before nightfall. The men unloaded the cargo as quickly as possible, then took the ship out into the gulf, set fire to her, and sent her to the bottom. Her old timbers blazed for twenty minutes before they were swallowed up by the waters. By morning there was not a trace of the ship called the *Mary Rose*.

We did no real celebrating that night. Instead, we prepared ourselves to repulse an attack. Dominique knew that the British would retaliate. They had to; the whole scheme had been so audaciously planned and so cleverly executed, and it had humiliated them badly. They would see Jean Lafitte's fine hand behind it all, and they would, as Jean had foreseen, come down on us hard. Dominique warned that the Americans might even join the British in a effort to wipe us out. Governor Claiborne was eager for a chance to destroy the Lafitte empire.

The attack came two days later, at dawn. As soon as Dominique's lookout spotted the first sail on the horizon he sounded the alarm bell and the men rushed to their battle stations. The mansion and warehouses were set far back enough from the shore on the gulf side of the island that enemy fire would not penetrate unless their ships were well within striking distance of our own guns.

Dominique manned his big gun on one of the fortifications on the southernmost tip of the island, and when two British warships and two frigates began to fire on the island he was ready to respond at once. He did better than he had with the rafts. His very first shot struck its mark, and one of the warships caught fire and had to retire from the fight. For every twenty shots of theirs that missed their target, one of Dominique's inflicted some damage on their ships.

Then Pierre and a crew manned one of our own warships and prepared to give chase. In a matter of a few hours we had routed the enemy and put them to flight. Dominique told me later that it would take many more ships and men to raze Grand Terre than the British had available at that time.

At least no American ships had joined the raid. Relations between the two countries were so tense that when the British lost a ship in American waters, the Americans would not readily leap to their defense. Feelings were running high against the British in most American ports in those days anyway, for the British industrial machine, being older and more sophisticated, could turn out goods and sell them in the United States at prices American manufacturers could not better.

We lost a handful of men and one warehouse in the attack. Although the island was not in real danger, most of the women and children fled to a remote part on the north side for safety, but when the warehouse burst into flames and the men were too occupied to help put out the fire, some of the women returned to carry the buckets of water. I liked my second taste of battle no better than my first. The thunder of cannon fire, the smoke, the flames, and now the added hysterical screams of some of the women and the slaves trapped in their pens made me sick and distraught. I had no desire to fire a cannon, but I helped Lily behind our line of guns, carrying drinking water and food to the gunners, taking messages from Dominique to the others, and nursing the wounded.

At the end of the day my face was black from soot and smoke and streaked with sweat. Every muscle ached, and I could have cried with exhaustion. I dragged myself to the house and soaked for an hour in Jean's great tub. Just as Dominique had said, I swore to myself that I was through with pirates and swords and guns. Would I change my mind again? Surely I was too revolted by the last few days to want to experience such violence ever again.

Jean returned from New Orleans a week after the battle at Grand Terre. At twilight someone saw his pirogue coming towards the island through Barataria Bay, and by the time he landed, four hundred men with torches were waiting to greet him. They set up a loud cheer as he stepped ashore, then crowded around him, clamoring for news.

As I stood at the back of the crowd watching him, my heart turned over. I had forgotten how handsome he was, how graceful, how free. I wondered momentarily if the outlaw was the only member of society who is really free. He might lose that freedom at any moment, perhaps pay for it with his life, but perhaps the risk was worth it. Jean Lafitte was his own man, doing what he wanted in spite of the consequences, and I loved him for it. I did not regret my association with him, nor the course I had chosen. Somehow, ironically, my journey to America on a slave ship had been my journey to freedom.

Lafitte waved his hat at his men. "Well, *mes amis*," he said warmly, barely containing his excitement, "I am delighted to find you in fine spirits. Have you perhaps enjoyed some recent success that I have not heard about?" They roared approvingly. "You must let me tell you about the strange stories that came to my ears in New Orleans, friends. 'Tis rumored that an English merchant ship was plucked from under the very noses of two well-armed frigates and a warship." Cheers. "The crew is said to have taken an unprecedented opportunity to enjoy a lovely touring excursion in some bayou skiffs. No one can say that the Baratarians are not hospitable."

The men danced and cheered, bragging about our victory over the British retaliation and describing the rich spoils from the *Mary Rose*.

Jean lifted his voice. "A moment, just a moment, my friends. In the most interesting tale I heard, the British captain was captured and held at bay by a fierce young lad with flashing dark eyes, the merest stripling, whose voice had not even matured." There was much laughter at that. I hung back in the shadows. I knew Jean would be furious, but I had not expected him to chastise and embarrass me

publicly. He went on. "The Captain, apparently, was not
the only victim of this young Hercules. He is said to have
slaughtered as many as eighteen British sailors, and the
Captain himself has set a price on the lad's head. Twenty
pounds, hard money, if he is brought in alive."

The men whistled and stamped and shouted merrily. I
cringed and stayed well away from them. Oh, it was
humiliating, this display of his. If he wanted to scold me
for what I had done, why didn't he do it privately? God
knows it had been a shocking and gruesome experience,
but at least I had come through it alive. Did he have to set
them laughing at me? Couldn't he leave me even a shred of
pride?

Lafitte's face grew more serious. "Now, this offer of
twenty pounds is not one to be taken lightly. And while I
was visiting the parish jailhouse for a few days, due to a
misunderstanding with the Governor, I gave a great deal
of thought to the identity of this youth. I have to agree with
the Captain that such a bloodthirsty youth should not be
allowed to live among civilized men, but for the life of me
I don't know who he was. I can only conclude that he was
sent by the gods to aid our cause, and there we must let the
matter rest."

I couldn't listen to another word. I fled to the house, my
cheeks flaming. He had every right to be furious. I had
acted impulsively, meddled in his business without con-
sulting him. I might have endangered the whole mission. I
might have been captured and tortured, and forced against
my will to tell everything I knew about Jean and his
contacts. He must hate me; he would ask me to leave
Grand Terre. Perhaps I should leave before he asked, but
the thought nearly broke my heart.

I went into the library and huddled in an armchair,
knowing he would seek me out. After a while I heard him
outside with Dominique and Pierre. I felt relieved: he

could not banish me in front of them, for they would
defend me. Then, with something like despair, I heard the
other two go away from the house and Jean come in alone.
I fought back a desire to run for the shelter of my room. I
had wanted to be as good as any man, hadn't I? Then I
would take my punishment like a man. I pulled myself
together and rose to greet him.

"Hello, Elise," he said warmly. "I missed you on the
beach. Have you been terribly bored in my absence? You
would have enjoyed the Governor's ball. I found myself
watching the other women there, and do you know, not
one of them, not the prettiest Creole beauty, could touch
you for looks. The Governor and I snubbed each other, of
course. He must have been wondering how I got my hands
on an invitation, but—"

"Oh, stop it, Jean," I snapped. He looked surprised.
"You don't have to heap coals of fire on my head."

He shrugged and turned his attention to the ledgers on
top of his desk. "No, that's true. You have promised to
come with me to New Orleans another time, and it was
rude of me to make you wish you had come along. What
would you have done while I was in jail?"

I put my hand to my mouth. "You—you were in jail?
Why?"

"Why, because the Governor thought I might have
information concerning the brigands who captured the
*Mary Rose*. It wasn't too bad, though. I couldn't help
him, and he had to let me go after two days. The food was
passable, but the bed! I'm glad to be home. Did you and
Pierre get to inventory the cargo yet?"

"Yes. It's on the desk."

He picked up the sheet. "Very nice, very nice indeed. I
like especially this little casket of sovereigns. Intended for
official bribery, I have no doubt. Can nothing be done
honestly these days? You seem to have kept things up to

date in my absence, Elise. Admirable. But I suppose you had little else to do. I'm sorry. You must have been bored.''

I could not detect the barest glimmer of a smile on his lips or in his eyes, and the anger rose within me. He was going to torment me by not bringing it out in the open. He was letting me off lightly this time because he saw that I was terrified of him, that I was quaking in my boots like a schoolgirl who had just been caught putting a frog in her neighbor's bed. What a devious mind! What a villain! Having escaped punishment this time I would doubtless behave myself in the future. And always this would hang over me. If I ever again expressed a desire to do anything he thought unseemly, he would throw this at me, threaten to punish me belatedly, and *voilà,* and put me in my place. Damn him! I would not permit it. I had nothing to be ashamed of, anyway. I had done what I wanted to do, and I wasn't sorry.

''If you must know, Jean,'' I said coldly, ''I was not bored. I spent my time killing English sailors and capturing the Captain of the *Mary Rose,* to satisfy my lust for blood and to bring you that casket of gold sovereigns.''

Jean Lafitte sat down in the armchair and smiled at me. ''I thank you for them.''

''You had damned well better thank me,'' I said stiffly. ''And do you know what else? I'm not sorry. No, I'm not.'' I was close to tears. ''It was wonderful, just wonderful. I like being a pirate and I shall go on being one as long as I feel like it. And if you try to stop me, I'll—I'll go off with some men and I'll start a rival band. A rival band of pirates, and we'll take all the ships and you won't get any, and, oh, I'm so sick of pirates! Why did I come here?''

He caught me as I ran past him and pulled me onto his knee. ''Rival band, indeed,'' he said gruffly. ''What a little idiot you are, Elise. Why on earth are you crying?

Did you think I was going to beat you? You're no better than a child. You are—remarkable.''

I buried my head in his shoulder and wept thankfully for some minutes. ''You're not angry with me, then?'' I asked in a small voice.

''Of course I am angry. Can't you tell?'' He dabbed at my wet cheeks with his handkerchief.

''What—what are you going to do, Jean? Are you going to punish me?''

''Punish you?'' He voice was surprisingly gentle. I looked into his face, transformed by the film of my tears into something glowing and saintly. ''Punish you?'' he said again, with amazement. ''If I am not mistaken, you have been punished enough for this rash escapade. Unless you really have a fondness for fighting. I have lost my taste for blood lately, and I cannot believe that you actually like killing. Wasn't shooting a man, two men, enough punishment for you?''

''Oh, Jean,'' I said softly, ''you know, then. You know how it was. Not what I imagined at all, but—awful.''

''I know what it is to fight, Elise, and perhaps now you will believe me when I tell you that it is not a fit thing for a woman.''

I sighed deeply and leaned my head again on his shoulder.

''One thing makes me sad, though,'' said Jean. ''The fact that you dreaded my return. You didn't want to face me, because you were afraid of me, Jean Lafitte, the man who has been father and brother and friend to you. For shame, Elise.''

I hung my head. He was right. I had known nothing but kindness and generosity from him, and yet I had behaved towards him as though he had been an ogre. Other men, many others, had given me good reason to tremble. But Lafitte was different. He ruled by love rather than fear, by understanding rather than intimidation. His whole concept of womanhood was different from any I had ever known. To Jean Lafitte a woman was not just a necessary nuisance, but a person who complemented his own personality, a friend who deserved to be cherished and loved for her own sake.

My heart swelled with gratitude and love, and I clasped him tightly. He was my friend, my only friend. "I'm sorry, Jean," I whispered.

"For what?"

"Because—because," I floundered. "Oh, you know why."

He grasped my shoulders and held me away from him so that he could look into my face. "Yes," he said with a little smile. "I know why."

Something in his eyes made me tremble. I became acutely aware of the pressure of his hands on my arms, and warmth spread through me, igniting the small flame of desire that I thought had been extinguished forever. I felt shaken to my very core, for I had not experienced that sensation since I—since Garth McClelland had been taken off the *Charleston Belle*. A lifetime ago, two, three lifetimes ago. How was it possible that I had existed so long without wanting a man?

I looked at Jean Lafitte, and I saw him for the first time not as a pirate, a scholar, an outlaw, a benefactor, but as a man. My mouth felt dry and my heart began to pound. I held my breath, waiting.

He lifted his hand to my face to brush back my hair. I shivered, and brought my own hand up to cover his. Touching him delighted me. I wanted his kiss, his tongue, his fire. I closed my eyes.

The fragile anticipation of that moment was shattered by sounds of stumbling and crashing in the hallway. I heard Dominique call my name. He was joined by Pierre and several others.

Jean laughed ruefully and set me on my feet. "I hope they remembered to wipe their feet," he said. "Come on, I think they want you to help celebrate. Now you can see the other side of piracy, the good side. Are you afraid?"

"Of course not," I said. "They are my friends, as you are." I kissed him quickly on the cheek.

"A year ago you would not have been so eager to claim the most celebrated thieves in the western hemisphere as your friends."

We heard pistol shots and the splinter of glass. Lafitte groaned. "They're shooting at the chandeliers," he said. "Damn them, they do it every time."

When Dominique and Pierre and their companions saw me they howled with delight and demanded that I join their party. I laughingly assented, although I really had no choice in the matter, and they hoisted me to their shoulders and carried me out of the house to the beach. Huge bonfires were blazing merrily, and from a distance I could hear music and see figures dancing and moving around. They cheered my arrival, thumping me on the back and plying me with wine from a dozen different bottles. Already the Legend of Elise the Pirate was taking shape. The reality of the terrified, stupefied girl was supplanted by a splendid story of a beautiful witch of the Caribbean who could wish a ball to its target. Only later did I discover what a fluke the shot that disarmed the captain had been; our pistols were crude weapons, inaccurate even at close range, and Jean assured me that it couldn't happen again in a hundred years.

The pirates toasted me lustily, declaring that never again would they undertake a mission without me, for I had brought them luck. Then the question arose of who was to have me when simultaneous voyages were in progress. Blood would surely have been spilled had Jean not intervened, saying that tokens that had my blessing would be just as effective. Since they all half believed in the voodoo practices that had spread from Haiti to New Orleans, and into the bayous, they deemed this an acceptable proposal.

The small orchestra consisted of a concertina, a fiddle, and a flute. Delirious with drink and excitement, the pirates and their women whirled furiously across the sand, not bothering to keep time or even hearing the music, I suspected. The fires cast a warm ruddy glow on the happy faces, and I thought the flickering, dancing flames kept better time than the pirates.

I danced with everyone except Jean. Pierre was a capable dancer, but he made it clear that he thought dancing silly, and that he would have preferred to spend his time with me in other ways. I chided him and told him that anyone would think he was smitten with me from the way he talked. He twirled me around, declaring loudly that I was the bravest lass ever to set foot in Louisiana, and that he was madly in love with me.

Dominique was a terrible dancer, worse even than Vincent Gambie, who danced like a bull on the rampage. I ached to feel Jean's arms around me. I wanted us to glide as gracefully as two sea birds coasting on an air current. But he never approached me and seemed to avoid my gaze, while he was dancing with all the other women there, even some that moved, and looked, like alligators.

The highlight of the evening came well after midnight. Dominique called for silence.

"Gentlemen! Ladies! And the rest of you drunken sots, be quiet and listen. This celebration tonight is because Jean over there is the smartest man that ever set foot in a skiff." Shouts of laughter. "And this wench, Mademoiselle Elise, is the bravest lady in the swamp. Tonight we are going to name her Queen of Grand

Terre—no, Queen of all the islands. Mesdames and Messieurs, I give you Elise, Queen of Barataria!''

Then some of the men came forward and presented me with a beautiful gleaming sword with a ruby-studded solid gold handle and two of the lightest smallest pistols I had ever seen. I swished the sword around a few times, to their delight, and then I loaded my pistols and fired them at the moon. I missed, but the men roared with laughter, and once again I found myself sitting on a couple of brawny shoulders while they cheered me. I laughed delightedly and smiled and waved my pistols enthusiastically.

When I looked at Jean I saw he was smiling and applauding with the rest. He was king here, no one doubted that; and now I was his queen. I felt that the evening had been a betrothal of sorts, and that the pirates had given us to each other because I had shown myself to be worthy of their leader. I was overwhelmed by the distinctive honor, and by my love for Jean Lafitte. Yes, I loved him. I loved them all.

I spread my arms and made it known that I wanted to speak. The men shouted for silence. ''I just want to say one thing,'' I said breathlessly. ''I think—I think that no woman could have led a more exciting and interesting life than I have since I came here, and no woman could have been made to feel more welcome. I—I have experienced some cruel behavior among so-called civilized men, but you, whom they call outlaws and thieves, have shown me nothing but kindness. I am deeply honored that you have named me your queen, and—and this moment shall live in my heart forever!''

We all drank more wine and danced energetically. As the night wore on I began to feel quite dizzy and tired, and I was not surprised to see Lily at my side.

''You come on along to bed, child,'' she said gently.

"Mister Jean says you look tired, and you're not long past being sick and almost dying. Let's go now."

"Oh, Lily," I protested, "I'm not sleepy, I'm not. I don't want to go to bed. I want to—" I searched among the flushed and happy faces for Jean. I wanted to dance with Jean. I saw him standing apart from the crowd, deep in conversation with Dominique and Cut Nose Chighizola. He didn't even see me. I sighed deeply. "All right, Lily, I'll be good. Good night, everyone."

My friends wished me good night and I permitted Lily to lead me up to the house. I climbed the stairs and bathed and fell into my bed, but I lay awake for a long time listening to the waning sounds of merriment that floated in my window from the beach. What a curious day it had been. Now I was not only a full-fledged pirate, but I was Queen of the Pirates. I had proved myself, and I had won their respect and admiration. Why did I feel so sad?

As if in answer to that question a flash of desire came over me. I tossed uneasily, trying to keep back the image that hovered over me of Garth McClelland smiling cynically. I had loved him, he had taught me how to love, but that was all over. Garth McClelland was dead.

What is the matter with me? I asked myself. Surely that kind of need, if it goes unfulfilled, will disappear after a while. But it seemed only to intensify as the night deepened. Garth's image faded, and the evil face of Josiah Fowler took its place. I shivered. Had not the atrocities I suffered at the hands of Captain Fowler put me off men for life? Apparently not. What is wrong with me?

I knew all too well what was wrong. I was a queen and I needed a king. A woman who wanted a man.

## VIII.    The Belle of New Orleans


The revelers gradually quieted down, and peace settled over the house. I could still hear a few stragglers putting out the fires and some house servants bumping around downstairs, laughing and telling each other that Grand Terre had never had a night like this before, and never would again. Then I heard footsteps in the hallway. The door to the room next to mine opened and closed.

I sat up and threw back my light coverlet. So Jean Lafitte, mighty King of the Pirates, had finished dancing for the night and was taking his gamboling heels to bed. I breathed deeply and tightened my fists as I pictured him undressing and crawling under the sheets, settling down for a nice, long sleep, alone. I hoped he would suffocate in his pillow!

I flounced out of bed and threw on a thin wrapper. No doubt he would sleep like a baby. I certainly wouldn't, in spite of all that wine. I was fully awake now, and I was profoundly angry.

Jean Lafitte, leader of men. Lover of women. A daring, dashing, capricious, devil-may-care corsair. My king? My friend? My nothing. He hadn't danced with me, he hadn't even looked at me the whole evening. I had thought he was about to kiss me when I was sitting on his lap in the library. Couldn't he see I was willing? All too willing. And yet he had given not a word, not a sign—why?

And then I knew. The truth came to me in a flash and left me gasping. He didn't find me attractive. On the contrary, he thought of me as a tragically unloved, ugly, little orphan. What an idiot I was! He was not to blame. I practically threw myself at him, and he behaved as he always had, with the utmost gentleness and propriety. His actions said clearly, this is as far as we go, you and I. Friends. Oh, yes, he would be all things to me—father, uncle, brother, comrade—but never lover. No, not that.

I hadn't lost my looks. I turned up my lamps and ran to my mirror to reassure myself. No, if anything I was more beautiful than ever. Although the sun had browned my skin a little it was still soft and creamy. I stood erect and tried to study myself objectively. Elegant shoulders, breasts that were full and firm, tiny waist, womanly hips. I remembered how I must have looked when they found me. The difference was amazing. He couldn't help but remember, too.

Perhaps he remembered too well. He could only see me the way I was when they found me. Foul. Foul looking, foul acting, even foul thinking. Not only what I had looked like, but far worse, what I had been and what I had done. He knew how Josiah Fowler and his men had used me, and he was revolted. Jean Lafitte was a sensitive, cultivated gentleman, and his knowledge of my sordid past completely destroyed any desire he might have felt for me. I didn't blame him. The memories were still so shattering that they made me sick. I had been lower than the lowest whore. In his eyes I was still tainted. I was —filth. No man with his sensibilities could possibly associate himself intimately with—filth.

And yet he himself had denied that this was so. He had stood behind me as I looked at myself in the mirrors downstairs, and he had said—oh, he was a smooth talker, was Jean Lafitte—he had said that we are what we are and not what has happened to us. He had made it all sound so easy, so easy to forget. Ignore the nightmare, look ahead, be happy. But be happy alone, for no man will want you.

I turned my back on the image that had caused me so
much sorrow. Tears rushed to my eyes, but I brushed them
away angrily. I would not cry for a man who did not want
me. I would die first. Where was my pride? I was not
about to fall in love with a man who looked on me as dirt.
All of that fine talk, all those facile compliments, it all
meant nothing. He was made that way, that was all, made
to charm women with his words and his eyes. That charm
was as much a disguise as the fine clothes he affected, it
was part of his company attire, his public manner. Yes, he
was different from his men. Any one of them would gladly
have taken me into his bed with the least encouragement.
But Jean Lafitte would not sully his impeccable soul by
entering into intimate companionship with—someone like
me.

I paced the floor, fighting with myself, feeling utterly
wretched and unhappy. I couldn't blame him because he
had breeding and taste. I couldn't blame him, but I did,
because he had actually made me believe for a while that it
didn't matter.

I walked up and down, up and down, working myself
into a frenzy. He must know how I feel, I told myself.
Surely he could see it in my face tonight. I stopped in
my tracks and covered my face with my hands. Oh, what a
bitch I was! It wasn't Jean's fault that I suddenly craved
him.

I heard a light tap at the door and one of the servants
who was still working downstairs poked her head in.

"'Scuse me, Missy, but Mistuh Lafitte he say for me to
see you all right. He think all that walkin' means you have
a pain an' you need somethin'—"

"Tell Monsieur Lafitte that if he's so concerned about
me he may come and see me for himself," I snapped. She
looked frightened and backed quickly out of the room.

I felt irritable and I found the warmth in the room

oppressive. I opened the windows onto the veranda and stepped outside. For Heaven's sake, don't start yapping at the housemaids, I scolded myself. I knew better than to take out my anger on innocent servants.

The door opened again. Good, she had returned. I took a breath and turned back into the room, intending to apologize for my rudeness to her. Jean Lafitte stood in the center of the floor, watching me.

"Oh." I drew the thin silk of my wrapper over my breasts. "I'm sorry I disturbed you. Were you asleep?"

He smiled ruefully. "No. Someone in the next room seems to have been trying to wear holes in the carpet. Are you all right?"

"Of course," I said in a brittle tone. "Why shouldn't I be?"

"No reason, I suppose. The excitement and the wine are keeping you awake, aren't they? I just wanted to see—the maid thought you were upset about something, and that I should see—"

I stepped out of the shadows. "And what do you see, Monsieur Lafitte? Do I seem to you to be sick, well, or simply indifferent?"

"Not indifferent, Elise. Never that." His eyes swept over me. He looked concerned. "And you're not sick, I hope. Yet you're not well, either. I sense a restlessness in you tonight that I haven't seen before. What's the matter? Do you want to go away? Are you unhappy here? Naturally, you were appalled at the way my men behaved tonight. Please forgive them. They are crude, no better than ignorant ruffians. They don't know how to sip their pleasures like civilized people do. No, they gulp at life, like doomed men. And perhaps they are." He spoke sadly, and then pulled himself up and smiled stiffly. "I don't know what's the matter with me. The hour, I suppose. I find that at three o'clock in the morning it is very easy for my thoughts to drift into uncharted waters. What was I saying? Oh, the men. They have never learned how to restrain themselves when they're having fun.''

''That is something I have not yet learned, either. Please don't feel that you need to apologize for them. I meant what I said tonight. They are my friends, and I was touched by what they did.''

''You made them very happy, Elise. It's not often someone tells them how good they are.'' After a long pause he said, ''Then if you're not angry with them it must be me. It is, isn't it? Won't you tell me, Elise? I won't bite you.''

He was using his most fatherly tone. I could have throttled him. But what was I to say? I'm angry because you didn't dance with me tonight? I turned away from him and said in a very controlled voice, ''I think I should go away.''

''If that's what you want, Elise, so be it. You can be on your way to New Orleans tomorrow. You'll be fine there. I know many influential people who will take you to their hearts, as we have. Of course it won't hurt that you are a noble Frenchwoman, nor that our sainted Napoleon is your godfather.''

''Sainted—rubbish,'' I muttered under my breath.

He came up behind me. ''Won't you at least tell me what is troubling you before you go, Elise?'' I kept silent. Then he said, ''You've fallen in love, haven't you?'' He saw me stiffen. ''I knew it! Who is it, Pierre? I heard what he said tonight when he was dancing with you. I shall speak to him—''

''Don't you dare!'' I faced him. ''Oh, how can men be so stupid? Idiots, morons, all of them! And I swear, Jean Lafitte, you are the worst. I wonder that you have come as far as you have. But of course, you deal with men in your business and not women, and it's a good thing. Fools, cretins, all of you! Get out of here at once, get out, I say!''

I flew at him with such a vengeance that he fell back a step with an expression of stupefied amazement on his face. ''But—but Pierre—I thought—you—''

''You thought!'' I said disgustedly. ''Well, you can stop your thinking, and if you're going to do any speaking you might as well speak to yourself, Monsieur, not that any good will come of it. You might as well admit to yourself that I'm not good enough for you. Those men out there—'' I waved my arm, ''—you're not fit to shine their boots. At least they know a good thing when they see it, and they don't preach one thing while they're thinking another, like some people. Even Pierre—I'm good enough for Pierre, but not for you, am I, Your Highness.'' I bowed mockingly. He put out his hand in a gesture of placation. ''Don't you dare tell me to be calm,'' I sneered. I roamed the room like a hungry tigress.

''I could kill you for the way you have treated me! I'm so sick of your politeness and your perfect manners that I could scream. I might as well have fallen for a marble statue with all its arms and legs broken off. For the love of God, stop treating me like a daughter. If any daughter felt about her father the way I feel about you, why, Hell itself would open up and swallow her.

''Oh, God, what am I saying?'' I looked at him beseechingly. ''I am not ungrateful, Jean, but must I feel gratitude towards you all my life and nothing else? Must we continue to be victim and savior, father and child, friends?'' I stopped suddenly. My rage drained away as quickly as it had come, leaving me feeling spent and humiliated. In a quieter, more subdued voice, I said, ''I have been a fool, Jean, to think that you would really want me after all that has happened. I know now that all I

did—that business with the swords and the pistols and the
*Mary Rose*—I did for you, to make you forget the Elise
you brought here, to make you want me. I'm sorry. I know
you can't buy love with deeds or daring or courage. Some
things go—deeper.''

"Elise—"

I breathed a long shuddering sigh. "Please go now," I
said weakly. "I am bitterly ashamed of myself, and I have
embarrassed you enough for one evening. I'll make my
own arrangements about leaving. You won't have to see
me again.''

I walked briskly out to the veranda and clung to the
railing, gulping in great lungfuls of sea air. I swallowed
back the tears with a great effort.

"I am sorry, Elise," he said softly from the open
doorway.

"Please don't say anything, Jean." My voice was almost steady. "It's all my fault. I'll never be able to look
you in the face again. I'm—I'm so ashamed.''

"It is I who should feel ashamed, Elise. For not seeing
what was under my nose, for causing you so much needless distress—"

"Don't you dare pity me, Jean Lafitte," I said, choking
on my tears.

"Pity you! For what? Because other men have found
you beautiful and have desired you? Because they took
you, like animals? I have wanted to do that a hundred
times, a thousand, but because I thought you would be
afraid and would hate me I fought it. I forced myself to
behave towards you in a gentlemanly and grotesquely
fatherly manner, but believe me, the thoughts in my mind
were far from fatherly!

"Look at me, Elise." I shook my head and kept my
eyes fixed on the stars. He came to me, and pulled me
around gently. He lifted my chin to face him. "Look at

me. What do you see, a man who despises you for something that happened to you long ago, through no fault of
your own? No, you see a man who desires you very much
indeed, and who always has, but who has been too much
of a fool to tell you so.''

I dropped my head to his shoulder and felt his arms go
around me. ''Oh, Jean, you are the most unlikely pirate.''

''I know. We must keep this quiet or I'll be drummed
out of the profession. You know, the only reason the
others have kept their hands off you is because they are
certain that you have been my mistress from the very
start.''

''Really?'' I lifted my head. ''Then we mustn't disillu-
sion them, must we?''

We went indoors and sat on the edge of my bed. Jean
put his arms around me and bent his head to kiss me, but as
I reached up to return his embrace, my body broke into a
cold sweat; my passion shriveled instantly within me and I
felt completely dead and cold. All the old horrors had
returned.

''No!'' I gasped and pulled away from him. All my
desire had fled, and I couldn't bear the thought of a man
touching me.

''Elise.'' He came towards me again, and I forced
myself to hold still as he stroked my face, then put his arms
around my waist and buried hs face in my neck. A great
wave of nausea and suffocation came over me. I choked
and screamed, terrified, and pushed him away. I was
hysterical, out of my mind, and I threw myself face-down
on the bed, my body sweating and shaking, while great
racking, tearing sobs convulsed my frame and threatened
to rip my chest apart.

When my terror and my sobbing began to subside, I
became aware of Jean, sitting on the bed, holding my
hand.

"Oh, God, I'm sorry, Jean," I gasped out, between my sobs. "I'm so afraid, I'm—I'm afraid, Jean. I wanted you, I did, you know I did, but—but—oh, God, I keep remembering, Jean. It was all so horrible." My sobs renewed in vigor, and I held tightly onto his hand.

"Don't apologize, Elise. You don't owe me anything. You don't owe anything to any man, except what you feel you can give him. It's all right, Elise. After all, it's been a long time for you, hasn't it? Just let me hold you, Elise. I love having you in my arms. You are so soft, so sweet, so lovely."

His tenderness seemed to melt away my fear, and I let him hold me. Gradually my tears ceased, and I clasped him tightly. We lay quietly for a long time. I felt great comfort in his nearness, in the smooth slim body underneath his robe. I snuggled against him, and he kissed me lightly, and then again, over and over. I grew hungry for his love and returned his kisses. His hands moved slowly over my body, gently caressing and exploring me. His tongue danced into my mouth, and desire flamed in me anew. I rolled over on the bed, pulling him on top of me. His expert caresses grew less gentle, and he undressed me slowly, revelling in my body. He threw off his robe, and the lamplight played on the taut muscles of his chest, arms, and thighs as he embraced my nakedness to his own. I felt the smooth suppleness of his gentle strength, and I opened the depths of my soul to his love.

As he mounted me, the curtain of my fear again came crashing down between us. A vision of Josiah Fowler swam before my eyes—horrible, grotesque, leering—and I screamed. Once again I experienced a choking sensation and an inner deadness that I could not control. I felt like I was suffocating, drowning under his weight and bulk, choking on the staff of his virility. I clawed at him, and a cry of desperate terror, in a voice I couldn't even recognize as my own, came tearing out of the nightmarish depths of my being. As he pulled away from me I drew my legs up and lay panting like a wounded beast. Then I buried my head in my arms and sobbed bitterly.

So that's what Josiah Fowler had done to me, that was his legacy to me: he had destroyed me as a woman. I could almost hear him laughing at me from the canyons of the Hell to which he had gone.

Jean stroked my hair and held my hand tightly until I was calmer.

"Oh, Jean, forgive me, forgive me. Please understand, I never never dreamed this would happen. Oh, dear God, what has happened to me?" I wailed. "I could die, die. Why don't you kill me?"

"Stop that," he said crisply. "It's not your fault, Elise. I was too hasty. I acted like a green schoolboy, and I should have known better."

"But it's—it's so unfair to you," I said through my tears.

He said wryly, "I suppose I'll live. Go to sleep now, my darling. We don't have to rush things. We have all the time in the world."

I tossed my head on the pillows. "It won't get any better, I know it won't. I'm—I'm a cripple!"

"Why, even cripples can be healed, or haven't you read your New Testament lately?" He kissed me tenderly and said, "Don't be frightened, Elise. I promise you, it will be all right."

I clung to him. "Don't leave me tonight, Jean, please. I don't want to be alone. Please stay with me."

He cocked his head. "You want me to sleep here with you?" I nodded. "You don't kick or have screaming nightmares or long toenails, do you?"

"No."

"Then I suppose I must." He sighed deeply. "How

these women take advantage of one's good nature." He moved around the room, extinguishing all the lamps. Then he slid into the bed beside me, but the space between us felt as wide as the Atlantic Ocean.

We lay for a long time in silence. I could tell from his breathing that he was still awake, as I was.

"Are you asleep?" I whispered.

"Certainly I'm asleep," he said crustily. "What do you want?"

I said, "I want you to hold me in your arms again."

"Oh, dear God," he groaned. "All right, come on."

I rested my head on his naked shoulder and snuggled close to him. "Are you always so grouchy in bed?" I asked.

He squeezed me hard. "Always. Women, I think, thrive on abuse."

"You're a darling, Jean. You know, I used to think you were the only man I had ever met who didn't know how to tease." I kissed his cheek and rubbed my thigh over his.

He slapped it with his hand. "If you don't stop that I shall beat you," he threatened.

I promised solemnly to behave myself. After a while I asked, "Jean, do you really have sixteen mistresses?"

"Oh, yes."

"And do you keep them all in the same house in New Orleans?"

"Certainly, Elise. Each of them has her own room, and when I go to the city I have to visit them all, one after the other."

"That must be exhausting."

"Yes, it is," he agreed, "but one has a responsibility to one's dependents, after all. I plan to put you in that house, you know."

"That's very kind of you. And what number shall I be? Shall you visit me first or twelfth or—seventeenth?"

He thought for a moment. "Well, as one goes on one's stamina decreases, you know, and thus the expertise of one's partner ought to increase proportionately. Therefore, I save the best for last. Since you are a beginner you'll have to start at the bottom and work your way up. First is an enviable position, too, though, because you'll get the best of me before I'm all used up."

I rolled on top of him and tugged his hair playfully. "I won't start at the bottom. I refuse. I want to be the first and the last and the best, Jean. I want to be so good that you won't even look at the others. You shall come to my room and take me sixteen times, and I'll get better and better each time, you'll see."

I could feel his manhood growing under my loins.

"You'll regret this, Elise," he said warily. "You know what you are doing and what it will lead to."

"Oh, yes, I know, Jean," I whispered. "I know exactly where it will lead."

He flipped me over on my back and lay on top of me, framing my face with the palms of his hands. "Are you going to cry like a baby?" he demanded. I shook my head. "Or scream like a virgin?" No. "Are you going to try to relax and enjoy it?"

"Yes, Jean. Oh, yes."

He brought his mouth down firmly on mine and at the same time he plunged into me. The fear welled up in me again and again, the nightmare reeling with evil, lusting faces and disembodied limbs and salivating lips and harsh animal breathing. And that face, that face. Oh, God, I said to myself, am I to see Josiah Fowler whenever I close my eyes for the rest of my life? I fought, as hard as I have ever fought anything, and eventually my disgust lay quiet, although I was still aware of it inside me, weighting me down like a stone.

This is Jean, I kept telling myself, Jean. I concentrated

on him alone. I bit my lips to keep from crying out, and I pressed my fingernails deep into the palms of my hands. He was as gentle as he could be, and he didn't prolong it, and when he had finished I felt a wave of relief and gratitude sweep over me. Tears filled my eyes and I hugged him tightly. Our love hadn't been good, I knew, but at least it had been possible. I was still a woman. He had given that back to me.

"If you cry I shall kick you out of bed," he said gruffly.

"I'm not crying, Jean, really, I'm not."

"That's good. Now suppose you tell me something. What on earth am I going to do with all those empty bedrooms?"

"Oh, Jean!"

Because he was patient and kind and he cared about me, Jean Lafitte helped me to forget the fears that haunted me and he exorcized the visions of Captain Fowler and his crew that plagued me. The process of teaching me to love freely again was a long one—but enjoyable enough (more fun than giving fencing lessons, according to Jean)—and the genuine delight we took in each other's company more than made up for any inadequacies on my part early in our relationship.

I felt my womanhood flowering under his care and attention. I was nearly nineteen, but the experiences of the past year and a half that had matured me too fast in some ways had left me a child in others. Now, as Jean Lafitte the benefactor was superseded in my life by Jean Lafitte the lover, I felt the last vestiges of childish behavior slipping away from me. The Elise of France was a stranger to me. Now I was Elise of Louisiana, Queen of the Pirates, mistress and friend of the country's most reknowned blackguard. I tried hard to please Jean as associate and assistant, and I tried even harder to please him as a woman and a lover.

In spite of the horrors I had experienced on the *Charleston Belle*, my sessions with Josiah Fowler had taught me that the routes to physical pleasure offered limitless variety.

"Really, Elise," gasped Jean, his senses reeling, for once losing his calm control as pleasure exploded into ecstasy, "ladies of quality don't do that sort of thing."

I laughed and caressed him again. His body jumped violently at every touch. "But you love it, don't you!"

"I can hardly bear it, I love it so much!"

"I like it, too. That must mean I'm no longer a lady, wouldn't you say?"

"No, I wouldn't say." He grasped me to him and kissed me soundly. "It means that you are an exceptional lady."

Whether I was an exceptional lady or not, I had an exceptionally good time with Jean. Visions of the *Charleston Belle* and Josiah Fowler no longer leapt into my focus when Jean made love to me. He thawed the icy pillar in my womanly depths; my involuntary stiffness and horror disappeared.

I loved nothing better than to surprise Jean bathing in the huge tub I had noted on my first inspection of the house. I would tiptoe up behind him and splash water in his face, then tumble into the tub with him. We would splash around like young muskrats, then I would scrub his back, his lean buttocks, his hard chest and thighs. When I gently soaped his soft sleeping tool of love and the little leathery pouch that held his man-jewels, I could feel him awakening, growing, rising in my hands. Then Jean would soap and caress me all over, playing with my breasts until the tips stood out as firmly as his own awakened desire, stroking and probing in the softness between my legs until the small spark of my passion became a roaring fire. Then I would feel his warm, wet, soapy body slipping over and around and into my own, and we would drown ourselves in the hot foaming sea of love.

We went to New Orleans for Christmas and the Mardi Gras season. Jean owned a little house on Dumaine Street. The rooms were spacious and cool, and a walled garden with a fragrant sweet olive tree gave us a place to go for peace and privacy outdoors. An elderly French couple whom Jean had rescued during the uprising in Haiti lived in the house as caretakers, tending to the gardening and the cleaning, and Lily came with us and acted as cook and my maid.

I loved being in a French city again, but I would have loved New Orleans had it been Spanish, Italian, or Portuguese. Its elegant homes with spreading lawns lined wide tree-shaded streets that were treacherously muddy in wet weather. I loved the warmth of the people, the colors and smells of the markets, the ever-blooming flowers. We had roses at Christmas and perfect camellias when my birthday came in February.

That night, when I was nineteen, Jean and I celebrated at home, just the two of us. I realized for the first time that I had missed my eighteenth birthday completely. A year before I had been less than human, a slave lower than the lowest slave, and I had not even remembered my birthday. For the first time in my life I had not celebrated—worse, I had not even known I had a birthday. And I wept a little, knowing that the delightful little Elise Lesconflair who had gotten so much out of her birthday parties was gone forever.

Lafitte introduced me to all his friends, distinguished or otherwise; he escorted me to balls and to the theater; and he let me accompany him on visits to his buyer and merchant friends. The days went by in a whirlwind of activity.

Jean's business, as New Orleanians jokingly called it,

gave him an entrée into the city's most exclusive homes.
No hostess would dream of giving a party without inviting
the charming brigand. Jean took advantage of those invitations, as much for his own sake as for mine, for he loved
good talk and good food, and he enjoyed showing me off.

"I have no illusions about why they ask me," he told
me once. "If the day comes when I have nothing left in my
warehouses to offer them, they will knock me down and
step right over me. But until that day we will continue to
use each other for our own reasons, and everybody's
happy with the arrangement."

I was the scandal and sensation of New Orleans during
the winter and spring of 1812. Although Jean carefully
introduced me as Mademoiselle Elise Lesconflair, newly
arrived from France, and my credentials of nobility in this
French city were undeniably genuine, everyone in the city
seemed to have heard some part of my story—how I had
been a captive on a slaver and been rescued by Lafitte's
men. Word of my subsequent exploits on the high seas
leaked out, thrilling the citizens. And the fact that I lived
openly as Lafitte's mistress added luster to my image as an
adventuress.

Men desired and admired me because I was beautiful
and supposedly shameless. Their women could not ignore
me for the same reasons, and also because my connections
with the Bonapartes made me the closest thing they had to
visiting royalty. So they could not afford to exclude me
from their parties. Even the most conservative Creoles
took me into their homes, and after I made it clear that I
posed no threat to their sons and their husbands, they even
made me feel welcome.

I felt happy in these days, less involved with my own
problems, and I began to think more and more about my
family, about Uncle Theo, and Philippe and Honoré.
Should I write to them? They must have given me up for

dead. I didn't want to go back to France. I still felt uncertain of the future, and I could not face my brothers' questions about the past until I had some answers for myself about the future. Would Jean Lafitte and I remain lovers forever? I didn't think so. Would I marry him if he asked me? Would he ask me? I didn't know.

I enjoyed being back in society again. Although New Orleans was not as sophisticated and exciting as Paris, it was a good deal more lively than country society around the Chateau Lesconflair had been. The upper-class French Creoles were cultured and educated, and I found their company amusing and stimulating. Much of the talk concerned the adventures of their ancestors: their grandfathers and great-grandfathers had been the first French settlers in Louisiana early in the eighteenth century.

The stodgier Creoles still considered themselves French, in spite of the changing ownership of the city over the years from French to Spanish to French and finally to American. Over the years the Creoles had intermarried with Spaniards, Englishmen, and Americans, and this cosmopolitan mix lent a distinctive flavor to their gatherings. Current talk was unabashedly political: possible war with England and Louisiana's recent statehood were prominent in their discussions.

The Creole mammas protected their sons and daughters with a provincial ferocity, however, and they saw me as a potential corrosive influence. Whenever I saw their eyebrows lift disapprovingly at me I would launch into an account of the Lesconflairs at the Crusades, or My Father General Lesconflair, Friend of Napoleon, and the tension in the room would dissolve. These things in my past were no longer important to me, but I enjoyed using them, I confessed to Jean, because I was so amused that they made effective social weapons.

"It's wonderful, Jean," I said gleefully, "I am the

wickedest woman in the city, but because of General Lesconflair and the title and estates and old Napoleon I am actually socially acceptable. Where else in this benighted country would that be possible."

His put his arms around me and hugged me until my spine cracked. "Then the Fates must have brought you to these noble lands. They knew that here in New Orleans we appreciate beauty."

"Here in New Orleans you are snobs, pure and simple. Really, Jean, everyone is aping my dresses, my hair style—suddenly all the girls have cropped their hair à l'Elise, have you noticed? And I'm trying to grow mine long again! And they are even naming foods after me: Souffle Elise, Sauce Lesconflair! I have never heard of such nonsense."

"Ah, the poor Americans, Elise. Even the Creoles. They are unsure of themselves. They think they are inferior to their European cousins, and they try their best to compete. But don't tell me the Europeans don't have crazes. Why, a few years ago the ladies were chopping their hair off so that they would resemble Marie Antoinette on her way to the guillotine."

"Oh, all right, Jean, I do like being adored by them. But more than that I like being adored by you. You never make impossible demands, never criticize the way I act, and no matter how much money I spend you don't complain."

"Why should I? It's not my money."

I looked at him and burst out laughing, and he joined me. "Oh, Jean, sometimes when I am with you I feel happy, really happy." I hugged him tightly around the waist.

"Thank you, my dear. I consider that a true compliment."

His tone was serious and I glanced up at his face. I saw a sadness in his eyes and something I hadn't seen before: Jean Lafitte was in love with me. For some reason this knowledge didn't make me as happy as it should have, and when I was alone I asked myself why. I knew the answer: I wasn't in love with him, not that way, and it was the sorrow of my life. Oh, I loved him dearly. He was my whole life, the center of my existence. I loved his intellect, his style of living; I loved his gentle ways; and I loved his sensual body. But in spite of everything I felt for Jean Lafitte, I was still my own woman. I would never belong to him wholly, passionately, deliriously, instinctively, uncontrollably. I had felt like that about only one man. Garth McClelland.

He did not deserve it—Jean was worth a dozen Garth McClellands. But I would never love Jean or anyone else the way I had loved—and hated—Garth.

Sometime in February, about a week before Mardi Gras, the Arceneaux family gave a masked Pirates' Ball in our honor. Jean and I decided we ought to appear dressed as real pirates: shoeless, hatless, ruthless, and dirty. We amused ourselves for hours imagining how we would look, and how the Creole snobbery would look at us. Eventually, however, we decided not to further besmirch our reputations, and we arrayed ourselves in gorgeous formal attire. Jean looked resplendent in white satin knee breeches and a dark green velvet frock coat, and I wore a high-waisted jade green silk gown with large puffed sleeves, and white camellias strategically placed in my bosom to soften the effect of the scandalously low décolletage. When we were masked we both looked splendidly and delightfully mysterious.

Just as we were about to leave we had an unexpected caller: Pierre arrived from Barataria with urgent questions

about a Spanish ship due to arrive from Brazil. Jean
disposed of the business with his usual quick efficiency,
but the delay made us rather late to the party.

"Oh, my dears, how *naughty* of you to be so late but
how *lovely* of you to come at all and how *sweet* you both
look," Madame Arceneaux twittered. "Elise, my dear,
the men have been *panting* for you. Look, Andre, Elise is
here at last. You don't mind, Monsieur Lafitte, if Andre
has the first dance with Elise? He is *smitten* with her,
simply *smitten*."

I blew a kiss to Jean as Andre Arceneaux, masked but
unmistakable, guided me carefully onto the dance floor
and positioned his arms around my waist. One, two.
Bump, two. Turn, two. I smiled bravely at him as he went
through his paces. Andre was eighteen and painfully shy. I
heard him speak a complete sentence on only one occasion, and that had caused heads to turn and mouths to fly
open in astonishment. He had told me that I looked beautiful, but a group of onlookers, which included his mother,
had behaved as though he was an infant just forming his
first coherent words. Since that time Andre had never
spoken to me again, but he always smiled charmingly and
seized every opportunity to be near me.

At the end of our dance a cluster of young men surrounded me, each begging me for the next dance, which
was to be a waltz. I laughed merrily at their squabbles, and
decided to end their arguments by closing my eyes and
choosing at random.

I pressed a gloved hand over my mask. "Very well,
gentlemen, I am sufficiently blind. Now if you will arrange yourselves in a circle around me—" The music
started. I spun slowly and just as I stretched my finger out
and stopped turning I felt myself being swept away by
strong arms into the sea of dancers.

I looked up. "Why, Monsieur, you are too precipitous!'' I exclaimed. ''You were not, as I recall, even one of the candidates for this dance.''

His blue eyes gleamed coldly at me through the black domino mask he wore. He was tall; indeed, he towered over most of the men in the room, and his thick hair was like shining gold—

I felt the blood drain away from my face. It couldn't be— I would have fainted but his arm gripped me tightly and kept me on my feet until the dreadful moment passed. He compelled me to step and whirl like a machine, even though I longed to run away, far away, anywhere to escape the chilling light in those eyes.

''Perhaps you will tell me with whom I have the honor of dancing, Monsieur?'' I asked with assumed brightness. His eyes did not even flicker.

We danced on. I did not speak to him again, and he made no effort to converse. As we circled the floor the memory of another night, another ball, another waltz filled my mind. Who was this man if not the Devil himself come to haunt me? I moved like an automaton in his arms, and it seemed to me that we were revolving slowly, more slowly than the music, twisting together in a dream world of fear and sorrow and memory.

When the waltz ended he bowed stiffly over my hand, and as he stood up he plucked one of the camellias from my bosom. I gasped at his daring and looked down at the place where the flower had nestled. When I raised my eyes he had gone, vanished into the crowd. I felt queasy and I pushed my way out of the ballroom and up the stairs to the ladies' dressing room. Tearing off my mask, I fell back into a chair and uttered one, long shuddering sigh. No, it wasn't—it couldn't have been he. Dead. He was dead. God, how my ghosts plagued me.

''Why, Elise, are you ill?'' Madame Arceneaux leaned over me and put her hand on my forehead in motherly fashion. "You're as white as a ghost, you poor dear. Can I get you some brandy?"

When she had fortified me with liquor and I had regained my speech, I asked, "Who is that tall man downstairs in the black coat and black domino mask? He has —blond hair, I think, and he's very tall."

Madame Arcenaux frowned. "Why, I don't know. Andre has light hair. You don't mean Andre, do you? Did Andre fool you? Oh, he'll be thrilled! Wait until I tell him!"

I smiled weakly. "Isn't that silly of me? Yes, do tell him—tell him I thought him very handsome and mysterious."

She patted my hand. "Oh, I will. He's smitten, Elise, simply *smitten*. Well, I must get back to my guests. You rest here as long as you like. I'll have one of the girls bring you some coffee, would you like that? Oh, I *must* tell Andre."

She bustled out, and I sat back and threw my arm over my face. No, no I was dreaming. I was tired, that's all. Too many parties, too much excitement. Just tired.

I did not see him when I regained sufficient courage to go downstairs an hour later, nor at midnight when the guests unmasked. What had happened to him? I tried to reassure myself that it had been a dream after all. I could not bring myself to enter into conversation with Jean on our way home. He looked at me curiously, but he asked no questions. Later, when we were in bed, I pulled him to me, locking my fingers in his hair and covering his face with kisses. "Make love to me, Jean." He did, softly, gently, warmly. We did not speak again.

A few days later word came that pirates had captured a Spanish ship. This was no news to us, but Spanish officials complained to the government of the United States in the person of William Claiborne, and the Governor issued an order for Jean's arrest. Notices were posted all over town offering a reward of five hundred dollars for the delivery of Jean Lafitte to William Claiborne.

Jean took a special delight in this new phase of their eternal warring, and he brought me a notice as a souvenir. Then he sat down to compose another notice of his own, in which he offered a reward of five thousand dollars to anyone delivering Governor Claiborne to him at Grand Terre. After they were printed Jean sent out a squad of men to post them all over the city. The good citizens of New Orleans, who had more fondness for their resident outlaw than for their cold Yankee governor, loved the joke.

Jean and I continued to appear in public and no attempt was made to arrest him. At first I was terrified that he would be snatched away from me and sent to prison.

"Don't worry," he assured me. "No one will lay a hand on me. They're too fond of their coffee and their cheap cinnamon and slaves, not to mention the silk stockings I can get for them at nine dollars a pair instead of twenty. Believe me, the people of this city are better off if I'm free. Now come on and get dressed. We have dinner and the opera tonight, remember?"

"I think we should stay home."

"No." He put his hands on my waist. "Do you want them to think Lafitte is afraid to show his face?" He slid his hands down to my buttocks and kneaded them gently. His voice lowered meaningfully. "But perhaps we can compromise, and miss dinner."

Later, before we left for the Opera House, Jean presented me with a pearl necklace. I touched the perfect round beads that encircled my throat and said, "They're beautiful, Jean. Was I that good?"

He kissed my hand and held it fast. "You're the best, *chérie*, you know that. You said once that being with me

made you happy. Well, being with you has made me
happy, too, very happy. I shall never forget you, Elise, do
you believe that?''

I was puzzled. "Why, of course I believe it, Jean." I
caressed his face. "Maybe we should miss the opera, too.
Two strings of pearls are better than one." He smiled, but
not with joy, and I went on more seriously, "I shall never
forget you either, Jean. But don't be sad, my darling."

"We can't go on forever, Elise."

"Why not?" I demanded. "Who's going to stop us?
William Claiborne or President Madison or Napoleon
Bonaparte can't come between us. No one can." Even as I
said it a cold shiver traveled up and down my spine. No,
no one could ruin what Jean and I had. I made a silent vow
to myself. "This isn't the moment of our final good-bye,
is it, Jean?"

"No, of course it isn't. I must be a little feverish, that's
all. It was just a feeling."

"*Tristesse*, Jean?" I asked archly. "Surely you're not
sad after making love to me!" I kissed him. "Now let us
go to the opera."

The first act of Mozart's *The Marriage of Figaro* had
already started, and we slipped into our box quietly so as
not to disturb those around us. Jean had taken the box next
to the Governor's for the season, so they could take mutual
delight in ignoring each other during the intermissions. I
loved *Figaro* and I kept my eyes glued to the stage.

The first intermission had begun, then, before I glanced
over at our neighbors and discovered that it was not
Governor and Mrs. Claiborne next to us at all.

The months flew away from me and I was once again
sitting in the forests of the Lesconflair estates, trying
desperately to cover myself from a pair of smiling blue
eyes. The blood rushed to my head and forced a small
strangled noise out of my throat. Slowly he turned his

head. He fixed his eyes on mine for a long moment—the same cold blue eyes, but without a trace of the smile —before nodding coolly; then he turned and spoke to his companion, a tall, striking blonde woman. She craned her neck to inspect Jean and me. Jean nodded to her politely, but she tilted her chin up and swivelled her head away from us again.

"Hm, another snub," Jean remarked. "It must be that box."

I sat frozen in my seat, but as the second act began I heard the woman say something about the Witch of Barataria. The man laughed—Garth McClelland laughed. I felt myself grow suddenly hot and then cold. A blackness settled over me and my limbs felt dead. I could see the Countess beginning her aria, but the thunderous roaring in my ears drowned out all the music. Those blue eyes had turned me to stone.

"Elise, what's the matter?" I heard Jean ask anxiously. "Let me take you out of here."

"No, no," I croaked, "what will people think?"

"What do we care what they think? Let them think I'm taking you home to bed, which I am."

The people in the boxes that flanked ours must have heard him, I thought despairingly, as he led me out. They must have. I wished I were dead.

The journey home through the night air restored my equilibrium somewhat, but when we were alone in our room I embraced Jean with a ferocity that surprised us both.

"Take me, Jean. Take me, right here, right now."

Without a word he dragged me to the floor and leapt on top of me. Never before had we been so violent, so pain-giving in our love. He took me with no tenderness, no caresses, and I wanted it that way. I fought him at first, viciously and senselessly, but when he forced his way into me I gripped him tightly. I wanted to feel close to him, so close that not even death could separate our fused flesh.

As he reached the height of his frenzy, I raked his back and dug into his hard buttocks with my fingernails until he cried out in pain. The storm broke over my body like a raging volcano. Shocks and tremors split my being as a bolt of lightning fells a great tree. In a few minutes we were spent, numb. We lay panting, our bodies gleaming with sweat.

"Don't send me away, Jean," I implored him. "Please don't ever send me away."

"Don't be foolish, Elise," he said impatiently. "I shall not send you away until you want to go."

"Oh, Jean, let's go home. Home to Grand Terre. Now, tonight." I knew that I would feel safe only when we were miles away from New Orleans, from—him.

"Not tonight, Elise," Jean said tersely. "We have other things to do tonight."

He picked me up and carried me to the bed. He kissed my breasts and sank his teeth into my neck and shoulders. I cried out. Then he tore into me again with a mad fury that I had never seen in him before.

# IX. The Duel

The next morning Jean and I packed our things and made arrangements to return immediately to Barataria. We hardly looked at each other, and we spoke little. I wondered if Jean suspected anything about Garth, but I told myself that the snubbing, along with my real concern about the price on Jean's head, were reason enough for my worry and distraction.

Soon we were safely back on Grand Terre, busily sorting through the welter of business details and problems that had accumulated in our absence. Although neither of us mentioned the madness that had possessed us the night before, we both knew that something had changed between us. The gentle warmth had fled from our lovemaking, leaving behind it a desperate urgency and an insatiable hunger. Passion alone could not dispel the tension that existed between us.

One afternoon when we were working in the library, Jean said quietly, "I want to get caught up so that you won't have too much to do while I'm away."

"Away?" I looked up from the column of figures I was adding. "Where are you going, Jean?"

He waved his hand. "Who knows? Out to sea. I am bored with bookkeeping, Elise. I am not a banker, I am a pirate! Since we came back to Grand Terre I have felt as though I were—waiting for something. But what it is, I don't know. I don't like the feeling, Elise. I feel trapped, nervous. Life has gone dull and stale for me. I need to get away."

"It's my fault, isn't it?" I asked softly. "Somehow I'm to blame. Things are different. You've felt it, too. Tell me, Jean, what happened? What did I do wrong?"

He sat beside me and put his hand over mine. "Nothing, my darling. You are as perfect and beautiful as ever. I suppose I haven't outgrown my thirst for danger, that's all."

I looked at him squarely. "Take me with you, Jean."

"No, Elise, it's too—"

"Please."

He walked to the fireplace and stared up at his cherished Rembrandt.

"I feel it, too, Jean," I said. "The boredom, the nervousness. Don't leave me behind. If we are together, perhaps we can recapture—" I paused.

"Recapture—what, Elise?" He didn't turn his head. There was an undertone of bitterness in his voice.

"Whatever it is that we've lost," I said firmly. "You're a stranger to me, Jean. You're so distant and damnably polite that I could scream! Please don't shut me out any more. Take me with you."

He lowered his head. We were silent for some minutes, then he said, "Of course I shall take you with me, my darling."

"Oh, Jean!" I ran to him and he held me close.

"We'll set the gulf aflame with our bravery and boldness, Elise," he said with a touch of his old swagger. Then he threw back his head and laughed. "Ah, I feel like a boy again! We must leave at once. It will be good to sail again. God knows I've missed it. I was never meant to be a—a clerk!"

Jean had a frigate overhauled for our use, and he renamed her *Elise*. We sailed forth into the Caribbean and for three months we terrorized English and Spanish merchant ships, accumulating a fortune in prizes. I was no longer the elegant darling of New Orleans society, but a pirate's wanton: wild, dangerous, and free. Occasionally I put on a gown for our evening meal together, as a kind of cynical concession to propriety and the old days on Grand Terre, but the rest of the time I wore a loose blouse and form-fitting breeches like the men. Jean taught me to be a pretty fair sailor—although I never could learn to navigate properly—and he delighted in watching as I manned the wheel and climbed the rigging.

When we were engaged in battle I took my place by his side, and he made no objections. My thirst for danger, my lust for adventure, everything I had dreamed about as I practiced with my swords and pistols came true, and the nightmare of that violent sea battle had vanished, the addiction for danger now deep in my blood. Jean and I gulped at life's pleasures like doomed men, as if we knew that our days together were numbered.

In the course of one particularly bitter struggle for a British brig loaded with cinnamon and indigo, a pistol ball wounded me slightly. It went cleanly through the flesh of my upper arm, but the pain and loss of blood were minimal. The incident, however, drove Jean into a deep depression. The ball, which hardly bothered me, seemed to lodge in his vitals and gnaw away at his enthusiasm. His manner with me and the men became strained, and finally he insisted that I go below decks whenever we were engaged in combat.

"It's madness, Elise, sheer madness," he said angrily. "I was a fool to let you come at all. Look at you, with your wild hair and man's dress and now this—this wound! You have no business here. I forbid you to show your face above deck when another ship is in sight."

"Jean, I'm here because this is where I want to be. You couldn't have stopped me, you know that. I am a pirate, Jean, and a good one, with no fears and no scruples.

Besides, I'm hardly hurt at all. You see, I can still move
my arm.'' I winced slightly as I did so. ''And it won't
affect our lovemaking, I promise you.''

''God help me, what have I done to you!'' he exploded.
''You even talk like a whore now. What happened to the
sweet girl who used to dance through the halls of the house
on Grand Terre in a muslin dress?''

I laughed and held him close. ''She grew up and became an outlaw, that's what happened to her. Oh, Jean, do
you think Governor Claiborne will put a price on my head,
too? I think I would like that.''

But Jean was adamant about my not appearing above
deck during battles. Whenever a foreign ship came into
view, no matter how small it was, I sulked in our cabin
with my pistols in hand, raging at his stubbornness.

One day we sighted a sail on the horizon and gave
chase. When we approached the vessel we discovered that
it wasn't a merchant ship at all, but a small schooner flying
an American flag. The two ships circled each other warily,
and even though Jean decided that she was unarmed and
not aggressive, he ordered me to go below. Furious, I
obeyed him, and I paced the floor of our cabin while I
wondered what was going on above my head. No shots
were fired, but I knew someone from the other ship had
come aboard, for I heard the splashing of oars and a bump
as a small boat came alongside and tied up to the hull of the
*Elise*.

The ship was very quiet. I felt distinctly nervous, and I
was about to go up and investigate when I heard an
unfamiliar step outside the door. I jerked my pistols up and
waited for the intruder to enter. The cabin door flew open
and Garth McClelland stood on the threshold. The old
sardonic smile played on his lips.

I pointed my weapons at his heart. ''Don't come any
further, Monsieur,'' I said in a low voice. ''What are you
doing here? Where is Lafitte?''

"Your precious Lafitte has given me permission to speak with you privately, Mademoiselle Pirate," he said. "May I come in?" Without waiting for my reply he entered the cabin, looked around, and calmly sat on the edge of the berth. "Not bad. Much better than the accommodations we shared on the *Charleston Belle,* don't you agree? I wonder where she is now?"

My aim never wavered. "She is at the bottom of the sea, along with her Captain. If you don't get out of here you will join them, I promise you."

He glanced at my pistols. "How fierce you sound, Elise. I trust you know how to use those things. Firearms can be dangerous."

"I know how to use them," I said grimly.

"Then put them down. They have served their purpose, inasmuch as I am impressed by your bravado and have duly taken note of your intention to repulse my advances. Your pirate friend assured himself that I have come in good faith—unarmed. Won't you trust me that much?"

"No." I moved to the table, where I could rest my arms and still keep him covered.

He shrugged. "Suit yourself. Naturally, the Scourge of the Gulf would not let down her guard for an instant. You should hear how New Orleans is buzzing with the news of your exploits. Jean Lafitte and his Pirate Queen, the black-haired witch of Barataria. The Spaniards are particularly impressed with you. They call you the Lady Devil. I am not surprised. I always knew you had it in you to be wicked, really wicked."

I ignored the amused glint in his eye. "What did you do with my camellia," I asked coldly, "press it in your Bible?"

"Ah." He smiled. "You should have seen your face that night. As white as the flowers you wore. I couldn't help myself."

"What do you want with me?" I demanded. "Did you

come here to tell me how shocked and surprised you are at the way little Elise is conducting herself on the high seas? I don't want to hear it. I am here by design, not by accident or coercion. I am a pirate and a good one. Piracy suits me.''

"Piracy may be the death of you.''

"So what?'' I tossed my head. "I have lived more intensely in the past two years than I did in the seventeen years that preceded them.''

"And loved more intensely?'' he asked slyly.

"Yes, if you must know.'' We watched each other for a while. I was wary and suspicious, he was calm and indulgent, willing to bide his time. "Well, you have seen what you came to see. I hope your curiosity is satisfied. Please go now, Monsieur. Your company bores me. I find you dull.''

He smirked. "You didn't always, Elise. I remember times when you found my company very stimulating indeed. In fact, you couldn't get enough of it.''

I flushed and said quickly, "What do you want with me, Garth?''

He gave a little shrug. "I have business with Lafitte. I thought I'd pay a call and see how you were getting along.''

"That's very touching,'' I sneered. "But I don't believe you.''

"I can't help that,'' he said lightly. He stood up and came towards me. "My intentions are strictly— dishonorable.''

I lifted my guns high. "If you come any closer I vow I will blow your head off. That's no idle threat. I've done it before.''

He stood at the opposite side of the table from me. "I don't doubt it, Elise.''

I jumped up and backed around the table. "Stay away from me, I tell you, stay away!"

He moved closer, backing me into a corner. My finger twitched on the trigger, and at the last moment I lowered my pistol and fired at the floor in front of his feet. The ball went wild and grazed the side of his boot, barely missing his leg. He leaped at me and gripped my shoulders in his huge hands. My wound pained me so terribly that I cried out and dropped both my pistols. He crushed me to his chest and kissed me, and I felt again the sharp stab of pleasure in my middle and the drowsy heaviness that settled in my limbs whenever I was close to him. I melted into his arms. The time that had passed since I watched them take him away to the *Eureka* was like nothing. Nothing had changed. I wanted him. He was like a maelstrom, a whirlwind, a fire storm. He possessed me and consumed me as no one else could, ever.

I clung to him, whispering, "Garth, oh, Garth!"

At that moment the door was pushed violently open and Jean Lafitte burst into the cabin. He stopped short when he saw us. "Forgive me," he said politely. "I thought I heard a shot."

Garth released me and I moved away from him. "Elise was demonstrating her accomplishments," Garth said. I glared at him. "Such remarkable talents!"

Lafitte smiled. "She is a remarkable woman, Monsieur. I can attest to that."

"I'm sure you can," said Garth. He grinned at me. I felt myself growing red with anger. "We shall meet again, I trust. On Grand Terre?" Garth addressed Lafitte.

Jean nodded. "If you wish it, Monsieur. If your business is so pressing perhaps we should discuss it here and now."

"No, no hurry. I can find my way out, Lafitte." Garth

sauntered towards the cabin door. "Mademoiselle is bleeding. I seem to have reopened an old wound." He grinned at me and went out.

Jean helped me off with my blouse. "I should have warned you against violent exercise," he said wryly.

"Oh, the—the bastard!" I said heatedly. "How dare he come here and demand to see me privately! He is rude. He is impossible! I hate him!"

"Really? I would never have guessed." Jean dabbed at the blood on my arm with his lacy handkerchief. "You know," he said casually, "he has first claim on you. You belonged to him—"

"Belonged! Claim!" I pulled away from Jean's kindly ministrations and stared at him coldly. "You talk as if I were a piece of property, or an animal that you found wandering loose in the fields! No man has a claim on me, Jean Lafitte, not even you!"

"Oh, I know that," Jean said hastily. "But he has come back into your life, Elise, and you cannot ignore him."

"Damn you!" I said fervently. "Damn all men! You knew, didn't you, Jean? You've always known that Garth McClelland was the man responsible for my being on the *Charleston Belle*. Yet you let me think it was my little secret."

"It was your privilege not to reveal his identity, Elise. The association was painful for you, and if you did not wish to be reminded of him—well, I could not blame you for that. But sailors talk, and Captain Fowler did a lot of talking before he died. Even if I didn't know before, I could have guessed after we saw Garth at the opera that night. You know how I feel about you, Elise," he said tenderly. "But he has a lot to offer a woman."

"Does he?" I asked dully. "I don't even know who he is."

Jean helped me into a clean blouse. "Well, he is the grandson of a Scottish-Irish adventurer named Stephen

McClelland who came to Louisiana many years ago. He made a fortune and married a rich Creole. His son Sean also married well, and your Garth is the issue of that union. The McClellands are well established and awesomely respectable. They own vast acres of prime land about forty miles to the north of New Orleans. His father is dead, but I believe that his mother is still alive. I have heard that Highlands is a very beautiful plantation, but I have never been invited to see it.''

"I don't believe it, Jean. He's no gentleman. He can't possibly be what you say he is. He has always treated me horribly. He is a brute and a bully.''

Lafitte chuckled. ''Perhaps you bring out the worst in him, my darling. I sense that he is not exactly immune to your charms nor are you immune to his.'' I snorted. ''He is rich and powerful. He was instrumental in winning statehood for Louisiana, and he has friends in all the right places: the Governor's mansion, Washington. When the time comes for Louisiana to choose her representatives to Congress he will certainly be elected.''

"What on earth was he doing in France?'' I wondered aloud.

"Who knows? From what you have told me I would guess that he was spying on Napoleon for President Madison. The French had a strong foothold in Haiti until a few years ago, when Jefferson's federal troops kicked them out. I suspect that Napoleon wanted to try again to establish an outpost over here, a power base. Madison must have thought him a genuine threat, one that he would do anything to subvert.

"McClelland, I imagine, must have been an obvious choice to undertake an undercover role in France. He does not lack courage, he is fluent in French, and he is familiar with the political situation in this part of the world. He is an ideal spy.''

"You don't like him, do you, Jean?''

Lafitte shrugged. "What can I say? We are like summer and winter, fire and ice. We are different in every way but one, I think: we both want you, Elise. He thinks I am a greedy, opportunistic bandit. I think he is ambitious, ruthless, and egotistical. We have had very little to do with one another up to now. If we ever clashed, I suspect one of us would die."

I leaned against him and hid my face in his frilly shirt front. "Oh, Jean," I sighed wearily, "what am I going to do?"

"Listen to your heart, Elise. Just listen to your heart. We have been good comrades, you and I, haven't we? If things don't work out you can come back to me. You're a first-rate pirate, you know. I wouldn't hesitate to give you a job."

"I don't want to leave you, Jean," I whispered.

"And I don't want you to go. But nothing remains the same. Times are changing, Elise. McClelland told me that Congress has finally declared war on England. There will be a dearth of merchant ships in this area for many months to come. I suppose I could become a privateer for the United States rather than a pirate. That's almost respectable. You don't want to stay around and watch Lafitte become respectable, do you?"

I couldn't answer him.

Two days later we anchored at Grand Terre. I saw as we entered the harbor that Garth's schooner was already there. He was waiting to greet us on the beach. Two of Lafitte's men stood near him with their pistols drawn.

"Ah, Monsieur McClelland, welcome to Grand Terre," said Lafitte graciously. "You must forgive my men. They were unsure if you come here as friend or foe, and they wisely waited for my return to find out. Will you come up to the house?"

We walked up the beach together. I wasn't fooled by Jean's casual manner. I knew that he was as tense and uncomfortable with Garth as I was. Garth, as always, remained a mystery to me. He seemed relaxed and unconcerned about Lafitte's armed warriors, and when I looked up at him I saw that he was gazing down at me with a curious little smile on his lips. I stiffened and turned my attention once again to Lafitte.

We entered the house. Garth glanced around quickly and lifted one eyebrow. I supposed that he was impressed by the richness and grandeur of a pirate's dwelling; everyone was when he saw it for the first time.

"My humble house is yours," said Lafitte. "Lily will show you to your room. You may want to bathe and change before dinner."

"There is no need to trouble yourself," Garth said. "What I have to discuss shouldn't take long."

"Oh, but we must dine first," Jean told him. "I hate to talk business on an empty stomach. Besides, Mademoiselle is tired and so am I. We need to refresh ourselves."

"Of course." Garth bowed slightly. "Until dinner, then." He followed Lily up the stairs to his room.

"Why did you invite him to stay?" I hissed at Jean when Garth had gone. "Why don't you just hear him out and then get rid of him? I—I don't want him here."

"Elise, my dear, I would not like it said that Lafitte ever refused his hospitality to anyone, particularly a friend of yours."

"He's no friend of mine," I said quickly. "I hate him!"

Lafitte grinned. "You have a peculiar way of showing your hatred. To throw yourself into your enemy's arms like that: what a clever strategy!"

"That was an accident," I said impatiently.

"I see." His tone was grave. "The boat lurched and threw the two of you together."

I looked at him, exasperated. "I never could fool you, could I, Jean?"

"No, my darling. You may be a fine pirate, but you are a terrible liar."

We had sherry in the library before dinner. Jean still resolutely avoided any talk of business, and so the three of us chatted about nothing in particular—politics, painting, the forthcoming opera season. I suspected that Lafitte was trying to unnerve his guest by postponing their confrontation, but Garth was unperturbed. He ate well, complimented his host on the fine food and wines, and seemed quite willing to let Lafitte make the next move.

I tried hard to hide the uneasiness I felt. I knew I looked my best—I was wearing a superb gown of blue watered silk with a scandalously low décolletage—and I was glad that Garth could see how I was thriving as Lafitte's mistress. But halfway through dinner my wits deserted me. I was so preoccupied with what I thought was the real purpose of Garth's visit that I contributed hardly anything to the conversation. Finally Jean suggested that we adjourn to the drawing room.

"Perhaps Mademoiselle would prefer to be excused," Garth suggested. "Our discussion might bore her."

Jean looked at me fondly and smiled. "Elise is my partner and my confidante. She knows all my secrets, and I greatly value her advice."

"Really?" Garth seemed surprised. "Then by all means, if she is willing—"

"Yes, of course," said Jean, "if you are willing, Elise."

I was annoyed. "I wish you would stop this nonsense.

Of course I am quite willing to hear what Monsieur McClelland has to say. I wouldn't miss it for the world."

I led the way to the drawing room. Jean handed around brandy and offered his guest a cigar. When we were settled in our chairs, Jean blew out a cloud of smoke and said, "Now, then, Monsieur, what brings you to Grand Terre? How may we help you?"

Garth studied the amber liquid in his glass. "Monsieur, not three weeks ago you captured a ship called the *Mont Olive,* did you not?"

Jean frowned and looked over at me. "Did we, Elise? I cannot recall."

"Yes, we did, Jean," I said. "She was sailing under a Spanish flag, remember? Carrying cocoa, coffee, cinnamon and indigo."

"Ah, yes, I remember now." Lafitte nodded briskly. "A fine ship. In fact, she is lying in my harbor at this very moment. I liked her lines and her speed. She wasn't fast enough to outrun the *Elise,* but she made a valiant try."

Garth smiled wryly. "I am glad she met with your approval. However, that ship and her cargo are mine. I must ask you to return them."

I felt as though a heavy weight had been lifted from my shoulders. Garth hadn't come here to claim me, as I had feared, but to talk about his silly ship. I was safe from him.

"Return?" Jean peered through a blue haze of cigar smoke. "But my dear sir, I do not understand. This was an American ship flying a Spanish flag, was it not? To me this means only one thing: that she was engaged in smuggling. I am truly sorry that the loss was yours, but when one thief falls victim to another thief, who can pity him? This is a chance you took when you decided to engage in this rather nefarious sideline, *mon vieux.* I can only wish that next time you may have better luck."

I sipped my brandy. "It seems to me that Monsieur McClelland is taking rather a chance, Jean, confessing to smuggling when an election is so close at hand. Whatever would your good citizens think, Monsieur, if they found out that the man whom they intend to elect to the United States Congress is no better than a common—pirate?" I smiled slyly. At my side Lafitte chuckled.

Garth took a long pull on his cigar. "Sin is a very attractive prospect for most mortals, Mademoiselle, as you have surely learned. I would hope that the voters would allow me to indulge my little hobby and not think too harshly of me. However, I had a great deal invested in this enterprise, Monsieur and Mademoiselle, and at the moment I can ill afford the loss. I must ask you once again to return the ship and her cargo to me."

Lafitte spread his hands. "Monsieur, you ask the impossible. Your goods have already been converted to cash. And I have taken such a liking to the *Mont Olive* herself that I must reluctantly refuse to part with her."

"When one plays with fire, he should not be surprised if he gets burned, right?" said Garth with a little laugh. "You will forgive me for saying so, Monsieur Lafitte, but you have a rather ungenerous spirit."

I took a breath. For a guest to say such a thing to the man who has just entertained him in grand style is unforgivably rude. I half expected Lafitte to order him out of the house.

But Jean only shrugged his shoulders and said, "I regret that you find me so, Monsieur, but there is nothing I can do."

"Monsieur McClelland's pride has sustained a rather serious blow, I suspect," I observed coolly. "He has forgotten his manners."

Garth favored me with a chilly smile. My heart thumped. "I realize that it is impossible for you to restore

my possessions to me, and I can understand that. But
perhaps you will consider a form of—compensation.''

''I might consider it, Monsieur.'' Lafitte drained his
brandy. ''What are you asking?''

''Jean!'' I spoke sharply. ''He doesn't deserve a *sou,*
you know that.''

Garth said calmly without looking at me, ''I would
accept—Mademoiselle Lesconflair.''

I could feel my color rising. ''What audacity!'' I
breathed. ''How dare you!''

Lafitte was shaking his head. ''That won't do, I fear.
You want to be paid in kind.''

''Not necessarily. I think Elise for the *Mont Olive* and
her cargo is a fair exchange. After all, you won her as the
spoils of war, did you not? And I think she wants to come
with me, don't you, Elise?''

I jumped out of my chair. ''I don't! You lying bastard!''

Garth grinned wolfishly. ''Come, come, Elise, let's not
descend to name-calling. Monsieur Lafitte is a fair man.
He won't keep you against your will.''

''I warn you, Monsieur,'' Lafitte said with dangerous
calm, ''you are being insulting. I must ask you to leave my
house.''

''But you will consider my request.'' Garth stubbed out
his cigar.

''Certainly not. Mademoiselle has said that she does not
wish to accompany you, and that is that.''

''Then,'' said Garth, rising slowly, ''if you will not
compensate me for my loss, Monsieur, I must demand
satisfaction. You are a thief, Lafitte, and I was your
victim. You have insulted me by robbing me. I cannot in
good conscience allow this slight to my honor to go
unredressed.''

''Your honor!'' I cried. ''And when did you become so

concerned with honor, Garth? Your whole life has been a mockery of honor!''

''How do you come to know so much about my whole life, Elise?'' His blue eyes flashed. ''Well, Monsieur,'' he said to Lafitte, ''will you give me satisfaction?''

Lafitte rose and tugged at his cuffs. ''With the greatest pleasure, Monsieur. Swords or guns?''

''Your choice.'' Garth sounded uninterested.

''No!'' I grabbed Jean's arm. ''This is madness, Jean. Don't let him trick you into fighting. This is what he's wanted all along, surely you can see that? This business about the ship was just a ruse. He came here to kill you, Jean!''

Lafitte looked at me sadly. ''My poor darling, do you think I am stupid? I knew this was inevitable that night we saw him at the opera. He wants you and I have you. This quarrel is as old as mankind. Don't be frightened.''

''Frightened!'' I gasped. ''I am not frightened at all. I am simply aghast at your childishness. Both of you! I am not a slave or a piece of chattel. How dare you fight over me, like two dogs over a bone? I don't want either of you, do you hear me? I refuse to allow this. I won't go with Garth and I won't stay here another minute. Stop this nonsense at once!''

Lafitte said to Garth, ''I should like the thrill of running you through, Monsieur. I suggest swords. I have a splendid collection. I am sure you will be able to find a blade that will meet with your satisfaction.''

''Shall we arrange a time?'' Garth asked off-handedly.

''Time? The time is now, Monsieur. Unless you feel that you would like to issue a more formal challenge through your seconds—''

''Not at all.'' Garth looked amused. ''I find the rigid formality of duelling tiresome. I prefer to fight, not to negotiate.''

''Good,'' said Lafitte approvingly. ''So do I. Will you

come with me, Monsieur? My ballroom is a fine place for duelling, as Mademoiselle knows. Elise, I will ask you to wait here.''

"I shall do no such thing!" I said furiously. "This —this *worm* has maneuvered you into a trap, Jean. How could you let him do it? I wash my hands of both of you! I hope you kill each other!" I clutched his arm. "For heaven's sake, Jean, be reasonable!''

Jean cupped my chin in his hand. "Elise," he said softly, "you are a fine pirate, as brave as any of my men, but at this moment you are acting just like a woman. Have you so little confidence in me? Don't you know by now that I would fight to the death for you? Now, if you don't stop your nagging so that I can concentrate on the fight I shall lock you up, is that clear?''

"Oh, Jean!" I stamped my foot. "Please listen—"

But he didn't listen. He was too bent on slaughtering his enemy to pay any more attention to me. The two men pored over Jean's collection of weapons for nearly an hour, discussing the merits of each blade as though there was a sale in the offing and not a killing.

Jean hefted a broadsword. "This is my favorite. She sings when she cuts the air, Monsieur. Listen to that. I have killed a hundred men with this sword.''

"They must have been very slow-footed men if they couldn't avoid getting stuck with that thing," Garth remarked. "It's as big as an oar.''

"Perhaps," said Lafitte, "but it can lop off a man's head with a single swipe, cleanly and swiftly. A sword like that is more like an ally than a weapon.''

"It is indeed," Garth admitted grudgingly. "May I?''

"Of course.''

Garth balanced the sword in his hand. His eyebrows moved up a half an inch. "God, it must weigh a good ten pounds.''

"Fifteen, Monsieur. But of course, if you prefer something lighter, I have some very fine rapiers."

"No, I like this one, I think." Garth slashed the air with the heavy broadsword. I cringed: I could almost feel the blade cutting into me. "I think it would be only fitting to decapitate you with your own sword, Monsieur Lafitte. I would not want you to suffer unduly."

"Have no fear of that, Monsieur McClelland," Lafitte laughed. "This thing cuts deeply and fatally. You will not escape with just a prick or a shallow wound." He shed his coat and his frilly white stock and picked up another broadsword. "Where would you like me to dispatch the remains?"

"There is no need for you to trouble yourself about that, friend," Garth told him. "I plan to live a good long life and die in bed." He flexed his brawny arm. "Would you like to bid farewell to your lady?"

"I think not." Lafitte smiled at me. "I shall enjoy her favors more after I have rid us of the nuisance that has plagued us these many months. Shall you give me a kiss for luck, Elise?" he asked gaily. I just shook my head, not trusting myself to speak. I did not want to upset Jean: any needless distraction might cost him the fight.

They saluted each other and lifted their blades. *"En garde,* Monsieur Smuggler," said Lafitte through his teeth. All traces of humor were gone now. "It is with the greatest pleasure that I hasten your journey to Hell."

"You will get there first, Monsieur Pirate," said Garth grimly. "And I pray you will hold the door for me."

I closed my eyes briefly and prayed for an earthquake or a hurricane, anything to stop this madness. I did not want Lafitte to die. He was everything to me: love and friendship and trust. And yet, when I heard the first deafening ring of their blades, I knew that I did not want Garth to die either. I didn't want to lose him again. I needed him. I desired him.

They circled each other warily at first, testing each other. I feared that Garth might have the advantage in size and strength, but I had forgotten just how quick and deadly Jean could be. He was beautiful to watch, graceful and agile as a cat. But even as he fended off the first of Garth's mighty blows I could see his arm quiver. The fair-haired man was as fierce as a lion and as strong as a bear, and I believed that it was only a matter of time before he wore Jean down.

Each man wore a look of intense concentration on his face. Once, when he dodged a deadly sweep of Garth's blade, I saw Jean beam joyously, but that was the only time he allowed himself any show of satisfaction. Garth drove him mercilessly. His mouth was set in a grim, determined line. He wanted Lafitte's blood, but Jean showed no fear. Jean was truly brave and fearless. He would go to his death thinking that no man could equal his strength and skill with a sword. I wished I had his confidence.

They began to tire. Jean wearied first, for Garth's aggressiveness put him immediately on the defensive. He had to parry and block Garth's hacking blows, but every once in a while he managed to get in a thrust of his own. His victory would come with one of those cunningly placed thrusts, if he could get close enough. Garth's face began to show signs of strain after they had been fighting for ten minutes and he hadn't even touched Lafitte. He pursued the pirate with great leaping strides. I had to admit that he was a magnificent animal, sleek and hard and ferocious. His muscles rippled under the tight dove-gray breeches that fit him like a skin. He, too, would go to his death thinking himself unequalled in battle.

Soon their white shirts were sodden with sweat. They were panting, their steps were slower, but as yet neither man had scored a touch on his opponent. My body was so tense and tight as I watched them that it ached, but I couldn't relax. I felt that two sides of my own nature were warring and that I was being torn apart.

Then Garth lunged at Lafitte, who skipped lightly to the side. The point of Garth's blade caught Jean under the ribs. He began to bleed.

"Do you surrender, Lafitte?" Garth demanded in a breathless gasp.

Lafitte shook his dark head. "To the death, *mon vieux*. I can accept nothing less, because I do not know when I have enjoyed a duel so much."

Garth charged again. Instead of backing up this time, Jean dodged to the side and transferred his sword to his left hand. He ducked down and thrust his blade at Garth, who turned nimbly and brought his own sword down on Lafitte's head as if it were an executioner's axe. I screamed, but I'm sure neither of them heard me. Lafitte slithered away from the attack and switched hands again, and this time he was close enough to his opponent to administer a swift thrust. Garth saw it coming and jumped aside, but the top of Lafitte's falling sword caught his thigh. Garth stumbled but did not fall, and blood oozed out of his wound and trickled down his leg to his boot.

"*Touché,*" Jean breathed. "And now I will finish you."

As he leaped to the attack I saw him falter. His shirt was crimson, soaked with blood. Garth's sword had cut him deeper than he knew. I saw that Garth, too, was beginning to sway unsteadily. They were hurt and exhausted, but they continued to chop away at each other with maniacal dedication. I couldn't watch them any longer.

I threw myself between them and raised my arm to fend off one of Garth's deadly blows. He caught himself just in time and flung his sword away. "Stop it!" I shrieked. "Stop it at once!"

I fell against Jean, who groaned and muttered something incoherent. His sword fell heavily to the floor.

"Stop it," I cried. "For the love of God! I'll go with you, Garth. Now, tonight, any time you say. I promise you!"

"Swear it," he wheezed. "Swear it, Elise!"

"Yes, yes, I swear. I'll swear anything, only stop this foolishness. You are no better than savages. For shame, both of you!" I turned to Jean, whose eyes were glazed and who was beginning to shiver. He had lost a lot of blood. I ripped off the ruffle of my petticoat and pressed it to the hole in his side. "Dear Heaven, Jean," I sobbed, "what good are you to anyone if you're dead?" I helped him to a chair.

I shouted at the servants who were clustered in the doorway to bring blankets and some brandy. Lily seemed to be the only one who had her wits about her, and she ran to obey. I looked around to where Garth was leaning heavily against the wall, panting.

I knelt in front of him. "You're a damn fool," I said heatedly. I shredded another strip from my petticoat and tied it around his thigh. "Why did you come here? Why couldn't you leave us alone? We weren't harming you, except for your old stupid ship, and that was your own fault. If you don't know how to arm a merchant ship properly, you shouldn't be in the business."

He laughed hollowly. "I'm no businessman, Elise. I've never owned a merchant ship in my life."

I stared at him. "You—you liar!" I pulled the bandage tightly around his thigh. He winced and sucked in his breath. "You ought to be shot. Scheming, spying vermin! I wouldn't go with you if—if it meant that I was going to be Empress of China. I refuse!"

He took hold of my arm and drew me up so that I was

facing him. He slid his arms around my waist. "You promised, dear Elise," he said huskily, "and I know you are a woman of honor."

He kissed me quickly. I pushed him away. I could hear Lafitte laughing weakly.

"So you have won her after all, my friend. I am happy to see you know how to claim your reward. She is a fine woman, but rather lively. You will need a firm hand."

I whirled on him. "Oh, he will, will he, Jean Lafitte? You have won, too, because if I had to stay with you for one more day I swear I would pick up one of these swords and chop your silly laughing head off. Winning, losing! And what have I won, may I ask? A cripple! I have won a cripple and lost one, and if you ask me, I'm right back where I started. I hope you bleed to death, both of you!"

Lafitte tried to laugh, and then he grimaced and held his side. "Ah, my darling, you are a lioness. I shall miss you, Elise. Take care of her, Garth."

"I give you my word, Lafitte." Garth slid down the wall to the floor and closed his eyes. "It was a fine duel, my friend. Next time I hope you have the sense to die. I must say, your size is deceptive. I never thought you would hold out so long."

I bundled Jean in a blanket and tilted the brandy bottle to his lips. Then I knelt at Garth's side and offered him the bottle. He drank deeply, then gripped my wrist and held it tightly. "We're going to have fun, you and I," he whispered. "I confess I have found life—and women—to be rather dull since I saw you last, my sweet. Pack your things. We're leaving immediately."

"Rubbish," I said impatiently. "You're not going anywhere tonight, except up to your room. Lily, call some of the men. We have to get these two morons to bed."

"Yes, Ma'am," said Lily. "An' then we got to get in here and scrub up the mess. It looks like there's been a pig slaughterin' in here!"

"Elise," Lafitte whispered plaintively. He sounded drunk. "Stay with me tonight. This one last night. I beseech you, Elise."

"You can sleep alone tonight, Jean," I said callously. "I have no desire to lie with a sick man."

"You are so cold, so unsympathetic," he complained.

"She's only obeying her sense of duty," Garth put in. "She will warm my bed tonight, won't you, Elise? You are mine now."

"Oh, hold your tongues, the two of you," I said crossly. "I'm sick of the sight of you." I swept out of the room and up the stairs to my room.

I could hear bumping and shouting as Lafitte's men brought the two combatants up to their rooms. They were calling to each other and praising each other's prowess with the sword, calling each other friend, and extolling my virtues as a mistress.

Lily came in when things were quiet to brush my hair. "They finished the brandy," she told me. "If they feels poorly tomorrow, it'll be from that drinkin' more than the fightin'."

"They're no better than children," I muttered. "Deadly enemies one minute and fast friends the next. I don't suppose either of them is in danger?"

"No," Lily chuckled. "Mr. McClelland lost a little more blood than Mr. Lafitte, but I guess he's got more to lose. Lord, but he's a big fellow. Good-lookin', too. You goin' with him, Miss Elise?"

"Yes, Lily," I said wearily, "I'm going with him. And God help us both."

Both men made an effort to appear at breakfast the next morning. Garth was limping badly, and Lafitte's right arm was weak and he seemed uncomfortable sitting up in a chair, but they were determinedly cheerful. Their comradeship of the night before was undimmed.

"Garth, you must stay here until you are well," Lafitte

pressed his guest. "My house and servants are at your disposal. At least let me show you around Grand Terre."

"Not this time, Jean. I need to get back to New Orleans. Governor Claiborne has asked me to report on British naval activity in the gulf. Have you seen anything?"

"Very little," Lafitte told him. "I imagine they are trying to solidify their position in Canada."

"You're probably right." Garth chewed a brioche thoughtfully. "But I suspect the Delta won't be spared. They're just biding their time." He looked up at me. "More coffee, please, Elise."

I glared at him and poured the thick steaming liquid into the cup he held out to me. "So the real purpose of your cruise around the Caribbean was not to find us after all, was it, Monsieur?" I asked coldly.

"I am a firm believer in killing numerous birds with one stone, Elise," Garth replied. "I promised myself a talk with you if the opportunity arose, and so it did."

"How convenient," I remarked acidly.

"Yes, I thought so. And now both my missions have been accomplished. I can return to New Orleans with an easy mind—and a light heart."

"You insist on leaving at once?" Lafitte asked.

"Yes. Mademoiselle and I shall sail this morning. Have you any messages for William Claiborne when I see him?"

Lafitte grinned. "Yes, tell him I shall put a bigger price on his head if he raises the price on mine. It's humiliating to be told that one is worth so little. Five hundred dollars, indeed! It is an outrage!"

Garth said, "Perhaps I can put up the extra money myself."

They laughed heartily. I stood up quickly. "I have to pack," I said hurriedly, and I turned away before either of them could see the tears in my eyes.

Jean came to my room while Lily and I were finishing

packing. He sat on the bed and nodded at Lily. She slipped away, leaving us alone.

"Well, Elise," he said softly, "our voyage together has come to an end at last."

My eyes clouded over. "Don't, Jean," I said. "Don't talk that way. I feel so strange about it. I'm not happy and I'm not sad. I don't know what I feel. Look at this." I swept my hand over the clothes and accessories that lay strewn over my bed and chairs. "If it wasn't for you—. Perhaps I should leave it all behind, for your next pirate-in-residence."

"No," he said firmly. "No one will ever take your place, Elise, you know that. And you have earned everything you possess. Your share of our takings has made you a rich woman." He shifted his weight and groaned. "Ah, this damned cut! You were very angry last night, Elise. I hope you have forgiven me. I didn't want to let you go—without a fight."

"You were magnificent, Jean," I said truthfully. "I shall always remember how brave, how gallant you were. You might even have won if—." I knelt in front of him and rested my head on his lap. "Oh, Jean, I wish it didn't have to end. You believe me, don't you?"

He stroked my hair. "Yes, I believe you. I know that you are torn apart inside. Your loyalty to me, and what you have always felt for him."

"But I hate—"

He put his fingers on my lips and shook his head. "I have always known that when he appeared I would have to give you up. He was my rival long before he came here. You don't hate him, Elise. I know that. You're not afraid of him, are you?"

"No," I whispered.

"Good. He is a hard man but—"

Lily tapped on the door and told us that Garth's boat was ready to leave.

"I hardly know him," I said. "I only know that I—I want to be with him. And perhaps we don't belong together at all. I may be back under your feet sooner than you think."

"You are always welcome here, Elise. And you will be seeing me soon, I promise you. I shall call on you when you are settled, all right?" I nodded. "Come, kiss me good-bye now. I won't go down to the beach with you. The temptation to pick up a sword again, just to keep him from taking you away, might be too strong to resist."

We kissed slowly, tenderly. Then I stood up and walked out of the room without looking back. I knew that when I left Grand Terre I would be leaving the best friend I had ever known for an uncertain future with a man who was still a stranger to me.

Lily and I walked down to the beach. Garth was waiting for us.

"Well, Garth," I said, tying on a wide-brimmed bonnet to protect my face from the glaring sun, "you see, I have kept my promise."

"You've led me quite a chase, Elise," he said. "Shall we go?"

I kissed Lily good-bye and bade farewell to the crowd of pirates who stood watching from a distance. Dominique was there, and Pierre, and all my friends from the *Mary Rose* adventure and from those last glorious weeks on the *Elise*. As Garth helped me into the small boat that would take us out to his schooner I turned and waved at them. They set up a loud cheer, and fired their pistols into the air. I ducked my head so that Garth wouldn't see the tears that came to my eyes. His men pushed us off from shore. He told me he would send the boat back for my things.

I turned my back resolutely on Grand Terre and Lafitte and looked hopefully towards the gulf and the horizon.

## X.  The House on Rue St. Charles

Garth escorted me to the small cabin on his schooner where I was to sleep.

"Not so gránd as the *Elise,* nor so humble as the *Charleston Belle,*" he said with a wave of his hand, "but it should do for a three days' sail."

I looked around. The furnishings were rough and simple but the room was clean.

I untied my bonnet and tossed it on the berth. "Thank you," I said politely. "I'm sure I shall be quite comfortable."

"The berth's not really wide enough for two," he said mischievously, "unless they're willing to endure some small discomfort in the interests of enjoying the greater pleasures—"

"I would prefer to sleep up on deck, if you don't mind," I told him briskly. "I have done it before."

He grinned. "I'm sure you have, but it won't be necessary, Elise. You may have the cabin to yourself. I won't bother you."

I raised my eyebrows. "Don't tell me you've reformed."

"No, but you have. If I tried anything here I might get my head blown off. I'm sure you brought your swords and pistols, and you have already demonstrated that you know how to use them." He walked to the cabin door. "Make yourself at home, Elise. I can wait. Longer than you, I'll wager."

I sat on the edge of the berth and combed my fingers

through my hair. "You would lose your wager, Garth. As you say, I have reformed. But I wonder, why do you want me after all this time? Is it merely curiosity, or does your taste naturally run to common thieves and pirates?"

He crossed his arms and leaned against the closed door. "My taste runs even lower than that, my dear, depending on where I am and what's available. You know, Elise, I have always felt sorry for the man who earns his living training horses for other men. He sweats and curses and earns kicks and blows from his charges, he is thrown and trampled, and when his colts mature into fine, disciplined racers he has to stand back and watch them being taken over by others who might not understand and appreciate them as he had. I break and train all my horses myself. That way I know their moods, their limitations, their temperaments."

"Oh?" I tried hard to suppress the anger I felt. "And do you always keep in touch with the virgins you have mangled, to see how well they have learned their lessons?"

He gave a shout of joyous laughter. "That would be impossible! There are far too many. But you, Elise, were my prize pupil. I was genuinely delighted to find you were still well, and looking, I must say, more beautiful than ever." He flashed me an impudent grin and went out.

My rage boiled up inside me. I tore off my slippers and hurled them at the door. "Odious dog! Vile worm!" I shouted. Then I took a breath. What was I doing? He hadn't changed a bit, and when I was with him it was as if the bad times with Fowler and the good times I had enjoyed with Lafitte had never been. I became young and hot-headed again, responding violently to his malicious teasing and his rude, pointed barbs.

For three days and two nights, as long as it took to sail upriver from the Delta to New Orleans, he made an elaborate show of keeping his distance. I sensed that he was willing to bide his time and wait patiently until I fell into his arms again. I was determined not to accommodate him; he could wait until his hair turned gray, I told myself. He would not catch me off my guard again.

On our second night out I noticed he was still limping. "Has anyone looked at your wound?" I asked him.

"No. My private physician doesn't like sailing. I've been tending to it myself."

"I'll look at it if you like," I offered.

"Oh?" he looked surprised. "I would have expected you to be squeamish about such things, Elise. But then you had these motherly impulses even on the *Charleston Belle*, if I remember correctly. Shall we go below?"

"If you like," I said calmly. "At least I know you're in no condition to chase me around the poop deck."

He took off his boots and trousers and sat on the berth. I bathed away the crusted blood and examined the wound closely. His skin felt dry and hot, and I suspected he was feverish. The old bemused smile never left his face as he watched the proceedings.

"Am I going to live?" he asked as I bathed the cut thoroughly and bandaged it again.

"I'm afraid so," I said, smoothing a strip of muslin over his firm, muscular thigh. It felt good to touch him again, I found myself thinking. Then I shook myself inwardly and administered a harsh, silent scolding. You don't feel anything for him, I insisted, nothing at all. See, your hands aren't even shaking. "I think perhaps you ought to sleep here tonight," I said. "It's warmer."

"Ah." His smile widened. "That is an unexpected invitation, Elise. I accept, gladly."

"Good." I gathered up my things and threw a shawl around my shoulders. "I prescribe brandy to help you sweat out your fever. Good night."

"I hope you never have occasion to nurse me again," he said sourly. "You've grown quite heartless, Elise."

I paused at the door. "Perhaps I have," I said thoughtfully. "But then, you've always been that way, haven't you, Garth?" I left him alone and went up to watch the banks of the Mississippi slide past as the wind caught our sails and carried us towards New Orleans. I turned my face into the breeze and laughed aloud. I seemed to have learned something from my adventures after all: for once I had had the last word when I was with him, and I loved it!

When the schooner anchored at the bottom of Canal Street we disembarked and Garth hired a carriage to take us to the Hotel Marengo on Rue Chartres. As the vehicle rumbled over the rutted, muddy streets Garth said, "At least I am spared showing you the city. You probably know it better than I do by now."

I fanned myself. "Well enough, I suppose."

"At least you were lucky enough to fall in with a man who has taste. Tell me, did Lafitte really find you clinging to a spar in the gulf after the *Charleston Belle* went down? I must have heard a hundred different versions of how you came to join him."

I shrugged. "Which version do you like best? Surely that's not important now."

"No, it's not important. I simply want to know the truth."

I said slowly, "Lafitte's men took me off the *Belle* when they boarded her. I was very ill, and Jean took me into his house and nursed me until I was well again. He was very kind to me. That's all."

"How charming. And our friend Josiah Fowler?"

"His body is at the bottom of the sea, I trust. And may his soul burn in Hell for all eternity." I could not conceal the bitterness and hatred I felt for the man, even though he was dead. I turned my face away from Garth and gazed out the window.

"I see your affection for him didn't grow after I left," Garth said laughingly.

My cheeks flamed and I whirled on him. "No, it didn't,

Garth. It's a shame you couldn't have been there to enjoy my total humiliation and degradation. You would have laughed yourself silly, I'm sure."

"Dear Elise," he said soothingly, "I didn't mean—"

"I know what you meant," I said. "It's all a great joke to you now, isn't it? Well, it's not a joke to me. That man raped and beat me. He treated me like an animal, worse than any black in that hold. When he had had enough of me he turned me over to his crew, and when they had finished with me I was almost dead. I lost the child I was carrying. That was very amusing, Garth. It was your child, and Doctor Hawthorne said I would probably never have another. If you want to know any more of the lurid details, ask me now, because in the future I will not discuss that ship or that captain or the crew."

My hands were trembling and my voice sounded brittle and sharp in my ears, but I didn't care. I plunged on. "I'm not afraid of you, Garth. I'm not afraid of any man because nothing could happen to me that could be worse than what I endured on that death ship. I asked Jean and Dominique to teach me to kill, and now I can deal out life and death just like any man. I have seen a lot since I saw you last, Garth, and I have learned a lot." I gave a short laugh. "You will be disappointed in me, I fear. The child you kidnapped from her brothers is no more. And I say good riddance to her."

His face was impassive during my recital, and when I had finished he sighed deeply and said, "Yes, I can see that you have changed, Elise." We rode on in silence for some minutes, then he said, "I misjudged you, I must confess. I thought your piracy was a parlor game, something the bored mistress of a vagabond played at because she found it amusing. But you were serious about it after all. Remarkable."

The carriage halted in front of the hotel. Garth climbed

down and offered his hand to help me. I looked up and saw Lydia Arceneaux and her son, Andre, emerging from the lobby. Her mouth dropped open.

"Why, Elise! Fancy, I haven't seen you in ages, my dear. And Monsieur McClelland! What—what a surprise. How is—ah, dear Georgette?"

"She is quite well, thank you." Garth was cool and polite.

"Please give her my regards when you see her," said Madame Arceneaux lamely. Andre blinked at us and worked his mouth soundlessly. "Such a surprise!"

"I'll do that." Garth bowed to them and took my arm. "Good day, Madame. Monsieur." We went inside.

The manager of the hotel ran over to us. "Ah, Monsieur McClelland, your suite is ready. If either you or Madame requires anything—"

"I should like a hot bath, a bottle of champagne, and a personal maid," I told him. He bowed delightedly and scurried away. I turned to Garth. "No home in the city, Garth?" I chided him. "How shocking for a man of your stature and reputation."

He smiled. "It's full of carpenters and painters at the moment, my dear. Most annoying."

"I'm sure. You know, I never saw Lydia Arceneaux at a loss for words like that before. She seemed quite surprised to find us together. Tell me, who is this Georgette she asked about?"

The manager came running up again, rubbing his hands with satisfaction. "Everything is ready, Monsieur, Madame. Your trunks are on their way up, and a young lady named Savannah has been assigned to Madame for the duration of her stay here."

"Excellent, Gaston," Garth said approvingly. "Elise," he turned to me, "I shall call on you a little later. I have some business to attend to now."

He started to move away but I rested my gloved hand on his arm and restrained him. "Who is Georgette?" I asked him again. I knew what his answer would be, but I had to hear it from his own lips, the lying traitor. "I'm too curious, I know."

He pressed my hand to his lips. "Georgette? Why, she is my wife, dear child. *Au revoir*."

Thunderstruck, I gaped after him as he left the hotel. I felt deaf, dumb and paralyzed, and I only dimly heard the manager requesting me to follow him up to my suite. When I was alone in the sitting room I stood for a full five minutes at the long window that overlooked the courtyard below. I saw nothing. My brain was tumbling around and around and I was calling myself every kind of fool. What an idiot I was! But I had never thought, never even guessed. My heart was pounding furiously and breathing was difficult. I wondered irritably if I was going to faint. I felt hot all over, then cold, then sick with fury.

I threw myself into an armchair and tried to think clearly. Damn these men! Damn Lafitte, who was so Frenchified that he took marriage for granted and never thought to mention that Garth had a wife. He must have known about her, and he must have known that Garth wanted me for his mistress, nothing more.

Well, what had I expected? That Garth would claim me for his own true love and marry me? I laughed bitterly, and the laugh became a sob that stuck in my throat. I wept silently for a few minutes. I didn't want to be his kept woman, his possession. I didn't want to be known to the citizens of New Orleans as Garth McClelland's mistress. Oh, I had been Lafitte's mistress, it was true, but my relationship with Lafitte was different, special. He was my savior and my friend. He was not married, he loved me, he had never paid for my services. I winced as I thought of the word. We had served—and loved—each other. What had I been thinking of? Why, why had I left Jean for Garth? And I couldn't go back. I was too ashamed and too embarrassed to admit that I had been so naive.

I drew myself up and said aloud, "It isn't as though I love him." But even as I spoke to the large empty room I knew that what I felt for Garth came dangerously close to love. I still wanted him, even though he had never shown me an ounce of respect or consideration. Oh, I was a fool.

There was a light tap at the door that connected the sitting and bed rooms. A thin, light-skinned Negress with clear blue eyes and pock-marked cheeks poked her head into the room.

" 'Scuse me, Ma'am, but your bath is ready."

"Thank you." I stood up and dried my eyes, thankful that I had gotten it out of my system before Garth returned. He would never see me crying for him. I would die before I showed that much weakness. "You must be Savannah?"

"Yes, Ma'am."

"Savannah, after I'm in my bath I want you to open the champagne and keep my glass filled."

"Yes, Ma'am!"

I went into the bedroom and stripped off my traveling clothes and pinned up my hair. I stepped into the steaming tub and let the blissful warmth soak the strain and sorrow out of my body. The bath and bubbling wine relaxed me, and I closed my eyes and wondered what to do next.

"Do you want me to unpack your things, Ma'am?" Savannah asked.

"No, Savannah," I said decisively, "I won't be staying here. Just look in that smaller trunk, will you? You'll find a white silk wrapper on top, and underneath there's a mauve gown and accessories. I shall need only those things and nothing more tonight, if you please." I sighed deeply. "And pour me some more champagne. I find it has a soothing effect."

"Yes, Ma'am. You sure has some beautiful things, Ma'am. You is lucky."

Lucky? I thought. Perhaps. Oh, why hadn't I known when I was well off? For a moment I hated Jean for letting me go, and then I realized that he had justly left the decision up to me. He and Garth would have fought until they were both dead, and I had intervened because —because I had really wanted to go with Garth. I stirred impatiently and watched the ripples in my bathwater lap against the sides of the tub.

Garth entered the bedroom casually, without knocking, as if he had every right to be there. I saw that he had changed into evening clothes. He poured himself some champagne, then he sat on a chair near the bath and crossed his legs nonchalantly.

"You may go, Savannah," I said softly. "I won't need you any more tonight."

She slipped silently out of the room. Ignoring Garth, I proceeded to finish my bath as though he wasn't even there. When I rose dripping out of the water, however, he came over to me and wrapped a soft towel around my shoulders. I took it without saying a word and stepped out of the tub without even glancing at the hand he extended to assist me.

I dried myself languidly, then slipped on my wrapper and sat down at the dressing table. I splashed myself liberally with *eau de cologne*, then unpinned my hair and let it cascade to my shoulders. I brushed it with strong, vigorous strokes. I was keenly aware of him sitting there, watching my every movement with those damnably cool, fathomless eyes. I sipped my wine and dawdled over my toilette, arranging my hair into ringlets around my face and drawing the rest into a fluffy chignon at the crown.

I drew on my silk stockings with slow, voluptuous movements. My wrapper was hanging open to the waist but I made no attempt to close it. Let him look, I thought. That's all he's going to get.

"I'd forgotten how really magnificent you are, Elise," he said softly. "You've grown up."

"What did you expect?" I demanded acidly before I could stop myself. "One cannot remain a whimpering virgin of seventeen forever."

Our eyes met in the mirror over the dressing table and I quickly looked away. "No, thank God," he said lightly, "even virgins can be cured."

I threw off my wrapper and slipped on a sheer organza undergarment with fine transparent lace panels over the breasts. I slid my feet into tiny kid slippers, tied the bodice of the chemise tightly so that my breasts swelled up over the top, and put on the gown that Savannah had laid out for me. It fit perfectly, hugging my bust and flaring away at the hips, but I had some difficulty with the fasteners on the back. I had dismissed Savannah prematurely, I realized with annoyance.

Garth came up behind me and pushed my clumsy fingers away. "Allow me."

"Please don't bother," I said stiffly. "I don't need any help."

"Of course you do." His fingers worked slowly and lazily. "I see that you haven't unpacked yet."

"I'm not staying."

"Oh. I'm sorry the suite doesn't meet with your satisfaction," he said calmly. "I'll ask for another room, if you like."

"It's not the suite and you know it!" I said angrily. I took a breath and forced myself to regain my self-control. "Aren't you finished yet?"

"No. Next time you want to show me how you can dress yourself, you might choose a gown with fewer than a hundred fasteners." I gritted my teeth and took in another deep breath. "Ah," he said rapturously, "your breasts still quiver when you are angry. Now don't pull away, Elise, or I'll never get you hooked up. This color suits you. I must buy you a diamond and amethyst necklace to wear with this gown. Yes, Lafitte does have taste, I'll give him that much. In clothes, women—"

"You may keep your amethysts," I said icily. "I don't care for them. And I chose this gown myself and paid for it myself. Lafitte did not have to buy my—." I bit my lips and tried to control my anger. Why did I have to let him see how much he annoyed me? Why did I always have to rise to the bait?

"Excellent," he said approvingly. "I like a girl who wants to make her own way in the world. There, done."

I put on a diamond necklace and fastened matching clips to my ears. Then I drew on my gloves and picked out a mauve silk and ivory fan. I swept past him. When I reached the door he ducked in front of me and rested his hand on the knob.

"Don't you think we should talk before we dine?" he said.

"I have no intention of dining with you," I informed him. "And as for talk—" I heard the quiver in my voice and struggled to get it under control, "as for talk," I said calmly, "we have nothing to discuss, Monsieur. Please let me pass."

"You have grown up, Elise," he marvelled. "In the old days when you were angry with me you would have thrown a vase at my head. I must congratulate you on this new maturity, my dear."

"I am not interested in your praise, Monsieur," I said levelly, meeting his gaze. "I am not interested in anything about you."

"Not even in my wife?"

My spine stiffened. Salty tears burned my eyelids.

"Why did you bring me here, Garth?" I asked in a husky voice. "To torment me? Didn't you have enough of that on the *Charleston Belle*? Do you want to punish me? For what? Because I survived that devil's madness? Why, why did you have to come back into my life at all? Why didn't the British kill you? I—I thought they had!"

He smiled grimly. "They tried, but I wasn't ready to die. Why are you so distressed, Elise? I am merely an old friend who decided to pay a call and see how you were faring." He touched my cheek. "You decided to come with me, after all."

"Bah! Liar!" I slapped his hand away. "Don't spin me any of your fairy tales. Old friend, indeed! You never felt any friendship for me at all, ever! You make me sick, you greedy bastard. I know all about men like you, Garth. You see something that attracts you and you start scheming about how to get it before you are even sure that you want it or that it will be good for you."

"I know what's good for me," he said slyly.

"You're a dog in the manger!" I shouted. "You don't really want me for yourself, but it killed you to see me with Lafitte, didn't it? What kind of idiot do you think I am? Do you think I can ever forget what you did to me? Would I have suffered any of those torments on the *Charleston Belle* if it hadn't been for you? I shall never forget those days, Garth, and I shall never forgive you. You think you can install me as your mistress in some dingy little house on a back alley, or in a room in a second-class hotel, and then come around and visit me twice a month or whenever you feel like it. No, my fine friend, I am not about to sacrifice the freedom and luxury I enjoyed on Grand Terre for that. I am my own woman now. No man owns me and no man tells me what to do. When I am ready to choose a lover *I* will choose, not he. And I would have to be a true imbecile and blind before I chose you. Let me pass!"

He shook his head. "You're as stubborn and willful as ever, Hellcat. But I let you have your say. Now I shall have mine."

He grasped my shoulders and spun me around so that my back was against the door. He towered over me and lowered his face to kiss me. I looked around desperately for a way to escape, but I was trapped. I scratched and pawed at his face, but my gloved hands made no impression at all. He laughed at me as I struggled vainly, and he captured my face between his cool hands and kissed me roughly. I bit down on his lip as hard as I could. He drew back and instinctively put his hand up to his mouth, and I seized my chance and kicked him as hard as I could on his wounded thigh. He sucked in his breath and I saw that his face was white and drawn with pain. I darted across the room, out of his reach.

"Don't come near me," I gasped. "I swear, Garth, I'll kill you if you touch me."

"You still need taming, woman," he breathed. He came towards me slowly, limping slightly on his hurt leg. I saw the dangerous light in his eyes and I fell back against the dressing table.

My groping fingers found my hairbrush and I threw it at him. It bounced off his shoulder and deterred him not at all. I felt around and grasped a heavy perfume flask. I sent it flying after the hairbrush. Then I hurled a vase, a champagne glass, a figurine. He loomed over me, his arms outstretched. I dodged one way and when he moved to follow I ducked under his arm and ran in the opposite direction.

In a panic I rooted among the stockings and lacy undergarments in my open trunk until I found the case that contained my two prized pistols—both loaded. I wrenched the lid open and snatched up one pistol. The smooth wood of the butt felt good in my hand, familiar. I whirled around and faced Garth, who was almost on top of me.

"I'll fire," I warned him breathlessly.

He lunged at me. As I pulled the trigger he knocked my arm upwards and sent the gun spinning out of my hand. The ball of the pistol buried itself harmlessly in the ceiling, sending down a shower of plaster dust. I fell backwards and he came crashing down on top of me. Stunned and winded, I closed my eyes for a minute and tried to catch my breath. When I opened them again I saw him standing astride me. He was naked and his bandage was blood-soaked. I had broken the wound open when I struck him.

I shrank away from him. "Stay away from me, Garth. I'm warning you."

Kneeling over me, he grasped the front of my gown in his two hands and rent it in two from top to bottom in one swift, strong motion. He lay panting on top of me and plunged his fingers into my dishevelled hair. I glared at him through wild eyes.

"I'd forgotten just how stimulating your company could be, Elise," he said breathlessly.

"Someday," I fumed, "someday I really will kill you. I swear it."

He made a purring noise far back in his throat and kissed me. I braced myself, certain that he was going to hurt me, but his mouth was surprisingly tender.

"Why so stiff, Elise?" he asked with an amused shake of his head. "Surely you're not afraid of me?" I muttered an obscenity. He frowned disapprovingly. "Poor little Elise. Still a wild creature with no manners, aren't you?" I prepared to spit in his face but he covered my lips with his mouth and kissed me again.

He moved his mouth slowly on mine, exploring, rediscovering. His hands began to move languidly over my body. They were cool and smooth and knowledgeable. A spasm of pleasure passed through me, leaving me limp and flushed with excitement. I felt myself relaxing under his gentle touch and a little ecstatic sigh escaped from my lips. I stirred against him. I could feel the moist stickiness of the blood on his thigh. His mouth traveled over my whole body—over my breasts, my abdomen, my thighs—to the core of my being. The old flame of longing roared up and engulfed me. I had missed him. God, how I had missed this man.

"Garth, oh, Garth," I murmured softly. I caressed him tenderly.

"Bitch," he said warmly. "Sweet, sweet bitch."

He drove his angry manhood deep into me and I took him greedily. We fused together, hot molten flesh that only an earthquake could sunder. I felt an enormous fissure opening inside me and I was sucked into breathless, pulsating darkness. There was no one like him. There would never be anyone to match him. We knew each other so well in the darkness. Why, why did we ever have to come up into the light again?

"You've learned your lessons well," Garth said later, rubbing his cheek against my hair. "Lafitte must be an excellent teacher."

"I wish you'd stop giving Jean Lafitte all the credit," I said testily. "I taught him a few things, too. You, on the other hand, haven't learned a thing since I saw you last. And you're still dreadfully hard on ladies' garments."

"They still insist on wearing clothes," he said. "That's not my fault."

I took a breath and said, "I won't be your mistress, Garth."

"I don't remember asking you," he said drowsily.

"No. No, you didn't ask. I suppose you were waiting for me to volunteer."

"Something like that." He licked my ear and nuzzled my face and neck.

"Well, I won't! Whatever I am, I'm not an adulteress." He grunted. "Was that Georgette at the opera that night?" I asked.

"Yes." He kissed the hollow of my throat and my breasts.

"Stop that! I'm trying to talk to you."

He laughed. "Forgive me, Elise. Whenever I'm with you my manners desert me. You were saying?"

"We were discussing Georgette. She's—she's rather attractive," I conceded. "Have you been married long?"

"Twelve forgettable years."

"That long?" I was astonished.

He said with mock seriousness, "I am nearly thirty-three years old, my dear little chit. Our marriage was arranged for us in accepted Creole fashion by our fathers when we were children."

"Oh." Yes, I could understand that. I recalled my ill-fated betrothal to the Baron. "Do you—do you love her?"

He sighed. "You women and your questions!" I realized then that all his women probably asked him the same thing. "Love never entered into it," he said patiently. "I married an enormous dowry and nearly two hundred thousand acres of prime land. Our plantations adjoined, you see. The McClellands went from being merely rich to being fabulously wealthy. Money is a great consolation, Elise, in a loveless marriage. You can do a lot when you have money."

"Oh, yes, I know that," I said. "You can buy yourself a seat in the Senate, and a box at the opera, and a string of mistresses a mile long." I drew away from him and pulled on my wrapper. "But you can't buy me, Garth," I said,

crossing the room to the window. "Not that you've offered, of course, but it might have come to that eventually.
I am on my own, Garth. I'm free."

"Of course you are," he agreed. "And just what do
you intend to do with your freedom, if I may ask?"

I fingered the velvet curtains at the window. "I'm not
sure yet. I have some money. I shall probably buy a little
house in town with some of it, and speculate with the rest.
Sugar or cotton—something. Jean would be happy to
advise me, I'm sure. And when I am very, very rich I shall
return to France. 'Oh, Elise,' everyone will say, 'how
well you look. You have prospered!' And I shall live in
grand style in Paris and entertain only the most important
people, like the Emperor and his brothers and advisers,
and generals in the army."

"They'll all think you made your money from whoring,
instead of from wise investing," Garth warned, laughing.

"Let them," I said tartly. "I don't care what they think.
And for lovers I shall choose only young men," I said
pointedly, "and I shall be very heartless and discard them
when I am tired of them." A light breeze was blowing
from the river. I could smell the scent of coffee and roses
and the intoxicating fragrance of sweet olive blossoms.

Garth laughed. "*Touché!* I wouldn't have told you my
true age if I'd known you would be put off by it."

I thought a minute. "It's not your age, Garth. It's
your—your coldness. For some reason it wouldn't matter
so much if you had a wife if I thought you loved her. That
sounds strange, I'm sure. But if you could love anyone,
then I might believe that you could even come to care for
me in time. If you cared for me," I said softly, more to
myself than to him, "I could forgive you anything. But as
it is, nothing has changed between us. You are still callous
and cruel, and you still take pleasure in hurting me. You

haven't learned that a woman has more to offer than a pair of breasts and soft lips and—and a warm place between her legs.''

"Then you still hate me?" Mocking laughter lurked just under his words.

"Yes," I said fervently. "With all my heart."

He came over to me and put his arms around me. "Poor Elise. You're homesick for Grand Terre, you're angry with me because I didn't tell you I had a wife, and on top of everything else you've come down with a bad case of *l'amour tristesse*. Come back to bed—''

I looked into his eyes. "It's easy enough for you to get me into your bed, Garth, but you would never be able to keep me there for very long. With all your stamina and your skill and your steed-like strength, you're no bigger inside than—than that thing you flaunt like some kind of trophy. You're dead inside. Dead, cold, and hollow, and you'll go to your grave never knowing what it was like truly to love a woman. I am sorry for you. Thank God I knew Lafitte. He was kind and selfless, and he knew how to love. If I thought that all men were like you and Josiah Fowler I would kill myself right now.''

"I wouldn't blame you one bit," he said, kissing me gently.

"You just don't understand what I've been saying, do you?" I said despairingly.

"Of course I do. You want me to ask you to be my mistress. Very well then, I'm asking. Shall we be lovers, you and I, dear Elise? Shall I call on you every day and sweep you into bed—like this—and make fierce, passionate love to you—like this?''

"No, Garth," I whispered, "you can't afford me. The only thing I want from you, you don't have to give.''

"Too bad," he said lightly. "It could have been—rather amusing."

We ate breakfast together the next morning in the sitting room.

"What are your plans for the day?" he asked. He sounded bemused and indulgent, like a father asking his child at a fair what he would like to do next.

I sipped my coffee. "First, I shall look for a house. And then I think I shall go to the Commodities Exchange and buy sugar. Lots of it."

"Really? Sugar is rather high now. Perhaps you should wait." He helped himself to a brioche and coffee.

"It will go higher," I said confidently. "The weather has been too dry for us to expect any kind of decent cane crop this year, and with the embargo on West Indian sugar, supplies will be short this winter, I think. Lafitte has a warehouse full, of course, but he won't sell if I ask him not to. By the time spring comes I shall have doubled my money."

"When did you figure all that out?" he asked, amazed.

"Last night, while you were making love to me," I said cruelly. "It wasn't hard. Lafitte was rather a pirate on land, too, and I learned a lot about business from him. That much you may give him credit for. More coffee?"

Garth shook his head. "Most remarkable. Will you permit me to accompany you today, Elise? I think I might learn something."

I shrugged. "Do as you please. But perhaps you don't want to be seen with me, Garth. It might damage your reputation."

"Oh, Lydia Arceneaux has already seen to that, I expect. Besides," he grinned impudently, "these scandalous romantic escapades only serve to enhance my reputation rather than to damage it. I'll meet you back here at eleven. You know, Elise, it has just occurred to me that there's a house you might like on Rue St. Charles. I believe the owners perished in a boating accident and that there are no heirs.''

I looked at him suspiciously. ''What are you trying to do, Garth?''

He looked genuinely hurt. ''Nothing, my dear. It was merely a thought. You don't even have to look at it if you don't want to. God knows, I don't want to interfere with your plans.''

I was somewhat mollified. ''All right, I'll look at it,'' I said. ''Thank you for remembering it.''

''Not at all.'' He tossed down his napkin and stood up. ''Until eleven, then?''

The house was perfect. Two stories high, set far back from the muddy avenue with shaded gardens and a wide veranda. And it was completely and tastefully furnished with everything I could possibly need. I fell in love with it at once.

''It's simply charming,'' I said to Monsieur Perrault, the estate agent for the deceased owners. ''How much are you asking?''

''Well, Madame, you understand we need to settle the estate as quickly as possible. There are so many legal complications after an unfortunate happening like this that it is best if we can liquidate everything as soon as possible.''

''Yes, yes,'' I said impatiently, ''but how much are you asking?''

Perrault lifted his shoulders. ''The market is very bad this time of year, Madame. And the house is completely furnished; of course, you don't have to take the furnishings, but if you do,'' he paused to pull down his waistcoat. I could hardly contain myself. ''The price for everything is two thousand dollars.''

''Two thousand!'' I exclaimed. ''But Monsieur Perrault, that is very reasonable indeed. I shall take it. House, furnishings, everything.''

He bowed. "Excellent, Madame.''

"I shall see my lawyers this very afternoon. Good day, Monsieur.'' Garth and I walked back to our carriage. "Oh, Garth,'' I said excitedly, ''it's exactly what I wanted. Small, but lovely, and convenient, and—oh, thank you so much for telling me about it. How fortunate, how delightful! I can hardly wait to move in!''

"It was a bargain,'' Garth admitted, ''although you could probably have persuaded him to take less. He seemed very eager to sell.''

"No,'' I said firmly, "I am quite satisfied with my purchase. It's truly charming,'' I raved as we rode to the lawyer's office. "And comfortable. The woman had taste, you can tell. This must be my lucky day. Jean would be pleased, I know he would.''

"Will you invite him to visit?'' Garth asked.

"Of course! I shall have parties and soirées, and perhaps I shall become renowned throughout Louisiana for my wit and hospitality. I shall have a salon, I think, and all the great minds in the country will call on me and admire me. Artists shall paint my portrait, musicians will write songs to me, and poets will do whatever it is poets do—oh, yes, they'll compose sonnets and ballads.''

"And you'll have lots of lovers,'' Garth said slyly.

"Lots? Yes, indeed,'' I laughed, ''but only one at a time! And servants. What shall I do about servants? A couple will do. I wonder if Savannah would like to come with me? I must buy her, do you think? I certainly won't own slaves. I shall buy her and set her free. We French must set an example for you crude barbarians. I wonder how much one ought to pay a maid and a butler these days? Running a house can't be that costly, can it? Jean has promised me a share of some goods that he has not yet sold. I'm sure I can manage until the spring. I must.''

I chattered on happily while Garth sat silently at my side, wearing that bemused expression on his face. He came with me to the lawyer's office and made several valuable suggestions about the best way to transfer funds and how best to expedite the purchase of the house. I was grateful for his presence, for there were times when I felt that the whole business was beyond my comprehension. Afterwards we had lunch at an elegant little tearoom not far from the St. Louis Cathedral.

He ordered champagne to celebrate. ''Tell me,'' he said, ''will you invite me to your house once you are settled?''

I swallowed some champagne. ''I shall certainly invite you to my first big party, Garth, but after that—. I'm afraid it won't be possible for me to receive you. You —you understand, don't you?''

''Certainly, knowing the way you feel about me. It's a great pity, though. You'll never find a man who understands you as I do.''

I bridled. ''What arrogance! You think you understand me, do you?''

''Where it counts, Elise. In bed.''

I dropped my fork with a clatter. The other diners looked around. ''How dare you say such a thing to me! I—I appreciate the help you've given me today, Garth, but for you to assume such a grossly possessive manner—''

''I am merely amused by the vision you have of yourself as patroness of the arts, Elise,'' he said. ''That sort of thing is all right for flat-chested, horse-faced women like De Staël who have been endowed with more brains than they need to compensate for their lack of beauty, but we both know where your talents lie.''

''I am furious with you,'' I said under my breath. ''I'm

glad you decided to pick a fight because it will make bidding you good riddance that much easier. Thank you, I can pay for my own lunch." I dug into my purse. "I don't want to owe you anything, Monsieur."

We rose to go. "Don't be an idiot, Elise," he said. "Next you'll insist that I present you with the hotel bill after you move out of the Marengo."

"Perhaps I'll do that," I said coldly.

"Don't let it get around that you're distributing your favors for nothing," he said, "or you'll have to beat the swains away from your door with a stick. Tell me, if one of them offered you a diamond necklace, would you take it?"

"I would accept it gladly," I told him, "but I won't take anything from you. Not that you would ever consider giving me anything: obviously you consider your body the most precious gift a woman can receive from you. But I don't want to feel that I am in your debt, Garth. I don't want to give you that—that advantage."

He bowed me into the carriage and told the driver to take us to the Commodities Exchange. "I won't argue with you, Elise. A woman who doesn't ask for things is as rare as snow in these parts. Now let us see if you can conquer the world of commerce."

I was the only woman on the floor of the Exchange. Trading actually stopped for a few minutes as all the men turned their heads to stare at me. Amused, I stared back boldly and unselfconsciously. I caught sight of Lafitte's agent, Pierre Montague. He saw my wave and came over.

"Monsieur Montague, I want you to help me corner the market."

The man laughed. "We would all like to do that, Mademoiselle! My guess is the only person who has even a remote chance of succeeding is Lafitte. The embargo hasn't affected him one bit. His warehouses are bulging while half the stores in New Orleans are short of goods. This war is going to make him rich."

"If you are going to accuse Jean of profiteering," I said, "then you must accuse me of the same. This war is going to make me rich, too. Is today a good day to buy?"

Montague smiled at Garth over my head. "Any day is a good day to buy, Mademoiselle Lesconflair, if you have the money."

"Good. Then I want you to act as my agent." I explained my plan. "I shall write to Jean at once, telling him everything. Your share of this venture will make you rich, too, Monsieur Montague. *Au revoir.*"

"Are you sure Lafitte will cooperate?" Garth asked when Montague had moved away. "If his warehouses are bulging, he might be rather anxious to sell, just to open up space."

"He will do better if he hangs on to his goods," I said wisely. "Suppose the British decide to blockade the river? No, the situation will not improve in the very near future, and I shall tell him so."

Garth looked impressed. "You terrify me, Elise," he said solemnly. "I should make you my business manager if I don't want to be a pauper."

"Garth, how are you!"

A young man of about twenty-five had called out the greeting as he approached us. He was tall and slender, elegantly dressed in a dark gray coat, pearl-colored trousers that fit to perfection, and a black silk waistcoat. His hair was dark brown with gold highlights, and he had fine black eyes that glowed warmly when he looked at me.

"Hello, Jacques. Elise, may I present Jacques Fournier? Jacques, Mademoiselle Lesconflair."

Jacques bowed low over my hand. "You won't remember me, Mademoiselle,'' he said with a rueful smile, ''but I competed for your hand at Madame Arceneaux's ball last spring.''

I did not remember him, but I said, ''I thought I recognized you, Monsieur Fournier.'' His face lit up and I was glad I had told him that little lie.

''Mademoiselle is moving to town, Jacques,'' Garth said conversationally.

''I am glad to hear it! We New Orleanians have long been envious of Jean Lafitte for monopolizing your company, Mademoiselle,'' Fournier said gallantly. We chatted amiably for a few minutes. At length he said, ''Perhaps I may be permitted to call upon you—''

''I would be delighted to receive you, Monsieur.''

When we were alone in our carriage Garth said, ''You'll have half the young pups in New Orleans camped on your doorstep, Elise. You won't be able to leave or enter your house without trampling them.''

''I thought he was charming,'' I said. ''His manners were exquisite.''

''Huh. Manners are something beardless boys affect when they have no—''

''Oh, for Heaven's sake, Garth,'' I said sharply, ''must you be so damnably smug all the time? Anyone who heard you would think you were the only man in Louisiana who knew what to do with a woman, and that the rest were just ignorant babies.''

''That's true enough,'' he confessed modestly.

''I suppose you have sired at least a hundred children by now?''

''Oh, twice that many, but sadly they are all illegitimate,'' he said cheerfully. ''Georgette doesn't care for children.''

''And you don't care for Georgette.''

"Very astute of you, Elise. You're right, I don't care for Georgette—as a bed partner. At other times she is a very lively companion."

I was surprised at the stab of jealousy I felt. "So are most women, given half a chance," I remarked.

"Certainly, if you like hearing about their aches and pains, their children's bathroom habits, their servant problems, or how difficult it is to find a decent milliner. Don't laugh, Elise. You have spent the past few years in the company of ruffians and vagabonds, and you have forgotten how really dull women can be. Now I prefer a woman who can converse intelligently about serious matters, like real estate and commerce—"

"You're making fun of me," I said, bristling.

Unexpectedly, he reached over and squeezed my hand apologetically. "Yes, I was," he said simply. "I'm sorry, Elise." The carriage pulled up in front of the hotel. "I seem to have left my tobacco pouch in your rooms. Do you mind if I come up for a moment?"

"Not at all." But when we got upstairs and I searched the two rooms for the tobacco I couldn't find anything. "Perhaps you left it at the lawyer's—"

"No, here it is." He drew the pouch out of his inner pocket. "Careless of me."

"If this is some kind of ruse," I began angrily.

"A venerable old trick that never fails, Elise. You've probably used it yourself."

"I haven't—"

"I merely wanted to say my farewells privately, without a curious crowd of onlookers gaping over my shoulder."

"Your—"

"I can understand the resentment you harbor against me, Elise, and I want you to know I respect your feelings even though I don't approve of them. I'm not a boor,

Elise, and I won't inflict myself on you if I am not wanted.
I'm leaving for Baton Rouge tomorrow—there's an election coming up and I'm afraid I have rather neglected the
voters lately. If you will allow me, I will avail myself of a
single visit to you in your new home when I return."

"Of course," I said weakly, confused by this sudden
shift in his strategy.

He cradled my hand in his and said, "You were right to
fight me. I would only have upset your life and made you
miserable. We're really no good for each other, I'm
afraid." He kissed my hand and then my cheek. "Good-
bye, my dear. I wish you all the luck in the world."

And then he was gone. I gazed after him with a puzzled
expression on my face. I felt cheated somehow, and
vaguely disappointed. I had thwarted his plans for me, but
I didn't feel at all triumphant. I sensed rather that he had
won this skirmish after all, although I couldn't explain
how, or why, or what he had won.

## XI.  The Demimondaine

For the first time in my life I was truly independent. I had my own house, my own servants, my own income.

"I'm glad you are happy, Elise." Jean Lafitte and I were having tea on the veranda one afternoon about a month after I had moved into the house on Rue St. Charles. "But tell me, where does our friend McClelland come into this?"

"He doesn't, Jean, that's the whole point." I tried hard to sound nonchalant. "It wouldn't have worked out between us. Too many bad memories, too much resentment. He had no part in this at all—except that he helped me find the house. Isn't it lovely?"

"Not half so lovely as its owner," Jean said warmly. "You have enough money, Elise?"

"Oh, more than enough," I assured him. "But are you quite sure that my share of the profits from our last voyage was really that great?"

"Do you doubt the accuracy of my bookkeeping?" he challenged me.

"Yes, now that you no longer have me to watch over you," I said.

"You are as insolent as ever, Elise." Jean bit into one of Savannah's frosted cakes and chewed thoughtfully. "I hear that Garth is seeing that little quadroon, Marie Duplessis. Poor fellow. His wife is very jealous, you know."

I stiffened. "No, how could I know? Really, Jean, I have never known you to take an interest in idle gossip. I don't care a whit who Garth is seeing or what his wife

299

thinks about it. And he's no more a 'poor fellow' than you are!''

"He is very good to his mistresses," Jean said.

I was amazed at the stab of jealousy that I felt. "Oh, for Heaven's sake, Jean, what are you suggesting? That I would have been better off if I had let him keep me? You don't understand, Jean. I—I didn't want it that way. I didn't want to feel as though I belonged to him.''

"Did you feel as though you belonged to me?" he asked gently.

"No. No, I didn't, but it was different with you, Jean. I don't know how to explain it.''

"You weren't in love with me," he said a trifle wistfully. "Therein lies the difference.''

"That's nonsense," I said scornfully. "It's simply not true. Only a fool would fall in love with a man like that. I am quite sure that Garth McClelland can be sweet and charming and loyal to a woman, but I have never seen that side of him. How could you allow yourself to be taken in by him? I thought you were a better judge of character than that.''

Lafitte grinned. "Very often one's judgment becomes clouded by other emotions. I disliked Garth before we met because he represented the sole threat to my love for you. Looking back, I can see now that I was mistaken, that the clarity of my thinking was disturbed by the turmoil in my heart. You may think you hate and resent him, but—''

"The idea!" My cheeks reddened. "Why, I haven't seen him in weeks, months! I am surprised at you, Jean. It's not like you to meddle like this in my affairs!''

"Forgive me, my darling." He leaned over and kissed my cheek. "I have your best interests at heart, believe me. I don't want you to be lonely.''

"Lonely!" I scoffed. "I am never lonely, Jean. Why, Jacques Fournier calls on me every day, and he writes beautiful letters as well. And he's not the only one. I get at least six letters every morning—''

Jean shook his head. "Boys, Elise, children. You are a woman, and a woman needs a man to make her happy."

"Jean, in another monent I shall have you ejected bodily! You're—you're being disgusting. I am sick and tired of you virile cavaliers who think you are the only ones who can satisfy a woman's needs. Can't a woman enjoy a friendship with a sensitive, gentle young man without you assuming that she's withering on the vine? I don't want to hear another word about it."

Savannah appeared at the French door. "Monsieur Fournier, Ma'am."

Jean sighed and stood up. "Time for me to be going, Elise. Every time I see that young whelp simpering over you I want to kick him from here to Grand Terre. I shall never understand you women, never."

"Poor Jean," I said, kissing him fondly. "He's not that bad."

Jacques came out of the house. He and Lafitte bowed formally to each other. Lafitte stayed for a few minutes chatting politely, then he excused himself.

"He hates me," Jacques said sagely, "because he is still in love with you himself. I can understand that, Elise. I don't see how a man could ever stop loving you."

"Don't talk nonsense," I said. "Jean doesn't hate you, he doesn't hate anyone. He's a very busy man, you know that."

"I'm busy, too, Elise. I've labored all morning on a poem for you. Would you like to hear it?"

I said I would, and as he read his seemingly interminable ode to my beauty I fixed an interested expression on my face and permitted my thoughts to wander. So Garth was seeing the Duplessis girl, was he? I had caught a glimpse of her at a ball one night. She was quite beautiful, and young—only sixteen. I wondered if I had begun to lose my looks. Great Heaven, I was nearly twenty! That horrid man. He was nearly old enough to be her father. I had been rather surprised that he hadn't bothered to call even once since I had moved into the house on Rue St. Charles. His actions had been typical, the scoundrel. He had used me for a night, and then gone on his way. He didn't care about me, he never had. I was delighted that I had foiled his little scheme, delighted that I would never be his whore. And I certainly didn't love him, I was sure of that. Jean was becoming just like an old woman. How could anyone love a man like Garth, especially if they knew, as I did, that he could not return that love?

"Did you like it, Elise? I meant it, every word."

I pressed Jacques' hand warmly. "It was lovely, Jacques. Simply beautiful. I am so flattered. You have such style, such wit."

"Do you think so?" He was pathetically eager for my approval. Suddenly he was on his knees in front of me, with his hands clasping mine tightly. "Elise, I love you! You must know it by now. I have never loved a woman before, not the way I love you. You are so beautiful, so much in command of yourself. You are a magnificent woman, the most gorgeous creature God ever created!"

"Dear Jacques," I protested gently, "please get up, I beg you. Of course I am very fond of you, but—"

"Marry me, Elise," he said passionately. "Right now, today! Marry me and come home to La Rêve as my wife. I want you desperately, my darling. Give me a sign, just a word. Let me hope. I beg you, Elise, say you will be mine!"

I shook my head. "It's impossible, Jacques, impossible! You are so young—"

"I am older than you are!" he cried. "I'm nearly twenty-six. I'm not a boy, Elise. I'm a man and I know what I want. I am determined to have you. You'll have everything you want, I promise you. Carriages and servants and clothes. You can give parties and balls every day if you want. Only say you will marry me. Please. Marry me!''

"Get up, Jacques," I urged him. "Can't you see that it would be a grave mistake for you to marry me? I'm not even respectable."

"That's not true!" he declared staunchly. "And even if it were it doesn't matter. Why, only yesterday I heard one of Mother's friends saying that when one was closely connected with royalty it didn't matter if one was well behaved or not. Everyone knows you're nobility, that you're Napoleon's goddaughter. Why, you'd be a brilliant match for anyone, and if you choose me, Elise, you will make me the happiest man on the face of the earth. I want you, Elise." He buried his face in my lap and murmured, "If you only knew how much I love you."

"Get up at once," I said tartly. "You—you mustn't do this, Jacques."

He raised his head. "Promise me you'll consider it, Elise. That's all I ask. Just think about what it would be like. You don't have to give me your answer today. I can wait a week, a year, a thousand years, if I know there is hope. Just give me a sign, a nod. Say that you'll think it over, my dearest. If you refuse me, I—I don't know what I'll do!''

I sighed wearily. "I will think about your offer, Jacques, I promise. Now please go. I have a slight headache and I would like to lie down before dinner."

"You're having guests this evening and you didn't invite me," he accused sullenly.

I said, "I didn't invite you because these are not very respectable people, Jacques. They're from the theater—"

"You're much more concerned with respectability than

I am,'' he grumbled. ''I have done a great many scandalous things that I wouldn't dare tell you about, Elise.''

I stifled a smile. ''I'm sure you have. Now please,
Jacques—''

''I won't go until you promise again to consider what I
have asked you.'' He squeezed my hands so tightly that
they felt numb.

I looked down at his upturned face. He was so young, so
handsome, so ardent. Perhaps I could—but no, it would
be wrong, terribly wrong. Did I really care so much about
respectability? Did I want so much to live in society again
instead of on the fringes with courtesans, actresses, quad-
roons? Since I had come to live in New Orleans alone the
best homes were closed to me. The families who had
entertained Jean Lafitte and me in grand style the year
before now snubbed and shunned me because they thought
I was something I was not, and I hated them for thinking
it. I thought ruefully that all those years I had spent at
the Chateau with the word 'honor' ringing in my ears
must have influenced me more than I knew.

Poor Jacques, gazing up at me so passionately, with all
the love he felt for me shining out of his eyes. If someone
else had looked at me like that, just once, I would have
done anything for him, gone anywhere, been low and dirty
and savage, and I would have gloried in it. But he didn't
love me. And Jacques did.

''You have my solemn word,'' I said. ''Write to me
tomorrow, as always?''

''I swear it!'' He kissed my hands and wrists. ''Oh, my
darling, we can be so happy together.''

When he had gone I closed my eyes and inhaled the
sweet fragrance of roses in the garden. I felt tired, besieged.

''That boy has it bad, if you ask me,'' Savannah
opined as she cleared away the tea things.

"They are so difficult today, Savannah," I said. "First Jean, with his absurd gossip and ridiculous suggestions, and now Jacques—. If these people give me any trouble tonight I shall scream."

Savannah grunted. "They ain't all in love with you, like those other two." She picked up the tea tray. "Seems to me the only fellow you care 'bout ain't never come here yet, and that's eatin' away at you and makin' you mean."

"Oh, Savannah," I moaned, "not you, too!" I stood up and took in a deep breath. "Once and for all," I announced to the bobbing rose heads, "I do not care about him. I shall be witty and charming and gay tonight and forget that I ever heard his name. So there!"

Savannah was not convinced. She went into the house, muttering about certain fools who couldn't see what was right before their eyes.

My party that night was a great success. The players from the French repertory company were full of theatrical gossip and amusing stories about life on the stage, and I had invited several of the dashing bloods in town who made it clear that they wanted nothing more than to be asked to stay after the party ended. I finally managed to get the last of them out the door.

"At least they was walking," George, Savannah's brother who acted as my butler and general handyman, remarked. "Some nights I has to carry them out to their carriages."

"I tried to get them out a little earlier than usual, George," I told him. "God, I'm tired. You can leave all this clearing up until morning if you like. Thank you so much for your help."

"Any time, Ma'am. Good night to you now."

"Good night. If you see Savannah, tell her that she needn't bother to come up." I climbed the stairs to my room. Instead of exhilarating me, the wine and talk and laughter had left me feeling limp and exhausted. I wanted nothing more than to crawl into my bed and let my brain drift into nothingness.

A single candle was burning on my dressing table. I removed my jewels from my ears, neck and wrists and put them in their case. Then I took off my gown and draped it over a chair so that Savannah would know that it had to be cleaned and pressed before I wore it again. I kicked off my shoes thankfully and peeled down my stockings. I massaged my legs. I felt tired to my very bones. I brushed my hair out quickly and then walked to the bed, where Savannah had laid out a fresh nightgown.

A low voice came out of the shadows. "I'm glad you didn't ask me to your party. I find theater people so dull."

I froze. "Who are you? How did you get in here?"

He was reclining on the lounge in the farthest corner from the light. I couldn't see his face. He stood up and stretched lazily. I whirled around and sat on the bed, and held the nightdress over my naked breasts.

"Surely you're not afraid of me, Elise."

"Garth!" My tiredness vanished. I was wide awake and angry. "How did you get in here? I shall call George at once!"

He laughed. "Come now, Elise. You promised me one visit, remember? But you didn't stipulate either the time I should call or the duration."

"The time is outrageous and the duration will be very brief, my friend," I said grimly. I slid the sheer gown over my head and stood up.

"Do you like your house?" he asked, ignoring my protestations. "I find it charming. What a fine-looking bed. I hope you haven't been lonely in my absence."

"Lonely!" I spat. "I have counted every day that I haven't seen you as a blessing. Why did you come here? Aren't the arms of that child Duplessis strong enough to hold you?"

"Ho! You've heard about *la belle Marie*! Yes, she is charming and beautiful. I have found her company most amusing."

"Then I suggest you return to her at once. You will find no amusement here."

"Elise," he said with mock sorrow, "you are so inhospitable. I am deeply disappointed in you. I have called on you as an old friend—"

"Bah!" I paced the floor angrily. "If you had any friendship for me at all you would have called at a more reasonable hour. I am tired, Garth, and I have had a really dreadful day. I want to go to bed—alone. Please get out of here. Oh, where have I put my pistols? I shall drive you out of here with a stick if I have to! You can't leave me alone, can you? You must take special delight in plaguing me because you know I hate you."

"Be careful, Elise," he cautioned. "If you get yourself all worked up you won't be able to sleep."

"Sleep! Sleep! Who can sleep with burglars and robbers in the room? Oh, I could spit, I am so furious." I walked right up to him and spat in his face. He calmly mopped his cheek with his handkerchief. The arrogant smile never left his lips for a moment. "Brigand! Fiend!" I raged. "Very well, Monsieur, you may sleep here tonight. The room is yours. Help yourself to anything you see—dresses, jewels, perfume—." I grabbed up a pillow and a light blanket. "I am going elsewhere."

He bounded after me and threw his arms around me before I could reach the door. "Why not wait until morning to kick me out of bed?" he asked.

"Let me go, Garth! I don't want you here. I don't want you at all. Can't you understand that?" I was practically crying with frustration.

"No, I can't understand it at all. You have brought me nothing but trouble from the first moment I set eyes on you, Hellcat, but I still want you." He gathered me roughly into his arms. "Can I help it if the Fates keep throwing us together?"

"Fates! One devil keeps throwing us together—you! Oh, dear God, how much more must I endure?" I dropped my head onto his chest with a despairing moan.

He laughed softly. "Don't think of it as enduring, Elise, but as enjoying." He stroked my hair tenderly. I trembled. "Come now, Elise, admit it. Aren't you the least bit glad to see me?"

"No," I muttered into his shirt front. I could hear his heart beating under my cheek. He felt so warm, so safe, so strong. "I despise you."

"Oh." He pushed me away gently. "I don't want to stay where I'm not wanted then." He walked towards the balcony. "Good night, Elise. Pleasant dreams."

"Come—come back here, you big bastard," I sputtered. "You might break your stupid neck!"

When Savannah came up with my breakfast coffee in the morning she brought two cups.

I frowned at her, but Garth grinned and said, "Morning, Savannah."

"Mornin', sir. Lovely day today. How you feelin' this mornin', sir?"

"Why don't you just ask him if he hurt himself climbing over the balcony last night?" I grumbled. Savannah giggled and hurried away. "I am surrounded by traitors, Judases!" I said. "But then even Judas didn't work for nothing. How much did this little adventure cost you?"

"That's my secret. Don't be too hard on them. I was very hard to resist."

"I'm sure you were," I said dryly. "I hope it was worth it?"

He folded his arms behind his head. "Well worth it, Elise, to have been able to help you baptize this bed."

I gasped. "Spies! Wretches! But don't think I've been waiting for you to call, because I haven't. I just don't go to bed with every man who wiggles his—eyebrows at me."

"Of course not. You've just been waiting for the right man to come along and here I am. I'm honored."

"I had very little choice in the matter, if you recall."

"Really?" He feigned concentration. "I seem to remember your calling me back as I was about to leave—"

"That doesn't matter," I said defensively. "You shouldn't have been here in the first place."

"Are you sorry I came?"

I looked at him. His fair hair was tousled from sleep. The sunlight that filtered through the blinds gleamed softly on his lean naked torso. His eyes were shining. I tossed my head. "You'll never get me to admit anything, Garth McClelland. Will you have some coffee?" I reached for the pot.

He intercepted my arm. "No. First things first, and I believe the best way to start the day is—"

"You really are—very hard—to resist."

He came again that night, and the night after that. I fought him, even when I was longing to throw myself in his arms, because I knew he would lose interest in me when he felt sure of me. But now I was still the quarry and he was the hunter, and he would stalk me until he had captured and tamed me.

One night he handed me a small velvet case. Inside lay an emerald and diamond ring, the most stunning piece of jewelry I had ever seen. The emerald was large and square cut, and when I held it up to the light I could see magical blue lights dancing in its mysterious depths. Even Lafitte's trove of magnificent objects contained nothing half so perfect.

I put the ring back in its case. "It's lovely." I tried to keep my voice casual. "What did you do, rob a pharaoh's tomb?"

"No. Aren't you going to try it on?"

I would have loved to see how it looked on my hand, but I swallowed and said, "No, I don't think so. I find emeralds rather overbearing and cold. Who is it for? Little Duplessis? She'll be charmed, I'm sure."

He lifted his brows. "Oh, she'd love it. But it's much too good for her. No, it's yours, Elise. Take it."

"How lovely of you, Garth," I said sweetly. "But I couldn't. Is it real?"

"Don't be a fool," he growled. "Of course it's real. Don't you want it? Are you mad or simply stupid?"

My eyes flashed. "Neither, I hope. But if I accept anything from you then I will be your mistress, don't you see?"

"No, I don't see. What have we been doing for the past three days, playing whist? If you're not my mistress what are you, my sister?"

"I am a woman of independent means and independent spirit," I said. "I have chosen to avail myself of the dubious pleasure of your company lately. So? I would not ask what that makes me, but what it makes you, my friend. You have served me very nicely indeed, but I think I might even be tiring of you—"

He stared at me, unbelieving. "Damned bitch," he breathed after a moment. "I've never known any woman like you."

I lifted my shoulders. "You and I meet on equal terms in bed. But I would not consider giving you anything to buy your loyalty. Why should you buy mine?"

"What in God's name are you talking about, Elise? Giving a token of—of friendship is not the same as negotiating a purchase—"

"It is when you are the giver, Garth. You want to dominate your women. That's easy, if they love you. But if they don't—and I don't—then you need to try another approach: brutality, seduction, or bribery. If I take anything from you, anything at all, then I put myself in the position of being a supplicant, a dependent."

"You're raving!" He laughed sharply.

"No, I'm not. I know what you're trying to do, Garth. If I thought you had a conscience I might be tempted to believe that you were trying to compensate for taking me away from my home and family. But you don't care about that. You never did. What bothers you is knowing that there is a woman living who has had the grand privilege of sharing a bed with you, and who still will not fall at your feet and sing your praises."

He crossed his arms over his chest. "I'm not a boy, Elise. I don't give a damn for your opinion of me—"

"But you do want a hold over me, Garth, and you're furious because I won't give you one."

He smirked. "But I have a hold over you. The strongest hold any man could have over a woman."

"Only because I let you have it. I'm not ashamed of enjoying your lovemaking, and I am delighted that you enjoy mine. But that's all there is to this—this relationship of ours, my old friend. I am the one woman who shall never be at your beck and call, never torment herself because she's afraid of losing you to another, never want to kill herself when you have left her for good. I know better than to give my heart to one who has no heart."

He sighed and got laboriously to his feet. "You are a child who has some remarkably quaint ideas, Elise. But at the moment I find them more tiring than amusing. I'll be going, I think."

"What?" I smiled coyly. "So you won't be staying for

a late supper and champagne? Lafitte sent over a case of some very fine—''

"I think not. I don't like playing in another man's leavings." He bowed a trifle stiffly. "Good night, Elise."

"Good night, Garth," I said coolly. "I hope Duplessis likes her *bijou*."

Savannah came in and closed the drapes and plumped up the sofa cushions. "You is plumb crazy," she said under her breath. "You is the craziest woman I ever seen. He's treatin' you like you was a queen, and givin' you jewels, and you send him away like he was dirt. His face was as white as that handkerchief you is waving in the air. He took his hat and he took his stick and he didn't say a word to me, like he usually does. That's the last we seen of him, mark my words."

"I don't know why I don't ask you and George to come in and take tea with us," I said frostily. "Then you wouldn't have to strain your ears at the keyhole."

"It didn't take no strainin' to see that you has let him get through your fingers," she retorted.

"You think so?" I rested my cheek on my palm and smiled. "I don't agree. That ring will burn a hole in his pocket. Even if he does give it to his whore—which I doubt—he'll think of me every time she wears it. In fact, every ring he sees on a woman's hand for the next week will remind him of me."

"I don't see how you can treat him like that," Savannah said. "It just don't make sense."

A full month passed before I saw him again. I forced myself not to think about him and I threw myself into a frenzy of social activities and a few casual love affairs. But when I entered a ballroom one evening on the arm of one of my faithful admirers, there he was, looking as cool and as handsome as ever. My heart leaped up to my throat when I saw him, but I nodded at him politely and smiled encouragingly, and when we danced later I was as warm and alluring as I could be.

"You haven't called on me for ages, dear Garth," I twitted him gently. "Savannah has missed you. I hear you have won your election. I am so glad. When are you leaving for Washington?"

"Not for a few months yet. You're looking well, Elise. The independent life of a demimondaine seems to agree with you."

I ignored his light sarcasm. The dance ended and he escorted me to the edge of the floor. "If I don't see you before you go," I said, "I want to wish you luck in your new career. I know you will make a success of it."

"I'll try to call on you before I leave," he said politely. I was sure he told everyone he met the same thing.

"Any time," I said airily. "You know the way. And come to the front door." I smiled mischievously and tapped his arm with my fan. "It isn't proper for a senator to climb balconies. *Au revoir.*" The orchestra struck up a cotillion and a new partner swept me away.

He came late that night. I half expected him and sent my escort home early. While I was dressing I heard voices at the front door, then he bounded up the stairs and burst into my room without knocking.

"Garth, what an unexpected pleasure," I cried gaily. "So kind of you, with your busy schedule, to come calling—"

He crushed me to his chest. "Be quiet, bitch," he said, grabbing my hair and jerking my head back. "If you say one more word I'll blacken your eyes."

We undressed each other quickly, then he hoisted me up on his shoulder and tossed me on the bed and came down on me so forcefully that I was afraid I might break apart.

The fury of his attack left me breathless but I held my tongue. I knew his capability for violence all too well, and I could tell that he was genuinely angry.

"I could strangle you," he said through his teeth. "I could twist your little head right off your stupid neck. You're nothing but a slut, a brainless flirt—"

I raked my fingernails across his naked back and sank my teeth into his shoulder. He writhed and ground his loins into mine.

"Slut." He pressed his hands around my throat. "You don't accept gifts from me because you're the first woman I've ever met who has a fair idea of her own worth," he hissed. "You're nothing, Elise. I should have tossed you to the sharks long ago."

A spark of anger flickered through me. "You did. You tossed me to human sharks and I survived. I came back from the dead, Garth, and I'll haunt you. You'll never be free of me. Never."

"I am free of you! You're nothing to me, Elise. You're a soulless bitch who distributes her favors mindlessly and cheaply. I'm finished with you."

He was determined to possess me. I was just as determined that he would not. When morning came and Savannah appeared with our coffee, he said to her, "Mademoiselle is not at home to callers today, Savannah, and she won't be going out. Is that clear?"

I sat up quickly. "I beg your pardon, Garth, but I have accepted an invitation to tea and one to a musicale this evening. Certainly I am at home, Savannah. Please put out my ivory walking dress and my parasol."

Savannah looked first at me, then at Garth. "Yessir," she said enthusiastically. "Anything you say!"

"See here, Savannah," I said loudly, "you are dismissed, fired! I shall tolerate no insubordination in my house. And George, too. You may tell him so."

Savannah smiled gamely.

"Savannah," Garth said, "if you put your head into this room just once before I call you, I'll shoot it off. Understand?"

"Yessir, I understands!"

"This is absurd," I said hotly after she had gone. "What gives you the right to dictate to me? You got what you came for, didn't you? What more do you want? Applause? Congratulations? Very well, I congratulate you. You were remarkable, superb, magnificent. There isn't a man in New Orleans who can match you."

"You should know." He lifted my hand. "A new ring. Who gave it to you?"

"I can't remember," I said vaguely. Actually it was one I had bought myself. "I think it was Pierre Moreau. Do you like it?" I flashed the little circlet of diamonds.

"And what did you give him?"

I snatched my hand away. "What do you think? I certainly didn't spend this past month hanging over my balcony, waiting for you to put in an appearance, dear Romeo. Besides, it's none of your business whom I see and what I do. You have no right to give me orders, Garth. I don't owe you a thing."

His eyes blazed. "You owe me everything. I didn't—find you this house so that you could entertain half the men in the city in your bed."

"It's my house and my bed and I shall entertain whom I please," I said angrily. "And if you don't like it you know what you can do."

He smiled grimly. "I do indeed."

"You're so naive, Garth," I said with a saucy toss of my curls. "I am not going to attend daily Mass and dose myself with saltpeter while you are away. You can't control my actions."

"I can and I will, if it means I have to chain you to my

side twenty-four hours a day. I know damned well what you're trying to do, Elise. There isn't a woman alive who can beat me at this game. I've been at it a lot longer than you have, and I've invented some of the very tricks you're using. You can't make me jealous and I will not be your willing slave. But I don't like being made a fool of. I shall have you yet, woman. On my own terms."

We quarreled and loved for a whole day and night. When he left me I knew that I had come perilously close to giving in to him, to promising him that I would be his mistress and that I would be faithful to him for as long as he wanted me. But I also knew that if I could keep my head I would win him. He would be mine, on my terms.

Later that day Savannah announced a visitor. "She says her name is Mrs. McClelland, Ma'am."

She ushered Georgette McClelland into my sitting room. I rose to greet her. She was about thirty, tall and well built, with a handsome alabaster face and corn-colored hair. She was fashionably but simply dressed in a lavender frock and shawl that made her skin seem sallower than it was. Her glance was imperious as it swept over me. She did not offer her hand and I did not offer mine.

"I came to see you because I was curious," she said bluntly.

"Won't you sit down? Perhaps you would care for coffee, Mrs. McClelland?"

She sat stiffly on the edge of a chair. Her long fingers plucked nervously at the fringe of her shawl. I thought she looked tired, and older than her years. They must have been a beautiful couple, I told myself. Then I drew myself up. She had come here because I represented a threat to her love for Garth. I would need all my wits.

"No coffee, thank you." Her eyes flickered over me. "You are much smaller than I remembered."

I couldn't resist saying, "And you are much larger."

"I don't want to fence with you, Mademoiselle," she said sharply. "My husband has spent a great deal of money on you. I wanted to see again what you were like, what he found so attractive."

"You have been misinformed, Madame," I told her. "I know your husband, yes. But he has spent no money on me, I can tell you with absolute certainty."

She pulled down the corners of her mouth. "You are a liar as well as a slut! He bought you this house, for one thing." I opened my mouth to protest. "Oh, yes, I have heard how you supposedly purchased it from the estate of some people who are now deceased, and how you paid only two thousand dollars for the house and everything in it. Two thousand!" She brought her fist down on the arm of her chair. "This house was empty until three months ago, when Garth bought it and furnished it from top to bottom. I don't know what kind of game you two are playing, or who you think you're fooling with this charade of yours. You are his whore, and the things he has given you rightfully belong to me."

"You're joking," I said slowly. "This house is mine. Mine! I—I bought it—"

"Everyone else in this city knows whose money paid for this house," she said. "You can't deny it." She stood up. Her hands were shaking violently. I felt suddenly, inexplicably sorry for her. He must have put her through Hell, I thought. "I—I hate you for this," she said thickly. "I would never have believed that he would have taken up with the castoff whore of that rascal Lafitte. It's so laughable, so—so degrading." She put her hand over her eyes and swayed unsteadily.

"You are ill, Madame," I said. "Let me get you a glass of water."

"No!" she shrieked. "No, I don't want anything from
you! I just wanted to see you face to face, I wanted to tell
you—"

She ran clumsily out of the sitting room. I heard the
front door slam. I ran to my desk. "Savannah!" I called.
"Savannah, come here at once!"

I sat down and scribbled a hasty note to Jacques: "My
dearest Jacques, I would be deeply honored to become
your wife. Don't delay in this, I beg you. I want to be
married as soon as possible." I pursed my lips and added,
"my darling. Your loving Elise."

I folded the note and handed it to Savannah. "Find a
messenger and have him deliver this to Monsieur
Fournier's house at once, immediately, now!"

She nodded wordlessly and scurried out of the room.

So he had tricked me after all. That devil must have
been laughing at me all along, every time I launched into a
splendid speech about my independence, and about how
he couldn't own me because I wouldn't let him. Let him! I
had been a blind fool, a dupe, and now I was a laughing-
stock. And my sugar speculation! I had recently received
word from Pierre Montague that my profits would be
enormous. Of course they would: as enormous as Garth
McClelland wanted them to be. Buying me, buying me
right under my very nose! Fixing it so I would be so deeply
in his debt that I could never refuse him anything. How
could I, if I didn't want him to evict me from this house?

My brain was spinning. We weren't equals at all. How
could we be? With his wealth and power he could arrange
my life to suit him, and I would have very little to say
about it. Three months! He must have had the house ready
for me when he brought me back from Grand Terre. He
hadn't been stymied when I refused to let him keep me;
oh, no, he had simply arranged things so that he could
keep me without my knowledge and consent.

"Savannah! Pack my things at once. Pack everything that wasn't here when we moved in, and leave the rest, just as it was. We must be out of here tonight."

"But Miz Elise—"

"I don't want any argument from you, do you hear me? You've probably been in on the joke from the very start, haven't you, Savannah? I suppose he's been supplementing your salary, too. Spies deserve something extra, don't they?"

"Missy, don't talk like that," Savannah said sorrowfully. "I don't know nothin' 'bout nothin', 'cept that you love him—"

"Love! What a laugh! I do not love him now, I have never, never loved him, I would kill myself if I loved him. He's a monster, an ogre, a scheming, lying devil. He always gets everything he wants, the black-hearted bastard, and this is one time he will fail. He isn't capable of being straightforward, and he doesn't know how to be honest." The black girl came over to me and put her arms around me. I rested my head on her shoulder and cried harshly. "Oh, Savannah, if he had loved me I would have done anything for him, anything! But it's not fair. I wanted to be free. He knew I wanted to be free, and he—he used me and betrayed me!"

"There, there, Missy, everything will work out fine, just you wait and see—"

I blotted my eyes and straightened my shoulders. "I am not waiting for anything. We are leaving tonight. When he comes here again this house is going to be empty, and it will look just as it did when he tricked me into buying it. He can give it to his mistress, with my blessing. Come on, we have a lot of work to do."

Jacques appeared while we were folding my gowns into a trunk.

"My dearest angel," he cried, "I came as soon as I

could! I'm so happy, Elise, I can hardly believe you've accepted me!''

"People will talk, Jacques," I warned him. "They'll call me names, and they'll say I married you for your money and your social position and your name. It won't be easy for you. And your family won't like it one bit, I'm sure.''

"But I don't care about them," he said earnestly. "I love you, Elise, and I'll spend the rest of my life making you happy, I swear it.''

I looked up at his happy, shining face. "I know you will, Jacques," I said softly. "How soon—"

"Tonight, Elise!" He clasped my hands. His palms felt cold and clammy and I had to force myself not to pull away. I concentrated on his fine, handsome face with its brilliant black eyes, deep set under finely arched brows, his sensitive mouth, his lean cheeks. He was good, he was kind, and he loved me. "I spoke to Father Jules at the Cathedral as soon as I received your message and he has promised to arrange everything for me. There won't be any problems. I'll come for you at eight, my darling.''

"No, that's too late," I said quickly. I was afraid Garth might return before I left the house. I didn't want to see him again. "I shall have my things sent to the Marengo and you can meet me there. Go now, Jacques, please. I have so much to do.''

"Yes, of course, I understand." He gazed deeply into my eyes and leaned towards me. He kissed me on the lips for the first time. His kiss was clumsy, awkward. I felt nothing. He was nervous, I told myself. Perhaps I was, too. "Good-bye, dearest Elise," he whispered. "I adore you.''

The ceremony took place in the dark, eerie cavern of the St. Louis Cathedral. Candles flickered in front of the side altars, and although the night was warm I was shivering. Jacques' hands trembled as we exchanged our vows. He was feverish with excitement and thrilled by the secrecy. I had the impression that he had never done anything furtive in his life until now, and that he was finding the experience exhilarating. Savannah and George were the only two witnesses to the ceremony. Jacques and I signed the proper documents and the other two made their marks, then I slipped my hand through Jacques' arm and we left the church.

Garth was waiting for us in the foyer. He looked at me sharply, then glanced at Jacques, then turned to me again. "What's all this?"

Jacques cleared his throat. "Congratulate us, Garth. We have just been married."

"That's absurd," Garth said to me. "What sort of trick are you trying to pull now?"

"It is no trick," I said. I drew closer to Jacques, seeking his protection and support.

Garth said, "You must be out of your mind, Elise."

"Monsieur," said Jacques stiffly, "may I remind you that you are addressing my wife?"

"Be quiet, Jacques." Garth's eyes never left my face. "Take pity on the lad, Elise—"

"I am tired, Jacques," I said. "Please take me home."

"Of course." Jacques tweaked my shawl higher around my shoulders with proprietary tenderness. Garth looked on, amused. "Good night, Garth. Please call on us at La Rêve. Mother is always glad to see you."

"I'll do that." A lewd grin split his face. "You may be sure that I shall call—as soon as it is decently possible."

Then he flung his head back and laughed long and loud.

As we climbed into our carriage I could still hear his laughter echoing along the dark, empty street. I moved closer to my new husband and swore silently that I would put Garth McClelland out of my mind and heart forever.

## XII.  Mistress of La Rêve

La Rêve, the Fournier plantation, stood on a knoll overlooking the Mississippi River halfway between Baton Rouge and New Orleans. We made the trip by boat, because in late summer the roads were ribbons of mire, virtually impassable.

Jacques stood at my side as we rounded the last bend in the river and I had my first glimpse of the sprawling white house with its encircling balcony and white colonnades. A regiment of gigantic live oak trees flanked the drive from the river road that led to the house. I could see a large group of Negroes gathered on the wharf at the foot of the slope. Some of them were waving their arms and shouting. Our boatman tooted his whistle in reply.

"They know about us, Jacques," I said, surprised.

"I decided to send word ahead," he said. "I—I wanted to prepare Mother. She'll be upset enough as it is."

The knot in my stomach tightened. I felt nervous and apprehensive about meeting his family, more nervous for Jacques than for myself. He was only beginning to realize what marriage to me meant. I squeezed his hand reassuringly, but received no answering pressure. He was still so deeply ashamed and embarrassed that he could hardly bring himself to look at me.

Our wedding night had been a farce, a travesty. We were both unnerved by our encounter with Garth at the Cathedral, and I attributed Jacques' shaking hands and stilted manner to his dislike of scenes. We decided to spend our first night together at the Hotel Marengo, away from the prying eyes and loose tongues of the family

servants who lived at the Fournier town house on Rue St.
Anne. I dismissed Savannah and George for the night. I
saw that someone had sent up champagne.

"What a lovely idea, Jacques," I exclaimed. "You are
always so thoughtful. Will you open it, please?"

"I didn't order champagne," he said dully. "Perhaps
the management—"

As we toasted each other I thought of Garth. What was
it he had said on the long ago wedding night at the
Chateau: "The object of champagne in the bridal chamber
is to alleviate embarrassment, calm the nerves, and dull
the pain."

I nearly choked on the wine. But Garth couldn't have
known about the marriage! He had seemed genuinely
surprised when he met us at the Cathedral. When he
discovered that I had left the house on Rue St. Charles, he
probably guessed that I had checked into a hotel. He came
to my room at the Marengo with champagne to appease
me, but I wasn't in my room. He asked where I might have
gone, and someone must have told him about the
Cathedral. No doubt Savannah had left word with her old
friends on the staff, just in case Garth appeared.

And now, ironically, I was drinking his champagne
with my new husband. I emptied my glass and held it out
to Jacques for more. Oh, I hated Garth McClelland, but I
had beaten him at his own game. I savored the sweet taste
of triumph.

"I am rather weary, Jacques," I said. "Will you help
with the fasteners on my dress, please?" I turned my back
to him and lifted up the coil of hair on my shoulder.

"I—you—" his hands twitched nervously. "You
shouldn't have sent Savannah away so soon," he said
hesitantly.

I smiled sweetly. "But my dear Jacques, I have a
husband now. I no longer require a maid to undress me."

He obliged me, although his hands were trembling so violently that the simple task took him nearly ten minutes. When he had finished I thanked him and said softly, "Don't keep me waiting too long, my dear." He made a squeaking noise far back in his throat and forced himself to smile.

He came to me nearly an hour later, reeking of spirits and laughing to himself. He was wearing a voluminous nightshirt with ruffles at the neck and on the cuffs. I thought he was joking.

"You look beautiful, my lord," I said teasingly. "And your costume! Most becoming. Who is your tailor, pray?"

That kind of banter would have amused Lafitte or Garth, but Jacques blushed fiercely and said, "This was a gift from my mother. She embroidered the border herself."

I tried to restrain my humor and I examined his mother's handiwork. "Why, it's beautiful, Jacques. She does exquisite work. I've never been any good at it myself. I was always running off to play with my brothers when I should have been sewing. Come, blow out the candles and come to bed. I know you must be exhausted. You've had a very trying day."

"Yes, yes I have," he agreed readily. He extinguished the candles in the room and crawled into bed. He lay there stiffly, breathing as heavily as if he had run a race. I put a hand on his arm and felt his muscles tense.

"Please try to relax, Jacques," I said. "I won't bite you. I—I love you, and I shall try and be the best wife I can be." I meant it. I would show Garth McClelland that I didn't need him to be happy. I would be mistress of La Rêve. I would help Jacques to use his brains and talents to make something of himself. If Garth could be a senator, then Jacques could be president! "Do you believe me,

Jacques?'' I asked. I moved closer to him and rested my head on his shoulder. He was as stiff as a tree trunk.

"Yes, of course I believe you, Elise. I'm tired, that's all. It's been a very exciting day for me. I've never done anything like this before."

We lay quietly for a long time. I could feel him gradually relaxing. He shifted and drew me closer to him, and I could feel his breath on my hair. He gulped, sighed, and told me that he loved me.

"Are you afraid of me, Jacques?" I asked him. "Even a little bit? Don't be. I—I won't force you—"

"What are you talking about!" he said angrily, raising himself up on his elbow. "Of course I'm not afraid of you. I've had women before, lots of them. Don't think I'm as innocent as I appear, Elise. Just because a man doesn't act like a bully or a brute, like Garth McClelland, doesn't mean he's not a man."

"I quite agree with you," I purred. "You are a true gentleman, Jacques, not an animal. I love your gentle ways, and your poetry. I could never marry a man like Garth. Never."

He touched my cheek hesitantly. "I know that," he said. "I know who you really are, Elise. You are kind and generous and you appreciate the really fine, beautiful things in life. You're not like other women. We like the same things, Elise." He licked his lips and kissed me.

I lay close to him, wondering why I felt so dead inside, so cold. I found his kisses rather repulsive: too soft, too wet, too shy. But I braced myself inwardly and told myself that I shouldn't be unreasonable and stupid and expect every man to be like Garth McClelland in bed. And then I cursed myself for thinking about Garth. I hated him. I wanted to forget him.

Suddenly Jacques sucked in his breath and rolled over

on his side with his back to me. "It's very late," he mumbled. "Good night, Elise."

"Good night, Jacques." I lay staring into the darkness long after his slow, regular breathing told me he was asleep. Hunger for a man gnawed at my vitals. I felt annoyed but not really angry. He was young. He needed time. But was he so young? an inner voice demanded. Can you imagine Garth at the age of twenty-six, rolling over on his belly and saying he was too tired to make love? A lusty animal like Garth would no more treat a woman like that than—. Oh, leave Garth out of this, I thought crossly. Garth, Garth, Garth. I'm sick to death of Garth!

The next morning Jacques told me he wanted to leave immediately for La Rêve, within the next two or three days. I agreed, thinking he might feel better about what he had done when he was on familiar ground, and we set about making arrangements for the journey. Savannah was eager to accompany us, but George told me he had received an offer from a fine gentleman in the city. I wished him luck and bade him a reluctant farewell.

And now, as I saw the pillared façade of the mansion at La Rêve shimmering above me, I prayed that we would be happy here, that I could make Jacques happy.

We stepped off the boat and the blacks swarmed around us, laughing and shouting and tugging at our hands. Jacques greeted them warmly and introduced me. Madame Fournier. I liked the way it sounded. Already marriage had given me a new name, new security, and a new home. What more could I ask? I looked past Jacques and saw a young woman running down the drive from the house. She was wearing a yellow muslin frock, and her auburn hair swirled loosely around her head.

"Jacques! Jacques!" she called excitedly. The slaves parted to let her through, and she threw herself into his arms and wrapped her thin arms around his neck. "Oh, we've been waiting for you for days, Jacques! Maman is rather perturbed by the whole thing, of course, but *I* am delighted. You must be Elise. How do you do? I am Colette, Jacques' sister. I'm sure he hasn't even mentioned me, because half the time he forgets I'm alive, don't you, Jacques?"

My husband looked happier than he had for three days. "I think about you constantly, little demon," he said. "But I couldn't tell Elise about you: she might not have married me if she knew that La Rêve had such a scamp living there."

We walked towards the house. Colette chattered constantly and danced around us like a fairy. I could feel Jacques' tension disappearing. She is good for him, I thought. I liked her a lot, but I wondered if I could possibly have been that giddy at sixteen. A great deal had happened to me in four years. I was no longer a girl, but a woman.

"Oh, Arnold is here," Colette announced with a little pout. "He rode up this morning, and I told him you had gotten married and that we were expecting you to come today sometime. He decided to wait around and kiss the bride."

Jacques mumbled something I couldn't catch. I looked at him and was surprised to see that his face was chalk white. I reached out and pressed his hand, but he pulled away from me.

"They're all gathered in the drawing room," Colette went on. "Maman and the aunts and Uncle Robert and Arnold, of course. But I was the only one who wanted to meet the boat, even though they all said I was crazy to come out in this heat. It's not that hot under the trees, is it? Elise, Jacques said in his note that you were French. I have never been to France, although Maman said I could go, but now that there's a war I don't suppose I shall ever be able to see France. Is it as beautiful as Louisiana?'' I assured her that it was. "I was afraid of that," she sighed pathetically. "I have never been out of Louisiana. I have never been anywhere except to New Orleans. You must tell me about all the places you've seen, Elise. Perhaps Maman will let us travel together sometime. Would you like that?''

I told her laughingly that I would. We mounted the steps under the portico at the front of the house. The door was opened by a black footman resplendent in red livery, and Jacques ushered us inside. The center hallway was cool and elegant, painted white with a few portraits of Fournier ancestors hanging on the walls. The footman led us directly to the drawing room.

"They told me to bring you in immediately," Colette whispered to me. "I guess they want to look you over before you get a chance to fix yourself up from the trip."

"Do I look really awful?" I wondered aloud.

"No, you look beautiful. I'm so glad you're a beauty. Papa used to say he could forgive a woman anything if she was beautiful."

Jacques' mother was seated on a sofa in the center of the room with her two sisters, Aunts Celine and Henriette. All three were dressed in black, and reminded me of crows sitting on a fence. An uncle, Robert Devereaux, was leaning languidly against the mantelpiece, smoking a cigar. As we entered the room a young man with thinning blond hair stood up from the piano at the far end of the room. He had been playing, and the silence that fell over the gathering when he stopped was thick and uncomfortable.

"Hello, everyone. This is my wife, Elise," said Jacques a little too loudly. "I hope you will make her feel welcome at La Rêve, and that you will come to love her as I do." He led me first to his mother, who nodded stiffly and did not extend her hand. The aunts looked right through me, and one of them turned her head to the side and coughed into her handkerchief. They looked like they had just smelled a most unpleasant odor. The waves of hatred and disapproval that engulfed me were so strong that for a moment I felt as though I couldn't move

Uncle Robert cast an approving eye over my breasts and hips and slowly raised my hand to his lips. He was about fifty, the husband of Aunt Celine. He held on to my hand much too long while he said jocularly to Jacques, "Well, you young scoundrel, it seems we can't trust you out of our sight for a minute." He laughed robustly. No one else joined him.

The young blond man was Arnold Charpentier. "A good friend and neighbor," Jacques explained when he introduced us. Arnold bowed over my hand. He looked familiar, but I was certain we had never met.

"I've been telling the Fourniers about your exploits, Madame," he said lightly. "I hope I haven't been too presumptuous, but we have never met a real pirate before. The experience is a most welcome one. Surely you will find marriage a rather dull proposition after the exciting life you have led."

Jacques emitted a strangled noise. I looked at him sharply. His face was white except for two red spots that burned on his cheekbones.

I drew my hand away from Arnold's icy grasp. I disliked him and distrusted him, and I felt that he wanted it that way. Why else had he brought up my past?

"Even pirates grow tired and want to retire," I told him. "A steady diet of excitement can be rather wearying, you know."

"I'm sure it can. Well, my heartiest congratulations and best wishes to you both, Monsieur and Madame Fournier. Let us hope we won't have to wait too long for an heir to La Rêve. That really will be a joyous occasion."

Everyone gasped at the ill-bred remark, but I noticed the aunts were smirking behind their fans. Colette was looking at Arnold with a distressed expression on her face, as though she couldn't quite understand his bad behavior. I hoped she wasn't falling in love with him.

"I'll be seeing you soon," said Arnold as he prepared to leave. "I'm sure Georgette will want to have a ball or a party of some sort to welcome you to these parts. Everyone will be so eager to meet you, Madame."

"Georgette?" Of course, the resemblance should have told me something. Her brother?

"My cousin, Georgette McClelland. I believe you have met her husband. He has just been elected United States Senator from Louisiana." His eyes gleamed wickedly. So he knew about Garth. She had told him. "Their plantation is the next one up the river from La Rêve. Highlands. I imagine this will give you and Garth an opportunity to become, ah, better acquainted," he said mischievously.

I bit back a retort. I didn't want to antagonize the senior Fourniers any more than I already had. Life at La Rêve wasn't going to be as easy as I had hoped. I knew I would have to work hard to win their affections, and I wasn't even sure that I wanted to be bothered. After Arnold left I pleaded weariness from our journey and asked Jacques if I could go to my room. Colette volunteered to show me upstairs, and I could have cried with relief when we closed the drawing room door on Jacques and his relations.

When we were alone in the hallway Colette impulsively threw her arms around my neck and said, "I'm sorry they were so dreadful to you, Elise. They were just a little surprised that Jacques would do such a thing, that's all. It's totally unlike him, you know. He's always been such—a paragon."

"And I'm not the kind of wife they would have chosen for him," I said a trifle bitterly. "They made that quite clear."

We went upstairs. My room was at the front of the house, overlooking the river. It was spacious and elegantly furnished in the modern French manner. The late afternoon sun was streaming in through the long windows that opened onto a balcony, and it bathed the whole room in a soft, golden glow. Colette pressed my hand and left me alone with Savannah, who was unpacking my things. I sank into a chair and let my head fall back.

"They're horrid, Savannah," I groaned. "Three wicked old ladies, a lecherous old man, and Georgette McClelland's cousin, Arnold, who is a viper with legs. I can't bear any of them. I can hardly bear Jacques right now. What on earth came over me?"

"That man came over you," Savannah grumbled. "And you was too proud and silly-minded to see that he was crazy in love with you. You think he would go to all that trouble to buy you a house and then hide it from you if he didn't love you? I never seen such a crazy woman before, never in my whole life!"

"Oh, don't scold, Savannah. I'm so tired of people who don't approve of me. Why did I come here? Why didn't I go back to France when I had the chance?"

"That man—"

"That man has never loved anyone but himself," I said sharply. "And please stop talking about him. I don't even want to hear his name, do you understand? Just one mention of Garth McClelland and out you go!"

"I don't know where I'm gonna go, less you want to send me to the slave cabins out there and make me a slave jest like the rest of these poor folks." Savannah closed a bureau drawer with unecessary force. "I'm the only free black on this place and I don't like it. I ain't no slave, and they knows that I'm not going to want to associate with the likes of them. Who am I going to associate with, you white

folks? If you holler at me again, Missy, I am going to jump
in the river and swim right back down to New Orleans.''

I went over to her and put my arms around her thin
frame. ''Don't leave me, Savannah,'' I pleaded. ''You're
the only one here I can talk to. I'll go mad if you leave me.
Please stay, and I'll promise to behave myself. It wasn't
fair of me to take it out on you.''

She patted my hand. ''We is in this together, Missy, but
I sure wish we was someplace else.''

I stood at the window, watching the setting sun casting
its fiery gleam on the shimmering water. Why did he have
to be so close? Highlands. I liked the name. Just up the
river, just out of reach. Five miles? Ten? It might as well
have been a thousand. We were separated forever now, by
barriers more insurmountable than distance.

Dinner that night was a dreary affair, and an accurate
sample of things to come. We all assembled in the drawing
room at seven-thirty for sherry. We ladies were rationed to
one small glass, but I suspected that Madame Fournier and
her sisters had already fortified themselves before they
came down. Uncle Robert had the perpetual glow of
spirits on his nose and his flushed cheeks, and I was sure
that he had whetted his appetite with whiskey before
joining us.

When James, the butler, announced dinner, Jacques
immediately took his mother's arm and led the way to the
dining room. Uncle Robert would have taken me in, but
his wife intercepted him before he got to me and I was left
to bring up the rear with Aunt Henriette and Colette. I was
furious with Jacques for attending to his mother rather
than to me. As his wife I was now mistress of La Rêve, not
she, and I would insist on being treated deferentially.

Conversation at the table was hardly scintillating: Uncle
Robert droned on and on about the war with the British and

the hardships it was bringing; Aunt Celine complained about the food, Aunt Henriette about her gout. Colette giggled occasionally and was reproved sternly by her mother. Jacques sat at the head of the table, looking truly handsome and poetic in evening dress, but his stilted speech and stiff manner betrayed his discomfort. If I had hoped that he might feel more at ease with his family than he was in New Orleans, I was disappointed.

We plodded from course to course. I drank more than my share of wine—I had a friend in James, who kept my glass filled—and the aunts' eyebrows rose and fell each time I raised or lowered my glass. I didn't care: even with my wits dulled by wine I found their company unbeliev- ably boring.

"Elise," said Jacques during a lull, "why don't you tell Maman about the Chateau Lesconflair. I am sure she would be very interested."

"Oh, yes, do, Elise," said Colette, bouncing in her chair.

"It's very large and falling apart," I said. "Uncle Theo never had enough money to keep it up, and when my brother's gambling debts made us paupers overnight, Uncle decided to sell off some of our more precious possesions."

Someone coughed. Maman lifted her water goblet to her lips. "How—ah—interesting."

"No, it wasn't very interesting," I said flatly. "The first thing to go was me. Uncle Theo sold me to a fat baron. Think of it, Jacques, you've married a would-be- baroness. Isn't it thrilling?"

Colette giggled. Frowning at her, Maman rose ab- ruptly. "Perhaps the gentlemen will excuse us." She nodded to her daughter and her sisters, who obediently followed her example. Jacques and Uncle Robert were on their feet, too. I remained stubbornly in my seat, clinging to my wine glass. "Aren't you coming, Elise?" Maman asked. "Jacques and Robert will join us for coffee in the drawing room after they have had their port."

Jacques was imploring me silently to cooperate. His eyes were suspiciously bright, and I suspected he was close to tears. I decided for his sake not to antagonize them further. I pushed back my chair and followed the other women out of the dining room.

They addressed not one word to me while we were waiting for Jacques and Robert. Aunt Celine, who had captured Colette and taken her to the opposite corner of the room from me, was talking loudly and incoherently about a niece of theirs who was born an idiot, and who still managed to marry the son of the richest Creole family in New Orleans. Maman toyed with some embroidery. Aunt Henriette complained about the sharp pain in her foot. I yawned profusely into a handkerchief. At last I heard Jacques and Uncle Robert approaching the door.

Jacques entered first. He cast me a beseeching look, then started across the room to where his mother was sitting on a long couch by herself. I jumped up and threaded my hand through the crook of his arm.

"Oh, Jacques," I twittered, "we have been having the most enchanting conversation. I love your family!"

He still insisted on proceeding to his mother's side, and when we were ready to sit I quickly positioned myself on his right so that I would be in the middle, between him and Maman. The heavy silence in our part of the room was happily broken by the arrival of coffee and a tray of sweetmeats. Then Aunt Henriette suggested a game of whist.

"I'm so tired, my darling," I said to Jacques in a husky voice that everyone else could hear. "Couldn't we go to bed?"

"Yes, of course, Elise," he said quickly. We bade his

family a hasty good night. Everyone nodded coldly to me but Colette, who hugged me so tightly that I couldn't breathe and told me in a rushed whisper that she loved me, even if the others did not.

When Jacques and I were alone in my room he turned on me with a fury I had never seen before.

"Elise, I am ashamed of you! You behaved abominably towards them, and—"

"They passed judgment on me before they even set eyes on me," I informed him tartly. "They have behaved rudely to me and have made it clear that I am not welcome at La Rêve. Why, they couldn't even bother to feign politeness for your sake, and you the master of the house! And you have not even tried to take my part, Jacques. How dare you take your mother into dinner and leave me behind with your sister and your aunts! You have hardly spoken a word to me since we came here, and you act like you don't want to look at me. Have I suddenly grown fat and ugly or old? What's the matter with you, Jacques?"

He said in a tight voice, "Nothing. Nothing is the matter with me. I was merely hurt and surprised that a lady of your breeding would act so brazenly. Why, you practically boasted of being Lafitte's companion."

I laughed. "And why not? I am not ashamed that I was his mistress. I'm not ashamed of anything I have done. I would like to see the women in your family try boarding an enemy ship. They wouldn't last a minute."

Bewildered, he shook his head. "I hardly know you, Elise. You're different. You've changed."

"It is you who have changed, Jacques. Not I. When you were away from them you played the part of the adoring lover to the hilt. You were impulsive, passionate, and eager. Why can't you be proud of me instead of feeling that you have to apologize for me?" His lips tightened. He started to leave. I grabbed his hand and held him back.

"Oh, listen to me, Jacques. Can't you see that they want to separate us? We can't let them do that. We have to present a united front. If we help and support each other, we can have a good, strong marriage that nothing, no one can shake. Please, Jacques—"

He pulled away from me and said brusquely, "I don't know what you're talking about, Elise. They're not trying to do anything of the kind. You don't understand them. And you don't understand me." He went to his room, which adjoined mine, and closed the connecting door.

I flopped into a chair and sighed deeply. I felt bruised and battered, as if I had been tossing around in the hold of a ship in a storm. Why, oh why—. But I must not look back. No regrets, no resentment. I had leaped into a hasty marriage with Jacques and I would make the best of it.

Much later, when I saw that the crack of light under his door had disappeared, I slipped on a peignoir, dabbed some perfume on my neck and shoulders, and went into his room. I could tell from his breathing that he was not asleep. and I sat on the side of his bed and put my hand lightly on his arm. He flinched slightly.

"Jacques, don't be angry with me, please," I said. "I—I want us to be happy. We mustn't quarrel like this."

"I'm sorry, Elise," he mumbled. "I should never have brought you here."

"Don't talk like that," I said. "I am here and we can be happy together, I know we can. Can't you forget everything else and remember that you love me? Please, Jacques."

He sat up and put his arms around me. His heart was thumping wildly. We sat for a long time, saying nothing, then I stroked the back of his neck and kissed him softly, again and again. His body was taut and unresilient, as though he expected me to hurt him.

"Don't be afraid, Jacques," I said. "Let me—"

I slid my hand under his nightshirt and rubbed his thigh lightly. He was so tense that he started to tremble. I persisted, working higher and higher, and suddenly, with a loud sob, he brought his hands up to my chest and pushed me away from him so violently that I almost fell off the bed.

"Leave me alone," he yelped. "Don't touch me! I—I can't stand it. Don't touch me!" Disgust filled his voice.

He rolled off the bed and stumbled across the room to the window. He leaned heavily against the panes of glass, drawing in breaths in long, shuddering gasps. I stared at him, too stunned and appalled to speak. Then I got up and went back to my own room. I saw that my hands were shaking, and that tears of shame and humiliation were coursing down my cheeks.

I had known a lot of men. Many of them had desired me, wanted me. But no man had ever been repulsed by my nearness. Had I gone too fast? Had I been too forward? But I was his wife! What had happened? I did not understand.

Then I remembered his peculiar, strained manner when he had introduced me to Arnold. I remembered Arnold's strange coldness, his pointed remarks to me, the way he had rudely wished for an heir to La Rêve. I felt cold and weak and I thought I was going to be sick. Arnold. Arnold and Jacques. No, it wasn't possible! It wasn't fair! Perhaps Jacques was just shy—. But no. The disgust and revulsion in his voice had been unmistakable. He had loved me from afar, but the prospect of intimacy with me had terrified me. I knew fear when I saw it.

I laughed weakly. What a joke. What a horrible, hideously funny joke. Our marriage wasn't a marriage at all, would never be a marriage. Oh, Garth, Garth. I remembered his laughter when he learned that Jacques and I were married. Had he known that—. No, he couldn't have known. He must never know. I had made a mistake, but I would never give Garth McClelland the satisfaction of admitting it. The marriage would have to go on. I would take my place as mistress of Jacques' plantation. I would carve out a life for myself, a position of prominence in society. I could do all these things, I knew I could. But how was I to still the persistent aching in my loins for a man?

I assumed command of the house the next day. The lines were drawn and the battle of wills between Maman and me began. It never ceased and often threatened to break into open war, but gradually I gained control of my rightful domain. I planned menus, saw to the training of new house servants, ordered new furnishings for the dining and drawing rooms. One day I asked Jacques to show me how the plantation was run.

"You wouldn't be interested in that, Elise," he said. "You wouldn't understand it."

"Then what's the harm in showing me?" I asked him. "You know I'm interested in everything about La Rêve."

We toured the grounds and the outbuildings, the slave cabins, the fields, the warehouses, the cane sheds and refining houses. Everything seemed neglected and shabby. Jacques explained apologetically that the harvest for the past few years had been poor, and that they didn't have enough slaves to work the estate properly.

"Then buy more," I said. "Or better yet hire extra men for the cutting and planting seasons only. Surely there are men willing to travel upriver from New Orleans, or down—"

"Yes, there are laborers for hire," he admitted, "but I can't afford to pay them as much as—as much as some of the other planters around here."

"You mean Garth?"

"Yes, Garth. In fact, I've been considering selling off some land to Garth if we can't make the place pay by next year. And I could sell most of the slaves, too, and we could live quite comfortably—"

"Until the money ran out," I said impatiently. "That's ridiculous, Jacques. Why don't you have a manager, an overseer, someone who can persuade the workers to try harder. Surely you have enough slaves right here."

"I had a manager," Jacques said defensively. "He went to work for someone who could pay him a better wage."

"Garth?"

"Well, yes."

"Listen to me, Jacques." I faced him. "You must never, never sell to him. You can't let him absorb La Rêve, you can't give in to him without a fight. I know he's vastly wealthy and we're not, but we can do it if we try harder. He's greedy, avaricious, venal. He'll do anything to get richer, I can see that now."

I knew in my heart that that wasn't true; Garth wasn't greedy, he was just strong and Jacques was weak. He would be a perfect fool not to buy Fournier land if it went up for sale, and Garth McClelland was no fool.

Jacques shook his head. "Don't concern yourself with this, Elise. I have done the best I could. The land is used up, depleted, that's all. Father didn't leave enough to keep us going. Please don't—"

"No. I will not allow him to take us over. Who is that big fellow over there, the one with the red scar on his throat?"

"Oh, that's Amos. Some whites in Mississippi tried to lynch him. I got him cheap."

I called the slave over. "Amos, Monsieur Jacques is going to sell off some of his land if we can't make a profit by next year. And he's going to sell you slaves, too. You know what that means?"

The big man nodded. It meant separation, heartache, a journey to a new master and a new life that might be even more difficult than the old.

"We are going to make you manager of La Rêve, Amos. We need to work longer and harder, all of us, but if we do make a profit on the crops, even this year, then I'll divide it with you. Half for the masters and half for the slaves. You can have it in cash, food, clothes, whatever you want. I'll do this every year, and eventually it will even be possible for you to buy your freedom. Do you understand what I'm saying?"

"Elise!" Jacques gasped.

"We are not going to sell to Garth McClelland!" I cried. "I'll do anything, anything to keep this land out of his hands. We can do it, Jacques, I know we can. We've got to!"

Jacques dismissed Amos curtly and said through his teeth, "This has got to stop, Elise. You've taken over the house, and upset Maman terribly in the process, but I won't let you meddle in affairs that don't concern you."

"They do concern me," I snapped. "I have no desire to be a pauper. And I have to get something out of this marriage, after all."

He flushed. "I'll—I'll divorce you. You're going too far, Elise. I'll have the marriage annulled."

"On what grounds, dear husband? Do you want me to tell the world the truth about you and Arnold Charpentier?"

He gripped my shoulder. "That's a lie! A vicious lie!"

"Is it?" I shrugged him off. "Then why haven't you touched me since our wedding night? Why do you blush and go pale at the mere mention of his name? I know love when I see it, Jacques. Love—or lust, it's the same thing.''

He slapped me sharply across the face. I pressed my hand to my burning cheek. I could feel loathing for him welling up inside me. He stared at me, his eyes burning. Then he lowered his head. ''Forgive me, Elise. I—I didn't mean to do that.''

"Let me have my way, Jacques,'' I said evenly. ''Let me try to save La Rêve. You have nothing to lose and everything to gain. And I won't interfere with your life. What you do is your business. Only let me run the plantation.''

''All right,'' he said sullenly. ''But I don't think it will work.''

I worked from early morning until late at night, trying to salvage that year's cane crop and planning for the years to come. The fields that were under water half the year anyway I decided to put into rice. Amos and his men worked so hard at harvest time that even Jacques was forced to admit that he had never known the task to be completed so quickly and efficiently. I changed my plans about redecorating the drawing and dining rooms and cancelled my orders for new drapes and carpets through-out the house. I kept an even stricter eye on the household budget and ruthlessly eliminated waste wherever I found it. Uncle Robert had to go without his usual vast quantities of whiskey, the ladies made do with last year's gowns, and once the servants understood that thieving and pilfering might cost them dearly—in cash—they began to police each other. The family chafed under my authoritarian rule, but by the end of the year 1812, La Rêve was less deeply in debt than any of the Fourniers would have dreamed possible.

At Christmas Senator and Mrs. McClelland invited us to a ball at Highlands. It was the first and only invitation

we had received since I came to La Rêve, and I knew that
Garth was responsible. He was undoubtedly curious about
Jacques and me, and since he had nothing to lose by
associating with us he had pressed Georgette to invite us.

I welcomed the opportunity to get away from the crushing responsibilities at La Rêve, even for one evening. I
found myself looking forward to the ball as eagerly as if it
were my first. I would not admit that I was excited by the
prospect of seeing Garth after so many months, but I chose
my gown and accessories with great care. Savannah and I
finally decided on a sleek and simple gown of sheer ivory
silk. The bodice was cut dangerously low, and the big
puffed sleeves hung well off the shoulders. The skirt fit
tightly across the front of my body and gathered into a
graceful fullness at the back, allowing ample room to
dance. At my neck I would wear only the string of
pearls Lafitte had given me, and smaller pearls on my
ears.

When I came upstairs on the afternoon of the ball, I
discovered that someone had slashed my beautiful gown
to ribbons.

"I never seen who it was, Missy," Savannah wailed.
"I went downstairs to see about your bath, and I never
even looked in your wardrobe until now. Oh, Missy, what
are we goin' to do?"

"It's all right, Savannah," I said quietly. "I have other
gowns. I wonder if perhaps it wasn't modest enough for
one of the older ladies in the house?"

Except for Colette they all hated me. To them I was
the interloper, a tyrant and a bully. And one of them had
decided to exact this petty revenge. I threw open the doors
of my wardrobe and contemplated its contents. "I want
something sheer and indecent, like—like mosquito netting. Ah, here we are." I held up a sheer, flimsy gown of
black pleated silk.

"But—but that a *nightie*," Savannah giggled. "An' it's black!"

"I can see that. What's wrong with wearing black? The aunts wear it all the time. I'll wear a white chemise underneath, and I'll poke a single red camellia—here, help me put it on." I tore off my muslin dress and slipped the wisp of a garment over my head. Only two narrow black ribbons held up the bodice, which was cut square and very low. My breasts billowed over the top of the gown, the white flesh providing a stunning contrast to the dark fabric. The skirt hung in soft folds over my hips and thighs, and when I whirled around the millions of tiny pleats opened and the dress fanned around me like a black cloud.

"Yes," I said grimly, "that's the effect I want, all right. We'll tear off this lace—there!—and sew on some black velvet ribbons for trim and for a sash, and we'll let the ends trail down in back. Hurry, Savannah, I don't want to be late. I have slippers and gloves to match somewhere. And look, here are some black stockings! Yes, I remember, Garth liked those. No jewelry, though. Just a simple black velvet ribbon at my throat. I certainly don't want to spoil the simplicity of the gown."

"You is goin' to look like the Debil's sister," Savannah declared. "Those aunts ain't goin' to like this at all!"

"Good," I said with deep satisfaction. "They're going to be sorry they started it, Savannah."

I wore a black velvet cloak over my gown during the drive to Highlands. I saw that Maman was watching me attentively, with just the slightest suggestion of a smirk on her lips. I sat back in the carriage and smiled benignly at all of them, biding my time.

Highlands wasn't at all what I had expected. Instead of the usual sprawling home that betrayed Spanish or French influences, the house was a masterpiece of Georgian symmetry. It was red brick, an unusual choice for that part of the country where lumber was so plentiful, and it reminded me of the English country homes I had visited as a child. In the gathering darkness I could glimpse formal gardens with marble statuary, a sweeping driveway that circled around a gorgeous marble fountain, and a gazebo perched on a knoll that overlooked the river. Highlands was the home of a wealthy, aristocratic man who had a solid belief in his own tastes. I wished it had been otherwise: I wished I didn't have to envy Georgette her home as well as her husband.

We ladies were shown immediately to an upstairs bedroom where we could divest ourselves of our wraps and make any adjustments to our costumes that were necessary. A maid helped me off with my cloak and I heard a horrified gasp behind me.

"What's the matter, Maman?" I asked without even turning my head. "Don't you care for my gown?"

"It's indecent, girl! Wicked!" she said in a voice choked with anger. "I cannot allow you to appear in front of our hosts dressed like some kind of—of siren!"

"Then you should have left your scissors in your sewing basket. My gown needed no alteration, thank you."

"That's a lie," she sputtered. "You can't—"

"Don't be a fool. Of course I can." I swept passed her, out of the room. Colette ran after me.

"Oh, Elise, I'm sorry," she said. "I saw her going into your room, but I never dreamed—"

"It's all right, Colette. I'm rather glad it happened. It might teach them a lesson. But forget about me and have a good time. I rather think I'm going to enjoy myself tonight."

Jacques and Garth were standing together at the foot of the broad center staircase. Jacques saw me first and he went white. I descended slowly, my skirts billowing softly around my legs. Garth looked up, and when our eyes met I could feel a rush of warmth passing through me. The hallway was jammed with guests. A gradual hush fell over the assembly, and then scattered murmurs rattled through the chamber like dry leaves on an autumn day. I paused in the middle of the staircase and smiled triumphantly. They had all treated me like a thief, a pirate, a siren. And now they could see for themselves that I was everything they had expected—and more.

"Madame Fournier?" Garth offered his hand. I rested my gloved hand on his. "Your husband has been telling me about your plans for La Rêve. Remember, any time you're willing to sell, I'm willing to buy."

"I'm sure you are, Senator," I said. "I'm eager to buy, too. How much are you asking for that swamp land at the southwest corner of your property?"

"Why?" He smiled. "Are you going to turn it into a rice field?"

"I might. Will you sell?"

"I'll consider it. It hasn't taken you long to become an expert planter, I see."

"I had to learn quickly," I said. "I made a bad bargain with some property once, and I don't want to be cheated again."

He laughed heartily, and that seemed to dissolve the tension in the room. Garth excused himself momentarily to attend to his other guests. I casually looped my hand under Jacques' arm and we went into the ballroom.

"This is a disgrace, an outrage," he muttered under his breath.

"It is indeed," I agreed. "He has no use for that land. I don't know why he won't sell."

"I'm not talking about the land. I'm sick of land, sick of La Rêve, and I'm sick of you. I'm talking about that obscene thing you're wearing. Have you no shame?"

"Not very much," I said placidly. "But then, neither

have you, dear husband. You've been sneaking out of the house to meet your lover, haven't you? Why be so furtive? Why not invite him to move in?''

''You—you've been spying on me,'' he hissed. ''I'll never forgive you for that. I could kill you, Elise!''

Garth and Georgette led the ball with the first dance, a cotillion, and he claimed me for the waltz that followed.

''I wouldn't want you to be a wallflower,'' he said with a little grin. ''All the wives and sweethearts in this room have given strict orders to their men to leave you alone.''

''Perhaps the gentlemen will follow your bad example,'' I said. ''Did your wife give you strict orders?''

''Do you think I would have paid any attention to her if she had?''

His arm tightened around my waist and we went spinning around the room. ''Every time I see you I'm always surprised and delighted all over again at how beautiful you are, Elise,'' he said. ''When we're apart I'm too busy fuming over your insults and your loose behavior and your mad schemes to give much thought to your beauty. Take this marriage, for instance. Fournier, of all people! I hope he treats you well, although I don't think he's man enough for you. I'm sure you're working yourself so hard during the day so you'll be too exhausted at night to think about what you're missing.''

This was so close to the truth that I stopped dancing abruptly and faced him angrily. Another swirling couple barged into us, and we all nearly went sprawling in a heap.

''How dare you talk to me that way!'' My eyes flashed fire. ''I—I'm a married woman now—''

He laughed sharply. ''Hah! And you think that marriage automatically makes you immune to assault from me, right? I'm no great defender of marriage vows, Elise. I have never respected my own, and I'm certainly not going to respect yours.''

''I won't dance with you. Let me go at once.''

He picked me up and whirled me around. My feet never touched the floor. ''Don't kick so, Elise,'' he scolded. ''They are all watching; they'll think I'm trying to carry you off to bed. If we fight like lovers they'll assume you're willing, and they would be right.''

''For Heaven's sake, put me down,'' I implored in a whisper. He obeyed and once again we circled the floor sedately.

''Do you remember that night at the opera? I knew you had come in even before I saw you.'' His lips were very close to my ear. I closed my eyes and let myself drift in his arms. ''I could feel you, smell you, sense you. I knew then that I had to have you, Elise. And when Lafitte loudly informed the entire audience that he was taking you home to bed, I wanted to run him through then and there. Sheer animal envy, I suppose. He was right—a quarrel as old as mankind. You bring out the worst in me, Elise. You always have. And I bring out the best in you.''

''You are still as arrogant as ever.'' I tried to keep my voice calm.

''I certainly hope so. Why don't you fan yourself briskly and ask me to take you out for some fresh air?''

''I'll do no such thing. I don't take orders from you!''

''Still the same, stubborn Elise,'' he chuckled. ''Do as I say or I swear I'll take you right here in the middle of the ballroom floor.''

I smiled up at him. ''Your ancestors will be shocked, Monsieur.''

''They will be delighted. My grandfather was a stable-boy, as was his father before him. There are no heroes, no crusaders in the McClelland family, and no honor to uphold. Come.''

We made our way through the crowd and went out through open French doors to a small garden. The cool of the December evening was refreshing after the warmth

and stuffiness of the ballroom. Garth led me to a marble
bench in a secluded corner of the garden.

"Ah, this is delightful," I exclaimed. "Will you bring
me some champagne, Monsieur?" I asked coyly.

"No." He took me in his arms and crushed me to his
chest. He buried his face in my neck and kneaded my flesh
roughly. I whimpered softly. "I've missed you, Elise,"
he said. "God knows I've missed you."

"Why?" I demanded, gasping. "Are there no women
in Washington?"

"None like you." He ravished my mouth with his
tongue, and I felt my legs turning to water.

I caressed his cheeks and combed my fingers through
his hair. Arching my back, I pressed close to him, so close
that I could hear the firm thudding of his heart and feel the
hardness of him pushing insistently against me. I had
never known that desire could be so agonizing, so painful.
I craved him with every ounce of my being, with all my
heart and soul. I knew he was only toying with me,
playing with me. I hated him for it and I hated myself, but I
was powerless to fight the passion that held me in its grip.

From a long way away I heard a footstep crunch on the
gravel and a sneering voice. "I beg your pardon. I seem to
have interrupted something."

Garth cursed under his breath and I looked up. Arnold
stood on the path, his arms crossed over his chest and an
expression of mild amusement on his face. Georgette was
standing a few paces behind him. I slid off the bench and
turned my back on them. I was still shaking with frustrated
desire, and now with shame and fury. I hated Garth for
compromising me like this. I hated all of them.

"Really, Garth." Georgette's voice was heavy with
loathing. "Couldn't you even wait five minutes before
you and your trollop ran off to the bushes?"

"Apparently not," he said lightly. He put his hand on

my arm. "Come, Elise, shall we go back in? It seems that Georgette and Arnold are also looking for a private place."

"You filthy liar!" Georgette hissed. "How dare you insinuate that I am like—like this little slut. Oh, I could murder you, Garth McClelland. Murder you!"

I walked swiftly towards the house. Garth caught up with me. "We're a fine pair," I said bitterly. "Jacques has already wished me dead, and now your wife—"

"They're just jealous," he said lightly. "Would you care for some of that champagne now?"

"No, thank you. I'm going home. I have no wish to be sniggered at for the rest of the evening. At least let them do it after I'm gone."

"I'll drive you."

"Don't bother. I'll send the carriage back for the others. Why spoil their evening? Oh, why did I come here? I should have known it would be like this!"

"Elise, I want to see you again."

I stopped on the path outside the ballroom and looked at him. "No, Garth, you'll have to get yourself another plaything," I said dully. "This is wrong, and sad. I don't want to cause the Fourniers any more embarrassment. No one calls on us as it is, and it's all because of me. Do you think I enjoy being the scandalous, wicked Madame Fournier? I don't. I just want to make some kind of life for myself, but every time I see you my plans fall apart because I fall apart. You've had your fun with me, Garth, but it has to end. Whatever you might think of me, I am not like those horses you spoke about: you have trained and broken and ridden me, but I will not come when you whistle. I have my own life to lead. Good night, Garth."

I passed through the ballroom and into the hallway. As I ascended the stairs to the dressing room I could hear Garth asking his butler to call the Fournier carriage. When I came down I saw that Jacques was there, too, wearing his usual worried expression.

"What's the matter, Elise?" he asked anxiously. "Are you ill?"

"No, Jacques, I am not ill. I am never ill. There isn't any time for illness. I am going home because I want to go, that's all."

"At least let me—"

"No, don't come with me. I'll send the carriage back. You'll need to attend to your mother. She'll be hearing some things that will probably make her faint."

Without another word to either of them, I walked down the front steps and stepped into the waiting carriage.

# XIII. The Plot

I rode alone every day after breakfast. There was less to do on the plantation between harvest and planting time than at any other time of the year, and in order to avoid being confined all day in the house with people who hated the sight of me, I would don my riding habit, choose a fast horse and then ride until I was exhausted and the furious gnawing desire within me was quelled, at least for a short time.

I hated my life at La Rêve. Not a day went by that I didn't consider riding out of their lives forever. Nothing was holding me to the plantation but my own stupid pride: I wanted to show them all that I could turn La Rêve into a paying operation, and I wanted Garth McClelland to see that I could exist very well without him.

Jacques and Arnold were growing bolder. Arnold was a frequent visitor, and if Maman or the aunts ever suspected what was going on they gave no sign. I was worried that Colette was falling in love with him. I knew the elder Fourniers would welcome the match: the Charpentiers were an old, respected Creole family. Never mind that Arnold reeked of degeneracy and evil. He was a Charpentier, and therefore he could do no wrong.

Jacques was like a stranger to me. We avoided each other and only spoke when it was necessary. He gladly left the running of the plantation to me, for he had no real head for business. Except for complaining about the smallness of the amount I permitted him to have for spending money, he never conferred with me or seriously challenged any of my decisions.

I had never felt so lonely, or so sad. As I rode out of the stable yard one gray morning I saw that huge black thunderheads were gathering on the eastern horizon. I felt suddenly wretched and oppressed, as though black clouds were gathering around me as well.

The storm broke when I was crossing one of the eastern cane fields, not far from the line that divided La Rêve from the McClelland lands. Almost instantly, it seemed, the field became a sea of mud. I urged my mount, an energetic young stallion named Beelzebub, towards a distant rise that promised dryer ground and surer footing. I was soaking wet, and my heavy woolen habit hung on me like a leaden shroud. A biting wind of hurricane strength tore over the fields, drenching us both thoroughly. Beelzebub plodded gallantly through the muck with his head lowered against the elements. When the ground felt harder under his feet he picked up speed and made a mad dash up the slope. I made no attempt to check him, but let him gallop furiously into the wind.

Ahead of me I saw a cane cutter's cottage nestled back among some pine trees. Beelzebub saw it, too, and we careened towards the shelter, slipping and slithering in the mud. When we reached the cottage I led my mount to the lee side, where at least he would be protected from the full fury of the driving wind and rain. I ran up on the front porch and squeezed some of the water out of my skirts. The porch roof was as leaky as a sieve, and after dodging rivulets for a few minutes I decided I might as well see if the interior of the cabin was any dryer.

I pushed open the door, which hung from its frame on one hinge. Then I heard a scraping noise that sent chills up and down my spine. When my eyes became accustomed to the gloom I could make out a figure squatting in front of the fireplace. It was Garth, and he was trying vainly to light a fire with a flint and some damp straw.

I stood rooted to the spot. He stood up when he saw me.

The rain was drumming on the roof and the wind roared in the pines. The storm was right on top of us, and the rolling thunder shook the little cottage. We didn't even try to speak. He came slowly towards me and took my hand. His touch was tingling, magical. With a little moan, I fell into his arms and let his kisses sear through me.

He peeled off my sodden clothing, pulled off my boots and let my hair down. Then he rubbed me all over with a dry woolen cloak until my flesh was glowing. He spread the cloak on the floor and we lay down on it. He entered me at once, and I welcomed him with a joyous sob. We were vicious, hungry, and impatient. Down and around we plummeted into love's black bottomless maelstrom. I didn't want to come into the light ever again. I wanted the darkness, the heat, the power of love that had been denied me for so long to go on and on.

When it was over I wept softly. Garth didn't laugh at me, but held me in his arms and stroked my hair. We loved again, and then we lay quietly for a long time wrapped in his cloak, listening to the fury of the wind and rain outside the cottage.

He stirred. "I'll try and light the fire again."

"It will smoke," I protested. "We'll suffocate."

"We'll lie close to the floor where the air is pure," he said. His flint worked now, and soon the fire was blazing merrily. The golden light shone on his lean haunches and strong back.

"You look like you've been cast in bronze," I said softly.

He grinned at me over his shoulder. He picked up my riding habit and draped it over the back of a rickety chair in front of the fire to dry.

"It will take hours before it's fit to put on," I said.

"That's all right. We have hours." He lay down beside me and enfolded me in his arms once again.

"Why are you here?" I asked him.

"I'm taking shelter from the storm, the same as you. At least I had sense enough to get under cover before it broke. Didn't you look at the sky before you came out this morning?"

"Yes, but I didn't care. I liked the way the storm made me feel free and brave." I gazed at the glowing embers in the fireplace. "And then I fell into your hands like an overripe plum. How you must have rejoiced to see me standing there, so soon after I'd made a grand speech about living without you."

"I never pay any attention to what women say. You also told me once that whatever you were, you weren't an adulteress."

"I remember. Do you always get what you want?"

"Yes, because I'm a patient man. I'm willing to wait."

"It's not fair," I pouted.

"Yes, it is. You got what you wanted, didn't you?"

I didn't answer him, I just moved closer to him and hid my face against his shoulder.

"I'm leaving for Washington tomorrow," he said.

"How long will you be gone?" I asked casually, as though it didn't matter.

"It's hard to say. It's a long trip, and I don't really have anything to come home to."

Drops of rain fell down the chimney and sizzled on the glowing logs. I got up and started to put on my damp clothing. He lay back on our makeshift bed and watched me. The cool, cynical smile hovered on his lips. I was waiting for him to ask me to come away with him, and I knew he wouldn't. And I wouldn't beg him. I hadn't sunk that low.

"Elise, come here tomorrow," he said in a silky, seductive voice that made me weak all over again. "I want to see you again. I must."

I didn't trust myself to speak. I shook my head. The rain

had slowed to a steady drizzle. I opened the door, and the wind caught my skirts and whipped them around my legs. I went out of the cabin without looking back.

Beelzebub cast me a look of deep misery when I approached him. I patted his nose and mounted him. When we passed in front of the cottage I saw Garth standing in the open door.

"I'll be waiting, Elise," he called. "Tomorrow morning."

He was so confident that I would come, so sure of me. I pulled Beelzebub up sharply, but the impatient horse had had his fill of standing in the rain and he wheeled sharply and reared. I brought my whip down hard in his flank and dug my heels into his sides. We galloped off towards home.

James, the butler, opened the door for me.

"It's mighty wet out there, Ma'am," he said. "Did you get caught?"

"I certainly did, James. Where is everyone?"

"The ladies is in the drawin' room, Ma'am, and the gentlemen—"

I heard a burst of raucous laughter. Looking around, I saw Jacques and Arnold coming down the grand staircase together.

"Ah, she returns!" Jacques cried jubilantly. "Elise, give me an advance on my allowance, will you? I need some new clothes." He and Arnold giggled like two schoolgirls.

"Why, are your old ones worn out with too much sitting?" I asked him.

"Oh, naughty Elise," clucked Jacques. "Isn't she naughty, Arnold? To scold poor Jacques for not working hard to save this wretched swamp? You have a temper, Elise. I didn't know you had a temper when I married you."

"The extent of your ignorance when you married me does not astonish me, Jacques," I said crossly. I started up the stairs and met them halfway. "If you'll excuse me, I'd like to get to my room and get out of these wet garments."

"No." Jacques was drunk and surly. Brandy had given him courage to stand up to me. "I won't get out of your way, Elise." He swayed unsteadily and clutched at Arnold for support. "If you want to go upstairs, you may use the servants' stairs at the back of the house. These are my stairs. This is my house, not yours." He and Arnold linked arms, barring my way.

I stood on the step below them and said angrily, "Stop being childish, Jacques. I am tired and wet and cold and I want to go to my room."

"It's not your room," Jacques said assertively. "It's my room, in my house. You can go sleep in the stables, whore—"

I lifted my riding crop and struck him across the face. He gasped, then raised his foot to my midriff and shoved with all his might. I fell backwards down the stairs and landed heavily at the bottom. I could hear them sniggering nervously. I heard a woman's scream, and James saying, "Lordy!" Garth's face filled my vision for one sweet, agonizing moment, and then I fainted.

I heard whispering. "Good God, Jacques, I hope you haven't killed her."

"Of course I haven't! It was an accident, you saw what happened."

I opened my eyes. James was bending over me, holding a glass of brandy to my lips. Arnold and Jacques were standing a short distance away. Colette was holding my hand, patting it nervously.

"Oh, Elise, please wake up. Say you aren't dead!"

I managed a weak smile. "No, I'm not dead." My voice sounded like it was coming from a long distance. I looked at Jacques and said, "I—I could kill you for that, Jacques."

Arnold grinned and said, "What are you talking about, Elise? You tripped over your skirts and fell down the stairs. That wasn't Jacques' fault."

"Nobody would believe that," I said. "James, you saw what happened, didn't you?"

The black man was shamefaced. "No, Ma'am, I didn't see anything. I was in the dinin' room, polishin' the silver."

Old loyalties are stronger than new, I thought. He knew Jacques as an infant, and Jacques was master of La Rêve. I was the stranger, the interloper.

"James, help me up," I said weakly.

"Ma'am, you've been hurt," he said in a frightened voice. "We ought to send for the doctor."

"He'd never get here," I said firmly. "The roads are mud. Help me up. I'm all right. Colette, help me, please."

"Are you sure she should be moved?" It was Maman's voice, shrill and imperious. So she, too, was witness to my downfall.

Colette and James helped me to my feet. I reeled and covered my eyes with my hand. The room was spinning and I felt sick. James supported me while I breathed deeply a few times, and then we started towards the stairs. I pushed him away.

"I'm fine, thank you, James. I want to go up by myself, please." I walked slowly and regally across the hall. I paused in front of Jacques and Arnold. Jacques gulped. He was frightened, and trying not too successfully to conceal it. Arnold wore his hatred of me like a badge, proudly and defiantly. I wished I had my swords and pistols. I could cheerfully have slaughtered them both. I mounted the first few steps and turned around to look at them. Three old women dressed in black regarded me hostilely from the drawing room door. Their expressions held only dislike and disgust. Two young men, perverted lovers, watched me silently, their expression barely concealing their hatred of me, one because I had nearly ruined his affair, the other because I had emerged as the stronger, dominant partner in a farcical marriage. The face of the young girl reflected only love and concern. She stood on the threshold of adulthood, unsure of herself and her heart. Had I been like Colette when I was sixteen, frightened and eager and passionate? Of course I had been; I was still like that, even though I felt as though I were a hundred years old. And the third man, the slave, who had to depend on people he must hate for his very life, dropped his eyes when they met mine. Poor James. He was a prisoner, too, as I was. Only he could never escape.

They watched me: cautiously, fearfully, worriedly, gleefully. I turned my back on them again. I couldn't bear to look at them anymore. Clinging to the bannister, I managed to get up the stairs to my room. Then I collapsed on the floor and wept silently. I hated them, I hated them all.

Savannah found me and crooned over me while she undressed me and put me to bed.

"Oh, Missy, we got to leave this place. This place is evil, and these folks is evil. We got to get out of here."

After Savannah left me I fell into a deep sleep. The house was dark and silent when I awoke. I had a headache and a slight chill, and I felt jittery and frightened. I needed something to calm my nerves, and I decided to go down to the library for a glass of brandy. Perhaps I could even find a soothing book that would distract me enough so that I could get back to sleep.

I went silently down the stairs on slippered feet, taking no special pains to be quiet but not wanting to draw the attention of the whole house to my nocturnal wanderings. I had my hand on the door of the library and was about to enter when the sound of voices inside stopped me.

"Don't be a fool, Jacques, it's the only way." I recognized Arnold's voice, clear, sober and intense.

"No, no, it's—it's unthinkable, Arnold," Jacques moaned. "There must be a better way. Violence—"

"It's the only way. What are you afraid of? It's a good plan, the only reasonable plan. She doesn't deserve to live, not after what she's done to you."

"I don't want to talk about it any more!" Jacques was almost sobbing. "It's horrible, frightening! You've got to stop talking like a madman, Arnold. You—you frighten me. Here, have some more brandy—"

"Will you be quiet and listen to me?" Arnold sounded angry and impatient. "That slut has brought you nothing but trouble and unhappiness. And your family, too. They hate her, you know they do. They would be grateful to you—"

"No! No one must ever know we even discussed it, Arnold. Arnold!"

I heard a sound like a slap and Jacques began to whimper. I could picture him, eyes wide and imploring, hands fluttering, his beautiful face twisted with the agony of making a decision. I knew he would never make a decision for himself. He would waver and whine and complain until Arnold forced his own will upon him.

"You're a yellow coward," Arnold snarled. "I don't know why I bother with you. I'm leaving, Jacques, and I'm not coming back."

I ducked into the shadows as his footsteps approached the door. The door opened a crack and an arrow of light cut through the darkness of the hallway.

"Arnold, please, don't leave me. I couldn't bear it if you left me. Please, I'll do anything you say, only—"

The door closed again. I didn't wait to hear any more. I ran back up to my room and sat on the edge of the bed, trying to stop my violent trembling. Think. I had to think. Their hatred of me went much deeper than I thought. Arnold—Arnold wanted me dead, and Jacques did, too, although he had been too weak and frightened to admit it. I was convinced they were plotting my death, and I didn't know what to do. I could hardly carry my pistols with me everywhere I went. It could happen any time. Tomorrow—or a year from tomorrow. Arnold was shrewd. He would choose his time wisely. Accidents were so easy to arrange.

I knew I had to get away, as soon as possible. Garth. I would meet Garth at the cottage in the morning and tell him I was going with him. He wouldn't refuse me. He would be pleased and flattered. I wouldn't have to tell him I was running for my life, only that I wanted him and needed to be near him. That part would be true enough.

I slept no more that night, but sat awake planning and thinking until a few hours before dawn. Than I dressed in traveling clothes and packed a small valise with the things I would need. I couldn't take Savannah. I hoped she would understand.

I wrote a note to Jacques, telling him that I could no longer continue in a loveless marriage and that it would be better for both of us if I went away. I left the note on my dresser with all the cash I had in my room. Savannah would find the note and take it to the family and keep the money for herself. She would need it to get back to New Orleans.

Before I left the house I went into the study on the first floor that I had used as an office. I opened the safe on the wall and took out all the money that was there, about five hundred dollars. I put a hundred in my valise and the rest into a small sack. Then I walked through the house and out

the back door. The sun was barely showing itself in the
eastern sky. I had no time to lose.

I ran to the stables and saddled Beelzebub. I led him
away from the plantation buildings and stopped at the last
cabin in the row of slave dwellings behind the barns. I
thumped the door lightly. It swung open and Amos
emerged, fully dressed and wide awake.

"Miz Elise, what you doin—"

"There isn't time to explain, Amos," I said quickly.
"I—I have to go away. I won't be coming back, ever.
Here." I put the sack with the money into his hands.
"This is for you to give to the others. I'm sorry my plans
didn't work out for all of you. Maybe you can have shoes
for the winter, or—or weapons." His nostrils widened
and he jerked his head up. "I'll ask Mr. McClelland to buy
you all when Jacques sells the plantation. He'll do that for
me, I know he will, and perhaps then I can think of some
way to free you. I have to do it this way. If I stayed
someone would be hurt, I can feel it. Good-bye, Amos."

I extended my hand. He took it and held onto it for a
moment. "Good-bye, Missy. Good luck to you, and God
bless you."

I mounted Beelzebub and rode away from La Rêve to
freedom, to Garth. As we skirted the low knoll I saw again
the cane cutter's shack. It looked different in the pale light
of early morning, bleak and uninviting. Nevertheless the
memory of the previous day made me quiver with delight.
I longed to see Garth again, to hold him.

A soft wind was blowing over the fields. As we drew
near the cottage, Beelzebub began to prance nervously,
and when I tied him to the porch railing he tossed his head
and pawed the ground. I patted his flank reassuringly and
told myself that he must sense my own apprehension.

I picked my way over the rotten boards on the porch.
The wind sighed mournfully in the pines, and somewhere

in the distance a lonely dove called to its mate. It really was a lonely, desolate spot. I felt afraid, and told myself sternly not to be a fool. There was no danger here. I had left the danger behind me.

The door was ajar, still hanging from its single hinge. I slipped into the cabin. A musty, unpleasant smell greeted my nostrils and I wrinkled my nose. A dismal enough place for a lovers' rendezvous, I thought. But at least no one would find us here. A little daylight seeped through the cracks in the walls and the torn greased paper on the windows. I could see particles of dust floating in the shaft of light that came through the open door.

And then I saw the body lying on the floor in the center of the room.

My stomach turned over and I screamed. The echoes of my terror rattled the walls. I forced myself to approach it, to see if it was Garth. I bent over him, peering at the face in the gloom to see if it might still be breathing. The twisted features seemed to glow in the shadowy room. I imagined it was leering at me, mocking me. Then I turned away from the gaze of the dead eyes and retched at the stench that drifted up from him. It was Jacques.

I saw the wound in his head, in the temple over his right ear. I steeled myself to feel for his pulse, even though his awful stillness and grotesquely staring eyes told me he couldn't possibly be alive. I lifted the hand and let it fall back again. I have never gotten used to the feel of dead flesh. Death has no resilience, no warmth. A dead limb feels extraordinarily heavy and leaden. The presence of death in that small room sickened me and made me feel limp and lifeless myself. I sat back on my heels and stared stupidly at the corpse.

Jacques. Had he come here to kill himself? Why here? He must have known about Garth and me. The cottage was airless, suffocating. I ran out into the dazzling morning brightness and clung to the shaky porch railing. Beelzebub snorted unhappily. He had known what we would find here. The wind had carried the smell of death to his nostrils, and he had been justifiably afraid. I looked around helplessly. The cane fields flowed away from the cottage in an unbroken vista of greens and browns. There was not another house in sight, not another living being. And Garth might not arrive for hours yet.

What was I to do? Clearly I would have to ride for help. The McClellands' plantation was the closest, but I didn't want to go there. No, I would have to go back to La Rêve now. It suddenly occurred to me that there was no longer any reason for me to leave.

I went back into the cabin. I searched the room, and then the body, for a pistol and I didn't find one. I felt shaken to my very core, and afraid. Jacques couldn't have committed suicide, or I would have found the gun. He had been shot by someone else.

The evil of the place overwhelmed me. I closed his eyes and bid him a brief, silent farewell.

I heard a step on the porch and a figure blocked out the light that came in through the door. I uttered a strangled, fearful cry and stood up quickly. My heart was thumping so loudly that I could hardly think. Then I gave a relieved sigh. With the light at her back I couldn't see her face, but I knew from her size and stance that it was Georgette.

"Paying your respects, Elise?" she asked.

"Oh, thank God you've come, Georgette," I babbled. "Jacques has been killed, murdered. We have to do something, quickly."

She stepped into the room. "And just what do you suggest we do?"

"Why, ride for help immediately," I said. She didn't move. I stared at her. What had she said when she came in? Something about paying my respects? "You—you knew he was here! You knew before you even came in!"

She stood over the body and prodded it with her foot. "Yes, I knew. Arnold told me. Poor stupid Jacques. Well, his worries are over now, aren't they?"

"I don't understand you," I said impatiently. "How did Arnold know?"

"Why, he was here when Jacques—killed himself."

"And I suppose he took the pistol with him? There is no gun in the room. I looked."

"Did you? My, you're alert. Garth would be so proud of you. Always the little heroine." She coughed delicately. "Let's get out of here, shall we? The air is rather close."

We went out. Arnold was standing on the ground with the horses. He grinned up at me.

"Hello, Elise," he said easily. "You're up early, aren't you?"

"Tell me what happened," I said. "Why did he do it? Did you quarrel?"

"He was so excitable," Arnold shrugged. "And so fond of brandishing weapons about. It was an accident."

My mouth felt dry. "It was no accident. You killed him, didn't you?"

Arnold laughed. His imperturbability was more terrifying than any energetic display of violence could have been. "And you'd like to see me hang for it, wouldn't you, Elise? I don't think I want to do that, though. I have too much to live for."

"You're mad, Arnold," I said. "He never harmed you in his life. He—he loved you, and you don't even seem to care that he's dead."

I didn't see Georgette's upraised arm until it was too late to block her attack. She brought a heavy rock down on the side of my head. The last thing I saw was her beautiful, evil, grinning face.

My head throbbed painfully. I lifted my hand to my forehead and rubbed the ache, but it didn't go away. When I opened my eyes I felt sick, and I vomited.

"Good. You're awake."

The mist in front of my eyes cleared. I was inside the shack, lying on the floor under a window. The body was gone. A short candle was burning on a small table. Georgette was standing near the door. She was holding a pistol in her hand.

"Arnold's gone to make arrangements," she said.

"Water." I tried to sit up. Once again nausea swept over me. "Water, please."

"Be still!" she barked. "You can sit up, but don't attempt to stand or I'll shoot you dead. Don't think I won't."

"Oh, I wouldn't doubt it for a moment." I leaned back against the wall and closed my eyes. "Isn't that the whole idea? A nice double murder?"

She smiled. "No. We have something even better in store for you. A really appropriate fate for a whore. I devised the idea some time ago and confided it to Arnold. He was enchanted by it."

I swallowed. "Garth wouldn't approve of this," I said.

"Garth! Ha! He won't even know. He's gone to Washington, my dear. He left last night, and he won't be home for a long, long time. Certainly no one would be surprised to learn that you ran away after killing your husband, least of all Garth. He told me about you. He laughed at you, Elise, when we were together. We laughed together. He said you were like a bitch in heat, that no man was big enough for you."

I knew she was lying, but in my weakened state I half

believed her. He had to come. He had said he would come.

"You're a liar," I said.

"Am I?" She gave a short dry laugh. "Don't you believe it. Garth loves me, Elise. He has always loved me, ever since we were children together. And I love him."

"Is that why you've given him so many children?" I asked maliciously.

"Hold your tongue! That—that couldn't be helped. And it never made any difference to him, I know it. You were just a temporary nuisance, Elise. I am the kind of wife he needs. I know what Garth wants out of life, and I know how to help him get it. I'm an asset to him, but you're the worst thing that could have happened to him at this point in his career. You're a scandal, a disgrace. You're vulgar and shameless! He's sorry he ever laid eyes on you!" Her tone was a crescendo of hatred.

"You're pathetic," I said with a little laugh. "You're just angry because you aren't enough woman to hang on to him. Do you think he ever would have looked at me if you had been any kind of wife to him?"

In two strides she crossed the room. She began to beat me around the head and neck with the pistol, screaming hysterically all the while. I fended off her blows and managed to aim a good, strong kick at her middle which sent her flying. She fell heavily. I jumped up and tried to snatch the pistol out of her hands. Then I heard a bumping noise on the porch. Arnold had returned.

He rushed at me and threw me down, then held his pistol to my head while Georgette caught her breath and got to her feet.

"Let me kill her now," the woman panted. "Let me—"

"No!" Arnold held her back. "I know the temptation is very great, Georgette, but be patient. I promise you, my way is better. She'll suffer for it, you won't be disappointed.''

"No, it won't work," Georgette said. "She'll get away, she'll come back—''

"I swear to you, you'll never see her again," said Arnold firmly. "Please, cousin, trust me." He turned to me. "You were very clever, weren't you, Elise? I see you obligingly packed your bags this morning, and I'll wager you even left a note. They'll find that note, and later today when they find Jacques they'll just assume you made good on your threats of yesterday. We all heard you, Elise. Even James would testify that you wanted your husband dead. They'll try and find you, but they never will. You'll be as good as dead, though. And I'll marry Colette and make La Rêve mine.''

"So you want La Rêve. That's all you've ever wanted, isn't it, Arnold? But you'll never be able to make it pay. You haven't the guts and the ambition.''

"Oh, Georgette will lend me some money from time to time until I get on my feet.''

"Why go to all this trouble?" I asked. "Why couldn't you just marry Colette, and you and Jacques could have lived happily together forever.''

He shook his head. "I didn't anticipate his marrying you, Elise. You nearly ruined it all. But now everything has fallen into place. Jacques is gone, La Rêve is mine if I want it, and you won't be around to cause trouble.''

Oh, God, I thought, he's mad, completely mad. "Quite an elaborate scheme," I remarked calmly.

"It had to be," he said excitedly. "Georgette thought up the best part, I give her credit for that, even though she's sorry now and would much rather kill you. But I persuaded her with little difficulty that death was too good for you. You need—to suffer before you die. And so we compromised. You must appear to be dead, and we shall dispose of you so that you can never be traced. It's a difficult problem, but not insoluble if you know the right people. And Georgette does. She knows a lot of really evil people.''

''You're crazy, both of you.''

Georgette laughed. ''Perhaps we are at that. Crazy with hatred for you. But don't say any more, Arnold. We don't want to spoil the surprise for Elise, do we?''

Arnold's eyes flickered dangerously. ''No. No, we don't.'' He checked his pocket watch. ''Nearly four o'clock. We'll have to work fast. We still have a lot to do. Take off your clothes, Elise. Everything.''

''You're a disgusting animal, Arnold,'' I said through my swollen lips.

''Why? Oh, you think I want to make love to you! No, my dear, not now. Strip, or I'll tear off your things piece by piece.''

I spat in his face and was rewarded by a forceful slap on the cheek. I sucked in my breath. Tears smarted in my eyes.

''You're managing her very well, Arnold,'' said Georgette admiringly. ''I could never have done all this. But then if it had been left to me I would have killed her, and that wouldn't have been nearly so much fun.''

Arnold hit me again, and I started to undress slowly. He wet his lips as he watched me, but he made no move to touch me. When I was wearing only my flimsy chemise I heard Arnold make a wheezing noise in his throat.

Georgette sniggered. ''Take off the chemise, slut. Arnold wants a better look. What do you think, Arnold? Would you like me to go outside for a few minutes?'' She laughed crudely.

I watched them both warily, hugging myself to cover my nakedness and to protect myself from his unexpected drooling lust. Georgette came over to me and ripped the chemise off my back. I gasped with fury and whirled to confront her, my clenched fists upraised. I struck her once in the face before Arnold threw himself on top of me and dragged me down. Georgette watched us wrestling and cried out gleefully.

"Go ahead, Arnold," she urged feverishly. "Take her. What are you waiting for? What are you afraid of? You want the slut, you know you do. Go ahead, Arnold. Do it."

I wriggled in his arms, hating the feel of his moist hands on my naked flesh. He cuffed me once again, so viciously that the room went completely black for a moment. He thrust his knees between my thighs and fell groaning on top of me, pushing his puny tool into me. He strained and sobbed in a kind of delirious fit. Through the fog of my pain and shame I could hear Georgette shouting encouragement, laughing excitedly, urging Arnold to hurry, hurry. The rough floor boards dug into my back. I tried to push him away but my arms had no strength.

"Hurt her, Arnold," Georgette shrieked. "Make her scream!"

Finally Arnold rolled away from me. He was panting and his eyes were bright and glazed. Suddenly Georgette was standing over me with her riding crop in her hands. She brought it down on my breasts and once again on my abdomen. I shrank away from her and drew my knees up to my chest, but her blows continued to rain down mercilessly on my back, my buttocks and my thighs. I swore that I wouldn't give her the satisfaction of screaming. The lash bit into my flesh, raising welts, drawing blood. I clenched my fists and bit my lips as pain enveloped me, and then, just when I thought I could stand it no longer and that I must cry out or go mad, something stayed her hand.

"That's enough, Georgette," Arnold cried. He grappled with her. "Stop it, stop it before you kill her."

"I want to kill her!" Georgette roared. "I hate her! I hate her! She deserves to die!"

"No, no! Stop! She'll pay, I swear it, Georgette. But we have work to do now, before it gets too dark to see properly. Please, do as I say."

She leaned breathlessly against the wall of the cabin, her whip hanging uselessly at her side.

"I'm glad I did that." She sounded exhausted but triumphant. "I'll remember for the rest of my life how good it felt. I only wish Garth had been here to see it and that I could have killed her."

"My way is better," Arnold said briskly. "You'll see." He was in control of the situation again, and he bustled around the cabin in a sudden fury of activity. "Did you bring the things I asked for?"

She nodded and went out of the cabin. In a moment she was back, carrying a shapeless bundle which she tossed at my feet. "Put these on," she ordered.

I looked through them. A worn-out chemise, a torn petticoat, a faded muslin dress, a moth-eaten shawl that had once been a pretty lavender. No shoes, no stockings. A square of unhemmed fabric that was probably a head scarf. I dressed quickly, glad to be able to cover my nakedness.

When I finished Arnold nodded approvingly. "Good. Very good, indeed, Georgette. Most convincing."

"Yes, isn't she? We have to go now. Someone will remark on our absence, and La Rêve will be in an uproar over Jacques' death. We need to be home so that we can offer advice and comfort. Tie her up and we can go."

"You don't have to come back tonight," Arnold told her. "I can do the rest myself."

"Oh, but I want to come back." She smiled coldly. "I wouldn't miss it for the world."

She watched while Arnold bound my hands and feet and pushed me down in a corner, then she left the cabin. Arnold checked his handiwork carefully to see that I couldn't free myself, then he extinguished the candle and walked out of the cabin, closing the door tightly behind him.

I strained futilely at the cords, but Arnold had done his work well and I quickly realized that I had no chance of escape. I screamed long and loud for help, even though I knew it was useless. No help came. The two conspirators had chosen their spot well, as well as the two lovers had the day before.

I lay in that stinking cottage for the rest of the day. When darkness settled over the cabin I started fearfully at every sound, fully expecting them to return at any moment. Another darkness, like black despair, settled over my soul. I didn't know what they had planned for me; or perhaps I did know, deep in my heart and didn't have the courage to acknowledge my fears. I did not want to admit it, to say the words that might make it real. I shut my mind to everything but my own discomfort. I didn't think about anything, not even of Garth.

Hours passed. My cramped arms and legs pained me terribly at first, then they grew numb and cold and began to ache with a deeper, more agonizing pain. I might have slept briefly. At last I heard a step outside the cabin and a beam of lantern light sliced through the darkness.

"Still here?" It was Arnold. I blinked into the glare. He leaned over me and cut the cords that bound my feet. "Get up." He hauled me upwards until I was standing. The rush of blood to my limbs hurt me so that I whimpered and sank back down again. He cursed and kicked me.

"Everything is all right?" Georgette had kept her promise. She had come back.

"Fine. Our lady friend is finding it a little difficult to stand up."

"Get her up," Georgette snapped. "I don't care how much it hurts." Arnold obeyed, pulling and prodding me until I stood, swaying and moaning. "Are we ready?"

"Yes." Arnold tied a rag around my mouth and pushed me towards the door. I stumbled and fell to my knees. He pulled my hair until I stood again, and he shoved me along in front of him. The splintery boards on the porch pricked the soles of my feet as I moved along. The night was dark, moonless. A few crickets chirped in the undergrowth, and an owl hooted in the pines. We crossed the cane fields. The rough stubble from last year's crop cut into my feet like so many knife blades. Swinging dizzily, the lantern cast crazy shadows on the faces of my tormenters.

We made our way towards the river road. When we reached the place where the drive to Highlands met the road we halted. Arnold extinguished the light. We were left with only a glimmer of starlight. We stood waiting, for what I didn't know. I felt cold and sick, and I knew that however terrible their treatment of me had been so far, the evening would surely bring even worse punishment. The whole day seemed like a deadly, terrifying dream. If only I could wake up.

Georgette became nervous and impatient. "You're sure he knows where to come? He won't miss us?"

"Of course not," said Arnold. "I know how to arrange things. Please give me a little credit for brains, dear Georgette. If you want to go home—"

"No," she said stubbornly. "I'm staying. I'll stay until dawn if I have to."

A light gleamed faintly in the distance. We fastened our eyes on it and watched as it drew closer. Soon we could

hear the creak and rattle of wheels and the slow plodding
of horses. An open wagon approached us, swimming in
the pool of light from a lantern that hung from a post near
the driver's seat. The light glowed eerily on our upturned
faces when the wagon came to a halt. Georgette had deep
shadows under her eyes and nose. She looked malevolent
and powerful, the very embodiment of evil.

"Put that light out," Georgette ordered the driver. "Do
you want someone to see us?"

My flesh crawled as I looked at him. I knew who he
was. His name was Bose Niles and he was known to
everyone in the vicinity as the Flesh Peddler. He made the
rounds of the plantations every six months or so, looking
for old, sick, or worthless slaves that no one else would
buy. Some plantation owners who felt they couldn't afford
to care for a slave who could no longer earn his keep would
sell them to the Peddler for just a few dollars. A better
bargain, they said, than paying for a coffin. He would be
sure to recognize me. I had ordered him off La Rêve at
gunpoint one day.

The man drawled, "Well, Ma'am, it don't look to me
like there's anyone around here to be seein' us anyways.
Horse got to be able to look where it's going. Just calm
down now. This won't take too long. This her?" He
jerked his head at me. "Got her mouth all tied up, I see.
She must be a talker."

"She's a screamer," Arnold said quickly. "We didn't
want to attract any undue attention, you understand. The
land around here is fairly flat, and sound carries."

"Sure, sure. Well, I won't let her have her say until
we're far away from here." He reached behind him. "But
right now I'll jest truss her up a little better." I could hear
the dull clanking of chains. He held up some shackles.
"These'll do, I reckon."

I made an hysterical screeching noise back in my throat.

Georgette chuckled. "Oh, I like them. Perfect, perfect. Put them on right now. At once."

"Hold on to your hat, lady." Niles climbed down from the wagon and knelt in front of me. I danced and kicked at him as he tried to fasten the hideous bracelets around my ankles.

Arnold cuffed me so hard that I fell backwards and struck my head on the hard ground. I lay stunned long enough for Bose Niles to lock the cold heavy rings around both legs. Then Arnold cut my bonds and dragged my hands around to the front. The stab of pain in my shoulders was excruciating. I felt the tears sliding down my face, soaking into the gag on my mouth. Then Niles manacled my hands with expert efficiency and dragged me to my feet.

" 'Course, the best way to do this is to have a 'smith fire the metal," he said conversationally. "But you folks probably know more about that than I do. You've owned a lot more than I'll ever see. Come on, Slave Gal." He led me towards the back of the wagon. I shuffled along slowly, unaccustomed to the weights on my wrists and legs. Arnold helped him lift me into the wagon. "She got a name?" the man asked Arnold.

"Her name is Eliza," Arnold said a trifle stiffly. "She's—she's a quadroon from Haiti. We're getting rid of her because, well, because she's mad. She'll tell you a lot of strange things, but believe me, none of them is true."

The Flesh Peddler laughed. "Doesn't matter to me. I don't care none if she's crazy or not. Where she's goin' it might even help her some."

At the word quadroon I started to scream, kick, and thrash. The shackles felt as though they were made of lead, and they seemed to be growing heavier by the minute. I panted and sobbed and almost choked on my own tears and mucus. After a moment I lay quietly at the bottom of the wagon, my energies spent.

I heard Georgette's voice at my head. Looking up I could see her face peering at me over the side of the wagon. Her eyes were shining.

"This is worth the Hell you've put me through," she said. "I hated you the first moment I saw you; no, from the first time I heard he had made you his whore. I could have killed you, you bitch. But Arnold was right. This is better, much better. You're a slave now, Elise. You'll live a slave and you'll die a slave, far from here. I'll never see you again, but I'll remember this night forever. Good-bye, Elise." The triumphant light of victory shone in her eyes. "I won't remember you to Garth. Too bad he can't be here."

I rolled my head to the other side so that I wouldn't have to look at her. Absurdly, I thought that she must have been the kind of nasty little girl who liked to torture smaller creatures: insects, dogs and cats, younger children. She felt very superior to me tonight because she had tortured me successfully, and I was sure she would relish this triumph until she died. I was sorry that I could give her that satisfaction.

The wagon rocked as Niles climbed up and released the brake. He bounced a sackful of coins in his palm.

"Real nice doin' business with you folks," he said cheerfully. "If I'm ever back this way I'll look you up, hear?"

He laughed heartily, then clucked his tongue at his horses. The wagon jerked into motion and the lantern bobbed. I fancied I could hear Georgette and Arnold laughing uproariously as I was driven away into the night.

## XIV.  The Master

The wagon jolted over a bump and I opened my eyes.
The expanse of sky over my head was blue, broken by
feathery tree tops. I struggled to sit up. Every bone, every
tendon in my body throbbed painfully.

My mouth was dry under the rag that still gagged my
mouth. I had tried without success to tear it off before I fell
asleep, but my fingers were so cramped and stiff that I
could not make the slightest impression on the knot. I
swivelled my head towards the front of the wagon. I saw a
brown-clad back topped by a fringe of dirty gray hair and a
disreputable wide-brimmed hat. I grunted loudly to attract
Bose Niles' attention. I got no response at first and wondered if he was sleeping. I tried again. He turned his head.

"Oh, you're awake," he said over his shoulder. He
pulled the horses up and climbed down, and walked to the
back of the wagon. He had to cut the gag with his knife, so
tightly had Arnold knotted it. I lifted my shackled hands
and rubbed the bruised corners of my mouth where the gag
had bitten into them. "You want to go off in the bushes?"
he asked. I nodded. "Go on then. Don't try to run. You
won't get too far with them things on your legs. When you
get back I'll give you a little water and some meat."

The irons on my legs made walking difficult and slow,
and it was some minutes before I got back to the wagon.

I said breathlessly, "Listen to me, Niles. I know who
you are and what you do. How much did they pay you? I'll
give you more, more, do you understand? I'm not a slave.
I'm Jacques Fournier's wife, Elise, from La Rêve.
We—we met once before. If you take me back to New

379

Orleans, I'll give you twice what they paid you. That's good business, isn't it? You'll be collecting twice for the same merchandise."

He tilted his ugly face to the side and said, "Lady, I don't care if you're the Queen of Arabia. I said I would do a thing, and I'm goin' to do it. Man's got a reputation to uphold, don't he? That's what I call good business, stickin' to your contract."

"But you don't understand—"

"I understand you threw me off your place without even givin' me a hearin'," he said. For an instant his hatred of me showed in his eyes, then it was gone. "Stop your fussin' now. We got a long way to go today, and I ain't had much sleep."

"I won't go with you." I backed away from him. "I won't go! Stop! Take your hands off me!"

He picked me up and threw me into the wagon, then said with unruffled calm, "There's some water in that jug, and here's a piece of meat. It's all you're goin' to get, so I'd think twice before I throwed it away."

I stared horrified at the man who was treating me like a slave, transporting me to another part of the state, another part of the country. He climbed into the wagon again, flapped the reins, and spoke to his horses. We were under way again.

I was tempted briefly to smash the water jug and to toss the food in his face, but I was hungry and I believed what he had said about this being all I would get. I gnawed the dried meat he had given me, which was salty and tasted slightly moldy, and washed it down with long pulls of tepid water.

The food restored my confidence and I began to think about escape. I examined the shackles. They were heavy iron rings hinged on one side and fastened on the other by a sort of padlock which seemed to require a key to open it.

Weighty chains with two-inch links were soldered to each of the rings, permitting my feet and hands a spread of only two feet.

My wrists and feet were small. I tried to pull them through the rings. The attempts were futile and painful, and I soon gave up. I flounced impatiently. My situation was hopeless, desperate. And if I couldn't escape soon it would get worse.

"Finished playin' with them things?" my jailor asked jocularly. "You won't make a dent in 'em, honey. Stronger men than you have tried and they couldn't budge 'em."

I nearly wept aloud with frustration. The morning sun beat down mercilessly and sapped the last of my strength. We were traveling north, and not on the river road, I saw, but on some desolate track that was so little used that tall grass grew out of the ruts. Any hopes I had of seeing someone I knew in passing were quickly dashed. Not, I reflected mournfully, that they would know me anyway. They would not even look beyond their first impressions of black hair and eyes and ragged clothing. A slave was a faceless entity, not a woman with feelings and hopes and desires. Arnold and Georgette had planned their revenge well.

I scolded myself. I was slipping into servility already. I could not let that happen, could not let my spirits falter. I must not let my determination to escape waver for an instant. I was not a slave. I would never be a slave, no matter what they did to me. I thought back to the *Charleston Belle*. The slaves in her stinking hold had been free once, too, until white men had forced their ways upon them. There was no escape for them now, none. No, no, I mustn't let myself think like that. No matter what happened to me I must remain strong and confident of myself. I had been tested before, and I had survived.

I thought of Jean Lafitte. More than anyone else, he had helped me become a woman, proud of my beauty and accomplishments, secure in the knowledge that I could do anything a man could do if I had to, a free spirit who had truly achieved a measure of independence that was rare for a woman.

And what lay ahead now? A journey to a new life with an ugly, amoral man who treated me like a load of goods. I was certain that nothing I could say would persuade him to abandon his task. I would certainly try hard to win him over, but I suspected that I would be wasting my time. No, if I wanted to escape I would have to use a little more ingenuity. I couldn't expect to talk my way out of this predicament.

The wagon rumbled along over the dry, deeply-rutted road bed. The horses seemed to know their way, and the man's head bobbed loosely, as though he were sleeping. If I slipped off the rear of the wagon while he was dozing, I thought, I could hide in the bushes until it was dark and then make my way to some civilized place—a house, a plantation—and beg for sanctuary.

We went a little farther. He still seemed to be sleeping. Hoping that the creaking and rattling of the wagon would cover any noise I made, I jumped off the back. The shackles made it impossible for me to keep my balance and I fell clumsily onto the hard road. But I scrambled to my feet and ran for the shelter of the undergrowth. I didn't even look back.

I hid quietly, not daring to breathe. After a few minutes I heard the crunch of footsteps on the road. He came closer, closer, and stopped about two feet in front of where I was hiding. I could see the scuffed toes of his boots.

"Why don't you come on out of there?" He sounded unperturbed. "Might be snakes back in those weeds. Hate for you to die of snakebite. Terrible way to go." He parted the brambles with his calloused hands and looked down at me. "Come on," he said wearily. "I don't want to stand here all day."

I emerged from my thorny hiding place and accompanied him back to the wagon, which stood about two hundred feet up the road.

"I thought you were asleep," I said wryly.

"I was. But I got ears, don't I? Besides, when you fell out of the wagon the whole thing shook near to pieces. Well, you won't get nowhere, gal. Not so long's I'm haulin' you."

"They really must have made it worth your while," I remarked with bitterness. "And you'll still collect on me twice, no matter who you sell me to, right?"

"Yes, I will."

"Is it much farther?" I asked, hoping to learn my destination.

"Oh, I guess so. Part of the deal was to take you so far from 'em that they'd never see you again. What did you think, that I was gonna sell you to the plantation next door so's you could run away and git in their hair again? No sir. I'm a man of my word. Keepin' your word's good business."

When he lifted me into the wagon he nodded and said, "See those ring bolts there on the sides?"

I looked around. "Yes."

"Well, if you disturb my sleep any more I'm gonna shackle you to one of them ring bolts. It'll be mighty uncomfortable ridin', but I don't care about that. It's up to you."

"I won't try anything," I muttered sullenly. I couldn't face being chained like a slave to the walls of this mobile prison.

We avoided main roads and settlements. Occasionally I caught glimpses of the Mississippi through the trees. I had already started to scheme about the coming night and how I could wrest the key away from him while he slept. But as night fell he merely lit his lantern and hung it aloft next to his seat and pushed ahead, never even stopping to eat or drink or rest his weary horses.

I slept briefly and woke when we jerked to a halt. He took his lantern down and came around to the back of the wagon.

"Are we here?" I mumbled sleepily.

"We're someplace," he grunted. "Get down."

I swung my legs over the back end and hopped down. I would have fallen, but he caught my arm. We walked down a slope. I heard the gentle lapping of waves against wooden pilings, and soon I could see the light from his lantern reflected on the surface of the water. We walked to the end of a deserted pier and sat down to wait. I couldn't see any signs of civilization, only this rotting pier in the middle of nowhere.

"We're a little early," Niles said. "Made good time on that cowpath. Good thing it was dry. River's high, though. Always is this time of year. The thaw up north."

"What are we waiting for?" I asked him.

"A boat."

I couldn't get any more information out of him. At least I knew we weren't going to travel over land indefinitely. Escape would be impossible on the water. I could never swim, weighed down as I was with my iron bracelets.

After a long time we saw a gleam of light far down the river and heard a low, roaring noise.

"What's that?" I asked wonderingly.

"Steamboat."

"Oh." I hadn't seen too many of the iron monsters that were just beginning to navigate the river. I knew they were dangerous and unreliable, prone to explosions and fires.

"I seen men get their whole heads taken off when one of

them boilers goes,'' Niles said encouragingly. ''Terrible. But they make time against the current, not like them keelboats.''

He waved his lantern and received an answering wave of a torch. As the monstrous thing hove into sight I could make out shadowy figures moving around on her single deck, which was about thirty feet long and fifteen wide. The center third of the boat was taken up by a furnace that belched flame-tinted smoke. Stacks of firewood were piled in the stern, along with barrels and sacks of goods that would be sold upriver—coffee, sugar, rice, whiskey, barley. The thing slowed down and anchored in front of us, about thirty feet out from the pier. Two men lowered a dinghy and rowed towards us.

''Howdy, Bose,'' called one.

My captor jerked his head. ''Jake.''

''What you got for me this run?''

Bose gave me a little shove. ''Quadroon slave. Friend of mine wants her far away, Jake. He doesn't want her to come back.''

''I'm not a slave,'' I shouted angrily. My chains rattled, belying my words. ''I'm not! It was a trick, an evil plot against me because they hated me. Won't you listen to what I'm saying? I'm not a slave, I'm a Frenchwoman—''

Bose gripped my arm warningly. ''Jest shut your face,'' he growled. ''Don't interrupt when a man's talkin' business.''

''You got a live one there, Bose,'' Jake laughed. ''How much you askin'?''

''Two hundred,'' said Bose calmly.

''Two!'' Jake spat into the water. ''She looks a little scrawny, even in this light. I'll give you a hundred, Bose, and I got some fancy liquor on board, straight from New Orleans.''

''You don't say so?'' Bose drawled. ''Two hundred, Jake. I got all the liquor I can use right now.''

"Aw, Bose," Jake said sorrowfully, "you ain't no fun to bargain with anymore."

"You'll get a lot more for her up north," Bose told him. "I can't let her go for less. Come on, honey, you and me'll try someplace else."

"I'm not going with you," I bawled. "Let me go!"

Jake laughed. "A hundred and fifty, Bose. And not a cent more."

Bose nodded. "Sounds good to me. She's all yours now, Jake." Hard money changed hands. "So long, gal. Hope he don't blow you up on that fool thing. I wouldn't travel on her, I know that."

They lifted me into the dinghy. I protested loudly, and when no one paid any attention I began to thrash and kick. When one of my kicks nearly overturned the dinghy Jake cuffed me and I sat down in the bottom of the boat. My head buzzed and I felt sick.

"You got a key for these things?" Jake called to Bose before we pushed off. He reached over and rattled my leg irons.

"Nope," said Bose. "Never carry a key. You'll have to get a 'smith to hammer 'em off."

Jake cursed. "We'll leave 'em on, then. I ain't goin' to no smith with this piece of trash. Ain't got the time. Well, so long, Bose. See you next time we're down this way."

Bose picked up his lantern and waved it at us as he walked back to his wagon. Jake rowed us out to the wheezing steamboat and lifted me up over the low side. Strong arms on deck hauled me aboard and I fell panting on the crudely-hewn deck. Jake and his mate climbed up and dragged the dinghy up, then made her fast. Jake shouted orders to his men to stoke the furnace, and after enough pressure had built up inside the boiler, the pistons began to pump up and down and the large paddled wheel on the port side started to turn, churning the river water. We moved slowly up the Mississippi.

"When we get up a nice head of steam we can do about five miles an hour against the current," Jake roared at me over the din. "Come on, I'll show you where you can sleep."

We skirted the furnace, which radiated an intense heat. The night was already uncomfortably warm, and I noticed that the three men, Jake and his two helpers, went shirtless and that their bodies were shiny with sweat. Jake led me forward to the prow. A small lean-to had been erected to provide a minimum shelter against the wind and rain. Blazing torches mounted on poles on either side of the craft illuminated the way ahead sufficiently so that floating trees and other obstructions could be avoided.

"There's only one blanket in there," Jake said. "Don't be scared if somebody nudges you a little later. We keep going night and day when the river's this high, and we take turns sleepin'. It's all right as long as there's two fellas workin', one to stoke and one to navigate. This is my boat," he said proudly. "The *Golden Eagle*." He gazed at me and moistened his lips. The torchlight flickered on his broad, seamed face. He reached out and grasped my shoulders and pulled me close to him, and tilted my face towards the light. "You're not bad-lookin' for a quadroon," he said. "What's yer name?"

I stiffened and lowered my eyes. He reeked of grease and smoke and whiskey. His hands were huge and so rough that I could feel the callouses on his palms through the thin fabric of my dress and shawl.

"Alligator got yer tongue?" he asked. "You need to loosen it up if you want to enjoy this trip. Folks on the river don't take kindly to mean-faced slave bitches. They'll beat your head in if they don't like your fancy ways. Come here."

He pressed me close to his oily chest, which seemed to radiate an unbearable heat. We fell back into the lean-to and he shoved my skirts up to my waist and wriggled around on top of me. I tried to hold my breath, just so I wouldn't have to smell him. I nearly passed out, and wished that I could faint and lose consciousness while he was straddling me. But I didn't.

He groaned as he relieved himself. My eyes were closed but I didn't have to see him to know what he was doing when he was finished with me. I had seen too many men strutting as they closed their breeches, gloating over their manliness. I hated them, all of them.

"Don't you worry none," Jake reassured me. "I won't let those other two pigs near you."

I would have laughed in his face if I hadn't been so choked with anger.

We nosed our way upriver, stopping often to replenish the supply of wood that the dragon devoured greedily, and to trade some of Jake's New Orleans whiskey for supplies. Jake worked me hard during the day and used me hard at night, or whenever he felt like it. The other two, although they must have resented Jake's decree, never laid a hand on me. I hated life on the river and I hated the River Rats, as they called themselves, but at least I was still alive. And as long as I lived I could dream of escape and revenge.

When we reached Memphis, Tennessee, Jake unexpectedly sold me.

"I need the money, Frenchie," he explained. He held an impromptu auction on the docks. I was wearing a tattered boy's shirt and a skirt made of sacking. The shirt had lost its buttons and I had knotted it together under my breasts. I was dirty and I smelled bad. My jaw was swollen from the last time Jake had beaten me, and my hair was so matted and tangled that I knew I couldn't have gotten a comb through it if I had owned one. I looked awful, but the men who sailed the keelboats and arks and rafts on the Mississippi thought I was beautiful.

"I got me a fine high-yeller whore from Haiti," Jake

bawled. "She's as pretty as a peach and as tough as nails." That much was true: life on the river had certainly toughened me, and I was as strong as any boy. "Come on, boys, take a look. Just step right up here. Smile for the boys, Frenchie. You look as mean-faced as a water moccasin."

Interested parties began to gather.

"What are you askin'?" someone called.

"Three hundred dollars, hard cash," Jake said. "Come on and take a better look. Say something, Frenchie. Let the fellas hear how nice you talk."

"I'll promise five hundred dollars to the man who delivers me to Jean Lafitte in New Orleans," I said. "I'm not a slave—"

Their laughter drowned me out. Jake clapped me on the back.

"See, boys? Ain't she a fine little bitch? Talks just like a real New Orleans whore."

The men crowded closer. One squeezed my breast while Jake's back was turned. I cursed at him and struck him on the face, and Jake obligingly knocked him down.

"I'm a Frenchwoman of noble birth," I shouted. "I was married to a rich planter. My enemies conspired against me. Please, please listen to me!"

But no one listened. They thought I was amusing, if a little crazy, and they commiserated with Jake when he told them he hated to part with me.

The bargaining was intense. Finally two hulking brothers who owned a keelboat bought me for two hundred and eighty dollars. They intended to sell me when they got to Illinois, where slaves commanded higher prices. They took turns beating and raping me, and by the time we reached Cairo, Illinois, where the Mississippi and Ohio Rivers merged, I was nearly dead. From Cairo I traveled upriver with my new owner, a hawk-nosed man

named Starker who talked a lot about repentance and the
evils of the flesh during the day, and who raped me every
night before he went to sleep.

Not surprisingly, none of my owners had my shackles
removed. They must have sensed that I would try and run
away as soon as I was free of them. I heard myself called
mulatto and quadroon and octoroon, and "fancy-house
whore from New Orleans," and even "high-class house
slave." I found the last appellation the most amusing. To
each and every new owner, in fact, to everyone who
would listen to me for just two minutes, I told the story of
my wealthy husband and my abduction. I promised my
listeners rich rewards if they would return me to New
Orleans. They would all look at me pityingly, and soon I
became known as the "crazy fancy-house slave from New
Orleans." They treated me like a slave because I looked
like I had never been anything else, and because I wore
chains on my wrists and ankles. Nothing I said could
persuade them otherwise.

Starker planned to take me to Wheeling, West Virginia,
and trade me for furs, which he would then take back to
New Orleans and sell at a handsome profit. We reached
Wheeling at the end of June, 1813. Starker hurried me
towards the wharf where the fur-trading warehouse stood,
and he cursed me because I couldn't walk any faster. I
pointed out that the shackles on my legs, which had cut
and bruised my flesh so badly that I could feel the blood
oozing around my feet as I walked, were the real impedi-
ments to my progress, and I suggested that he have them
removed. He cursed and cuffed me, and seemed enraged
when I continued to smile calmly and shuffle along at a
snail's pace behind him.

Wheeling seemed to be no different from so many of the
frontier towns I had seen on my journey up the river from
Louisiana. The buildings were little more than shacks, and

streets were hard earth or muddy channels, depending on
the weather, and towering forests and mountain ranges
came right up to the fringes of this mean civilization,
making me think that these Americans were not so far
removed from living like savages after all. The men were
crude and loud-talking, and the women, when there were
any to be seen, were gaunt and tired-looking. A goodly
proportion of the populations of these towns seemed to be
transients who spoke with undimmed hope of finding a
better place and a profitable role in this vast, untamed
country.

We passed a smithy, which I eyed hopefully, a saloon,
and a few stores. People stared at me as we shambled
along. I saw no pity in their eyes, only curiosity. We
reached the warehouse and Starker dragged me inside.
Furs were piled in bales and sorted according to grade and
type, and several men were walking around the piles,
picking up pelts, examining them, arguing with each other
about their cost and quality.

"Damn you," Starker said under his breath, "we're
too late. This is the tail end of the season, the dregs! The
best quality furs are gone, gone, and it's all your fault.
You damned bitch. I knew I should have left you to those
two bastards at Cairo. You're so damned slow—"

"It's not my fault you wasted all that time plowing me
when you should have been traveling," I said with a
superior smile. So great had been his last-minute hurry to
get to the trading center that we hadn't even had breakfast
that morning.

He slapped my face and barked at me shrilly for talking
back to him. The other traders fell silent for a moment, and
turned their heads to see what was going on. As soon as
they saw that it was only a man beating his slave they
returned to the business at hand, and once again the sounds
of commerce filled the air.

Starker dragged me from trader to trader. Each time he offered me in exchange for a good-sized bundle of furs, the owner would shake his head and say, "Sorry, fellow, hard money only." He grew more and more irritable as the day wore on. Finally he left me sitting on a bale of rabbit skins near the door while he went across the street to the tavern.

A burly, black-bearded man stepped into the vast room. He carried a pile of pelts on his back, not rabbit, but muskrat, beaver and mink. He was almost as tall as Garth, but he was thick and broad where Garth was lean and hard and he must have weighed half again as much. His face was red and furrowed with seams and scars above his beard, and his eyes were small and so pale in color that they seemed to disappear into his head. He wore the usual odd combination of clothing for a frontiersman: a fur cap, a stained deerskin coat with fringe at the bottom and on the sleeves, a knife in the belt, some rough woolen trousers and heavy black boots. He looked around the warehouse. When he saw me he set down his bundle and came over to me. He took a stance in front of me and studied me wordlessly through his pale eyes. There was something in his gaze, something inhuman and cold, that frightened me, but I looked at him boldly and fearlessly.

I lounged on one elbow on my soft perch. "Would you like to see my teeth?" I asked tartly. He made no reply. "What's the matter?" I twitted him, growing braver in response to his silence, "haven't you ever seen a woman before?"

His eyes flickered. "Who owns you?" he asked. His voice was deep and rasping. The sound seemed to reverberate through the enormous chamber of his torso before it came out of his mouth like rumbling thunder.

This time I made no answer, but swung around on my bale so that my back was to him. He chuckled.

"You stink to high heaven, girl," he said. I heard him walk away.

Starker came running up. "Who was that man? Who were you talking to?"

"Some filth who says he wouldn't give you three rabbit skins for me," I said.

"You're a goddamn liar," Starker hissed. "I'm going to ask him myself."

I shrugged elaborately and lay down.

In a few minutes Starker came back with the man in tow. "Get down," my owner squawked. "He wants to look at you."

"He's already had his look," I said sullenly. Starker yanked at the chain between my legs. I felt the blood drain out of my face and I bit back a yelp of pain. "All right, all right," I said grudgingly. I slid off the bale and faced them boldly. "I don't smell any better up close," I told the bearded man. "You might want to step back a little."

He bared his teeth in what I took to be a grin, but Starker squealed and hopped up and down. "Hold your tongue, you black bitch," he said in my ear, "or I'll beat the daylights out of you. Mr. Hennessy's gonna give me his furs for you, and by God if you spoil this I'll kill you!"

I turned my head slowly in his direction and spit right in his eye. Starker howled with rage and blotted his face, then drew back his hand and swung at me. The bearded man caught his arm and bent it backwards. Starker wriggled helplessly in his grasp like a worm on a hook.

"Don't do that," the big man said. "I don't pay for damaged goods. My pelts are in better shape than she is right now. Take 'em and get out of here. Come on," he said to me. "Let's go."

I followed him out of the warehouse, dragging my chains. He made a face at them and said, "We'd better get those things off you. I can't stand the noise."

He took me to the smithy, and he and the blacksmith pounded and hammered at the rusted irons for nearly an hour until I was free of them. With every stroke, every blow of the hammer, I cringed and quivered but told myself that soon I would be free, free of the hideous trappings of slavery. The irons rubbed my wounds until they were really raw, and by the time the last bracelet had fallen off I was white and sick with pain and the effort of not crying out. The blacksmith applied some smelly ointment to my sores. Hennessy gave him a few coins and led me out into the sunshine.

"Wait here," he said, and he disappeared into the general store next to the blacksmith's shop.

I looked around me, amazed. He had actually gone away and left me alone. It was a miracle, nothing less. I peered up and down the dusty street, then I ran for the river as fast as I could go. My feet and ankles throbbed as I ran and I started to limp after the first hundred yards. I cried with anger at my body's frailty, and I paused to rest for a moment not far from the place where Starker had left his canoe. I knew how to paddle it. I would steal it, go upriver a while, then take to the woods. They would never find me.

When I had caught my breath I plunged on. I could feel the interested glances of the people I passed, but I ignored them. I was running for my freedom, for my life. By the time they came to their senses and realized that I was a runaway slave, I would be long gone.

So intent was I on my escape that I never even heard the horse and rider coming up behind me. Hennessy's voice crashed like the thunder of doom in my ears. "You won't get far that way," he chuckled mirthlessly. "How about a ride?"

I stopped in my tracks and buried my face in my hands. The despair that filled me was so deep that I couldn't even cry. I looked up at him for a moment and was immediately aware of how futile my attempt to escape had been. He loomed over me on his mount. He had strength, weapons, serviceable clothing. I didn't even have shoes. I collapsed onto the ground and lay there, too heartsick even to move. He dismounted, picked me up and slung me over his horse's back. I clung to the animal's mane and pulled myself into a sitting position. Then he climbed up behind me and we rode out of town into the forest.

We traveled until it was almost dark. We made camp in a clearing near a stream. He had shot a rabbit; now he threw the carcass at my feet and told me to cook it.

"If you don't want to eat the fur and innards you'd better give me a knife," I told him. He grinned and reached for his hunting knife. He flicked his wrist sharply and the next moment I saw the knife handle, still vibrating, protruding from the rabbit's side. He laughed heartily, and stood over me with his musket pointed at my heart while I skinned and gutted the animal.

When I had finished he said, "Give me that knife back now," and he jerked his musket slightly. I longed to plunge the blade into his fat belly, even if it meant that he would kill me, too. But I told myself that there would be a better time to escape. I would have to be patient, and choose my time well. I tossed the knife into the dirt at his feet. He picked it up and shoved it into his belt.

I built a fire, spitted the rabbit on some green sticks, and walked to the stream to fill a pan with water for coffee. He watched my every move, pulling at a flask of whiskey and wiping his mouth with the back of his hand. I could hear the change in his breathing—it became low and deep, like a series of longing sighs—and I braced myself for the onslaught I knew would come. He attacked me suddenly, bellowing fiercely and violently like a maddened bull. I hit the ground forcefully, and then he was on top of me. The smell of him sickened me. I struggled and strained against him, then my fingers found the handle of the knife in his belt. I prayed I could drive it into him before he was even aware of what I was doing.

"What's this?" He yanked at my hand and twisted my arm so viciously that I thought he would wrench it from its socket. He roared angrily, "So you're a fighter, are you, bitch? Well, so am I."

I huddled on the ground, sick with pain and fury and the longing to kill him. He was Josiah Fowler reincarnated, but my captivity was even harder to endure that it had been on the *Charleston Belle*. On the ship there had been no thought of escaping. But here, in the wilderness, the promise of freedom was so near, so tantalizing.

He never let me out of his sight. I cursed myself for moving too swiftly and losing his trust. If I had been docile, perhaps, he might have been lulled into thinking that I was helpless and weak. But now he followed me everywhere when we were camped, and even my most private acts were not hidden from his watery, evil eyes.

"Starker said you were from New Orleans," he said one rainy night as we crouched near a smoking campfire. "I bet you worked in a whorehouse in New Orleans. I was there once. Fine town. Prettiest women I ever seen."

I disdained to answer him.

"You're French, ain't you? Let me hear you talk some French."

I maintained a haughty silence. Suddenly he reached over and cuffed me hard on the side of the head. I fell backwards.

"You are the dirty son of an ass who mated with a snake," I said in rapid French. "May you begin to rot and putrify before you die. May your limbs fall off. May you become like a eunuch—"

He threw back his head and roared appreciatively. "I

don't know what you're sayin'," he said, "but I bet you're cursin' me up one side and down the other. Go 'head and curse me all you please, Frenchie, if it makes you feel better."

"I know how you can make a thousand dollars," I said in English. "Maybe more."

"Yeah? Where?" He devoured a haunch of rabbit in a single mouthful and swilled some whiskey. I had to turn my face away. Just watching him eat made me lose my appetite.

"New Orleans," I said. "You have heard of the pirate Jean Lafitte? Well, he is a good friend of mine. He would give a thousand dollars for me if you took me back there. I am not lying to you, Mr. Hennessy. A thousand dollars!"

He shook his shaggy head doubtfully. "I never heard of no slave bitch goin' for a thousand dollars."

"But I'm not a slave," I insisted. "I am a free woman. I swear it's true." I launched into my story. He listened impassively. "Please believe me. I'm telling you the truth."

"No. You're mine now, Frenchie. I paid good money for you, and I'm gonna work you until you drop. Make no mistake about that."

"How much were those pelts of your worth?" I asked him.

"About five hundred dollars," he said, chewing thoughtfully.

I laughed loudly. "You were cheated then, you fool. I wouldn't bring much more than two hundred and fifty on the block, maybe not even that much. You didn't see anyone else begging to buy me at Starker's price, did you? Right now he's laughing his head off at you for being a damned fool."

A strange expression flitted across his face momentarily, and then it was gone. "It wouldn't change things for you if I had paid five dollars for you instead of five hundred," he said slowly. "You're mine until you die, or until I decide to sell you or kill you."

Or until I run away, I thought. Our eyes met over the fire.

"You better not try runnin' away," he said, reading my mind. "I'd find you pretty quick, gal, and I'd fix you so you'd never run anyplace again." His words were horrible but his tone was dry and flat. It made me shiver. "Starker was no fool," he grunted. "He knew that if he took those leg irons off you you'd be gone before he knew what happened. I'm no fool either. I took 'em off because we couldn't make time while you had 'em on. But don't figure you'll be able to get away. I knew you'd try it back there. I could see it in your face at the 'smith's. But I figured I'd test you. I wanted to know just how bad you wanted to get loose."

"And so now you know," I said dully.

"I know. You may think I've been cheated, but I haven't been. You've got a lot of years left in you, and a lot of hard work." He laughed and said to himself, "Yep, I'm gonna get my money's worth out of you, bitch. You can bet on it."

I looked at him. In the firelight he looked bear-like, evil, a creature from the darkest places of these primeval forests. "So now we know where we stand," I said with forced lightness. "You have a lot of slaves?"

"About fifty."

"And they don't run away?"

"I bring 'em back and they don't try it again," he said flatly. "I've never lost one yet."

I huddled in my blanket near the dying embers. Disembodied faces whirled around in my head. Uncle Theo, Fowler, Garth, Jake, Arnold—and now this man. When I fell asleep I dreamed of the *Charleston Belle*. I was a slave in the hold, the only slave there, and Edward Hennessy was the captain. I woke myself with my panicked sobbing and I couldn't sleep. I lay on the hard ground and listened to the sounds of the night and to his breathing. My hatred would keep me alive, I knew. After a long time I managed to fall asleep.

He prodded me awake long before dawn. We ate cold stew and drank coffee, then we set out across the mountains. Rain fell steadily all through the day, but we plodded on, climbing the steep wooded slopes with difficulty. We managed to cover about twenty miles a day through the mountains. Hennessy told me that he owned a plantation in Shenandoah County, Virginia, about four hundred miles from Wheeling. He used the word plantation proudly and boastfully, and I conjured up visions of a place like La Rêve or Highlands: beautiful and gracious, with rich land that produced abundant crops.

Our journey took a little over three weeks. Every day was the same: we would climb to the top of a wooded rise, only to confront a seemingly endless vista of green mountains; then we would descend once again into a dense wooded valley. At night, after we had eaten and he had abused me, if he felt like it, he would bind my hands and feet so tightly that I could hardly move. He would free me when morning came and it was time to travel again.

I had brought that punishment on by trying to kill him when we were a week out of Wheeling. One night as he lay snoring by our campfire, I decided that I would have to kill him in order to get away, and I knew how to do it. While he slept I crept over to a large flat rock that I had seen while I was building our fire. I lifted it. It was heavy and deadly. It would crush his skull like an eggshell, and then I would have his horse, his weapons, and my freedom.

I moved towards him silently on bare feet with the rock cradled in my hands. I crouched near his head and raised my bludgeon. Just as I brought it crashing down some sense of danger woke him and he rolled aside.

With one violent sweep of his arm he sent me sprawling on the ground. I could taste the blood in my mouth.

"Tryin' to kill me, are you?" he shouted deafeningly. "I'm too smart for you, Frenchie. I got ears like an Injun and I'm quicker than a rattlesnake. You're gonna be mighty sorry you tangled with Edward Hennessy, bitch."

He beat me until I vomited blood. Then he bound my hands and feet with a single leather thong. I groaned and tossed restlessly on the hard ground. He kicked me and sneered, "That ought to stop you from gettin' any more fancy ideas while I'm sleepin'."

The day came when we crossed the last mountain and he said, "That's it. That's my plantation."

I saw a small white frame house standing on a bleak, windswept hill. The few regular green patches on the rocky hillsides were tobacco, he said. On another brown slope a small herd of cattle grazed somnolently under the burning summer sun. The earth looked parched, lifeless. A few weathered buildings, slave shacks and tobacco-drying sheds and barns, surrounded the house. They were unpainted, as brown and weathered as the ground they stood on. Dead, I thought. The whole plantation looked dead and empty.

It was a pathetic contrast to La Rêve. As we approached the buildings some dogs that were tied near a tilting smokehouse set up an hysterical barking. Hennessy was humming lightly, echoing their high, angry tones. He spoke sharply to the dogs and they subsided a little. A handful of chickens in the yard scattered as we approached the house. We came to a halt at the door. A pale thin woman appeared. Two wan little girls clung to her skirts.

"Edward! Did you get a good price?" she called. When

she saw me step out from behind the horse her mouth fell open.

"This is Frenchie," Hennessy said. I was startled by the gleeful note in his voice and I looked at him. He was grinning widely at her, daring her to challenge him. The little girls whimpered.

The woman pushed a strand of hair out of her eyes. "I don't understand," she said. "You were—"

"She's a new slave, Martha," the man explained gruffly.

Martha Hennessy stepped into the sunlight and shaded her eyes with her hand. "But—but the money, Edward," she said hesitantly. "We needed it so badly. The crops —I—I don't understand. Isn't there any money?"

"No." He hooked his thumbs in his belt and cocked his head at her, daring her to say anything more. She stood gaping at me, and after a moment he said, "This is all, Martha. I traded the furs for the girl. They were worth five hundred dollars. She was a bargain, was Frenchie. Step up, girl. Show yourself off. Isn't every day Martha gets to see a woman worth that much money."

Two desolate tears ran down his wife's thin cheeks. She gulped. "I suppose we can put her in with old Annie," she whispered. She almost gagged on the words.

"She's to have the spare room," he told her. "She's a fancy house servant, Martha. A helper for you. What's the matter? Can't you appreciate what I've done for you?"

She shook her head wordlessly and ran into the house. He bolted after her, almost falling over the two terrified children, who wailed and looked at me fearfully, then followed their parents inside. I heard angry voices, his deep and biting, hers high and shrill. The children were crying. Then I heard a shriek, followed by a short silence, followed by more wails and shouts. He had struck her.

I stood alone in the hot, shadeless yard. So he had brought me here to torment his wife. He was mad and hate-filled, and we were all his victims. The need to be free was so strong in me that it was almost painful and I had to stop myself from crying out. I knew I would escape him somehow. I had to.

## XV.   The Brand

Blinking my eyes against the rising clouds of steam, I plunged my arms into the hot soapy water and kneaded the dirty clothes energetically. Then I dragged each piece out of the water and scrubbed it over the fins of a washboard before I set it aside for rinsing.

"Do you like being a slave, Frenchie?" Jenny asked. She was eight, and even the terrible tension that filled her life could not dampen her natural curiosity.

"Not much," I said gruffly. I didn't want to grow fond of the children. I didn't want to become attached to the farm or the Hennessys in any way. I tried to rebuff them when they wanted to get close to me, but it wasn't easy. They were sweet little girls, and although they had some of their mother's shyness and timidity, they had none of their father's meanness. "I would rather be far away, in a place where I wouldn't have to do any washing or scrubbing or cooking," I said, punctuating my words with vigorous strokes on the washboard. "Far, far away."

"What would you do then?" Sarah, who was six, was picking up her sister's habit of questioning.

I thought a moment. "I would go sailing. Yes, I think I'd go sailing under the blue sky and the stars. I'd have a strong wind at my back and a wide, empty sea in front of me and all around me. Sailing alone in a fine shiny boat with sails as white as clouds, and smooth decks and a little cabin filled with good wines and lots of food. And I'd have lots of warm blankets for when it got cold."

I wished for all the things I did not have: privacy, good

food and wine, warmth against the chill of Virginia's autumn nights. And freedom.

"Papa says you're from France," Jenny said.

I glanced at their thin faces peering at me over the edge of the washtub. "Yes, that's right."

"Is France far from here?"

"Quite far. First you have to get to the coast, and then you cross the ocean in a big ship. And then you get into a golden carriage and you ride until you get to Orléans. That's a beautiful city, very old. Jeanne d'Arc is from Orléans. And after that you ride south a little ways. The land is rolling and wooded, but not like it is here. Things are smaller, and simpler. And the estates are lovely, older and more beautiful than American plantations." I could almost see the Chateau Lesconflair in the steam that rose up from the hot water. "And life there is very good, very good indeed." I clamped my teeth down on my lower lip and viciously rubbed one of Martha Hennessy's faded housedresses on the washboard.

"Would you like to go back there?" Jenny's blue eyes were sad.

"To France?" I stifled a bitter laugh. Ever since Hennessy had brought me to this place I had thought of nothing else. Sometimes the longing for my home was so strong that I could hardly bear it. I would have given anything to be able to go back. "Yes, I guess I would like to see my home again."

Edward Hennessy's large frame filled the doorway of the wash house. "Go play someplace else, girls," he said to his daughters.

The girls turned their frightened eyes to him for a second and then slipped past him and ran into the yard.

"Gettin' homesick?" he asked gleefully, leaning against the doorframe.

I didn't look up. "What if I were?"

He said, "What the hell difference does it make whether you're French or whether you're the bastard bitch of some white planter and his black whore?"

"Obviously it makes a great deal of difference to me," I retorted.

He advanced into the room and stood next to me. I could feel the heat thrown off by his body and smell the traces of tobacco and sweat that clung to his clothing. I hated him so much that his nearness made me shake with loathing. I didn't try to hide it.

Rivulets of perspiration trickled down my face and neck. In the close heat of the tiny shed I had unbuttoned my blouse and permitted it to hang open over the tops of my breasts. Now I pulled the fabric together and held it closed with my hand while I stood waiting patiently for him to leave.

His big laugh filled the cramped shed. "You're a rare bitch, Frenchie," he said, stepping closer to me and yanking my hand away from my blouse. "I knew the first minute I set eyes on you that you were the kind of woman who could appreciate a real man, and I was right. But you got to watch yourself. You're gettin' to be as cold and mean as Martha."

"Then the fault must be yours," I observed tartly. "Any woman who works as hard as we do can hardly be expected to have any outside interests."

He wrenched my blouse open and cradled my breasts in his gross hands. I tried to pull away. "No," I said through clenched teeth. "Get out of here. Don't you care anything about the children? If they saw—"

"I'll whip them if they try to come in," he said. "Come here—"

We struggled. He tried to put his arms around me and when I resisted he struck me in the face with his open hand. I felt as though I had been hit with a sledge hammer.

My eye started to swell immediately and I knew it was
turning black. He rubbed his knee against me and slid his
hand under my skirts. While I fought him weakly he
started to drag me down to the floor.

"Mas' Edward, one of the mules has gone and busted
her leg!"

A Negro named Ira stood panting in the doorway,
watching us.

"Goddamn it, get out of here!" Hennessy bellowed.
"Where?"

"North field, Mas'," the man said, shifting uncomfortably and staring at the floor. "She fell in a hole and she
went down like she was dead. Now she's jes' lyin' there,
breathin' heavy."

"I'll be there in a minute. Now get the hell out of here."

"Yes, Mas'."

The slave disappeared. Hennessy clenched his fists. He
seemed to grow large with fury. He roared thunderously
and with one sweep of his arm he sent my heavy steaming
tub and washboard flying. Water flooded the shed floor
and clean clothes lay with dirty ones in pools of mud on the
rough boards. He whirled on me, daring me to say just one
word. I gazed back woodenly. I knew better than to open
my mouth. He hurled himself out of the wash house and
ran towards the north field.

I stood for two solid minutes ankle-deep in hot dirty
water. Tears of hatred and shame streamed down my
cheeks, mingling with sweat and the blood that oozed out
of the cut he had opened under my eye. I had never felt so
low, so degraded. I swore I would have my revenge on
him, on all the people who were responsible for my being
here: Georgette, Arnold, Garth. I blamed Garth, too, for
not keeping his word to me, for not meeting me that
morning and taking me away before any of that could
happen. I pulled myself up and walked briskly towards the

kitchen. I tried not to think about him. It was too sad, too painful. I had enough to worry about without letting my mind dwell on the past.

I told myself that it could be worse: I could be Martha Hennessy. Even now she was out in the tobacco fields working as hard as any of the blacks, helping to harvest the crop and to carry the tied bundles to the drying sheds. She never spoke an unnecessary word to me, and only addressed me when she had to give me orders about my duties around the house. I couldn't blame her. I could tell that the very sight of me made her sick with hatred and jealousy. I tried to avoid her, as she avoided me. I had decided that Hennessy must be the wickedest man alive, for he was intelligent enough to know how to torment people mentally as well as physically, which made him an even worse devil than Josiah Fowler.

I crossed the yard, pressing the corner of my apron to my bleeding cheek. I would have to dress my wound, and then I would need more hot water to rinse my soiled laundry. On my way I met Isaac, a black boy of about fourteen who was in charge of the kitchen garden and the poultry.

"Good morning, Isaac," I greeted him with forced cheerfulness. He grinned in reply. "How are you feeling today?"

"Better, Missy, a mite better." He bobbed his head and limped away, using a branch cut from a tree as a crutch.

I watched him go and a heavy sadness settled over me. When I first came to this benighted farm, Isaac had been a spry, light-hearted lad—inasmuch as it was possible for anyone to be light-hearted on Hennessy's land. Then one day he had run away. Hennessy took the dogs and went after him. When they returned the boy was a cripple. One of his legs had been horribly mangled. Hennessy said the dogs had done it, but Isaac told the other slaves that the

Mas' had deliberately severed his Achilles tendon as punishment for running away. Now his foot curled inwards and was almost useless. Isaac would not try to run away again, it was true. He could barely hobble.

The slaves had been unsure at first of the way they should treat me. They knew that I was a white woman, yet I was clearly as much Hennessy's slave as any one of them. We were all abused and downtrodden, and I'm sure not one of them envied my place in the Master's bed at night. Hennessy was trying to make a living from land that was rocky and unyielding and utterly unsuitable for farming. He had no money to spend on frivolities like shoes for his workers in winter and any but the poorest rags for their backs.

I heard a faraway shot. He had killed the maimed mule, I guessed.

I had soon realized that the cooks at La Rêve had thrown away better scraps than Hennessy's slaves got to live on. Most of the women were chronically ill, the men were gaunt with hunger and undernourished, and their children's bellies were distended with hunger. The master beat them all harshly when they did not work hard enough to suit him, and once he tied a man to a stake in the center of the yard on the hottest day of the summer and left him there for two days and nights without food or water. I tried to give the man some water and Hennessy caught me. He had knocked me flat with one swipe of his huge hand. If he had balled that hand into a fist he would have broken my jaw.

I looked every bit as scruffy and ragged as the rest. My nails were broken and my feet and hands were calloused and so dirty that they never really came clean no matter how much I washed them. I wore a scarf around my head most of the time, just like the other slave women, because it kept my hair out of my face and also absorbed some of the perspiration that poured off my forehead when I worked. I often thought about the rich, easy life at La Rêve, particularly when I had to do my turn in the fields at harvest time, whacking down tobacco and picking the cotton bolls that grew so sparsely on the starved anemic plants that grew out of the barren soil.

The slaves were a little better fed since my arrival, thanks to my cunning in the kitchen. Hennessy had decreed that I would have to learn how "to cook decent" so that his wife would be free to use her energies in the fields. I smuggled food out to the cabins whenever I had the opportunity and if I was sure the food would not be missed. As yet I had not been found out, even though Hennessy kept a sharp eye on the stock in the larder, which he usually kept locked until I asked him for certain items for the day's meals.

When I finally finished the laundry and hung it out to dry, I went back to the kitchen to prepare lunch, the main meal of the day. I heated the oven and baked some loaves of bread that I had put to rise earlier. I paused for a moment to gaze out the kitchen window at the mountains in the distance, from which I had come to this place with my new master. I never used that title when I addressed him, but always looked at him boldly and said whatever I had to say without needless pleasantries.

The green and blue mountains glimmered through the haze beyond the parched hardness of the farmland. They seemed so distant, so unreachable, like the Promised Land, or a mirage. I longed to run to them, to escape this horrid existence. If only there were some way I could get away from him. But I was never out of his sight long enough: he watched me closely during the day and would notice my absence immediately, and he never failed to come to my room at night.

I saw the little girls racing down the hill towards the

house. Both were in tears and were shrieking wildly. I looked past them. Edward Hennessy was coming across the yard with his wife in his arms. Her head and limbs were drooping limply, and even from a distance her face looked as pale as death. I ran out of the kitchen.

"Mamma's dead, Mamma's dead," the children sobbed, clinging to my skirts.

"Go inside at once, girls," I said briskly, "and make sure your Mamma's bed is turned down. Will you do that for me?" They obeyed. "What happened?" I asked Hennessy. I grabbed her hand and felt for her pulse.

"She fainted, that's all," he growled. "No need for all this excitement. She ain't dead yet."

I followed him inside and up to her room. He dumped her on the bed. I sent the girls for a basin of water and a cloth, and when they returned I told them to go outdoors and sit in the shade until I called them. Then I undressed the unconscious woman and bathed the grime of the fields off her face and arms. Hennessy watched silently from the doorway.

"She'll be all right," he said brusquely. "It's time for lunch. Leave her."

I said savagely, "She will not be all right. You'll have to get someone else to take the place of your dead mule. And you can damn well get your own lunch."

He smirked. "Maybe you'd like to take her place in front of the cart?"

I ignored him and continued to minister to the woman. I slapped her face lightly until she began to jerk and moan, then I helped her into a sitting position and tilted a glass of water to her lips. She choked and fell back on the pillows. I heard a noise behind me and looked up. Her husband had left the room.

"Drink it," I urged her. "Please try. It's all right now, he's gone."

She licked her lips and murmured harshly, ''No. Leave me alone. Get out of here. I don't want you in here. Get out.'' I made no move to leave her, however, and after a moment she accepted a drink of water. ''What happened?'' she asked dazedly. ''I feel so awful.''

''You fainted,'' I told her.

''Oh. Yes, I remember now. I felt so sick all of a sudden, and then—everything turned inside out. It—it must have been the heat.''

''It wasn't the heat,'' I said bluntly. ''You're pregnant, aren't you?'' she closed her eyes and sighed deeply. ''Are you crazy, working like a beast of burden in heat like this?''

''Do you think I have any choice?'' she demanded tearfully. ''Oh, I don't even care any more. It would be better if I died.''

''Don't say that,'' I snapped. ''That's no way to talk. Do you want him to win after all? Do you really want him to have the satisfaction of killing you? Think of the children if you can't think of yourself. And the baby. How far along are you?''

She laughed and sobbed all at once. ''Five months. You'd think I'd be past getting sick, wouldn't you?''

''You're not past killing yourself. Does he know?''

''What do you think?'' I tried to wipe her face with the damp cloth. She pushed my hand away. ''He hasn't looked at me since he brought you back here. Why should he? I suppose I should be grateful to you—but I'm not. Go away and leave me alone.'' She buried her face in her pillow.

I served lunch to Hennessy and the girls. The children had been upstairs to see for themselves that their mother was really all right and had just been ''overcome by the heat,'' as I told them. They were even more subdued than usual, and they picked listlessly at their food. I hated to see them like this. It was unnatural for children this young to be so quiet and sad. Most children don't have fathers like Edward Hennessy, however. He seemed to be unaffected by his wife's sudden illness, and he ate and drank greedily and spoke to me and his daughters as though nothing out of the ordinary had occurred. I don't think I ever hated him as much as I did that day.

That night he came to my room as usual. I had stopped trying to resist him after he knocked me unconscious one night and used me anyway, even though I was as limp and unresponsive as a wet dishcloth. He finished quickly and was soon snoring heavily. I turned my back to him and drew as far away as I could. Once again the nightly ritual had been accomplished. His wife never protested. He had blackened both her eyes that first day, and she knew that her next complaint would bring an even worse punishment. I thought about the child she carried. How would this monster react when he found out? In most families the arrival of a new member was an occasion for rejoicing, but that wouldn't be the case here. Another child would mean another mouth to feed and another soul to torment.

I covered my ears with my hands against his raucous snoring. I couldn't stay to watch what would happen. I wanted no part in this new tragedy. I had to get away, soon.

The next day Hennessy announced that he was going into Henderson, the village about fifteen miles away from the farm, to buy a new mule. He would be gone overnight. I felt that my prayers had been answered. Immediately after he left, I went up to Mrs. Hennessy's room and told her that her husband had ordered me to work that day in the fields. She was still feeling ill and had decided to take advantage of his absence by spending the day in bed. She nodded listlessly when I told her I would leave a cold lunch set out for her and the girls in the dining room. I made my preparations carefully but quickly: I assembled a parcel containing food, a strong knife, and a blanket. At about eight o'clock in the morning I was ready to go. The farm was quiet. The slaves had been working in the fields for two hours already. The children were playing in their mother's room. I left the house and ran for the shelter of the woods.

I walked swiftly all through the day, stopping only long enough to eat some food and drink some water. I was thankful that my feet had developed thick callouses on the bottoms, for the terrain was rocky and often treacherous. I knew that Hennessy would set the dogs after me and so I followed creek beds as much as I could in order to throw them off the scent. I had heard the slaves talking about that one night soon after young Isaac had been captured. Isaac had used the trick and he had been taken anyway. I tried not to think about that, or the dogs, or the possibility of ever going back to that place. Nevertheless, a picture of Edward Hennessy's brutal, ugly face stayed in the front of my mind all day long, spurring me on whenever I felt tired.

I traveled south, towards Louisiana. I had no knowledge of the geography of that part of the continent. I only knew that it was rough and mountainous and that I might travel for many days before I reached a town or settlement. I started preparing a story to explain my ragged appearance: I was going west with my husband and child, we were attacked by robbers who stole everything we owned and killed the rest of my family, leaving me for dead. I would win their sorrow and their sympathy from the start and never give them reason to suspect that I was a runaway slave.

I heard the dogs at early evening. A shock of fright passed through me and I stopped and stood absolutely still, straining my ears to listen to their mournful baying.

They couldn't be Hennessy's dogs, I reasoned. They just couldn't be! He was gone, gone until tomorrow. Their frantic howls sounded closer, ringing through the silent forest like hellish chimes. I ran. I scrambled over rocks and fallen trees, became entangled in sharp briars and heavy undergrowth, and twice I fell heavily when my feet caught in natural traps of vines and branches. As I extricated myself for the second time I began to sob, wasting precious energy and breath. I fancied I could hear the animals' breathing as well as their excited barks and cries.

I needed to use my hands to help clear my path, and I dropped the bundle that contained my knife. Only a moment later did I realize that I could have used that knife now, and that I could use it as a weapon when the time came, as it surely would. The dogs were calling to each other. I heard the crash of hooves and a man's voice encouraging them. A deep bass voice, the voice of Edward Hennessy. I lunged forward blindly, not daring to look behind me.

I didn't want the starved deprived beasts to devour me whole. When I came to a clearing and saw a fir tree whose limbs hung close to the ground I began to climb as quickly as I could. The dogs burst out of the undergrowth and dashed for the foot of the tree. Their din sounded in my ears like a death-knell, but I kept my eyes upward and climbed steadily. I could hear them snapping at my feet, scrambling at the bottom of the tree, whining and yowling with frustration. I looked down. The whole earth below me seemed to be filled with red, lolling tongues and white wet teeth and shiny, hunger-crazed eyes. I cried out fearfully and inched my way further up the tree. They clawed at the bark, and I could almost feel the moist heat of their breath on my legs. I imagined how their fangs would feel when they tore into my flesh.

Hennessy rode out of a thicket and lashed at the frenzied dogs with his whip.

"Come on down from there," he called to me.

I shook my head. "You'll have to shoot me down. I won't let them eat me alive."

He chuckled, a low growl that I could hear over the dogs' clamor. "They won't eat you. They're trained to scare, not to eat. Get away from there, you bitches." He tossed them a dead rabbit that he had slung over the saddle. They fell on it with hungry snarls and soon they were tearing it to bits. I could not believe that they would have spared me.

"Come down," Hennessy called again.

I locked my arms around the rough, sappy trunk of the tree and shook my head vigorously. I was terrified of him. He would surely kill me, I knew he would kill me. Or maim me, as he had maimed Isaac.

He dismounted and walked over to the tree. Very calmly he tested his foothold on one of the bottom branches and he began to climb up after me. Several branches snapped under his weight but somehow he kept himself from falling. He came slowly and steadily. I had climbed as far as I thought I could go before the thick growth of branches at the top of the tree prevented me from going higher.

I looked down at his upturned face. An excited gleam shone in his eyes, and he was grinning and salivating, just like his dogs. I screamed loudly and begged him incoherently to let me go free. He stretched his arm up and grabbed at my naked ankle. I tried to kick his ugly face in, but he held me fast and began to drag me down. His strength was terrific, and I was exhausted from a day's running. I felt myself being dragged down, down, and although I tightened my grip on the branches over my head I soon felt my fingers being ripped away from their hold.

Then we both fell and landed on the hard dry earth under the tree. He grappled with me silently, clamping a huge hand over my mouth to still my incessant deafening screeches. I thought for a moment that he was going to rape me as a way of celebrating his victory over me, but then I saw that the light in his eyes was not lustful but angry and full of mad hatred. He unstopped my mouth and when I screamed again he drew back his hand and hit me hard. Everything grew dark for a moment, and I could taste my own blood on my tongue.

He hauled me to my feet. "Bitch. Damned bitch," he hissed.

I swayed dizzily. "Why—didn't—you—kill—"

"You're surprised to see me, ain't you, bitch? I didn't have to go to Henderson after all. Found a neighbor with a mule he wanted to sell. Good thing, too. You didn't have time to get very far. Get up on that horse."

"I—"

"Get up!" He picked me up and set me on the saddle, then climbed up behind me and whistled at the dogs, who, appetites appeased, now regarded me with a more casual interest.

We retraced the path I had carved with my own scratched and scarred body. When Hennessy saw the bundle of things I had stolen he muttered an oath and retrieved it. The journey back to the farm took such a short time, and I had felt as though I had gone a hundred miles since early morning. It was nearly dark when we reached the farm. As we rode into the yard I felt sick and faint with fear. I was sure that he would not let this transgression go unpunished. He could have tortured and beat me in the forest, but he didn't. He was saving me for something worse.

He shouted to the frightened slaves who came out of their cabins to build a fire in the middle of the yard. They hurried to do as he ordered, bringing armloads of wood and scraps of lumber. Soon a good-sized bonfire was blazing at the heart of the homestead, bathing the shabby buildings in a pink glow and casting tall, eerie shadows all around. My heart was thumping madly. I looked around me desperately, searching for some means of escape, but Hennessy stood next to me and when he saw my panic he grinned and put a heavy hand on my shoulder.

Then he turned to face me and tore the clothes off my body. I flinched and shuddered as he stripped me naked, shouting at the Negroes to watch.

"Get 'em out here, all of 'em," he bellowed. Soon a forest of dark bodies closed around us.

I hung my head with shame, even though there was no joy, no interest in their faces, only deep sorrow and pity. Hennessy bound my hands in front of me and forced me to kneel.

"Please," I said to him, "please let me go. I won't try to run away again, I swear it."

His mouth tightened. "You call me Master. Say it. Say, 'I'm sorry, Master.' Say it, damn you!" He locked his hands around my throat and pressed hard, and as he choked the life out of me he pushed his leering face close to mine and repeated, "Say it, or I swear I'll kill you right here and now."

"I'm—I'm sorry," I gasped.

"Master!" he thundered. The pressure on my throat tightened.

The bizarre scene became even more distorted to my bulging eyes. The sea of black faces seemed evil now. His own face was diabolical, hideous and satanic. Then a blackness began to press in from the periphery of my vision. I couldn't breathe. He was killing me—

"M—Master," I croaked.

He released me and I fell panting to the ground. I was aware of figures moving around between me and the fire. After a while, Hennessy took hold of my hair and pulled me up to my knees.

"Somebody hold her," he barked. "You, Ira and Jess, take her hands."

They raised my arms over my head. I twisted my head around to see what was happening. I saw Hennessy pull a red-hot iron out of the fire. He carried it towards me.

I screamed so loudly that it felt like my life was being wrenched out of my body by that scream alone. I was still screaming when I heard the sizzle of the iron on my flesh and smelled the sickening odor of charred skin. Pain shattered my whole body and exploded in my brain. I sank into merciful oblivion.

When I awoke I was immediately aware of the burn, which hurt so badly that I was sure I must still be on fire. I tried to speak but no words came. When I cried no tears came. I opened my eyes. Martha Hennessy was standing over me, holding a glass in her hand.

"Drink this," she said kindly. "It will numb the pain."

She and a tiny black woman, old Annie, helped me to sit up. I drank some of the brandy and it helped to clear my head. I saw that I was lying on a pallet in Annie's cabin. Martha's face swam into my field of vision once again as she knelt in front of me. I saw no hatred in her eyes now, only a haunting look of the deepest despair.

"You've been sick for days," she told me. "You've had a fever. We thought you were going to die." Annie peeled the bandage off my back. I groaned and clutched at Martha's hands. "We have to change the dressing. Please try to bear it. He—he shouldn't have done this. He had no right. You're not even—" she lowered her voice and I felt Annie's hands pause in their work, "you're not even a black woman," Martha finished in a whisper. "He's inhuman, a fiend. He was furious when he found you were gone. I thought he was going to kill me. He must have thought I had helped you. Oh, may God forgive me. God forgive and help us all." She bowed her head over our clasped hands and cried.

I looked away from her. The burden of my own self-pity was too much for me to bear. I couldn't begin to sympathize with her.

"I should have known when I married him," she said brokenly. "He was stubborn and hot-tempered then, but I thought it was romantic. He—he worked for my father. We were well off, rich, I suppose. My father was an important man. Edward wanted to prove himself. He made some money in a scheme and he came back for me. Father hated him. We ran off together. We haven't had one happy moment since, not one. He's trying to prove something, I guess, by scratching a living out of this worthless land with his own hands. He doesn't want to owe anybody, he says. But he never loved me, I know that now. He couldn't believe it when Father died and didn't leave us anything, not even a penny. I thought Edward would go mad. He was counting on that money, even though I told him that Father was hard, that he would never relent. But I was glad in my heart, glad that he was hurt so much. I hated him then. I hate him now."

When she had gone I said to Annie, "The next time I'll need help to get away. You'll have to cover up for me. I'll pretend to be sick. I'll go now. He doesn't come here. He'll never find out."

Annie said sternly, "He comes in here every day, jes' to look at you, grinnin' like the Debil. You want us all to get branded, Missy? Now you jes' lay back and close your eyes. You is crazy with pain and grief, that's all. You hush and I'll fix us some nice soup. Don' you go talkin' 'bout runnin' away again. Next time he'll kill you for sure."

"I hope he does," I said dully. "I can't live like this. I'd rather be dead."

I closed my eyes. This was Josiah Fowler's revenge, I thought bitterly. I could almost hear his laughter echoing up from Hell. Yes, he had found a worthy successor in Edward Hennessy.

In time the wound from the branding healed. I could trace the scab with my fingers: a letter "R", for Runaway, I supposed. I was branded for life, branded because I wanted to be free. Branded because Georgette and Arnold hated me. Because I had loved Garth McClelland, and he had betrayed me. By loving him I had brought the full wrath of the gods down on me. I knew I would never see him again, and I wasn't sorry. He was at the root of all my sorrow, all my pain.

Winter was upon us. We slaves spent most of our time trying to keep warm in our drafty cabins. Annie and I huddled together near our little fire, rubbing our hands to get the chill out of our fingers long enough so that we could caulk the cracks in our walls and tack up old bits of sacking over the windows and door to shut out the icy blasts from the north and west. The wind out of the mountains cut us to the core. When the farm was buried under six feet of snow sometime in January, influenza broke out in the cabins. Hennessy lost half his slaves and one of his children, little Sarah. I suspected he grieved more for his slaves. He stayed away for weeks at a time, trapping and shooting so that when spring came he would have furs to sell in Wheeling. He didn't have to worry about our escaping in wintertime: he knew we would never survive.

Sometimes the slaves would gather together in our cabin on cold evenings. We would talk and sing and exchange stories and tales. I told them about France, the slave ship *Charleston Belle* and her captain, Josiah Fowler. He was a character they recognized. They all marvelled at the changes in fortune I had experienced. I told them about the Chateau Lesconflair and described its beauties in detail. They were delighted with my stories about my pirate days, and Jean Lafitte became a kind of hero to them, as he was to me. And I told them a bit about La Rêve's gracious beauty and the comparatively easy life the slaves there enjoyed.

I told them, too, about the slave rebellions in Haiti, and how the blacks there had thrown out their oppressors and made a country of their own. Those slaves had not had to run away to freedom: they had seized it, wrenched it away from their white masters, won it with their own blood and pain.

When I had finished my story of the Haitians, the eyes of my listeners were shining with hope. Then Ira said, "But there was hundreds of them. And there's only twenty-some of us left." And the dream of freedom died in them as they thought about Hennessy and his guns and dogs.

I looked around the shabby room. "What are you talking about?" I cried. "He's only one man! One man, and you couldn't find a more inhuman fiend anywhere. Why are you so cowardly?" They kept silent as I harangued them. "You all know what he's capable of doing," I went on. "You've seen it with your own eyes. We live like pigs and eat like pigs. Isaac can't walk. Millie can hardly pick up a straw, she's so weak from hunger and sickness. Ira, he broke your arm last year, didn't he? Just snapped it in two. And you, Jess, you're branded, too, just like me. Don't you hate him? I do. I hate him with every ounce of life left in me."

Ira said slowly, "They kill you if you so much as lifts your hand against your Master, Missy. I seen 'em hangin' from trees, 'cause they did what you want to do. 'Cause they killed their Master and ran away."

I said intensely, "He's no master of mine. I'm free, do

you hear me? No matter what he's done to my body, my soul and my mind are free! I'll get away from him yet, I promise you.''

I walked to one of our tiny windows and shoved aside our sack curtain. A light snow was falling outside. I felt desperate and alone with my hatred. One by one the slaves went away, back to their own cabins. When we were alone Annie said, ''Talkin' like that won't bring us nothin' but trouble, Missy. If the Mas' finds out—''

''I don't care if he finds out,'' I said passionately. ''Can't you see that? What's the matter with all of you? You're like sheep, lambs to the slaughter. I'd kill him. I would. And I'd be proud of it. And I dare them to hang me for it!''

She looked at me. ''They wouldn't hang you,'' she said quietly. ''You is white. They don't hang white women.''

We faced each other. My anger at them drained away. ''I'm sorry, Annie,'' I said. ''I don't know why I spoke as I did.''

''You ain't been a slave your whole life, that's all,'' she said. ''It's harder once you know what it is to be free.''

I raged inwardly at my situation for the rest of the winter, while the cold and the misery deepened and we felt as though we would never be warm again. Hennessy came around to the slave cabins every day when he was home, just to count heads. He never spoke a word to me and I was thankful. But occasionally he would send Annie away and rape me. My hatred grew, and I amused myself with thoughts of his death while he was abusing me.

Annie went up to the house in December to help with the new baby.

''He's a scrawny, sickly-lookin' little mite,'' she told me. ''She don't have no milk for that child, not a drop. An' that baby don't want cow's milk. Makes him colicky. He ain't gonna live out the winter.''

When the baby died Martha Hennessy nearly lost her mind. We could hear her mournful wailing and his outraged shouting down in the slave cabins.

Edward Hennessy didn't take his furs to Wheeling that year, but sold them to a trader who was passing through. He seemed reluctant to leave his farm for even a day. I thought I detected a growing irrationality in his behaviour. His moods seemed to shift hourly, he began to contradict his own orders and then to punish us when we didn't obey him. He was violent and loud one moment and sullen and secretive the next. He ceased to make any effort to keep himself clean, and he drank heavily.

When the ground thawed we were all forced into the back-breaking work of preparing the fields for planting. I hacked at the stiff clods of rocky earth with a hoe one afternoon, cursing him under my breath with every blow. When I looked up I saw that Martha was working only ten feet away from me. Wife or slave, black or white: Edward Hennessy made no distinctions. He worked us all with no regard to bodily health or sanity.

"I'm sorry," I said impulsively. "About the baby."

She blinked into the glare of the sun. "Sorry? Don't be sorry. He's better off dead. I only wish I had died, too."

"It can't go on like this much longer," I said. "It can't! Something will happen and things will change."

"You think so?" Her voice was lifeless and defeated. "I've lived like this for ten years. Every day I told myself that it wouldn't go on, that God would surely put an end to my misery. But He never did. The end comes when you die, not before."

The end came in June. Bob, a strapping young black whom Hennessy had bought in April with the money the trader had given him for his furs, tried to run away. Hennessy went after him with the dogs and brought him back a few hours later. He stripped the lad and lashed him to a fence post not far from the barns at the edge of the fields. Then he called us all in from our labors to watch the punishment. We gathered around in a tight, silent knot. Hennessy came out of the house and strode purposefully across the yard. He was carrying an enormous bull whip, and he had shoved a pistol into his belt.

The sun was hot, the air was still and soundless except for the boy's panicked breathing and the stirring of our bare feet in the dust. Martha was there, but I saw no sign of Jenny. I was glad Martha had kept the child away.

Hennessy raised his whip and brought it down across the boy's bare back with a loud crack. The lad screamed. A streak of red appeared on the flesh where the whip had fallen. At once my mind flew back to another whipping, another slave, another tyrant. Hennessy lifted his arm again, and I saw not a vicious, black-bearded dirt farmer, but that evil worm, Captain Josiah Fowler. The crowd that pressed around me was peopled not with slaves but with rough-talking seamen. The boy at the post—not Bob, but the slave I had named Joseph. Joseph, whom I had nursed in my cabin until Fowler took him away.

Fowler's second lash tore a sobbing cry out of my throat. He was wicked, wicked beyond all description.

"Villain," I shrieked tearfully. "Evil, bloody bastard!"

He turned to face me for a fraction of a moment. His eyes shone in his head like red embers, and he barked at me to keep silent. I saw the inhuman hatred in his look. He was a madman, an inhuman, blood-crazed fiend.

Annie put her hand on my arm. "Hush, now," she hissed. "You want to be next?"

Images of Josiah Fowler and the *Charleston Belle* danced in front of my eyes, obscuring reality, intensifying the horror of the experience for me.

Another heart-rending cry from the boy spurred me into

action. I shook off Annie's restraining hand and threw myself between the master and the slave.

"Stop it! Stop it!" I cried, grabbing at the whip in his hand.

He glared down at me and threw me away from him with one easy motion as easily as if I had been an annoying insect. I lay panting on the ground for a moment. I heard him laughing, and looking up I saw the whip coming down on me. I rolled to the side and it spent its force in the dust.

"Stay out of this, bitch," he warned, "or I'll flog you, too."

He brought the whip down on the boy's back once again. The lad's screams were growing weaker. His back was a maze of bleeding welts. Blood streamed down his buttocks and legs. He was bathed in blood.

My eyes lit on the pistol jammed in Hennessy's belt. I leaped at him again, and this time when he shoved me away I had the pistol in my hand. I fell back on the ground. Hennessy lifted his whip arm and cracked the bull whip once in the air before he lashed out at me.

"Now you're going to die, bitch," he snarled, "I've been waiting a long time for this."

Unconsciously, automatically, I raised the pistol and fired at him.

A small red hole appeared in the center of his powder-blackened forehead. A bubble of blood started to ooze out and trickle down his face. Someone screamed as he swayed drunkenly and then fell sideways onto the blood-stained earth at his slave's feet.

I stood up and looked down at him. Hatred welled up within me. I felt no sorrow, no remorse. Screwing up my mouth I spat on him, once, and looked up defiantly at the stunned, silent crowd. My eyes met Martha's, and I thought I could read forgiveness and relief in her look. Then I tossed the pistol aside and shouldered my way through the group of slaves. I walked briskly towards the forest and I didn't look back, not even when I heard hysterical shouting and screaming and smelled smoke, and guessed that the slaves were burning the farm buildings and slaughtering the dogs in a frenzy of hatred and euphoria.

# XVI.  The General


I crossed the freshly plowed tobacco fields and broke into a run. Free! I was free! I didn't want to think about why or how I had done it. It was enough for me that I could escape into the shelter of the trees without fear of being captured. No one would follow me now. The dogs were dead, I knew, just as their master was dead.

A gigantic black man stepped out of the trees into my path. Filled with guilt and fear at what I had done, I gave a startled scream and dove into the underbrush.

"Miss Elise!" he called after me.

He came after me and caught me around the waist with his two strong arms. I kicked and struggled but he held me fast.

"Hey, hey, don't kick so, Missy," he said, laughing. "You sayin' you don't know me?"

He let me go. I stumbled back from him and stared.

"You—you're Joseph!" I said, unbelieving. "But you can't be—! Joseph?"

"Yes, Ma'am, I am. Joseph McClelland, at your service."

My strength deserted me. I sat down on a log and gaped at him. "Joseph!" I whispered. "Oh, dear God, you don't know what's happened—"

"I saw it," he said. "I was watching from behind the barn. Passing through on my way to Richmond this morning. I saw the crowd of folks over yonder near that field, and I wanted to see what was going on. I saw you shoot him. I got out of there pretty fast and followed you."

I covered my face and said with a little moan, "I didn't

even think. I just—shot him, Joseph. I've been aching to murder him for so long—and now that lt's done, I feel—. I don't know how I feel. But it's wrong, wrong to murder a man!''

He said firmly, ''You saved two lives when you killed him: your own and that boy's. And maybe more than that. Your Mr. Hennessy had a reputation for meanness, Missy. But we've got to get out of here right quick. Those slaves have gone crazy with hate. This is an uprising and you started it. The white folks around here are going to come looking for you. They'll need to hang someone for this.''

''He—he branded me, Joseph,'' I said. ''I have the brand of a runaway slave on my back. If anyone saw that, they'd suspect something. They might even make me be a slave again.'' I moaned softly. ''Oh, God, will it never end? I can't go back, I can't!''

Joseph took me to his waiting horse. I was shaking violently from shock and anguish and sheer physical and mental exhaustion. He unfurled a rolled-up blanket and wrapped it around me.

''I heard from the slaves in these parts that he had a white woman for a slave,'' he said, shaking his head. ''But I never would have guessed in a hundred years that it would be you! The Lord sure works in strange ways. I heard about you some from Garth.''

''Garth?'' I cocked my head. ''I don't understand.''

''In his letters. He said that he had found you and that you were alive. I was mighty glad to hear that. I was sure that Cap'n would kill you.''

''He very nearly did. You astonish me, Joseph,'' I said weakly. ''Garth wrote you letters?''

Joseph laughed. ''And sent money, too. For my mission among the slaves. I'm a man of God now, Missy. I'm working to make them free. I'm a wanted man myself.''

"You called yourself McClelland. Did Garth adopt you?"

"In a way. He said that in this country a man was better off with two names. After we escaped from the *Eureka*, Garth gave me money and helped me get to a friend of his in Philadelphia. A Quaker minister and his wife. They took me into their home and treated me like their own son. Richard Hedley taught me about the Lord, and about how the Lord loved all men equally. He taught me to read and write and speak English. Why, I remember yet how Garth and I had to communicate in signs and grunts on the *Eureka*. Garth taught me a lot, too. We were on that ship nearly a year, but I guess he told you all about that. They beat him and starved him and nearly killed him, but he never gave in to them. They couldn't break him. He had the fever and he talked to me for hours, and I didn't even know what he was saying. I heard your name. That was one word I recognized."

I shook my head in amazement. "He never told me any of that. He was so evasive and flippant about it, like he always was about everything. How did you get away from the British?"

Joseph grinned. "Well, they couldn't keep us in irons if they wanted us to work, right? When we got to Kingston, Garth managed to set fire to the ship. In the confusion we jumped into the water and swam for shore. They looked high and low but couldn't find us. Some lady friend of Garth's hid us in her bedroom all that day and into the night."

"I'm sure Garth didn't object to that," I said.

"Lord, no!" Joseph laughed infectiously, and for the first time in months I found myself smiling. "Late that night we found some smugglers to take us to Cuba, and then we got a boat to New Orleans."

"And the *Eureka* sank?"

Joseph spread his arms. "Gone to her eternal rest at the bottom of the sea. Amen!"

"Just like the *Charleston Belle*," I said. I told him about Fowler's treatment of me, and about my rescue by Lafitte's men. "Lafitte saved me then, and you've saved me now, Joseph. I had to shoot Hennessy. He was so evil, so much like—"

"Now, don't you get all worked up about it," said Joseph sternly. "We have got to get away from here. Neighbors might see the smoke and come running. And if they catch you, they'll hang you for sure."

My teeth were chattering and I started to giggle. "No, they won't. They can't hang me because I'm a white woman."

Joseph lifted me onto his horse's back. "You were a slave, Miss Elise. And you committed the worst crime a slave can commit: you killed your master. Let's go. We can talk more later, after we put some miles between us and this place. I'll feel better when we're far away from this devil's land."

He climbed up behind me and we rode away from the place where I had endured such misery and pain for a whole year. I kept telling myself over and over that I was free now, that I was no longer a slave, but I didn't really believe it. Both Joseph and I knew that I was branded for life, and that I would have a hard time convincing anyone that I was a white woman, not a slave. If they caught me they would prosecute me and hang me for murder and for inciting slaves to rebellion. In this country no one cared that a slave owner might be cruel, bloodthirsty and mad: on his own lands he was a despot, and God help the poor slave who tried to escape or to curb that oppressive madness by force.

We rode east, avoiding towns, farms and settlements. Joseph knew that if white men saw us together they would

become suspicious. We couldn't very easily disguise ourselves. At that time I resembled a fine lady no more than
Joseph resembled a slave, and we could not have passed
for mistress and servant. Joseph seemed even taller and
broader than I remembered. He wore a black jacket and
white shirt and stock, black breeches with shiny black
boots. He might have looked just like any prosperous
Virginia planter—if he had been white. He planned to take
me to Philadelphia, to his friend and mentor, Richard
Hedley, who would help me return to France. I had told
him that I had no desire to go back to New Orleans, the
scene of my greatest triumphs and my greatest shame.

"You don't want to see Garth's wife and that fellow,
Arnold?" Joseph asked me.

I stared at my clenched hands. "No, Joseph," I said
grimly. "I'm afraid of what I might do to them. I'd kill
them, I know I would."

"Sometimes it's kind of hard to know what you're
going to do before you do it," Joseph observed.

"I'm half-Corsican, Joseph," I said fiercely. "Corsicans never let wrongs go unavenged. My Uncle Theo used
to say we were savages. And I'm proud of being a savage,
if it means that I have the courage to punish the ones who
betrayed me. But the other half of me knows that revenge
is wrong, and that I'd be sorry afterwards. I'm not a
murderess. I just want to go home, back to my family,
back to the place where I was happy. I haven't been happy
since I met Garth."

"He probably thinks you're dead," Joseph said.
"Don't you—"

"Let him think so," I said brusquely. "We're both
better off."

France. I longed to see my home and family again. Why
hadn't I permitted Lafitte to send me away from America
as soon as I was well enough? Why had I ever thought that

I would be happier away from my home? I ached to see them all again: Uncle Theo, and Françoise, and Philippe and Honoré. They had loved me and I had been safe there. Until Garth McClelland came along.

Our journey was not too taxing at first. Game and wild fruits abounded in the forests in mid-summer, and at least Joseph and I were well-fed. But towards the end of July I became ill with a fever that even Joseph, who had more than a rudimentary knowledge of medicine, could not cure with his concoctions of herbs and grasses. I grew steadily weaker, and he became worried. We were camped near a town in northeastern Virginia, about a hundred miles from Washington, when he insisted that I had to have a decent place to stay until I was well.

"I can't do anything else for you, 'Lise. If you don't get help soon you're going to die, and I don't want that. Please let me find—"

"No," I said firmly. "We can't trust anyone. If they saw the—the mark on my back they would send me back to Shenandoah County to stand trial. You know they would. Please, Joseph, I beg you, don't tell anyone about me."

"I'm going to go into town and get some medicine," he said. He frowned deeply and tried to hide his worry. "I'll come back alone, I promise. Maybe I can find a doctor who can give me something to help you. Now don't make yourself feel worse by fretting. Lie back and stay warm. I'll be back as soon as I can."

He mounted his horse and rode away. I lay on my bed of pine needles and leaves and slept. Joseph was very late in returning. I grew worried, and as darkness began to fall I became almost frantic. The night closed in around me, filling me with dread and terror. I believed that the monsters I had dreamed about would emerge from the shadows and drag me to Hell.

When I heard the thumping of hooves on the dry ground I screamed. Joseph's reassuring voice came out of the night.

"It's only me, 'Lise, don't be afraid. I got some whiskey—it's all they had in that little place, but it will help sweat the fever out of you." He knelt by my side. "I've been with some Negroes, 'Lise. Some free men. They know a man in Washington, a Quaker doctor name Barker. They say he'll help us get to Philadelphia, and if you're sick he'll let you stay with him until you're well. He's a good man, they said, and an honest one. He won't turn us in. We should start tomorrow morning, just as soon as it's light. I'll make you a litter—"

"No, Joseph, a litter would only slow us down. I can ride, really I can."

"We'll double up as usual, then, like we been doing. We can make it in two days if the weather holds, maybe three. If you can hang on 'til we get there, 'Lise. Just try and hold on until we get to Washington, and Doctor Barker."

The trip to Washington was a nightmare. I was sick and weak, yet I forced myself to sit upright in the saddle for ten and twelve hours a day. The late August heat was terrific, even in the shadowy depths of the woods. Several times I fainted and would surely have fallen off if Joseph hadn't held on to me.

On the morning of the third day of our journey, when we were about fifteen miles from the city, we smelled smoke.

"It's so dry," Joseph remarked. "Someone's started a brush fire and I bet it got out of hand."

Then we saw some people coming towards us through the trees. They were the first persons I had seen since I left Hennessy's farm and I was frightened. Joseph left the trail so that we wouldn't have to meet them, but they called to us and begged us to come back. They told us that the British had attacked Washington, and that they were sacking and burning the city. Houses, shops, inns, government buildings—everything was in flames. This family had fled with their portable goods when the attack began, and like many others they had sought the safety of the trees.

The children were crying. Their faces were dark with smoke and dirt.

"We've got to go on, sir," Joseph said grimly. "I have a sick woman here and I've got to get her to a doctor. Perhaps you know where we can find him? Doctor Barker?"

The man said, "No, we don't know any doctor by that name. But you're crazy to want to go there now. The town will be ashes by the time—"

My head lolled against Joseph's shoulder. He kicked at our horse and said, "We've got to go. Good luck to you folks, and may the Lord watch out for you." We moved along at a quicker pace. "I think we can use the main road now," Joseph said to me. "It will be faster, and I expect folks will be too excited about this attack to pay any attention to us."

Further on we met some Negroes who told us that the British had promised freedom to all slaves once they were in full control of the country.

"They're trying to buy our help," Joseph said when we had left them. "They figure this will make us want to fight for them. I wouldn't trust them, though. I've seen how they treat men who are supposed to be free. No reason why they would treat us any better."

As we neared Washington we could see clouds of smoke hanging over the town. We met countless groups of people who had piled wagons and carts and horses with everything they could carry in an effort to save some of

their possessions from the pillaging, looting British soldiers. Joseph was right: they gave us not the slightest
attention as they trudged along. Some of the women were
weeping and moaning loudly, but most were silent, their
faces set into stern sorrowful expressions of bitterness and
defeat. The men roundly condemned the failure of the
militia to save the city. They told us that Washington had
fallen with hardly any show of resistence, and that the
swinish invaders had even burned the President's house.

When we entered the town, Joseph wrapped me in
blankets and protected my face and eyes against the foul
air. We passed through the smoke-filled streets, searching
for Dr. Barker's house. British redcoats ran to and fro,
carrying torches as well as bayonets. Whole areas of the
city had been destroyed in the previous day's fires, and
now, on the twenty-fifth day of August, the British were
finishing their job of destruction. Gangs of soldiers
emerged from private homes and offices with their arms
filled with loot. Many were drunk and were wantonly
smashing windows, mirrors, and glassware, and shred-
ding bedding and pillows so that feathers filled the air in
front of some of the houses. Other soldiers were openly
carrying on with the only women left in the city, the
prostitutes.

We stopped in one street and Joseph asked a harried-
looking citizen if he knew Dr. Barker's house.

"House?" the man yelped. "The whole street's gone,
not just the bloody house. I haven't seen Barker for days.
Joined what is laughingly known as the militia, I think.
They burned me out, the bloody bastards! Burned me out!
That damned fool Madison's not worth a cent."

Joseph allowed himself a small sigh of despair.

"Leave me here, Joseph," I said weakly. "I'll be all
right."

"No. We've got to find Barker. We've—"

"Hey, Black Fella," a crude Cockney voice shouted at Joseph. "What you got there?"

Joseph's arms tightened around me. "A sick woman, friend. If you know where I can find Dr. Barker—"

"Doctor, eh?" I felt a hand plucking at the blankets that covered me. "Let's see this sick woman of yours, Blackie."

"Keep your distance," Joseph warned. "She has smallpox."

"Smallpox!" The man fell back. After a second he said, "You wouldn't be holding her so close if she had the pox." Joseph tried to ride through the gang of soldiers that had gathered around us. Someone caught the reins and held us in check. One of the soldiers ripped the blanket away from my head. "She ain't got no pox," he bawled. She's a white woman, too. Where you going with this pretty lady, mate? Don't hog the goods, now."

Rough hands seized us and dragged us off the horse. I moaned as they tore me out of Joseph's arms, and I could hear him shouting loudly for them to free us in the name of the Lord. The soldiers laughed and shouted, and one of them fell on top of me and started to fumble with the blankets that enfolded me. I screamed again, and Joseph plucked my attacker off me and tossed him aside as easily as if he had been a feather bolster. The soldiers ganged up on him then. He tried to fight them off, his huge fists falling on them like a shower of cannonballs. They scattered for a moment and then renewed their attack on him.

I scrambled to my feet and ran to an English officer who was watching the imbroglio with an expression of disdainful amusement on his face. I fell on my knees in front of him and babbled in French, "In the name of God, *mon géneral*, make them stop! Please save him! He is good, kind. Please call off your barbarians!"

He looked into my eyes. His face was lean and weathered, with a prominent hawk-like nose and a square chin and clear blue eyes. I clutched at his hands to plead for Joseph's life.

"You are a civilized man, Monsieur, a gentleman. I can see it in your face. Don't let them do this. They are attacking a man of God. I beg you—"

He strode decisively into the mob and shouted some orders in a sharp, penetrating voice. When the men saw the bars on his shoulders and the rich plumes on his hat, they fell silent and quickly came to attention. Breathing heavily, I stood up. Joseph stumbled towards me and we clung to each other.

"Thank you, sir," said Joseph to the officer. "We were looking for a doctor who used to live in this street. The lady is ill with a fever—"

"Please accept my most sincere apologies for this incident," the officer said crisply in English. Then in French he said to me, "What is your name, Mademoiselle? How do you, a Frenchwoman, come to be here in this ruined city?"

"Please sir," said Joseph, "she is very sick."

"She will be cared for. Mademoiselle?"

"My name is Elise Lesconflair," I said thickly through my parched lips. I struggled to hold my head up and I was grateful for Joseph's support. "Evil people made me a slave, and this kind man has saved my life. Please let us go, sir. We mean you no harm."

He growned. "Lesconflair? But I know that name."

"My father was a general in Napoleon's army, Monsieur."

"Of course! I knew him well. He visited London on a diplomatic mission between the wars. I was attached to Wellington's general staff at the time, so it must have been—1802? My name is Ross, Robert Ross. And you are—Elise. He often spoke of you. You were attending school there, weren't you? And I remember your mother very well. You are like her. Forgive us, Mademoiselle. This was an outrage. You, men, call my carriage! I will take you to my house at once and my personal physician will attend you, Mademoiselle.''

I managed a weak smile before I fainted dead away.

When I awoke I found myself in a real bed in a beautifully furnished room. Light streamed in through small-paned windows, and everything was clean and soft. I sighed thankfully and slept again.

Before the British occupation of Washington, General Ross's house had belonged to a Justice of the United States Supreme Court. Ivy Cottage, as it was called, was a small brick dwelling that stood on a wooded area overlooking the Potomac River at the edge of the little village of Georgetown, not far from Washington itself. There General Ross, leader of the British invasion forces, entertained Admiral Cochrane, commander of the British fleet, and other officers and their wives, who had accompanied them on this trip. Ross was forty-eight, a veteran of the American Revolution and campaigns against Napoleon. He was confident that his experienced soldiers could easily defeat the Americans this time, and his confidence was shared by Admiral Cochrane. It struck me that the whole invasion had a holiday air to it.

Ross was tall and handsome in the way that only well-bred Englishmen can be handsome. His dark hair, which he wore powdered and beribboned on the most formal occasions, was only slightly touched with gray, and he was lean and fit for his years. He was a great favorite among his men, who found him to be a just and compassionate leader. I was delighted to have found someone who could tell me about my father, for my memories of him were cloudy. I ignored the streak of cruelty that I sensed in him, the kind of cruelty that would let a man watch smilingly while a pack of his men boisterously attacked a black man and a sick woman. I told myself that men at war behave differently than they do in peacetime. And he was never cruel to me. He was kind and thoughtful, and although military matters kept him occupied he always managed to spend several hours with me each day.

Joseph never visited me at Ivy Cottage. Ross insisted that he had given the black man permission to call on me, but I never saw him. I fretted over his disappearance, and I was certain that something horrible had befallen him. I prayed that he was well and safe, but beyond that there was nothing I could do.

A British army physician dosed me with physic and bled me twice, and prescribed beef tea and laudanum and a long bed rest. I improved in spite of his regimen. In a few days I was able to receive visitors, and in a week I was able to accompny General Ross on daily walks in the small formal garden behind the house. Ross found dressmakers who were willing to work night and day to supply me with a new wardrobe, and he escorted me to parties and balls on the Admiral's flagship, *Royal Oak*. He grew more attentive with each passing day, and I blossomed under his attentions. It had been a long time since a man had flattered and pampered and petted me. As my health improved I felt that I could once again be called beautiful, even though I was still too thin and I tired easily.

"I am delighted to find a truly civilized woman among all these barbarians," the General told me one evening as we circled the garden before dinner. "And a beautiful civilized woman at that!"

"You are only a guest in this country, dear General, the same as I," I admonished him playfully. "You mustn't be so critical of the natives. But then I, too, am your enemy, am I not?"

"Enemy?" He laughed. "No, my dear, France and England are at peace, at long last. Bonaparte's government has fallen, you have a new king on the throne, and the little General is resting comfortably on a miserable little island called Elba."

I stared. "You're joking! Napoleon, gone? What about the Empress? And the King of Rome? I—I can't believe it."

"It's true, my dear. Marie Louise and her son are in Vienna, I believe, and the rest of the Bonapartes have scattered to the four winds, probably to dream of a restoration that will never come to pass. Where have you been all this time?"

I flushed and turned my face away. "I've been rather out of touch."

"Oh, I'm so sorry, Elise. I have no manners, none. The doctor told me you had been—ah, branded. It's shocking, really shocking! These people are beasts, animals! They must be!"

I smiled bitterly. "But the people responsible for my enslavement were educated and well-born. It seems to me that acts of savagery transcend lines of birth and wealth, General Ross. History is full of stories of the atrocities committed by nobility against the poor and against each other. The Roman Emperors, the Borgias, your Richard III. Why, even twenty years ago French aristocrats could easily procure *lettres de cachet* against their enemies, who would then be tossed into the Bastille and left there to rot. I have been unfortunate, yes, but at least I have survived."

I led the conversation to other topics, but we talked again about my life as a slave two weeks later as we walked in the garden at twilight.

Robert Ross said, "Surely you can't be so Christian as to forgive them for what they did to you!"

"No, dear General, I am no saint. If I saw either of them

again I would kill them, I am sure I would. But I have no wish to make a career of murder." I swallowed. "I have already killed. It was a frightening experience."

Ross took my hands in his and guided me to a stone bench. "Elise, you must come away with me. As soon as we win this wretched war we'll go to England together."

I said, "You are very kind, General Ross—"

"If you don't stop addressing me as General I shall go mad," he exclaimed with mock rage. "Why can't you call me Robert? And I'm not kind, not really. I took you in not only because I knew your father, but because—because I knew when I saw you for the first time, dirty and sick and ragged as you were, that you were someone special, someone a man could worship."

I drew my hands away. "Dear Robert, I have been very troublesome to every man I have ever known. And the ones that worshipped me have fared worse than any. You would be happier if you had let your soldiers have me."

"You mustn't say that!"

"It's true. I want to go back to France, Robert. I want to go home. Nearly four years have passed since I left, and I want to see my family again."

He gazed warmly into my eyes. "I understand, Elise. If you come with me on the *Royal Oak* back to England, I promise I shall take you to France as soon as possible. I'll have some leave coming to me after this campaign. Please, say you'll come back with me. I can't bear the thought of leaving you in this awful place."

"I'll consider it, Robert," I said softly. "That's all I can tell you right now."

"All right, my dear. But don't wait too long to decide. We'll be leaving Washington soon and I'll need to make arrangements."

Ross's batman came out of the house. "Admiral Cochrane to see you, sir."

Ross made a face. "Will you come in to greet my Lord Admiral, Elise?"

"No, thank you, Robert. I'd rather stay out a little longer. I don't think your Admiral approves of me, you know. He thinks I am distracting you from your duties."

Ross smiled and pressed my hand to his lips. "You are, Elise. Your beauty is becoming increasingly distracting—and attracting—every day. Don't stay out too late, will you? I don't want you to take cold."

"I'll be careful," I promised.

"I just hope he doesn't feel he has to accept an invitation to dinner," the General grumbled. He squeezed my hand and then walked briskly up the gravel path towards the house.

I followed him with my eyes. When he had gone inside I sighed deeply. Here it was, then, my passage to France. On an English warship with an English general who had known my father many years ago. And now the wars between France and England were over for good. Napoleon was no more. Life was funny, bizarre. But I could go home. Home.

I strolled to the edge of the garden. The evening was warm and a soft breeze was blowing from the river. Crickets and cicadas rattled and chirped in the trees beyond the Justice's carefully manicured garden. I closed my eyes and remembered the Chateau on a summer evening. Dinner with Uncle Theo and his guests in the great dining room, with the long windows open to catch the breeze. The smell of ripening grain and sun-baked fields. Light muslin dresses, as thin as air, and satin slippers with ribbons. Trips to the seaside. Games on the lawns and cool drinks. And laughter. The kind of warm, honest laughter that one can only share with the members of one's own family.

As I stood watching the lengthening shadows I heard a

crackle of twigs behind me. As I turned I was seized roughly and dragged into the bushes. A huge hand clamped down over my mouth so that I couldn't cry out. I squirmed helplessly in my assailant's arms.

"If you scream I'll break your neck," a voice hissed in my ear. "Do you understand?"

I jerked my head in assent. The hand slid off my mouth and I twisted around to face him. I felt the blood drain away from my face.

It was Garth McClelland.

As I opened my mouth to speak he pressed his fingers over my lips. "I mean it, Elise," he said grimly. "I'll kill you if you scream. If you want to get back to your dear General Ross tonight you won't attract any unwelcome attention."

He took his hand away. I wiped my hand over my mouth and glared at him. "Still the gallant cavalier, I see," I said caustically.

The corner of his mouth twitched. "Still complaining about my manners, I see. You do turn up in the oddest places, my dear. So did your poor husband. Did you really have to kill him? I know he was an abominable lover, but no man deserves death just because—"

"He wasn't any kind of lover at all," I said hotly. "And I didn't kill him. Let me explain—"

"That's not important now," he said brusquely. "The point is you're here and I might as well make use of you."

"What are you doing here?" I demanded.

"I would ask what you're doing here, but it's rather obvious. You are in the employ of the British. I am here in the service of my country."

"As a filthy spy," I jeered. "Still doing what you do best, I see."

He grinned slyly. "And so are you. You know, I feel sorry for poor Fournier. Little did he guess when he married you that he was signing his own death certificate. But then you were always a little too eager to show off your skill with firearms. You're as weak and willful as ever, Elise. When you find yourself in a situation you don't like, you run away. When you find yourself married to a man who doesn't satisfy your needs, you murder him. Like a spider that devours her own mate—"

Rage blurred my vision. Claws bared, I leaped at his face. I could have killed him for talking to me that way. He caught my hands and wrestled me to the ground. I struggled futilely, cursing him freely. He pinned me down and covered my mouth with his hand again.

"Listen, bitch," he growled. "I've got no time for one of your tantrums now. I'm not interested in the men you've killed and I'm not interested in your whoring, only in how you can best use it to my advantage."

My eyes blazed at him. I tossed my head, as if to say, "Go to Hell."

"Your good friend Joseph is my prisoner, Elise," he said. "If you don't do as I say we'll kill him. Now settle down and listen to me."

He jerked me into a sitting position and squatted next to me. I gazed at him with horror.

"You're a monster," I breathed, "a madman. Joseph is your friend, too."

"This is war," he said. "In wartime morals are suspended and nice little institutions like love and friendship have to go hang. Don't think I wouldn't kill Joseph if I had to. You know me well enough by now, Elise. I don't make idle threats. Your lover Ross has a dispatch case. He wears the key on his watch chain. I want the information in that case, and I want it tomorrow. You're going to get it for me tonight, copy it, replace the documents in the case, and deliver your notes to me in the morning. He has a field drill and maneuver at eleven o'clock and he'll be away from the house then. Under no circumstances must he suspect that the case has been tampered with. He and Cochrane might change their plans and all our efforts will have been for nothing.''

I was transfixed with anger. Finally I gave a short harsh laugh and said, ''You seem to have thought it all out so brilliantly. Why don't you just finish the job?''

''Because as his mistress you're in a better position to get the information without raising his suspicions.''

''But I'm not his—''

''Don't bother to explain, Elise. You can't help yourself. It was inevitable that a woman like you would end up being a camp follower. It's the only way you can get enough to satisfy you.''

The cold hatred in his voice left me speechless. Clearly Joseph hadn't told him what had been happening to me. He didn't know anything about Georgette's plot, the Mississippi River Rats, or Edward Hennessy. He didn't know I had been kidnapped, enslaved, branded. And I was glad he didn't know. I was grateful to Joseph for keeping my secret. Now, when this distasteful spying business was done, I would return to France with Robert Ross. And at last I would be truly free of Garth McClelland.

I said stiffly, ''And suppose I can't get the plans tonight?''

Garth dug into his pocket for a small twist of paper, which he tossed into my lap. ''Here's a powder. He'll sleep like a baby and awake feeling rested and refreshed. Of course he'll have your skills in bed to thank for that. And the wine you'll drink together before you—sleep. If he suspects anything, Elise, you'll be to blame. So use all your wiles, lady, as an actress and a whore.''

My breast heaved. I bowed my head and bit my tongue

to keep from lashing out at him again. I believed him. I believed that he really would kill Joseph if I failed him in this.

"And—and when it's all over?" I asked. "What will become of me then?"

"I don't give a damn what you do then, Elise. You can go where you please, with whom you please."

He stood. I looked up at him. His blue eyes shone brightly through the thickening dusk. He was handsomer than ever, bronzed like a classical Adonis, with his fair hair flowing away from his forehead like strands of golden thread. He wore tightly-fitted breeches and knee-high boots, and his billowing white shirt was open to the waist. His sleeves were rolled up above the elbows, and his forearms were smooth and muscular. Even though I loathed and despised him, he still had the power to make me tremble.

I dropped my eyes. He was too awful, too god-like. He had passed judgment on me without knowing any of the facts. He was headstrong. He was stubborn, arrogant, arbitrary, and—impossible! And he held Joseph's life in his hands.

"I have no choice, it seems," I said dully.

He grunted. "Don't make it sound so distasteful, Elise. I'm not asking you to do anything that goes against your character. I'll be here tomorrow morning at eleven. Don't be late. And don't try any tricks. If Ross takes me prisoner or kills me, Joseph will die anyway. Just do your job. I am primarily interested in their plans for the Delta region and New Orleans. If you're running short of time and have too much information to take down, concentrate on that. If there are maps, note down key points and place names, and if you don't understand certain designations just sketch them down and I'll figure them out later. If you don't let your lovemaking get out of hand you should have plenty of time. Ross gets up at six. But you know that.''

I hadn't known it, but it was pointless to argue with him. I nodded wearily.

He studied me for a moment. ''Whoring is ruining your looks, Elise. You're too pale and thin. I know it's a strenuous life, but—''

''Elise, where are you?'' Ross's voice came from the garden.

I scrambled to my feet. ''Here I am, Robert.'' I walked quickly to meet him at the end of the path. Garth melted into the shadows, but I could feel him there, listening to every word we said. ''Oh, I'm so silly, Robert,'' I said, taking his arm, ''I thought I would explore the woods a little and I got lost! I walked in circles, around and around, and I might have been walking still if you hadn't called to me.''

''Poor darling, you've soiled your gown.'' We started back towards the house.

''I know,'' I said disgustedly. ''I tripped over a root and I shall have to change. Is Admiral Cochrane staying to dinner?''

''No, thank God. What an infernal bore that man is.''

''You only think so because he is a sailor and you are a confirmed landlubber,'' I said lightly. ''I don't know how you two manage to communicate at all.''

We went into the house. I went upstairs to my room to change for dinner. The shock of meeting Garth again made me shake so violently that I had to sit down. I was strongly tempted to give way to tears, but I stopped myself. He wasn't worth it, and besides, I was supposed to seduce a man that night and I didn't want to spoil my looks.

I tore off my dress and slipped on a flimsy peignoir.

Then I sat at my dressing table and ran a brush through my hair. I looked at myself critically as I began the age-old woman's ritual of making myself beautiful for my lover. Yes, the torments I had endured had stripped away some of my youthful glow and exuberance, but as for losing my looks—no, Garth was wrong about that. A few more weeks of good food and rest and I would be as beautiful as ever. I liked the new maturity in my face. But I would have to get the bitter sadness out of my smile, and the glimmer of fear out of my eyes. I smiled coyly at the reflection in the mirror, and suddenly my vision was fogged by tears.

I hated this stupid charade! And Garth must hate me to make me do it. He really believed I was capable of prostitution and murder. What was I doing, letting him use me like this? How could I demean myself like this?

I heard a soft knock on the door. I mopped my eyes and splashed my temples and neck with *eau de cologne*. "Come in, please," I called.

General Ross poked his head in. "Are you ready—? Oh, forgive me, Elise. I thought you would have finished dressing by now." He started to leave.

"Don't go, Robert," I said quickly. "Please, come in and close the door."

He obeyed and sat down on a chair not far from the dressing table. I smiled at him. "I've been rather silly," I confessed with a wan smile. "I started to dress, and then I began to think about many things, and some of them made me sad. I even started to cry! Now my face is ruined and my appetite is gone, and I must beg your forgiveness. I cannot dine with you tonight."

"Forgiveness?" At once his face was filled with concern. He stood next to me. "Oh, no, Elise, please don't apologize. Tell me what has made you unhappy. Is it something I've done?"

"Oh, no, Robert," I cried, "of course not! You have

been so good and kind to me. I'm just being childish. I wanted to tell you first that I have decided to go back to England with you. I would be honored to accompany you."

"But that's wonderful!" His face creased into a smile. "I hinted to Cochrane that you might be traveling with us. He was delighted."

"Oh, Robert, he wasn't. I don't believe you."

"He was," Ross insisted. "Said you were a damned pretty wench, or some such thing. But he did hint that I was a trifle old for you." I laughed. "It's good to hear you laugh, Elise. But surely the thought of coming to England with me didn't make you sad. What else, my dear?" He knelt in front of me and held my hands.

"I don't have any suitable clothing. England is very cold, even in the summer."

"I'll buy you a boatload of dresses before we go. What else?"

"I thought I had lost all my beauty."

"Lost it!" he cried. "Great Heavens, girl, you're the most beautiful woman I've seen on three continents. No, I take that back. Five. Five continents!"

"But you didn't know me before—before——" I faltered.

"Nonsense! I know you now, don't I? Believe me, Elise, a soldier's eye can be trusted in these matters."

"You're not too jaded, then?" I teased.

"Certainly not. But is there anything else? Come now, out with it. I'm getting hungry."

I touched his face with my fingertips and said softly, "Yes, there was one more thing. I was thinking about how difficult it would be to seduce you."

He sat back on his heels. His mouth hung open. "Well, I'm damned," he said at last.

I toyed with a few objects on my dressing table. "Do

you think I'm terrible? I suppose I am, talking like that.
But I felt lonely and sad. And I did rather hate the idea of
forcing myself on you.''

Suddenly his arms were around me and he was kissing
me passionately, saying my name over and over again
between kisses. ''Silly, silly darling,'' he murmured
warmly.

I managed to endure his embrace without flinching. I
had been so downtrodden, so badly used for so long
that I wanted no part of men and their lovemaking. What
Lafitte had cured long ago had been fear, terror of what
men like Josiah Fowler could do to me. But I felt no fear
now, only a dead coldness, anger, and revulsion. Brutes
like Jake and Edward Hennessy had finally succeeded in
killing the part of me that desired a man's caresses, a
man's warmth. But Joseph's life might depend on the
success of my deception, and I thanked God that I was
experienced enough in genuine enjoyment that I would
have no trouble feigning pleasure I did not feel.

''You're not angry with me?'' I asked slyly.

''Angry!'' He shouted with laughter. ''Yes, I'm angry.
With myself. For not having the wits to take the initia-
tive.''

I began to unbutton his uniform jacket. I saw the small
key dangling from the watch chain, right where Garth had
said it would be.

''Well, Monsieur,'' I said with a plaintive little sigh,
''you know what they say about French girls. We are very
brazen. Do you need help with your boots?''

''I do indeed, little witch.''

His rough soldier's hands traveled over my naked body.
I sighed ecstatically and wriggled around the way any
normal woman would have under the circumstances. I
gave a thousand times more pleasure than I got, but I did
not care. He never suspected that inwardly I was seething

and managing only with the most stupendous force of will not to scream out my disgust and throw him out of bed.

We dozed briefly, then had our supper in my room. When we had dined and drunk our fill of wine we made love again. Before we slept I told Robert that I wanted to toast him with champagne, and so he had a bottle chilled and brought up to us. We toasted each other lovingly. I watched him drain his glass of wine and sleeping powder, then I drained mine and refilled them both. Later I blew out the candles and lay beside him. He groaned happily and gathered me into his arms. Soon he drifted into a sound sleep.

He did not stir when I squirmed out of his grasp and fumbled around in the darkness for the key that I had seen on the chain. I slipped out of the room and went down-stairs to the library. I knew where the dispatch case was; I had been with him on two occasions when he had opened it. He kept it in the bottom drawer of the desk, and the drawer had no lock.

I moved as quietly as I could, for Ross's batman, Perkins, slept on the first floor in a room off the kitchens. Creeping soundlessly through hallways and rooms in a house with which I was still unfamiliar, I finally reached the library. I went to the desk and felt the inside of the drawer. It was empty. I sat frozen with despair on the floor in front of the desk and pondered what to do next. The house seemed alive with creaking sounds and noises that sounded like footsteps. I forced myself to keep calm, to think about where the case might be. Had Cochrane taken it with him? No, that wasn't sensible. It was Ross's case. No one else would use it.

Perhaps he kept it in a different place at night. In his bedroom, in his trunk or chest of drawers. I crept upstairs again and went into the bedroom across the hall from mine. I saw that a small fire had been burning in the grate, and that a few embers were still glowing. I found a candle and lit it from an ember, then methodically searched the room. I found the case at last, on top of the armoire. I set it down on top of a small table near the window and fitted the key into the lock. The lid sprung open and I lifted the documents and papers out slowly so that I would re-member how they were placed inside.

I found several messages from an Admiral Bush regard-ing possible American defenses of Baltimore and the Chesapeake Bay, an outline of a plan to capture Baltimore signed by F.C.—Forrester Cochrane, several letters from England signed "your loving wife, Ruth," and finally, at the bottom of the case, a fistful of maps, directives, letters and plans, all referring to the invasion of New Orleans and the capture of the Mississippi Delta region.

I made one more foray into the library for pen, ink, paper and more candles. Then I began to copy all the information about the Delta operation. One sentence in particular caught my eye: "If possible communicate with smuggler Jean Lafitte. Good potential ally." Potential ally! They didn't know Jean Lafitte as I did, I thought. He would never join forces with the British to conquer New Orleans, never.

Much of the material seemed meaningless to me and perhaps even trivial, such as names of ships and the numbers of guns they carried, but I copied it anyway. The hours slipped away. I worked feverishly until I heard the clock in the room below striking five. Then I returned the papers to their box and restored the case to its rightful place on top of the armoire. I took my pen and ink back to the library and finally tiptoed back to my room. Robert Ross was snoring softly. After I concealed my copies behind the washstand, I slid into bed beside him and lay waiting for the dawn.

I was still awake at six o'clock when Ross moaned and sat up. "God, I haven't slept so well in years. You have remarkable powers, Elise."

"Who is Ruth?" I asked him.

He stared dumbly. "Where did you hear about Ruth?"

"You said her name in your sleep," I said smoothly.

"Did I? Hmm. Ruth is my wife, Elise. I meant to tell you about her—sometime."

"Is she still alive?"

"Oh, yes. This won't change anything, Elise. It can't. Well, I have to go now. I'm reviewing the troops at eight o'clock. I should be home at eleven." He climbed out of bed and started to pull on his clothes. "We can talk then."

And Garth had been certain that Ross would be gone at eleven. "But I thought—." I sat up and raked my fingers through my hair.

"What, darling?"

"Oh, I thought you—you never told me you had a wife, Robert," I said.

He seemed embarrassed. "I know I didn't. I suppose I should have said something. I'm very sorry, Elise. I love Ruth, after a fashion, but I'm in love with you. Please try to believe that. You—you aren't sorry about last night, are you?"

We looked at each other. I felt nothing for him. Not even gratitude. I forced myself to smile. "No, I have no regrets, Robert. Come and kiss me before you go."

He leaned over the bed and I kissed him tenderly. "You won't let this change your mind," he said. "About coming with me? I should have told you. I imagined it wouldn't have mattered—to a girl like you."

I was stung. "I don't know," I said honestly. "It wouldn't be fair to her, to your wife, if I came with you. I'll have to think about it."

He smiled humorlessly, kissed me again, and left the room. I heard him cross the hall to his own room and I hoped fervently that everything was as he would expect to find it.

I couldn't go with him. I didn't want any part of his "love" or his lovemaking. Love brought pain, and I had had enough pain to last me a lifetime. I had to find Joseph, had to go to Parson Hedley in Philadelphia. He would help me return to France, I was sure of it.

I washed and dressed myself, and after the maidservant had brought my breakfast I stuffed my dresses and lingerie and the gifts Ross had given me into a carpetbag. I was sorely temped to leave them all behind, but I told myself that this was not the time to be proud if I didn't want to wear rags. I took everything, and the things that didn't fit in the satchel I threw into a large square shawl that I knotted into a bundle. I fastened the packet of plans under my bodice and arranged a ruffled *fichu* over my bosom to hide the lumps. At ten o'clock I left the house by the side door. I took my things to the woods and hid them behind some rocks.

I had left a note on General Ross's bed, expressing my thanks for his kindness and wishing him well. I thought ruefully that my career as a camp follower had been a remarkably short one.

# XVII.   Patriot's Navy

I waited anxiously for Garth to appear. He had promised to meet me at eleven o'clock, and Ross expected to be home by eleven. When he found me gone and read my note he might search for me, perhaps even call out his soldiers. Garth might be captured as well, and I would never find Joseph, never see France again. I stood on the spot where Garth and I had argued the previous evening. I felt tense and nervous. I had to tell him that he would have to take me with him. He would refuse and we would argue, and I hated arguing with him because he always bested me. And this was one argument I had to win.

Suddenly he was beside me. I jumped. "Where did you come from?"

He grinned boyishly. "I spent half my boyhood practicing to be an Indian. I never dreamed that my skills might come in handy, but then well-learned skills usually do. I hope your skills served you well last night? May I see the papers?"

"You're very sure of yourself, aren't you?" I said coldly. "Unfortunately your information was wrong about one thing: General Ross expects to be back here by eleven. You said he would be gone."

He shrugged. "So? Hand over the papers and you can run home to your lover."

"He's not my lover and I'm not going back to him," I said. "I'm going with you. I want to see for myself that Joseph is all right."

He looked grim. "No. Joseph is in good health and he will remain that way, unless you continue to play your little game and waste my valuable time. Is this a trick to get me captured?''

"Of course not. I've written Ross a note, telling him that I've left him for good,'' I said. "But he might look for me. Oh, God, there he is now.''

We heard a door slam. "Elise! Elise, where are you?''

"Goddamn you, Elise,'' Garth muttered. "Give me the papers, now.''

"Damn yourself,'' I said boldly. I knew I had the upper hand. "You'll have the papers when I see Joseph. Not before.''

Steps crunched on the gravel path. Garth put his hand on my shoulder and shoved me down behind a thicket. Ross called again plaintively, "Elise, come back, I—I want you,'' he added in a forlorn voice. We heard his steps turn again towards the house.

"Damn you,'' said Garth through his teeth. "Come on, let's get out of here.''

I retrieved my possessions and followed him through the woods. A fine black horse was grazing deep in a grove.

I climbed into the saddle without Garth's assistance, even though the horse was so tall that I could hardly lift my leg high enough to reach the stirrup. Garth handed up my carpetbag and bundle and mounted behind me. As he put his arms around me to catch the reins I could feel from the tension in his forearms that he was stiff with fury. I didn't care. I had won this small skirmish and I felt jubilant and rather proud of myself.

We crossed the Potomac River at a place called Little Falls and then rode south. We traveled for hours without speaking a word. Once or twice I felt myself dozing off. My head dropped back on his chest and I would jerk it up and pinch myself to stay awake. It was nearly dark by the time we reached our destination, a little cottage near the mouth of the river. The area was thick with tall grass and a few scrubby pines. A good-sized boat lay beached on the riverbank above the tide line.

We hadn't stopped for food or rest all day, and I felt hungry, cold, and stiff. We dismounted and Garth asked again for my papers. I snapped at him, "Not until I see for myself that Joseph is all right."

He glowered at me. "Joseph!" he bellowed.

The cottage door flew open and the voice I knew so well said, "Oh, you're back at last, Garth. Did the beautiful Elise cooperate?"

"Why don't you ask her yourself," Garth said, amused.

With a cry of delight Joseph came towards me, his arms outstretched. "Oh, 'Lise, you look so much better! That general's doctor did a fine job, I can see that—"

"Don't you come near me, you black bastard," I said angrily.

He stopped in his tracks. "What?"

"You heard me. You don't look any more like a prisoner than—than *he* looks like a saint! Traitors! Liars!"

"Now, Missy," said Joseph calmly, "you just settle down. There ain't nobody here that's a prisoner. Nobody here at all, except us."

"I am all too aware of that," I said. I didn't even try to control the rage I felt. I fumbled in my bodice for the packet of papers I had laboriously copied, thinking all the while that with them I was buying Joseph's life.

"So that's where they were," Garth said. "I thought you looked even more ample than usual, my dear."

I threw them in his face. "Take them and be damned, both of you!" I strode to the beach and glared at the calm water. I was quivering with anger. They had used me, tricked me, betrayed me. I could have murdered them both.

I heard them conversing in low tones, then Joseph came

up behind me and said, "Don't take on so, Missy. He didn't mean any harm, and neither did I. I didn't know Garth was telling you lies about me."

"Oh, don't play the injured innocent with me, Joseph! You knew all the time that he was in Washington, and it was part of your divine plan to bring me here, wasn't it? Just so he could see me and gloat over me. You must have been delighted with Ross's offer to take me in. You let him take me away and you never came to see if I was all right. You—you didn't care if I lived or died! I hope you feel very proud of yourself."

Joseph said, " 'Lise, it was my intention from the first to take you to Philadelphia. You know we came to Washington only because you were so sick and I couldn't care for you any more. I didn't even know Garth was here until I saw him one day in the forest near the American camp."

"And he didn't lose any time, did he, in taking advantage of where Fortune had so conveniently placed me? I suppose he told you what I had to do to get those papers? If I wasn't a whore before, I'm certainly one now, because of what he made me do! And all because I thought he was going to kill you! Did he tell you that? He's a bloody, heartless bastard, and so are you! I wish he had killed you!" I sobbed wretchedly for some minutes. "And I suppose you told him all about where you found me and what I had been?" I said accusingly between sobs.

"I didn't tell him anything," Joseph said quietly. "Only that you were sick and being cared for in General Ross's house. Everything else was his idea. Your life is your business, 'Lise. You can tell him the truth about yourself, or you can keep it secret. I think it would be a good thing if you told him, myself."

"No!" I said vehemently. "I'll never tell him a thing, ever! I—I want him to go right on thinking I am the kind of woman he believes me to be. I certainly don't want to spoil any of his precious illusions. And don't you say a word, Joseph. Not a word! I just want to get away from him, back to France—"

"I won't say anything," Joseph promised. "Come on inside now and I'll get you something to eat. If I know Garth he didn't stop to feed you, did he?"

"Ha. The bloody bastard has more regard for his horse than he does for me. God, how I hate him!"

Joseph led me towards the cabin. The interior was crudely furnished with a cot, a table and a lantern, and a few rough benches. Garth was seated at the table, poring over my copies in the dim light.

He didn't look up when we came in, but said, "It's a good thing you came along, Elise. Your handwriting is abysmally bad. I thought French girls were supposed to be well-educated?"

I tossed my shoulders and growled, "Only in the arts of whoring and seduction, Monsieur. Although some of us actually do learn to read and write—in our spare time. I hope you go blind reading those things. I nearly did in writing them. And you'll get no help from me in deciphering them, either."

"Tut, tut, Elise," Garth said pompously. "Do you want Joseph to see how ill-tempered you really are? He thinks you're an angel, you know. But then he hasn't known you as long as I have."

"We're all entitled to our illusions," I retorted.

Joseph laughed, a low, rolling rumble. "She looks like an angel and she fights like a devil," he said happily. "When I marry it will be the other way around."

"Yes, by all means don't marry for looks, Joseph,"

Garth advised sagely. "You'll only regret it later. She'll get uglier and mean-spirited as the years pass. Marry for money and you can't go wrong."

"Joseph," I said coldly, "I thought you brought me here for food, not insults."

"Oh, yes," he chuckled. "Fine rabbit stew, coming right up. And Garth even laid in some fine wine. We patriots don't have to starve in the service of our country, do we? Here we go now." He set a plate of stew in front of me, on the table across from Garth. "Eat up. You'll feel better."

I took my plate and my spoon and sat on the edge of the cot. "You know, Joseph, food is not the only solution to problems," I said.

"No, it's not," he admitted, "but it sure helps you see your problems in a better light."

The stew was delicious—Joseph was a much better cook than I was—and I ate two heaping plates full and drank half a bottle of wine. My spirits improved. When I had finished eating I felt extremely sleepy, for I had had no rest the night before and had endured a particularly difficult day on the road with Garth. I thanked Joseph for the food and stretched out on the cot. Within minutes I was fast asleep.

When I awoke a few hours later I lay still, enjoying the warmth and comfort of my bed. I saw that someone—I'm sure it was Joseph—had covered me with a blanket. I could hear Joseph and Garth at the table a few feet away, talking in low voices.

"But if this information is correct," Garth was saying, "they may try to invade New Orleans from the sea and not from land. We don't know when they'll strike, but my guess is they won't get down there before November if they're planning any more activity in this area. We could warn Claiborne now. He'd have plenty of time to prepare defenses. We have to get a message out. Right now. Tonight.''

"They've got us surrounded," Joseph said. "It might take a rider two months to get down to New Orleans—if he don't get caught first.''

"We'll take the boat. It's much faster, and we'd only have to go as far as Naval Headquarters down on the Virginia coast, and they'll take the plans the rest of the way. Claiborne must be expecting an invasion, but detailed plans like this would be invaluable to him. Look at this, Joseph: the name and strength in guns of every ship in the fleet, manpower, numbers of infantrymen they'll be carrying. Elise was very efficient last night.''

I thought I detected a bitter note in his voice. I continued to feign sleep.

"The whole river's blockaded, Garth," Joseph protested. "And the bay, too. We'll never be able to get past them tonight with this full moon.''

"We've got to try, Joseph," Garth insisted. "It's vitally important.''

"I know that. But there's going to be a good, thick fog tomorrow night if the cold from the north settles in. I don't know if you can navigate through it, but if you can, they'll never see us.''

"If you can produce fog, Joseph, I can navigate through it." I heard the rustle of papers. "Excellent. We'll leave tomorrow night. The trip to Norfolk shouldn't take more than three or four days. The hardest part will be getting through that line of warships at the mouth of the river. We can probably avoid scouting vessels in the bay if we keep our eyes open.''

Joseph dropped his voice to a whisper. "What about—'Lise—trip—''

"—just have to leave her behind," Garth murmured.

I strained my ears to catch every word. Joseph was

silent for a minute, then he said more vehemently, "No, I won't let you do that to her. You've hurt her enough already, Garth."

"Me? I didn't do a damn thing to her. For the love of God, Joseph, you know better than to listen to what a woman tells you—"

"If she stays behind, I stay."

"You don't understand women like Elise, Joseph," Garth argued. "They land on their feet every time. They're—"

"She's a fine lady, and she's been through a lot that no woman should have to go through." Garth made a disparaging noise, but Joseph went on. "I'm not going to add to her troubles. She's coming with us, or I'm staying. Besides, I owe her my life."

"She was just a child then," Garth said peevishly, "a crazy, impulsive girl who would have helped anybody just so she could tell herself that she was being a glorious martyr to humanity."

"She helped me," Joseph said, "and risked that Captain's anger. I'll never forget it, and it's my turn to help her. I promised her."

Garth tried to reason with him. "She can take care of herself, Joseph. Look, I'll take her back to Washington tomorrow while you're working on the boat. She'll be all right there. She'll find someone to latch on to. But we cannot take her with us. She'd only be underfoot."

Joseph stood firm. I had never been so grateful for anyone's friendship. And I had never disliked Garth McClelland more. He finally agreed to take me along. They extinguished the lantern and Garth left the cabin. Joseph lay down on the floor near the cot. I wanted to thank him for what he had done, but I didn't.

Joseph started working early in the morning, getting the boat into shape. When I saw Garth at breakfast I asked him if he was planning a journey. He narrowed his eyes at me.

"We're going to do a little blockade running tonight, that's all. It could be dangerous."

"Oh, Garth," I said slyly, "you know how women like me thrive on danger. May I come along?"

He scowled deeply and said curtly, "I don't care what you do, Elise. I told you that. Of course, if you're frightened of the British—"

"Frightened!" I laughed. "Why, Admiral Cochrane is my favorite lover—next to General Ross, of course. The British are my friends, remember?" I leered seductively. "They have never shown me anything but—kindness."

I smiled coolly at him and strolled over to the water's edge to visit Joseph. "I hear we're going on a trip tonight," I said, kicking off my shoes and sitting down on the bank. The warm water licked around my ankles.

Joseph applied a paddleful of sticky tar to the bottom of the boat. "You hear right, 'Lise. I hope you like sailing."

"I like it very much. Garth doesn't seem particularly pleased that I'm going along. I'm surprised that he's letting me come at all. I don't suppose that's any of your doing, Joseph?"

"Might be. He'll get used to it, I expect."

I tilted my face up to the warm September sun. "Joseph, why does Garth have to be such a—a monster? He wouldn't treat his worst enemy the way he treats me. If I were his rival in politics or war, he would be gallant and cunning and very polite. But I'm only a woman, and therefore lower than dirt in his eyes. He's never shown me a moment's tenderness or consideration. He uses me and then he drops me. I hate him. I'll never forgive him for exploiting me the way he did. Camp follower, indeed!"

Joseph's face split into a wide grin. "A man does funny things when he's jealous—or in love," he said.

"In love! Listen, Joseph, where I come from a man in love doesn't abuse, bully, tyrannize, and insult his woman."

"He might, if he was afraid."

I squinted at him. "You certainly have caught on quickly to American ways, Joseph," I remarked. "Your thinking is becoming remarkable subtle."

"Oh, we Africans can be subtle, too, 'Lise. We fall in and out of love, just like white folks."

"Were you ever in love, Joseph?" I asked.

"I was married."

I felt embarrassed. "Oh, I'm so sorry, Joseph. I didn't know."

"How could you know? My wife and son died when they burned our village and took us all for slaves. Some-day maybe I'll go back to that village. I'll carry the Lord's word to Africa, right, 'Lise?" Joseph worked silently for some minutes, then he said, "I had a brother, older than me. He always had to run faster and shoot his arrows straighter and walk taller than anyone else. He didn't have any close friends. He didn't need them. He always liked to go out hunting alone. And he liked danger. Said he liked to feel the heat of the lion's breath on his face before he killed him."

"What happened to your brother?"

Joseph laughed. "Oh, he married a little woman from a distant tribe. She showed him a whole new way of living. He stopped going out alone so much, and when my father died he became chief of the tribe. He was a good ruler and a wise man. We lived at peace with our neighbors and with each other."

I sighed deeply and lay back on the soft grass. "Why does everything always have to be so difficult?" I mumbled crossly.

"It only seems that way because you're older," Joseph said. "You're doing more thinking. Come on, 'Lise, want to help me sew up some of the holes in these sails?"

Joseph and I worked and talked together for the rest of the day. Garth stalked around the cottage and the beach, making preparations for our voyage. He didn't speak to me and I made a point of ignoring him.

We sailed a little before sundown that evening. I took my things on board and looked around for a place to stow them. Garth had stocked the cabin of the schooner with food, blankets, lamps, some weapons—mostly rifles, pistols, and knives, and huge rolled charts of the river mouth and Chesapeake Bay. Our boat was a chunky two-masted schooner which had been used for fishing and carrying light cargo on the bay. Somewhat wishfully named the *Sea Demon*, it made up in strength what it lacked in speed and grace. One man might have difficulty handling her in rough weather, but a two man crew would certainly be adequate. I had no intention of volunteering my services to Garth as a crewman, even though by experiences with Lafitte's ships made me well qualified. If Garth wanted me to help he would have to ask, and even then I would probably refuse him.

Joseph's prediction of fog came true. We skimmed down the Potomac to the bay without being challenged by a single unfriendly vessel. When the time came to pass through the line of warships that made up the blockade at the mouth of the river, Joseph pulled in our sails to cut our velocity and we crept through. I could see lanterns winking on the decks of the great ships, and we came so close to the *Royal Oak* that when I raised my head I could see the black cannons poking like snouts through the gunwales on her sides.

Garth warned me—quite unnecessarily—to be quiet, and after favoring him with an icy stare I retired to the prow of the schooner where I would be out of his way. I would have liked to hide from him completely, but the boat was too small. The cabin had two narrow bunks, but the air below deck was close and hot, and the room was barely large enough for me to turn around in.

We spent the night anchored in a marshy cove where we

could wait safely until the fog lifted and we could head out to the open sea. I lay on deck with a single blanket covering me. I fell asleep to the strange night sounds of the creatures that lived on the shoreline, and when I awoke before dawn, when the tide was high and Joseph and Garth were setting sail, I saw a gathering of snowy egrets feeding on tiny fishes in the shallows not twenty feet from where our boat lay. High grasses concealed us perfectly from any roving ships that might have been scouting the bay. The world was still and peaceful, and I hated to leave the place.

The rising sun quickly burned away the fog and a brisk wind carried us towards the naval station at Norfolk. I lifted my face into the wind and salt spray. The sun blazed down, warming my body, salving my hurts, searing away the ugly memories of Edward Hennessy, the men on the Mississippi cargo boats, the agonizing journey to Washington, the humiliating encounter with Garth in the woods near General Ross's commandeered house. I took the pins out of my hair and let it whip freely around my head. I thought that if only Garth weren't there I would feel really free and happy. I didn't know what would happen after we delivered our messages to the navy. I supposed that we would sail north to Washington again and that Joseph and I would proceed to Philadelphia while Garth resumed his duties as a senator and a patriot.

Whenever I swung around to speak to Joseph I saw Garth watching me. His face was taut, hard and expressionless. And when I turned my back on him I could feel his cold eyes boring into me. I tried to ignore him, but I was constantly aware of his hard strength and beauty, of the power he used to have over me.

Over our midday meal Garth and Joseph discussed the war, the weather, British strategy in the south. I didn't particularly want to be close to Garth and I remained aloof from them, returning to my place in the prow as soon as I had finished eating. Towards evening we anchored in a natural harbor not far from a fishing settlement called Sandy Bottom, near the mouth of the Rappahannock River. I fished from the schooner and caught several fine sea trout. Garth decided to visit the village to ask about recent British naval activity in the area. Joseph and I stayed with the *Sea Demon*. We built a fire on the shore and roasted our fish and a few potatoes in the coals and boiled water for tea.

After an hour Garth returned. He had bought some flour and whiskey, and the storekeeper had told him that British naval vessels had been thick along the coast a month ago, raiding villages and settlements for supplies. Sandy Bottom had been spared. He crouched near the fire and warmed his hands, for the September evenings were growing chilly. Then he reached into his pocket and brought out a small parcel. He tossed it at my feet.

"Fish hooks," he said. "I noticed you were having trouble finding one this afternoon. If I had known you were such an avid sportswoman, Elise, I would have been better prepared. But I hope you'll find these satisfactory."

"I have never been able to understand how you Americans can regard hard tack and beef jerky as food," I retorted. "Surely in the midst of so much abundance—" I unwrapped the hooks and my mouth fell open. I swallowed hard and mumbled my thanks, unable to pull my eyes away from the paper the hooks had been wrapped in.

It was a cheap handbill, the kind they printed up by the thousands on traveling printing presses to advertise medicine shows, slave auctions, impromptu sales and offerings of property in the west by the United States Land Office. It was crumpled and faded into near-illegibility, but the words seemed to jump out at me: "Wanted for murder and inciting slaves to rebellion in Shenandoah

County," it read. "Light-skinned octoroon known as Frenchie, eighteen years old, branded R on left shoulder."

There was more but I couldn't read it. Joseph reached over and took the thing out of my hands, and spreading it out on his knee he read it slowly. Then he dropped it in the fire and we watched as it blackened and turned to ashes. My mouth felt dry. My hands were shaking and my hot tea was spilling out of my mug. I looked at Garth. He was enjoying his meal, taking an occasional pull of whiskey to wash down the potatoes and fish, not even watching me. I sighed inaudibly and hoped I hadn't given myself away.

"More tea, 'Lise?" Joseph offered, taking my cup. "How about a tot of this whiskey here?" I nodded. "Yes, I think this tea would be improved with some liquor in it." He shoved the cup into my hands and I drank. My hands stopped shaking.

Garth stood up and stretched lazily. "I'll sleep on the boat tonight," he said. "We'll get an early start tomorrow, before dawn. Don't stay up too late." He moved away into the vast darkness that lay beyond the rim of cozy firelight.

"Why did he do that?" I whispered at Joseph when he had gone. "Why did he bring that thing here if he didn't suspect something? He—he might betray me to those people! I wouldn't put it past him. He hates me so—"

"Stop it," said Joseph sharply. "It was just a coincidence, nothing more. And so what if he did find out? He wouldn't turn you over to the slave catcher, 'Lise."

"You—you don't know him, Joseph," I said. "He'd like nothing better than to see me hang. Then he'd be rid of me for good. I—I wonder if he knows already! Perhaps he even put Georgette and Arnold up to it! I didn't think of it before, but he must have! Why didn't he come to the cottage that morning? Why was he in such a hurry to leave for Washington? Because he helped his wife concoct the whole scheme, and then he left before anyone could involve him. His money paid for everything, Joseph!''

''Why are you talking crazy, woman? I know he wronged you, 'Lise, but that's no reason to take on like that. Garth wouldn't sell you. He thinks too highly of you.''

''Oh, Joseph, don't be ridiculous. Thinks highly of me? No, he's evil and cruel. He did it, I know he did!'' I began to tremble again. ''He hates me and wants me dead. And so do you, Joseph! You've brought me out here to kill me! Oh, God, what am I going to do?''

Joseph snorted disgustedly. ''You're tired and upset by seeing that thing. Just go to sleep and forget this foolishness. Good night, 'Lise.''

I fell on the sand and buried my face in my arms. I was badly frightened. Just when I had thought I was free Garth had managed to remind me that I wasn't. I was a branded fugitive, a murderess, a hunted criminal. I wasn't safe anywhere. I couldn't trust him. I couldn't trust anyone, not even Joseph.

I moaned aloud. What was the matter with me? I was losing my mind. Joseph was my friend, even if Garth was not. Joseph would protect me from Garth. And I would have to be watchful and protect myself.

My nerves were taut and strained. For the next two days I was silent and suspicious, keeping to myself, glowering at Garth and daring him to say something, anything that would give me an excuse to fly into a magnificent, glorious rage that he would never forget. I half convinced myself that he was responsible for my enslavement, and that his attitude towards me reflected his anger that I hadn't perished at the hands of my masters.

He returned my baleful looks, his light blue eyes shining eerily out of his deeply tanned face. When the weather was fine he shed his shirt and boots. The sun played on his tawny gold skin and on his smooth, rippling muscles. He looked handsome and threatening, like a demon prince, and sometimes I was amazed that I had ever desired him. I feared and loathed him now, and he felt the same about me.

We were caught in a violent storm when we were about thirty miles north of Norfolk. Our small schooner rocked and pitched violently in the high winds. When Joseph was wrestling with the wheel, Garth shouted at me to help him take in the mainsail. I crossed my arms over my chest and glared at him silently, making no move to obey his orders.

"I've tied the wheel down," shouted Joseph over the roar of the wind. He came over to us. "I'll help you—"

"No." Garth silenced him angrily. "She can help us or she can swim for it. You have a choice, Elise. Either pull your weight on this boat or—"

"Look, Garth," Joseph said reasonably, "I'm responsible for Elise. Don't—"

"This isn't a pleasure cruise, Joseph," Garth told him. "This storm is getting worse, and goddamn her, it's about time she did something around here besides acting like a goddamn queen bee. She can help out or she can go hang." I stiffened at that. "Well, Elise?"

I took a breath and prepared to tell him to go to Hell. A huge wave swamped the deck. I lost my footing and went tumbling over the side into the icy water. I went under immediately, then surfaced, gasping, then went under again. Tons of water pounded at me, twisting me around so that I quickly became disoriented and dizzy. Whenever I bobbed up to the top I gulped some air and looked around desperately for the *Sea Demon*, but I couldn't see over the waves. The water dragged at my skirts and when I tried to tread water I found that my legs were imprisoned. I tore at the clothes that entrapped me, but my fingers were already stiff and numb and the waves pulled my hands away from my garments whenever I got a hold on them. I shouted lustily once or twice, inhaling gallons of seawater with every cry. Soon I felt myself growing weaker. I began to slide under the waves into black, chilling oblivion, and I couldn't save myself. I thought wonderingly and a trifle sadly, "So this is how it's going to end."

Then I heard Garth's voice over the wind. "Elise, over here!"

I opened my eyes and saw him swimming towards me. He was only a few feet away. I stretched out my hands towards him, then the waves grabbed me again and sucked me down.

He reached me. I felt him tugging at my hair, pulling me out of the silence into the din once more. I clutched at him desperately and wound my arms tightly around his neck. He choked and we went under together, wrapped in each other's arms. When we came up again he was in back of me, gripping me tightly across the chest. With his free hand he ripped at my skirts and disposed of the tangle around my legs. Then slowly he started to drag me back to the boat. Joseph was shouting at us. I couldn't tell where his voice was coming from, but Garth seemed to know and to follow it. After an eternity we reached the *Sea Demon* and Joseph hauled us aboard. I lay face down on the madly tilting deck while Garth worked over me, beating the life back into me. I meekly muttered a protest which he ignored. Finally he eased up and helped me to sit while Joseph poured whiskey down my throat. I choked and vomited and drank more whiskey. It felt like fire and tasted like bile, but it spread welcome warmth through my frozen limbs. I shook my head and looked at Garth through bleary eyes.

"Go to Hell," I said before lapsing into semi-consciousness.

He picked me up and carried me down to the cabin. I was nearly naked, except for a short chemise that clung wetly to my flesh. He tore it off with a single sweep of his hand, then wrapped me in a rough blanket and tossed me none too gently onto a bunk. He went up on deck, and I could hear him and Joseph shouting at each other although I couldn't make out what they were saying. I didn't care anyway. I felt bruised and exhausted, and I fell asleep.

We rode out the storm with no real damage to the schooner. When we reached Norfolk the next morning I was feeling almost normal again, although I didn't try to show my face above deck until Garth had gone ashore. When he returned a few hours later he glanced at me impatiently and made no reference to the episode the day before. His face looked drawn and weary.

"Our navy, such as it is, is gone," he said bitterly. "They were attacked by the British a couple of weeks ago and many of their ships were lost. The rest are under repair or on their way up the Chesapeake to Baltimore. There isn't anyone who can take a message for us, I'm afraid. Damn. We can try to get a crew, but I don't think we'll have much luck. I think we three will have to manage by ourselves."

Joseph shook his head doubtfully. "It's a long way, man. Nearly two thousand miles around Florida and up the gulf."

"Not that far," Garth corrected him. "Fifteen hundred at the most."

"This is the worst time of year for this kind of trip," Joseph pointed out. "You know that."

"What do you expect me to do about it?" Garth exploded. "Fly my report by carrier pigeon? I'm not exactly looking forward to the prospect of a month's sail on this tub." He scowled at me. I tilted my chin up and faced him without blinking. "All I know is we have to reach New

Orleans before the British do, and we don't even know how much time we have.''

"You're crazy!" I told him. "I don't care what you do or where you go, but don't think that I'm about to go with you, because I'm not! I'm going to Philadelphia. Joseph, you promised me! I don't want to go back to New Orleans and I don't want to sail with you. I'll run away. I'll go to Philadelphia alone!''

Joseph said quietly, "You'd never make it past Virginia, 'Lise.''

I knew what he meant. The handbills. The description. I would be caught and hanged if I tried to travel alone. As long as I was in this part of the country I was in danger. I had no choice. I would have to go with Garth to New Orleans.

"But—but the *Sea Demon* is too small," I protested. "Unseaworthy. We'll drown, all of us, and your precious papers will drown, too. Are you some kind of madman, Garth McClelland? Don't you know when a thing's impossible? We'll be caught. We—we need more men, a bigger ship!''

Garth sighed and shook his head, "You're all the extra crew I'll need, Elise, if you do what you're told and behave yourself. Surely being a pirate taught you something about boats, and I'll teach you the rest. And the *Sea Demon* is perfectly seaworthy.''

I was trapped. I said despairingly, "I won't go with you! You can't force me. I won't go!" But I could tell from the set of his jaw and the steely glint in his eyes that argument was futile. I looked to Joseph for support. He was trying to look sad and sympathetic, but I could tell that he really wanted to go. The promise of adventure was just too tempting, too exciting. He was aching to strike at the British.

"Oh, you—you men!" I sputtered angrily. I stalked

down the beach and cursed the waves and the sky and the madness that makes men want to be one with them. A vision of a month on that small schooner with Garth McClelland loomed in front of me. I knew what I was in for. Two men. A boat. The wide, wide Atlantic Ocean. And me. What a crew. What a stupid scheme. What a nightmare.

Joseph and Garth decided that the next two weeks would be wisely spent overhauling the boat, getting her ready for the trip to New Orleans. I did not suffer their madness in silence, but my complaints and logical objections meant no more to them than the bits of flotsam that floated around the pilings of the pier at Norfolk. I slept on the boat at night. Garth suggested that I might be more comfortable at the inn in town, but I was afraid of meeting anyone who might connect me with the Frenchie of the handbill. He had no reason to avoid civilization, however, and frequently spent whole nights away from the schooner and came back at dawn reeking of whiskey, cigar smoke and cheap perfume. I told myself that I ought to be grateful: as long as he was giving the local ladies the pleasure of his company he would be unlikely to bother me. But I still felt irritated and annoyed when I saw him returning after a night's absence.

"I thought you were in a hurry to get to New Orleans," I said one morning as he poured himself a cup of coffee from the pot that I kept on the campfire on the beach.

He sipped slowly. "I am."

"Then why don't you spend more time working on your boat and less with—with those tarts."

He looked up at me. "Angling for customers, Elise? I'm a charitable man. You should have told me you needed the money. I'm always glad to oblige a lady."

I flushed. "How—how dare you talk to me that way? What gives you the right to slander me, Garth McClelland!"

He stood up, smiling. "What gives you the right to poke your little nose into my business, Madame?" He ducked and laughed as I hurled the coffee pot at his head. "Just let me know when you're available for business. What is it they say: charity begins at home? I would assume your rates are reasonable—"

I picked up a crowbar and charged him. He wrested it neatly out of my hand, and before I even knew what was happening I was lying on my back on the sand.

"You—you tripped me!" I fumed.

"And you tried to stave my head in. That makes us even." He offered his hand to help me up. "Truce?" he grinned.

I spat at him. He walked to the boat, whistling cheerfully. Soon I could hear the sound of hammering. Cursing, I got to my feet and collected the coffee pot and crowbar and wondered why I had started a fight with him so early in the morning. I knew damned well I couldn't win, and it just ruined my whole day.

Finally we were ready to sail. Garth remodelled the cabin, enlarging the space somewhat and building storage lockers under the bunks. The hold, forward of the cabin, and lockers were stuffed with dried meat, potatoes, apples and oranges, flour, salt, sugar, tea, coffee, whiskey, gunpowder in waterproof tins, blankets, warm clothes, and small casks for fresh water. The *Sea Demon* was even armed: Garth had found a small cannon, a twentypounder, which he had mounted in the prow. I had armed myself with a fine dagger and sheath that I bought from a peddler in Norfolk with money I borrowed from Joseph, who had to borrow from Garth. I couldn't bring myself to ask Garth for it, and even so he had great fun calling me Madame Buccaneer and offering to teach me how to throw my knife. I made a point of wearing the weapon at all times, jammed in the waistband of the tight-fitting cord breeches I had made myself for the journey.

Garth had equipped himself with compass, sextant, and other navigational tools, and with charts of the coast down to Florida. He studied these diligently and marked what looked like good hiding places. He would stick close to the coastline most of the way in order to avoid meeting any enemy ships on the open sea, where we would have no hope of outrunning them. We would have a better chance of escaping them if we were close to the dangerous shoals and shallows that they would wish to avoid. And we could easily put into shore at any time for fresh water and game.

We left Norfolk and sailed into the Atlantic on a misty morning in early October. Word had reached us of the attack on Baltimore, and Garth was sure the British would head for the Gulf Coast next. I soon learned that tempers on board the *Sea Demon* mirrored the mood of the sea. When the skies were clear and a brisk wind from the north carried us swiftly down the coast towards New Orleans, we were buoyant and cheerful. Garth was inclined to overlook my shortcomings as a sailor, and I managed to temper my dislike of him enough so that an uneasy truce existed between us. But gathering clouds dampened our spirits, and in heavy winds and high seas emotions rose accordingly.

Joseph was caught squarely in the middle. He tried his best to act as counselor and mediator when Garth and I squabbled, but his success was usually short-lived.

"Damn it, Elise, don't let that boom swing around like that," Garth shouted at me one day when he were bucking a strong headwind and I was fighting with the foresail.

"The rope slipped out of my hands," I retorted. "It wasn't my fault."

"It's always your fault when something goes wrong on this boat," he snapped. "Don't let the rope slip out of your hands. Why can't you hang on to it?"

"Because I can't!" I yelled. I could feel my cheeks

growing red, as they always did when we quarrelled. "It's not as though I haven't tried. My hands are rough and bleeding from trying. Look, look if you don't believe me." I shoved my upturned hands in front of his nose. "I have cuts and splinters and bruises on every part of my body. I hate this wretched boat and I hate you. Why did you make me come? I know why! So you could torture and browbeat me! If I didn't loathe you so much I wouldn't make mistakes!"

"By all means blame your clumsiness on me," he said with heavy sarcasm. "I'm only trying to teach you."

"Teach me!" I flung my head back. "What a joke! You couldn't teach a fish to swim."

"So I'm a miserable bully because I don't give in to your whining and sniveling," he snorted impatiently. "I have better things to do than pander to a woman who thinks everything should be made easy for her because she's—." He swallowed the word, turned his head and spat into the ocean.

"Beautiful?" I finished for him. "Is that what you were going to say? Don't make me laugh, Garth. I've paid for my beauty every day of my life since I met you. I've paid and paid and I'm sick of it. I'm sick of men and I'm sick of you. You have the impudence to sneer at me, Garth McClelland, because you just happened to be the first man to take advantage of me. Bravo, McClelland, for getting there first. Bravo! For being the first in a long line of greedy—pigs!" I hurled the word at him.

We were breathing hard, both of us. I watched his face go pale under his new growth of beard, then dark with anger.

Just then Joseph strolled over, moistened his forefinger and held it up between us. "I thought I felt a little squall blowing up," he said. "Strong winds and fifty-foot waves. But I think it will pass, don't you, Garth?"

Garth and I glared at each other. Then he laughed humorlessly and turned his back on me. My face was burning. I took a breath and was about to shower him with insults when Joseph rested a warning hand on my arm. I looked up at him, and he shook his head gently.

"Save some of that for later," he advised. "We got a long way to go yet."

I scowled at him. "We're trapped together on this miserable leaking washtub like two fighting cocks in a pen," I fumed. "We keep pecking and clawing at each other. I hate the sight of him, Joseph, and he hates the sight of me. We'll destroy each other, I know we will." Joseph sighed deeply. "Oh, Joseph, I'm sorry! I know this is hard on you. I wish—I wish it didn't have to be this way. I should never have come. I should have stayed with Robert Ross. Why didn't I?"

Joseph said, "It only hurts me because I love you both, 'Lise. And because there's really no need for you two to carry on like this. Tell him, 'Lise. Tell him the truth about what happened to you. He'll understand, I know he will."

"No," I said stubbornly. "You think that would change anything? You don't know him, Joseph." I raised my voice so that Garth, who had taken the wheel, would hear me. "He would still treat me like a whore because he's always treated me that way. He treats all women like whores."

Garth stiffened and glared at me. Joseph rested a kindly hand on my shoulder and said, "You'd better go below for a little while. You're tired, I know. We're all tired."

His gentleness brought tears to my eyes. "Oh, Joseph," I whispered, "I can't take much more of this." And I dove down the short ladder to the privacy of the cabin.

A severe storm overtook us when we were three days out of Norfolk. Clouds gathered all through the day and by evening the winds became stronger, but Garth insisted on waiting to put into shore until night fell or until the storm worsened.

"It's going to be a pretty bad blow, Garth," Joseph argued. "Some of these gusts feel like ninety knots."

"We'll find an inlet where we can ride out the storm before it breaks," Garth said. "There's time yet."

"But we're fighting a headwind anyway," Joseph said. "We're working like dogs, doing only about three miles an hour. Why don't we just put in now—"

"No," said Garth tersely. "Damnation, Joseph, can't I get any cooperation from anyone on board this boat? Please do as I ask and make sure everything is battened down."

Joseph shrugged and went about his duties. Our little schooner bobbed around on the huge swells like a cork in a bathtub.

"Garth," I called over the roar of the wind. The boat heeled sharply and I found myself skittering perilously around on the deck. "Garth, there's a bad leak in the hold. The water is coming in faster than I can bail it out."

"Take the wheel," he ordered. He went below.

I peered over the helm and saw a white sail on the horizon. The *Sea Demon* reared and plunged on the waves and I lost sight of it for a moment but as we rode the crest of another swell I saw the sail again, coming closer. I called to Joseph. He took the wheel and told me to get Garth at once.

I plunged down the ladder into the cabin and moved foreward to the little trap door that led to the hold. "Sail on the northeast horizon," I shouted at Garth. "It's approaching us fast."

We went up on deck. Garth followed my arm and saw the sail. He reached for his spyglass and peered at it.

"British," he said. "She's coming straight towards us.

We'll put into shore immediately." He shouted orders and Joseph and I ran to obey. This was no time for argument. We pulled the *Sea Demon* about and headed for the Carolina coast. I heard a faint rumble and saw small puffs of smoke hovering around the pursuing vessel. They were firing at us. The first cannonball fell far short of us, the second went wide of its mark.

"It's all right," I shouted to Joseph, "their gunner has no aim." I felt a red-hot ball whiz past my ear. I yelped and threw myself face down on the deck.

Joseph laughed. "That must have been his lucky shot, 'Lise. Garth, ain't we awful near Cape Fear?"

"That's what I'm afraid of," Garth answered over the wind. "If we can just make it around the point and into the inlet he wouldn't dare follow. The rocks are treacherous around here and they know it."

The boat lurched and heeled over so violently that if Joseph hadn't thrown his arms around me I would have gone over. We heard a sickening crunch and a scraping noise, and we saw Garth wrestling with the wheel, which was spinning madly in his hands.

"We're on the rocks," Garth yelled. I ran to assist him while Joseph started shifting the sails so that the wind would carry us away from danger. Garth soon abandoned the wheel to help Joseph with the sails. A long look at the horizon assured me that the British had given up the chase when they thought we had run aground.

We struggled for what seemed like hours to get away from the rocks. When Garth felt we were out of danger he lowered the anchor a few feet to help give our wildly pitching boat some stability, then we limped towards a sheltered inlet south of Cape Fear to ride out the storm. We were all drenched to the skin, and we huddled shivering in the cabin, sipping whiskey to ward off the numbing effects of the wet cold. Joseph and Garth took turns with the deck watch. I offered to take my turn, too. Garth ignored me

and left the cabin abruptly, while Joseph told me soothingly to sleep, if I could. Sleep was impossible. I started
awake each time the men changed their watch. We were
riding lower in the water because of the water in the hold,
and with every pitch and lunge I thought we would be
swamped. The cabin floor was ankle deep in water, the
bunks and blankets were sodden, and I was too scared and
cold to close my eyes even for a minute.

The next morning we found a good spot behind a
breakwater to anchor and we beached the boat for repairs.
Garth and Joseph scoured the shoreline for driftwood logs
that they could use as rollers, and after I helped them
unload our gear to lighten the weight of the *Sea Demon*
they maneuvered her out of the water and braced her up so
that the damaged rudder was exposed.

I spread our blankets out in the sun to dry and built a fire
to heat water for making tea and washing clothes. I scrubbed and scoured my shirts and breeches and spread them
over tufts of dune grass to dry. By mid-morning the sun
had banished the deep chill I had felt since we had left
Norfolk. After lunch I took a clean skirt and blouse, a
blanket, a comb and brush and small piece of soap, and
walked along the beach to search for a place to bathe. The
tide was high, and I found the ideal spot: a small pool
where the sun had warmed the trapped water to bath
temperature. I soaked and soaped myself and washed the
accumulation of salt and sand out of my hair. I put on my
skirt and slipped on my blouse but didn't button it, then
spread out my blanket on the warm sand and started to
comb out my wet hair. After a while I stretched out and fell
asleep.

"Elise? Elise, where are you?"

I sat up and reached instinctively for my dagger. Garth
was calling me. I got to my feet and gathered up my
things, sticking my knife into the waistband of my skirt.

He came over the crest of a dune and stopped. "Where

in hell have you been?'' he demanded angrily. ''You know better than to go wandering off without saying anything. What's the matter with you?''

I had had a very pleasant day and I didn't want to spoil it. So I just shrugged and said, ''Don't be absurd, Garth. Are you afraid the Indians might get me?''

''May I remind you that this is not Fontainebleau, Madame,'' he said tightly. His eyes went to my open blouse and his lips curled into a sneer. ''This land is wild, vast, and untamed. There's no telling—''

''Oh, for God's sake,'' I interrupted him impatiently, ''there's no one around for miles and miles. Any fool can see that.'' I folded my blanket over my arm and started to walk past him.

''Damn you, Elise,'' he said through his teeth, ''I'm just telling you for your own good—''

I turned on him. ''That's a lie,'' I said. ''You've never done anything for anybody's good but your own. You looked around and saw that your little slave, Elise, was out of earshot and you decided to drag her back so she could wait on you. Well, I am not your servant, Senator McClelland, and I am not at your beck and call. I go where I please when I please, and if I want to get away from you for a few hours, who can blame me?''

He put his hand around my upper arm. ''Listen to me, Elise,'' he said evenly. ''No one regrets your presence on this trip more than I, but I want to make it clear that I expect—''

I dropped my things and drew my dagger out of its sheath. ''Take your hand off me, Garth, or I swear I'll castrate you!''

His eyes gleamed strangely and his lips curved slowly into a leering grin. Without saying a word he grabbed my wrist and twisted it hard until I dropped my weapon. Then he hooked his leg behind me and came down hard on top of me.

"You haven't learned a damned thing," he muttered under his breath.

He pushed up my skirt. I felt his rough sailor's hands on my thighs and a cold, sick dread came over me. I strained and struggled, but I only succeeded in exhausting myself. It was useless to fight him. I raged at my powerlessness, my weak, helpless femininity.

He unleashed his fiery weapon and thrust it into me. I shuddered and went limp. I remembered the days when I would have swooned with pleasure, delighting in the lovely weakness and warmth that always engulfed me when he had me in his power. But no more. I felt dead and cold inside, and I was enveloped not by delirious pleasure but by a leaden hatred that sat on me like an incubus, weighing me down and suffocating me.

He threaded his long fingers through the hair at my temples. "What's the matter, bitch," he said savagely, "isn't this what you've been waiting for? Praying for? You used to thrill to the merest touch of my hand, Elise. Remember? You were alive then, girl. Alive. More exciting than any woman—." He gripped my jaw with his fingers and plundered my mouth with his tongue. "I suppose," he said between kisses, "that having lain with generals you no longer wish to dally with a mere politician, is that right?"

"You—sicken—me," I said breathlessly.

He shrugged. "And you are beginning to weary me, Madame Slut. But a starving man cannot beg for caviar when someone offers him stale bread, can he? I just hope you're not diseased, wench."

I bared my teeth at him. "Stinking vermin!" I spat. "Scum! It is you who is diseased, in your heart and in

your mind!'' I swivelled my head, trying to bite the hands
that held me prisoner.

He lifted his hand. I thought he was going to strike me.
Hazy visions of Edward Hennessy danced in front of me,
and I sucked in my breath and closed my eyes.

"Don't hit me," I moaned, "I beg you, don't hit me
again."

I felt him stiffen and pause only for a moment, then he
renewed his attack on me. I bore it all silently, limply.
Finally he grunted and lay quiet for a moment before
rolling off me.

"I'm not surprised that you looked like you were starving in Washington," he remarked. "I wouldn't pay you
two cents for a performance like that, my sweet. And you
a professional!"

"You filthy bastard," I breathed, raising myself up on
my elbow. "You'll pay for that, Garth. You will die! You
can't watch me all the time. You have to sleep. And some
night I swear I'll drive my knife so deep into that hollow
shell you call a heart—"

He clucked his tongue. "Always the little firebrand, eh,
Elise? You like to stir up trouble, and then you get angry if
no one quenches the fires you set. But you have lost some
of your verve, your splendid spirit. You disappoint me,
child."

I stood up slowly, painfully. My hair was tumbling
around my shoulders in wild disarray, and it was so full of
sand and sweat that I would need to bathe all over again.
He turned his back on me and started to walk away. I saw
my knife lying in the sand where it had fallen when he
attacked me. In a split second I had it cradled in my hand.
Its fine steel blade gleamed wickedly in the sunlight.
Murmuring a prayer to the gods of vengeance I sprang
after him, my knife poised to plunge into his heart.

He anticipated my attack. He swung around swiftly and

warded off my deadly blow, which was propelled by a maniacal strength that surprised me, but not before I felt the blade cut into the flesh of his sweeping forearm. I gave an exultant cry and darted away from him, ready to defend myself. But he had grabbed at me as I moved away, and I heard the tearing of fabric as he pulled my blouse away from my back.

I gave an agonized whimper and tried to cover my nakedness with the tattered garment. He was watching me closely, paying no attention at all to the river of blood that cursed down his arm. He stepped towards me and I raised my blood-stained knife.

"Don't come any closer, Garth! Get away from me. Get away!"

This time he chopped at my wrist as he lunged and my knife went spinning. Clutching me around the waist, he spun me around so that my back was towards him. He held my blouse away from the brand and traced it lightly with his finger.

"Let me go!" I sobbed. He released me and I stumbled away from him, trying vainly to cover my breasts with the torn blouse.

"Where did you get that?" he asked in a low voice.

I backed away from him, shaking my head soundlessly.

"Tell me!" His face was quite pale but his eyes were burning with a fanatical light. He grabbed me by the hair and pulled me close to him. He jerked my head so that my face was close to him. "Tell me!"

"How do you think I got it?" I sneered. "I did it myself. Branding is all the rage on the really good plantations this year, Garth. Where have you been?"

He was breathing deeply, glaring at me. Then he let me go and almost pushed me away from him.

"You'd better tell me everything, Elise," he said. "From the beginning. Did you kill Jacques?"

I was weeping and trembling with shock and anger. "Oh, yes, I killed him. I have many talents, Garth: whoring and murdering not the least among them. He was beginning to bore me and so I drove a knife through his heart."

"He was shot," Garth said tonelessly. "Did you quarrel?"

"Why should we? We weren't lovers. He had a lover long before I met him. Your wife's cousin."

"Arnold? Arnold killed him? You—you didn't do it?"

"No, I'm afraid not. Are you disappointed, Garth? I seem destined to disappoint you today, don't I? I'm glad. You've been entirely too satisfied with yourself lately. It feels good to deflate you a little. A pity I couldn't deflate you with my knife, but you can't say I didn't try, can you? Maybe I can have the pleasure of murdering you tomorrow."

"Arnold killed Jacques and then arranged for you to disappear," Garth said to himself. "Everyone would assume you were guilty—"

"Yes, wasn't he clever? Only don't give him all the credit. Your dear wife had a hand in it all. You would have been very proud of her, Garth. She very nearly destroyed me. She and dear Arnold sold me to Bose Niles. Do you know him? They call him the Flesh Peddler." His head jerked slightly. I knew he had heard about Niles. "I had a lovely trip up the Mississippi with some really charming men, Garth. So thoughtful and kind, you Americans. But you're always in such a hurry. When there is no time to woo or love a woman, voilà, you rape her. And it's so convenient to have a woman on board if you're sailing. Any time you feel like it, day or night—"

"Stop it, Elise," he said sharply.

"Stop?" I looked puzzled. "Why, don't you want to hear what happened next? I must be a very bad storyteller,

Garth, if I can't hold your attention with a sordid little tale like this! Then I will be brief: the brand that caught your eye a few moments ago was the gift of another generous American, my last owner. He'll never brand anyone again, though, because he is dead. I shot him with his own pistol. So fitting. Lafitte would have been proud of me. Bang, one shot, right between the eyes. He would have called it luck, but it wasn't luck. It was salvation to me, a reprieve from certain death. That handbill you picked up at Sandy Bottom was fairly accurate about the details, except for my name and age. They called me Frenchie. Very imaginative, you people.''

Garth frowned. "Handbill? What are you talking about, Elise?''

"I'm a runaway slave, Garth,'' I explained with mock patience. "Here's your chance to be rid of me once and for all. All you have to do is turn me over to the slave catchers when we reach New Orleans. You might even get a reward. To compensate you for your disappointments.''

He stared at me for a long time, impassively. Then he said softly, "Let's go back to the boat, Elise. We can discuss this later.''

*"No!"* I roared. I stood in front of him with the palm of my hand on his chest. "I want to talk about it now, Garth. What gives you the right to play God, Mr. Senator? You passed judgment on me, remember? You condemned me without having a scrap of evidence. But now you've seen evidence, haven't you? What now, Garth? Will you pardon me, Garth? Even make me your mistress again? Surely you won't let this pass and do—nothing! Are you going to forget it, pretend that it never happened? I can't forget. I can't pretend that nothing has happened, that nothing has changed. Everything has changed. I have changed! I am sick of being treated like a mindless piece of meat, a whore, a slut. You never cared about me. You

used me because when we lay together it was good, magical almost, and you could forget everything else: your grotesque wife, your responsibilities, your problems. You could even forget me, Garth, and you did, time and again. Did you know I found Jacques in the cottage where we had made love in the rain? The place where you said you would meet me, and you never came. I—I was ready to go with you, Garth. But you didn't come. Only death came. And evil.''

"Elise." His eyes were sad. He covered my hand with his. I moved away quickly, as if I had been burned. "I want to tell you—"

"Don't!" I said, sobbing. "Don't talk about it. I'm not interested in anything you can say to me, Garth McClelland. I just want to go home to France where I can forget the horror I have seen in this country, where I can forget—you!''

My fists were clenched, tears were streaming down my cheeks. I was half-naked, dirty and dishevelled, crazy with anger and with sorrow, but I didn't care. I didn't care what he saw when he looked at me. I wiped my eyes with grubby hands and retrieved my scattered possessions. I restored my dagger to my waistband. I paused in front of Garth, who was standing immobile, watching me, and I spat into the sand at his feet. Then I returned to camp.

Joseph looked up from the brace he was carving for the broken rudder. The smile on his face faded when he saw my tattered clothes and tear-stained cheeks.

" 'Lise, what happened?'' He stood up slowly and came towards me.

"I—I'm all right, Joseph," I said in a calm voice that barely concealed my hysteria. "I—I fell down.''

He wrapped a sun-warmed blanket around my naked shoulders and led me to the fire. He sloshed some whiskey into a tin cup and put it into my hands.

"He shouldn't have done that," he said slowly. "He shouldn't have."

"I cut him," I said with grim satisfaction. "Badly."

The beach was quiet. I could hear the muffled roar of the surf on the other side of the sand bar that protected our harbor. A few scattered gulls swooped and dived into the sea for crumbs, and came up squabbling and screeching. The sun was setting, casting its fiery gleam on the shimmering water.

"Elise."

Joseph and I looked around. Garth stood a few feet away. His left arm was drenched in blood. He had made no attempt to bandage it.

Joseph shouted angrily and charged him. Garth wasn't prepared and he fell back on the sand with an astonished grunt. The two men grappled together, groaning and panting. Garth stumbled to his feet and swung his fist, catching Joseph, who was coming up from a crouch, under the chin. The black man went down, but only for a second. He bounced up swiftly, thundering like a lion, and he tore into Garth with a ferocity and determination that must have been Heaven-inspired. Garth, who was weakened by the loss of blood, staggered and fell. Joseph fell on top of him and they rolled around on the blood-spattered sand.

"Stop it! Stop it at once!" I shouted, throwing off my blanket and dashing up to them. They paid no heed. I snatched up one of the rifles we always kept loaded in case of attack and fired into the air. The two men fell apart. I ran over to them and threw my arms around Joseph before he could hammer Garth again. "No, Joseph, please," I cried. "Are you trying to kill each other? Do you think I'm going to sail this leaky bucket to New Orleans by myself? Stop it now, please."

Joseph stood up slowly, rubbing his jaw. "You shouldn't have done that, Garth," he said. "There was no need. The next time you touch her, by God I'll kill you for it.''

Garth was panting. ''You—you should have told me, Joseph,'' he said thickly.

''I asked him not to,'' I said. ''It was none of your business anyway, Garth. Would you really have treated me any differently if you'd known? I don't think so.'' I passed my hand over my eyes. ''Oh, God, I'm tired. I'm so tired.''

Three days later—three days of cold silences, murmured instructions, resentful, sidelong glances—Garth and Joseph finished repairing the rudder. We reloaded the *Sea Demon* and launched her at floodtide, not long after noon. The skies were gray and leaden and a sharp, cruel wind was blowing from the northwest. I had the feeling that autumn was upon us.

# XVIII.  Cape Fear

Life on board the *Sea Demon* was not the same. My relationship with Garth deteriorated even more, to the point where we didn't even address each other directly but used Joseph as an unwilling intermediary. Garth and Joseph were barely civil to each other, and the easy camaraderie they had enjoyed was gone.

"You shouldn't have fought him, Joseph," I said one day. "It wasn't worth it."

"It was worth it to me. He had no right to treat you that way, 'Lise."

I shrugged. "He would disagree with you, Joseph. He would say he had every right, and if he had the chance he would do it again, you know he would."

Garth was still favoring his wounded arm. He had attended to it himself and he probably wasn't as careful as he should have been when he cleaned the wound. I resisted the temptation to ask him to let me look at it; he would have refused me anyway, and at least I was spared that rebuff.

"I hope he gets gangrene," I muttered to myself. "It would serve him right."

Joseph noticed the stiffness and swelling, too, and he was concerned.

"That arm of yours looks a mite sore, Cap'n," he said to Garth one day. "You'd better let me see it."

"No." Like most strong men Garth was impatient with his own illnesses. "I changed the bandage this morning. It's all right."

Joseph was not easily dissuaded. "I'd like to see that for myself, if you don't mind." He made Garth sit down and he carefully removed the clumsy bandage. "You'd make a poor doctor, Garth. This looks real bad. 'Lise, come over here."

The cut hadn't healed at all in a week. The wound was still swollen and red, and it looked infected.

"What did you do, Elise, dip your knife in poison?" Garth asked me.

Joseph laughed. "If she had we would have seen the last of you, Garth. Why, in Africa a little drop of poison on the tip of an arrow can kill an elephant."

"I'm sure if Elise had had some of that she would have used it," Garth remarked acidly. "I'm sorry I couldn't oblige you by dying, Elise."

I said, "I'm a very patient woman. We still have a long way to go."

"We're going to have to lance it and drain it, 'Lise," Joseph said. "I know a good poultice to make out of moss and roots. Some Indians taught me. We'll put into shore tonight—"

"No," Garth said quickly. "We're going to take advantage of this wind for as long as we can. We can't stop."

Joseph protested vigorously, but Garth stubbornly held firm. He allowed us to lance the infection and to cleanse and bind up the wound again, but he refused to make camp on shore just so Joseph could gather the ingredients for his "jungle witchcraft," as Garth called it.

We rode the wind for the next two days, and then suddenly we were becalmed in mid-ocean without even a breath of air to rattle our slack sails. We floated on gentle swells for four days. I spread our clothes and bedding all over the schooner to dry, and the men tried to find tasks to occupy their time. Garth cursed and fretted at this period of enforced inactivity.

On the fourth day as I was climbing the short ladder from the cabin to the deck I saw Garth coming down. I backed down again so that he could pass. Neither of us spoke. I was about to go up when he caught my arm and pulled me back.

"What's the matter, Elise?" he asked when I tried to jerk away from him. He was breathing heavily and he sounded drunk, but when I looked at him more closely I could see that he was feverish, ill. "Afraid that I'll rape you?"

"No, I'm not afraid of you, Garth," I said calmly. "Please let me pass."

He placed his hands on the bulkhead on either side of my head to brace himself. "It's no disgrace to be afraid, Elise," he said thickly. "Everyone is afraid of something."

"Oh, really? And what are you afraid of, Garth?" I tried to hide the uneasiness I felt at his nearness. I didn't want to be close to him. I felt as though I couldn't breathe, that I was drowning.

"I'm afraid of crazy girls who wear knives, for one thing." He glanced down at the weapon I always wore in my belt. "But that doesn't mean I intend to maintain a respectful distance between us forever, Elise. The best way to conquer fear is to confront it."

His eyes were unnaturally bright and I could feel that his body was radiating intense heat. Any other man would have been flat on his back by now, but not him, I thought resentfully.

"All right, Garth, I'll confront you," I said evenly. "Here we are, face to face, head to head. I'm not afraid of you. I don't look frightened, do I? *Bon*, I have conquered my fear! May I go now, please?"

He touched my cheek very gently. I stiffened and pressed my back against the bulkhead. He laughed softly. "Not afraid? But you're trembling, my dear. You're terrified. You may not fear me, but the mere thought of a man's touch makes you grow white with horror.'' He looked sorrowful. ''What a shame. Those men have a lot to answer for.''

''And so do you,'' I said angrily. ''If you don't mind, I don't wish to discuss this matter—or any matter—with you. Get out of my way.''

''Meet your fears head on, Elise,'' he coaxed, ''and you'll soon discover that they don't exist. If you like, I'll try to cure you of this terrible—affliction.''

''I am not afflicted and I don't require help from you, Garth McClelland. Although I'm sure you are expert in this sort of thing. I would rather join a convent than submit to a cure from you!''

He closed his eyes and moved closer to me. He rested his hands lightly on my shoulders, then slid them down to my waist. I felt none of the old, deep stirrings, only slight nausea and an all-consuming rage that seemed to envelop my brain like a mist.

The schooner gave a sharp lurch and I heard Joseph calling, ''Wind, Garth! From the southeast.''

Garth released me and went up on deck. I sat on my bunk and clasped my hands together in my lap. I felt no desire, no warmth towards him, nothing but sorrow and self-pity and anger. I wished with all my heart for the voyage to be over so that I could leave him behind me forever and take up the strands of a new life.

By evening Garth was unsteady on his feet, his face was flushed and his breathing labored. Joseph and I exchanged a long, meaningful glance, and Joseph announced loudly that we were going to have to put into shore for fresh water, for the days of calm had almost wiped out our supply. Garth gave him no argument, and so we headed towards the Georgia coast and sailed up a wide inlet that seemed to be the mouth of a river. We anchored in a deep channel between the banks, and Garth stayed on board the *Sea Demon* while Joseph and I waded ashore to shoot some game and fill our casks.

"Dear God, he looks terrible," I said to Joseph when we pulled ourselves up on the riverbank. "He—he isn't going to lose that arm, is he?"

"No, I don't think so," Joseph said. "But the poisons in the arm have got into the rest of his body and made him mighty sick. Maybe my medicine will help and maybe it won't, but we have to give it a try."

The wooded areas along the river consisted of a thick cover of short, scrubby pines and brambles. The earth underfoot was sandy and soft. Joseph had to penetrate rather deeply into the undergrowth to find the mosses and leaves he needed for his poultice. I shot a couple of ducks for our supper and finally located a stream where the water ran clear and fresh and tasted free of salt. I filled the casks and left them for Joseph to carry back to the schooner, then I returned to the riverbank. The evening was calm and serene. The setting sun shone orange on the furled sails of the *Sea Demon*, making them look not unlike slim pillars of fire. I could see Garth moving around on her deck. He had a rifle in his hand. When he saw me he paused and raised his arm in a mocking salute. In the evening light he looked like a Viking warrior about to sail into battle.

Just then the air was split by a blood-curdling scream and the sound of gunfire. I whirled around to see Joseph stumbling towards me from the dense curtain of the forest.

"Get back, 'Lise," he shouted. "Get back to the boat and get out of here!"

I froze for a second then ran towards him. Two painted savages burst out of the woods and flung themselves at me. Joseph intercepted one of them and dragged him to the ground. The other was on top of me before I had the wits to raise my rifle and fire at him. Joseph leaped on his back and yanked him off me. The Indian made a choked, gurgling noise far back in his throat and slumped to the ground. I gaped at him. He was wearing the cotton tunic and deerskin leggings of the peaceful Seminoles I had seen around New Orleans, but his face was daubed with paint and he looked weird and inhuman.

"Run, 'Lise," Joseph gasped. He was reeling from a bloody wound in his chest. His blood-stained knife fell out of his grasp.

"Joseph!" I rushed to help him. Then about a dozen Indians came out of the trees. They were all yelling and brandishing rifles and knives. Joseph charged them, his knife slashing and cutting. They soon overpowered him and I watched with horror as he fell under them and lay still. I fired once and one of the attackers clutched at his stomach and pitched forward onto the ground. But I had no time to reload. I threw my rifle aside and raced towards the riverbank. I plunged into the water and swam towards the *Sea Demon* as fast as I could.

Something grabbed at my ankle. I twisted around and saw that an Indian had followed me into the water. I took a lungful of air before he dragged me under water, and I felt in my belt for my knife. I had it in my hand when we surfaced again and when he pulled me towards him I stabbed at him with all my strength. He released me and floated backwards, a ribbon of red flowing from his side. As I looked towards shore I could see an army of savages plunging into the river after me. I heard a shot over my head. Garth was firing at them, holding them off until I could reach the boat. One shot from our small cannon scattered and panicked them. They left the water and ran for the shelter of the trees. I swam furiously; when I reached the boat Garth reached over the side and helped me up. Shots from the Indians' rifles spent themselves in the water, but as I fell on the deck I heard Garth grunt and mutter a curse. One of the bullets had found its mark.

We were drifting downstream towards the sea. Garth must have pulled in the anchor just before I reached the boat.

"Take the wheel and guide her, Elise," he said hoarsely. "We can hoist our sails when we're out of the channel."

He crouched in the stern and fired at the Indians. I felt the boat sway and looking over my shoulder I saw two of them climbing aboard. They carried no rifles, but were armed with hatchets and knives.

"Garth!" I screamed. I snatched up a loaded pistol and fired. One of them snarled and leapt at me, then dropped at my feet. The other threw himself at Garth and wrestled him to the deck. I saw that Garth was bleeding badly from a wound in his shoulder. He struggled valiantly with the Indian but I knew his strength was deserting him. Sobbing, I reloaded my pistol and took careful aim at the enemy's head. I fired, and he staggered and fell over the side.

Garth moaned and lay spread-eagled on the deck. There was another wound, a knife wound, in his side. I threw myself on my knees beside him. He tried to sit up and I pushed him back down.

"We're safe now, Garth," I told him. "We're out of their range and we're safe. Just lie still until we're under way and I'll be back."

"Renegade Creeks," he said, gasping. "British arms. Bastards. Shouldn't—shouldn't have—Joseph—." He closed his eyes and sighed deeply. My heart was pounding and I felt for his pulse. He had fainted. He was still alive. I staunched the bleeding and left him momentarily.

I hoisted the sails and guided the schooner out of the inlet and into the ocean, wondering all the while what I would do if Garth died. I thought of Joseph, slaughtered by Indians while on an innocent healing mission. I thought my heart would break.

When we were well out to sea I secured our lines and lashed the wheel so that it wouldn't spin and let us drift with the tide. Garth was still unconscious and starting to shiver. I wrapped him in blankets and tried to make him comfortable until I could get him down to the cabin. I could never move him like this. I would have to wait until he woke up. There was still one dead Indian to dispose of. I hauled and lugged him to the side of the boat and tipped him over. The leaden splash as his body hit the water and sank under the waves filled me with a grim satisfaction.

Garth moaned and stirred. I knelt by him. His flesh was burning hot and dry. I moistened a cloth and bathed his forehead and gave him a sip of water.

"Garth, listen to me," I said in his ear. "I need to get you below, to the cabin. But I can't do it alone. I need your help. You're going to have to stand, Garth. I know it will hurt but you have to try, just this once. Please."

I tugged at his hands. He grimaced and groaned and I helped him sit up. I kept talking to him, urging him, and somehow I managed to get him down that ladder and into a bunk. The darkness of a moonless night threatened to swallow us up, and I lit a lantern and hung it from a hook on the ceiling. It swung dizzily over our heads, casting wild, dancing shadows on the cabin walls.

I knew I would have to take the rifle bullet out of his shoulder and sew up the gash in his side, but I couldn't do it now, tonight. All I could do was keep him warm and dry. I fell asleep kneeling on the floor near his bunk.

The *Sea Demon* drifted in mid-ocean for five days while Garth hovered between life and death.

While he lay unconscious in his bunk on the day after the attack, I cut into his shoulder and extracted the bullet, fighting down nausea every second. I disinfected his wounds with whiskey, bathed him in cool seawater, and bandaged him loosely. That night his fever shot up and he became delirious, moaning and calling my name and shouting orders to a band of invisible men.

I kept cold compresses on his forehead. "Garth, Garth, it's all right," I said soothingly. "The battle is over now. You can rest. Try to rest."

"Indians!" he shouted, struggling to rise. "Powder dry! The flames, the brand. The brand! Too late. Go—go to France."

I tried to hold him down. As sick as he was, his strength was almost too much for me.

He tossed his head and murmured. "Elise. Damning—damning black eyes. Little Hellcat. Savage. Fire. Firebrand." Then he opened his eyes and said lucidly before closing them again, "Will you have some wine, Mademoiselle? It's a splendid vintage, a very good year, as I recall." He sighed and started to shiver violently. "Cold." His teeth were chattering. "Cold."

I was at my wit's end. "Oh, dear God," I sighed wretchedly. I piled blankets on top of him and when his shivering didn't lessen, I bundled all our clothing around him, everything I could find. Finally I held him in my arms, trying to give him some of my own warmth.

I knew that we would have to go ashore soon for water, for we had lost all our casks but one in the Indian attack. I scanned the skies eagerly every day, but saw no signs of rain. I dreaded the thought of landing on the coast. I could probably handle the schooner if the seas stayed calm, but the memory of those screaming savages was still fresh in my mind. I could never fend off an attack by myself.

For the first few days I hardly slept. I tried to nap while Garth was resting quietly, but at the slightest unusual movement of the boat or sound of distress from him I awoke instantly. I knew I couldn't manage both the nursing and the sailing. So far my luck had held and the weather had been good, but I was sure that in the event of a storm we would sink to the bottom at once. And I knew Garth would be more comfortable on land. His wounds weren't helped by the bumping and buffeting they received in the cabin. Finally I put us on a westerly course and hoped we would sight the Florida coast before too long.

Occasionally I felt inexplicably sick and weak myself. I would vomit over the side and then lie on the deck in the sun, gasping and shivering. The seas were calm and I didn't feel really seasick. I told myself that it was lack of sleep and proper nourishment.

Every so often I would go below and find that Garth had thrown off all his covers and was trying to get up.

"Got to warn them," he shouted incoherently. "Tell them. Too late. Too late! Get out of my way!" He put his hands on my throat and started to choke me. "Got to tell them. Don't stop! Don't stop!"

I managed to break his hold and persuade him to lie down. "It's all right, Garth," I told him. "I'll warn them, I promise. But you have to rest. Do you understand that? Rest! Lie back and be quiet, please. Everything will be all right."

He fell back exhausted and I covered him up again. I sat on the other bunk and sighed deeply. I didn't know how much longer I could endure this. Would he ever be well? Had the fever damaged his brain? Suppose I were trapped on a boat in the middle of the Atlantic with a madman? There was no escape. My nerves were frayed and I was so tired I could hardly stand, but I was too worn out to sleep.

"Elise." He was calling me. "Elise!"

"Yes, Garth, I'm here, what is it?"

He clutched my hand. His eyes were wild, bloodshot. "Don't leave me. I—I have something to tell you."

"Shhh, I'm here. What is it? What do you want to tell me?"

"The story of my life," he whispered conspiratorially.

"About Grandfather, and Highlands. And Georgette, too.
You have to know about her. Never—never loved—. The
women. Never loved any of them, Elise. You were right. I
couldn't love them. Grandfather was a stable lad. Ran
away. Shall we go there together? Come with me, say
you'll come with me."

"Of course I will, Garth." I stood up and tried to pull
my hand away. "You ought to sleep now. And I—I have
things to do."

But he wouldn't release me. I sat on the bunk and he
talked, talked for hours, telling me all the things I had once
wished he would tell me so that I could know him better.
Everything was garbled and out of sequence, but soon I
was able to piece together a picture of his whole life, from
childhood on, until he met me. I was in his ramblings, too.
I was the French Bitch, the Girl with the Damning Black
Eyes, the Hellcat, the Savage, the Firebrand. I tried occasionally to slip away but he held me fast. I was forced to
relive our meeting in the forest, our farcical marriage, the
voyage on the *Charleston Belle*. I heard about his other
women: the Maries and Louises and Annettes. I seemed to
have been the only Elise among them. There were women
in every city and town in the Americas and in Europe as
well. And there were duels, debts of honor paid by sword
and gun, nights spent whoring and gambling, hard rides
over rough roads on secret missions, kisses stolen from
countesses, princesses, schoolgirls and shopgirls. There
were enemies, real and imagined, in Louisiana, the United
States Congress, the British infantry. General Ross qualified as an enemy on two counts, as a British soldier and as
my lover. There was the wistful longing for a son, the
soaring love of his country and his home, his eagerness to
serve his President. And underlying it all was a deep
loneliness. Joseph had known about it, had sensed it. And
until that night I hadn't believed him.

He forced me to listen while he laid himself bare and

stripped away all the pretense and posturing that he had always used to disguise himself when he was with me. Several times I cried out, "Stop, Garth, please! I don't want to listen to this. I don't! Please let me go—." But he ignored me and kept on, alternating between lucidity and complete irrationality.

"I was born at Highlands. The ancestral home. I was the first and only son of an only son. Grandfather bought the estate in England where he had worked as a boy. I've been there: drafty halls and wind-blown hills. They told me it was beautiful country. That the woods were full of grouse and the streams brimming with trout. That's true, to a point. But her beauty pales beside America's. You can see in Europe what centuries of war and plague and famine have done to civilized countries. America is still intact, still pure and whole. It's wild and free. Wild and free."

He had grown up the pampered only son in a family of four children. He had had tutors and slaves of his own, but at twelve he had left home and run away to sea as a cabin boy on a French merchant ship. His father brought him home and extracted a promise that he would not run away to sea again. He ran away, but not to sea: the next time he lived for a year with the Choctaw Indians, learning their language and their ways. His despairing father told him that he was free to live as he chose, after he finished his schooling. Garth attended the University of Virginia and read law for a while, then he volunteered his services to President Jefferson as a scout on the Louisiana frontier.

Family business took him abroad for a few years after his father died. He lived in Paris and London and became familiar with the manners and modes of living in the world's more sophisticated capitals. He traveled extensively, to Russia and the Orient, to India, Africa, Egypt. His facility for languages stood him in good stead, and his wits and intelligence made him an invaluable man for his fledgling government to have in their employ. When he returned from Europe he married his neighbor, Georgette Charpentier. It was his father's dying wish that their two plantations be merged, and Garth wanted to gratify the last request of the man whom he felt he had disappointed by his way of living.

"I didn't want to step into another man's shoes. Had to make him see that the role of gentleman planter didn't suit me. Bored by that society. Farming is a bore. Georgette was attractive. And intelligent. At the time I thought that's what one looked for in a wife. Have to take one's pleasures elsewhere, with the others. Dull woman. Mean. She loved Highlands. I didn't mind paying for her pleasures. Better than giving her—" His voice faded.

"—part of yourself," I finished for him. I looked at him. He had fallen asleep, his fair hair falling over his forehead like a little boy's. He must have been an impossible child, spoiled and undisciplined and selfish, but a determined individualist and lovable in spite of himself. Would I want my son to be like him? I pulled myself up with a start. There would be no son, there couldn't be. I drew away from him, torn between regret and thankfulness.

His fever broke that night. He stopped thrashing and fell into a deep, heavy slumber. He lay so still that I thought he must be dead. I touched him. His skin felt cool for the first time in days. He would be all right now. He would live.

He opened his eyes and said my name. "Elise."

"Yes, Garth, I'm here." I knelt near the bunk and tilted a cup of water to his lips. He drank thirstily.

"Where are we?" He was weak and exhausted, but he sounded rational.

"Somewhere off the Florida coast, I think," I told him.

"Joseph? Where's Joseph? We should be—"

He was becoming excited. I put my hand on his arm and said, "Joseph is dead, Garth. Don't you remember?"

He closed his eyes. "Indians. I—I remember now. We

shouldn't have gone there. I should have known. My fault.''

"It's not your fault, Garth. It's nobody's fault. You're alive. That's all that matters now. You'll get stronger every day and soon we'll be on our way again.''

"Joseph." He sighed deeply. "A good man. My—my friend. I'm sorry we had to fight. He was a good friend until then.''

"His friendship never stopped, Garth. I know that. He never hated. He didn't know how to hate. He was better than both of us.''

He slept again. That day I sighted the coast and scouted around for a likely-looking campsite. I found a wood-fringed inlet and dropped anchor. Through the spyglass I studied the shoreline for any signs of Indians. I saw none, but then they would hardly be waiting to greet us. I would have to be on my guard. Garth was calling me. I sighed and went below.

I saw that he was trying to sit up. "Save your strength," I told him. "We're going to have to go ashore for water, and I've decided to make camp until you're well.''

"No," he said. "We can't afford the time. You have to take us to New Orleans, Elise.''

I looked at him. He didn't remember anything about last night. He was behaving just like the old Garth: arrogant, imperious, demanding.

"I don't think so, my friend. This is my ship now, and I say that we're putting ashore until you're well. I can't sail this thing and look after you at the same time, Garth. We're just lucky we didn't have any heavy weather while you were ill.''

"How long—how long since the attack?" he asked.

"Almost a week.''

"A week! No, we can't, it's impossible! We have to get to—''

"Stay where you are until I tell you to move," I said firmly. "If you don't I'll tie you down, Garth. I mean it."

He glared at me. "You wouldn't dare."

"Oh, yes I would. I have enough to do without you getting under my feet. Try to get some sleep now. It's the best thing for you." I started up the ladder.

"Where are you going?"

I didn't even pause but said over my shoulder, "I'm going to pitch a tent."

It was low tide and I started to carry the things we would need ashore. I waded through the shallows with my goods piled on my head. The undertow wasn't strong but there were occasional tricky cross-currents, and once I was swept clear off my feet and my load fell apart in the water. Fortunately, I wasn't carrying food on that trip, only clothing and a canvas sail. For several days after that I found stray items of lingerie and underclothing washed up on the beach.

I found what looked like a suitable place to build our shelter in a spot just off the inlet. A broad sward of silky grass was surrounded by tall pines and hemlocks. There was a stream of fresh water about a hundred yards away. The beach at that point was full of driftwood for fires, and I saw fish and waterfowl in abundance. All I had to do was build a waterproof shelter, I thought, and Garth and I could live quite comfortably during the weeks of his convalescence.

The invalid needed to be kept warm. I toyed with several designs for our shelter, and finally decided to construct an Indian-type wickiup like those I had heard about from trappers on the river who had been west. This was to be a cone-shaped dwelling with a vent at the top for smoke so that we could have a small campfire inside the tent. I felled and stripped five sturdy saplings that afternoon and lashed them together at the top with ropes from the *Sea Demon*. The most difficult part was draping the stiff canvas sails over my framework, lashing them to the upright poles, and driving stakes into the ground at the bottom to keep the skirts from blowing up in a high wind.

It was nearly sunset by the time I finished my task and swam out to *Sea Demon* for the night. I was proud of my handiwork. Our dwelling was about ten feet high at the center and twelve feet at the base, with plenty of space for two sleeping pallets—at opposite sides of the floor—and for storing our food and clothing and ammunition. Plans were whirling around in my brain. I would build a bed of stones under the campfire. The stones would hold the heat from a small blaze very well, and would serve as a sort of stove. Tomorrow, after I got Garth settled, I would explore the woods for herbs and grasses that I could use to season our food. Joseph had shown me which ones to look for, and I hoped they grew this far south. I would also keep a sharp eye out for traces of Indians. I should have done that first thing: if I saw any we would have to pull up anchor and move to another spot.

I pulled myself aboard our little schooner. My arms ached and I was shivering slightly, for the heat of the day had disappeared with the sun. I went down to the cabin to change into some dry clothing. Garth was awake, I saw, and he had lit the lantern.

"Why did you get out of bed?" I demanded angrily. "I told you not to."

He grinned weakly. "Call of nature, my dear. How did your day go?"

"Splendidly, unless I've landed us in Indian territory," I said. I stripped off my wet clothes and dried myself with a scrap of muslin. He was watching me closely but I didn't care. He was too sick to be interested in doing anything more than look, and privacy was too much to ask in these circumstances. "I'm moving you ashore tomorrow morning, Garth,'' I told him. "It won't be easy, but I'll help you all I can. The tide will be low at mid-morning and you can wade in without too much difficulty." I dressed and moved around the cabin, putting things away, preparing another load to take ashore in the morning. I set out soap, water, and a shaving brush.

"What's that for?" he growled.

"Haircut and shave," I said. "There's no point in bathing you until we're on land and I can heat your water, but this can't wait." I mixed up some soap in a cup until I had lots of lather.

"It certainly can wait," he said sharply. "You're not going to bathe or shave me. I don't need a bath. I don't—"

I said briskly, "You stink, Garth. And besides, I'm the one who has to look at your face, not you. I like it better clean-shaven. You don't want to get lice, do you?"

He narrowed his eyes until they were the merest slits. "You think this is very funny, don't you? You think I'm at your mercy, that you can do what you like to me now! Well, Madame, you're wrong. Get away from me!"

I applied a brushful of lather to his furry cheek and he knocked my hand away. The next time he opened his mouth I stuck the soapy brush into it. As he sputtered and growled I said with icy calm, "I don't find this one bit amusing, Garth. If I had wanted to take revenge on you I would have let you die of your wounds and thrown your body to the fish. But I kept you alive so you could get me to New Orleans, and after that I don't care what happens to you. We have a long way to go together and I want to make it as easy for myself as possible. I don't want to fight with you and I expect you to be sensible about your illness. You were sick, very sick. You very nearly died, and you won't be well any time soon. You'd better get that through your stupid head. You're making it harder for yourself by fighting me, and every time you waste energy arguing with me you're prolonging your convalescence. I won't ask you to do anything unreasonable, and when you're better you can take care of your own toilette. But I have to live with you and wait on you, like it or not. The least you can do is cooperate with me.''

I let him rinse his mouth. "Goddamn you, Elise," he muttered.

"He did damn me, Garth. When he sent you into the forests of the Lesconflairs four years ago. Close your mouth now—.''

In the morning I helped him dress. We only spoke when it was necessary, and then just a few syllables. He was still angry with me over the shaving business. He wasn't used to being thwarted by a woman. He crossed the cabin floor without my help, but by the time he mounted the ladder to the deck he was out of breath and had to sit down and rest.

After a minute he lifted his head and said, "All right, Madame Slave Driver.''

"You can rest a little longer," I told him. "There's no hurry."

"No." He sounded determined. "Let's get this nonsense over with. I suspect I'll be resting for a long time."

He leaned heavily on me as we crossed the deck. I helped him over the side and into the ocean. We slogged through the waist-high waves with agonizing slowness. Finally we came out of the water and he collapsed on the beach. I had sun-warmed blankets already waiting and I wrapped him up immediately. His face was pale and pinched looking and his chest was heaving. We waited until he felt rested, then he nodded at me and signalled his readiness to go on. I led him to the cove where I had erected our tent. When he saw it he stopped short and stared. His eyebrows went up and he looked down at me. He didn't say a word.

The inside of our dwelling was warm and dry. The opening flap faced away from the prevailing winds. We could hear the surf rumbling softly over the sand. Home. Until Garth was well again. I hoped he would mend quickly.

When I helped him into dry clothes I saw that the wound in his shoulder had broken open and was oozing blood. As I changed the dressing he said irritably, "What did you do to me, Elise? Bury one of your razors in my flesh?"

He lay back on his grass-filled pallet and I drew the blankets over him. "You didn't know I was a surgeon, did you?" I said lightly. "I saved the bullet for a souvenir. Remind me to show it to you sometime. I was quite proud of myself."

"I'll bet you were. You must have derived great joy from digging the point of your dagger into me. I can just see you: lips curved into a malicious smile, eyes shining with the prospect of inflicting pain without meeting any resistence from me. And now you can gloat over me, can't you? You like seeing me this way, helpless and weak. Well, don't expect me to thank you for your dutiful attentions, Madame. None of this would have happened if you hadn't been so hysterical when you thought your honor was being slighted."

"You'll have to forgive me, Garth," I said, "if I don't agree with your conception of rape as a kindness. I'm not sorry I tried to kill you. I'd do it again."

"Get out of here," he snarled. "I'm sick of the sight of you."

I picked up my rifle and left the tent. I told myself that he wasn't really angry with me, that he was just annoyed at himself for being sick and for showing weakness. Impatiently, I brushed away a tear that had started to roll down my cheek. He must hate depending on me for everything. He hated and despised me. I knew him so well now, well enough to understand his cruelty, if not to forgive it.

That night I prepared a fish stew and opened a bottle of burgundy.

"Burgundy?" the invalid muttered. "Surely I had some pinot—"

"You'll need a lusty wine to make this stew palatable," I informed him. I dug at the cork with the tip of my knife.

"Dear God, and you're going to taint it with cork besides! Let me do that." I handed the bottle over to him.

"You must be feeling better," I remarked. "Your temper is improving."

He tasted the stew. "You astonish me, Elise. Your cooking is as bad as ever. You seem to have mastered everything else: navigation, sailing, nursing, even tent-building and hacking a living out of the jungle. How is it you didn't teach yourself to cook?"

I tried to control my anger. I was unsuccessful. I picked up the pot of stew and hurled it out into the night, and did the same with the bottle of burgundy, his cup, his plate, and his spoon.

"You bloody arrogant bastard, you can eat dirt for all I care!" I shouted. I hoped he starved to death. I gathered up some blankets and my rifle and stormed out into the darkness. I slept on the grass outside the tent that night, with my hand clutching the stock of my rifle. I dreamed of Indians and death, and slept poorly.

When I entered the tent the next morning I saw that he was asleep. His arm was thrown over his face, and his blankets had slipped down so that his entire upper torso was exposed. He looked deceptively innocent and vulnerable. I drew the covers up and tucked them around him. He opened his eyes and grasped my hand.

"Good morning," he said.

"I thought you were asleep." I tried to pry his fingers loose. "You have remarkable strength for a sick man."

"Aren't you even going to ask how I'm feeling today?"

"No. I don't give a damn how you feel." I reached for the knife in my belt. "Now let me go before I cut your hand off."

He sighed and released me. "Life has made you hard, Elise."

"Is that so surprising? Life hasn't been easy for me. But I've survived."

"You'll have trouble finding a ship that will take you to France, you know. This is wartime."

"I don't care. I'll find some way of getting away from this wretched country if I have to swim." I heard an animal howl in the depths of the forest. "I hate this land of yours," I said, shivering. "If I ever get back to Paris, I swear I'll never leave it."

He smiled. "You'll find Paris dull after all this, Elise. The men there are as pale and as weak as women. All they care about is the latest gossip from the theater and from court, who is being cuckolded and by whom, who has been seen on whose arm. Surely you don't miss all that?"

"All that and more. I would like to sleep in a real bed and eat real food. I want to be warm and dry and safe from savages. We'll probably be attacked at any minute. Not that you care."

"Oh, I'm sure you'll be able to fight them off, Elise," he said airily. "You're rather a tigress yourself. But the Seminoles that live this far south are generally peaceful. I could probably persuade them not to slaughter us."

"You speak their language?"

"I could make myself understood. The Seminoles were originally Creeks in exile. Wanderers. They speak a Creek dialect."

"I thought you were more familiar with the Choctaw dialect," I said without thinking.

He blinked. "That's true. How did you know about the Choctaws?"

It would be so easy to use his rambling confessions as a weapon whenever I was angry with him. Easy and unfair. I said, "I don't recall. Perhaps it was Jacques who told me. You lived with them when you were a boy, didn't you?" I picked up our water buckets and walked out of the tent before he could answer.

I made my way to the stream. While I was bending over I suddenly felt dizzy and sick, and I had to sit with my head on my knees until it passed. What was wrong with me? This was no seasickness. And I couldn't be—pregnant.

No, it wasn't possible. It couldn't happen. It would be so unfair, so unthinkable. I wasn't supposed to be able to get pregnant again. I assured myself that I was just tired and weakened by anxiety and overwork, that I was upset with Garth, and that I might even have caught a touch of some kind of Florida jungle fever. Yet deep in my soul I knew it was true. I threw myself on the ground and wept until I was weak.

"Damn him. Damn him to Hell!" I sobbed.

I wanted to kill it, to kill myself. Why, why did it have to happen now, when we were so near the end? After we reached New Orleans I would never see Garth again. And when I got back to France my belly would be big with his child. Oh, God, it was so unfair, so cruel.

I dried my eyes. He must never know, never. I wouldn't tell him. He would only laugh at this new twist of fate, as he had always laughed at my troubles. Mother of his child! This would give him a new hold over me. He might not let me go home! Oh, I hated him, I hated him!

I could hardly bring myself to look at him for the rest of the day, I was so angry and so ashamed. I answered his questions with one-syllable replies, gave him his meals without fuss or comment, and failed to respond to his barbs.

"You can't wait to get away from me, can you?" he said at dinner. I gave a short, bitter laugh. "You'll miss me, Elise. I've been a challenge to you, haven't I? I'll hate going back to dear Georgette. Something must be done about her. I can't permit her to go about enslaving my mistresses, can I?"

"Why don't you divorce her?" I asked softly. "You don't love her."

"No," he admitted, "I don't love her."

I set down my plate. I had hardly touched my food. "You'll never leave her, Garth. Marriage is a very safe institution. You don't have to get too involved with anyone else because you're a married man. The Creole mammas in New Orleans can't pester you, your mistresses can't plague you to marry them, and because you are rich and good-looking you can have any woman you fancy, just for the asking. Or even without asking."

"Except you," he said. "You've given me more trouble than any twenty other women."

"Your Maries and Louises and Annettes?" I said viciously before I could stop myself. His mouth was open with astonishment. I bit my lip. "Bloody bastard," I muttered, and I ran out of the tent into the cool night air.

Rain fell all the next day and night. I hated being confined with him, and so I busied myself with mending and cooking and a hundred other distractions in the hopes that I could avoid conversing with him. He watched me closely, watched my every movement without saying a word. I fancied I could feel the heat of his gaze on me even when my back was turned. I became self-conscious and tense. My movements were awkward and clumsy and my hands began to shake. Finally I whirled on him and cried out, "Stop watching me, can't you? Leave me alone!"

He looked hurt. "Surely a sick man should be allowed

some entertainment, Madame. What do you want me to do, turn my face to the wall and dream about my Maries and Louises and Annettes?''

''I don't care what you do,'' I said angrily. ''Just stop bothering me.''

''I beg your pardon, Madame Fournier,'' he said with mock politeness. ''By the way, isn't it time for my bath?''

''You'll get no more baths from me,'' I told him. ''If you're well enough to plague me you're well enough to take care of yourself.''

''I'm making remarkable progress,'' he said complacently. ''Your beauty is having a wonderful effect on me. I find the black tangle of your hair so charming, and I love that revealing tear in your blouse and the smudge of dirt on your cheek. You are truly a goddess, Elise.'' He laughed softly.

I stared at him. My eyes were wide and my cheeks were flushed from the stuffy warmth in the tent and with anger. ''You—you swine,'' I whispered hoarsely. ''If you think for one minute that I enjoy slaving for you—in this muck and slime and stink——'' Tears started to spill. The rain was falling in torrents outside the tent but I didn't even see it as I ran outside and stood in the downpour, shaking and sobbing. I was so lonely—and so sad. In a minute I was soaked to the skin. My hair was hanging lankly around my face and shoulders, and my blouse—the blouse with the revealing tear—clung to my body.

I did not hear him approach. All at once his arms were around me and he was saying, ''Come back inside, Elise. I shouldn't have teased you. Forgive me, Elise. My poor darling, dear Elise.''

My heart split wide open. I let him hold me close, and I buried my face in his chest and clung to him. We stood in the pouring rain, holding each other while thunder rolled ominously around us and occasional flashes of lightning illuminated the clearing with a searing white glare.

Finally I came to my senses. "And just what do you think you're doing out of bed?" I said fiercely. "Do you want to kill yourself, you damned fool? If you think I need your comfort and consolation you're wrong, I don't."

We walked slowly back to the tent. Garth was bent over slightly, holding his side. When we got under shelter again I threw another log on the fire and helped Garth change into dry clothing. Then I went over to my side of the tent and stripped off my sodden garments.

"Elise," he said softly. I ignored him. I toweled my head vigorously and combed out the tangles. "Elise," he said again, "lie with me tonight." He wasn't whining or begging, he was just asking: lie with me tonight.

I wrapped myself in a blanket and went over to him. "I suppose you're going to tell me you're cold," I said.

"No, but you are. You're still shivering. Please, Elise. Just for tonight. I won't hurt you."

My eyes filled with tears. "I—I can't," I whispered.

"Just tonight. I won't ask again."

We didn't speak another word. I slipped under his blanket and lay with my back against the curve of his body. Every part of my body felt stiff, as though someone had wound me up with an invisible spring. I felt sad and frightened of the future, and I found his nearness more comforting than any words. He fell asleep with his arm loosely draped over my waist, and I continued to stare into the smouldering embers. A revelation more shattering than any other had come to me when he held me in his arms in the rain. I loved him. I had always loved him, from the very first moment I saw him, and I would never love another.

The rain stopped before dawn. I slipped away from him to add some fuel to the fire, then I dressed and went out to greet the first light of day.

Later that morning I changed his bandages. When I was finished I sat back on my heels and said, "Listen to me,

Garth. About last night. I don't want you to think that there will be any repetitions. I won't allow you to use me to ease the boredom of your convalescence. I—I'll sleep on the *Sea Demon* and let the panthers have you.'' I knotted my hands together. ''I felt—distraught—and I needed someone, that's all. But it can't happen again. Not here, and not when we're at sea. I'm not going to beg or threaten you. I'm just asking you to give me your word that you will respect my wishes and keep your distance. You—you owe me that much, I think.''

''Of course, Elise,'' he said. ''Whatever you say.'' He reached for my hand and I saw the old arrogant gleam in his eye. ''You have my word. I'll wait for you to make the first move.''

I drew my hand away and said with the old aplomb, ''You will have to wait a long time, my friend. Perhaps forever.''

''I'm a patient man. When I know a thing is worth waiting for.''

Garth grew stronger day by day. He insisted on doing as much for himself as he could, and one week after we made camp he managed to walk a few hundred yards down the beach and back again without my assistance.

''Well, I'm fine now, Elise,'' he said briskly. ''We'll break camp tomorrow and set sail—''

''You're being a little hasty, aren't you?'' I said. ''Give yourself more time.''

''I've had enough time!'' he exclaimed impatiently. ''How long has it been since the attack? Nearly three weeks! It's practically November, and we still have a thousand miles to go!''

''Don't be idiotic, Garth,'' I said crisply. ''You know how difficult sailing is when you're in the best of health. Do you think I want you to collapse over the wheel and leave me in sole charge of that wretched schooner? No, thank you.''

"I'll be perfectly all right," he said irritably. "I am not a child, Elise. I've been wounded before, lots of times. Nothing is gained by babying oneself." He turned on his heel. "We leave tomorrow morning."

"Very well," I said calmly. "You may leave, but I shall remain here. I will not sail with an incompetent captain."

"Incompetent!" His face darkened. "All right, stay here and let the alligators eat you alive, if the Indians don't get you first."

"*Bon voyage,* then. You might want to start dismantling the tent now. You'll need the sails."

"Damn you, Elise," he said grimly. I noticed that he was looking pale and shaky. We stood silently for some minutes, watching the waves breaking out past where the *Sea Demon* was anchored in the inlet, listening to the sigh of the wind in the hemlocks and the raucous calls of the brightly-colored birds that flew and wheeled over our heads. After a while he said, "God, I'm tired. I hate this—this boredom. I hate—doing nothing!" He balled his hands into fists.

Impulsively, I put a sympathetic hand on his arm. I wanted him to know that I understood his frustration and anger. He brushed me off and stepped away from me. "I don't want your comfort, Elise. Any more than you want mine." He walked up the beach to the tent and disappeared inside.

Why did it have to be this way? Why did we have to be either raging hot or deadly cold? Why did our relationship have to be a thing of violent extremes instead of gratifying serenity?

Heavy rainstorms and strong winds confined us to our tent for the next four days. Garth told me, rather unnecessarily, that winter was the rainy season in this part of the country, and that we had been remarkably fortunate in the good weather we had enjoyed so far.

"I have never seen rains like this," I grumbled one afternoon as I peered through the open tent flap at the torrents of water that poured out of the sky. "I can't imagine why this whole country doesn't just melt into the sea."

"Surely it rains in France," he said distractedly.

"You're not even listentling to me," I said irritably. "Oh, I know only boors and strangers have to resort to the weather to find a topic of conversation—"

He chuckled. "And which are you, Elise?"

I sniffed. "I am not a boor, therefore I must be a stranger."

"You don't look like a stranger. You look like a girl I once knew. She had fine large breasts and damning black eyes, and she was most beautiful when she was angry, which was most of the time. I made it a point to annoy her constantly because I loved her best that way."

My heart gave a queer little jerk when he said that, but I cocked my head and said, "Well, I won't be angry with you again if you like it so much. You may tease me as much as you like. I won't rise to the bait and I won't let you upset me."

"Excellent. No more tantrums, no more flying objects, no more sullen dark looks and pouting lips. No more stumbling out into the rain and crying on one's shoulder. And if I should steal a kiss or squeeze one of those lovely breasts—"

"You wouldn't dare!" I said hotly. "You promised!"

He laughed aloud, a rich, warm sound. "You see how rash it is to make promises you can't keep?"

I tossed a piece of driftwood on the fire. "I really despise you, Garth McClelland," I muttered. "I liked you better when you were almost dead. At least I had some power over you then."

"But you do have a power over me, Elise," he said in a

different voice. "You always have, and I'm only beginning to realize it."

I felt the blood rise to my cheeks. I stirred the ashes of the fire with a stick and thought bitterly. You are the one with the power, Garth. You can still reduce me to jelly with a look and a word, and there's nothing I can do about it.

"What shall we talk about next?" he asked. "Love?"

"I don't think either of us has very much to say on that subject," I said dryly.

"And why not?"

"Because I have never been in love," I lied, "and you don't know how to love."

"Is that so?" he mused. "I had several wildly exciting affairs in my youth. And I discovered eventually, as most youths do, that passion is not love, although I guessed that love was probably passion. But I haven't thought that part through yet."

"I'm not surprised. I wouldn't think you had too much time to think about such things," I said.

He laughed. "Well done, Elise! You're quite right. I don't think about them at all, or I haven't until recently. Must be a sign of advancing age."

I smiled at him. "Are you willing to share your discoveries with an amateur, Monsieur? What do you think about love now?"

"Oh, love is arbitrary, unexpected, and annoying. But like a case of sickness or a bothersome itch, it will soon go away if it is ignored. And you, Elise. What, in your opinion, is love?"

I gazed at him thoughtfully over the tongues of flame that licked at the piece of driftwood. "Love?" The chasm in my heart widened slightly. "Love is pain."

Several minutes passed. "Love is rather hard to describe, I fear. Go to sleep now, Elise," he said. "If the weather is clear tomorrow we'll pull up anchor and sail. I'm tired of this place.''

I didn't argue with him. He was assuming command again and I was happy to relinquish it.

The next day dawned bright and clear and Garth was true to his word. We dismantled the tent and carried our belongings out to the *Sea Demon*. We spent the rest of the morning bailing water out of her hold and preparing her to sail. I had some misgivings about Garth's ability to endure the rigors of a voyage so soon, but I didn't voice them. He was determined to sail, and I was just as eager to be on my way to New Orleans. I looked forward to the remainder of the journey with a mixture of hopefulness and dread, and I felt almost sad about leaving our little Paradise. He would not be so tolerant of me once we were under way, I knew. His mission would take precedence over everything else. And the tensions of the voyage would be very hard for him to endure without some sort of release, especially when there was a woman on board.

We had been at sea about a week when I looked down at myself and shuddered. I looked like a slattern. My blouse was hanging open so that my breasts were practically spilling out. My sleeves were rolled up over my elbows like a common laborer's. My breeches were stained and torn and I was still carrying my dagger in my belt, as though I were some kind of buccaneer! And my feet were so grimy and rough that they might have been a boy's.

Somewhat impulsively I scrubbed myself vigorously with seawater and lavender soap, put on a dainty green frock, and dabbed myself with perfume. My hair was hopeless, frizzy and dry from the dampness and exposure to the sun, but I brushed it until some of the gloss had returned, and put it into two braids which I pinned up on top on my head. Little black tendrils escaped and waved around my face, but on the whole I looked much neater and rather pretty, I thought. I had to go barefoot because my kid slippers had been corroded with mildew and my sturdier boots would not be appropriate with my gown.

I swirled around the tiny cabin, curtsying to invisible gentlemen, pretending I was in Paris at last, the toast of Napoleon's—no, Louis'—court. I wondered how much fashions had changed. I would have so much to catch up on, so many people to see. Parties and balls, the opera, the theater.

"Elise, where are—?" Garth swung himself down the ladder and stopped short. "Well!" He let out his breath in a long sigh. His eyebrows lifted a full half inch and he smiled appreciatively.

Suddenly I felt absurdly shy and ridiculous. "I—I couldn't bear the way I looked," I stammered. "I wanted to see what it felt like to be a woman again," I rushed on. I raised my skirts to show off my bare feet. "I'm thinking of starting a new style for spring. Suitable for the country only, of course. Do you think it will catch on in Paris?"

I chattered on mindlessly, nervously, while he crossed the floor and took my hand. I fell silent immediately.

"You look beautiful, Elise," he said. "But you manage to look bewitching even in your breeches and blouses. I see that you've abandoned your dagger. Are daggers out of fashion this year?"

"Quite," I said with a little smile. "But I don't need it any more, since you gave me your word."

"Ah." He sounded disappointed. "I thought you were giving me a sign."

"A sign?"

"That you were ready to release me from my promise." His eyes looked very dark and fathomless, like the ocean that surrounded us.

It would be so easy to say, "Yes, I release you," so tempting. I would have loved to feel his arms around me again, to lose my fears and forget my troubles, if only for a little while. Then I thought ahead to the end of our voyage together. I would be leaving him forever, and letting myself feel close to him now would only make that more difficult. I was going to have his child, I was certain of it now. Loving him had already brought me enough sorrow and pain. I had to be strong, to maintain the crucial distance between us.

"I think not," I said lightly. "The idea holds no attraction for me whatsoever."

He raised my hand to his lips. "As you wish. Poor little hand. It wasn't meant for work like this."

"Oh, are you offering to let me retire in exchange for a life of pleasure and ease?" I asked him.

"I wish I could, but—"

"You can't. I am a sailor first and a woman second, right? Very well, Monsieur, I understand."

He studied my face. I found myself blushing under his scrutiny. "You know, Elise, you're a coward."

I swallowed. "You're right, Garth, I am."

He went up on deck again. I took off my frock and packed it away. I would not take it out again until we were ready to land. I slid into my breeches and pulled on my blouse. The boat heeled sharply. A strong wind was blowing up, perhaps a squall. He would need my help with the sails. I started up the ladder and then I paused. I ran back to my bunk and snatched up my dagger, and stuck it back into its accustomed place in my belt.

# XIX.  The Battle

We reached the islands of the Mississippi Delta early in December, 1814. We entered the main channel of the river as evening fell and immediately sighted a British flagship anchored in the middle. Garth turned the *Sea Demon* about before they saw us, and slipped into a narrow channel that led to the gulf.

"Bloody bastards," he cursed under his breath. "We'll have to go up to Lake Borgne and then cut overland, but I'll bet anything they have that way blocked, too."

"That leaves Barataria Bay as the only possible route," I said. "Let's go to Grand Terre, Garth. Jean will help us get to New Orleans."

"If he hasn't joined forces with them," he grumbled.

"He wouldn't do that! I know him, Garth. He hates the British."

"They have undoubtedly stationed ships at the pass between the gulf and the bay," Garth argued. "We'll be sailing right into a trap."

"I know these islands," I told him. "Trust me, Garth. We can avoid the British and approach Grand Terre from the bay side. Yes, I remember now. We're just south of where I captured the *Mary Rose*. My first exploit as a pirate. I was terrified!"

"Piracy is like love," Garth observed dryly. "The first time is usually the worst."

We sailed through the southwest pass and up past Point au Tigre and Bay Bastien towards Grand Terre. While Garth kept watch through his telescope, I guided the *Sea*

*Demon* through the pass between Grand Isle, the smaller island southeast of Grand Terre, and the mainland.

"There are a couple of British flagships anchored about a half mile from the island in the gulf," Garth said after checking with his telescope. "I'm surprised your friend Lafitte hasn't blown them out of the water, if he's as patriotic and loyal as you say he is."

"He must be planning something," I said staunchly. "You may be sure he would not permit them to anchor if he didn't have a good reason for doing so, my friend."

"Suppose Lafitte is tired of warring with Governor Claiborne over his right to do business in the State of Louisiana," Garth suggested. "He might feel that he would have more freedom under British rule."

"That's absurd!" I declared hotly. "Jean is no traitor. I would never believe such a thing. Never!"

Garth made a noncommittal noise. He was unconvinced. "Lafitte has a loyal friend in you, Elise," he said. "Would you be so fiercely loyal to me, I wonder?"

I shook my head. "Lafitte never betrayed me. He never abused me, or forced me to do anything I didn't want to do, or raped me, or tyrannized me. I would trust him with my life, and I would give my life for him, I know I would."

"He's a lucky man," Garth said after a moment. He raised his telescope to his eye again.

Darkness and a heavy fog had fallen when we approached the northern shore of Grand Terre.

"The water is very shallow here," I told Garth. "We may run aground if we're not careful."

Garth played out the anchor. "She's struck bottom. We're in about two fathoms of water. How far from shore are we, can you tell?"

"I'm not sure. It's so dark, and I can't make out any of the landmarks I used to know."

"Well, it's time for a little swim, Elise. I hope there are no alligators in these waters." He stuffed the waterproof pouch with his documents into his shirt.

"There are hundreds," I said. "Why don't you give me the papers while you decoy the alligators?"

He laughed and we prepared to leave the *Sea Demon*. Suddenly Garth reached for my hand in the darkness. It was the first time he had touched me in weeks. "It's almost over. Afraid?"

My heart was pounding, but not from fear. "No, of course not," I said calmly. I climbed over the side of the schooner and slid into the water.

We waded ashore together and I led Garth towards Lafitte's mansion. We didn't speak a word, but after we had gone about twenty feet up the beach I felt a knife prick my side and I heard a low growl. "Halt, if you don't want me to smear your innards all over this beach."

"Auguste?" I thought I recognized the voice. One of Jean's burly guards. "Is that you?"

"Mam'selle Elise?" he said wonderingly. "Mon Dieu, look at this, Jean-Paul," he called to his companion, who had captured Garth. "It's Mam'selle Elise, come home again! What are you doing, you little wench, sneaking up on us like that? Do you want to get yourself killed?"

"No, Auguste, we've come to see Jean. It's vitally important. Please take us to him."

"Tell us if they've attacked New Orleans yet," Garth demanded.

Jean-Paul said in a low growl, "Who is this fellow, Elise? Are you his prisoner?"

"No, no, Jean-Paul, it's quite all right. He is—a friend. Tell us what's been happening? The gulf is alive with British warships."

"You'd better ask the boss," Auguste grunted. "He's got a party of 'em up at the house right now."

"Probably selling them arms," Garth said under his breath.

"He's not!" I cried. "Oh, let's hurry!"

We reached the mansion and I raced up the front steps and burst into the main hallway. Lily was going towards the library with a tray that held a brandy decanter and three snifters. When she saw me she shrieked loudly and threw up her hands. Decanter and glasses splintered on the marble floors with a deafening crash. In a moment I was engulfed in her broad bosom and she was sobbing, "Mis' Elise, Mis' Elise! I don't believe it! Oh, wait 'til Mister Lafitte sees you! Oh, child, this is a great day. We thought you was dead! And here's your man, too!"

I could hear Lafitte's voice behind the closed doors of the library. He was saying, "I suppose I'd better see what's the matter. Dependable servants are so hard to find these days. Excuse me, gentlemen?"

He stepped into the hallway and closed the door behind him. He stood stock still when he saw me. I was wet and ragged, and I gave him a sheepish smile. He opened his arms and I flew into them. "Thank Heavens, Elise," he murmured softly. "I thought—." Then he saw Garth.

He held me away from him and put a finger on his lips. He gestured towards the library and said in a whisper, "Take Garth upstairs, Elise. You will want to wash and change. Lily will help you. Go now, hurry. I'll come for you as soon as my guests have gone."

I smiled at him gratefully. He pressed my hand to his lips and then went back into the library.

"These women are so excitable," I heard him say. "A tiny lizard—"

Garth and I followed Lily upstairs. She was bubbling over with excitement. "I'll have some bathwater up here in a jiffy," she said in a whisper loud enough to be heard all over the island. "And I'll fix you some food, too. You folks must be starvin'. Lord, Mis' Elise, you look like you been livin' like some riffraff in the bayou! You come along and get yourself cleaned up now, and I'll take this nice gentleman to Mister Lafitte's room and fix him right up.''

Garth came into my room while I was putting the finishing touches on my toilette. He was wearing dove gray trousers and a frilly white shirt.

"She actually had some things that fit," he said. "I can't believe it."

"Lily probably raided one of the warehouses," I said. "Who knows, Garth, you might be wearing the costume of some Spanish grandee, or an English lord."

He lounged in a chair. "You look lovely, Elise. That garment was made for you, I'll warrant."

I pulled on a tiny white slipper. "Yes, it was. I thought Jean would have disposed of all these things by now."

"Touching," Garth remarked. "The traitor has kept a shrine to your beauty."

"Don't call him that," I said sharply. "You don't understand him. You never will. Just because you have never felt deeply enough about someone to want to keep a reminder—"

"Why should I need a souvenir? I got the real thing."

"Well, you won't have me for very long," I said. "I'm sure you'll be happy to see the last of me. You won't want to be reminded of all the dreadful times we've shared."

"You found them dreadful? I rather enjoyed them, myself," he drawled.

Jean tapped on my door and came into the room. "Ah, please forgive me. I didn't want my distinguished guests to feel as though they didn't have my undivided attention. Have you eaten yet?"

"I think you'd better tell us what's going on, Lafitte," Garth said impatiently.

"Not until you are fed, my friend. Come along. I'll have Lily serve your trays in the library. Then you can tell me all your adventures."

"This isn't a social call," Garth said. "I need to see Governor Claiborne as soon as possible."

"Of course. I quite understand."

They faced each other. "Are we your prisoners, Monsieur Lafitte?" Garth asked quietly.

"Dear Heaven!" Jean seemed surprised and a little hurt. "Certainly not. You may come and go as you choose, Garth. You are my honored guests. Please, come downstairs and I will explain everything." He offered me his arm.

"Monsieur McClelland thinks you are a collaborator, Jean," I said. "I haven't been able to persuade him otherwise."

Jean shook his head. "Because I have been forced to entertain two miserable red-coated ruffians in my home? My dears, how else could I find out what their plans were for me and for New Orleans unless I pretended to consider their proposal?"

"Proposal?" Garth was interested. "I suppose they want you to supply them with arms?"

"No, my vast supplies of arms and powder are my gift to General Jackson, if he will accept them. These British think that because I am French, I should resent the American government for intruding on my affairs and forcing me to carry on my business without their sanction. They want me and my men to join them in a fight for our independence! Come, I will show you their letters to me."

We went into the library. Lily brought in steaming bowls of crayfish bisque, hot bread, and ice-cold champagne. While we ate Garth pored over the letters from the British command to Jean Lafitte.

"You see," said Jean with a wry chuckle, "they hint strongly that if I do not choose to cooperate with them in this matter they will destroy Grand Terre."

"Oh, no, Jean!"

"It's all right, Elise, I have already made arrangements. My papers, my slaves, my most valuable merchandise have all been moved to the Temple warehouses." The Temple was the strip of land that lay between the north end of Barataria Bay and New Orleans. "These gentlemen came here tonight to demand a reply. I pleaded for more time, telling them that half my men were still strongly opposed to the idea because they thought they would be imprisoned after the battle. I said I thought I could persuade them, but that I would need at least two more weeks. They assured me that if they were victorious, which they are sure they will be, my men will be granted a full pardon."

"And I suppose you want Jackson to top their offer," Garth said.

"Not at all," Jean said. "We will fight to the death for America, all of us. But Governor Claiborne has already rejected my offer of assistance once, and so now I must do my dealing directly with General Jackson, who is a soldier and understands better the need to suspend petty differences in times of crisis. I leave for New Orleans tomorrow to take this up with him. My men have brought me detailed information about the strength of the British forces, and even if the dear General refuses to let us fight for him, he might be grateful for a little intelligence, no?"

"I knew you would never join them, Jean," I said warmly.

He shrugged. "Governor Claiborne and I have had long-standing differences of opinion but our affections are the same. We both love this land and we want to remain free. I have no wish to live in a British colony. And now, suppose you tell me how you come to visit me in the middle of the night, on the eve of battle?''

"We have additional details about British infantry and naval strength," Garth said. "We're probably too late for it to be of any use—"

"I don't think so," Jean said excitedly. "What do you have? Show me."

Garth hesitated only the merest fraction of a second before he produced his packet of documents. He and Lafitte went over them piece by piece. From time to time Jean uttered delighted exclamations.

"This is astounding, remarkable! Your spy must have been living in the hip pocket of the Admiral's staff!"

"She was," said Garth.

"I should have known, Elise," Jean said admiringly. "She is a fighter, isn't she, Garth? You were lucky to have her on your side. There is no better companion, no stronger friend. But you have certainly learned all this for yourself."

"Yes," Garth said softly. He looked at me penetratingly. "Yes, I have."

"We Americans thank you, Elise," said Jean. "You are really one of us now."

"No, not really. The outcome of this battle will make very little difference to me one way or the other. I am planning to return to France at the earliest possible opportunity."

Jean looked from Garth to me. "So that's the way of it," he sighed. "You make such a beautiful patriot, Elise. I shall be sorry to see you go. Won't you, Garth?"

Garth made no reply.

"France needs her patriots, too, Jean," I told him. "Now more than ever, because she has lost her battles and her leaders."

"You may rely on me to render you every assistance," Jean said. "I am so delighted to see you again, Elise! I heard that your husband died and that you simply —disappeared. I was quite worried and I made extensive inquiries. My agents could discover nothing."

Extensive inquiries. Dear Jean. Garth had not bothered to inquire. He had simply assumed that what he heard was true.

"I didn't kill him, Jean."

"I know you didn't, my darling. If you had you would have stayed, not run away. You are not a coward."

I smiled at him and kissed his cheek. "Thank you, Jean," I whispered.

Garth stood up abruptly. "I'll go tonight," he said. "I've got to see Jackson as soon as possible."

"My friend, you cannot go anywhere tonight. The bayou is covered with a dense fog, and not even my best men, the ones who know these swamps well, would be willing to take a chance on getting lost in the mist and finding not New Orleans but quicksand. No, you must wait until tomorrow, I'm afraid. We shall all go together at first light. Dominique will stay here with a band of men. If the British become suspicious of my delaying tactics and decide to retaliate, he has orders to fire the warehouses and abandon Grand Terre. After he gets in some damaging shots at their ships, of course. You agree, Garth? We'll take our skiffs across the bay tomorrow, and perhaps we can call on the good General together. He will want to congratulate Madame Elise on her success and render her thanks, I am sure."

Garth shrugged. "I seem to have no choice." He walked to the door. "I need a breath of air. I'll smoke a cigar outside, if you don't mind. Good night, Elise." He went out, leaving me alone with Jean.

I gazed after him, then sighed deeply and rested my

head on my hand. Jean sat next to me and put his hand on
my arm.

"Elise, what's wrong? You seem so sad tonight, so
lost. Please, tell me what is troubling you."

"I never could hide anything from you, could I, Jean?
I'm—I'm going to have a baby."

"But that's wonderful news, my darling! And we
thought you couldn't. Ah, this is wonderful, delightful!
I'm sure Garth is very excited about it."

"He doesn't know, and I'm not going to tell him," I
said. "I just want to get away from him, from this country.
Oh, Jean, I'm so unhappy."

"But why?" Lafitte lifted his shoulders and looked
genuinely amazed. "You love him, don't you?"

"Yes, yes, with all my heart. I'll love him until I die.
But he doesn't love me. He doesn't love anyone."

"Bah! Nonsense! Of course he loves you. Do you think
any man would battle Lafitte for a woman he didn't
love?"

I smiled and held Jean's hand tightly. "You are wonderful, Jean. But I don't want to burden you with my
troubles. I'll go up now."

"No, sit down," he insisted. "Here, have some of this
excellent brandy that Lily managed not to spill. Dear God,
what a racket she made! Like she had seen a ghost, which
of course she had. Come, tell me everything that has
happened, Elise. You need to talk to someone, and I am
proud to be your confessor."

I told him what had happened at La Rêve, and afterwards. Jean listened with a sorrowful expression on his
face, and from time to time he made comments like,
"How horrible! Ah, Elise, I would cut off my arm if it
would help you," and "Garth McClelland is a fool, a
blind fool to let you go."

"We could never be happy together," I said. "Because of Georgette and what she did to me. Because of the way he has treated me. Because of all the things that have happened to me. Oh, Jean, I can't be sure of him. I can't trust him, you see that, don't you? Women are nothing to him. And he doesn't love me. He's never given me a word or a sign. He's the kind of man who has no room in his life for women. And I don't want to be his mistress. I don't want to live on leftovers—and uncertainty."

"But he doesn't love his wife," Jean said. "He would belong to you, Elise, to you alone."

"No, Jean. He belongs only to himself. I would rather take my bastard home to my family and live out my life in disgrace and scandal than have to beg for his love."

Jean said sadly, "You are so proud, Elise. I'm sure if you told him about the child—"

"I won't! Do you think I want to bind him to me with false ties?"

"A child of love is hardly a false tie," Jean said.

"But it isn't a child of love! It's a child of sorrow and anger and—and rape. Do you think I could hold him with a weapon like that? And I don't want my child to be a weapon, Jean. I would rather lose Garth forever than have him resent and pity me. And don't you dare tell him! Promise me, Jean. Promise you'll keep my secret."

I began to weep. He put his arms around me and patted me soothingly. "Your secret is safe, Elise. You know that. Oh, he is a fool. A fool!"

I was awakened late that night by someone entering my room through the balcony door.

"What's that?" I whispered. "Who is it?"

"Garth."

"Oh." I sank back on my pillows. "We've played this scene before, as I recall."

"With a difference," he said, sitting on the edge of the bed. "I didn't have to climb tonight. I'm in the room next door."

"Really?" I laughed softly. "Lafitte is probably trying to play Cupid. I should have told him he would be unsuccessful."

"You two were very cozy tonight. He told me later—in a very nice way, of course, no slight intended—that I was a fool. What lies have you been spreading about me?"

"No lies." I leaned up on my elbow. I couldn't see his face in the darkness, only the barest outline of his figure. But I could feel him, sense him. "I told him the truth. He formed his own opinions. I'm sorry he thinks you're a fool—he shouldn't have told you. But Jean is rather irrepressible, I'm afraid."

"Do you agree with him?" He began to toy with a lock of hair that had fallen over my shoulder.

"What if I did? Would you change?"

"No. I have been foolish, but I'm no fool. What are you going to do in New Orleans?"

"I'll stay at Jean's house on Dumaine Street until the war is over, I suppose. And then I shall take the first boat to France. Who knows, if the British win I may even take my friend General Ross up on the kind offer he made me in Washington." He rested a hand on my breast. I shrank away from him and pushed him back. "Why don't you go now, Garth. It's so late—"

"I'm not going, Elise. I'll spend this last night with you, if you don't mind."

"But I do mind! Please, Garth, you promised—"

"Everything comes to an end, my dear. Voyages, love affairs, promises."

A sinking, swirling sensation started in my middle and spread to every part of my body. He threw off my coverlets and slid out of his robe. He was naked. Covering me with his body he showered my face and neck with kisses. I managed to wriggle out from under him and I stumbled out of bed and ran across the floor. He came after me and grabbed me around the waist. I twisted around and went for his eyes with my fingernails. He grabbed my wrists and held them behind my back. I struggled and kicked.

"You never learn, do you?" he said through his teeth.

I cursed him feelingly. He ripped open my gauzy night-dress and sank his teeth into my nipple. I cried out in anguish as he forced me down on the floor. His lips seared my flesh, and even as I fought I could feel myself growing warm and languid under him.

"Please let go of my wrists," I said breathlessly. "You're hurting me."

"So you can claw my eyes out? No, thank you, Elise. I know the tricks a woman uses to defend herself."

"Garth." I stopped struggling and lay still. I could feel the rapid pounding of his heart on mine. "Garth, please let me go." He waited a minute, then he freed my hands. I lightly stroked the hard muscles in his thighs, buttocks and back. He jerked convulsively and sucked in his breath. I traced the line of his jaw and his mouth. I memorized the contours of his nose, his cheeks, his forehead. I laced my fingers through his hair and pulled his face close to mine so that our lips were nearly touching. "Why do we always fight?" I asked him wistfully. "Why can't we be lovers instead of combatants this time? I want you—"

He said, "What difference does it make? I intend to have you, woman, here and now, whether you like it or not."

"It makes all the difference in the world to me," I murmured. "I want to remember this night forever. Please be kind to me, my darling."

He held me tightly and growled, "Sometimes I swear I could kill you, Elise." He stroked my neck. "I could put one hand around this lovely white throat of yours and crush the life out of you.''

"Why? Am I in your blood, Garth?"

"You know damned well you are,'' he said gruffly. We shared a slow, languorous kiss. He thrust his throbbing manhood into me. I gasped and choked back a terrified sob. He must have felt me stiffen. ''Are you afraid?''

"Would—it make any difference—to you if I were?" I asked hoarsely.

He did not say anything for a long time. He lay still, sheltering me with his fine body, stroking the hair away from my face. Finally he answered. "Yes." His whisper was faint, almost inaudible. Then he said again in a stronger voice, "Yes, damn you, it would."

I shook my head. "I'm not afraid—only—only that I won't be able to—"

"Yes, you will." He began to move slowly in me, lulling and soothing me.

"Is this your famous cure, Doctor?" I asked him slyly. "What if I don't respond?"

"You'd better," he laughed, "if you don't want to be here all night."

I lay back in his arms with a contented sigh and let the flames of his love flicker over me. We slept very sporadically that night, so great was our hunger for each other. Somehow he had banished the awful ache I had carried in me since the last time we had made love in the cane cutter's cottage at La Rêve. I closed my mind to the future. The present was all that mattered.

Just before dawn he tightened his embrace and said, "You're not going back to France."

"But Garth—"

"I won't let you go. Don't argue with me, Elise."

"But you don't—"

A deep kiss drowned my protests. We held each other

close and I heard him murmur, "I need you. God, how I
need you."

The future would take care of itself.

Soon after dawn we were poling across Barataria Bay in
skiffs. Jean and Pierre rode in the first skiff with a stalwart
crew and a few of Jean's favorite possessions: his Rembrandt, some gorgeous silver goblets that had been destined to belong to William Claiborne and had somehow
been sidetracked, and some simple brass candlesticks that
had belonged to his family in Haiti. Garth and I followed
in a skiff manned by Auguste and Jean-Paul and three
other burly crewmen. Another skiff followed behind us,
carrying the last of the precious cargo that Jean did not
want to leave to the loofing British.

I was wearing a simple gray dress with a shawl over my
shoulders to ward off the dampness. As he was helping me
into the boat Garth said, "Your friend Lafitte is gloating
like a cat this morning."

"That makes two of you," I said. "You're looking
fairly smug this morning yourself, Monsieur."

"It's always nice to know that one need not be branded
a fool for life if he has only been a fool part of the time."

I looked over at Jean, who grinned triumphantly and
gave me a Gallic nod of approval. He even rubbed his
stomach and mouthed, "Did you tell him?"

"What's he doing now?" Garth asked.

"Perhaps he missed his breakfast," I said distractedly.
I formed my mouth into a silent "no" that Jean could see.
He shrugged and threw up his hands.

The remnants of fog hung over the water in patches.
Even though it was December the air was close and thick
and the day promised to be warm and muggy. The only
sounds we could hear were scattered birdsongs and the
sucking of our poles in the mud that lay under the shallow
water.

Suddenly the quiet was shattered by the sound of rifle fire. I peered ahead to Jean's skiff, but it had become enshrouded in a thick patch of fog and I couldn't see him. Garth and the other men were tense and alert, their weapons in readiness.

"For God's sake, somebody give me a gun," I hissed. One of the pirates slapped a knife into my outstretched palm and another gave me a loaded pistol.

The shots came again, closer this time, and I could hear shouts and see flashes of red around us.

"British scouting party," Garth said in a low voice. "They probably expected Lafitte to try something after their visit last night."

They were everywhere. There seemed to be hundreds of them, coming at us from all directions. Our little skiff rocked and tipped as they brought their own boats alongside and tried to board us. Then I heard more shots and a rapid exchange of gunfire close at hand. Pirates. Reinforcements. Once again Lafitte had anticipated the enemy's movements and had been ready for them.

The skirmish raged around us for some minutes. I could see Garth, his golden head shining, firing and reloading with quick and deadly efficiency.

He looked over at me. "Get down, Elise," he shouted. "Do you want to get your damned head blown off?"

I grinned at him. Dear Garth. Always so thoughtful and polite.

While we were repulsing the attack our skiff had drifted until it struck a small hummock, one of the small lumps of ground that abounded in the bay. I looked up to see a fierce-looking redcoat bearing down on me. I plunged my knife into his belly and he fell into the brackish water. Then a dozen more British soldiers appeared out of the mist and came towards us.

"Garth!" I shrieked.

He saw them and leaped to my side. He fought them hand to hand. Then one of them struck him on the side of the head with the stock of a rifle. Garth slumped to the bottom of the skiff. The soldier was about to drive his bayonet into him when I raised my pistol to his head and fired. He fell back out of the skiff and hit the water with a splash. As I bent over Garth to examine his wound, I felt a strangling pressure around my throat. I pried at the fingers but couldn't loosen them. The world began to grow black. I could feel rough masculine hands dragging me out of the skiff, over the coarse grasses of the hummock. A burst of laughter. And overwhelming silence.

I was drowning. I choked and sputtered. Then I coughed and tried to sit up. A strong wave of nausea forced me back down, and I lay with my eyes closed, trying to decide if I was alive or dead.

"When she comes around bring her to my quarters."

"Yessir."

Someone was hitting me in the face. "Come on, lass, wake up now. You're not dead, you've just had a nice sleep."

I pushed their hands away and opened my eyes. Strong arms lifted me to my feet.

I was on a ship and the men who surrounded me were British sailors. They wore blue jackets and hard flat hats like soup plates. Their faces were ugly, grinning.

"She's the little demon that knifed that sergeant back there in the swamp," one of them said. "She must be one of them Louisiana wildcats we heard about."

"Come along, little lady," the largest of them said. "The Admiral wants to see you."

I remembered the voice I had heard as I was waking up. "Admiral—Cochrane?"

"The very same. Why, you know him?"

I brushed my hair back and straightened my dress. "We have met," I said. "In older and happier times."

They laughed at that. My escort clapped me on the back and said, "What a charmin' coincidence, isn't it, mates? Let's go, Ma'am. I'm sure you're just as eager to see him as he is to see you." More guffaws. We went up on deck. Over the starboard side I could see the hazy outline of Grand Terre.

We were on board the Admiral's flagship, *Royal Oak*. General Ross had taken me aboard several times while the ship had lain at anchor in the Potomac River. The Admiral had given parties and balls on her for his officers and their wives. My escort, a bo'sun named Kirby, led me to the Admiral's cabin and tapped at the door. A voice bade us enter.

Kirby saluted sharply and said, "Brought the prisoner as you requested, Admiral, sir."

Forrester Cochrane looked up from the table where he was seated. His blue eyes were cold, and with his sharp features and shock of white hair he reminded me of a hawk, dangerous and predatory. For the first time I felt a stab of fear.

"Well, Madame, this is a remarkable coincidence," he said. "When last we met you were the houseguest of General Ross, and now I find you here, in the company of brigands and thieves. Your friendships take in an astonishing array of men, but that doesn't surprise me. Women like you are not particular, I understand."

I said stiffly, "Both Lafitte and General Ross were my friends. How is the General, if I may ask?"

"General Ross died a hero's death at Baltimore."

I felt ill. "Oh, I'm sorry," I said lamely.

"So was I. But I am sorrier for you, Madame, because you thought you would have a friend in this camp and now you find you have none, only men who know you for what you really are. I am not sorry that Ross died before he learned that he had nurtured a traitoress to his bosom.''

"I don't know what you mean."

"I mean finding you here, in Louisiana, in the camp of a common thief.''

"I told you, Lafitte is an old and dear friend," I said, trying to match his coolness. "I see nothing remarkable in the fact that I choose to visit an old friend.''

"Perhaps not. But I know that Robert had in his possession copies of plans for the British invasion of New Orleans. I know that a few days after you disappeared suddenly and without warning, Robert remarked to me—with incredible naiveté—that he thought his papers had been disturbed. I know that Lafitte has been strangely unreceptive to our overtures—''

"That is no fault of mine!"

"So unreceptive, in fact, that one would almost think that he had knowledge of them in advance!" Cochrane said vehemently. "Did he, Madame? Did you warn 'your friend' that we might approach him? Did you warn the Governor of this state and his assistants that we would descend on them and wrest control of the city from their hands? I was suspicious of you from the very beginning, wench. I am not a stupid man. I saw how you were worming your way into the affections of a simple soldier, alienating him from his wife, from his duties!''

"That's a lie!" I cried. "He was an old acquaintance! He knew my father!''

"Ah, yes, your celebrated father, one of Napoleon's generals, wasn't he? I find that an unlikely tale, Madame. I suppose Wellington himself dandled you on his knee when you were an infant? I am calling you an artful liar and a spy. I find it not so incredible that General Ross might have befriended a visiting officer in London, but that the daughter of this foreigner would suddenly appear on his doorstep in the midst of war with the Americans! Preposterous, I call it!''

I shrugged elaborately. "You have seen enough of life to know that coincidences are indeed preposterous and remarkable, Admiral. How can I convince you that I am innocent of your charges?''

"You can't,'' he said bluntly. "Nothing you could say would alter my opinion of you, Madame. You could tell me that the sky was blue and that water was wet, and still I would not believe you. You are an American agent, a French-speaking native of Louisiana. You were sent to General Ross with that ridiculous tale, claiming kinship with a man whom you never even met—''

"He was my father!''

"—spying on us and carrying away with you important information that would be invaluable to that rascal Jackson if it fell into his hands. I am not going to have you searched. It is too late for that. And I am not going to prolong the agony of this interview. You are a spy, Madame, and you will hang for it.''

"You can't do that!'' I said. "You have no right! I am a citizen of France, not an American—''

"Spies have no citizenship,'' he barked hoarsely, "and they have no rights. This is wartime, Madame, and you will get no trial, no hearing. I am in charge of this operation. I am master not only of this ship but of these waters and of this territory. I call you spy, I sentence you to death, and I will see that the execution is carried out. Take her away, Kirby. The sight of her sickens me.''

Kirby put his hand on my shoulder. I shrugged him off.

"And when is my execution to take place?'' I demanded.

"At my discretion. Perhaps even tomorrow morning, at dawn.'' Cochrane smiled cruelly. "I'm taking no chances that you might escape and warn our American friends of the forthcoming attack on their city.''

"It's too late already, dear Admiral," I said gloatingly. "They have been warned. And they will be ready for you. I hope you and your ships go up in flames!"

"Take her below, Kirby, and put her in chains," Cochrane bellowed. "At once!"

"He is a boor," I sniffed when Kirby and I were alone in the passage. "He is crude and ignorant. A Frenchman would never treat a female prisoner like that, even one that was scheduled to die at dawn. He would show his appreciation for her beauty—and her other good qualities—and express his regrets for having to end so charming a life. Well, you heard him, Monsieur. Take me below and lock me in irons, and take care that I don't knock you down and make my escape. I can be very violent and dangerous, you know."

Kirby chuckled. "Orders is orders, Ma'am. Now, if it was me—"

"You should be the Admiral of this fleet, not he," I said graciously as we went up on deck. "Pooh. He is a petty tyrant." A soft breeze rustled the sails and the shrouds and blew my hair gently around my face. I breathed deeply. "Ah, let me say farewell to my freedom," I sighed ecstatically. "The air is soft and beautiful. I am sorry to be leaving this life. And the life that I carry, too—you know, I am going to have a child. It would have been a little son, I know, and he would have cherished his freedom as I have cherished mine." Tears coursed down my cheeks. I felt the grip on my arm loosening ever so slightly. "Your Admiral is a double murderer, my dear friend. With no more thought than that," I snapped my fingers, "he boldly snuffs out not just one life but two!" I began to weep noisily, heartbrokenly. "Oh, my son, my son."

Kirby shuffled his feet with embarrassment. His hold relaxed still more, and in a flash I wrenched myself free and threw myself over the side of the *Royal Oak*.

I plunged into the chill waters of the gulf. While I was still submerged I worked feverishly stripping off all my cumbersome outer garments so that I could swim for shore. I surfaced right under the ship's hull. I could hear the sound of running feet and angry voices over my head. The creaking of tackle told me they were going to lower a boat and come after me. I drew in a few long breaths and then dove under the waves and swam away from the ship. I was grateful for the hard work I had done on the *Sea Demon* for I was strong and I knew my endurance was good.

I bobbed to the surface about fifty yards from the ship. I cast a quick look behind me. The decks seemed alive with activity. Then I heard a thunderous booming noise and a cannonball splashed into the water about twenty feet away from me. I gasped and dove again and swam with long strokes towards Grand Terre. They fired again. This time the ball came down in front of me and I could hear the sizzle that the hot sphere made as it entered the cool water.

Just then I heard answering shots from ahead of me. I peered intently over the water. I could barely make out a sail on the horizon near Grand Terre. I swam towards it, praying that they would see me. They approached me swiftly. I shouted and waved my arms frantically. It was the *Tigre*, and as she drew nearer I even thought I could see Dominique at the helm. I hailed them wildly. I wasn't sure that they had seen or heard me, for they were diligently returning the *Royal Oak*'s fire. Just when I thought they were going to run me down the vessel sheered off and then came about.

I swam towards them and grabbed at the line they tossed me. They hauled me up on deck where I lay gasping like a beached fish. Someone poured whiskey down my throat and rough hands wrapped me in a blanket.

"I told you boys we didn't have any time for fishin'!" I heard Dominique's hearty voice. The men laughed. "What is all this?" He knelt by me and tweaked my wet hair.

"Hello, Dominique," I panted. "They were going to hang me for a spy and I decided to swim for it."

The pirates roared with laughter. Dominique said, "Did you, now? Those slimy bastards, I'll show them who they're playing with! Give 'em a volley, boys, and aim for her middle."

His men ran to obey and soon I heard the deafening thunder of guns.

"We were attacked this morning, Dominique. Lafitte and Garth—"

"I heard all about it. Our men rousted the redcoats and sent 'em back to the swamps. Jean and Pierre got off all right. I don't know about that other one." Dominique was jealous of Garth.

"I saw them hit him and he fell. I don't know if they finished him off," I said miserably. "Dear God, Dominique, we're wasting time! We have to get word to New Orleans at once. They're planning to attack by land and sea both! What if Jean didn't get through? Someone has to warn General Jackson."

"It's all right, child. You just calm down. We're not boys at this game. Look."

He helped me to my feet and turned me towards Grand Terre. Thick black smoke lay like a pall over the island, and I thought I could smell the reek of burning timbers even a mile out to sea.

"She's in flames," I breathed. "The whole island! Oh, Dominique!"

"That's right, we've set her on fire, just like Jean said.

And now we're going to join Jackson's army. They're grouping on the plantations south of New Orleans. Jean thinks the British will attack from the west first. They've built a road overland from Lake Borgne. And when they come we'll be ready. Jackson's brought in men from all over the country, from as far as Tennessee. Sharpshooters and scouts and Indians, too. And now he has us—he can't lose. Let's find you some dry clothes, Elise. Lord have mercy, I didn't expect to find you swimming out here! We heard the gunfire and thought they were attacking, and so we set fire to the island and came 'round to see if we could sink a few of His Majesty's ships before headin' into battle.''

The *Royal Oak* gave half-hearted chase and gave up when we slipped through the pass between Grand Terre and Grand Isle. Dominique hid the *Tigre* in the bayou off Barataria Bay and found the skiffs he had hidden to take him and his men to New Orleans.

We beached the skiffs at the Temple where Jean had warehouses and dwellings. ''We've got a ton of gunpowder stored there,'' Dominique told me proudly. ''Enough to blow the whole damned fleet out of the water. I hope that old hornet Jackson appreciates it.''

We reached New Orleans on the evening of the fourth day after my capture by the British. Dominique took me straight to Jean's house on Dumaine Street. Lily opened the door and I fell exhausted into her arms.

''Mister Jean, come quick!'' she shouted.

Jean ran to me and held me close. ''Thank God, Elise!''

''You can thank me and the boys,'' Dominique growled. ''We're the ones that fished her out of the water.''

''After I had the wits to get away,'' I put in smugly. ''Jean, is Garth all right? I've been so worried—''

Jean's expression was grim. ''I don't know, Elise. He

disappeared after the attack. We combed the area and we couldn't find him. I think he must be—''

"No!" I said quickly. "He isn't dead. He can't be. You don't know him, Jean. He's practically indestructible. He isn't dead! I would know if he were, somehow I would know." I started to cry.

Lily led me upstairs and put me to bed. She tried to console and reassure me, but I knew she didn't believe he was alive. None of them did. I felt that I would know for certain if he were dead, because a part of me would die, too.

There was an air of excited anticipation and elation in the city, almost as if people were expecting a fair or a carnival instead of a battle for their homes and possessions. Exotic-looking Indians from the north mingled with lanky woodsmen wearing caps of fur and costumes made of skins and decorated with feathers. Jean and Pierre and Dominique had left to join Jackson's army, leaving Lily and me alone in the house.

"You better stop breakin' your heart over a dead man," Lily said one day.

"Don't say that, Lily!" I flew at her in a rage. "I won't believe he's dead until someone shows me his corpse, do you hear?"

"You ain't never goin' to see it if it's sunk in the mud of the bayou," she said matter-of-factly. "You better stop your broodin' and look ahead."

"No. I know he's alive and I'll find him, you'll see."

I wandered the streets of New Orleans disconsolately, hoping to catch sight of him. One day I saw Georgette, riding in a carriage down Rue St. Charles, past the house I had lived in. She saw me too, standing at the gate.

I heard the carriage approach and slow down. I turned around and we faced each other for the first time in nearly two years. Neither of us moved a muscle. Her face gave nothing away. Then she spoke sharply to her driver and drove on. I didn't even look after her, but turned my thoughts once again to the house and my memories. She couldn't hurt me now.

The Battle of New Orleans began on January 8, 1815. We could hear muffled gunfire, and Lily and I climbed to the top of the house and looked towards the south. We could see occasional puffs of smoke that the wind carried upwards before they disintegrated in the air. I couldn't stand the waiting and I visited our old haunts and begged for news of the battle.

The Americans were victorious. Jackson and his motley army marched into the city and were besieged by deliriously happy citizens who showered them with flowers and kisses and coins. I scanned the faces of the returning soldiers for Garth, and I studied lists of the dead and wounded, terrified that I would see his name. I shouldered my way through the excited throng, asking everyone I knew and even people I didn't know if they had seen him. They all shook their heads and returned to their celebrations.

I walked down every street and alley in the city, searching for him. I didn't even know if Jean had survived the battle, or if the Baratarians had distinguished themselves. I only wanted Garth, and as the day of victory wore on I felt a sense of urgency that told me he was alive and that he was near. I was frantic, certain that as soon as I had left one street he would appear there. I pictured him eluding me unknowingly, and I feared I would travel around and around in feverish circles while he stayed in one place, or while he traveled in larger or smaller concentric circles. At the end of the day, weary with searching and weak from hunger and despair, I decided to abandon my search and return to Lafitte's house. I brushed off the eager hands of jubilant soldiers and made my way towards Dumaine Street.

Just as I reached the corner of the street about five blocks away from Jean's house, I felt a huge stinking hand clamp down over my mouth and another pass around my waist. I was dragged upwards, up a flight of stairs into a rotten-smelling room over an inn. I thrashed and kicked at my unknown captor but I was unable to deter him. When we reached our destination he kicked the door closed behind us and released me. I whirled around to face him.

*It was Josiah Fowler!*

His face was horribly scarred, almost beyond recognition, but I knew him. I was paralyzed. My worst dreams had come true. The nightmare that had plagued me, the fear that had haunted me for the past four years had become reality. He was alive and he had found me. I couldn't move, couldn't speak. I could only stare and stare while waves of sickening memory washed over me. The monster lived. He lived, and he had found me at last.

"Surprised to see me, ain't you, lady? Thought I was dead, didn't you?"

The voice was the same, the stench was the same, the crazed gleam in his watery eyes was the same. My mouth opened and shut soundlessly.

"Your pirate boyfriend thought he was doing you a kindness, puttin' me and the *Belle* out to sea to rot together. But I'm no fool. I found a flint in the hold and I made a spark, and I lit a fire that burned my ropes and sent the *Belle* to the bottom. I almost went with her. You're sorry I didn't burn, ain't you? I nearly did. That's how this happened." He touched his hideous face.

I shook my head wordlessly. He came closer. I shrieked and moved back hastily.

"You don't like my good looks," he growled. "You

don't think Josiah would be just as good in the dark, even
though his face has been burned off? What good's a face
anyways? You look like you done mighty well for yourself, bitch. You're a fine lady now, ain't you? And you
don't cotton to the likes of me. You know how I been
livin' these past few years? Like an animal! Like a mangy
dog that no one even wants to look at." He lunged at me.
"Come here, wench, and let Josiah kiss you!"

I scrambled away from him, looking around frantically
for a weapon, anything that I could use to fight him off.
The room was almost bare of furniture. I hurled a candle-
stick at his head. It glanced off his forehead and he yowled
with pain. He came at me blindly, like an enraged bull. I
raced towards the door, shouting for help at the top of my
lungs. Festive noises still drifted up from the street below.
No one would ever hear me.

He grabbed my skirt and pulled me down, clambering
on top of me and ripping my bodice open. He reeked of
urine and sweat and the accumulated filth of years. I
tried unsuccessfully to twist away.

I called out Garth's name over and over as though it was
a magic word that would somehow protect me.

"You quit callin' for your pretty boy," Fowler snarled.
He struck me across the face. "Your pretty boy ain't here
to help you now."

"Garth!" I bellowed.

As Fowler placed his gross hands on my thighs and
wrenched my legs apart, I heard footsteps pounding up the
stairs.

"Elise!" He had come, he had found me. "Elise, are
you in there?"

"Gar—"

Fowler's fist stopped my mouth. My head was whirling
and I gasped for air. The repulsive creature stood up and
stumbled to the door.

"You get away or I'll kill her," he shouted. "You hear me, pretty boy? I'll kill your whore!"

I heard the splintering of wood. The door burst open and Garth came into the room. Fowler attacked him at once and wrestled him to the floor. I saw the glint of steel in Fowler's hand.

"Garth," I cried, "he has a knife!" Dragging myself to a corner, I watched the fight through dazed eyes.

Fowler slashed mindlessly at Garth, who skipped lightly out of reach time and again until his adversary gave an enraged howl and attacked him blindly. Then Garth tripped him up and the knife went flying. They both went after it, and Fowler got there first. Garth brought his fist down on the horrid creature's wrist, and when the knife dropped to the floor he gripped it and plunged it into Fowler's chest. The Captain lurched and stumbled towards me. I could see blood and spittle drooling down his chin. Then he dropped like a felled tree, slowly and not ungracefully, and lay spread-eagled at my feet.

Garth gathered me into his arms. "Oh, dear God, Elise, are you all right? I've been looking everywhere for you. Lafitte told me you were alive. Alive. Oh, Elise, oh, my darling."

I hid my bruised face in his neck. "I knew you weren't dead," I whispered. "I knew you would find me. I love you, Garth. I've always loved you. I don't care what you do with me. If I could see you just once a year, from far away, that would be enough for me. I'll never love anyone else."

He picked me up and carried me out into the street. The crowds seemed to part when they saw us coming. Several soldiers began to cheer, and soon the whole mob took it up.

"That's the way to do it, soldier," someone shouted. "Don't ask the gal, just take her!"

"That's always been your way," I said softly in his ear. "I love you so much! Where are we going? To Jean's?"

"No, we're going home."

"Home? Where's that?" I asked him.

He didn't answer but continued to stride forward. Soon we were on Rue St. Charles, and then we reached the house, our house. Savannah flung the door open.

"Mis' Elise! Oh, Lord, what's happened to you?"

"Hello, Savannah." I stretched out my hand. She grasped it and held it to her cheek. "I—I've missed you."

"Oh, mercy, Mis' Elise, you come on upstairs with me and I'll get you cleaned up. Who did this to you? I'll—I'll shoot him, that's what I'll do! Was it one of them Northern riffraff? Damned no-accounts, don't know how to behave!"

Garth laughed and swept me up the stairs. "Stop your complaining and bring up some hot water and some cold champagne, Savannah," he called over his shoulder. "I'll take care of the rest."

## XX.  The Trial

I peered at my face in the looking glass.

"Three days and it's still swollen, Garth," I said dole-fully. "I'm not beautiful anymore. How can you still want me when I'm not beautiful? I shall have to join a convent," I declared.

"Stop fussing over things that aren't important and come back to bed," he grumbled.

I cocked my head. "I shall not even consider your invitation, sir. Do you realize that we've only been out of this house once in the past four days, to meet General Jackson? How can you, a man of action, be content to spend your days in idleness while the world passes you by?"

"As you say, I'm a man of action, Elise. That should answer your question." He raised himself up on his elbow and ran his fingers through his hair. "Are you coming or do I have to come and get you?"

I brushed my hair languidly. "You're so impetuous, Garth! Anyone would think we were a hot-blooded youth and his first mistress instead of a steady, reliable public servant and the woman who has been his constant companion for four months—and his bane and despair before that."

He grunted. "If I were a young man I would drag you back to bed by force. But because I am old and white-headed I can only lie here pleading with you."

"Oh, well, in that case," I strolled over to the foot of

the bed and pinched his toe, "I most certainly won't join you! I am not interested in old men—"

He lunged at me. I squealed and tried to escape him, but I caught my slipper in the carpet and stumbled, and we both fell to the floor, laughing and kissing each other fiercely.

"Oh, I love you so much," I murmured happily. "I wish—I wish it didn't have to end."

"It won't end," he said. "But I thought you were going to be quite happy looking at me once a year from afar? What happened to that resolution?"

"I'm so weak," I said. "And so greedy. I love you too much. I'd kill you before I'd let you do that to me!"

"Silly child, you were doing it to yourself, as I recall. I had nothing to say about it."

"But you have a wife and a home and a responsibility to your voters—"

"Damn them. Damn Georgette and Highlands and the United States Senate. Do you think I'd let any of them keep me from having you? We'll go away. We'll go west, to parts of the country that no white man has ever seen. I'll sit back in the sun while you fight off bears and Indians and wolves—"

"Oh, Garth, stop teasing me."

"I'm not teasing you. I admire you, Elise. I never could have gotten that information to Jackson without you. And the way you went after those redcoats! Like an angry mother to the defense of her young. 'Somebody give me a weapon!'" he mimicked. "Magnificent! Superb! If all women were like you we men wouldn't have to fight at all. I do feel a bit sorry for Cochrane. He not only lost the war for Britain, he lost his prize catch, the wicked Louisiana-French spy!" He laughed. "I can just see that poor sailor's face when you jumped ship."

"You would have jumped ship, too, if they had informed you that they were going to hang you at dawn,'' I said sourly. ''I'm glad my ferocity amuses you. Just be thankful I fought on your side, not theirs.''

''Oh, I am, lady, I am.'' The laughing expression on his face softened and he kissed me deeply and tenderly.

''This is the longest time we've been together without quarreling,'' I observed.

''I know. Perhaps you're growing up.''

''Me!'' My eyes snapped and I tried to sit up. Then I saw the laughter in his eyes and I had to smile. ''Why do you goad me into attacking you? Suppose I were armed?''

''I would disarm you.''

''I would fight you anyway, with my bare hands.''

''I would conquer you.''

''By force?''

''By love.''

Much later when we lay clasped tightly in each other's arms I felt that I was ready to tell him about our child. I felt so close to him, and I thought I could trust him not to hurt me.

''Garth, listen to me. I have something important—''

Savannah tapped at the door. ''There's some men downstairs to see Mis' Elise,'' she called. ''They want to see her right away.''

''Tell them to go away and come back next week,'' Garth shouted.

''I did tell 'em,'' she said, ''and they said they ain't goin'. They say they is goin' to wait until the Missy comes down.''

''What do you suppose they want?'' I asked Garth. I climbed out of bed and started to dress.

''God knows,'' he said. ''They're probably old lovers waiting to welcome you home.''

I felt strangely nervous. My hands shook as I drew on my stockings and picked out a dress to wear. I chose a modest pale blue morning dress with long sleeves and a matching fringed shawl, and as I left the room I heard an inner voice say, "You'd better take a bonnet. They might not let you come back."

They were standing at the foot of the stairs, three men, two in the uniform of Claiborne's militia and one in a black morning coat. Garth had said he would be down in a few minutes, and so I faced them alone now.

"Madame Fournier?" the one in the black suit asked.

"Yes, I was Madame Fournier. My husband is dead."

"We have come to arrest you for the murder of Jacques Fournier, Madame. You may bring anything with you that you might need while you are in prison, of course—"

I felt an explosion inside my head. Dizziness swept over me but I did not faint. I clung to the bannister and breathed deeply.

Savannah was shrieking, "She didn't do it! I swear it, the Missy didn't do it! I—I was there when they found him, and I know she didn't! Mister Garth! Mister Garth!" She ran screaming up the steps to our room.

"Are you coming, Madame?" the man asked softly.

"Give—give me a few minutes, please?" I asked quietly. "I promise you, I won't try to run away." I nodded at some chairs in the hallway. "Won't you sit down?"

All three men looked embarrassed and uncomfortable. "No, thank you, Ma'am."

I heard Garth on the stairs behind me. "What's all this?" he demanded angrily. "This charge is a fake, a fraud. It's nonsense! Now get out of this house before I throw you out!"

The two militia men stuck out their chins and rested their hands on their swords.

I put my hand on Garth's arm. "No, Garth, I have told

them I would go with them. Please, don't make it any more difficult for me.''

"This is ridiculous, Elise!" he said. "We both know who's behind this action, and she can't get away with it.''

"She has gotten away with it," I told him sadly. "Even if they find me innocent, and I don't see how they can, she will have caused you great embarrassment. Perhaps she would even have made you doubt me. It wouldn't have worked out—"

"No!" He clenched his fists. "We'll fight it, Elise. I know lawyers, the best in the country. I won't let her—"

I put my arms around his waist. "Hold me, Garth. Hold me close. Remember, I'll always love you. Always." Then I ran upstairs to collect the things I would need.

They took me to the Cabildo, the Spanish-era prison not far from the St. Louis Cathedral where Jacques and I had been married. Savannah insisted on coming with me. My cell was damp and chill, and we tried hard to make it bearable.

"I sure hope they ask me about that man," Savannah fumed, referring to Jacques. "I could tell them a thing or two about him and that rat, Mister Arnold.''

"Don't be too vehement, Savannah," I cautioned her. "You'll just be giving them the reasons why I should have killed him sooner.''

"He deserved to die, everyone knew that!" I didn't agree, but I didn't argue with her. "An' then not ten days after he was in the ground, that Mister Arnold married Miss Colette and moved right in and started actin' like La Rêve was his! I didn't stay around to see more; he was actin' crazy-like and sellin' everything he could lay his hands on, and I was afraid he might even try and sell me. So I took the money you left and lit out for New Orleans and got my job at the Hotel Marengo back again. I stayed there until Mister Garth came and got me, sayin' 'Mis' Elise goin' to need you some more, Savannah.' Oh, Missy, I sure hope they don't hang you. You tell him about the baby yet?''

"No, I didn't.'' I had meant to, and now I was glad I hadn't. He liked me well enough, I knew that, and he would be sorry to lose me. We had been good comrades as well as lovers. But in the depths of my heart I didn't really believe he loved me, that he was capable of love. The child wouldn't have meant anything to him, just another illegitimate bastard he had fathered. ''And I don't want you to tell him, either, Savannah. I'll beat the living daylights out of you if you breathe a word to him!''

A lawyer came to see me immediately. His name was Howard Livingston, and he was tall and fair, with thin, pinched cheeks, kind brown eyes and a warm, worried smile.

"I've known Garth a long time. We were in school together, that is, when he deigned to attend school. He swears he'll split me in two if I don't get you off. I've never seen him so angry. Suppose you just tell me what happened, Madame Fournier—''

''You'd better call me Elise,'' I told him with a weak smile. ''I'm not terribly fond of the Fournier name right now.''

He grinned. ''Elise. A beautiful name, for a beautiful woman. Now, your story, please.''

I told him everything I could remember about that last, dreadful day at La Rêve. Then he started to ask questions about my life with Jacques. I confessed that our marriage had been a sham and a fake from the beginning, and that Jacques had had a deep passion for Arnold Charpentier.

Livingston shook his head slowly. ''We can't prove any of that. We have no witnesses to their plot against you, only you and Madame McClelland—Georgette. And she swears she doesn't know anything about Jacques' death.''

"Of course she doesn't," I said bitterly. "And neither does Arnold, I'll bet."

"You win your bet. They have witnesses, Elise, who will testify to having heard you threaten to kill Jacques. The family is eager to tell the world about how you wrested control of La Rêve out of poor dear Jacques' hands, how you humiliated him and exploited his good nature, how you embarrassed him in public by carrying on with a certain notorious neighbor. You had a hundred reasons to want him out of the way: complete control of the plantation, hatred, jealousy, your affair with Garth.''

"It's preposterous!" I said. "If I was such a devil, why didn't I arrange the murder more cleverly? Why didn't I stay and inherit what was mine, instead of disappearing into thin air?''

The lawyer lifted his thin shoulders. "You were frightened, upset by what you had done. Perhaps you felt remorse. Perhaps you ran off to join your lover. You and Garth have been seen together in public, and already the story of your voyage from Washington to Grand Terre is making the rounds. In the eyes of the citizens of this city you are Garth's mistress, and you were even before you married Jacques. The Fourniers can prove that, too. There's a deed to a house on Rue St. Charles with Garth's name on it, and a hundred people can testify that you lived in that house.''

"I can see Georgette's fine hand in this," I said. "She saw me at the house a few weeks ago. I should have known—''

"She hates you, Elise. I met her socially not long before your arrest, and she started talking about you, vilifying you. She'll do anything in her power to destroy you. She'll

try to protect Garth if she can—she's too fond of Highlands and of being a senator's wife to want to sacrifice him
to the wolves—but sacrifice him she will if she has to, to
get rid of you.''

"You—you don't believe that I killed him?" I asked
softly.

"No, I don't think you did, but Garth and I are about the
only people in New Orleans who don't believe it. Don't
you see, Elise, even your association with Lafitte is
against you. You were a pirate, and therefore you are a
violent woman accustomed to getting what she wants by
the use of force. You know how to use weapons, and you
have used them. The prosecution can probably produce
witnesses who can swear they've seen you shoot a snake's
eye out at a hundred paces.''

I smiled grimly. "I can do it, too."

He threw up his hands. "You see what I mean!"

"What about the time I spent as a slave?" I asked him.
"My—my brand?"

He thought hard for a moment then said, "It's a possible point in your favor. But there's always the chance that
someone will connect you with the 'Frenchie' who killed
her owner in Virginia, and that would only enhance your
reputation for violence. It's too big a risk, Elise. The
prosecution could claim that it was just your misfortune to
be mistaken for a quadroon and made a slave. He would
make it look like there was never any plot against you.''

"But if you found Bose Niles, Jake—"

"The only way we could get the jury to believe them
would be if we could persuade Arnold or Georgette to
confess. And they'll never do that. I'm for you, Elise, but
I don't want you to build on false hopes. This won't be an
easy case, and it will probably become a celebrated one.
Public opinion has a strong influence on the outcome of
cases like this.''

"You mean cases of murder and adultery?" He nodded. "Yes, I can understand that. It's such a simple thing to judge, not like disputes over property or—." My voice died away. I hid my face in my hands and sighed deeply.

"I'm sorry, Elise," Livingston said gently. "There's more bad news. Judge Hall refused to set bail because of your connection with Lafitte. He's had Lafitte and his men up in front of him too many times to trust them. He's afraid they might help you to escape, and he's probably right."

"I wouldn't go," I told him. "I am not a coward. I want to stay and see this thing through."

"I admire your sentiment, but I can't say I would feel the same if I were in your shoes. It would be very tempting to get away—" He stood up. "Well, I'll leave you now, Elise. I want you to try and think of any time when the jealousy between Arnold and Jacques might have erupted in public. Perhaps we can attack them from that angle. And Elise—"

"Yes," I said wearily, lifting my eyes.

"Garth wants to see you. He says you've refused to see him, and—"

"No," I said firmly. "I don't want him to see me here. I don't want to drag him down with me. It would be too painful for me, to see him and touch him and know I'm losing him forever. Tell him I love him. Tell him—tell him that it would damage my case for him to come here. You'll do that, won't you, Howard?"

He nodded and kissed my hand. "Yes," he said, "I'll do that. Good-bye, Elise."

A bleak despair settled over me. I had lost Garth, and Georgette had won. She had succeeded in keeping us apart, perhaps forever. I could picture her gloating triumphantly, her pale face twisted into a delighted grin, as it had been when Bose Niles took me away. She must have been furious when she discovered that not only was I alive, but that Garth and I were together again.

I sighed deeply. I felt too despondent to cry. Life was so

unfair: just when I thought that the last of the nightmares had been vanquished, another, more horrible than all the rest, rose up and threatened to—what was Livingston's word?—destroy. And I couldn't even battle this monster. What was the use? When I was free I would be Garth's mistress, nothing more. We would never run away together. That was just a lovers' dream, the frail kind of dream that melts away in the harsh light of duty and necessity. I would be his until he left me for another adventure, another woman.

If he really loved you, my inner voice declared, he would divorce Georgette and marry you. The scandal wouldn't matter to him. He'd give it all up, if he really loved you.

The days before the trial passed slowly. One was much like another. Lafitte was forbidden to visit but he sent baskets of food and wine every day, which the guards examined thoroughly before they delivered them. He also sent letters filled with gossip, books he thought I might enjoy, even French newspapers. But I never heard from Garth. He never tried again to see me, never sent a note or even a verbal message through Howard Livingston. Out of sight, out of mind, I thought bitterly. He was too vital, too energetic a man to wait for a woman who was rotting in prison. He probably had a new mistress, or a dozen. A Marie, or Louise, or Annette. Sometimes I hated him, hated him for being free.

The trial began on the second day of February. Livingston asked if I wanted him to try for a postponement, and I refused. I was in my fourth month of pregnancy, and I wanted to get the spectacle over with before anyone knew. I had no wish to let the child I carried become an object of pity and sympathy. I thought about where the baby would be born. In prison? Would they let it be born at all if I was condemned, or would they wait until it was delivered and then hang me? Should I tell Garth, ask him to make a home for my baby? I thought of my child growing up with Georgette. I would kill it and myself before I would let it come to that.

I could feel the ripples of excitement when I entered the courtroom on the first day of my trial. I quickly scanned the crowd for Garth, and when I didn't see him I sat down and ignored the proceedings as best I could. Until I heard a familiar voice bellowing at the rear of the room.

"Tell the bastards the truth, Elise, they'll have to believe you!" It was Dominique. His voice was joined by others I recognized.

"Don't let them hang you for something you didn't do!" one of them shouted. "We'll save you, Elise. Have no fear!"

I heard the sounds of scuffling and then some pistol fire. The pirates were trying to rescue me. They were repulsed by the courthouse guards after Judge Hall rapped his gavel repeatedly and gave orders for their arrest. That evening the prison authorities changed my cell, placing me deeper in the bowels of the Cabildo so that the pirates wouldn't be able to reach me.

"I know they meant well," Livingston said with a worried frown, "but they've damaged your case before the trial has even begun. Judge Hall is prejudiced against you, the jury is looking at you like you were the original Lilith, and the prosecuting attorney is grinning so widely that you could get an alligator into his mouth—sideways. And I don't even know where Garth is. I haven't seen him in days."

"It doesn't matter, Howard," I told him. "Don't be upset."

He stared at me. "I don't understand you, Elise. Don't you want to go free?"

I thought a moment. "I suppose I do, Howard. I mean,

prisoners are supposed to long for freedom, aren't they? But right now I don't even care. Garth doesn't care. If he cared he would be here, and he would be moving Heaven and Earth to save me."

"I'm sure there's a reason, Elise," Howard declared, not too convincingly, "there must be."

I smiled at him. "Of course, Howard."

He went away, shaking his head.

The parade of prosecution witnesses began the next day. James, the old butler at La Rêve, testified that he had heard me threaten to kill Jacques, and members of the Fournier family backed him up, even Colette, who gazed at me apologetically as she spoke her damning sentences. Livingston tried to reconstruct the incident on the stairs, but apparently none of them but Arnold knew that Jacques had pushed me, only that I had fallen and that I had shrilly blamed Jacques. Arnold lied, of course, and blandly suggested that I might have been slightly drunk, for he had thought at the time that he smelled whiskey on my breath. The day wore on, Livingston's expression grew more serious, the jury started nodding at the witnesses, as though they confirmed the general opinion that I was a whore and a schemer and that poor Jacques had been my innocent victim. I ceased to pay attention to any of it after a while. I could tell from the very beginning how the trial would end, and I found the details wearying and depressing.

After the third day of testimony Georgette McClelland came to my cell.

"So nice of you to receive me," she said, looking around her disdainfully.

"I wasn't consulted," I told her. "I suppose you bribed the authorities to let you in here, just so you could see for yourself what you've done to me? All right, you've had your chance to gloat. Now get out."

She drew her skirts around her and sat gingerly on the cot that I slept on. "I want to talk to you, Elise."

"I don't want to talk to you. Guard!" I called through the door. "Guard!"

"He won't come. When I bribe, I do it handsomely."

"I'm sure. Like the way you bribed Bose Niles to dispose of me, only he didn't do a very good job, did he?"

She shrugged. "I always say, if you want a thing done right—"

"And I suppose you've bribed all those nice witnesses we heard today. I never said or did half the things they're attributing to me. I suppose you even wrote out their scripts and coached them?"

She clicked her tongue. "Elise, you give me too much credit. I can't help it if these people have imaginations, can I? I couldn't begin to make up some of the stories they've told. But I'm not interested in them. I came here to make a bargain with you, Elise."

"Bargain!" I spat. "I don't make bargains with— devils!"

"Hear me out, please." She took a breath. "I don't want to lose Garth."

"Lose him!" I snorted. "You lost him long ago, woman. Do you think he'll even speak to you after this? He knows what you did to me. You'll be lucky if he doesn't shoot you down, like the dog you are."

Her cheeks reddened. "Don't talk to me like that, Elise."

"I'll talk to you any way I please," I said. "This is my home, and you are an uninvited guest. If you don't like my hospitality, leave, it's as simple as that."

She smiled unexpectedly. "People are saying that you have lost your interest in living, Elise. That you don't care if you go to the scaffold or not. I think that's a lie. You're still a scrapper, aren't you? A little wildcat. And you want to live. As each day of this trial passes and you see your chances for freedom becoming more remote, you want life more and more. I would imagine that at this point even a life without Garth McClelland would appeal to you, wouldn't it?'' I made no reply. ''As I was saying, I don't want to lose him. I don't want him to divorce me.''

My heart leaped. ''Has he—has he asked you—''

''Not yet. We have not met since he returned from Washington. I don't want to lose my home. Highlands is everything to me, Elise. You'll never know what it means to me until you have a home of your own. I've helped Garth build it into what it is today, and I won't give it up. And I would have to give it up if he left me, or if the scandal of his association with you drove him from public office. I've lived with rumors of him and his women for years, but he never showed any sign of taking those affairs seriously. He wanted his fame, the glory of being a daring adventurer and a friend and adviser to presidents. Our lives hardly ever crossed, but we were content with the arrangement. Until you came along. I've had to endure a great deal as his wife, but I won't endure that.''

''What are you talking about?''

''If you hang, the scandal would be so damaging to his career that he would have to leave office. If you go free, he might divorce me and marry you, and the result would be the same. I would have to leave my home.''

''You should have thought of that before you started all this.'' I waved my hand.

''No, you're wrong. This was all Arnold's idea. He was frantic when he heard you were back, and he decided to attack you before you could expose him. But I have a solution to all our problems, Elise.''

''You have already indulged in some rather extreme behavior, just to dispose of me, Georgette,'' I remarked calmly. ''Or did you come here to assassinate me?

Perhaps you can bribe one of the guards to take the blame. They say every man has his price."

"Listen to me, Elise," she said, getting up from the cot and striding over to me. "I'm offering you your freedom. Do you hear me? Your freedom! I shall go before the court tomorrow and tell the world that Arnold killed Jacques, that he came to me that morning and confessed what he had done, and that he begged me to help him."

I laughed. "Arnold isn't going to like being betrayed," I said.

She smirked. "I don't care about him. And he's guilty, isn't he? I'll only be telling them the truth."

"Surely—surely you won't tell them about Niles, about—"

"Why not? That was all part of Arnold's plan. I'll tell them that he forced me to carry it out, that he threatened to kill me if I ever breathed a word to anyone about Jacques or about you. He'll go mad, you'll see. I know my cousin well. He won't be able to listen to that without making some display that will convince them all that he's the guilty one, not you. And he'll be in court tomorrow, you may be sure. He hasn't missed a day of this trial. It's the best fun he's had in a long time. You may be sure I can make it look like I have been just another of his victims. If a little breath of scandal brushes me—who cares? You will be free and Garth will be free of you. We can pick up the threads of our lives again. Everything will be as it was before you came."

I wet my lips. "You haven't told me what I have to do," I said. "Surely you're not doing this because you don't want Garth's heart to be broken."

"Garth has no heart, Elise," she sneered. "You know that by now. He's like every other Scot I've ever known. He'll pursue a thing as long as it eludes him, but once he has it—. He's a stubborn man, and he's easily bored. The only reason you've been able to hang on to him this long is that you've been leading him a merry chase. But once he has you—he'll go on to something else.''

She had spoken my deepest fears. ''Another adventure, another woman,'' I whispered.

''Precisely. No, Elise, this is one scheme that can't afford to fail. I want to be rid of you once and for all. I want you to promise me that you'll leave Louisiana, that you'll return to France and never set foot in this country again. If you promise me that, then I'll do as I said and you'll go free. There's a merchant ship lying at anchor in the river right now. The *Etoile de France*. She sails for Marseilles tomorrow night. You can be on her, Elise. Think of it. You'll see France again in just a few weeks. You have family, don't you? You'll see them again. France. Home. Don't you want to go home, Elise?''

''Yes,'' I cried out. ''Yes, I want to go home! Oh, God, if I could believe you, if I could trust you—''

''Believe me.'' She gripped my arms with her gloved fingers. I could feel her claws digging into my flesh and I could see the mad gleam in her eyes. But I didn't care at that moment who she was and what she had done to me. She was offering me freedom, life. And I wanted to live. I wanted to see my child grow and become a man. I wanted to go home. ''Trust me. I'm telling you the truth, Elise. I have arranged passage for you already,'' she said. ''All you have to do is cross that gangplank to the ship and say good-bye to all of this. And there's extra money waiting for you in the Captain's keeping.''

I blinked. ''I don't want your money.''

''I'm not bribing you, Elise. Be sensible. You'll need to buy yourself some decent clothes when you get to France, and you'll have to pay for the rest of your journey. It's all taken care of, Elise. Think of it.''

I pushed her hands away. ''Suppose—suppose he follows me? Suppose he comes to France—''

"He won't," she said flatly, "if you use your head. Don't see him after the trial. Don't let him come near you. Just go directly to the ship and stay there until she sails. Listen to me, Elise. If anything goes wrong, if you betray me and go back on your word to leave the country, if he tries to find you, I'll make you sorry. I'll hurt you, even if it means destroying Garth in the process. You know I'd do it, Elise. You know how far I'll go to be rid of you, and to see him free of you. If you want him to be safe and happy you'll leave for France and never look back. Just tell Howard Livingston when you see him that I want to testify, that I *must* testify. And then leave it to me. In a few hours you'll be free again."

"All right," I said quietly. "Yes. I'll do it. I'll leave and I won't come back."

"Good." She permitted herself an icy smile. *"Bon voyage*, Elise." She called for the guard. "Don't bother to write."

The guard let her out of my cell. I sat on the cot for hours and thought about her plan. I would never see Garth again, but I would be alive, and I would have our child. I would thank God all my days for giving me that child, and for giving me even the brief happiness I had known with Garth.

Before the trial began the next morning I told Howard, "I had a visitor last night. Georgette McClelland. She's going to tell the truth about Arnold and the murder."

"What on earth!"

"You have to call her today, first thing. Ask her about that morning. She'll tell everything, even about Bose Niles. She's going to make it seem like it was all Arnold's idea, and pretend that he forced her to play along. Her testimony should be enough to free me."

"I don't believe this! She would never offer—. What did she get from you, Elise?" the lawyer demanded. "What did you promise her?"

I stared at him levelly. ''Nothing. Nothing at all. If anyone asks you about it, just tell them that Georgette's conscience got the better of her and that she didn't want to see an innocent woman hang. If they know her well they won't believe it, but tell them that.''

''But—''

There was a slight commotion at the back of the court-room. I didn't turn my head. Then I heard Howard say, ''Garth.'' I swivelled around in my chair. He was there, standing at the door in the back, with Bose Niles on one side of him and Jake, the River Rat, on the other. He was looking straight at me with a triumphant grin on his face. Howard went back to talk to him.

I faced the front of the room again and hid my face. He was trying to save me, moving Heaven and Earth. He hadn't deserted me, he hadn't abandoned me. I was a fool. I should never have doubted him, and now I had bargained him away. I had a sudden mad urge to run back and throw myself into his arms. I turned and caught Georgette's eye. It was no good. If I permitted myself any demonstration of affection or love she wouldn't testify, she would let me hang.

The judge entered the courtroom and called the session to order. ''Mr. Livingston, have you any witnesses to call for the defense?''

''I have, your honor. The defense calls Madame Georgette McClelland.'' The crowd buzzed excitedly as Georgette came forward and was sworn in. Livingston cleared his throat. ''Madame McClelland, do you recall the morning—''

She told her story in a strong, unwavering voice. She was an accomplished actress; I found myself half-believing her lies. I wondered if Garth would believe her. I could sense the undercurrent of amazement in the spectators' gallery, and when she said, ''Arnold told me he had just shot Jacques Fournier, and he wanted me to help him.

I was his cousin, after all—'' I heard an hysterical squeal and the sound of fleeing footsteps. Arnold was running for his life. Two sturdy bailiffs took hold of him and ushered him into a waiting room.

The prosecution asked Madame McClelland why she hadn't come forward earlier.

"Why, Arnold threatened to kill me if I ever breathed a word of what happened that day to anyone. I lived in fear of him, day after day. But I could not bear to have Elise punished for something he did. I know I was wrong to aid him in his mad plot against her. I know how she must have suffered at the hands of—those men. With the passage of time, the burden on my soul grew heavier, not lighter. I was delighted to discover she was still alive. I shall accept the pronouncement of the court in this matter. If the court decides that I have some punishable guilt, then I will pay and pay gladly. I only hope that Elise and the citizens of this parish will forgive me for keeping silent this long. I had no choice.''

Then Howard Livingston called Bose Niles and Jake. He allowed Bose to give only enough evidence to support Georgette's testimony without casting her in too villainous a light. The prosecution made no cross-examination. The courtroom was in an uproar and the judge finally despaired of restoring order and sent the jury out to deliberate. They returned in a few minutes with a verdict of not guilty and a recommendation to remand Arnold Charpentier for questioning. Howard embraced me. Out of the corner of my eye I saw Garth pushing his way through the crowd.

"Take me out of here, Howard, I beg you. I—I feel faint.''

"But Elise, don't you—''

"No, Howard. Please!''

He led me out a side door and into the sunshine—and freedom. A carriage was waiting.

"Georgette told me it would be here," Howard said. "She's thought of everything."

I rode away. When we were well away from the court-house I instructed the driver to take me to the docks, to the *Etoile de France*. I asked to be taken to the Captain, a courtly white-haired gentleman from Bordeaux. When I identified myself he personally escorted me to my cabin and drew a heavy pouch from his jacket pocket.

"My instructions were to give you this when you came aboard, Madame."

I thanked him cordially and he departed, informing me that we would sail with the evening tide. I looked around. I recognized the bags I had had with me in prison, and one I had left behind at the Rue St. Charles house. She really had thought of everything.

Hours passed. I did nothing. I felt nothing: no sorrow, no joy. Only a nagging eagerness to be under way. I would not feel safe until we were well out to sea. I could hear the rush and hustle up on deck as the sailors made ready to weigh anchor and hoist their sails. Suddenly the cabin door burst open and Garth strode into the room.

"What in hell do you think you're doing?" he demanded angrily. In the passage I could see Savannah's anxious face peering in at me. "Do you think I don't know that you and Georgette cooked up something between you? Give me a little credit, Elise. I know Georgette very well, almost as well as I know you."

"You don't know me, Garth," I said softly. "You've hardly given me a thought."

"What kind of thing is that to say? Come on, we're getting off this ship."

"No. I'm staying here. I want to go—I want to go home. Please leave me, Garth. Don't—"

He scowled at the open door. "Excuse us a moment, Savannah," he said, closing it. "Savannah insisted on coming with me. We had a hard time finding you. Of course you didn't confide in her because you knew she'd tell me. Savannah doesn't believe you're going to sail, and neither do I.'' He came closer to me. I drew back. His face darkened. "So that's the way it is. You can't wait to get away from me.''

"It's not you, Garth," I said wretchedly. "It's the whole terrible nightmare. My whole life since I met you—''

"I know, I know," he said impatiently. "Do you honestly believe that I'm as callous and cold-hearted as you seem to think I am? Do you really think that I have no respect for your feelings, for your pain? I'll give you some time to yourself, Elise, if that's what you want. But I'm not going to let you run away from me like this. I will not let Georgette arrange the details of my life—''

"It's not Georgette," I told him truthfully. "It's *me*. I want to get away, far away. *I* want to go home. *I* want to have my—" I swallowed, "my family around me again. Please, Garth, let me go——''

"You're a damned little coward," he said viciously. "You haven't the courage—''

"No! You're wrong, Garth," I said passionately. "Sometimes it takes more courage to run away than to stay. I'm not just thinking of myself. I—I don't trust you, Garth," I blurted out. "I don't trust you not to hurt and betray me again!''

He narrowed his eyes at me and stood for a long time staring at me, saying nothing. "So that's it. It seems we have different conceptions of what is cowardice and what is bravery, Elise. You don't make any sense, you know. A few weeks ago you loved me, you adored me, you told me you'd be grateful for crumbs. Make up your mind, Elise. You either want me or you don't. You're either coming with me now or you're staying. It's that simple.''

"Georgette told me you didn't speak to her of divorce. From the way you talked, about leaving it all—"

"There's time enough for talk later, Elise. Let's go." He put his hand on my elbow.

"No, wait. How much are you prepared to give up for me, Garth? How important am I to you?"

"Important? Don't be foolish, Elise. You know I want you."

"Want and love are two different things, Garth," I said slowly. "You want me now, but what about tomorrow?"

"Just like a woman!" He sounded exasperated. "You can't be begging me to marry you, Elise. You know as well as I do that the bonds of marriage are only as strong as the people involved. My marriage to Georgette never deterred me from going after the things I wanted."

"And marriage to me wouldn't be any different, would it? That's what you want to say. I'm not even sure if I want marriage. What I want from you is a commitment, a promise, a word. I want your love, Garth, and I think I'm asking the impossible."

"For God's sake, Elise, let's not go into that again! I want you. I want you more than I've ever wanted any woman. I love your will, your ferocity, your passion—"

"My damning black eyes, my beautiful hair, my soft lips—"

"Yes, all of you! You're a queen among women, little firebrand. I've never known a woman to touch you. Isn't that enough for you? Look, if marriage is so important to you, Elise, then we'll marry. But if you want sweet words and eternal vows, then you're asking the wrong man."

"Then I'll never hear you say, 'I love you, Elise'?" I asked gently. "That's all I want. It's not so much, is it, Garth? But it's too much to ask of you. You've never said it to any woman, and meant it."

We stood only a few feet apart, yet the distance between us was vast and bleak.

"Are you coming with me?"

"No, I'm not. We'll both be happier this way, Garth."

"Then go to the Devil," he said huskily. He threw the door open and disappeared into the dimly lit passage. Savannah crept into the cabin.

"Where you goin', Missy?" she asked.

"Home, Savannah. Home to France."

"Well, I ain't never been to France," she said. "I guess I'll go along."

"Savannah," I shook my head sadly, "it's such a long way. The language is different—"

"It's French, ain't it? I been around French-speakin' people all my life, and it never bothered me none. Now don't give me no argument, Missy, 'cause I won't be moved. You can't travel over this ocean all by yourself, an' you carryin' a baby an' all! I'll take care of you when your time comes, and for as long as you want me. I wonder if I can find me a husband in France?"

I started to laugh, and then I threw myself into her arms and sobbed.

"Oh, Savannah, I love him so much! Why does he have to be so stubborn?"

"Sounds to me like you is both too stubborn to live," she said. "Oh, Missy, the ship's movin'! Let's go up and see!"

I protested but she was adamant. She dragged me up on deck with her and waved her arms at the people on the docks below.

"Savannah, you don't know any of those people," I said.

"I can wave at 'em anyway, can't I?" she demanded. " 'Sides, I knows Mister Garth. Look, there he is."

I saw him then, leaning against a bale of cotton with his arms folded across his chest, looking perfectly impassive and cold. My heart rose up in my throat. I thought I would choke. I tried to pull away from the bulwark but Savannah blocked me amd made me stay.

"Don't go, Missy," she said firmly. "Don't let him see how sad you is. Be beautiful, Missy, and he'll remember you lookin' just like that, proud and beautiful."

## XXI.  The Last Adventure

"He is an angel!" Françoise cried.

"The sweetest little child that ever lived!" said Savannah passionately.

I looked at them. The coolness that had existed between them when I came home three years earlier had dissolved in their mutual adoration of my son.

"He is a demon," I said coldly, "and he needs to be beaten."

"No!" they cried in chorus, shielding the culprit behind their skirts.

"Yes!" I said in a voice like thunder. They trembled. "No wonder he's so spoiled. You both let him run wild, and when he's wicked you never, never punish him. He could have killed someone with that crossbow! Three years of age and a little warrior! I shall never be able to control him. Shame on you, Savannah, for filling his head with stories of Indians and voodoo—and God knows what else! And you, Françoise! You used to beat me often enough, as I recall, for misdemeanors much less serious than—attempted murder! Poor old Derain. I'm surprised he didn't die of shock, right there on the spot. Now stop protecting him. Etienne, come here, please. Mama wants to talk to you."

"I want my Papa," said a small voice from behind the bulwark of his two nurses. "Papa is coming today."

I sighed deeply and sat down. "What on earth has gotten into the child?" I demanded. "He's been like this for weeks. He has asked every man he has seen if he is his

Papa, even old Derain and the stable lads. I don't know what to do with him. I am at my wit's end."

The two women exchanged glances. Françoise spoke. "A boy needs a father," she declared. "I don't know why you don't marry that poor Marquis. You've caused him enough trouble, don't you think?"

"Pooh. Armand Valadon can take care of himself," I said. "I don't feel responsible for him. Besides, if he really wanted to be married he would have chosen a wife long before he met me."

"Now, child, you know that's not true," Savannah put in. "A man don't marry until his heart tells him to. That boy of yours needs a man." Françoise nodded agreement.

"What are Philippe and Uncle Theo, if not men?" I demanded. "He has all the men he needs." I knew that wasn't really true. My brother and uncle were far too indulgent with their nephew. They doted on him, spoiled him with gifts and toys, and instead of curbing his wild behaviour actually seemed to be encouraging it as the mark of a true Lesconflair. I threw up my hands. "You are all against me. What can I do?"

My son ran towards me and threw himself into my arms. "I'm not against you, Mama! I love you!"

I brushed the fair hair away from his face. He was beginning to look more like Garth every day, with his blue eyes and his golden curls, his strong, determined chin and his sturdy frame. The old hunger crept up on me and I pushed it down. Perhaps I should marry Armand. What was I waiting for?

We had met at Marseilles, where the *Etoile de France* docked after her voyage from New Orleans. Savannah and I were making our way through the crowds on the docks, trying to find someone who could take charge of our baggage and hire us a carriage. France! I felt dazed and rather overwhelmed at being back. Marseilles was so busy, so dirty and noisy and congested. Much different from the gracious, lovely city we had left a few weeks earlier.

"Perhaps I can be of some assistance?"

I looked up and saw a dark-haired gentleman of about forty smiling down at me. He was bowing slightly, holding his hat in his hand. His clothes were beautifully cut but plain, and his face was lean and ascetic, longish, and perhaps a bit sorrowful-looking. But his eyes were warm and kind, like his smile.

"No, thank you," I said a trifle stiffly, "we will be able to manage. Come, Savannah."

I can imagine how we must have looked: two frightened women, one obviously pregnant, both looking wide-eyed and apprehensive as they moved along the docks, trying to ignore the rude stares and coarse remarks of the stevedores and sailors and messengers. When we reached the street a huge dray pulled by an enormous workhorse bore down on us. Savannah shrieked, and when I tried to pull her to one side she tripped over an empty crate that lay crushed and broken in the gutter. The two of us would surely have fallen under the wheels of the conveyance as it rumbled by if the stranger hadn't called to the driver and stopped the horses himself.

He pulled down his cuffs and brushed off the tails of his coat. "I think you do need help, you know," he said with a kindly smile. "Please, let me introduce myself. My name is Armand Valadon, Marquis de Pellissier."

I blinked at him. I could feel the blood draining away from my face, and with a little cry I fainted dead away. He carried me to a nearby inn and revived me with a glass of brandy. I choked and opened my eyes. Savannah was chattering nervously in English and clumsy Creole French.

"Be quiet, Savannah," I said briskly. "Forgive me, Monsieur, but your name is not unknown to me."

"So it would appear, Madame," he said, "but for the

life of me I cannot remember where or when we have met.
How could I be obtuse enough to forget such a lovely
face—''

"We have never met, but we were married." He looked
astonished. "My name is Elise Lesconflair, Monsieur.
Have you heard of me?"

He blew out his breath in a long whistle. "I have
indeed, Madame. When I returned from Russia for the last
time—when was that? Three, four years ago?—I heard the
most amazing gossip about a wedding I was supposed to
have taken part in in one of the northern provinces. Lesconflair. Yes, that was the name of the girl. What a
remarkable coincidence this is, Madame. I am—I am
charmed to meet you at last."

"Indeed," I said wryly, "you have my sincerest
apologies for any embarrassment I might have caused
you, my Lord. And I apologize for having troubled you
today. I think we can—''

"But no!" he cried. "You cannot escape before you
have satisfied my curiosity about this affair. Who was the
impostor? Do you know?"

I stood up and smoothed down my skirts. "Yes, I
know. He was an American adventurer named Garth
McClelland." My hands lingered for a moment on the
mound of my stomach. "Good day, my Lord. And many
thanks for your kindness."

"Ah, Madame, it is I who should beg forgiveness for
having embarrassed you," he said, resting his hand lightly
on my arm. "I beg you, don't be angry with me. It all
becomes clear to me now. You—you are just returning
home from America, are you not? Ah," he shook his
head, "this is remarkable, incredible! McClelland, eh?"

"You knew him, then?"

Armand Valadon laughed. "Oh, yes, I knew him! We
were both concerned with the same problem, only we had

opposing points of view. I should have known—! God, the man was clever. And the audacity of his scheme!'' He saw my pinched expression. ''But how unfeeling you will think me, Madame, for taking delight in an incident which has undoubtedly caused you so much pain. Won't you let me assist you? To make reparation for the discomfort caused you by my, ah, American counterpart? I know an inn, not too bad for Marseilles, and we can proceed by easy stages to Paris whenever you feel ready to travel.''

I studied him. He was genuinely kind, and he sincerely wanted to help. I knew better than to think he was attracted to me in my present condition; his intentions could only be honorable. I smiled and gave him my hand. ''Thank you for your concern, my Lord. I am most grateful to you.''

He bowed over my hand and smiled up at me. ''And I am most grateful to you, Madame, for resolving a mystery that has plagued me for quite some time. Do you believe in coincidence? I do not. I believe in destiny.''

He arranged everything for me: clothes, hotels, travel, and he never permitted a word of protest. Armand Valadon became my friend and protector. He seemed to think that the gods had intended for us to meet. I decided it would be best if he did not accompany me to the Chateau.

''One shock at a time, Armand. Who knows? Uncle Theo might throw me out. If he does, will you take me in until I find a suitable place to live?''

I said it facetiously, but his answer was serious. ''If I took you in, Elise, I would never let you go.''

I laughed. ''Dear Armand, what a scandal that would cause! A pregnant woman, unmarried, recently returned from exotic places! We would be the talk of Paris.''

''My dear, at my age one no longer concerns himself with avoiding scandal, but with rejoicing in it when it comes. Just remember, I am at your service, Elise. Forever.''

He traveled with us as far as Orléans, then hired a carriage to take us to the Chateau. Savannah and I arrived one warm night in April. A new footman opened the door to us and gave us an icy stare. Then old Derain, the butler I had known since I was a child, came out of the dining room.

"Ah, Mademoiselle Elise!" he cried. And he literally ran back to the dining room, calling, "My Lord! My Lord!"

Françoise heard the commotion and raced screaming down the marble staircase. Without a moment's hesitation she swept me into her arms and wept noisily.

Then Uncle Theo and Philippe approached us. Françoise stepped back and Philippe embraced me and kissed me warmly. He was crying, too. He had lost an arm, I saw, and his empty sleeve was pinned up on his shoulder like some grim hero's medal.

"Oh, Philippe," I whispered, "what happened? What happened?"

He gave a gallant little laugh. "I left my poor arm in Vilan, during the Russian campaign, my dearest. Oh, Elise, Elise, it's so good to have you back!"

"The prodigal returns," I said sadly. I turned to Uncle Theo. "Well, Uncle, have you a word for your errant niece?" I removed my cloak so that he could see my swollen figure. "I'll go if you want me to, Uncle Theo. I have no desire to bring you further shame and scandal. But I wanted to see my home again—"

He came towards me. I was surprised to see how little he had changed. His hair was a little whiter, his clothes a bit shabbier, but he was the same in every other way.

"Oh, my child, my child!" he murmured, taking me in his arms. "Thank God. Thank God." He was weeping softly, everyone was weeping, even Savannah and the new footman, who couldn't take his eyes off her. "You have come home to us, Elise," Uncle Theo sighed, holding me away from him. "That's all that matters. The Lesconflairs have provided France with her greatest heroes, but they have also given her her most exciting scandals. In either case, posterity has much to thank us for. And who is this fine-looking woman?" He turned to Savannah.

"This is Savannah, my maidservant from America, Uncle Theo." Savannah and Françoise eyed each other suspiciously.

"America! Dear God, child, no wonder we never found you! America! Oh, Elise, you never wrote, never sent word," he said sadly. "We thought you were dead."

I pressed his hand. "I'm sorry, Uncle," I said. "I meant to write, many times, but things happened, bad things. I didn't want to disgrace you, to cause you any more pain. I suppose I thought it would be best for you to think I was—dead. But I have had many adventures, and I have survived them all. I think you will be proud of me. But wait? Where is Honoré?" I looked around the vast hallway. "In Paris? Has he married?"

Uncle Theo looked suddenly tired and old. Philippe said, "Honoré was killed in a duel, Elise, not two months after we lost you."

"Oh, no," I whispered, "it was my fault. Someone said something about me and—. Oh, his temper was always so wicked!"

"No, no," Philippe assured me hastily, "nothing like that. It was a girl. You know how he was. We didn't hear anything about it until it was all over, and it was too late."

"My poor dears," I said slowly, "I wish I had been here. I know how hard it must have been."

Françoise spoke up. "It's been hard enough all around, I expect," she said briskly. "But the wheel turns. The wheel always turns. You're looking entirely too pale and thin, Elise. Do you want that baby of yours to be a puny weakling?''

I laughed. "No, Françoise, I do not, and I don't think there's any danger of that as long as you have anything to say about it."

"You should have heard her when I came back from Russia," Philippe said. "She tore into me as if I had deliberately starved myself."

"Hmmph," Françoise grunted. "You can be sure that that runt Bonaparte wasn't skinny when he got back to Paris. And he didn't have frostbite and other pitiful diseases, either. I declare, I'm glad he's gone!"

"Françoise, for once I am inclined to agree with you," Uncle Theo said. "Come, Elise, you shall have your supper with us and Françoise will see to your Savannah. What a pretty name. America! I have always wanted to see it. Your great-uncle Pierre-Claude settled in America, you know."

"To escape the bailiff," Philippe explained dryly. "Why, Elise, you're crying!" He put a brotherly arm around my shoulders. "What's wrong?"

"Nothing!" I dried my eyes. "It feels so good to be back, so very good. Nothing has changed—and yet, I feel that everything must have changed. I feel like a foreigner, but everything is so familiar, so dear. I'm so glad I came home, Philippe. So very glad!"

My son was born in June, 1815. I named him Etienne, for Stephen McClelland, Garth's grandfather. Uncle Theo recalled that Etienne Lesconflair had distinguished himself at the Norman invasion of England in 1066, so that name was perfectly acceptable to him. I was in labor for a whole night and day, and in the sweat-drenched intervals between the tearing, agonizing pains I thought of Garth. His handsome face seemed to dance seductively in front of my eyes, and I could almost hear his voice saying my name. And when I heard the first cries of our son, I wept with joy and with sorrow. I would never lose Garth now. Part of him would belong to me until I died. But I would never see him again, either, and that knowledge almost drowned the delight I took in the birth of Etienne.

No, nothing had changed—and everything had changed. The Chateau, at least, was still the same. A bit dustier, a little shabby, like its owner, but still filled with the wondrous objects that had enchanted me as a child. But I worried over the state of Uncle Theo's finances when I noticed one day that the portrait of me as Diana was missing from its accustomed place above the fireplace in the library.

"Oh, Uncle Theo, you didn't!"

"Didn't what, child?"

"Sell the Diana! Oh, this is awful! We could have borrowed. Armand would have been delighted—"

"I am sorry, Elise." Uncle Theo's tone was grave. "I know how much you liked it. I did, too. But Davids are fetching splendid prices these days—." He shrugged. "I had no choice, my dear."

"You don't sound particularly upset," I observed coolly. It was my painting, after all. I supposed I had forfeited my right to it by disappearing. But he could have kept it.

"Money is often an acceptable alternative to sorrow," he said. "Someday when you're older, Elise, you'll understand."

Really, men could be most annoying.

"Mama! Mama!" The small hand that tugged at my skirts was insistent. "Please, may we go out? Please, Mama?"

I swept him up in my arms and held him struggling on my lap. "Out? Etienne, my darling, you have been in and out of the Chateau all day, and you find trouble wherever you go! Why do you want to go out?"

He smiled. "I want to go out with you."

"The crossbow! The Lesconflair crossbow!" Uncle Theo burst shouting into the room. "Missing! Stolen! Where is Derain? Where is—?"

"The crossbow is here, Uncle Theo, wrested from the hands of your infant nephew before he managed to do any real damage. Derain is resting in his room, secure in the knowledge that this little rascal might have failed to de-capitate him today, but that he will surely try again tomor-row. Poor Derain. Poor Uncle." I kissed his cheek. "I am taking him out now—"

"Where?" Uncle Theo asked quickly. "Where are you going, my dear?"

I looked at him, puzzled. "I don't know. Perhaps to the forest." Etienne shrieked delightedly when he heard that. "Why?"

"Oh, nothing, nothing. If someone comes to call—"

"No one will call. Armand is in Rome this week, remember? Come, little demon. Well, Uncle, what shall we do with the culprit? Shall I spank him?"

"Spank him!" Uncle Theo's brows rose alarmingly. "Certainly not, Elise. The child can't help his natural high spirits."

I smiled ruefully. "And neither could I help mine, but I remembered you encouraged me to try."

"Bah! Etienne is a true Lesconflair, an adventurous boy. You mean he really figured out how to work that bow all by himself? I can't believe it!"

"Then you may ask Derain to confirm it. Let's go, Etienne." I held out my hand and Etienne shoved his grubby fist into it. "Say good-bye to Uncle Theo, and to Françoise and Savannah." They all bent their heads so that he could kiss them. He was a demon, but he was also very loving and affectionate. "Where would you like to go, dearest?" I asked him as we walked with unaccus-tomed restraint down the great staircase.

"To the forest," he said quickly. He tugged impatiently at my hand. "I am going to kill Indians today, I think. I want to show Papa lots of dead Indians."

This Papa business again!

Victor, the footman, who was now married to Savannah, beamed at us and opened the front door. We stepped from the coolness of the hall into the warm sunshine. I released Etienne and he raced down the stairs and across the drive to the fountains.

"I wish I had half his energy!"

"Oh, Philippe." I smiled at my brother, who was just coming up from the stables. "I know, I think mothers should be endowed with twice the energy of their children instead of only half. Did you hear what he did today?"

"The crossbow?" Philippe laughed. "Yes, Derain couldn't wait to tell me. Said he'd never been shot at before! I don't think he liked the experience. I'll confess that I didn't either. Is that a dreadful thing for a war hero to say? Don't tell Uncle Theo. Lesconflairs never whine."

"How are you feeling today, Philippe?" Philippe had never completely recovered from his battle wounds and sickness. "I wish you could be well. I wish I could give you my health."

"No, my dear, I would refuse it. You'll need it all to keep up with him." He nodded at the demon, who was splashing in the pool at the bottom of one of the fountains, trying to catch goldfish in his bare hands. "I am quite well enough, thank you, and I daresay I shall outlive you and your son. And how are you, Elise? You look beautiful. Are you happy here?"

"Of course I am, Philippe! What a question."

"I would feel better if you were settled, sister. If you had a man to love and care for, a man who would love and care for you." I thought he was going to pressure me to marry Armand, but he said, "Elise, do you ever think of Garth?"

I was surprised. I was going to say, "Of course not!"

But instead I watched Etienne playing and said softly, "I think of him every day, Philippe. I hope that he is well and doing work that suits him. I hope he has found love and happiness, even small happiness. I wish him well."

"Ah," said Philippe, "you still love him. If you could see him—"

"I wouldn't see him. It would be too painful," I said abruptly. "Forgive me, Philippe, but I have promised to take Etienne to the forest. I don't want to wait too long."

I ran across the lawns to fetch my son, and as I looked back over my shoulder I saw that Philippe was grinning. I felt slightly irritated. What was the matter with everyone today?

Etienne left the pool without protest when I announced that it was time to scout for Indians. We tramped across the fields that smelled rich and warm and fertile in August. We found a patch of daisies. I made a chain and then a circlet of flowers, and knelt in the lush grass as Etienne crowned me Queen of the Indians. Finally we reached the pool where I had seen Garth for the first time. I hadn't planned to go that far—or perhaps I had. It was a long time ago. Eight years. When I was seventeen and as green and guileless as a girl could be. I told myself it was silly to think about that day, but memory never listens to the wishes of the brain, only of the heart.

"Oh, Mama, may I swim?" Etienne was hopping up and down excitedly.

"No, darling, not today. But we shall come back, I promise, when there's more time. I shall probably have to carry you home as it is."

"No, I can walk," he said stoutly. "If I can't swim, I'll play with my sword." He found a stick and charged a small rabbit, who scurried off into the briary undergrowth. He tilted at everything for about half an hour, then he climbed up in my lap and demanded a story. In a few minutes he was asleep. I held him for a while, then put him down on a sun-warmed bank on some soft grass. I would let him sleep for a bit, then we would start back to the Chateau. I smoothed the damp hair away from his forehead as he slept. He was a beautiful child and I loved him. I would not have surrendered him for anything, even if it meant that the incident of eight years ago would not have taken place.

I walked along the creek for a short way, watching how swiftly the water moved here, and how deep and cool the pool looked.

"If I didn't know better, I'd think I was dreaming. But no, I should have known you'd be here."

I saw him reflected in the pool, and I turned slowly. I knew that voice so well. I felt myself growing weak and pale even before I looked at him. He was seated on the back of a fine chestnut stallion. He hadn't changed much in three years. I thought I saw a touch of gray at his temples, the lines in his face were deeper than I remembered. My heart turned over.

"Hello, Garth," I said.

He dismounted but didn't approach me. Instead he stood next to his horse and gazed at me for a long time without speaking.

"You come here—frequently?" he asked.

I shook my head. "No, I haven't been here since —since I've been home. This is quite a coincidence, then."

"It was inevitable. You look beautiful, Elise. Even more beautiful than I remember."

I flushed, certain he was mocking me. I searched his face for some sign of the old arrogance that used to infuriate me, but I saw none. His eyes looked deep and dark, and his expression was quite serious. Self-consciously I reached up and removed the crown of blossoms from my hair. My gown was soiled and stained from playing in the fields with Etienne, and my neck and arms were bare of any decoration. Damp tendrils of hair kept falling in front of my eyes, and I brushed them away impatiently.

"You do not find me at my best, Monsieur," I said with strained levity. "We should have met at court—"

He smiled for the first time. "I don't think so, Elise. You look—just as I imagined you would look."

I couldn't meet his gaze any longer. I felt a slow blush stealing over my face and I dropped my eyes. My limbs felt heavy. I couldn't move.

"You are a long way from Louisiana, Garth."

"Yes. President Monroe has appointed me ambassador to France, Elise. I was on my way to Le Havre—I have business in London—and I thought a detour to the Chateau would not be too time-consuming. I am becoming remarkably sentimental in my old age, I suppose. I find that the memory of the afternoon when I first saw you is still fresh and vivid. I enjoy thinking about it."

"I have been remembering it, too," I said in a low whisper.

"And wishing for me to appear?"

I jerked my head up. "No, certainly not," I said tartly. "You didn't go to the house, did you?"

"And risk being shot down by one of your Corsican relations? No, thank you." He grinned. He was the old Garth again, arrogant and cynical. "Besides, my fondest memories are associated not with the Chateau but with this place. I had a hard time finding it."

"Then you were going to pass me by without calling?" I said airily. "For shame, Garth!"

"Yes, I'm afraid I was, Elise. Although your old friend Lafitte suggested that I drop in. We met for dinner before I left."

"Did you? How is Jean? I haven't heard a word from him."

"And he hasn't heard from you, but that hasn't dulled his affection for you, Elise. He is well, and talking about moving his operation to Galveston, Texas. I think he wants to retire."

"Retire! What nonsense. He's still a young man."

Garth shrugged. "Perhaps. But a life of crime and hair-raising adventure has a way of aging a man rather rapidly. And a woman."

I bit my lips. "If you are suggesting," I began hotly.

"I'm not suggesting anything," he said with an innocent laugh. "You have already heard me declare that you're still beautiful, haven't you, Elise? And I do not compliment women lightly these days. I am growing particular, I fear. Another price extracted by age."

"That's the third time you've mentioned age, Garth," I said with a sly smile. "Are you afraid of growing old?"

"No," he said, looking serious again. "I'm not afraid of it. I don't relish the idea. Georgette is dead," he said suddenly.

"Oh." I didn't know what to say. I wasn't sorry about it. "When?"

"Two years ago. Arnold was declared insane and committed to an institution. He escaped and found Georgette visiting La Rêve. He killed her and then himself. And burned the house."

The intrusion of murder and horror into the bright little world that I had been living in for the past few years frightened me. I felt again the terrors that I had experienced at the hands of men like Fowler and Hennessy. I had almost forgotten them, and now I was reminded again that evil existed and that I had lived with it once.

I covered my eyes. "That's horrible. Horrible. I—I'm sorry, Garth."

"Don't be," he said curtly. "Her death was swift and more merciful than she deserved."

I took a long breath. "You're as hard as ever, aren't you? Why don't you go now, Garth? You've brought a blight, a taint with you. You have reminded me of—of so many things I haven't thought about in years. That violent country of yours. Those dreadful men like Fowler and the rest. Slaves and death and suffering. Why, why did you come here?"

"So I've spoiled your perfect idyll, then. Are you happy, Elise?" His face was grave.

I wanted to say, Yes, I'm happy. I don't need you. I don't want you. But I couldn't say the words. I loved Etienne. I loved my family and my home. But I wasn't happy. I had permitted Armand Valadon and a few others to woo me because I liked the distraction their attentions brought. And the few months I spent in Paris each year brought another kind of frantic, cosmopolitain forgetfulness. I didn't think about happiness, didn't pursue it because I sensed it would always elude me.

"Are *you* happy, Garth?" I asked him.

He gave a little shrug. "I keep busy. I don't think about it."

"And neither do I," I told him. "I have never liked to brood about things I cannot change."

"You haven't married. I'm rather surprised at that. Are the French so blind to beauty?"

"Not at all. But my lovers are so numerous and so ardent—how is a woman to choose?" I demanded gaily. "By the most astonishing coincidence, Garth, the most ardent among them is an old friend of yours."

He looked interested. "Oh, really? Who?"

"Armand Valadon, Marquis de Pellissier."

"What?" He shouted with laughter. "What a joke!"

"Yes, we both found it quite amusing," I said. "You do know him, then?"

"Of course. One cannot successfully impersonate a man whom one has never met. We even crossed swords on one occasion. He almost bested me. I wonder how time has treated him?"

"He is kind, and very fond of Et—of all of us," I said. "Uncle Theo has hopes that the Fates may put everything right after all."

"I see." His cool eyes probed me. "And does he hope in vain?"

I felt my pulse quicken. Why didn't he go? Why did we have to meet here, awkwardly, in so secluded a spot? If we had met in Paris I would have been able to take refuge in any number of places, with any number of other people. But here—. We were alone, isolated. I felt vulnerable and a little frightened. Not of any physical assault, but of the keen ability of his mind to ferret out the cause of my uneasiness, the root of my sorrow. He would discover that I loved him still, and I didn't want him to know he could still wield that power over me.

"No," I said, "Uncle's hopes are not at all groundless. I am very fond of the Marquis." Right then I decided to marry Armand Valadon, if only to keep this man from knowing he could have me at any moment if he wished.

"I won't offer premature congratulations," he said with a wry grin. "As I recall, your wedding to that absurd Baron was almost a certainty until I appeared. Some men are spoilers."

"You have made a career of it," I said a trifle bitterly. "You may be sure if a wedding ever does come to pass that you won't be invited."

He chuckled. "Oh, no? I'm very respectable now, Elise. I came to France this time not as a spoiler but as a man of stature, with weighty diplomatic responsibilities."

"You can't fool me. You haven't changed a bit." I gazed at him intently for a long moment. I knew myself too well to think that I wouldn't live on this memory for weeks to come. "It is getting late, Monsieur l'Ambassadeur," I said softly. "You will miss your boat to England."

"Elise." He took a step towards me. All the levity had gone from his face and his eyes were dark and fathomless again. "I have never stopped thinking about you."

I caught my breath. "I know you too well to think you've been faithful to my memory," I said huskily.

He smiled. I saw a fleeting sadness flicker across his face. The sadness of loneliness. "And have you been faithful to me?" he asked.

"Yes. I—I haven't wanted any other men. I mean—I mean—." I was suddenly confused, like a girl of seventeen. "I don't want anyone now, not even you, Garth. I don't want—"

"I love you, Elise," he said. I broke off my tirade and gaped at him. My brain reeled and I couldn't speak. "I love you," he said again, slowly. Then he laughed. "There, that wasn't so hard to say. I've been saying it over and over again in my mind for a long time, but I never spoke the words before. I love you. It gets easier every time. Elise—"

"Oh, stop, stop!" I cried. "Why do you torment me? You didn't even intend to visit me! Our meeting here was accidental! How can you say you love me? I—I don't believe you, Garth." I turned my back on him. "Oh, why did you have to come here today? Why couldn't I have gone on as I have been, living on dreams? I don't believe you love me. You've just added one more weapon to the arsenal of things you use to seduce women. Go away, Garth, and let me forget I ever saw you. I'll tell myself I dreamed it—"

"Elise." His arms were around me and his lips were burning my neck. I drew in my breath to cry out, but the sound died in my throat, drowned by the rush of pleasure I felt in his arms. He whirled me around and lifted my face to his, then his lips found mine and the old fire devoured us both. He branded my eyes, my cheeks, my throat, my breasts with kisses, and I said his name over and over.

"Come away with me, Elise," he said breathlessly. "Now, today. Come—"

"No, no, I can't," I murmured, "I can't leave—"

"You must. Don't tell them, don't go back. Be my mistress, Elise. I'll take you to London tonight and you can send word—"

I felt as though he had doused me with ice water. "Your mistress," I gasped. "Your mistress! So, you think I'll follow you just like that!" I snapped my fingers. "And start the whole stupid business all over again! You still think all you have to do is murmur sweet, sweet words in my ear and I'll follow, just as I've always done, even when I fought you and fought you and swore I wouldn't? You think we can pick up where we left off, don't you? Well, we can't, Garth McClelland. Never! I'll never go with you!"

"Not even if I swear I love you?" His eyes were shining.

"No. What do I care for your love! I don't trust you. I can't!"

"Mama!"

I broke off and looked around. I heard it again, Etienne's piping voice, coming from very far away. Dear God, and I had thought he was asleep. I ran to the place where I had left him. He was gone.

"Mama, up here!"

I looked up. He was hanging by his knees on the limb of a tree, just out of my reach. His blond curls fell straight down from his head and his blouse had come untucked and was veiling his flushed face.

"Etienne! What on earth are you doing?" I reached up for him. "Come down from there at once!"

"I can't," he said with a grunt. "I can't pull myself up. I'm going to fall."

"Mother of God," I said despairingly. "What am I going to do with you? How am I going to get up there?"

I had forgotten all about Garth. I suddenly noticed him standing at my side, looking at the dangling boy with an expression of stupefied amazement on his face. He came to his senses and reaching up plucked my son out of the tree as easily as if he had been a ripe fruit and set him down at my feet. I crouched down beside him and dusted him off. I smoothed the hair away from his face and tucked his shirttails back into his breeches.

"Are you all right, Etienne?" I asked anxiously. "Were you frightened?"

"No," he said blandly. "I just couldn't get down." He was watching Garth through large, interested eyes.

"I declare, you are the worst behaved boy I have ever known," I said impatiently. "You could have broken your silly neck, and I wouldn't have been sorry! I don't know what I'm going to do with you!"

Etienne looked up at Garth. "You're my Papa, aren't you?" he asked.

Garth smiled. "You had better ask your Mama," he said, looking at me.

I lifted my chin and said defiantly, "What do you think? He was born nine months to the day after you—you took me on that beach in North Carolina. But you can't have him! He's mine, Garth, the only thing I have in my life! I'll never let you take him away from me!" I stood up to him, fists clenched.

He said slowly, "You couldn't wait to get away from me. It didn't make sense, your letting Georgette help you. You didn't want the world to know that on top of everything else you were to give birth to a bastard child, did you? Were you afraid it would hurt me? Or didn't you trust me not to hurt you?'' He put his hands on my shoulders.

"I didn't want you to leave me, and so I left you first," I said miserably. "And I was even afraid you would laugh at me—"

"Dear God, Elise," he cried, anguished, "did you think I would abandon you? What do you take me for? I love you, you silly wench. I've always loved you, but I was such a blind idiot—!" He held me close. I was crying softly. "Oh, my darling, what you must have been through. How lonely for you, how sad. Don't cry. Please. Look," he tilted my chin up and looked into my eyes. He was grinning devilishly. "I'll even marry you if you like. That's what you were fishing for, isn't it?"

"Certainly not," I said indignantly. "I wouldn't marry you now if—if—"

"Of course you'll marry me," he said confidently. "We don't want Etienne to be a little bastard for the rest of his life, do we?" He looked around. "Where has the boy got to?"

The boy was playing calmly under the belly of Garth's huge stallion, dangerously close to those enormous hooves. Gasping, I ran towards him and snatched him away.

Garth laughed and lifted Etienne onto the horse's back. "It's more fun up there than underneath, you'll find."

"He'll fall off," I protested.

"No, he won't. Not if he hangs on. That's the first thing you have to do when you're learning to ride, isn't it, Etienne?"

"Watch me, Papa!" Etienne kicked his legs. "I'm going to chase Indians now. And shoot them until they're all dead!"

"Stout lad," said Garth approvingly. He turned to me. "You're a terrible mother, Elise. In the space of just a few minutes your child has almost met his death twice, and all because of your negligence. He clearly needs a firmer hand than yours, my sweet.''

My cheeks blazed. ''How dare you—after three years —how dare—''

''A father has some rights, surely,'' he said innocently. ''How did you know my grandfather's name was Stephen?''

''I—I didn't know it at all. He is named for the Lesconflair who—''

''Yes, yes. You know, Elise, I don't think France will be able to hold him when he gets bigger. I've been west, to the Pacific. It's a magnificent country. I think we'll find a place between mountain ranges, where there aren't too many Indians—''

''But Garth, what about Highlands?''

''Oh, we'll keep it up. Stephen might want to live there some day, or perhaps one of his brothers.'' Garth picked up the reins and started to lead the horse out of the woods. He cautioned Etienne—Stephen—to hang on and kept his hand on his back to steady him. He slid his free arm around my shoulders. ''He'll have lots of brothers. Six or seven. And a few sisters to tease and torment.''

''Oh, will he?'' I asked. ''Have I nothing to say in this matter?''

He smiled down at me. ''Not much. You are quite capable of founding a dynasty, Elise. I don't suppose I can carry the two of you off right now?''

I shook my head. ''No. We must do it properly. I shall take you home and let the family look you over—again. You won't be able to persuade Uncle Theo to surrender his great-nephew, I'm afraid. They worship each other.''

''He may come and visit,'' Garth said grandly. ''There's room for all.''

''You'll have to build a very large house,'' I told him, ''to accommodate ten children and a host of in-laws.''

He waved his hand. "Anything you like, Elise. Fifty rooms? A hundred? Ah, it will be good to see Philippe again. Perhaps he would like to come with us to America when my duties here are finished. We'll find him a wife, a good strong Creole girl, perhaps. I was sorry to hear about Honoré. He was a good lad. Hot-headed, of course, like his sister, but he meant well."

I halted and glared at him. "Where—how did you hear about Honoré?"

"Oh, your Uncle Theo is a most amusing correspondent," he said. "I know everything. Philippe's arm. How splendidly Françoise and Savannah are getting along, and Savannah's marriage. The only thing he didn't tell me about was our lad here. I think he meant that to be a kind of *coup de grace*. It was Theo Lesconflair's revenge."

"Well!" I felt myself growing red. "Of all the—the duplicity! The arrogance of you men! How dare you scheme against me? How dare you!" I tried to shrug off his arm but he held me tight. "Oh, you men are villains. I can see it all now. The Diana painting. I suppose it hangs in a place of honor in your bedroom?" He laughed and nodded. "The odd looks I've been getting all morning, and the strong hints about marrying to give Etienne a father. And even Etienne, insisting that his Papa was coming today! They expected you, didn't they? Everyone knew about it but me. Why, you don't even have a satchel, or any kind of traveling bag. Liar! London, indeed. Oh!" I didn't know if I should laugh or cry, but I didn't have to decide. He put his arms around me and kissed me deeply.

"I wouldn't be surprised if your parish priest is waiting for us when we get back," he said softly, between kisses. "I told Theo that I wouldn't be responsible for what would happen if we didn't marry very soon. It would be a shame if Stephen's brother had to be conceived out of wedlock, too."

"Oh, you're very wicked," I scolded him gently.

pressed close to him, loving the familiar lean hardness of his body, the new tenderness in his manner, the lack of tension between us. He had changed since I saw him last. Garth McClelland had learned to love.

"You know," he murmured, "we could distract the child somehow and—"

I nodded past him to where Stephen and the horse were ambling away from us with unbecoming speed. "I think he is taking care of that himself," I said.

"Papa! Mama! Look at me!" Our son squirmed around in the saddle and waved at us. "No hands!"

"Mother of God," Garth breathed angrily, "when I catch that little monkey I'm going to warm his backside!"

Racing after them he pulled the horse up and lifted the boy high into the air. Stephen shrieked with delight.

"Well, my lad, so you like adventure, do you?" He lowered his son to his shoulder and looked at me. "I shall teach you about adventure, then, and your mother will teach you about love. She's the expert."

Garth stretched out his hand to me. I took it and held it to my cheek for a moment, brushing away a little tear that fell on it. Then Garth passed our son to me and took hold of the horse's reins, and we all went out of the gathering gloom of the forest into the brightness of the afternoon sun.